# GALACTIC
# EMPIRES

# GALACTIC EMPIRES

### EDITED BY
## NEIL CLARKE

*Night Shade Books*
NEW YORK

Night Shade books may be purchased in bulk at special discounts for sales promotion, corporate gifts, fund-raising, or educational purposes. Special editions can also be created to specifications. For details, contact the Special Sales Department, Night Shade Books, 307 West 36th Street, 11th Floor, New York, NY 10018 or info@skyhorsepublishing.com.

Night Shade Books® is a registered trademark of Skyhorse Publishing, Inc.®, a Delaware corporation.

Visit our website at www.nightshadebooks.com.

10 9 8 7 6 5 4 3 2 1

Library of Congress Cataloging-in-Publication Data

Names: Clarke, Neil, 1966- editor.
Title: Galactic empires / edited by Neil Clarke.
Description: First edition. | New York, NY : Night Shade Books, 2017.
Identifiers: LCCN 2016030371 | ISBN 9781597808842 (paperback)
Subjects: LCSH: Science fiction, American. | Imperialism--Fiction. | BISAC:
  FICTION / Science Fiction / Short Stories. | FICTION / Science Fiction /
  Adventure. | FICTION / Science Fiction / General.
Classification: LCC PS648.S3 G25 2017 | DDC 813/.0876208--dc23
LC record available at https://lccn.loc.gov/2016030371

Print ISBN: 978-1-59780-884-2

Cover illustration by Toni Justamante Jacobs
Cover design by Jason Snair

Please see page 622 for an extension of this copyright page.

Printed in the United States of America

# CONTENTS

For my parents,
Eamonn and Joan Clarke.

# Introduction:
## What's Going on Out There?

### *Neil Clarke*

When I think back on my life as a science fiction fan, there are various moments that I cherish. One of those occurred at age eleven in 1977, when my dad took us to see *Star Wars*. By then, I had had a long history with *Lost in Space*, Godzilla movies, and the occasional episode of *Star Trek*, but this was something different. We left the theater stunned and amazed. While walking to our car that night, my dad pointed to the sky and made some comment about what could be going on out there. I don't recall the words, but that sentiment has always stuck with me.

Since then, through film and television, the galactic empire has further reached beyond the science fiction community and into our broader culture. *Star Wars* wasn't the first, mind you, but it has become a touchstone across several generations. For many people, the mere mention of "empire" conjures "The Imperial March" and visions of Darth Vader. That inimitable franchise's propaganda wing has kept that particular link alive and kicking ever since. However, one arguable side effect of the success of *Star Wars* was the resurrection of *Star Trek* as a series of movies starting in the late seventies. The Federation also saw a return to television through several spin-off series that introduced new civilizations and, unlike *Star*

*Wars*, an empire portrayed as a force of good. Today, we have a modernized reboot of the original series in theaters and a promised return to television next year.

Galactic empires also play a significant role in shows like *Stargate, Doctor Who, Farscape,* and several others. However, the one that had the greatest impact on me was *Babylon 5*. While I enjoyed the rest, writer and producer J. Michael Straczynski approached *B5* differently. He believed that while science fiction literature had matured, its representation on TV had become stuck in the past: bad science; clear-cut good vs. evil; simplistic plots; and stories that wrapped up all too neatly, often without impact on future episodes. Straczynski's modern galactic empire story was complex, mysterious, gritty, and fun. It was a series of novels for TV and I was hooked for its entire five-year run.

Additionally, you can't look back at the recent history of the entertainment industry without noting the rise of the video game. There's a rich history of the galactic empire theme in this medium, but in the last fifteen years, it's become a force to be reckoned with. Perhaps one of the most successful of these is the Halo series, which launched in 2001. Focused primarily on the character Master Chief, the mechanized armored protagonist battles an array of enemies set against the backdrop of the remains of the Forerunner empire. Big dumb objects, fancy toys, and memorable characters have made Halo the much-emulated king of the hill. Not only popular on gaming consoles, it has spun off best-selling novels, graphic novels, a wide array of merchandise, and videos.

Another notable game series is Mass Effect. Much like *Babylon 5*, the game has an overall arc spread out over three installments. Featuring a complete and well-conceived story, the tale is set in a galaxy controlled by several empires that must inevitably come together to avoid extinction. For many, it sets the bar for character development, plot, and storytelling in video games. The decisions the player makes as Commander Shepard, the main protagonist, have direct consequences on the trajectory of the game's story, leading to multiple possible endings. Like Halo, Mass Effect has also crossed over into a number of successful novels and comics.

All that said, the galactic empire has had a much longer life in written form. By age twelve, I had discovered science fiction novels and stories and it would soon become an outlet for the seed my dad planted that day. What *is* going on out there? I turned to my local library and discovered Asimov's Foundation trilogy, Frank Herbert's *Dune*, and later, Brian Aldiss' two-volume anthology, *Galactic Empires*. For that time, this was probably the best possible introduction I could have had. Brian's anthologies introduced me to new authors and variations on the theme that I could spend years exploring. That journey took me through the works of E. E. "Doc" Smith, A. E. van Vogt, Clifford Simak, and many more.

As I grew older, my interests broadened, but I remained fascinated. I still encountered the occasional empire story, but my options were limited. It wasn't until I started meeting like-minded individuals in college that I started to pay closer attention to what was going on elsewhere in the world. Over time, it became clear that the really interesting works featuring galactic empires were coming from the UK. If your tastes lay a bit more to the modern side of things, it can be argued that Iain M. Banks was one of the most influential contributors to the galactic empire in recent times. Starting in 1987, Banks revitalized the empire theme with his much-beloved Culture stories and novels until his death from cancer in 2013. His work opened doors for even more innovation and experimentation across the field. In the extensive reading I did for this anthology, I could certainly feel the ripples of his influence even in works quite different from his.

Despite this loss, the current state of the galactic empire is strong and healthy in the hands of many, including Alastair Reynolds, Ann Leckie, Lois McMaster Bujold, Ian McDonald, and others. They are the ones influencing the future in all media through their writing, and even as direct participants in the development process of movies, books, comics, and television programs. And so the empire continues to be one of the most visible motifs in science fiction today and, if anything, we're experiencing a small period of expansion as its popularity across all media peaks. The stories in this anthology represent some of the best and the brightest from the empire as it exists in this century. So cue the music . . . and long live the galactic empire!

Neil Clarke
June, 2016

Paul McAuley is the author of more than twenty novels, several collections of short stories, a *Doctor Who* novella, and a BFI Film Classic monograph on Terry Gilliam's film *Brazil*. His fiction has won the Philip K. Dick Memorial Award, the Arthur C. Clarke Award, the John W. Campbell Memorial Award, the Sidewise Award, the British Fantasy Award and the Theodore Sturgeon Memorial Award. After working as a research biologist and university lecturer, he is now a full-time writer, lives in London, and can be found at unlikelyworlds.blogspot.co.uk. His latest novel, *Into Everywhere*, was published by Gollancz in April 2016.

# WINNING PEACE

## *Paul J. McAuley*

One day, almost exactly a year after Carver White started working for Mr. E. Z. Kanza's transport company, Mr. Kanza told him that they were going on a little trip—down the pipe to Ganesh Five. This was the company's one and only interstellar route, an ass-and-trash run to an abandoned-in-place forward facility, bringing in supplies, hauling out pods packed with scrap and dismantled machinery, moving salvage workers to and fro. Carver believed that Mr. Kanza was thinking of promoting him from routine maintenance to shipboard work, and wanted to see if he had the right stuff. He was wrong.

The Ganesh Five system was a binary, an ordinary K1 star and a brown dwarf orbiting each other at a mean distance of six billion kilometers, roughly equivalent to the semimajor axis of Pluto's orbit around the Sun. The K1 star, Ganesh Five A, had a minor asteroid belt in its life zone, the largest rocks planoformed thousands of years ago by Boxbuilders, and just one planet, a methane gas giant named Sheffield by the Brit who'd first mapped the system, with glorious water-ice rings, the usual assortment of small moons, and, this was why a forward facility had been established there during the war between the Alliance and the Collective, no less than four wormhole throats.

The system had been captured by the Collective early in the war, and because one of its wormholes was part of a chain that included the Collective's New Babylon system, and another exited deep in Alliance territory, it had become an important staging and resupply area, with a big dock facility in orbit around Sheffield, and silos and tunnel networks buried in several of the moons. Now, two years after the defeat of the Alliance, the only people living there were employees of the salvage company that was stripping the docks and silos, and a small Navy garrison.

Carver White and Mr. Kanza flew there on the company's biggest scow, hauling eight passengers, a small tug, and an assortment of cutting and demolition equipment. After they docked, Carver was left to kick his heels in the scow for six hours, until at last Mr. Kanza buzzed him and told him to get his ass over to the garrison. A marine escorted Carver to an office with a picture window overlooking the spine of the docks, which stretched away in raw sunlight toward Sheffield's green crescent and the bright points of three moons strung in a line beyond the great arch of its rings. This fabulous view was the first thing Carver saw when he swam into the room; the second was Mr. Kanza and a Navy officer lounging in sling seats next to it.

The officer was Lieutenant Rider Jackson, adjutant to the garrison commander. In his mid-twenties, maybe a year older than Carver, he had a pale, thin face, bright blue eyes, and a calm expression that didn't give anything away. He asked Carver about the ships he'd flown and the hours he'd logged serving in the Alliance Navy, questioned him closely about what had happened after Collective marines had boarded his crippled transport, the hand-to-hand fighting in the corridors and holds, how Carver had passed out from loss of blood during a last stand among the cold sleep coffins, how he'd woken up in a Collective hospital ship, a prisoner of war. The Alliance had requested terms of surrender sixty-two days later, having lost two battle fleets and more than fifty systems. By then, Carver had been patched up and sold as indentured labor to the pharm factories on New Babylon.

Rider Jackson said, "You didn't tell the prize officer you were a flight engineer."

"I gave him my name and rank and number. It was all he deserved to know."

Carver was too proud to ask what this was all about, but he was pretty sure it had something to do with Mr. Kanza's financial difficulties. Everyone who worked for Mr. Kanza knew he was in trouble. He'd borrowed to expand his little fleet, but he hadn't found enough new business to service the loan, and his creditors were bearing down on him.

Rider Jackson said, "I guess you think you should have been sent home."

"That's what we did with our prisoners of war."

"Because your side lost the war."

"We'd have sent them back even if we'd won. The Alliance doesn't treat people like property."

Carver was beginning to like Rider Jackson. He seemed like the kind of man who preferred straight talk to evasion and exaggeration, who would stick to the truth even if it was uncomfortable or inconvenient. Which was probably why he'd been sent to this backwater, Carver thought; forthright officers have a tendency to damage their careers by talking back to their superiors.

Mr. Kanza said, "If my data miner hadn't uncovered his service record and traced him, he'd still be working in the pharm factories."

Rider Jackson ignored this, saying to Carver, "You have a brother. He served in the Alliance Navy too."

"That's none of your business," Carver said.

"Oh, but I think you'll find it's very much *my* business," Mr. Kanza said.

Mr. E. Z. Kanza was a burly man with a shaved head and a short beard trimmed to a sharp point. He liked to think that he was a fair-minded, easygoing fellow, but exhibited most of the usual vices of people given too much power over others: he was arrogant and quick-tempered, and his smile masked a cruel and capricious sense of humor. On the whole, he didn't treat his pilots and engineers too badly—they had their own quarters, access to good medical treatment, and were even given small allowances they could spend as they chose—but they were still indentured workers, with Judas bridges implanted in their spinal cords and no civil rights whatsoever, and Mr. Kanza was always ready to use his shock stick on anyone who didn't jump to obey him.

Smiling his untrustworthy smile, Mr. Kanza said to Carver, "Jarred is two years younger than you, yes? He served on a frigate during the war, yes? Well, I happen to have some news about him."

Carver didn't say anything. He knew what had happened to Jarred, was wondering if this was one of Mr. Kanza's nasty little jokes.

Mr. Kanza appealed to Rider Jackson. "Do you know how long they last in those pharm factories before they cop an overdose or their immune systems collapse? No more than a year or two, three at the most. I saved this one from certain death, and has he ever thanked me? And do you want to bet he'll thank me when he learns about his brother?"

Rider Jackson said, "Don't make a game out of it. If you don't tell him, I will."

The two men stared at each other for a long moment. Then Mr. Kanza smiled and said, "I do believe you like him. I knew you would."

"Do what needs to be done."

Mr. Kanza conjured video from the air with a quick gesture. Here was Jarred White in a steel cell, wearing the same kind of black pajamas Carver had worn in the prison hospital, before he'd been sold into what the Collective called indentured labor and the Alliance called slavery. Here was Jarred standing in gray coveralls against a red marble wall in the atrium of Mr. Kanza's house.

Mr. Kanza told Carver, "Your brother was taken prisoner, just like you. One of my data miners traced him, and I bought out his contract. What do you think of that?"

Carver thought that the videos were pretty good fakes, probably disneyed up from his brother's military record. In both of the brief sequences, Jarred sported the same severe crew cut that was regulation for cadets in the Alliance Navy, not serving officers; when Carver had last seen him, his brother had grown his crew cut out into a flattop. That had been on Persopolis, the City of Our Lady of Flowers. Some twenty days later, Carver's drop ship had been crippled, and he'd been taken prisoner. Three days later, Jarred had been killed in action.

The Collective didn't allow its POWs any contact with their families or anyone else in the Alliance; Carver had found out about his brother's death from one of the other prisoners of war working in the pharm factories. Jarred's frigate, the *Croatian*, had been shepherding ships loaded with evacuees from Eve's Halo when a Collective battleship traveling at a tenth the speed of light had smashed through the convoy. The *Croatian* had been shredded by kinetic weapons and a collapsium bomblet had cooked off what was left: the ship had been lost with all hands. Carver had been hit badly by the news. Possessed by moments of unreasoning anger, he'd started to pick fights with other workers; finally, he attacked one of the guards. The woman paralyzed him with her shock stick, gave him a clinically methodical beating, and put him on punishment detail, shoveling cell protein from extraction pits. Carver would have died there if one of Mr. Kanza's data miners hadn't tracked him down.

After Mr. Kanza bought out his contract, Carver resolved to become a model worker, cultivate patience, and wait for a chance to escape; now, wondering if that chance had finally come, if he could turn Mr. Kanza's crude trick to his advantage, he stepped hard on his anger and held his tongue.

Mr. Kanza said to Rider Jackson, "You see? Not a speck of gratitude."

Rider Jackson turned his tell-nothing expression on Carver; Carver stared back at him through his brother's faked-up ghost.

The young lieutenant said to Mr. Kanza, "You're certain we can trust him?"

"I've had him a year. He's never given me any trouble, and he won't give us any trouble now," Mr. Kanza said, pointing a finger at Carver. "Can you guess why I went to all the trouble of buying out your brother's contract?"

Carver shrugged, as if it meant nothing to him.

Mr. Kanza said, "You really should show me some gratitude. Not only have I already saved your brother's life, but if everything works out, I'll void his contract, and void yours too. You'll both be free."

"Meanwhile, you're holding him hostage, to make sure that I'll do whatever it is you want me to do."

Mr. Kanza told Rider Jackson, "There it is. I have his brother as insurance, the tug will fly itself, and if he does get it into his head to try something stupid, I can intervene by wire. If worst comes to worst, I'll be the one short a flight engineer and a good little ship; as far as you're concerned, this is a risk-free proposition."

"As long as the Navy doesn't find out about it," Rider Jackson said.

"We've been over that," Mr. Kanza said.

Carver saw that there was something tense and wary behind Mr. Kanza's smile, and realized that he had worked up some reckless plan to get himself out of the hole, that he needed Rider Jackson's help to do it, and he needed Carver too.

"We've talked it up and down," Mr. Kanza told Rider Jackson. "There's no good reason why the Navy should know anything about this until you buy out your service."

Rider Jackson studied him, then shrugged and said, "Okay."

Just like that. Two days later, Carver was aboard Mr. Kanza's tug, cooled down in hypersleep while the small ship aimed itself at the brown dwarf, Ganesh Five B.

Mr. Kanza made extensive use of a data mining AI to track down skilled prisoners of war who were being used as common laborers, and to look for business opportunities overlooked by his rivals. The data miner had linked a news item about an alien and an astrophysicist who had disappeared after hiring a small yacht just before the beginning of the war with an academic article by the astrophysicist, Liu Chen Smith, that described an anomalous neutrino flux emitted by a pinpoint source within a permanent storm in the smoky atmosphere of a brown dwarf, Ganesh Five B. It was possible, the data miner suggested, that the alien, a !Cha that called itself Useless Beauty, had bankrolled an expedition to find out if the neutrino source was some kind of Elder Culture artifact.

Although most of the systems linked by wormhole networks were littered with the ruins of the cities, settlements, and orbital and free-floating habitats of Elder Culture species, these had been picked clean long ago by the dozens of species that preceded human colonization. Working examples of Elder Culture technology were fabulously rare and valuable. There was only a slim chance that the neutrino source was some kind of artifact, but if it was, and if Mr. Kanza could capture it, his financial difficulties would be over. He had one big problem: if the garrison that policed the Ganesh Five system found out about the neutrino source, the Navy would claim it for the state. That was where Rider Jackson, a criminal turned war hero, came in.

Rider Jackson had been born and raised on a reef circling a red dwarf star, Stein 8641. When their sheep ranch failed, Rider Jackson's father ran off on a trade ship and his mother committed suicide. At age sixteen, Rider Jackson, their only child, inherited the responsibility of honoring his family's debts. Our Thing, Stein 8641's parliament, ruled that he should be indentured to his father's chief creditors, the Myer family, until he had paid off all that was owed. Five years later, the day after war was declared between the Alliance and the Collective, he stole one of the Myer family's ships and lit out, abandoning the ship in the sprawling docks of New Babylon and turning up the next day at a Navy recruiting office in the planet's dusty capital, where he was promptly arrested for carrying false ID, a crime against the state that earned him ten years indentured labor. Soon afterward, having suffered two devastating defeats in quick succession, the Collective's armed forces rounded up everyone with freefall experience from the state's pool of indentured workers. Rider Jackson's sentence was commuted to ten years' service in the Navy. He fought in three campaigns in two different systems, and then his drop ship was hit by an Alliance raider and broke apart. Rider Jackson took charge of a gig and rescued seventy-eight warm bodies, including the drop ship's captain. His heroism won him his lieutenant's pip, a chestful of medals, and public acclaim, but his criminal history prevented him rising any higher, and at the end of the war, the Navy stashed him in the Ganesh Five garrison, with no hope of promotion or transfer, and nothing to do but listen to the self-pitying monologues of his commander, make random checks on ships passing between the wormholes, and file endless status reports. He still had seven years to serve, and after that he would be returned to Stein 8641, and the Myer family.

Mr. Kanza, knowing that Rider Jackson couldn't afford to buy out the unserved portion of his contract with the Navy, much less pay what he still owed the Myer family, had made him an offer he couldn't refuse: help chase the hot lead on what might be an Elder Culture artifact in return for fifty percent of any profit. Mr. Kanza brought to the deal the information he'd uncovered, a ship, and someone to fly it; Rider Jackson rejigged the garrison's tracking station to cover up the flight of Mr. Kanza's tug, and used its deep space array to survey the brown dwarf. He found two things. The first was a microwatt beacon from an escape pod in orbit around Ganesh Five B. The second was that there was no longer any anomalous neutrino flux within the brown dwarf. It looked like Dr. Smith and the !Cha had captured the neutrino source, but then had got into some kind of trouble that had forced them to abandon their ship.

No wormhole throat orbited Ganesh Five B; the only way to reach it was through real space, a round trip of more than sixty days. Rider Jackson couldn't take a leave of absence from his post and Mr. Kanza was unwilling to risk his life, and couldn't afford to hire a specialized, fully autonomous rescue drone because he was more or less broke and had exhausted all his lines of credit. His lightly modified tug, with Carver White riding along as troubleshooter, would have to do the job.

Carver learned all this while he helped Mr. Kanza prep the tug. He quickly realized that even if he brought back something that made Mr. Kanza and Rider Jackson the richest men alive, Mr. Kanza wouldn't keep his promise about freeing him; if he was going to survive this, he would have to find some way of exploiting the fact that he knew Mr. Kanza's story about holding Jarred hostage was a bluff. He also realized that he didn't have much chance of taking control of the tug and lighting out for somewhere other than the brown dwarf. He would be shut down in hyper-sleep for most of the trip, and the tug was controlled by an unhackable triumvirate of AIs that, sealed deep in the tug's keel, constantly checked each other's status. Not only that, but Mr. Kanza demonstrated with a ten-second burst of agony that he had hidden a shock stick in the tug too, and could use it to stimulate Carver's Judas bridge if it looked like he was going to cause trouble.

Carver's last thoughts before hypersleep closed him down were about whether he had done enough to make sure he could live through this; it was the first thing on his mind when he woke some thirty-one days later, in orbit around the brown dwarf.

The tug had discovered a scattering of debris, including hull plates, chunks of a fusion motor, and a human corpse in a pressure suit—it was clear that Dr. Smith hadn't survived the destruction of her ship—and it had also located the escape pod, which was tumbling in an oblate orbit that skimmed close to the outer edge of the brown dwarf's atmosphere before swinging away to more than twenty million kilometers at apogee. A blurry neutron density scan snatched by a throwaway probe revealed that the pod contained a !Cha's life tank, but its AI had refused to respond to the tug's attempts to shake hands with it, and there had been no response to an automated hailing message either: there was no way of knowing if the !Cha, Useless Beauty, was dead or alive.

The tug played a brief voice-only message from Mr. Kanza, telling Carver that he was to suit up and go outside and retrieve Dr. Smith's corpse.

"She may be carrying something that will tell me what killed her. Also, her relatives may pay a finder's fee for the return of her body."

The tug was already matching delta vee with the body. By the time Carver had sent an acknowledgment to the message (it would take five and a half hours to reach Mr. Kanza), eaten his first meal since waking, and suited up, the tug and Dr. Smith's corpse were revolving around each other at a distance of just a few hundred meters.

Carver rode across the gap on a collapsible broomstick. Ganesh Five B filled half the sky, a dim red disk marbled by black clouds spun into ragged bands by its swift rotation; Dr. Smith's corpse was silhouetted against the baleful light of this failed star, tumbling head over heels, arms and legs akimbo. Her pressure suit was ruptured in several places, and covered by fine carbon particles blown into space by eruptions in the brown dwarf's magnetosphere; a fog of dislodged soot gathered around Carver as he fixed a line between the dead woman's utility belt and his broomstick.

After he'd towed the body back to the tug and stowed it in the cargo hold, Carver discovered a long tangle of transparent thread thinner than a human hair wrapped around Dr. Smith's right arm. He couldn't cut off a sample with any of his suit's tools; he had to unwind the entire tangle before he could bring it inside the tug and feed one end of it into the compact automated laboratory. He'd brought the computer from Dr. Smith's suit inside too, but its little mind was dead and its memory had been irretrievably damaged by years of exposure to the brown dwarf's magnetic and radiation fields.

The lab determined that the thread was woven from fullerene nanotubes doped with atoms of beryllium, magnesium, and iron, and spun into long helical domains, was a room-temperature superconductor with the tensile properties of construction diamond: useful properties, but hardly unique. Even so, the fact that its composition didn't match any known fullerene superconductors was tantalizing, and although he told himself that it was most likely junk, debris in which Dr. Smith's body had become entangled after the destruction of her ship, Carver carefully wound the thread around a screwdriver, and shoved the screwdriver into one of the pouches of his p-suit's utility belt.

He had been hoping that the astrophysicist had survived; that she had been sleeping inside the escape pod; that after he'd woken her, she would have agreed to help him. He knew now that everything depended on whether or not the !Cha was alive or dead, and reckoned things would go easier if it was dead. Because if it was still alive, he would have to try to make a deal with it, and that was a lot riskier than trying to make a go of it on his own. For one thing, it was possible that the !Cha had murdered Dr. Smith because it wanted to keep whatever it was they'd found to itself. For another, like every other alien species, the !Cha made it clear that human beings didn't count for much. Ever since first contact, when the Jackaroo kicked off a global war on Earth and swindled the survivors out of rights to most of the solar system in exchange for a basic fusion drive and access to a wormhole network linking a couple of dozen lousy M-class red dwarf stars, aliens had been tricking, bamboozling, and manipulating the human race. In the long run, like other species before them, humans would either kill themselves off or stumble onto the trick of ascendency and go on to wherever it is the Elder Cultures have gone, but meanwhile they were at the mercy of species more powerful than them, pawns in games whose rules they didn't know, and aims they didn't understand.

Carver had a little time to work out how to deal with the !Cha; before it retrieved the escape pod, the tug spawned dozens of probes and mapped the brown dwarf with everything from optical and microwave radar surveys to a quantum gravity scan. Ganesh Five B was a cool, small T-type, formed like any ordinary star by condensation within an interstellar gas cloud, but at just eight times the mass of Jupiter, too small to support ordinary hydrogen fusion. Gravitational contraction and a small amount of sluggish deuterium fusion in its core warmed its dusty atmosphere to a little under 1500 degrees centigrade. There were metal hydrides and methane down there, even traces of water. Sometimes, its bands of sooty clouds were lit by obscure chains of lightning thousands of kilometers long. Sometimes, when the tug passed directly above the top of a convection cell, those huge, slow elevators that brought up heat from the core, Carver caught a glimpse of the deep interior, a fugitive flash of brighter red flecked with orange and yellow.

And at every tenth orbit, the tug passed over the permanent storm at the brown dwarf's equator, the location of the anomalous neutrino flux that had drawn Dr. Smith and the !Cha to Ganesh Five B. The storm's pale lens was more than fifteen thousand kilometers across; probes dropped into it discovered a complex architecture of fractal clusters crawling and racheting around each other like the gears of an insanely complicated mechanism bigger than the Earth. They also discovered that it was no longer emitting neutrinos, and it was breaking up along its edges—the tug's AIs estimated that it would break up in less than ten years.

While the tug swung around the brown dwarf's dim fires, Carver thought about the !Cha and what he had to do when the tug returned to Sheffield, and he lost himself in memories of his dead brother. He and Jarred had been close, two Navy brats following their parents from base to base, system to system. Although Jarred had been two years younger than Carver, he'd also been brighter and bolder, a natural leader, graduating at the top of his class in the Navy academy. The war had already begun when he graduated; the day after his passing-out parade, he followed Carver into active duty.

The last time Carver had seen Jarred, they'd spent three days together in the port city of Our Lady of the Flowers, Persopolis. It was the beginning of Jarred's leave, the end of Carver's. The night before Carver shipped out, they bar-hopped along the city's famous Strand. The more Jarred drank, the more serious and thoughtful he became. He told Carver that whichever side won the war, both would have to work hard at the peace if humanity was to have any chance at surviving.

"War only happens when peace breaks down. That's why peace is harder work, but more worthwhile."

"We defeat the Collective, we impose terms," Carver said. "Where's the problem?"

"If we won the war and imposed terms on the Collective, forced it to change, it would be an act of aggression," Jarred said. "The Collective would respond in kind and there would be another war. Instead of forcing change, we have to establish some kind of common ground."

"We don't have anything in common with those slavers."

"We have more in common with them than with the Jackaroo, or the Pale, or the !Cha. And if we don't find some way of living together," Jarred said, "we'll grow so far apart that we'll end up destroying each other."

He started to tell Carver about a loose network of people who were discussing how to broker a lasting peace, and Carver said that he didn't want to hear about it, told Jarred he should be careful, what he and his friends were doing sounded a little like treason. Now, in the cramped lifesystem of the tug, endlessly falling around a failed star, six billion kilometers from the nearest human being, Carver thought about what his brother had said on their last night together. Carver had gone a little crazy when he'd heard about his brother's death because it had been about as good and noble as an industrial accident. One machine had destroyed another, and Jarred and the rest of the *Croatian*'s crew had been incidental casualties who'd had no chance to fight back or escape. It was a brutal irony that Jarred's death could help Carver win his freedom.

At last, the tug fired up its motor and slipped into a new orbit, creeping up behind the escape pod, swallowing its black pip whole, then firing up again, a long hard burn to achieve escape velocity from the brown dwarf's gravity well. It pinned Carver to his couch for more than two hours. When it was over, following Mr. Kanza's instructions to the letter, Carver suited up, went outside, and clambered through the access hatch of the cargo bay.

The pod's systems were in sleep mode; careful use of a handheld neutron density scanner confirmed that apart from a !Cha tank, it contained nothing out of the ordinary. If Dr. Smith and Useless Beauty had retrieved something from the brown dwarf, either it had been lost with their ship, or it was hidden inside the !Cha's impervious casing.

Carver didn't attempt to contact the !Cha. He knew that his only chance of escape lay in a narrow window of opportunity during the final part of the return journey; until then, he wanted to keep his plans to himself. He fixed telltales inside the cargo bay in case the !Cha decided to try to break out, locked it up, climbed back inside the lifesystem, and sent a report to Mr. Kanza, and let the couch put him to sleep.

Carver was supposed to remain in hypersleep until rendezvous with Mr. Kanza's scow, but he'd managed to reprogram the couch while prepping the tug. It woke him twelve hours early, four million kilometers out from Sheffield.

The !Cha's tank was still inside the escape pod, the pod was still sealed in the cargo bay, and the tug was exactly on course, falling ass-backward toward the gas giant. In a little over two hours, it would skim through the outer atmosphere in a fuel-saving aerobraking maneuver; meanwhile, the bulk of the planet lay between it and the Ganesh Five facility and Mr. Kanza's scow.

Carver had less than an hour before Mr. Kanza regained radio contact with the tug. While the tug's triumvirate of AIs threatened dire punishments Mr. Kanza had not trusted them to carry out, Carver climbed into his pressure suit, blew open the locked hatch using its explosive bolts, hauled himself to the cargo bay, and took just under fifteen minutes to rig a bypass and crank it open and slide inside.

He'd dropped a tab of military-grade amphetamine (it had cost him fifty days' pocket money), but he was still weak from the aftereffects of hypersleep, dopey, chilled to the bone. It took all his concentration to plug into the external port of the escape pod, scroll down the menu that lit up inside his visor, and hit the command that would open the hatch.

Nothing happened.

Carver knew then that the !Cha was awake; it must have locked the hatch from the inside. He was crouched on top of the escape pod in the wash of the gas giant's corpse light with nowhere else to go. Blowing the hatch had compromised the tug's integrity; if it plowed into Sheffield's upper atmosphere, it would break up. And in less than thirty minutes, it would reestablish contact with Mr. Kanza's scow. Mr. Kanza would have to alter the tug's course to save it, and then he would torture Carver until Carver's air supply ran out. So Carver did the only thing he could do: he opened all the com channels and started talking. He told the !Cha who he was, told it about Mr. Kanza and Lieutenant Rider, explained why he needed its help. He talked for ten minutes straight, and then a flat mechanical voice said, "Tell me exactly what you plan to do."

Relief washed clean through Carver, but he knew that he was not saved yet. With the feeling that he was tiptoeing over very thin ice, he said, "I plan to keep us both out of Mr. Kanza's clutches. I'd like to surrender to the Navy, but Mr. Kanza partnered up with an officer in the garrison here, so our only chance is to escape through one of the wormholes."

"But you do not have command of the tug."

"I don't need it."

Another pause. Then the flat voice said, "You have my interest."

Carver explained that the escape pod's motor was small but fully fueled, that with the tug's delta vee and a little extra assist it should be able to get them where they needed to go.

"I hope you understand that I'm not going to give you the flight plan. You'll have to trust me."

"You are afraid that I killed Dr. Smith. You are afraid that I will kill you, if I know the details of your plan."

"It crossed my mind, but you're a better bet than my owner."

"If I wanted you dead, I would not need to do it myself. Your owner will do that for me."

Carver wondered if that was an attempt at humor. "He'll kill both of us."

"He will not kill me if he believes that I have something he wants."

"If you do have something, he'll kill you and take it. And if you don't, he'll kill you anyway."

Carver sweated out another pause. Then, with a grinding vibration he felt through his pressure suit, the hatch of the escape pod opened.

Carver powered up the pod's systems, moved it out of the cargo bay, and adjusted its trim with a few puffs of the attitude jets, then fired up its motor. Ten minutes later, the tiny star of the dock facility dawned beyond the crescent and rings of the gas giant. The comm beeped. Mr. Kanza said, "That won't do you any good, you son of a whore."

"Watch and learn," Carver said.

"Listen to me carefully. If you don't do exactly as I say, your brother is a dead man."

"My brother was killed in action, along with everyone else on his ship."

Carver had control of the escape pod and was out of range of the shock stick hidden on the tug: he could say whatever he liked to Mr. Kanza. It was a good feeling. When Mr. Kanza started to rage at him, Carver told him that he was going to have to find some other way of covering his debts, and cut him off.

Far behind the pod, the tug lit its motor; no doubt Mr. Kanza was flying it by wire, hoping either to bring it close enough to use the shock stick on Carver, or ram him. He told Useless Beauty that if whatever it had found at the brown dwarf could be used as a weapon, now was the time to let him know.

"And don't tell me that you didn't find anything: there's no longer a neutrino source in that strange storm. You fished out some kind of Elder Culture artifact, and it did a number on your ship."

"One of the Elder Cultures may have had something to do with it," Useless Beauty said, "but it was not an artifact."

The squat black cylinder of its tank was jammed into the space between the two acceleration couches, three pairs of limbs folded up in a way that reminded Carver of a praying mantis. He tried to picture what was inside, a cross between a squid and a starfish swimming in oily, ammonia-rich water, the tough, nerve-rich tubules that ordinarily connected it to puppet juveniles plugged into the systems of its casing. It was even harder to picture what it was thinking, but Carver was pretty sure that his survival was at the bottom of its list of priorities.

He said, "If it wasn't an artifact, a machine or whatever, what was it?"

"A mathematical singularity from a universe where the laws and constants of nature are very different from ours. A little like the software of your computers, but alive, self-aware, and imbued with a strong survival instinct. Perhaps an Elder Culture brought it through a kind of wormhole between its universe and ours. Perhaps it is a traveler unable to find its way home. In any event, it was trapped within the brown dwarf, and created the storm by epitaxy—using its own form as a template to make something approximating the conditions of its home, just as my tank contains a small portion of the ocean where my species evolved. Dr. Smith and I were able to capture it, but it broke free after we brought it aboard our ship. At once, it began to consume the structure of the ship. Dr. Smith went outside and successfully cut it away, but by then the fusion motor had been badly damaged, and it began to overheat. When Dr. Smith attempted to repair it, the cooling system exploded, and ruptured her suit. She died before she could get back inside, and I was forced to use the escape pod. I got away only a few minutes before the ship was destroyed."

"What happened to the thing you found?"

"If the neutrino flux is no longer detectable, I must assume that it was unable to return to the brown dwarf. Without a sufficient concentration of matter to weave a suitable habitat around itself," Useless Beauty said, "it would have evaporated."

It was a good story, and Carver believed about half it. He was pretty certain that the !Cha and Dr. Smith had captured something, Elder Culture artifact, weird mathematics, and that it had begun to destroy or transform their ship—it would explain why the composition of the thread Carver had found wrapped around Dr. Smith's arm didn't match anything in the library of the ship's lab—but Carver was pretty sure that Dr. Smith hadn't died in some kind of accident. It was more likely that Useless Beauty had murdered her because it wanted to keep what they'd found to itself and that prize was hidden somewhere inside its tank. But because he needed the !Cha's help—the casing of its tank was tougher than diamond, and its limbs were equipped with all kinds of gnarly tools, trying to fight it would be like going head to head with a battle drone—he didn't give voice to his doubts, said that it was a damn shame about losing Dr. Smith and the ship, he hoped to bring it better luck.

Useless Beauty did not reply, and its silence stretched as the escape pod hurtled toward Sheffield's ring system. Carver sipped sweetened apple pulp, watched the tug grow closer, watched the scow change course, half a million kilometers ahead, watched his own track on the navigational plot. He wasn't a pilot, but he knew his math, and his plan depended on nothing more complicated than ordinary Newtonian mechanics, a straightforward balance between gravity and distance and time and delta vee.

That's what he tried to tell himself, anyhow.

The rings filled the sky ahead, dozens of pale, parallel arcs hundreds of kilometers across, separated by gaps of varying widths. At T minus ten seconds, Carver handed control to the pod's AI. It lit the pod's motor at exactly T0. Two seconds later, the comm beeped: another message from Mr. Kanza.

Carver ignored it.

The tug was changing course too, but Carver was almost on the ring system now, falling toward a particular gap he'd chosen with the help of the escape pod's navigational system. He watched it with all of his concentration—he was finding it hard to believe in Newtonian mechanics now his life depended on it.

But there it was, at the edge of one of the arcs of ice and dust: a tiny grain flashing in raw sunlight: a shepherd moon. In less than a minute, it resolved into a pebble, a boulder, a pitted siding of dirty ice. As it flashed past, the pod's AI lit the motor again. The brief blip of acceleration and the momentum the pod had stolen from the moon made a small change in its delta vee; as it swung around the gas giant, the difference between the trajectory of the pod and the tug widened perceptibly.

The tug didn't have enough fuel to catch up with the pod now, but beyond Sheffield, Mr. Kanza's scow was changing course, and a few minutes later, a Navy cutter shot away from the dock facility, and the comm channels were suddenly alive with chatter: the salvage company's gigs and tugs; a couple of ships in transit between the wormholes; the Navy garrison, ordering both Mr. Kanza and Carver White to stand to and await interception.

Carver couldn't obey even if he wanted to. Less than a quarter of the pod's fuel remained and it was traveling very fast now, boosted by the slingshot through Sheffield's steep gravity well. With Mr. Kanza's scow and the Navy cutter in pursuit, it hurtled toward one of the wormhole throats. Carver had no doubt that the scow would follow him through, but he believed he had enough of an edge to make it to where he wanted to go, especially now that the Navy was involved. Someone in the garrison must have discovered Rider Jackson's deal with Mr. Kanza, and that meant the cutter would be more likely to try to stop Mr. Kanza's scow first.

The wormhole throat was a round dark mirror just over a kilometer across, twinkling with photons emitted by asymmetrical pair decay, framed by a chunky ring that housed the braid of strange matter that kept the throat open, all this embedded in the flat end of a chunk of rock that had been sculpted to a smooth cone by the nameless Elder Culture that had built the wormhole network a couple of million years ago. The pod hit it dead center, the radio chatter cut off, light flared, and the pod emerged halfway around the galaxy, above a planet shrouded in dense white clouds, shining pitilessly bright in the glare of a giant F5 star.

The planet, Texas IX, had a hot, dense, runaway greenhouse atmosphere—even Useless Beauty's tank could not have survived long in the searing storms that scoured its surface—but it also had a single moon that had been planoformed by Boxbuilders. That was where Carver wanted to go. He took back control of the pod and reconfigured it, extending wide braking surfaces of tough polycarbon, and lit the motor. It was a risky maneuver—if the angle of attack was too shallow, the pod would skip away into deep space with no hope of return, and if it was too steep, the pod would burn up—but aerobraking was the only way he could shed enough velocity.

Like a match scratching a tiny flare across a wall of white marble, the pod cut a chord above Texas IX's cloud tops. Carver was buffeted by vibration and pinned to the couch by deceleration that peaked at eight gees. He screamed into the vast shuddering noise; screamed with exhilaration and fear. Useless Beauty maintained its unsettling silence. Then the flames that filled the forward cameras died back and the pod rose above the planet's nightside.

The stars came out, all at once.

Useless Beauty's affectless voice said, "That was interesting."

"We aren't down yet," Carver said. He was grinning like a fool. He believed that the worst was over.

The escape pod fell away from Texas IX, heading out toward its moon. It was almost there when Mr. Kanza's scow overtook it.

Soon after it had formed, while its core had been still molten, something big had smashed into Texas IX's solitary moon. It had excavated a wide, deep basin in one side of the moon, and seismic waves traveling through the crust and core had focused on the area antipodal to the impact, jostling and lifting the surface, breaking crater rims and intercrater areas into a vast maze of hills and valleys, opening vents that flooded crater floors with fresh lava. That was where the escape pod came down, a thousand kilometers from the moon's only settlement, a hundred or so hardscrabble ranches strung along the shore of a shallow, hypersaline sea.

The scow, shooting past at a relative velocity of twenty klicks per second, had cooked the pod with a microwave burst, killing the pod's AI and crippling most of its control systems. Although the pod's aerobraking surfaces gave Carver a little leeway as it plowed through the moon's thin atmosphere, it smashed down hard and skidded a long way across a lava plain; despite the web holding Carver to the couch and the impact foam that flooded the pod's interior, he was knocked unconscious.

When he came around a few minutes later, the pod was canted at a steep angle, the hatch was open, and Useless Beauty was gone. Carver was bruised over most of his body and his nose was tender and bleeding, possibly broken, but he was not badly hurt. He clawed his way through dissolving strands of impact foam and clambered out of the hatch, discovered that the pod lay at the end of a long furrow, its skin scarred, scraped, and discolored, and radiating an intense heat he could feel through his pressure suit. Big patches of spindly desert vegetation burned briskly on either side, lofting long reefs of smoke into the white sky.

Useless Beauty's tank stood on top of a ridge of overturned dirt, its black cylinder balanced on four many-jointed legs, two more limbs raised as if in prayer toward the sky. Carver was surprised and grateful to see it; he'd thought that the !Cha had taken the opportunity to make a run for it.

"This is only a brief respite," Useless Beauty said, as Carver clambered up the ridge. "Your owner's ship has swung far beyond this moon, but it is braking hard. It will soon be back."

"Then we can't stay here," Carver said. "We have to find a place to hide out until someone from the settlement comes to investigate."

The tank's two upper limbs swung down, aiming clusters of tools and sensors straight at Carver, and Useless Beauty said, "This is the part of your plan that I do not understand. This moon is owned by the Collective. You are a runaway slave. Surely they will side with your master. And if they do not, they will claim you for themselves."

Here it was. Carver took a breath and said, "Not if you claim me first."

After a short pause, Useless Beauty said, "So that is why you needed me."

"As we say in the Alliance, one good turn deserves another. I rescued you; now it's your turn to rescue me."

Throwing himself on the mercy of the !Cha was the biggest risk of the whole enterprise. Carver had never felt so scared and alone as he did then, waiting out another of Useless Beauty's silences while hot sunlight beat down through drifts of smoke, and Mr. Kanza's scow grew closer somewhere on the other side of the sky.

At last, the !Cha said, "You are very persistent."

"Does that mean you'll help me?"

"I admit that I want to see what happens next."

Carver supposed that he would have to take that as a "yes." Low hills shimmered in the middle distance. The ruins of a Boxbuilder city were scattered across their sere slopes like so many strings of beads. He pointed at the ruins and said, "As soon as I've gotten rid of this pressure suit, we start walking."

The !Cha's four-legged cylinder moved with easy grace through the simmering desert. Carver, wearing only his suit liner and boots, a pouch of water slung over his shoulder, had to jog to keep up. The air was thin, and the fat sun beat down mercilessly, but he reveled in the feeling of the sun's heat on his skin and dry wind in his hair, in the glare of the harsh landscape. Everything seemed infinitely precious, a chain of diamond-sharp moments. He had never before felt so alive as he did then, with death so close at his heels.

As Carver and the !Cha climbed toward a ravine that snaked between interlocking ridges, a double sonic boom cracked across the sky. The scow had arrived. But Carver wasn't ready to give up yet, and there were plenty of places to hide in the ruins. Chains of hollow cubes spun from polymer and rock dust climbed the slopes on either side, piled on top of each other, running along ridges, bridging narrow valleys: a formidable labyrinth with thousands of nooks and crannies that led deep into the hills, where he and Useless Beauty could hide out until some sort of rescue party arrived from the colony. For a little while, he began to believe that his plan might work, but then he and the !Cha reached the end of a chain of cubes at the top of a ridge, and found Rider Jackson waiting for them.

The young officer put his pistol on Carver and said, "You led us a pretty good chase, but you forgot one thing."

He was wearing a black Navy flight suit with a big zip down the front and pockets patching the chest and legs; that know-everything-tell-nothing expression blanked his face.

"I did?"

"You forgot you're an indentured worker. Your Judas bridge led me straight to you. Your owner will be here as soon as he can find a place to park his ship. I reckon you've got just enough time to tell me your side of the story."

While the scow lowered toward a setback below the ridge, Carver told Rider Jackson more or less everything that had happened out at the brown dwarf. Rider Jackson knew most of it, of course, because he'd seen the footage and data the tug had sent to Mr. Kanza, but he listened patiently and said, when Carver was finished, "I didn't know he was lying about your brother. If I had, I would have put an end to this a lot sooner."

"He was probably lying about a lot of things."

"Like giving me a fifty percent share in the prize, uh?"

"Like giving you any share at all."

"You might well be right," Rider Jackson said, and looked for the first time at Useless Beauty's tank. "Care to explain why you came along for the ride?"

"I have nothing to give you," it said.

"I bet you don't. But that wasn't what I asked," Rider Jackson said, and that was when Mr. Kanza arrived.

Grim and angry and out of breath, he bulled straight across the roof-less cube and stuck his shock stick in Carver's face. Carver couldn't help flinching and Mr. Kanza smiled and said, "Tell me what the !Cha found and where it is, and maybe I won't have to use this."

Rider Jackson said, "There's no point threatening him. You want to know the truth, figure out how to get the !Cha to talk straight."

Mr. Kanza stepped back from Carver and aimed the shock stick at Rider Jackson. "You were indentured once, just like him. Is that why you're taking his side? I knew it was a mistake to let you go chase him down."

"You could have come with me," Rider Jackson said, "but you were happy to let me take the risk."

"He told you. He told you what that thing found and you made a deal with him."

"You're making a bad mistake."

The two men were staring at each other, Rider Jackson impassive, Mr. Kanza angry and sweating. Saying, "I bet you tasted the stick in your time. You'll taste it again if you don't drop that pistol."

Rider Jackson said, "I guess we aren't partners anymore."

"You're right," Mr. Kanza said, and zapped him.

Carver was caught by the edge of the stick's field. His Judas bridge kicked in, his muscles went into spasm, hot spikes hammered through his skull, and he fell straight down.

Rider Jackson didn't so much as twitch. He put his pistol on Mr. Kanza and said, "The Navy took out my bridge when I signed up. Set down that stick and your pistol, and I'll let you walk away."

"We're partners."

"You said it yourself: not anymore. If you start walking now, maybe you can find somewhere to hide before the cutter turns up."

Mr. Kanza screamed and threw the shock stick at Rider Jackson and made a grab for the pistol stuck in his utility belt. Rider Jackson shot him. He shot Mr. Kanza twice in the chest and the man sat down, winded and dazed but still alive: his pressure suit had stopped the flechettes. He groped for his pistol and Rider Jackson said, "Don't do it."

"Fuck you," Mr. Kanza said and jerked up his pistol and fired it wildly. Rider Jackson didn't flinch. He took careful aim and shot Mr. Kanza in the head, and the man fell sideways and lay still.

Rider Jackson turned and put his pistol on Useless Beauty's black cylinder and said calmly, "I don't suppose this can punch through your casing, but I could shoot off your limbs one by one and set you on a fire."

There was a brief silence. Then the !Cha said, "You will need a very hot fire, and much more time than you have."

"I have more time than you think," Rider Jackson said. "I know Dana Sabah, the woman flying that cutter. She's a good pilot, but she's inexperienced and too cautious. Right now, she'll be watching us from orbit, waiting to see how it plays out before she makes her move."

"If she does not come, then the settlers will rescue me."

"Uh-uh. Even if the settlers know about us, which I doubt, Dana will have told them to back off. I reckon I have more than enough time to boil the truth out of you."

Useless Beauty said, "I have already told the truth."

Carver got to his feet and told Rider Jackson, "It doesn't matter if it's telling the truth or not. All that matters is that we can escape in the scow. But first, I want you to drop your pistol."

Rider Jackson looked at the pistol Carver was holding—Mr. Kanza's pistol—and said, "I wondered if you'd have the guts to pick it up. The question now is, do you have the guts to use it?"

"If I have to."

"Look at us," Rider Jackson said. "I'm an officer in the Collective Navy; you're a prisoner of war sold into slavery, trying to get home . . . We could fight a duel to see who gets the scow. It would make a good ending to the story, wouldn't it?"

Carver smiled and said, "It would, but this isn't a story."

"Of course it's a story. Do you know why !Cha risk their lives chasing after Elder Culture artifacts?"

"It's something to do with sex."

"That's it. Back in the oceans of their homeworld, male !Cha constructed elaborate nests to attract a mate. The strongest, those most likely to produce the fittest offspring, made the biggest and most elaborate nests. Simple, straight-ahead Darwinism. The !Cha left their homeworld a long time ago, but the males still have to prove their worth by finding something novel, something no other male has. They have a bad jones for Elder Culture junk, but these days they get a lot of useful stuff from us too."

"It's lying about what it found," Carver said. "It told me it lost it, but I know it has it hidden away inside that tank."

Rider Jackson shook his head. "If it still had it, it would have killed you and paid off Mr. Kanza. And it wouldn't have called up the garrison back at Ganesh Five."

"It did? Is that why the cutter came after us?"

"Why do you think traffic control spotted you so quickly? It told them what you were up to, and it told them all about my deal with Mr. Kanza too. Dana Sabah told me all about it when she tried to get me to surrender," Rider Jackson said. "I guess our friend thought that involving the Navy would make the story more exciting."

"Son of a bitch. And I thought it was on my side because it owes me its life."

"As far as it's concerned, it doesn't owe you anything. The only reason it stuck with you is because you have something it needs. Something as unique as any ancient artifact, something it believes will win it a mate: the story of how you tried to escape."

"Your own story is just as good, Lieutenant Jackson," Useless Beauty said. "The two of you are enemies, as you said. Fight your duel. The winner will take me with him—I will pay well for it."

Rider Jackson looked at Carver and smiled. "What do you think?"

"I think the war is over." Carver was smiling too, remembering something Jarred had said. That peace was harder work than war, but more worthwhile.

Useless Beauty said, "I do not understand. You are enemies."

Rider Jackson stuck his pistol in his belt. "Like he said, the war is over. Besides, we both want the same thing."

Carver lowered the pistol he'd taken off Mr. Kanza's body and told the !Cha, "You're like Mr. Kanza. You think you own us, but you don't understand us."

"You must take me with you," Useless Beauty said.

"It wants to find out how the story ends," Rider Jackson told Carver.

"I will pay you well," Useless Beauty said.

Carver shook his head. "We don't need your money. We have the scow, and I have about thirty meters of a weird thread I took off Dr. Smith's body. It's superconducting and very strong, and I can't help wondering if it's something you and her pulled out of Ganesh Five B."

"I told you the truth about what we found," Useless Beauty said. "It escaped us and destroyed our ship, but it did not survive. However, I admit this thread may be of interest. I must examine it, of course, but if it is material transformed during the destruction of the ship, I may be willing to purchase it."

"That's what I thought," Carver said. "It may not be an Elder Culture artifact, but it could be worth something. And maybe the data from the probes I dropped into Ganesh Five B might be worth something too."

"I may be willing to purchase that too," Useless Beauty said. "As a souvenir."

"What do you think?" Carver said to Rider Jackson. "Think we'll get a better price on the open market."

"I can force you to take me," Useless Beauty said.

"No you can't," Carver said.

"And even if you could, it would ruin the ending of your story," Rider Jackson said. "I'm sure the settlers or the Navy will rescue you, for a price."

There was a long moment of silence. Then Useless Beauty said, "I would like to know what happens after you escape. I will pay well."

"If we escape," Carver said. "We have to get past the cutter."

"Dana Sabah's a good pilot, but I'm better," Rider Jackson said. "I reckon you are too."

"Before we do this, we need to work out where we're going."

"That's pretty easy, given that you're an indentured worker and the Navy wants my ass. Think that Kanza's old boat will get us to the Alliance?"

"It just might."

The two men grinned at each other. Then they ran for the scow.

Ann Leckie is the author of the Hugo, Nebula, and Arthur C. Clarke Award winning novel *Ancillary Justice*. She has also published short stories in *Subterranean Magazine, Strange Horizons,* and *Realms of Fantasy.* Her story "Hesperia and Glory" was reprinted in *Science Fiction: The Best of the Year, 2007 Edition* edited by Rich Horton.

Ann has worked as a waitress, a receptionist, a rodman on a land-surveying crew, and a recording engineer. She lives in St. Louis, Missouri.

# NIGHT'S SLOW POISON

## *Ann Leckie*

The *Jewel of Athat* was mainly a cargo ship, and most spaces were narrow and cramped. Like the Outer Station, where it was docked, it was austere, its decks and bulkheads scuffed and dingy with age. Inarakhat Kels, armed, and properly masked, had already turned away one passenger, and now he stood in the passageway that led from the station to the ship, awaiting the next.

The man approached, striding as though the confined space did not constrain him. He wore a kilt and embroidered blouse. His skin was light brown, his hair dark and straight, cut short. And his eyes . . . Inarakhat Kels felt abashed. He had thought that in his years of dealing with outsiders he had lost his squeamishness at looking strangers in the face.

The man glanced over his shoulder, and cocked an eyebrow. "She was angry." The corners of his mouth twitched in a suppressed grin.

"One regrets." Inarakhat Kels frowned behind his mask. "Who?"

"The woman in line before me. I take it you refused to let her board?"

"She carried undeclared communication implants." Privately, Kels suspected her of being a spy for the Radchaai, but he did not say this. "One is, of course, most sorry for her inconvenience, but . . . "

"I'm not," the man interrupted. "She nearly ruined my supper last night insisting that I give up my seat, since she was certain she was of a higher caste than I."

"Did you?"

"I did not," said the man. "I am not from Xum, nor are we anywhere near it, so why should I bow to their customs? And then this morning she shoved herself in front of me as we waited outside." He grinned fully. "I confess myself relieved at not having to spend six months with her as a fellow passenger."

"Ah," Kels said, his voice noncommittal. The grin, the angle of the man's jaw—now he understood why the eyes had affected him. But he had no time for old memories. He consulted his list. "You are Awt Emnys, from the Gerentate." The man acknowledged this. "Your reason for visiting Ghaon?"

"My grandmother was Ghaonish," Awt Emnys said, eyes sober that had previously been amused. "I never knew her, and no one can tell me much about her. I hope to learn more in Athat."

Whoever she was, she had been from the Ghem agnate, Kels was certain. His eyes, his mouth, the line of his chin . . . With just a little more information, Kels could tell Awt which house his grandmother had been born in. "One wishes you good fortune in your search, Honored Awt," he said, with a small bow he could not suppress.

Awt Emnys smiled in return, and bowed respectfully. "I thank you, Honored," he said. "I understand I must disable any communications implants."

"If they are re-activated during the voyage, we will take any steps necessary to preserve the safety of the ship."

Awt glanced at the gun at Kels' waist. "Of course. But is it really so dangerous?"

"About three months in," said Kels, in his blandest voice, "we will pass the last ship that attempted to traverse the Crawl with live communications. It will be visible from the passengers' lounge."

Awt grinned. "I have an abiding wish to die old, in my bed. Preferably after a long and boring life tracking warehouse inventories."

Kels allowed himself a small smile. "One wishes you success," he said, and stepped aside, pressing against the wall so that Awt could pass him. "Your belongings will be delivered to your cabin."

"I thank you, Honored." Awt brushed Kels as he passed, awakening some unfamiliar emotion in him.

"Good voyage," Kels murmured to the other man's back, but there was no sign Awt had heard.

Ghaon is a moonless blue and white jewel orbiting a yellow sun. Its three continents provide every sort of terrain, from the great deserts of southern Lysire, and the rivers and gentle farmlands of the north and west of that same continent, to the mountains of Aneng, still fitfully smoking. Arim, the third continent, is arctic and uninhabited. Aside from the sorts of industry and agriculture that support the population of any world, Ghaon produces pearls and ingeniously carved corals, which, when they find their way outside the Crawl, are highly valued. Flutes carved from the wood of Aneng's western forests are prized by Gerentate musicians.

According to legend, the first inhabitants of Ghaon came from a world called Walkaway, the location of which is unknown. There were thirteen original settlers, three agnates of four people each plus one eunuch priest of Iraon. The three agnates parceled out the world among themselves: Lysire, Aneng, and the surface of the sea. The priest blessed the division, and each agnate prospered and filled the world.

The legend is only that, of course. It is impossible that thirteen people would possess the genetic diversity required to populate a planet, and in any case studies show that the first human inhabitants of Ghaon, whose descendants now populate Lysire and Aneng, derived largely from the same populations that eventually made up much of the Gerentate. The ancestors of the sea-going agnates arrived several thousand years later, and their origins are obscure.

In any case, the first colonists must have either known about the Crawl before they arrived, or constructed it themselves. The latter seems staggeringly unlikely.

Gerentate explorers found Ghaon some years after that entity's expansionist phase had run itself out, and so the only threat they presented was a trickle of ill-bred, bare-faced tourists.

But the Radch was another matter. Every soul on Ghaon, from the smallest infant at the breast to the most ancient Lysire matriarch in her tent on the edge of the drylands, believed that the nefarious Anaander Mianaai, overlord of the Radch, had cast a covetous eye on Ghaon and contemplated how he might make it his own.

Fortunately enough, the ships and seemingly endless armies of the Radch, which had been the downfall of a thousand worlds and stations, could not traverse the Crawl. Only it stood between Ghaon and the Radchaai. Spies regularly probed this defense, the Ghaonish were certain, and the acquisitive minds of the Radchaai continually planned and plotted how best to breach it.

In vain did more sober minds point out that the worlds of the Gerentate were a larger and in some ways easier target, that the reward for defeating the Crawl was far outweighed by the difficulty of the task, that the sweeping ambition of the Radchaai could hardly notice this one, small, somewhat obscure world. The people of Ghaon knew these arguments were specious. The overlord of the Radch had set his mind on acquiring Ghaon—so its inhabitants believed.

Third watch was on duty, guarding the pilot's station and pacing the corridors of the *Jewel of Athat*. First watch was asleep. Second watch had finished their supper, and the small table held cups of tea and the remains of the bread. Inarakhat Kels leaned forward, elbows on the table. Ninan and Tris, his fellows on second watch, leaned against the bulkhead.

"A spy!" said Ninan, trying not to sound jealous. "Well, we were about due for another one." He leaned an elbow companionably on the table beside Kels'.

"How is it," asked Tris, "that their attempts are so obvious, and yet the Radchaai are so rich and powerful?"

"They are naturally perverse." Ninan picked up a teacup and peered at its contents.

"So one imagines," said Kels. "In any case, Anaander Mianaai must find some other way to pass the Crawl."

Tris grinned, teeth showing beneath the mask that covered his upper face. "And the others? What do we have to look forward to this time?"

"Chis Sulca," said Kels. He leaned back, feeling crowded by Ninan. They knew the Ghaonish merchant from previous trips. "A few others." He thought of Awt Emnys. "The usual sort. A tourist from Semblance." Ninan and Tris each made derisive noises. "A Faunt clanswoman on her wander. A young man from the Gerentate."

"Another tourist," groaned Ninan.

"No!" said Tris, half-laughing. "I spoke to that one. He's searching for his Ghaonish grandmother!"

Ninan laughed. "He'll find some runaway or some whore was his ancestress, and to what end?"

"Whoever she was, her grandson has money and time to indulge his curiosity," said Kels, stung.

Ninan shook his head in disapproval. "He expects to find some ancient, noble agnate, whose matriarch will acknowledge him as her cousin."

Tris nodded. "He'll hang an overpriced, tasteless mask on his wall and brag to his neighbors about his exotic and aristocratic blood."

"What if his blood truly is aristocratic?" asked Kels, knowing what the other two did not know. The Ghem agnate was among the most ancient, most prestigious of families. He reached forward, poured himself more tea.

"It hardly matters," said Ninan. "No agnate would be pleased to find a barefaced brute on the doorstep."

Under the mask Kels' eyes narrowed. "He can hardly be blamed for the customs of his people," he said in his most even voice.

Ninan turned to regard him more closely. "No doubt."

"It's been a long day," said Tris, conciliatory. "And Inarakhat has spent it dealing with passengers. But now we rest, at least until tomorrow."

"And a dull tomorrow it will be," said Ninan. "For which, thank Iraon."

"Thank Iraon," Tris and Kels echoed in agreement.

Ghem Echend was the most beautiful girl Inarakhat Kels had ever seen. Echend's mouth was firm and full, her skin a warm dark brown. Her hands were square, and strong, and graceful, as were all her movements. She seemed to laugh even when she merely spoke. But her chief beauty was her eyes, wide and gray and luminous. She never took to the fashion for masks that obscured them. Indeed, she had skirted the outer edge of acceptability, preferring masks that exposed and emphasized her eyes as much as possible.

She had kissed him on a moss-covered hillside by the river. The summer stars had been thick and silver in the sky, no other lights but the city below, and the boats passing, colored lanterns hanging in their masts, red and blue and green and gold. She tasted of flowers. It seemed to him that his heart stopped, and everything bled away from his awareness but her. He lifted a hand to touch her cheek, hardly able to believe his daring. She kissed him again, and taking that for approval he placed a single finger tentatively on the lower edge of her mask.

With both hands she shoved him hard in the chest, and he found himself lying on his back in the soft moss, with only the stars in his vision. "Not yet," she said, and ran away laughing.

He could hardly breathe with happiness. Not yet!

Never.

Within six months, the extent of his agnate's debts had been revealed, as well as the lengths to which his aunts had been willing to go to support their lifestyle, which had been beyond their means for quite some time.

When the expected letter, sealed in red and gold, had arrived, it had contained not an offer of marriage but a few curt lines informing him that if recently certain expectations had been raised, they were unfounded and it would be best if he realized this. It was not from Echend, but from the matriarch of her agnate.

He had stuffed a single change of clothes into a sack and gone down to the docks intending to offer his labor to whatever ship would take him farthest away from Athat. No ship would have him, so he made his way to the precinct employment bureau, where the civil servant on duty had judged him a fit candidate for the Watch. Next morning he was on a shuttle for Ghaon's orbiting station. He had not set foot on Ghaon since.

The Crawl is not detectable by sight, nor by any scanner yet devised. It is, however, ineluctably there. Its outer boundary is littered with the wrecks of ships whose captains disbelieved the warnings. Sometimes these are whole ships, with no sign of damage except their aimless drift. Some are collections of fragments, shining eerily in the light of the warning beacons placed at intervals along the limits of the Crawl. Occasionally a ship traversing the Crawl will come across a human body, rigid and frozen, spinning in the vacuum.

In order to survive the passage through the Crawl a ship must go slowly; it takes nearly six months. In another system it would be a matter of hours. And it is well known that the use of communications equipment within the Crawl has disastrous results.

It is less well known that the Crawl may only be safely crossed by particular routes, which the Ghaons had not recorded or marked in any way. Careful of their one defense, they had been at pains to be sure that knowledge existed only in the minds of pilots authorized to make the trip. The Watch was founded not only to prevent spies from boarding the ships and to enforce the ban on communication, but to ensure that no one meddled in any way with the pilot.

The lounge on second deck was small and narrow, a few tables and chairs along the wall on one side, ports for viewing on the other. Two travelers, one in the brightly-dyed, draped robe typical of the world Semblance, the other bare breasted and skirted in ochre, sat at one table, hunched over a game board, scooping counters out of hollows and placing them around, quickly, with a quiet word every few moves. At the other end of the space Awt Emnys stood, looking out on the void. His face was shadowed, a matter of both relief and disappointment to Kels.

The eyes were Ghem Echend's. He could not have been more certain if the two genotypes were laid out before him. Echend had not been Awt Emnys' grandmother, but certainly some aunt or cousin of hers had left Ghaon, gone to the Gerentate.

If Kels had married Echend, he would have had children. Or his co-husbands would, it was all the same. For the first time in years he allowed himself to wonder what that would have been like. He couldn't imagine an infant Awt with any clarity, but the dark-haired, gray-eyed young boy . . . a memory flowered in his mind, Kels and his father (so very tall and imposing then!) walking hand in hand down to the riverbank to see the boats come in.

Awt Emnys turned his head, displacing the shadows. He smiled as he saw Kels. "It's you again."

"One is always oneself," said Kels, unaccountably disturbed by the younger man's words.

"But you're not always on duty," said Awt, and came closer to where Kels stood at the other end of the viewing ports. "You all wear the same clothes, and the same masks, and I'm never quite sure who is who." He smiled, slightly, made an apologetic gesture. "I was speaking with the Honored merchant Chis," he said, as though it followed naturally on his previous words. "She is most gracious. She advises me to give up pursuing my ancestor and instead rent a boat and visit the coastal towns of Western Aneng, where she assures me I will find the most exquisitely beautiful scenery in all known space. Not to mention the finest arrak and the most reasonable prices on cultured pearls."

"Ah," said Kels, somewhat disdainfully. "She is from Western Aneng, and biased as a result. All of those are to be found in the vicinity of Athat."

Awt gave a wry smile. "I suspect her intent is to divert me from embarrassing my grandmother's agnate with my existence. But you advise me to tour Athat?"

"Certainly." Athat was the loveliest city on Ghaon, spread over the mouth of the river like an exquisite mask. "There is also a forest preserve, to the south of Athat, that you may be interested in visiting. Though," he said, frowning, thinking of Awt's luggage, "you may need to purchase some equipment if you intend to stay there long."

"I rarely camp on worlds I'm not entirely familiar with."

"Doubtless a wise policy. One would not advise doing so alone, anywhere on Ghaon."

"And why is that, Honored?" asked Awt.

"The vondas."

"Vondas?"

"They range from very small to . . . " Kels made a wide and shallow cup of his hands. "This large. With the tiny, common ones, a bite will itch for a few days afterwards. Some of the larger ones may affect a person more. Indeed, some of them are in demand for the intoxicating effects of their venom." He thought of the vonda-bars in the northern precincts of the city and made a soft, disgusted sound. "One doesn't recommend it. But the one you should be careful of is the tea vonda."

"It's dangerous?"

"It's called a tea vonda because from the moment it fastens itself on you, you have just enough time to prepare and drink a cup of tea before you die."

Awt raised an eyebrow. "That is, perhaps, not the wisest way to spend those few minutes. Have you ever encountered one?"

"I was bitten," said Kels. He had been fifteen, and his uncle had been to the market in Athat and bought a basket of berries and left them on a counter in the kitchen that ran long and narrow across the back of the house. The berries were at the height of their season, huge and dark purple, and when Kels had seen them he had reached out without thinking. Almost before his fingers had touched the fruit he'd felt an icy sting.

"What did you do?" asked Awt Emnys. "Not put water on to boil I presume."

"I panicked," said Kels. For a few, blinking moments he'd stood trying to understand what had happened, coldness creeping up his hand towards his wrist, and then his mind had registered the tea vonda fastened to his hand, berry-purple bleeding away from it. Its center was dead white, shot with streaks of silver. Its surrounding membrane pulsed and fluttered, the convoluted edges turning pink and then red as it dug its proboscis deeper into his hand. As he watched, his hand went numb, and the ice continued to inch past his wrist towards his elbow. He tried to scream, but no sound would issue from his throat. "I froze."

"What should you have done?" asked Awt Emnys.

"I should have taken the largest knife in the kitchen and cut off my hand." And he'd thought that far, had run along the length of the room to open the cabinet and draw out the knife, heavy-handled, with a blade three inches wide and fifteen inches long. Then he stood there unable to do what needed to be done, no coherent thought settling out of the whirl of fear and panic in his mind. His sister came into the kitchen then. She closed the distance between them at a dead run, grabbed the knife out of his hand and shoved him against the counter. Then, as though she were dressing game for a feast, she jerked his arm straight and swung the knife down in a fierce blow, crunching through bone and severing his arm just below the shoulder.

*Then* he'd screamed.

"What happened?" asked Awt.

"My sister found me and cut my arm off. It was very fortunate. I had been very foolish."

"Indeed." The skirted woman, from Faunt, spoke up. "Had I been your sister I would have left you to die."

"Come now, Honored," said her opponent. "Surely not. Anyone might panic in such a situation."

"Not anyone fit to survive," said the woman, with a curled lip. "It speaks poorly of the Watch that such a one would be selected."

"Surely your people would not be so cruel," said the man. "Surely not."

"Cruel? We are practical," she replied.

"I can't blame him," said Awt Emnys. "It's easy enough to tell yourself the doctor can replace it, but when it comes to actually doing it . . . " He shook his head. "It only makes sense that we should be reluctant to injure ourselves so grievously."

The woman scoffed. "I am now convinced that the Gerentate will fall to Anaander Mianaai the moment he turns his attention that way. You are all of you far too sentimental. Ghaon as well, despite the Crawl and the efforts of the Watch." Here she looked directly at Kels.

"Honored," said Kels. "There is no need to be rude."

"I say what I think," said the woman. "My people don't hide behind masks."

"You certainly do," said Awt, equably. "Your mask is rudeness and offensively plain speech. We only see how you wish to appear, not your true self. Mask or not, Watchman Inarakhat has been more honest than you."

The woman made her disgusted noise again, but said nothing further.

Kels looked out the viewing port for a moment, gathering his thoughts, settling himself. He wanted to leave the lounge, but felt that it would be a retreat of some kind. "Honored Awt, do you intend to approach your grandmother's agnate?" It wasn't what he had intended to say.

Awt Emnys seemed unsurprised by the question. "I don't know. Do you advise it?"

*Yes* and *no* and *I didn't mean* collided, tangled, blocked his speech. Ghem, who had balked at any association with his own ruined agnate, would be no more charitable towards Awt, and the thought distressed Kels. And also pleased him. Let Ghem see what they rejected!

Or perhaps they would be at least courteous to him. "One could hardly say, Honored. Only . . . "

"Yes?"

"If you do, buy a mask. Not at the shops near the shuttle port, nor even along the riverbank. Find a place on the third hill, behind the jeweler's district. And be sure to choose one that is neither very elaborate, nor very brightly colored."

"That would have been my own inclination," said Awt. "I thank you again for your advice." He paused a moment, as though undecided about something. "The merchant Chis is an inveterate gossip."

Behind the mask, Kels frowned.

Awt continued, quietly. "She tells a fantastic and romantic story of your youthful disappointment in love. Not, I'm sure . . . " Awt made a small, ironic gesture, "out of any disrespect for you, but to further discourage me from approaching my grandmother's agnate. Whichever that might be. But when I heard your story just now, I wondered. Have you held to something you should have let go? The daughter of a wealthy, noble agnate might not have chosen her first husband, or even her second. But the third would have been her heart's choice. Perhaps you didn't know her as well as you thought. She certainly behaved very badly, if what Honored Chis says is true." He bowed slightly, apologetic. "Forgive my presumption."

"Her agnate," Kels began, and Awt raised an eyebrow. Kels was glad of the mask. "It was a long time ago, Honored."

"I've offended you. Please believe it wasn't my intention."

"No, Honored," said Kels, in his most even voice, and then, at a loss, bowed and left the lounge.

Six months on a small ship is a long time. The view out the ports of the *Jewel of Athat* was the same as any ship. One can only play at counters so much, and one has only a limited number of potential opponents. Even betting on the games loses its charm a month in.

"It's fashionable to have a Ghaonish ancestor six or seven generations back," Awt said to Kels near the end of the first month. The Faunt woman had retreated in silent pique, Awt having defeated her at counters the third time in a row, and they were alone in the lounge. "Even farther back is better. Too near—and poor—and you're half-foreign, an outsider in your own family. My mother's relatives always suspected my half-Ghaonish father of mercenary impulses. They cared for me when my parents died, but more out of their sense of propriety than anything else."

"How different your childhood would have been, had your grandmother never left Ghaon!" Kels said, thinking as much of himself as of Awt.

"True, but then I wouldn't have been Awt Emnys."

By the second month of the voyage, the library of recorded entertainments that seems so large and varied at the start of the voyage becomes monotonous and dull. Fellow passengers who had seemed either exotically foreign or companionably familiar lose all their charms and become objects of irritation. The small spaces become ever-narrowing traps.

Ever since he had known them, Ninan and Tris, Inarakhat Kels' fellow Watch officers, had been more or less pleasant company, despite a certain distrust on their part; even ruined, his agnate was far superior to theirs. Near the end of the second month, their dismissive observations about the passengers became a burden to Kels, particularly their assessment of Awt Emnys. It was no different from jibes directed at previous Gerentate travelers looking for Ghaonish ancestors, and those had amused Kels in the past. But now he realized that his disdain had a different source and direction than theirs.

In the third month it seems as though there has never been any world but the ship, and the endless progress through the blackness. Life before the voyage is a distant memory, unreal and strangely textured. The idea of disembarking at some final destination seems untenable. During this month the wreck of the last ship to defy the ban on communications takes on an interest out of proportion to its significance.

"Just as you promised," Awt said to Kels as he watched the dead ship drift. Quietly, because the others—the fierce Faunt, the tourist from Semblance, even Chis Sulca, who had seen it before, were silent. "I wonder why they did it."

"They were fools," said Chis.

"They were driven mad by isolation," said the tourist from Semblance, by his tone of voice meaning a joke, but it lacked conviction.

In the fourth month desperate boredom sets in. The beige, undecorated walls, the black view out the ports, the nourishing but unvaried diet, become an undifferentiated background, and sensory deprivation forces the mind to produce all sorts of fantasies in an attempt to ward off starvation.

"Have you read Thersay?" asked Kels. He and Awt were alone in the lounge.

"*The Consolation of Insanity?*" Awt smiled. "No, I never have. And I've probably never met anyone who has, either, highly regarded as it is."

"I've tried," confessed Kels.

Awt smiled. "That bored?"

"You laugh," Kels said. "She began the work here, on this very ship, at that table, there, at just about this point in the voyage. What a strange and sprawling thing it is! She must have been half mad."

"It wouldn't surprise me in the least," Awt said.

The fifth month is much the same as the fourth, time having contracted into a single eternal moment.

In the sixth month, the mind awakes slowly to the realization that there will indeed be an end to the endless voyage. When the Watch announces that only one day remains before the ship will exit the Crawl and increase speed, feverish excitement runs through the passengers. The day ahead, and the few days after that it will take to reach the station orbiting Ghaon, seem unbearably long. In vain do passengers remind themselves that the time will surely pass without their watching. Everyone, whether openly or surreptitiously, will mark each interminable second and anxiously await the thunk and jar of docking.

It was during the last day inside the Crawl that disaster struck.

Kels had endured his shift, and a silent, tense supper with Ninan and Tris. He'd retired early, but after several hours of uncomfortable tossing he rose and dressed and went to the lounge. It was empty; he was vaguely surprised and disappointed that Awt Emnys wasn't there, though he'd known that the passengers were likely asleep at that hour.

Once Awt disembarked Kels might never see him again. It had been true of every passenger over the years, but it had never mattered to him before. This, then, was why he couldn't sleep. There were things he wanted to say, that he didn't know if he *should* say, or even if he possibly could.

He traced the path he would have on his rounds, but met no one, not even his counterpart on third watch. The passengers' cabins were shut, the ship felt deserted and lonely. He wished someone would come out and nod, or give some perfunctory greeting, just to break the unsettling feeling that he was invisible, a disembodied ghost alone on an abandoned and drifting ship.

It was because of this feeling that he did something he almost never did—he approached the two Watch officers standing outside the door behind which the pilot guided the ship.

He raised a hand in greeting, expected the same gesture in return, and questions about why he roamed the corridors at this hour. A perfunctory sentence or two about not being able to sleep was on his tongue, ready for the question, but the two officers stood masked and unmoving at the end of the narrow corridor.

He stopped, bewildered. "The days are longer near the end, are they not?" he essayed.

No answer. The feeling of invisibility increased, and for a moment Kels wasn't so much alarmed at the thought that something might be wrong with the guards as he was despairing of his own substantial existence. But common sense exerted itself. He put a hand on one silent watchman's shoulder. "Honored!" Nothing. He pushed gently, and the man turned slowly to the side, as though he were in some sort of suggestible trance.

Kels drew his gun, and pushed past the two unresponding men to open the door to the pilots' station.

The pilot was in his seat, back to the door, and before him were the ship's controls. A dark-haired figure in kilt and embroidered blouse bent over him, a small recorder in his hand. They were both close enough that Kels might have reached out to touch either man. Kels was on the verge of firing when Awt Emnys straightened and looked at him with Ghem Echend's eyes.

The moment of hesitation was enough. Awt grabbed the gun, pulling it upwards and away, twisting Kels' arm around painfully until he was forced to let go his weapon. Awt pointed the gun at Kels, and pushed him against the bulkhead.

"Why?" Kels gasped, his arm still hurting from Awt's grip.

"It's my job," Awt said. "Did you think warehouse inventory suited me?"

"Have you no regard for your own people?" asked Kels. "Or is the Gerentate truly our enemy?"

Awt smiled, a little sadly. "The Gerentate is not your enemy. The Radch, on the other hand . . . " He shrugged.

"Radchaai," Kels whispered in horror. "We are destroyed."

"On the contrary. To destroy any part of the world would be to destroy its value. No one who submits will be harmed. Those who don't submit . . . " He shrugged, gun still aimed at Kels. "They choose their own fate. But if you mean some indefinable quality of being Ghaonish, or that splendid pride and isolation . . . I would have thought that you of all people would have understood that it wasn't worth preserving." He cocked an eyebrow, sardonic. "It wasn't only you the Ghem agnate treated badly. I know more of my grandmother than I said."

Kels was dizzy, and breathing was difficult, as though the air had turned to water and he was drowning. Awt had understood, had already known the things that Kels had so wanted to say to him.

"I owe Ghaon nothing," Awt continued. "Nor the Gerentate. And the Radchaai pay me well for my services." He let go of Kels, who didn't move, still frozen with the revelation, and the threat of the gun. "Don't accuse yourself. Nothing would be gained if you had killed me. Do you think this is the first successful attempt? None of you will remember anything, just like every other time an agent has made this run." Awt put a hand on Kels' shoulder, gave a consoling squeeze. "I won't kill you unless you make me. And I would regret that very much." Then he turned away, gun still in hand, and resumed his quiet questioning of the pilot.

Kels' arm hurt, but distantly, as though the pain was part of some dream he would wake from shortly. He tried to make his breaths deeper, but only felt even more starved for air. Had he himself ever stood entranced beside the pilot's station as a Radchaai spy carefully probed for the keys to Ghaon's strongest defense? How many times? His failure was galling, even more so the thought that he had failed over and over again, and never known it. He was afraid to die, afraid to risk his life and indeed his death might well be purposeless, as his life had been. But what difference would it make? If what Awt had said was true, Ghaon was already doomed, and he himself would have no memories to reproach himself with.

Awt spoke to the pilot, quietly, and the pilot murmured in response. He recalled Awt speaking to him in the lounge, six months back. *Have you held to something you should have let go?* Awt had judged him well. *It speaks poorly of the Watch that such a one would be selected.*

"Awt Emnys."

Awt turned, one ear still towards the murmuring pilot.

"Don't do this. Destroy the recording, return to your cabin. I will tell no one." Without answering, Awt turned back again.

No more hesitation. This was the moment. Kels shoved himself away from the bulkhead, grabbed Awt's arm as he turned. The gun fired, the bullet grazing Kels' ear and burying itself in the bulkhead behind him. Alarms sounded, faint and distant beneath the pounding of Kels' heart. He brought his knee up hard between Awt's legs, yanked the gun from his hand, brought the muzzle up to Awt's head, and fired.

The alarms brought first and second watches. Blood was splattered on Kels, the still senseless pilot's body, the deck. Ninan was speaking but Kels could only hear the roaring silence that had followed the gunshot.

"  . . . in shock," said a distant voice. But Awt wasn't in shock, he was dead.

"He's not injured." Ninan's mouth moved with the sound. Ninan speaking. His mask was askew. "None of this blood's his. Iraon! Look at it all!" Someone made retching noises, and the need to vomit was overpowering for a moment, but Kels managed to suppress it.

"Lying bastard!" Tris. Kels couldn't see him. "I bet there's no Ghaonish grandmother at all. I knew he was no good, that kind never are."

"Inarakhat Kels, you're a hero!" said Ninan, and patted Kels lightly on his jaw. "Caught a spy!"

Kels drew in a long, ragged breath. Ninan was saying something about promotions and pay raises, and someone said, "Now they'll know they can't fool the Watch." They were all familiar and foreign at the same moment.

"Let's get you to your bunk," said Ninan.

"It doesn't matter," said Kels.

Ninan was pulling him up by his arm. "What?"

"It doesn't matter. It wasn't worth it." Ninan looked at him, uncomprehending. "None of you are worth it." Kels shook his head. Ninan would never understand, or Tris, or any of them. Awt Emnys might, but Awt Emnys was dead.

"Of course," said Ninan reassuringly. "It's upsetting. But he chose his own fate. You did nothing more than your duty."

"He wouldn't submit," said Kels.

"Exactly. A fatal mistake." Ninan clapped Kels on the shoulder. "But enough of this. Let's get you to your bunk. And something strong to drink."

"One thinks," said Inarakhat Kels, "that a cup of tea would be sufficient."

Gwendolyn Clare's debut novel—*Ink, Iron, and Glass*—is the first in a steampunk duology about a young mad scientist with the ability to write new worlds into existence, forthcoming from Imprint in 2018. Her short stories have appeared in *Clarkesworld, Asimov's, Analog,* and *Beneath Ceaseless Skies,* among others, and her poetry has been nominated for the Rhysling Award. She holds a BA in Ecology, a BS in Geophysics, a PhD in Mycology, and swears she's done collecting acronyms. She lives in North Carolina with too many cats, too many ducks, and never enough books.

# ALL THE PAINTED STARS

## *Gwendolyn Clare*

They are not the Brights, and so I hesitate to save them. Part of me is eager, and part of me ashamed.

Even through the haze of plasma blasts dispersing over their shields, I recognize the ship as a Bright construct—too much glass, arranged in sharp geometric panels so the entire upper surface glitters with reflected starlight. Still, I know the pilots must not be Brights. First, because they fly clumsily and appear not to know how to fire the main cannon. Second, because the Brights went extinct some twelve hundred solar cycles ago.

I decide to take a closer look at their attackers, and the fibers in my flesh tauten with anticipation—though I tell myself I will just *look,* not engage. Intent ripples down my middle tentacles to the interface between flesh and machine, and my little stellate-class fighter zips nearer. The attackers have seven mid-size cruisers, nothing so cumbersome as the Bright ship nor so whimsical—boxy and compact, and decked with weapons. I do not recognize the design. Some backwater species, no doubt. I am patrolling near the edge of protected space, so it is to be expected.

I choose a wide selection of frequencies and broadcast an audial message to all the ships in the vicinity. "Hostile vessels, please be informed you have entered protected space. Under the laws of the Sheekah, acts of genocide are punishable by death. Power down your plasma weapons."

The attackers do not respond. But then, if they do not know our laws, what is the chance they know our language?

I broadcast the same message in the Bright language, and then add, "You must provide evidence of personal grievance to a Sheekah enforcer prior to engaging in interspecies violence."

I wish I did not feel a surge of excitement at their silence, at the continued barrage of plasma fire.

I spin the fighter nervously, considering my options. The aggressor may hold a legitimate grievance and simply suffer from an onboard system too crude to translate the transmissions. Or they may have chosen to ignore me, assuming my tiny fighter poses no threat. A compromise then: I will destroy one ship at a time until they relent.

My neurochemical balance adjusts, heightening awareness and reducing reaction time, and I cannot help but enjoy the feel of neurons singing for battle. I trigger the thrusters and slice through the void toward the nearest ship, my body fibers tensing against the heavy acceleration. My fighter is a difficult target to hit—shaped like an eight-pointed geometric star, with just enough room for my core mass in the middle and a tentacle stretching down each ray of the star for interfacing. Stellate-class fighters are highly maneuverable, but I am still outnumbered six to one. This is why I am an enforcer: I am one of the few Sheekah violent enough to accept such odds with glee.

I fire my own weapons in quick, precise bursts, and the reactors of the first cruiser explode in a glorious ultraviolet light-show. Now I have the attention of the rest; two of the remaining cruisers break off from their engagement with the Bright ship to pursue me. I dance away like a comet on an eccentric orbit, there and gone again before they can look twice.

When I repeat the transmission, I should be saddened that they still do not cease fire, though in truth the challenge thrills me. I dart through their fleet and destroy two more cruisers, pausing between each explosion, but the remaining cruisers seem if anything incensed to further violence.

I am closing in on the fourth cruiser when my fighter is hit.

Stellate-class fighters are much too small to carry shield generators, relying instead on maneuverability to avoid getting hit. Ironically, it is not a plasma blast that finds my little fighter, but a shred of shrapnel from one of the cruisers I destroyed. Through the interface, I feel the shrapnel impact as if it were slicing my own flesh, and then one of my tentacles goes numb, a safety precaution against excess stimulation. I run diagnostics and discover that one ray of the star is badly damaged, the thrusters useless.

Well. This changes things.

My fighter has a Stillness Bomb installed, though I have never before activated it. Use of the Stillness is tightly regulated under Sheekah law—it is considered a last resort. But here I am, damaged and outnumbered, and the Brights were never formally removed from our list of treatised allies so I am justified in using the Stillness to defend the Bright ship. A technicality, of course, since I know the inhabitants aren't Brights, but it allows me to use the weapon nonetheless.

To save them, I need to maneuver into contact with their hull, a task I struggle to accomplish without my full array of thrusters. After long seconds of angling, I pass through the Bright shields and stab into the ship, one of the rays of my fighter penetrating the hull. The ray unfolds, sealing the two vessels together and leaving one of my tentacles dangling down through an open aperture into a hallway in the Bright ship. This fusion complete, I can now calibrate the Stillness Bomb to avoid the Bright ship and its occupants. When I am certain the weapon identifies the Bright ship as an extension of my fighter, I meticulously disengage three levels of safeties and activate the Stillness.

My fighter shudders, straining to stay attached to the Bright ship, then goes still. For a moment, nothing seems to have changed, and I wonder if perhaps the weapon was damaged in the firefight. Then the attackers' plasma weapons sputter and die out, and the four remaining cruisers start to drift very slowly out of formation. The motion is barely perceptible, but it fills me with a cold, sick dread. All those lives snuffed out, and what if my judgment was wrong? What a wretched Sheekah am I, who would choose this life of killing.

I do not have long to think on it, though, because the stress of activating the weapon has exacerbated the damage, and my fighter's systems are failing. I must abandon it or die with it. I consider the second option—after all, what am I without my fighter?—but the automated preferences are set for survival, so the fighter disconnects me without waiting for my decision.

As soon as the emergency disconnect triggers, I am blind and suffocating. I fall through the aperture of my fighter into the Bright ship, bits of metal interface still clinging to my tentacles, and I land hard. I flop helplessly on the deck, unadapted for artificial gravity, and without my fighter I sense nothing. My circulatory fluid is slowly turning toxic, and even if the atmospheric composition were appropriate, I have no organs designed for interfacing with air.

I need lungs or I will die. I need visual and auditory organs, too. Immobile as I am, I must wait for the telltale vibration of feet upon the deck, heralding the arrival of the aliens. I think I feel it now, I can't be sure—even my ability to feel the shudder of metal against my flesh is dulled without the electronic stimulus of my fighter.

I flail my tentacles, panicking, and find nothing but empty air. To calm myself, I focus on the task of slowing all nonessential bodily functions. This will buy me a little time, I hope. I cannot quite think rationally with all my neurochemical feedbacks screaming at me to adapt, to survive.

Again, I flail desperately, but this time one tentacle lands on bare flesh. Yes! I eagerly wrap my tentacle around the limb and begin probing for genetic information. Stem cells are ideal—they retain the broadest memory of how the organism as a whole works—though gametes provide a useful perspective, too. I do not dare to hope for embryonic cells, because that would require an incredible stroke of luck and my luck has not been good today.

The stem cells of this species have disappointingly limited potency, but I explore enough to start appropriating their genetic design. The toxin buildup in my circulatory system clouds my thoughts and slows my progress. I hope what I can glean from this individual will be sufficient.

I begin to understand this species as my body begins to integrate their design. They are bilaterally symmetric, endoskeletal, bipedal, endothermic, sexually dimorphic. (Definitely not Brights—if I had any doubts about that, they are gone now.) They have sensory organs for electromagnetic radiation, compression waves, and chemicals. I grow the lung tissue first, so I will be able to breathe as soon as my cellular respiration has altered, then I focus on retinas and cochleae.

As my new senses sharpen and stabilize, I gain awareness of the aliens. There are several of them encircling me, black handheld weapons cradled in their arms. They raise their weapons menacingly, and raise their voices as well; the one I am touching emits a shrill warning call. I begin to realize how very dire my situation is. Have I violated a taboo against physical contact? Perhaps they are a race of clinical xenophobes? I do not know what I have done to agitate them so quickly after I saved their lives.

I was never meant to be an ambassador—I do not have the training, and I am too violent besides. I have spent the last thirty-six solar cycles alone inside my fighter, engaging with other species only in my capacity as an enforcer of Sheekah law. And now I find myself in contact with a new species, trying to remember how to mimic physiology, to become one of them. I fear I have already ruined any chance of rapport.

When I am sure I have collected sufficient genetic data to survive in their atmosphere, I unwrap my tentacle, releasing the gene donor. I suck down my first lungfuls of oxygen through newly formed facial orifices.

And the difficult part begins.

They do not kill me right away. I take this as a good sign. They lift me onto a mobile platform and move me to a room with other platforms, some of them occupied by members of their own species. These ones do little in the way of moving or vocalizing, but they also leave me with two males holding weapons. I do not try to ask the killers for more gene donation.

Time passes. Other aliens—ones who do not carry weapons—are often present, watching me, waving diagnostic equipment over me, trying to communicate. I have no translating abilities without my fighter, so I must learn their language the slow way. I grow legs and arms, I learn to metabolize their sugars, I grow vocal chords and lips and a tongue to shape their words. I wonder if my fighter is irreparably damaged, which would mean all this effort to survive is a waste.

I am learning names. Mosby, Rosenberg, Liu; Ahmed, Levitt, Jones. But I do not know what to tell them when they ask for mine. I pause, they think I do not understand and gesture more vigorously towards me. Mosby Rosenberg Liu Ahmed Levitt Jones, they repeat, touching themselves with their hands, then they aim their digits at me and wait for an answer. What can I tell them? Sheekah are named when they choose their lifepath—as a pilot, my name is the name of my stellate fighter. Or at least it was. My fighter is damaged, I am no longer interfaced, and I have taken a new form, yet I am hardly in a position to ask them to name me as a true ambassador would. I cannot even communicate what the problem is.

"Ohree," I eventually say. It was my childhood nickname long ago. Fitting, because I am so like a child now—awkward and unplaced.

"Ohree," they repeat, and the name sounds distorted even though we share a vocal anatomy now.

I cannot explain anything, I cannot ask for anything. I can only point to an object and earn a garble of syllables for an answer. Does "medbay" describe the platform, the material it is made of, the function it serves, or the person lying prone upon it? Is "door" the word for an egress, or the object that blocks the egress? For the first time since I was a child, fumbling to find my lifepath, I feel hopelessly frustrated.

Liu and Rosenberg are in the room with me when I decide I no longer care about upsetting them. If they tell the killers to shoot me, then I will be shot, and at least that will be a change from what I am now. I slide off the platform, balancing uncertainly with my new bipedal body, and take careful steps toward one wall where there appears to be some kind of interface terminal. Rosenberg makes loud vocalizations, and I ignore her.

The terminal has a manual interface—buttons to be depressed by fingers, unthinkably primitive—which I rip out of the wall. I press one palm to the exposed circuitry and close my eyelids, concentrating on the task of growing a direct electronic interface of my own.

They still haven't shot me yet.

I learn this terminal was designed for accessing the medical portion of the ship's database, which is unfortunately not the portion that I need. I mentally slip behind the front-end processes and gain access to the database in its entirety. It is very large, and organized with the dubious logic of Bright minds, information twisting and twining back on itself like a jumble of vines grown together. Eventually, I access the language files for these aliens and use what little I know to identify "English" as the dialect I need to download.

When the task is done, I disengage from the terminal and resorb the interface into the flesh of my hand. "Now," I say, "this will be easier."

"Incredible," says Liu, shaking his head. The gesture makes me wonder if I should have looked for a file on nonverbal communication among humans.

Rosenberg stares at me, and then says, "Someone better get Mosby."

Upon my life, I do not know why it was so important to fetch Mosby. He asks the most inane questions, while Rosenberg holds her lips tight together and Liu backs away as if ceding the whole room.

Once I prove to Mosby that I am now conversant in his language, the first thing he says to me is, "We need to know about that weapon you fired." Mosby is the most important of their trained killers and holds the title of "colonel." He tells the other killers what to do.

I don't see the relevance, but I answer his question anyway. "It produces a sort of space-time whiplash that disrupts neurological functioning. Fatally so, in all organisms we've encountered so far."

"Is it still usable?"

I stare at him for a moment. "No, that's unlikely. The damage to my fighter is too extensive. Were you planning to commit genocide in the near future?"

Mosby's face scrunches up in an expression I do not understand. Rosenberg takes a step forward, places a hand on his arm, and says to me, "Of course not. The Colonel's just worried about defending the ship against another attack."

"That is no longer my concern," I say.

"What do you mean 'not your concern'?" Mosby says, his volume and pitch rising. "Aren't you supposed to be some sort of interstellar policeman?"

"I am no longer interfaced with my fighter."

Mosby says, "Listen, you—" but Rosenberg drags him by the arm out into the hallway.

They talk. I cannot quite hear, but I believe I have displeased one or both of them. I am not sure how—it was not my intention.

Liu, who seems to avoid standing in proximity to Mosby, comes closer again now that Mosby is elsewhere. "Don't judge all of us based on the likes of Mosby," he says. "There's a reason they put a civilian in charge of the expedition."

I don't know who "they" refers to, but I doubt it matters. "I am not here to judge you. The only judgment I am authorized to make is to determine the legitimacy of grievance in interspecies conflict."

Liu does something with the muscles in his lips. "I'm sorry, it's easy to forget you learned our language less than an hour ago. I meant that you must be forming impressions of what our species is like, and Mosby isn't representative. Not of all of us, anyway."

"I will take that under consideration."

Rosenberg returns alone. She apologizes for Mosby's behavior, though I would not have known he behaved inappropriately if she and Liu had not told me. Rosenberg is a leader, but not a killer, and seems to have incomplete authority over Mosby.

"So," Rosenberg says as she leans against the exam table next to mine. "You saved our butts out there, and now you're stuck with us. First of all: thank you. Second, if we could impose upon you further, we could use some help navigating this region of space."

Now I am truly confused. "You do not know where you are going?"

Rosenberg lets out a breath noisily. "The Brights left this ship in our home system a little over thirteen thousand years ago. When we discovered it, their recorded instructions were . . . cryptic, but the nav system came pre-programmed. We've been following the course they set for us, but obviously we're having some trouble with the locals along the way."

Her lengthy reply does not actually answer my question. I try to rephrase it to be clearer. "What is the purpose of your journey?"

"We're going to Bright space. It's not clear why they want us to come, but we couldn't pass up an invitation like this." She raised a hand as if to indicate the room, or perhaps the ship at large. "I've done some poking around in the database to learn about your species, so I know the Sheekah were allies of the Brights once. Would you consider helping them now, even if they're not here to ask for it?"

This surprises me. "You do not know?"

"Know what?"

"They are gone."

"Gone," Liu interjects loudly, before Rosenberg can answer. I do not understand why he repeats the word—perhaps I misused it.

"The Brights went extinct," I clarify. "They developed a genetic anomaly that spread from cell to cell throughout the body, causing widespread genomic degradation, and was, like a pathogen, highly transmissible between individuals. Many Sheekah were infected trying to help them before the Ambassadorial High Council declared quarantine."

"Gone," Rosenberg says and goes silent for a minute. (Does everyone need to say this word?) Something appears to be wrong with her, but I do not know what to do. Eventually, she says, "Did they know they were dying off when they left us the ship?"

I do a little quick math, converting unfamiliar units of time based on what I gleaned from the ship's database. "Given the age of the ship, that seems probable."

"I guess now we know why they named the ship *Legacy*." She puts her hand over her mouth, as if to hold in the words, but I can still hear her clearly. "We have to figure out where we're going, and why. Would you consider helping Ahmed with the database?"

I stare, not knowing how to respond. What happens to those I protect after I enforce the law has never been my concern. I wonder what it would feel like to be invested in their fate, but all I can feel is the absence of metal against my skin, the ghost-memory of tentacles I no longer possess.

"I am here," I say dispassionately. "I will help with what I can."

Days pass. I interface again with the *Legacy* database and develop a rudimentary understanding of the systems architecture. This helps, a little, to alleviate the ache of losing my fighter and my lifepath with it. At least when my mind is occupied, I am not dwelling on how wrong everything feels. I try and fail to explain the database to the technologists, who cannot grasp the Bright way of thinking. Whole sections of the ship are offline and locked down, and I am surprised they made it this far with such limited control.

I also learn more from the database about these humans; they live short lives, for instance, the equivalent of only nine or ten Sheekah solar cycles. I must seem ancient to them, though among the Sheekah I am considered young. They have so little time—this helps me understand why they seem so desperate to accomplish something, even if they do not know the nature of their task.

I grow irritated with the technologists. They are always near, bothering me with questions, even though they do not generally understand the answers. After the long cycles of solitude in my fighter, I am unused to tolerating so many individuals in such close proximity. I look for something else to do.

Instead I help the botanist, Keene, revive some of the plant species, the ones whose genomes indicate they will be harmless to humans. It is tiring but not particularly difficult work; I must grow a temporary interface with which to access the genomic database, and my body requires extra sustenance to provide the molecules with which to shape the seeds. Keene seems very pleased with the results. I care little for reviving extinct species from the Bright homeworld, but it also costs me little, so what does it matter either way? The Brights loved their botany and would not have wanted *Legacy* to fly with empty solaria. Indeed, from what I learned of the systems architecture, I suspect healthy solaria will prove important for restoring and optimizing certain functions elsewhere on the ship. Not that this matters to me.

I miss my old self. I think about fixing my fighter, but I can find only some of the tools and none of the spare parts I would need for the task aboard *Legacy*.

I consider ending my existence.

I sit on a bench in the aft solarium, which remains dark and unused and skeletal. In the central solarium Keene's seeds have begun to sprout, so I come here instead to avoid the curious visitors drawn in by the promise of green growth. Back here, if I hold very still, I can feel the subsonic hum of the main engines vibrating the hull.

Through the geometric panes of the ceiling and walls, the stars look strangely close, as if the hull were not clear at all but rather painted with the likeness of stars. I stare into space, remembering how this view used to belong to me every hour of every cycle. It's not the same, of course—these human eyes see such a narrow spectrum—but at least it feels familiar.

The aft solarium doors breeze open and Liu, the psychologist, enters. I do not look away from the stars but I can tell it is him from the way his soft gait whispers on the deck. He takes a seat next to me on the bench. Humans are highly social and require near-constant interaction and stimulation when conscious.

"How are you adjusting?" he says.

I think my habit of sitting here alone disturbs Liu. He does not understand me at all. "I do not know if I wish to adjust."

"Look—I know this isn't where you want to be, but the truth is, we could use your help here. The *Legacy* database is thirteen thousand years out of date and so huge we can't find what we're looking for most of the time anyway. We could use a guide who knows what they're doing."

I lower my gaze to look at him. Humans seem to desire a quite specific quantity of eye contact while communicating—not too much, not too little—though I have not yet mastered the exact proportion. "I am not an ambassador," I say. "I was trained to be an enforcer of the law. I cannot perform another life."

Liu's brows tighten and draw together. "Life?"

"Job," I say, to clarify. I have not yet discerned why they have two words for this concept.

Liu exhales forcefully and leans back against the bench, stretching his legs. If the gesture means something, it is lost on me. Humans rely heavily on nonverbal communication, much of it subconscious, and it frustrates my efforts to understand them. Or rather, it would frustrate me, if it were important for me to understand them. Which it is not. Because I think I will kill myself today.

After a while, Liu speaks again. "In the ship's logs, the Brights say they left us *Legacy* because they knew we would someday build conservatories."

I do not know the word. "Conservatories?"

"Places where we cultivate plants for aesthetic value." He points at the solarium ceiling. "The architecture usually looks something like this. Anyway, at the time when they left us the ship, humans had barely started getting a handle on agriculture. We didn't build conservatories until thousands of years later."

"Are plants of great cultural significance to you now?"

"They're not central to our society, no. Well—Keene might argue otherwise, but most people don't think twice about the cultural value of plants." He lifts his shoulders in an unfamiliar gesture. "I don't know. Maybe the Brights saw what they wanted to see in us."

"As you see what you want to see in me."

"The point is," Liu says, "you hardly ever get the ideal situation you're hoping for. But if you're lucky, you find something that will suffice."

"I am not an ambassador," I say again.

"No, but you're close enough for us."

Maybe I will wait until tomorrow to kill myself.

Tomorrow comes, but the humans distract me. Over the comm, they say they have desperate need of me in the systems control room. And what does it matter if I delay another hour, another day? So I go to them.

The systems control room lies buried deep in the ship, in one of the few areas with no view of the stars. The room itself is dimly lit and decagonal, a display and a crude manual interface affixed to each of the walls. Rosenberg and Mosby are there with Ahmed, the chief technologist, and a subordinate technologist whose name I do not recall.

I move too quietly for them to notice my arrival. (Always, these details I cannot seem to get right. I wear human skin, but it will never fit exactly.) To announce myself, I say, "What has happened?"

Four pairs of eyes look in my direction. As soon as they register my presence, everyone tries talking at once. Rosenberg and Mosby quickly turn on each other. These humans spend so much time arguing about what to do, it's amazing they ever get anything done.

Finally, the rest of them agree to quiet down so Ahmed can speak. "We're getting power fluctuations all over the ship. Life support keeps trying to shut down—we've had to force a restart three times in the past fifteen minutes. No idea what's causing it."

This does not surprise me. The Brights did not design their systems architecture to be solid and immutable, but rather flexible and adaptive. "I will look," I say.

I place my palm on an exposed patch of hardware, grow an interface, and begin sifting through the diagnostic reports. Bright diagnostics are so literal they are almost evasive—always describing *what* is happening, but never hinting at *why*. I skip past the reports and prod gently at the underlying systems, doing the command equivalent of poking life support with a stick to see if it twitches.

Life support seems raw and hypersensitive, overreacting to stimulus. The shields seem lethargic, the main engines argumentative.

I mentally pull back to give my analysis to the waiting humans. "*Legacy* is experiencing some sort of systems destabilization, possibly triggered by the introduction of plant life in the central solarium. The ship is attempting to re-evaluate resource allocation and re-integrate, but systems integration seems to require guidance." For clarity, I add, "Guidance from a Bright engineer."

Predictably, Mosby wants to know if the power to the main cannon can be restored, and Rosenberg starts arguing about prioritization. Humans are a confrontational and violent people, whatever Liu might say to the contrary. Perhaps I understand this better than any trained ambassador could. Sometimes I even see a little of myself in them. Were I still an enforcer, would I not take great care to restore my weapons systems? Of course I would.

But I tell him, "Systems integration is a very complicated process. I most likely will not be able to complete it at all, let alone to your desired specifications."

This silences them. They all stare at me, wide-eyed. Have I somehow misspoken? In a situation like this, am I supposed to ply them with false hope instead of giving an honest status report?

I do not know the Brights the way an ambassador would; I am too young to even have spoken to anyone with first-hand knowledge of the Brights. I have only a superficial understanding of their thought patterns, and this is a task best reserved for someone who truly knew them. If not for a Bright itself.

I cannot do what the humans expect of me. And yet, I must try.

I close my eyes to block the stimulus so I can delve deeper. Soon, I can visualize the interconnected web of the ship's systems, each hub enmeshed among the others as if held in place with thick, pulsing vines. The offline sectors and systems appear marooned and dark, disconnected from the vital flow of the web.

Concentrating, I examine the systems more closely. Here: movement, change. And here, and here. Everywhere I scrutinize, the deep structural connections are unraveling, senescing, peeling away like flower petals destined to be supplanted with fruit. It is a process I understand only with academic distance—from my examination of plant genomes, not from personal experience. Still, I recognize the patterns as organic design, organic thinking. Only the Brights would build a ship as convoluted and self-referential as a genome.

Back in the control room, the humans are getting restless. "What is going on?" demands Mosby.

I retreat from the depths enough to answer him. "The architecture you have now was never meant to last. It is . . . " I do not know why I pick the word: "juvenile."

Mosby opens his mouth but Ahmed looks at him says, "Less talk, more work."

I must agree with Ahmed.

Ignoring the sounds of the control room, I return my focus to the *Legacy*'s architecture. I pull myself deeper, down into the disordered conglomeration of systems, losing awareness of my physical body. I focus all my mental acuity to study the ship.

It wants to grow, to metamorphose, to mature. I can tell this much: growth could be good, but it also could be cancerous. The old connections run dry and slough off, and the systems sprout wild new vine stubs that quest in every direction. Left to their own devices, the systems will strangle themselves with malformed, overgrown connective structure. But how am I to guide this process, rife with botanical zeal only a Bright could comprehend?

I pause, thinking. Metamorphosis is an animal concept. They are not vines, they are tentacles—and tentacles I understand. I think of my stellate fighter, how cleanly designed it was, with its eight rays each encapsulating a tentacle, and all the neatly arranged interfaces. And at the center, my brain to process and control.

So, me—and by extension, the control room—at the nexus of the web. The strongest connections, thick and steady, direct from each system to the nexus. Lesser connections, flexible and mutable, exchanging information among the systems themselves. I weave the ship the way I would weave my own flesh, easing the nascent tentacles over a new growth template as if it were a foreign genome to be integrated.

When the connections have been laid, the most delicate part still remains to be done: I carefully extract myself from the center of the web, leaving behind the shell of the control room, not so much a vacancy as a resting state. I pull away, leaving all the connections intact, the hollow space waiting patiently for its next command.

It is done. And, if all is right, it will even be receptive to the humans' control.

I rise slowly, like floating up to the surface from the depths of an ocean, the lights and sounds of the control room wavering and resolving. I blink, eyes slow to focus as the ciliary muscles reawaken to their duties.

On every wall of the room, the display screens shine with dazzling varicolored light. My tear ducts water, my pupils hasten to contract. I see the humans shading their faces with their hands, so I know my body's reaction is not an oversensitive after-effect of deep interfacing. The screens are very bright.

Yes, I realize. The screens are Bright.

"They're beautiful," says Rosenberg, "even if it hurts to look at them."

Ahmed is still bent over a console. "There's an audio recording, too, but the frequencies are all ultrasonic."

Rosenberg asks, "What are they saying?"

"It'll take awhile for the translators to work it out," says Ahmed.

"Unnecessary," I say. I force some crude adjustments to the anatomy of my ears, expanding the range of my hearing. The recording is part-way through the message, but I wait until the end and it loops back to the beginning. "Roughly translated: the *Legacy*'s destination is a research base on a dwarf planet in the outskirts of the Brights' home system. They hope that, in the time it has taken your primitive species to develop interplanetary travel and discover *Legacy*, the pathogen will have gone extinct. The research base contains preserved samples of healthy Bright genomes. If you have the technology to restore plant biota from the genomic database and shepherd *Legacy* through the transition to maturity, you will be able to restore the Brights."

Everyone goes quiet. What have I done, meddling in the fate of these humans? An ambassador would have known better than to do for them what they cannot do themselves; I was a fool to think I could help without entangling myself. I feel nauseated, an unfamiliar physiological response to this upwelling of emotions inside me.

Ahmed is the one who says what they all must be thinking. "But it wasn't us who brought back the plants and guided the ship, it was you."

Which means the task of restoring the Brights falls on my shoulders, not theirs. "I know," I say, and rush from the room.

Hiding in the aft solarium, I stare out at the painted starscape. By human means of reckoning, this region of space was my home for three lifetimes:

cold empty death punctuated with tiny oases of energy and life. They all belonged to me, once. I felt at home in the void, satisfied with what I was, and now I am trapped behind this glass and can only yearn for that silent solitary existence.

At my core I am a fighter pilot—a thug, a killer. I was made to do what the rest of the Sheekah, with their delicate dispositions, could not. How can anyone expect me to resurrect a whole sentient species when all my training and experience has been in dealing death, not life?

I am no one's savior. It is too heavy a burden to bear.

Liu comes in: shuffle, shuffle, soft steps on the deck. He approaches hesitantly, hanging back as if he doesn't wish to intrude on my thoughts.

"Rosenberg sent you?" I say. I am learning how their hierarchy works.

Liu takes the words for an invitation and joins me on the bench. "She wants me to try talking with you."

"We have now spoken." I look at him. "You may report success."

"Why, Ohree, that was almost a joke. Are you growing a sense of humor to go with the mammalian physique?"

"Doubtful," I say, looking away again. Though maybe I am.

Liu lets out a loud breath. His vocal pitch drops lower. "You know what I'm here to ask you about."

"Rosenberg wants me to continue with you to your destination. Rosenberg wants me to revive the Brights."

"We can't do it without you, obviously."

"You do not understand. The process will not be a simple one, like with the seeds. Brights are very complex organisms. I will have to adapt my whole physiology, I will have to gestate the embryos inside me."

Liu is silent for so long that I give up my view of the stars and turn to face him. He is staring at me. "What exactly do you have on your to-do list that ranks more important than this?"

I pause. "If they made the smallest mistake, if even one gene region is tainted with pathogenic code, I will die."

"Since when were you more afraid of dying than of not having a purpose?" Liu's lips curl in an expression I now know to indicate amusement. "How human of you."

The words fall on me like a blow. He is right—only two days ago I was contemplating suicide. I fall back on an older argument. "An ambassador would be properly trained for such a task, which I am not."

"You thought you couldn't guide the *Legacy* through her transition, but you could," he said. "It doesn't matter that your own society marked you a castaway. It doesn't matter what life you had before. You are capable of things you haven't even dreamt of yet, and it would honor us to be the ones who help you discover those things."

I go very still. I do not dare to hope this could be true. It violates a paradigm so deep-seated in my psyche that I did not even suspect its existence until now.

Liu says, "Humans aren't in the habit of changing their given names. Surnames, though, were originally descriptive—you were named for your profession, or the village you came from, or your parentage." He pauses, the silence almost livid in the air. "You don't have a surname."

If I was frozen before, now I am a comet lost between the stars—even my molecules feel stuck. I am sure I could not look away if I tried. I know Liu knows how Sheekah naming works.

Liu smiles, though somehow the expression seems grave, as if he understands exactly what it is he's doing. "I think we'll call you Ohree Brightbearer, if the sound of it suits you."

"Yes," I say, hardly able to breathe. "Yes, it suits me fine."

I am named, and there is work ahead of me.

# FIRSTBORN

## *Brandon Sanderson*

While safe aboard his flagship, there were two ways for Dennison to watch the battle.

The obvious method relied on the expansive battle hologram that dominated the bridge. The hologram was on at the moment, and it displayed an array of triangular blue blips representing fighters flying about waist high. The much larger blue oval of Dennison's command ship hung a moderate distance above and behind the fighters. The massive and powerful but far less agile leviathan probably wouldn't see battle this day. The enemy's ships were too weak to damage its hull, but they were also too fast for it to catch. This would be a battle between the smaller fighters.

And Dennison would lead them. He rose from his command chair and walked a few steps to the hologram's edge, studying the enemy. Their red ships winked into existence as scanners located them amid the rolling boulders of the asteroid field. Rebels in name but pirates in action, the group had thrived unhindered for far too long. It had been five years since his brother Varion had reestablished His Majesty's law in this sector, and the rebellious elements should have long since been crushed.

Dennison stepped into the hologram, walking until he stood directly behind his ships. There were about two dozen of them—not a large force, by Fleet standards, but bigger than he deserved. He glanced to the side.

Noncommissioned aides and lesser officers had paused in their duties, eyes turned toward their youthful commander. Though they offered no obvious disrespect, Dennison could see their true feelings in their eyes. They did not expect him to win.

*Well, Dennison thought, wouldn't want to disappoint the good folks.*

"Divide the squadrons," Dennison commanded. His order was transmitted directly to the various captains, and his small fleet broke into four smaller groups. Ahead, the pirates began to form up as well—though they stayed within their asteroid cover.

Through the movement of their ships, Dennison could feel their battle strategy taking shape. At his disposal was all the formal military knowledge that came with a high-priced Academy education. Memories of lectures and textbooks mixed in his head, enhancing the practical experience he'd gained during a half dozen years commanding simulations and, eventually, real battles.

Yes, he could see it. He could see what the enemy commanders were doing; he could sense their strategies. And he *almost* knew how to counter them.

"My lord?" an aide said, stepping forward. She bore a battle visor in her hands. "Will you be needing this?"

The visor was the second way a commander could watch the battle. Each fighter bore a camera just inside its cockpit to relay a direct view. Varion always wore a battle visor. Dennison, however, was not his brother. He seemed to be the only one who realized that fact.

"No," Dennison said, waving the aide away. The action caused a stir among the bridge team, and Dennison caught a glare from Brell, his XO.

"Send Squadron C to engage," Dennison commanded, ignoring Brell.

A group of four fighters broke off from the main fleet, streaking toward the asteroids. Blue met red, and the battle began in earnest.

Dennison strode through the hologram, watching, giving commands, and analyzing—just as he had been taught. Dogfighting ships zipped around his head; fist-size asteroids shattered as he walked through their space, then re-formed after he had passed. He moved like some ancient god of lore, presiding over a battlefield of miniature mortals who couldn't see him, but undeniably felt his almighty hand.

Except if Dennison was a god, his specialty certainly wasn't war.

His education kept him from making any disastrous mistakes, but before long, the battle had progressed to the point where it was no longer winnable. His complete lack of pride let him order the expected retreat.

The Fleet ships limped away, reduced by more than half. From the statistics glowing into hovering holographic existence before him, Dennison could see that his ships had managed to destroy barely a dozen enemy fighters.

Dennison stepped from the hologram, leaving the red ships victorious and the blue ships despondent. The hologram disappeared, its images shattering and dribbling to the command center's floor like shimmering dust, the pieces eventually burning away in the light. Crewmembers stood around the perimeter, their eyes showing the sickly shame of defeat.

Only Brell had the courage to speak what they were all thinking. "He really is an idiot," he muttered under his breath.

Dennison paused by the doorway. He turned with a raised eyebrow, and found Brell staring back unrepentantly. Another High Officer probably would have sent him to the brig for insubordination. Of course, another commander wouldn't have earned such disrespect in the first place. Dennison leaned back against the side of the doorway, arms folded in an unmilitaristic posture. "I should probably punish you, Brell. I am a High Officer, after all."

This, at least, made the man look aside. Dennison lounged, letting Brell realize that—incompetent or not—Dennison had the power to destroy a man's career with a mere comm call.

Dennison finally sighed, standing up and walking forward. "But, you know, I've never really believed in disciplining men for speaking the truth. Yes, Brell. I, Dennison Crestmar—brother of the great Varion Crestmar, cousin to kings and commander of fleets—am an idiot. Just like all of you have heard."

Dennison paused right in front of Brell, then reached out and tapped the man's chest in the center of his High Imperial Emblem. "But think of this," Dennison continued with a light smile. "If *I'm* an idiot, then *you* must be pretty damn incompetent yourself; otherwise they would never have wasted you by sending you to serve under me."

Brell's face flared red at the insult, but he showed uncharacteristic restraint by holding his tongue. Dennison turned and strolled from the room. "Prepare my speeder for my return to the Point," he commanded. "I'm due for dinner with my father tomorrow."

He missed dinner. However, it wasn't his fault, considering he had to travel half the length of the High Empire. Dennison's father, High Duke Sennion Crestmar, was waiting for him in the spaceport when he arrived.

Sennion didn't say a word as Dennison left the airlock and approached. The High Duke was a tall man—proud, broad shouldered, with a noble face. He was the epitome of what a High Officer should be. At least Dennison had inherited the height.

The High Duke turned. Dennison fell into step beside him, and the two strode down the Officer's Walk—a pathway with a deep red carpet, trimmed with gold. It was reserved for High Officers, uncluttered by the civilians and lower ranks who bustled against each other on either side. There were no vehicles or moving walkways on the Officer's Walk. High Officers carried themselves. There was strength in walking—or so Dennison's father always said. The High Duke was rather fond of self-congratulatory mottoes.

"Well?" Sennion finally asked, eyes forward.

Dennison shrugged. "I really tried this time, if it makes any difference."

"If you had 'tried,' " Sennion said flatly, "you would have won. You had superior ships, superior men, and superior training."

Dennison didn't bother trying to argue with Sennion. He had given up on that particular waste of sanity years ago.

"The High Emperor assumed that you simply needed practical experience," Sennion said, almost to himself. "He thought that simulations and school games weren't realistic enough to engage you."

"Even emperors can be wrong, Father," Dennison said.

Sennion didn't even favor him with a glare.

*Here it comes,* Dennison thought. *He's finally going to admit it. He's finally going to let me go.* Dennison wasn't certain what he'd do once he was released from military command—but whatever he chose to do, he couldn't possibly be any worse at it.

"I have arranged a new commission for you," Sennion finally said.

Dennison started. Then he closed his eyes, barely suppressing a sigh. How many failures would the High Duke need to see before he gave up?

"It's aboard the *Stormwind.*"

Dennison froze in place.

Sennion stopped, finally turning to regard his son. People streamed to either side on the lower walks, ignoring the two men in fine uniforms standing on the crimson carpet.

Dumbfounded, it took Dennison a moment to begin to respond. "But . . . "

"It's a fine ship—a good place to learn. You will serve as an adjutant and squadron commander for High Admiral Kern."

"I know it's a 'fine ship,' " Dennison said through clenched teeth. "Father, that is a real command on an imperial flagship, not some idle playing in the Reaches. It's bad enough when I lose a dozen men fighting pirates. Need I be responsible for the deaths of thousands in the Reunification War as well?"

"I know Admiral Kern," Sennion said, ignoring his son's objections. "He is an excellent tactician. Perhaps he will be able to help you with your . . . problems."

"Problems?" Dennison demanded quietly. "Problems, Father? Has it never even occurred to you that I'm just not any good at this? It isn't dishonorable for the son of a High Duke to seek another profession, once he's proven himself unsuited to command. Goodness knows, I've certainly satisfied *that* particular requirement."

Sennion stepped forward, grabbing Dennison by the shoulders. "You will not speak that way," he commanded. "You are not like other officers. The High Empire expects more. The High Empire *demands* more!"

Dennison was taken aback by his father's lack of formality, and some of the passersby stopped to regard the strange sight of a High Duke acting with such passion. Dennison stood within his father's stiff grasp, reading the man's eyes. *It isn't the High Emperor, is it, Father?* Dennison thought. *It's you. One genius son isn't enough. For you, one success and one failure simply cancel each other out.*

"Go prepare yourself," Sennion said, releasing him. "The *Stormwind* is expecting your speeder in three days, and it's a seventy-hour trip."

"With permission, Your Majesty, I don't think this is the command for me," Dennison said, kneeling before the speeder's wallscreen.

The High Emperor was a middle-aged man with a firm chin and a full face. He was balding in a time when most men got scalp rejuvenations, but his refusal to enhance his appearance lent him a weight of . . . authenticity. He frowned at Dennison's comment. "It is an enviable post, Dennison. Most young High Officers would consider it an amazing opportunity."

"I am hardly like most young officers, Your Majesty," Dennison noted.

"No, that you certainly are not," the emperor said. "However, I would think that this post's near proximity to your brother would interest you."

Dennison shrugged. "To be honest, Your Majesty, I don't know Varion. I'm curious about him, but no more so than another person might be. I maintain my petition to be released from this commission."

The emperor's frown deepened. "You need to show more initiative, young Crestmar. Your pessimism has been a great annoyance to the High Throne."

Dennison glanced down—it was always bad when the emperor switched to the third person. "Your Majesty," he said. "I really have tried—I've tried all my life. But I received near-failing marks at the Academy, I never managed to even place in the games, and I've bungled every command given me. I'm just not any good."

"You have it in you," the emperor said. "You just have to try a little harder."

Dennison groaned softly. The emperor had obviously been speaking with his father again. "How can you be so sure, Your Majesty?"

"I just am. Your petition is denied. Is there anything else?"

Dennison shook his head.

Admiral Kern was not waiting for Dennison in the docking bay when he left the speeder, but that wasn't unusual. Though a High Officer, Dennison was still a junior one, and Kern was one of the most powerful admirals in the Fleet.

Dennison followed an aide through the flagship's passageways. They were surprisingly well decorated for a warship, adorned with the twelve seals of the High Empire. This was an imperial flagship, designed to impress inside and out. The aide led him to a large circular chamber with a battle hologram at its center. Though the air sparkled with miniature ships, only one man stood in the room—this wasn't the bridge, but a simulation chamber very similar to the ones Dennison had used at the Academy.

High Admiral Kern was young for one of his rank. He had a square face and thick dark hair, and he was large enough that one could imagine him as some ancient general with a horse and broadsword, yet he had the typical reserved mien of an imperial nobleman. He didn't look away from his battle as Dennison entered. The edges of the room were dim, the only illumination coming from the illusory ships and the glowing ring that marked the hologram's edge. Kern stood at the center, not directing the progress, just observing. The aide left, closing the door.

"Do you recognize this battle?" the admiral suddenly asked.

Dennison walked forward. "Yes, sir," he said, realizing with surprise that he did. "It's the battle of Seapress."

Kern nodded, face lit from below, still watching the flitting ships. "Your brother's first battle," he said quietly. "The beginning of the Reunification War." He watched for a moment longer, then waved his hand, freezing ships in the air. Finally, he turned eyes on Dennison, who gave a perfunctory salute—really more a wave of the hand. Might as well establish what he was like from the beginning.

Kern didn't frown at the sloppy greeting. He folded his arms, regarding Dennison with a curious look. "Dennison Crestmar. I hear you have something of a smart mouth."

"It's the only part of me blessed with such virtue, I'm afraid."

Kern actually smiled—an expression rarely seen on a High Officer's lips. "I suspect that was why your father sent you to me."

"He has great respect for you, sir," Dennison noted.

Kern snorted. "He can't stand me. He thinks I'm undignified."

Dennison raised an eyebrow. When Kern said nothing more, he continued. "I feel that I must warn you, sir, that I am poorly suited to this commission. I doubt that I will fulfill your expectations of a squadron leader."

"Oh, I don't intend to put you in charge of any ships," Kern said, laughing. "Forgive me, but I've seen your records. The only question is whether you're a worse strategist or tactician."

Dennison sighed in relief. "Then what are you going to do with me?"

Kern waved him forward. "Come," he said, motioning with his other hand and restarting the hologram.

Dennison stepped into the hologram. He'd seen the battle before—one couldn't graduate from the Academy without taking several courses on the mighty Varion Crestmar. Varion's ships were outlined in white. He had two command vessels—one a simple merchant ship, the other his imperial longship—and he controlled only four dozen fighters. Fewer ships than Dennison had been given to waste fighting pirates.

"Tell me about him," Kern requested, watching Varion's longship as it approached the battle.

Dennison raised an eyebrow. "Varion? He's more than twenty years older than I. I've never even met him."

"I'm not a parlor visitor asking about your family, Dennison. I'm your commander. Tell me about Varion the warrior."

Dennison hesitated. Varion's longship, the famous *Voidhawk*, slid forward. Varion's forces were laughably small compared to those of his enemy—the rogue planet of Seapress had boasted a fleet of five massive battleships and nearly a hundred fighters. Two decades ago, at the nadir of imperial power, such a fleet had been impressive indeed.

The Seapress ships, however, didn't form up to attack Varion. They simply waited.

"Varion is . . . " Dennison said quietly. "Varion is perfect."

Kern raised an eyebrow. "In what way?"

"He has never lost," Dennison said. "He was given his first command the very day he left the Academy. Within five years, he had risen to command the entire Imperial Fleet, and was charged with regaining control of the Distant Sectors. He's fought that war his whole life, and he's never suffered a single failure. Hundreds of battles, and he's never lost once."

"Perfect?" Kern asked.

"Perfect." Dennison said.

Kern nodded, then turned back to the battlefield. The blockish merchant ship had pulled ahead of Varion's flagship, and was ponderously making its way toward the Seapress array.

"It all started here," Kern said.

As the first in his class in the Academy, Varion had been offered positions aboard the grandest fleet flagships. He had turned them all down, accepting a lesser post aboard a ship commanded by a regular officer—one who wasn't noble.

Article 117 of the Fleet Code allowed a High Officer to use his rank as a nobleman—rather than his military rank—to take command of any ships where a low officer was in charge. It was an article rarely invoked, for if the nobleman fared badly, the emperor was permitted—even expected—to have the man executed.

Varion had used Article 117, taking command of the *Voidhawk* and its small fleet, the commoner captain becoming his XO. Varion's first action had been to ignore their standing orders, striking out instead toward the rebellious colonies on the Western Reaches.

"He took the merchant ship by force, you know," Kern said. "As if he were a pirate. I remember the High Emperor's fury. He ordered a half dozen longships to hunt your brother down. But Varion's ruse wouldn't have worked otherwise. Seapress—like most of the rebel factions—had spies in the upper ranks of the Fleet. They had to believe that Varion was going rogue. That was why he seized command so rashly and why he captured a merchant vessel, then towed it to Seapress as a 'gift.'

"Nobody on his ship resisted him. That is your brother's most impressive attribute, Dennison. He's not just a tactical master. He's also an amazing leader. And an amazing liar."

The image of the merchant ship rocked suddenly, its engines blasting with unexpected strength. It gained momentum as the Seapress capital ships began to turn, their commanders confused, their own engines firing belatedly. The merchant vessel rammed the Seapress flagship, then both ships twisted and rammed into a second carrier vessel.

"He's also void-cursed lucky," Kern noted.

Dennison nodded as Varion's line burst with motion, fighters streaking away from his flagship, his smaller gunboats moving to enfilade the three remaining Seapress command ships.

Kern held up a hand, and the ships froze. He turned toward Dennison. "All right," he said. "Your turn."

Dennison frowned. "You want me to take command?"

Kern nodded, leaving the hologram and typing a few orders into the control panel. "Let's see what you can do."

Dennison raised an eyebrow. "What will that prove?"

"Humor me," Kern said.

The simulation began again. The massive Seapress command ship rolled weakly to the side, the hole in its side belching flames as oxygen escaped into the void. Seapress should have blown Varion from the sky the moment he entered their space. An imperial longship, with a commander fresh from the Academy, committing treason? They should have seen through the ploy. But they hadn't. Somehow Varion had convinced them.

Dennison shot a look to where Kern watched from the shadows. What did he see? A young Varion? Dennison and his brother were said to be very similar in appearance. The biggest difference was their hair: Dennison's was black, but Varion's had started turning a silvery grey on his twenty-second birthday. By twenty-five, he had already acquired the nickname Silvermane.

"Launch the fighters in three formations," Dennison said, turning back to the hologram. "Order the *Darkstring* to mark four-seven-one and tell it to hold position, firing on any ships that try to escape those wounded flagships. I want the *Fanell* to take up position to my lower port flank, then provide cover if any fighters get too close."

The battle began, and Dennison fought. As always, he tried. He tried hard. The insubordination and cynicism disappeared whenever he entered a battle hologram. Standing within the fray, ships swarming around, above, and below him, he abandoned his habitual pessimism and really tried.

And he lost horribly. The Seapress ships cut down his fighters when Dennison failed to give them proper covering fire. He lost the *Darkstring* when the mortally damaged Seapress flagship rolled too close, then self-destructed. When he tried to retreat, enemy missiles tore out the back of his command ship, and left him to suffocate as life support fizzled. The hologram switched off.

Dennison sighed, turning back toward Kern.

"I've seen worse," Kern finally said.

"Oh?" Dennison said. "You've seen recordings of my Academy fights?"

Kern didn't respond. He stood, tapping his chin in thought. "You asked what you are doing here," he finally said. "Since you're not going to be given a command."

Dennison nodded.

"The High Emperor wants me to turn you into a leader," Kern explained. "But I don't intend to throw away any men on you. Therefore, I've found an instructor to train you."

"Who?"

"Your brother," Kern said. "Get used to this room, Dennison. You're going to be spending a lot of time here. I want you to go through every one of Varion's battles, studying his methods and his strategies. I want you to read every major profile written on him. You will become the empire's foremost expert on Varion Crestmar—you will memorize and you will practice until you can fight this battle, and any other, just as he would."

"You're kidding," Dennison said flatly.

"You should get busy," Kern said, then tapped his control pad. A list of dates and battles appeared on the wall. "You've got a lot of work to do."

"Lord Kern, sir," Dennison said, speaking with an attention to formality he rarely invoked. "I'm not my brother. I never will be."

"That's no reason not to try and learn from him."

"He destroyed my life," Dennison said. "From the first day I entered the Academy, I was fated to fail. How could I do otherwise, considering what others expected of me? Let me study someone else. High Admiral Fallstate, perhaps."

Kern thought for a moment, then shook his head. "You'll do as I order, son."

Each battle was a blow to his self-esteem. Even after studying Varion's tactics, even after watching the battles replay over and over, Dennison had trouble winning. The simulator had a random factor in its programming so that he couldn't just memorize and make the same moves that Varion had.

Dennison sighed, rubbing his forehead as he watched a holographic replay of his latest battle. His year aboard the *Stormwind* had passed quickly and with an odd sense of distortion. He felt removed from events in the empire. His entire world was shrunken to an endless replay of strategies, tactics, and failures, centered around a single individual.

Varion.

The replay of Marcus Seven continued. By this point, Varion's fleet had grown to several thousand ships, and had official imperial support. Varion hadn't even been at this battle in person; he had directed from his flagship many light-years away. The larger an object was, the longer it took to reach its destination via *klage*—so, while visual communications were essentially instantaneous, flagships could take months to travel between distant points of the empire.

These limitations frustrated Varion, so he had split his forces into two different battle groups, sending them in opposite directions. Dennison understood Varion's reasoning now—a year of studying the Silvermane had immersed him in the worldview of a man he'd spent his life trying to escape. Who was Varion Crestmar? He was perfect. Dennison could no longer say that with even a hint of sarcasm.

Every day spent living his sibling's life through battle brought the two of them closer. Dennison found himself spending his extra hours in the hologram room, looking over his recorded battles, then watching Varion's handling of the same conflict. He stopped looking for the strategies and instead focused on the man. What kind of person was this Varion Silvermane? He had been separated from his family for two decades, living in glorious self-imposed exile because the war effort required all of his attention.

Many of these early battles in Varion's campaign made perfect sense. Back then, Varion had still needed to persuade the emperor that he was worthy of trust and support. Dennison could see why the planet Utaries had had to be crushed quickly, because of its ability to rally other planets to its cause. He could follow the logical connection between subduing the Seapress people, then moving on to the less powerful—yet technologically superior—Farnight union.

As the Reunification War proceeded, however, Varion's choices grew baffling. Why had he gone after New Rofelos when doing so had exposed his forces to division? What had been the purpose of committing so many of his forces to conquering Gemwater, a planet of little strategic importance and even less military power?

Questions like these haunted Dennison. Varion's true genius was in his ability to connect battlefields, to lead his fleets from one victory to the next, always gaining momentum, expanding his war to second and third—then tenth and twentieth—fronts. He didn't just destroy or subdue, he converted. Before Varion's conquering began, the empire had barely held enough ships to defend its ever-shrinking border. By Marcus Seven, however, the Fleet had contained more ex-rebel ships than official ones.

Varion was bold and daring, willing to take risks. Yet he was also lucky, for those risks always brought returns. Or *was* it luck? Dennison's father would have scoffed. "Each man has responsibility for his own existence," would have been the characteristic pronouncement.

In the hologram, Dennison's flagship exploded in a spray of metal and light. Varion was perfect. And Dennison was perfectly incompetent. He didn't make this acknowledgement despondently or with self-pity. It was simply a fact. Varion had won Marcus Seven in barely two hours. The fiasco Dennison had just watched was a recording of his fourth attempt. He'd needed seven tries to win.

Dennison sighed, rising and leaving the hologram chamber. He needed to stretch. The lavish passages of the *Stormwind* were oddly empty, and Dennison frowned, walking along the carpeted corridor until he encountered a minor aide. The man paused briefly, saluting and showing the same discomforted confusion the junior officers usually gave Dennison. They weren't certain what to make of a High Officer who hadn't been given a command, yet was important enough to share dinner with Admiral Kern every evening.

"Are we in battle?" Dennison asked.

"Um, yes, sir," the younger man said quickly, eyes darting to the side.

"Be off with you then," Dennison said, waving the man away.

The junior officer eagerly dashed away. Dennison stood, frowning to himself. Had he really been so absorbed that he hadn't noticed the battle alarm? Not that Kern's flagship was really in any danger. This would be a minor battle; Varion's personal fleets handled all the serious fighting. Still, Dennison would like to have watched the fight. He headed for the bridge.

The *Stormwind*'s main bridge was larger than those of ships Dennison had commanded, but the central feature was still the battle hologram. Dennison left the lift, ignoring salutes as he stepped up to the railing, looking down. Kern himself stood in the hologram, but said little. He was a traditional commander; he left most of the local decisions to his squadron commanders, who flew in smaller gunships or longships that were in the thick of the battle.

Varion didn't use squadron commanders. He fought every battle himself, controlling each squadron directly. That would have been fool-hardy for anyone else, but Varion did it with the aplomb of a chess master playing against novices. Dennison shook his head. *Enough of Varion for the moment,* he thought.

Kern's own battle didn't look like much of a fight. The High Admiral's ships outnumbered the opposition by at least three to one.

The battle progressed as expected. Dennison felt a longing as he watched, a wistfulness that he thought he'd quashed back in the Academy. His study of Varion was awakening old pains. He could almost feel the moves on the battlefield. When the squad commanders made their decisions—the orders manifest in the movement of the holographic ships—Dennison instantly knew which choices were better than others. He could see the majesty of the entire battlefield. Kern's forces needed to press to the northeast quadrant, drawing fighters away to defend their command ships so that the gunships to the south would fall. That would let Kern's superior numbers drain the enemy of resources until the rebellious group had no choice but to surrender.

Dennison could see this, but he didn't know how to accomplish it. As always, he grasped the concepts, but not the application. He was not a practical, hands-on commander of the type the empire preferred. It wasn't so odd. Dennison knew of men who loved music, but couldn't play a note themselves. One could enjoy a grand painting without being able to repli-cate its brushstrokes. Art was valuable for the very reason that it could be appreciated by those of lesser skill. Remote leading and battlefield tactics were indeed arts, and Dennison would never be more than a spectator.

"Where are we, anyway?" Dennison asked an aide.

"Gammot system, my lord," the aide answered.

Dennison frowned, leaning down on the railing. *Gammot?* He hadn't realized that Varion had gotten so far, let alone Kern's mop-up force. He waved for an aide to bring him a datapad, then punched up a map of the empire and overlaid it with a schematic of Varion's conquests. He was amazed by what he saw.

It was nearly done. Varion's forces were approaching the last rebellious systems. *I really have been distracted lately,* Dennison thought. Soon there would be peace. And with that peace, commanders wouldn't be as important. They hadn't been, during the Grand Eras.

Why, then, was it so imperative that Dennison be forced into Varion's mold? Everyone—the High Emperor, Kern, Dennison's father—acted as if Dennison's studies were absolutely vital.

It had to be his father, pleading for Dennison's continued training—not because it mattered to the empire, but because Sennion didn't want a failed warrior as a son.

"Of course there will still be a need for commanders," Kern scoffed as a servant ladled soup into his bowl. "What makes you think otherwise?"

"The Reunification War is nearly over," Dennison said.

Kern's dining chamber was a compact version of one in an imperial mansion back on the Point, complete with marble columns and tapestries. The High Admiral's rank forbade his fraternizing with his other subcommanders, but Dennison's higher birth and relation to Varion Crestmar made him an exception. Kern seemed able to relax and dine with Dennison—as if he didn't see him as an underling, but rather as a young family member come to visit.

Kern snorted at Dennison's logic. "There will be insurrections for some time yet, Dennison," he said, attacking his soup. Kern lived like an imperial nobleman, but he was far less reserved than most. Perhaps that was why Dennison got along with him.

"Yes, but Varion and his officers will be free to handle them," Dennison said, ignoring his own soup.

"All men age, and new blood needs to replace them," Kern said.

"The empire doesn't need me, Kern," Dennison said. "It *never* has. Only my father's stubbornness keeps me here."

"I wouldn't be so sure about that," Kern said. "Either way, I have my orders. How is your training coming?"

Dennison shrugged. "I fought the Marcus Seven battle four more times today and lost twice. Still can't win it consistently."

"Marcus Seven," Kern said with a frown. "You're taking your time. At this rate, it'll take you another year to get through Varion's archive."

"At least I'm not complaining anymore."

"No," Kern agreed. "You aren't. In fact, you actually seem to be enjoying yourself."

Dennison took a sip. "Perhaps so. My brother makes for an interesting subject."

"When you first came on board, I could tell you hated him."

Dennison rested his spoon back in his bowl. "I suppose I did," he finally said. "At the Academy, I was never given a chance to succeed—the other boys challenged me to battles before I was ready, each one wanting the prestige of defeating Varion's brother. I became a loser before I could learn otherwise. I didn't choose my path—Varion chose it for me.

"But now . . . " Dennison trailed off, then looked Kern in the eye. "Could any man really hate him? How can you hate someone who's perfect?"

Kern seemed troubled. Finally, he turned back to his meal. "At any rate, you should soon have a chance to meet him."

Dennison looked up, surprised.

Kern took a sip of soup. "The Reaches are nearly subdued. In two months, Varion will meet with an Imperial Emissary on Kress, where they will hold a ceremony welcoming him back to civilization. You may attend, if you wish."

Dennison smiled broadly. "I do," he decided. "I do indeed."

Dennison was surprised by how bright the colors were. Kress was a sparsely inhabited world near the border of the Reaches. Its weather was obviously unregulated, for the wind blew strongly against Dennison's face as he stood in the speeder's door.

Dennison stepped onto the soft ground, sneezing and raising a hand against the bright sunlight. The vibrant green grass came up to his knees. What kind of world was this to greet a returning hero? A pavilion had been erected a short distance away, and Dennison made his way there. A local weather regulator had been set up, and the wind slowed as he entered the invisible confines of its influence. There, he unexpectedly found his father standing with a delegation of high-ranking ambassadors and military men. Sennion's perfect white uniform was a pristine contrast to the wild lands around him.

*A small pavilion on a rural world? Why not meet Varion with the adoring crowds he deserves?*

Dennison could see a dropship descending through the wild air. He stepped up beside his father. Dennison hadn't seen him in over six months, but Sennion barely nodded in acknowledgement. The dropship fell like a flare. It plummeted, slowing only when it neared the ground, its plasma jets carelessly vaporizing the grass. The weather sphere kept the wind of its landing from unsettling the pavilion's dignified occupants. Dennison edged a bit closer to the front, waiting eagerly as the dropship doorway opened.

He had seen pictures of Varion. They didn't do him justice. Pictures could not convey the confidence, the powerful presence, of a man like Varion Crestmar. With his silver hair and commanding eyes, he walked down the ramp like a god descending to the mortal realm.

When last seen on the Imperial Homeworld, Varion had been a smooth-faced boy. Now he bore the lines of combat and age; he was in the middle of his fifth decade. He wore an imperial uniform, but not one of a standard color. Dennison frowned. White was for nobility, blue for citizen officers, and red for regular soldiers. But . . . grey? There was no grey.

A group of officers walked down the ramp after Varion. Dennison recognized many of them. The woman would be Charisa of Utaries, a celebrated fighter pilot and squadron leader, one of the first rebel commanders who had joined Varion. The histories and biographies spoke often of her. What they didn't mention was the way Varion rested his hand on her elbow as they walked forward, the way he watched her with obvious fondness.

To Varion's right were Admirals Brakah and Terarn, two men who had been with Varion at the Academy, then had requested assignment under his command. They were said to be his most trusted advisors. They walked behind Varion as he approached, with the sure step Dennison had imagined. Varion stopped just short of entering the pavilion.

Sennion Crestmar, High Officer and Imperial Duke, stepped forward to greet his son. "In the name of the High Emperor, I welcome you, returning warrior." His words carried over the wind that still whipped outside the pavilion. "Accept this as a token of our esteem, and take your rightful place as the greatest High Admiral the empire has ever known."

Sennion extended a hand bearing a golden medal emblazoned with the double sunburst seal, the highest and most prestigious of the Imperial Crests.

Varion stood in the wind, looking down at the medal that swung from his father's hand. He reached out, taking the award in his hand, then held it up in the light, dangling it before his eyes.

All were still.

Then Varion let the medal drop to the grass.

Sennion's gun was in his hand in an instant. He pointed the weapon at his son's forehead and gave no opportunity for reaction. He simply pulled the trigger.

The energy blast burst just millimeters before Varion's face and then dissipated. The High Admiral hadn't moved. He was unhurt, and apparently unconcerned.

Around Dennison, the pavilion's occupants burst into motion. Flex-blasters and slug-drivers were pulled from holsters as men jumped for cover. Soldiers and officers alike drew. Dennison stood, immobile amid the yelling and the gunfire, and realized he wasn't surprised.

*The greatest High Admiral the Fleet has ever known . . . perhaps the greatest commander mankind has ever seen. Of course he wouldn't stop with the Reaches. Why would he? Dennison's father fired again, weapon held just inches from Varion's face. Again the blast evaporated, hitting some kind of invisible shield.*

*This is no imperial technology, Dennison thought, stepping forward obliviously as others opened fire. Energy bolts and slugs alike were stopped by Varion's strange shield. Twenty years on his own, autonomous and unfettered by imperial control . . . Of course! He captured the most technologically advanced worlds first. That's why some of those choices didn't make sense. He was planning for this even back then.*

Men called for Dennison's father to get out of the way. Some were firing at Varion's officers, but they too had the strange personal shields, and they stood calmly, not even bothering to return fire. Dennison continued to walk forward, drawn to his brother. He watched as Varion reached down, unholstered his sidearm, and raised it to his father's head.

"You are no child of mine," Sennion said, proudly staring down his son. "I disavow you. I should have done it twenty years ago."

Dennison froze as Varion pulled the trigger. The duke's corpse crumpled to the ground, a few wisps of smoke rising from his head.

A wave of gun blasts stormed from behind Dennison, ineffectively firing at Varion. The grass and earth before Varion exploded with fire and weapon blasts. Someone called for a physician.

Varion turned to regard the attack, raising a hand, waving his people back into the ship. Then he noticed Dennison. Silvermane stepped forward, carefully picking his way across the scarred ground. Dennison felt like scrambling back toward his speeder, but running would be useless. This was Varion Silvermane. He did not lose. People did not escape him. Those eyes . . . looking into those eyes, Dennison knew that this man could destroy him.

Varion stopped right in front of Dennison. The High Admiral's eyes looked contemplative. "So," he finally said, voice clear even over the gunfire and yells. "They *did* clone me. Well, the High Emperor will find that I am capable of defeating even myself."

He turned and left. Someone finally got a big repeating Calzer gun working, and it fired a blinding barrage of blue bolts. Varion's shields repulsed them. There should have been some blowback, at least, but there was nothing. Varion walked up the ramp to his ship as calmly as he had strolled down.

The Calzer soon drained the pavilion's energy stores, and the weather sphere collapsed, letting in the full fury of the winds. Dennison stepped forward through lines of smoke torn and then dispersed by the gale, ignoring the voices of angry, confused, and frightened men.

Varion's dropship blasted off, throwing Dennison to the ground. By the time his vision cleared, the ship was a dark speck in the air.

"We knew he had *something*," Kern said, watching the holo for the tenth time. "But his shield—where did he develop it? We put spies on each world. . . . "

"He brought them with him," Dennison said quietly, standing against the view railing.

"What?"

"The scientists," Dennison said from the side of the hologram room. "Varion doesn't trust anything he can't watch directly. He would have brought the scientists from Gemwater with him, probably on his flagship. That way he could supervise their work."

"Gemwater . . . " Kern said. "But he conquered that planet over fifteen years ago! You think your brother has been keeping secrets for that long?"

Dennison nodded distractedly. "He knew from that first battle at Seapress. He understood that by quelling the Reaches, he would make the High Empire stronger and harder to defeat when the time came. That's why he took Gemwater so early, to give its scientists decades to build him secret technology."

Kern watched the holo again.

The universe felt . . . *awry* to Dennison. His father was dead. Sennion Crestmar had never been loving, but he had instilled in Dennison a powerful will to succeed. He'd been demanding, rigid, and unforgiving.

Yet Dennison had hoped that someday . . . maybe . . . he would be able to make the man proud.

And now he never would. Varion had robbed Dennison of that.

*What does it matter? Dennison thought. The hologram below showed the fire-fight through smoke and verdant grass. Sennion wasn't even really my father. I have no father. Unless Varion was wrong.*

No. Varion was never wrong.

Only two men could verify the claim for certain. The first lay dead from an energy blast to the head. The other—the High Emperor, who had to approve all cloning petitions—had yet to respond to Dennison's request for an audience. But Dennison knew what the answer would be. The saddest part wasn't that Dennison was a fabricated tool, it was that he was a defective one. Genetically he was the same as Varion. He had even checked in the mirror and found a few silver hairs. Varion had started to go grey at twenty-three—Dennison's age now.

So many things made sudden and daunting sense. *You* cannot *be like other officers,* his father had said. *The High Empire expects more.* No wonder they had pushed Dennison so hard; no wonder they had refused to let him leave the service. He *was* Varion.

And yet he wasn't. Whatever Varion had, it hadn't been transmitted to Dennison. That confidence of his hadn't come from a random mingling of chromosomes. The victories, the power, the sheer momentum. These could not be copied.

*The High Emperor will find that I am capable of defeating even myself. Varion knew—knew that he was special, somehow.*

"Dennison," Kern said.

Dennison looked up. Kern sat below, in a chair just before the holo, looking up disapprovingly. He had paused the recording. The point he had inadvertently chosen showed a disturbing image. Varion's weapon raised, smoking, a corpse falling to the grass below . . .

"Dennison, I asked you a question," Kern said.

"He's going to win, Kern," Dennison said, staring at the holo. "The empire . . . to Varion, what is the empire but another collection of recal-citrant planets to be brought into line?"

Kern glanced at the holo, and—realizing where he'd paused it—turned off the image.

"We are High Officers, Dennison," Kern said sternly. "Such talk isn't fitting."

Dennison snorted.

"Varion *can* be defeated," Kern insisted.

Dennison shook his head. "No. He can't. And why should we bother, anyway? When does a man stop being a hero and start being a tyrant? If he had the right to bring the rebellious Reaches into line, then why shouldn't he claim the same moral right regarding us?"

Kern frowned. "Only the planets that raided us were conquered—at least at first, back when Varion was still nominally under control. This complete conquest of the Reaches was his own plan, done against the High Emperor's wishes. By the time we realized our mistake, he was already too powerful. We had only one option—gather strength and wait, hoping that he would be satisfied with taking the Reaches."

Dennison shook his head. "If you hoped that, then you never really knew him. He is a conqueror, Kern. It's like he feels some divine right to take the High Throne for himself."

Kern's frown deepened. He reached over, turning the recording back on. Once again, Dennison was confronted by the frozen image of his father dying, his brother . . . his other self . . . watching impassively.

"At least the High Empire believes in honor, Dennison," Kern said. "Is there honor in that face? The face of a man who would slaughter his own father?"

Dennison glanced away, shutting his eyes. "Please."

He heard the holo wink off. "I'm sorry," Kern said sincerely. "Here, let me show you something else instead."

Dennison turned back; the holo shifted to an image of Varion. This image, however, was in motion. Varion sat behind a broad, black commander's desk, a small datapad in his hand.

"What is this?" Dennison asked, perking up.

"The feed from a bug we have in Varion's ready room," Kern explained. "Aboard the *Voidhawk*."

Dennison frowned. "How—?"

"Never mind how," Kern said. "This is our only bug feed from the *Voidhawk* that didn't fuzz off within an hour of the incident on Kress. I doubt that Varion's scanners caught the other twenty but missed this one."

"He knows about it, of course," Dennison said. "But why would he . . . " He trailed off. Silvermane had left the bug because it amused him. Even as Dennison watched, Varion looked up—directly toward the ostensibly hidden camera—and smiled.

"That man  .  .  . " Kern said. "He wants us to watch him, to know how unconcerned he is by our spying. He's so arrogant, so certain of his victory. You would bow before this creature? Whatever the empire is now, it will be worse with him at the head."

Dennison watched Varion lounge in his ready room. *But I am him—an inferior knockoff, at least.*

Kern eventually snapped off the feed. "I'm giving you a subcommand, Dennison."

Dennison frowned. "I thought we had an understanding."

"We have too many fighters and too few officers. The time for study is over."

Dennison felt himself pale involuntarily. "We'll be facing  .  .  . him?"

"Just a minor battle," Kern said. "A preliminary skirmish, really. I doubt Varion will bother directing his side of it. It will happen some distance from the bulk of his fleet."

Dennison knew Kern was wrong. Varion directed all of his battles personally.

"This is a bad idea," Dennison finally said, but Kern had already turned back to his review of the Kress incident.

"Yes, son. It's true." The emperor looked  .  .  . weary.

"It's illegal to clone a member of a High Family," Dennison said, frowning as he knelt in front of the wallscreen image.

"I *am* the law, Dennison," the emperor said. "Nothing I do can be illegal. In this case, the potential benefit of a cloning outweighed our reservations."

"And I was that benefit," Dennison said bitterly.

"Your tone threatens disrespect, young Crestmar."

"Crestmar?" Dennison snapped. "Clones have no legal house or family."

The High Emperor's aged eyes flashed with anger at the outburst, and Dennison looked down guiltily. Eventually, the emperor's voice continued, and Dennison was surprised at the softness he heard in it.

"Ah, child," the emperor said. "Do not think us monsters. The laws you speak of maintain order in High Family succession, but exceptions can be made. It was your father's stipulation in agreeing to this plan. Your right of succession was ratified by a closed council of High Dukes soon after your birth. Even had your father not required this, we would have done it. We did not create a life intending only to throw it away."

Dennison finally looked back up. The weariness he had noted in the High Emperor's face was evident again—during the last few years, the man had aged decades. *Worrying about Varion would do this to any man.* "Your Majesty," Dennison said carefully. "What if I had turned out as much a traitor as he?"

"Then you would have gone to war against him," the High Emperor said. "For Varion would never be willing to share rule, even with himself. We hoped maybe you would weaken each other enough for us to stand against you. That, however, was a contingency plan—our first and foremost goal was to see that you did *not* turn out as he. It . . . seems that we were *too* successful in that respect."

"Apparently," Dennison mumbled.

"If that is all, young Crestmar, then I must be about the empire's business—as must you. The time for your battle approaches quickly."

Dennison bowed his farewell, and the wallscreen winked off.

Dennison paused in the doorway, the command bridge extending before him. This would be his first time commanding a real crew since he had begun studying under Kern's direction.

The bridge of the *Perpetual* was compact, as one would expect from a ship of its class. Kern's fleet had a dozen such minor command ships that traveled attached to the *Stormwind*. During a battle they were released and stationed across the battle space, allowing for a division of labor, as well as decentralizing leadership.

The bridge was manned by five younger officers. Dennison realized with chagrin that he didn't know their names—he had been too engrossed in his studies to mingle with the rest of Kern's command staff. Dennison walked down the ramp toward the battle hologram. The officers stood at attention. There was something odd about their postures. With a start, Dennison realized what it was. None of them showed even a hint of disrespect. Dennison had come to expect a certain level of repressed scorn from those under him. From these men, there was nothing. No hint that they expected him to fail, no signs that they were frustrated at being forced to serve with him. It was an odd feeling. A good feeling.

*These are Kern's men, Dennison thought, nodding for them to return to their stations. They're not just some random crew—they trust their ultimate commander, and therefore trust his decision to assign me to this post.*

The battle hologram blossomed, and a crewman approached with a battle visor. Dennison waved her away. She bowed and withdrew, showing no surprise.

*They trust me, Dennison thought uncomfortably. Kern trusts me. How can they? Can they really have forgotten my reputation?*

He had no answers for himself, so instead he studied the battle space. Varion's ships would soon arrive. His forces were pushing toward Inner Imperial Space, surrounding the High Emperor's forces in an attempt to breach the imperial line simultaneously in a dozen different places. Kern's forces were arrayed defensively—a long double wave of ships positioned for maximum mutual support. Dennison and his twenty ships were at the far eastern end of the line—a reserve force, unless they were directly attacked.

As seen in the holo, Varion's squadron suddenly appeared as a scattering of red monoliths disengaging from the *klage-dynamic*. Their *klage* wouldn't have been very fast—only a small multiple of conventional speeds—because of the large command ships at the rear. When traveling together, a fleet could only move as quickly as its largest—and therefore slowest—ships.

Just a moment after the command ships disengaged from *klage*, fighters spurted from Varion's fleet toward Dennison's squadron. So much for staying in reserve. Dennison's hologram automatically zoomed in so he could deploy his ships. He had twenty fighters and the *Perpetual*, a cruiser which could, in a pinch, act as a carrier as well. Directly to port was the *Windless*, a gunship with less speed and maneuverability but greater long-range firepower.

Kern would make the larger, battlewide decisions, and subcommanders like Dennison would execute them. Dennison's own orders were simple: hold position and defend the *Windless* if his sector was pressed. Dennison's crew waited upon his commands.

"Expand hologram," Dennison said. "Revert to the main tactical map."

Two of the officers shared a look at the unconventional order. It wasn't Dennison's job to consider the entire battle. Yet they did as he asked, and the hologram zoomed back out to give Dennison a view of the entire battle space. He stepped forward—bits of hologram shattering against his body and re-forming behind him—studying the ships in red. Varion's fleet. Though the Silvermane wasn't present personally, he would be directing the battle from across space. Dennison was finally facing his brother. The man who had never known defeat.

The man who had killed his father.

*You're not perfect, Varion, Dennison thought. If you were, you'd have found a way to bring our father to your side, rather than just blasting him in the forehead.*

Varion arranged his defense. Three prongs of fighters bracketing larger gunships formed the most direct assault in his direction. Something was off. Dennison frowned, trying to decide what was bothering him.

"Kern," he said, tapping a dot on the hologram, opening a channel to the admiral.

"I'm rather busy, Dennison," Kern said curtly.

Dennison paused slightly at the rebuke. "Admiral," he said, a little more formal. "Something is wrong."

"Watch your sector, Lieutenant. I'll worry about Varion."

"With all due respect, Admiral," Dennison said, "you just had me study him for months on end. I know Varion Crestmar better than any living man. Are you sure this is the time to ignore my advice?"

Silence.

"All right," Kern said. "Make it quick."

"The orientation of his forces is odd, sir," Dennison said. "His fighter prongs have been deployed to focus on the eastern sector of the battle. Away from you. But the *Stormwind* is by far the most powerful ship in this confrontation—stronger, even, than Varion's own capital ships. He *has* to deal with you quickly."

"He's used this formation before," Kern said. "Remember Gallosect IV? He focused on gunships first so that he could surround the flagship and take it from a distance."

"He had two-to-one advantage at Gallosect," Dennison said. "He could afford to expend fighters keeping the flagship busy. He's too thinly extended to try that here—by pressing to the east, he's going to expose himself to your batteries. He'll lose capital ships that way."

Silence.

"You wearing your visor, Dennison?" Kern asked.

"No."

"I thought not," Kern said. "Put one on."

Dennison didn't argue. The same aide walked back, proffering the equipment. Dennison slipped it on and saw a view from his fighter commander's cockpit.

"Here," Kern said, through the earpiece, no longer using an open channel. "Look at this."

The right half of Dennison's visor changed, showing a smaller version of the battle map. It was covered with arrows indicating attack vectors, and there were annotations around most of the vessels.

"What is this?" Dennison asked.

"Speak quietly," Kern said in a whisper. "Not even my bridge officers know about this feed."

"But what is it?"

"Intercepted *klage* communications," Kern said softly. "This image is being sent from Varion to his commanders here. It's how he commands—not verbally, but with battle maps outlining what he wants done."

"You can intercept *klage* communications!" Dennison said quietly, turning away to muffle his voice. "How?"

"Varion wasn't the only one who spent these last few decades working on technology," Kern said. "We focused on communications and may have gotten the better end of the bargain, since it appears his shields are only effective on a personal scale. Our scientists developed a special bug that can work on a klage transmitter. The bug in Varion's ready room, the one he thinks he's so clever to have found, is just a red herring."

"Can you intercept the responses from Varion's commanders?"

"Yes," Kern said. "But only if they come through the *klage* transceiver on the *Voidhawk*."

"And could we change the orders he sends?" Dennison asked.

"The techs say they might be able to," Kern said. "But if we do, we give away that we've been listening in. This gives us an edge. Read that map and tell me what you think."

Dennison zoomed his visor in on Varion's orders. They were succinct and clear. And brilliant. As the fighters engaged, he saw patterns emerge and interact. His brother made brave moves—daring, almost ridiculous moves. Here, a squadron of fighters was lured too close to another group. There, a gunship used its opponents as screens, keeping their cannons silent lest they destroy their own forces.

And he continued to push east. Varion didn't explain himself in his transmissions, but after just a few minutes of watching, Dennison had confirmed his suspicions. "Kern," he said quietly, drawing the admiral's attention back from his command. "He's coming for me."

"What?" Kern asked.

"He's coming for me," Dennison replied. "He's defeated every commander he's ever gone up against—and now he has a chance for what he sees as the ultimate battle. He wants to fight himself. He wants to fight me."

"Nonsense," Kern said. "How would he know where you are? He doesn't have our *klage* interception capability—of that, we're as certain as we can be."

"There are other ways to get information," Dennison said.

He stood quietly for a moment. And then he felt a chill.

"Kern," he snapped, "we need to retreat."

"What?" the admiral said with frustration. He obviously didn't like being distracted. "This whole battle is wrong," Dennison said. "He's planning something."

"He's *always* planning something."

"This time it's different. Kern, he wouldn't expose himself to the *Stormwind* like that. Not even to get to me. We need to—"

A blast—sharp, shockingly loud—sounded in Dennison's ear. He jumped, crying out.

"Kern!" Dennison yelled.

Chaos. Screaming. And then static. Dennison whipped off his visor, looking at his startled crew. "Raise the admiral!"

"Nobody's responding," said the comm officer. "Wait—"

". . . Lord Canton from the *Stormwind* reserve bridge," a voice feed crackled to life. "There has been an explosion on the main bridge. I am assuming command of the ship. Repeat. I am assuming command."

*Kern!* Dennison thought. He spun, looking at the holographic projection of the *Stormwind*. An explosion on the bridge—sabotage? An assassin?

A shot sounded. Several of Dennison's crew jumped—but this too had come over the comm.

"Lord Canton!" Dennison shouted.

Screams. Weapons fire.

He scanned the battle map. Kern's forces were in chaos. Even within the careful structure of the Imperial Fleet, the loss of an admiral was devastating. Varion's forces pressed on, fighters darting, gunships firing. Pressing toward Dennison.

*Kern might still be alive. . . .*

No. Varion's assassin wouldn't fail. Varion wouldn't fail.

"This is Lord Haltep of the *Farmight*," a voice crackled over the comm. "I am assuming command of this battle. All commanders secure bridges! Squadrons Six through Seventeen, press toward the *Stormwind*. Don't let the flagship fall!"

*That's what Varion wants, Dennison thought. He presses east, creates a disaster on the flagship, then cuts us in two.*

This battle could not be won. It was hard to see—technically, they still outnumbered Varion's forces. But Dennison could see the death of

Kern's fleet in the chaos of the battle space. Varion was control. Varion was order. Where there was chaos, he would prevail.

But what could Dennison do about it? Nothing. He was useless.

Except . . .

*I can't let Kern's fleet be destroyed. These men trusted him.*

"Open a channel to the commanders of every capital ship," Dennison said quietly to his crew.

They complied.

"This is Duke Dennison Crestmar," Dennison said, feeling a bit surreal as holographic ships burst and died around him. "I am invoking Article One Hundred Seventeen and taking command of this fleet."

Silence.

"What are your orders, my lord?" a stiff voice eventually asked. It was Lord Haltep, the one who had only just assumed command.

*These are good soldiers, Dennison thought. How did Kern, who seemed so relaxed about military protocol, command such respect from his men?*

Perhaps that was what Dennison should have been studying these last two years. Regardless, he had command. Now, what did he do with it? He stood for a moment, watching the battlefield in its chaos, and felt a twinge of excitement. This was no simulation. That was Varion, the real man, on the other side. This was what Dennison been created to do: to fight Varion, to defend the empire. Why else had he studied all those months?

*Why else did I study? So I could know that this battle was unwinnable. Our admiral dead, our forces divided. Varion would easily beat me in a fair battle.*

*And this one is far from fair.*

"All fighter squadrons to the eastern flank," Dennison said.

"But the flagship!" Haltep said. "Our forces have regained control inside. They're on the third bridge!"

"You heard my orders, Lord Haltep," Dennison said quietly. "I want the fighters back, arranged in a tight aegis pattern."

"Yes, my lord," a dozen voices came through the com. Their fighters and gunships complied, pulling back into what was known as an aegis pattern—the fighters defending the larger ships at very close ranges.

Dennison lost some fighters as they broke off from the enemy. *Come on,* he thought. *I know what you want to do. Do it!*

Varion's ships swarmed the *Stormwind*. It began to fire back, displaying awesome power, but without its own fighters, it was at a distinct disadvantage. Explosions flashed on Dennison's hologram.

"All ships to dock," Dennison said.

"What?" Haltep's voice demanded.

"Varion's fighters are busy," Dennison said. "I want all fighters to dock in the closest command ship. The gunships can even take a few, if necessary. We only have a few minutes."

"Retreat," Haltep spat over the comm.

*"Yes,"* Dennison replied. *I've certainly had a lot of practice.*

It worked. Varion realized too late what Dennison was doing—he'd already committed to taking down the *Stormwind.* It wasn't a mistake, but it was as near to one as Dennison had ever seen from his brother. Obviously he hadn't expected Dennison to concede and run so quickly.

As the larger ships began to *klage* away, Dennison watched the *Stormwind* finally break, its massive hull blowing outward from a ruptured core. Debris sprayed through his hologram as the mighty ship died.

*And so, I fail again,* Dennison thought as his own ship *klaged* away.

Dennison strode down the walkway, clothed in a crisp white uniform. It bore no ornamentation—no awards, no badges of service, no indications of commissions fulfilled. His speeder sat cooling in the dock; he'd spent nearly a week in transit back to the Point, thinking about Kern's death and the loss of the *Stormwind.* Why did the admiral's death bother him even more than his father's had?

A squad of six armed MPs met him at the foot of the ramp. *Six?* Dennison thought. *Did they really think I'd be that much trouble?*

"Lord Crestmar," one of them said. "We're here to escort you."

"Of course," Dennison said. He walked, surrounded by soldiers, still lost in thought.

What would have happened if he'd fought his brother? He couldn't have won, but Kern likely hadn't believed he'd beat Varion either. Kern had fought, rather than giving up. Rather than running. Now he was honorably dead, while Dennison still lived.

Lived after invoking a near-forbidden article and forcing an embarrassing retreat. Men had been executed for less. Men had deserved execution for less.

The guards led him through four separate checkpoints. Dennison's trip home had been spent in near silence, with sparse communications, so Dennison knew little of Varion's conquests during the last week. However, considering the events aboard the *Stormwind,* the extra security made sense.

His escort led him into a section of the imperial complex filled with bustling aides and officers. It was a testament to their worried state that not a single one paused to notice him, despite the color of his uniform and the crests that declared him to be an Imperial Duke. Crests that he probably wouldn't hold for much longer. After a few turns down hallways, the guards led Dennison to the Emperor's command center. They walked apart from him, so they didn't tread on the crimson carpet reserved for High Officers.

The soldiers at the door saluted, and Dennison's escort halted. "The emperor is inside, my lord," the lead MP said.

Dennison paused. This was looking less and less like an execution. Ignoring his pounding heart, Dennison walked into the command center. None of the guards went with him.

The first thing that struck him was the room's busyness. Ten huge viewscreens had been erected all around the chamber, and high-ranking officers stood before these, calling out orders. Aides and junior officers scurried about, and armed soldiers, their weapons drawn, stood in every corner of the room, watching the occupants with suspicion. Nearly everyone—guards and commanders alike—seemed haggard, their faces wan, their eyes red from stress and fatigue. The room was kept dim to make the glowing icons that represented ships more easily visible.

The viewscreens depicted ten different battles in ten different systems. Dennison caught a young officer's arm. "What is going on here?"

"The Silvermane," the woman said. "He's attacking."

"Where?"

"Everywhere!"

Dennison let the woman go. *Everywhere?* he thought, stepping forward. He recognized a few of the men giving orders. High Admirals, like his father. Scanning the screens, Dennison was able to piece together their situation. New Seele. Highwall. Tightendow Prime. These were important core worlds, each home to an imperial fleet.

The emperor had moved his other fleets out to protect his borders. Dennison knew the numbers; he knew how many ships the Fleet had. If Varion took these worlds, there would be nothing left to resist him. The empire would be his.

"And he's fighting them all at once," Dennison said aloud, looking up at the screens. "He's controlling all ten battles at the same time."

An aging admiral—one Dennison recognized from his Academy days—sat in an exhausted posture in one of the room's many chairs.

"Yes," the man said. "It's like we're a game to him. Defeating us one at a time isn't enough of a challenge. He planned it like this—he wants to destroy us all at once—to show us just how good he is. By the Seal, we never should have let him leave the Academy. We've doomed ourselves."

Dennison turned away from the screens. At the center of the room, on a platform elevated a few steps above the floor, the Emperor sat in a large command chair surrounded by ten smaller viewscreens showing the same ten battles. He was obviously making an effort to maintain an erect, confident posture—but somehow that only made him look wearier, like a warrior straining to bear armor that was too heavy for him.

Dennison stepped up to the chair.

"Dennison," the emperor said, looking at him with tired eyes, but smiling slightly. "You arrived just in time to watch your empire fall."

"I suppose executing me now would be pointless."

"Executing?" the emperor asked, frowning.

"For invoking Article One Hundred Seventeen and losing a flagship."

The emperor sat for a moment, blinking. "Dennison, I was actually thinking of giving you a medal."

"For what, Your Majesty? Most flamboyant waste of half a fleet?"

"For *saving* half a fleet," the emperor said. "Lad, you have always been too hard on yourself. Varion was an optimist all through the Academy; he believed that he could do anything. Why do you always assume that you are a failure?"

"I—"

"Varion struck six separate fleets the same day he attacked Kern's," the emperor said. "In each battle, he managed to assassinate the fleet admiral—and in four of the six cases, he killed the next man who took command as well. We still don't know how he got so many assassins onto our bridges—you can see that we've had to take a number of precautions here on the Point.

"Regardless, of those six fleets, only *yours* escaped. Three of the fleets managed to disengage, but Varion chased them down and destroyed them. If you hadn't abandoned the flagship as you did, you never would have been fast enough to get away."

Dennison regarded the emperor, then looked down.

"Even in victory, you doubt yourself," the emperor said quietly.

"It's no victory with Kern dead, Your Majesty."

"Ah," the emperor said, rubbing his forehead. He looked so exhausted. So worried. "Do you know what happens when a conqueror runs out of people to fight, Dennison?"

Dennison hesitated, then shook his head.

"It's always the same," the emperor mused. "Men like Varion cannot be content with peaceful rule. They make brilliant commanders, but terrible kings. His reign will be filled with unrest, rebellion, oppression, and slaughter."

"You speak as if his victory were inevitable," Dennison said.

"Do you honestly believe otherwise?" the emperor asked.

Dennison glanced back at the big screens. He could easily see why the emperor had set up this room. The threat from Varion's assassins had required a single secure command post—likely with backups, should this one be destroyed—away from the ships themselves. The men here would be blood loyalists of the emperor's household. From this room, the Imperial High Admirals could command the ten separate battles and work for victory right under the emperor's eyes. Unfortunately, they were losing. All of them.

*Such brilliance,* Dennison thought. *Like a master of games, sitting before his boards, playing ten opponents simultaneously.* Varion seemed to be most brilliant when he was stretched, and these ten battles must have stretched him greatly, because he was in rare form. He pressed his advantage on all ten fronts, and while the battles were by no means over, Dennison could see where they were headed.

"I can't let you take command," the emperor said.

Dennison looked back.

"If that's why you came back to the Point," the emperor said, "then I must disappoint you. I read our almost inevitable doom in these battles, and the men who fight them are good tacticians. Our best. I realize you must want to fight your brother, but we both know you don't have the skill for it. I'm sorry."

Dennison turned back toward the viewscreens. "I didn't come to fight him, Your Majesty. I fled that opportunity."

"Ah. Well, perhaps you will survive his attack, lad. In a way, you are his family. He might let you live."

"As he let his father live?" Dennison replied.

The emperor did not respond. Dennison turned to watch the screens, staring at Varion in his power, his perfection. "If he comes, I don't want to live," Dennison whispered. "He's taken everything from me."

"Your father and Kern."

Dennison shook his head. "Not just that. He's stolen my purpose. I was created to defeat him, and yet I am just as powerless as the rest of you. Nobody can face Varion. For the others, there is no shame in this—but *my* inability is a profound failure. I could have been him."

"You don't want to be that creature, Dennison," the emperor said, shaking a weary head, leaning back. "What has his life been? Nothing but success after success. That has bred an arrogance that will kill him someday. Better to be the failure who nobly strived than the success who never really had to."

Dennison closed his eyes. The words seemed foolish. Better to be Dennison the failure than Varion the genius?

*What could I possibly have that Varion does not?*

Dennison hesitated. Around him there were sounds—breathing, grumbling, called commands. One of the admirals cursed loudly.

Dennison didn't open his eyes. That admiral's curses—he knew what had caused them. "The battle for Tightendow Prime," Dennison said. "Varion just took the eastern fighter flank, didn't he?"

"Actually, yes," the emperor said.

Dennison stood with eyes closed. "On the fifth screen. He is pressing toward the gunships in the western screen-sector. He is taking them now, though moments ago they seemed safe. On the first monitor, he is pushing toward the flagship. It will fall within ten minutes. On the ninth screen, Taurtan, he is leading your fighters into a trap. They are being cut off somehow—I don't know how, but I know he is doing it. They are lost."

Silence.

"On the eighth screen, the planet Falna, he is collapsing the front line. After that, he will find a way to push the gunships into retreat, breaking their firing lines and opening the way for his fighters."

"Yes," the emperor whispered.

Dennison opened his eyes. "I don't know *how* he will do these things, Your Majesty. That is the difference between him and me. Somehow, he can make his dreams into realities." Dennison turned toward the emperor. "Do we still have the bug in Varion's *klage* transmitter?"

"For all the good it does," the emperor said. "We discover his orders only a few moments before they are carried out. Perhaps that has allowed us to survive this long."

"Just before he died," Dennison said, "Kern told me that you might have found a way to fake the transmissions coming in and out of Varion's ship."

"The long distance ones, yes," the emperor said, frowning. "But it's far better just to spy on him. If we started fabricating messages, it wouldn't take long for Varion and his men to discover the trick. We'd trade a long-term tactical advantage for a few minutes of confusion."

"Your Majesty," Dennison said, "there *is* no more long-term. If Varion wins this day, then we are all dead."

The emperor's frown deepened. He sat in thought for a moment, rubbing his chin. "What do you propose?" he finally asked.

*What am I proposing? Dennison thought. I've failed enough. Why pull the entire empire down with me?*

He started to tell the emperor he'd meant nothing by the comments, but something made him stop. Optimism and pessimism. He'd learned many things from watching Varion—tactics, strategy, how to manipulate a squadron. But it seemed he'd never learned the one thing that was most important.

Confidence.

"I'll need a crew of technicians and aides," Dennison said, "and these ten monitors beside your throne. Oh, and a tech who is familiar with that bugging system we have on Varion's *klage*."

The emperor continued to sit in his command chair for a moment, looking up at Dennison appraisingly. Then, surprisingly, he stood, calling to one of the admirals. A few moments later a young technician was ushered into the command center.

"You can hack the traitor's *klage* data lines?" Dennison asked the thin man. "Sending false information to Varion's ship?"

The technician nodded.

"How long can you keep it up?" Dennison asked.

"It depends," the technician said. "He has no reason to suspect a bug in his transmitter—he doesn't know about the technology. But changing his information will create some interference that his technicians should notice and pick apart. If I'd have to guess, I'd say maybe a half hour or so."

Dennison nodded thoughtfully.

"My lord," the tech continued. "It won't be a very useful half hour. We can send false messages in, and we can block the real transmissions from his admirals. But we can't stop orders going *out* from the *Voidhawk*, so the nine other battle groups will soon realize Varion no longer knows what is truly happening, and is relying on bad information."

"No matter," Dennison said. "Prepare to hack the line. I want you to make it seem that the fleets in the other nine battles are doing exactly as I say. Instead of the real reports Varion's commanders are sending, give him the fabrications I describe."

The technician nodded, gathering a small crew and moving to a set of consoles at the side of the room.

"What good will this do us, Dennison?" the emperor asked quietly. "Buy us a little time, perhaps? Sow a little confusion?"

"Yes," Dennison said. "Make certain your admirals make good use of it."

"What of the tenth battle?" the emperor asked. "That's the one where Varion himself commands in person. We can't fool his own eyes—and that battle is happening the closest to the Point. If he wins there, he comes here, and none of our fleets will be able to stop him."

Dennison turned, glancing at the tenth map. The *Voidhawk*, Varion's own flagship, flew there in its glory. Dennison looked away from the ship, scanning the screen, searching for a particular squadron of fighters. They were always at the forefront of the battles where Varion himself was present. It was led by a particular pilot: the woman who had walked beside Varion on Kress.

Dennison walked over to the admiral who was contending with Varion in this tenth battle. "My lord, I need you to do something for me. Take five squadrons of fighters, and make certain to destroy *every single fighter* in that unit at mark five-six-six."

"Five squadrons?" the admiral asked with surprise.

Dennison nodded. "Nothing else is as important as destroying those fighters."

The admiral looked questioningly over at the emperor, who nodded. The admiral turned to obey the order, and the aging monarch looked uncertainly at Dennison, who returned to his side. Then the emperor stepped aside, gesturing toward his command seat, which sat before the ten smaller screens. "You'll need this."

Dennison paused, then quietly sat down.

"I'm ready," the technician said.

"Interrupt the feed," Dennison said, taking a deep breath, "and show Varion exactly what I tell you."

The man did so, and Dennison took control of nine battles. Or, at least, he took *fake* control of them. The blips on his screens became lies. Fabrications, sent to Varion as a poisoned gift of knowledge.

The knowledge of what it was like to be Dennison.

Varion swung his fighters toward the gunship position on the planet Falna, intending to push back the imperial line. In real life, that's exactly what happened. However, in the simulation, Dennison made a few changes.

One of the imperial ships got in a lucky shot, and Varion's fighter line took a hit in just the wrong place. The fake imperial line rallied, destroying Varion's ships in a way that was unlikely, but not unreasonable.

Dennison made such changes to each of the nine battles. Here, a squadron attacked at the wrong angle. There, a command ship's engines failed at precisely the wrong moment. Individually, they were the kinds of small problems that happened in every battle. Nothing ever went *exactly* to plan. Yet all of these small bits of luck added up. As the nine conflicts raged in real life, Dennison sent Varion an increasingly invalid picture of his battle spaces.

Whatever Silvermane tried, it failed. Fighter squadrons collapsed. Gunships missed their targets and then were destroyed by a random stray missile. Command ships fell, and sectors were lost—all in a matter of minutes, and across all nine battles.

In Varion's own vicinity, the five squadrons of imperial fighters did their job. The ships Dennison had targeted were gone in under a minute, though the major redirection of firepower left a hole in the central imperial line, making it collapse. Dennison paid no attention to that losing battle, or to the reports that the others were really faring far worse than his simulated victories. He even ignored the emperor, who called for a chair, then sat quietly beside him, watching his empire tumbling down around him.

Dennison ignored all of this. For a moment, he was perfect. He was Varion, his every effort rewarded. His hopes were truth. His commands matched his dreams. He was a *god*.

*So this is what it is like to win, Dennison thought as his crew fabricated a victory for one of his squadrons, then sent it to Varion. This is what it is like to expect to win. Is this really what he feels all the time? Is he so sure of himself that he sees his entire life as merely a simulation, played out exactly as he desires?*

*Well, for a few moments, he'll have to live with being Dennison instead.*

Dennison made the tactical fabric of the conflicts collapse, caused Varion's forces to be routed. The only battle Dennison couldn't control was the one at which Varion himself was present. However, once the Silvermane was convinced he was losing in other parts of the galaxy, he began to make mistakes on his own front. He took more and more risks, struggling against the omnipotent force that was Dennison.

"Revenge," the emperor whispered. "Is this what you wanted, Dennison? Is all of this about playing a last cruel trick on your brother before he takes our empire from us?"

*Yes,* Dennison thought. *This* was his victory—his victory over Varion, his victory over a failed life. *This* was his moment: a perfect crescendo of battle, the entire universe bending to his will.

Then it ended.

"Someone must have noticed the bug!" the technician shouted as the viewscreens suddenly snapped back to the real battles. "The *klage* vibrations were a little irregular. I warned you!"

Dennison sat back in the emperor's command chair, releasing the breath he'd been holding. The room was growing quieter—the ten admirals hadn't gained much during their respite. *I've failed,* Dennison thought. The deception hadn't lasted long enough—Varion would now know he'd been duped. His communications now secure, he would easily retake command of the other battles.

"What have you done?" the emperor asked Dennison with a haunted voice.

Dennison didn't respond. He sat motionless, staring at the ten screens. For a moment he'd almost been able to convince himself that he *was* Varion. A victor.

"Your Majesty!" a surprised voice called from the back of the room. It was the aging admiral, pointing at the screen. "Look! Look at the Silvermane's forces. . . . "

In the tenth battle, the one that Dennison hadn't been able to falsify, several of Varion's fighter squadrons had turned away from their assault. Then the *Voidhawk* itself broke off its attack.

"Your Majesty, they're retreating!" another admiral said with amazement.

The emperor stood, turning toward Dennison. "What . . . ?"

Dennison stood as well, stepping forward, toward the viewscreen. *Could it be . . .* If Varion's technicians had found the discrepancy and fixed it on their own before telling Varion what was happening . . . extending for just a few moments the time in which Varion believed he was being defeated . . .

Dennison watched Varion's forces retreat, and in that moment he knew the truth. He could see it in the organization of the ships.

He had won. His trick had worked. "In all the things Varion discovered or was taught," Dennison said, a little stunned himself as he sat back in the chair, "for all his success, for all his genius, there was *one* thing he never learned. . . . "

Dennison paused, reaching over to his datapad and looking for a specific data feed. He clicked the button, bringing up an image on the main viewscreen: the image that showed Varion's ready room via the bug that Varion had always known about. The bug that he had allowed to remain because it amused him. It showed exactly what Dennison had hoped to see.

There, presented on the enormous screen, was an image of the High Admiral. Lord Varion Crestmar the Silvermane, greatest military genius of the age, sat behind his desk in the *Voidhawk*. In his limp fingers he held a gun, a smoking hole blown through his own forehead.

"He never learned how to lose," Dennison whispered.

# RIDING THE CROCODILE

## *Greg Egan*

I

In their ten thousand, three hundred and ninth year of marriage, Leila and Jasim began contemplating death. They had known love, raised children, and witnessed the flourishing generations of their offspring. They had traveled to a dozen worlds and lived among a thousand cultures. They had educated themselves many times over, proved theorems, and acquired and abandoned artistic sensibilities and skills. They had not lived in every conceivable manner, far from it, but what room would there be for the multitude if each individual tried to exhaust the permutations of existence? There were some experiences, they agreed, that everyone should try, and others that only a handful of people in all of time need bother with. They had no wish to give up their idiosyncrasies, no wish to uproot their personalities from the niches they had settled in long ago, let alone start cranking mechanically through some tedious enumeration of all the other people they might have been. They had been themselves, and for that they had done, more or less, enough.

Before dying, though, they wanted to attempt something grand and audacious. It was not that their lives were incomplete, in need of some final flourish of affirmation. If some unlikely calamity had robbed them of the chance to orchestrate this finale, the closest of their friends would never have remarked upon, let alone mourned, its absence. There was no esthetic compulsion to be satisfied, no aching existential void to be filled. Nevertheless, it was what they both wanted, and once they had acknowledged this to each other their hearts were set on it.

Choosing the project was not a great burden; that task required nothing but patience. They knew they'd recognize it when it came to them. Every night before sleeping, Jasim would ask Leila, "Did you see it yet?"

"No. Did you?"

"Not yet."

Sometimes Leila would dream that she'd found it in her dreams, but the transcripts proved otherwise. Sometimes Jasim felt sure that it was lurking just below the surface of his thoughts, but when he dived down to check it was nothing but a trick of the light.

Years passed. They occupied themselves with simple pleasures: gardening, swimming in the surf, talking with their friends, catching up with their descendants. They had grown skilled at finding pastimes that could bear repetition. Still, were it not for the nameless adventure that awaited them they would have thrown a pair of dice each evening and agreed that two sixes would end it all.

One night, Leila stood alone in the garden, watching the sky. From their home world, Najib, they had traveled only to the nearest stars with inhabited worlds, each time losing just a few decades to the journey. They had chosen those limits so as not to alienate themselves from friends and family, and it had never felt like much of a constraint. True, the civilization of the Amalgam wrapped the galaxy, and a committed traveler could spend two hundred thousand years circling back home, but what was to be gained by such an overblown odyssey? The dozen worlds of their neighborhood held enough variety for any traveler, and whether more distant realms were filled with fresh novelties or endless repetition hardly seemed to matter. To have a goal, a destination, would be one thing, but to drown in the sheer plenitude of worlds for its own sake seemed utterly pointless.

A destination? Leila overlaid the sky with information, most of it by necessity millennia out of date. There were worlds with spectacular views of nebulas and star clusters, views that could be guaranteed still to be in existence if they traveled to see them, but would taking in such sights firsthand be so much better than immersion in the flawless images already available in Najib's library? To blink away ten thousand years just to wake beneath a cloud of green and violet gas, however lovely, seemed like a terrible anticlimax.

The stars tingled with self-aggrandisement, plaintively tugging at her attention. The architecture here, the rivers, the festivals! Even if these tourist attractions could survive the millennia, even if some were literally unique, there was nothing that struck her as a fitting prelude to death. If she and Jasim had formed some whimsical attachment, centuries before, to a world on the other side of the galaxy rumoured to hold great beauty or interest, and if they had talked long enough about chasing it down when they had nothing better to do, then keeping that promise might have been worth it, even if the journey led them to a world in ruins. They had no such cherished destination, though, and it was too late to cultivate one now.

Leila's gaze followed a thinning in the advertising, taking her to the bulge of stars surrounding the galaxy's center. The disk of the Milky Way belonged to the Amalgam, whose various ancestral species had effectively merged into a single civilization, but the central bulge was inhabited by beings who had declined to do so much as communicate with those around them. All attempts to send probes into the bulge—let alone the kind of engineering spores needed to create the infrastructure for travel— had been gently but firmly rebuffed, with the intruders swatted straight back out again. The Aloof had maintained their silence and isolation since before the Amalgam itself had even existed.

The latest news on this subject was twenty thousand years old, but the status quo had held for close to a million years. If she and Jasim traveled to the innermost edge of the Amalgam's domain, the chances were exceptionally good that the Aloof would not have changed their ways in the meantime. In fact, it would be no disappointment at all if the Aloof had suddenly thrown open their borders: that unheralded thaw would itself be an extraordinary thing to witness. If the challenge remained, though, all the better.

She called Jasim to the garden and pointed out the richness of stars, unadorned with potted histories.

"We go where?" he asked.

"As close to the Aloof as we're able."

"And do what?"

"Try to observe them," she said. "Try to learn something about them. Try to make contact, in whatever way we can."

"You don't think that's been tried before?"

"A million times. Not so much lately, though. Maybe while the interest on our side has ebbed, they've been changing, growing more receptive."

"Or maybe not." Jasim smiled. He had appeared a little stunned by her proposal at first, but the idea seemed to be growing on him. "It's a hard,

hard problem to throw ourselves against. But it's not futile. Not quite." He wrapped her hands in his. "Let's see how we feel in the morning."

In the morning, they were both convinced. They would camp at the gates of these elusive strangers, and try to rouse them from their indifference.

They summoned the family from every corner of Najib. There were some grandchildren and more distant descendants who had settled in other star systems, decades away at lightspeed, but they chose not to wait to call them home for this final farewell.

Two hundred people crowded the physical house and garden, while two hundred more confined themselves to the virtual wing. There was talk and food and music, like any other celebration, and Leila tried to undercut any edge of solemnity that she felt creeping in. As the night wore on, though, each time she kissed a child or grandchild, each time she embraced an old friend, she thought: this could be the last time, ever. There had to be a last time, she couldn't face ten thousand more years, but a part of her spat and struggled like a cornered animal at the thought of each warm touch fading to nothing.

As dawn approached, the party shifted entirely into the acorporeal. People took on fancy dress from myth or xenology, or just joked and played with their illusory bodies. It was all very calm and gentle, nothing like the surreal excesses she remembered from her youth, but Leila still felt a tinge of vertigo. When her son Khalid made his ears grow and spin, this amiable silliness carried a hard message: the machinery of the house had ripped her mind from her body, as seamlessly as ever, but this time she would never be returning to the same flesh.

Sunrise brought the first of the good-byes. Leila forced herself to release each proffered hand, to unwrap her arms from around each nonexistent body. She whispered to Jasim, "Are you going mad, too?"

"Of course."

Gradually the crowd thinned out. The wing grew quiet. Leila found herself pacing from room to room, as if she might yet chance upon someone who'd stayed behind, then she remembered urging the last of them to go, her children and friends tearfully retreating down the hall. She skirted inconsolable sadness, then lifted herself above it and went looking for Jasim.

He was waiting for her outside their room.

"Are you ready to sleep?" he asked her gently.

She said, "For an eon."

## II

Leila woke in the same bed as she'd lain down in. Jasim was still sleeping beside her. The window showed dawn, but it was not the usual view of the cliffs and the ocean.

Leila had the house brief her. After twenty thousand years—traveling more or less at lightspeed, pausing only for a microsecond or two at various way-stations to be cleaned up and amplified—the package of information bearing the two of them had arrived safely at Nazdeek-be-Beegane. This world was not crowded, and it had been tweaked to render it compatible with a range of metabolic styles. The house had negotiated a site where they could live embodied in comfort if they wished.

Jasim stirred and opened his eyes. "Good morning. How are you feeling?"

"Older."

"Really?"

Leila paused to consider this seriously. "No. Not even slightly. How about you?"

"I'm fine. I'm just wondering what's out there." He raised himself up to peer through the window. The house had been instantiated on a wide, empty plain, covered with low stalks of green and yellow vegetation. They could eat these plants, and the house had already started a spice garden while they slept. He stretched his shoulders. "Let's go and make breakfast."

They went downstairs, stepping into freshly minted bodies, then out into the garden. The air was still, the sun already warm. The house had tools prepared to help them with the harvest. It was the nature of travel that they had come empty-handed, and they had no relatives here, no fifteenth cousins, no friends of friends. It was the nature of the Amalgam that they were welcome nonetheless, and the machines that supervised this world on behalf of its inhabitants had done their best to provide for them.

"So this is the afterlife," Jasim mused, scything the yellow stalks. "Very rustic."

"Speak for yourself," Leila retorted. "I'm not dead yet." She put down her own scythe and bent to pluck one of the plants out by its roots.

The meal they made was filling but bland. Leila resisted the urge to tweak her perceptions of it; she preferred to face the challenge of working out decent recipes, which would make a useful counterpoint to the more daunting task they'd come here to attempt.

They spent the rest of the day just tramping around, exploring their immediate surroundings. The house had tapped into a nearby stream for water, and sunlight, stored, would provide all the power they needed. From some hills about an hour's walk away they could see into a field with another building, but they decided to wait a little longer before introducing themselves to their neighbors. The air had a slightly odd smell, due to the range of components needed to support other metabolic styles, but it wasn't too intrusive.

The onset of night took them by surprise. Even before the sun had set a smattering of stars began appearing in the east, and for a moment Leila thought that these white specks against the fading blue were some kind of exotic atmospheric phenomenon, perhaps small clouds forming in the stratosphere as the temperature dropped. When it became clear what was happening, she beckoned to Jasim to sit beside her on the bank of the stream and watch the stars of the bulge come out.

They'd come at a time when Nazdeek lay between its sun and the galactic center. At dusk one half of the Aloof's dazzling territory stretched from the eastern horizon to the zenith, with the stars' slow march westward against a darkening sky only revealing more of their splendor.

"You think that was to die for?" Jasim joked as they walked back to the house.

"We could end this now, if you're feeling unambitious."

He squeezed her hand. "If this takes ten thousand years, I'm ready."

It was a mild night, they could have slept outdoors, but the spectacle was too distracting. They stayed downstairs, in the physical wing. Leila watched the strange thicket of shadows cast by the furniture sliding across the walls. These neighbors never sleep, she thought. When we come knocking, they'll ask what took us so long.

## IH

Hundreds of observatories circled Nazdeek, built then abandoned by others who'd come on the same quest. When Leila saw the band of pristine space junk mapped out before her—orbits scrupulously maintained and swept clean by robot sentinels for eons—she felt as if she'd found the graves of their predecessors, stretching out in the field behind the house as far as the eye could see.

Nazdeek was prepared to offer them the resources to loft another package of instruments into the vacuum if they wished, but many of the abandoned observatories were perfectly functional, and most had been left in a compliant state, willing to take instructions from anyone.

Leila and Jasim sat in their living room and woke machine after machine from millennia of hibernation. Some, it turned out, had not been sleeping at all, but had been carrying on systematic observations, accumulating data long after their owners had lost interest.

In the crowded stellar precincts of the bulge, disruptive gravitational effects made planet formation rarer than it was in the disk, and orbits less stable. Nevertheless, planets had been found. A few thousand could be tracked from Nazdeek, and one observatory had been monitoring their atmospheric spectra for the last twelve millennia. In all of those worlds for all of those years, there were no signs of atmospheric composition departing from plausible, purely geochemical models. That meant no wild life, and no crude industries. It didn't prove that these worlds were uninhabited, but it suggested either that the Aloof went to great lengths to avoid leaving chemical fingerprints, or they lived in an entirely different fashion to any of the civilizations that had formed the Amalgam.

Of the eleven forms of biochemistry that had been found scattered around the galactic disk, all had given rise eventually to hundreds of species with general intelligence. Of the multitude of civilizations that had emerged from those roots, all contained cultures that had granted themselves the flexibility of living as software, but they also all contained cultures that persisted with corporeal existence. Leila would never have willingly given up either mode, herself, but while it was easy to imagine a subculture doing so, for a whole species it seemed extraordinary. In a sense, the intertwined civilization of the Amalgam owed its existence to the fact that there was as much cultural variation within every species as there was between one species and another. In that explosion of diversity, overlapping interests were inevitable.

If the Aloof were the exception, and their material culture had shrunk to nothing but a few discreet processors—each with the energy needs of a gnat, scattered throughout a trillion cubic light-years of dust and blazing stars—then finding them would be impossible.

Of course, that worst-case scenario couldn't quite be true. The sole reason the Aloof were assumed to exist at all was the fact that some component of their material culture was tossing back every probe that was sent into the bulge. However discreet that machinery was, it certainly couldn't be sparse: given that it had managed to track, intercept and reverse the trajectories of billions of individual probes that had been sent in along thousands of different routes, relativistic constraints on the information flow implied that the Aloof had some kind of presence at more or less every star at the edge of the bulge.

Leila and Jasim had Nazdeek brief them on the most recent attempts to enter the bulge, but even after forty thousand years the basic facts hadn't changed. There was no crisply delineated barrier marking the Aloof's territory, but at some point within a border region about fifty light-years wide, every single probe that was sent in ceased to function. The signals from those carrying in-flight beacons or transmitters went dead without warning. A century or so later, they would appear again at almost the same point, traveling in the opposite direction: back to where they'd come from. Those that were retrieved and examined were found to be unharmed, but their data logs contained nothing from the missing decades.

Jasim said, "The Aloof could be dead and gone. They built the perfect fence, but now it's outlasted them. It's just guarding their ruins."

Leila rejected this emphatically. "No civilization that's spread to more than one star system has ever vanished completely. Sometimes they've changed beyond recognition, but not one has ever died without descendants."

"That's a fact of history, but it's not a universal law," Jasim persisted. "If we're going to argue from the Amalgam all the time, we'll get nowhere. If the Aloof weren't exceptional, we wouldn't be here."

"That's true. But I won't accept that they're dead until I see some evidence."

"What would count as evidence? Apart from a million years of silence?"

Leila said, "Silence could mean anything. If they're really dead, we'll find something more, something definite."

"Such as?"

"If we see it, we'll know."

They began the project in earnest, reviewing data from the ancient observatories, stopping only to gather food, eat and sleep. They had resisted making detailed plans back on Najib, reasoning that any approach they mapped out in advance was likely to be rendered obsolete once they learned about the latest investigations. Now that they'd arrived and found the state of play utterly unchanged, Leila wished that they'd come armed with some clear options for dealing with the one situation they could have prepared for before they'd left.

In fact, though they might have felt like out-of-touch amateurs back on Najib, now that the Aloof had become their entire *raison d'être* it was far harder to relax and indulge in the kind of speculation that might actually bear fruit, given that every systematic approach had failed. Having come twenty thousand light-years for this, they couldn't spend their time day-dreaming, turning the problem over in the backs of their minds while they surrendered to the rhythms of Nazdeek's rural idyll. So they studied everything that had been tried before, searching methodically for a new approach, hoping to see the old ideas with fresh eyes, hoping that—by chance if for no other reason—they might lack some crucial blind spot that had afflicted all of their predecessors.

After seven months without results or inspiration, it was Jasim who finally dragged them out of the rut. "We're getting nowhere," he said. "It's time to accept that, put all this aside, and go visit the neighbors."

Leila stared at him as if he'd lost his mind. "Go visit them? How? What makes you think that they're suddenly going to let us in?"

He said, "The neighbors. Remember? Over the hill. The ones who might actually want to talk to us."

## IV

Their neighbors had published a précis stating that they welcomed social contact in principle, but might take awhile to respond. Jasim sent them an invitation, asking if they'd like to join them in their house, and waited.

After just three days, a reply came back. The neighbors did not want to put them to the trouble of altering their own house physically, and preferred not to become acorporeal at present. Given the less stringent requirements of Leila and Jasim's own species when embodied, might they wish to come instead to the neighbors' house?

Leila said, "Why not?" They set a date and time.

The neighbors' précis included all the biological and sociological details needed to prepare for the encounter. Their biochemistry was carbon-based and oxygen-breathing, but employed a different replicator to Leila and Jasim's DNA. Their ancestral phenotype resembled a large furred snake, and when embodied they generally lived in nests of a hundred or so. The minds of the individuals were perfectly autonomous, but solitude was an alien and unsettling concept for them.

Leila and Jasim set out late in the morning, in order to arrive early in the afternoon. There were some low, heavy clouds in the sky, but it was not completely overcast, and Leila noticed that when the sun passed behind the clouds, she could discern some of the brightest stars from the edge of the bulge.

Jasim admonished her sternly, "Stop looking. This is our day off."

The Snakes' building was a large squat cylinder resembling a water tank, which turned out to be packed with something mossy and pungent. When they arrived at the entrance, three of their hosts were waiting to greet them, coiled on the ground near the mouth of a large tunnel emerging from the moss. Their bodies were almost as wide as their guests', and some eight or ten meters long. Their heads bore two front-facing eyes, but their other sense organs were not prominent. Leila could make out their mouths, and knew from the briefing how many rows of teeth lay behind them, but the wide pink gashes stayed closed, almost lost in the gray fur.

The Snakes communicated with a low-frequency thumping, and their system of nomenclature was complex, so Leila just mentally tagged the three of them with randomly chosen, slightly exotic names—Tim, John and Sarah—and tweaked her translator so she'd recognize intuitively who was who, who was addressing her, and the significance of their gestures.

"Welcome to our home," said Tim enthusiastically.

"Thank you for inviting us," Jasim replied.

"We've had no visitors for quite some time," explained Sarah. "So we really are delighted to meet you."

"How long has it been?" Leila asked.

"Twenty years," said Sarah.

"But we came here for the quiet life," John added. "So we expected it would be awhile."

Leila pondered the idea of a clan of one hundred ever finding a quiet life, but then, perhaps unwelcome intrusions from outsiders were of a different nature to family dramas.

"Will you come into the nest?" Tim asked. "If you don't wish to enter we won't take offense, but everyone would like to see you, and some of us aren't comfortable coming out into the open."

Leila glanced at Jasim. He said privately, "We can push our vision to IR. And tweak ourselves to tolerate the smell."

Leila agreed.

"Okay," Jasim told Tim.

Tim slithered into the tunnel and vanished in a quick, elegant motion, then John motioned with his head for the guests to follow.

Leila went first, propelling herself up the gentle slope with her knees and elbows. The plant the Snakes cultivated for the nest formed a cool, dry, resilient surface. She could see Tim ten meters or so ahead, like a giant glowworm shining with body heat, slowing down now to let her catch up. She glanced back at Jasim, who looked even weirder than the Snakes now, his face and arms blotched with strange bands of radiance from the exertion.

After a few minutes, they came to a large chamber. The air was humid, but after the confines of the tunnel it felt cool and fresh. Tim led them toward the center, where about a dozen other Snakes were already waiting to greet them. They circled the guests excitedly, thumping out a delighted welcome. Leila felt a surge of adrenaline; she knew that she and Jasim were in no danger, but the sheer size and energy of the creatures was overwhelming.

"Can you tell us why you've come to Nazdeek?" asked Sarah.

"Of course." For a second or two Leila tried to maintain eye contact with her, but like all the other Snakes she kept moving restlessly, a gesture that Leila's translator imbued with a sense of warmth and enthusiasm. As for lack of eye contact, the Snakes' own translators would understand perfectly that some aspects of ordinary, polite human behavior became impractical under the circumstances, and would not mislabel her actions. "We're here to learn about the Aloof," she said.

"The Aloof?" At first Sarah just seemed perplexed, then Leila's translator hinted at a touch of irony. "But they offer us nothing."

Leila was tongue-tied for a moment. The implication was subtle but unmistakable. Citizens of the Amalgam had a protocol for dealing with each other's curiosity: they published a précis, which spelled out clearly any information that they wished people in general to know about them, and also specified what, if any, further inquiries would be welcome. However, a citizen was perfectly entitled to publish no précis at all and have that decision respected. When no information was published, and no invitation offered, you simply had no choice but to mind your own business.

"They offer us nothing as far as we can tell," she said, "but that might be a misunderstanding, a failure to communicate."

"They send back all the probes," Tim replied. "Do you really think we've misunderstood what that means?"

Jasim said, "It means that they don't want us physically intruding on their territory, putting our machines right next to their homes, but I'm not convinced that it proves that they have no desire to communicate whatsoever."

"We should leave them in peace," Tim insisted. "They've seen the probes, so they know we're here. If they want to make contact, they'll do it in their own time."

"Leave them in peace," echoed another Snake. A chorus of affirmation followed from others in the chamber.

Leila stood her ground. "We have no idea how many different species and cultures might be living in the bulge. *One of them* sends back the probes, but for all we know there could be a thousand others who don't yet even know that the Amalgam has tried to make contact."

This suggestion set off a series of arguments, some between guests and hosts, some between the Snakes themselves. All the while, the Snakes kept circling excitedly, while new ones entered the chamber to witness the novel sight of these strangers.

When the clamor about the Aloof had quietened down enough for her to change the subject, Leila asked Sarah, "Why have you come to Nazdeek yourself?"

"It's out of the way, off the main routes. We can think things over here, undisturbed."

"But you could have the same amount of privacy anywhere. It's all a matter of what you put in your précis."

Sarah's response was imbued with a tinge of amusement. "For us, it would be unimaginably rude to cut off all contact explicitly, by decree. Especially with others from our own ancestral species. To live a quiet life, we had to reduce the likelihood of encountering anyone who would seek us out. We had to make the effort of rendering ourselves physically remote, in order to reap the benefits."

"Yet you've made Jasim and myself very welcome."

"Of course. But that will be enough for the next twenty years."

So much for resurrecting their social life. "What exactly is it that you're pondering in this state of solitude?"

"The nature of reality. The uses of existence. The reasons to live, and the reasons not to."

Leila felt the skin on her forearms tingle. She'd almost forgotten that she'd made an appointment with death, however uncertain the timing.

She explained how she and Jasim had made their decision to embark on a grand project before dying.

"That's an interesting approach," Sarah said. "I'll have to give it some thought." She paused, then added, "Though I'm not sure that you've solved the problem."

"What do you mean?"

"Will it really be easier now to choose the right moment to give up your life? Haven't you merely replaced one delicate judgment with an even more difficult one: deciding when you've exhausted the possibilities for contacting the Aloof?"

"You make it sound as if we have no chance of succeeding." Leila was not afraid of the prospect of failure, but the suggestion that it was inevitable was something else entirely.

Sarah said, "We've been here on Nazdeek for fifteen thousand years. We don't pay much attention to the world outside the nest, but even from this cloistered state we've seen many people break their backs against this rock."

"So when will you accept that your own project is finished?" Leila countered. "If you still don't have what you're looking for after fifteen thousand years, when will you admit defeat?"

"I have no idea," Sarah confessed. "I have no idea, any more than you do."

V

When the way forward first appeared, there was nothing to set it apart from a thousand false alarms that had come before it.

It was their seventeenth year on Nazdeek. They had launched their own observatory—armed with the latest refinements culled from around the galaxy—fifteen years before, and it had been confirming the null results of its predecessors ever since.

They had settled into an unhurried routine, systematically exploring the possibilities that observation hadn't yet ruled out. Between the scenarios that were obviously stone cold dead—the presence of an energy-rich, risk-taking, extroverted civilization in the bulge actively seeking contact by every means at its disposal—and the infinite number of possibilities that could never be distinguished at this distance from the absence of all life, and the absence of all machinery save one dumb but efficient gatekeeper, tantalizing clues would bubble up out of the data now and then, only to fade into statistical insignificance in the face of continued scrutiny.

Tens of billions of stars lying within the Aloof's territory could be discerned from Nazdeek, some of them evolving or violently interacting on a time scale of years or months. Black holes were flaying and swallowing their companions. Neutron stars and white dwarfs were stealing fresh fuel and flaring into novas. Star clusters were colliding and tearing each other apart. If you gathered data on this whole menagerie for long enough, you could expect to see almost anything. Leila would not have been surprised to wander into the garden at night and find a great welcome sign spelled out in the sky, before the fortuitous pattern of novas faded and the message dissolved into randomness again.

When their gamma ray telescope caught a glimmer of something odd—the nuclei of a certain isotope of fluorine decaying from an excited state, when there was no nearby source of the kind of radiation that could have put the nuclei into that state in the first place—it might have been just another random, unexplained fact to add to a vast pile. When the same glimmer was seen again, not far away, Leila reasoned that if a gas cloud enriched with fluorine could be affected at one location by an unseen radiation source, it should not be surprising if the same thing happened elsewhere in the same cloud.

It happened again. The three events lined up in space and time in a manner suggesting a short pulse of gamma rays in the form of a tightly focused beam, striking three different points in the gas cloud. Still, in the mountains of data they had acquired from their predecessors, coincidences far more compelling than this had occurred hundreds of thousands of times.

With the fourth flash, the balance of the numbers began to tip. The secondary gamma rays reaching Nazdeek gave only a weak and distorted impression of the original radiation, but all four flashes were consistent with a single, narrow beam. There were thousands of known gamma ray sources in the bulge, but the frequency of the radiation, the direction of the beam, and the time profile of the pulse did not fit with any of them.

The archives revealed a few dozen occasions when the same kind of emissions had been seen from fluorine nuclei under similar conditions. There had never been more than three connected events before, but one sequence had occurred along a path not far from the present one.

Leila sat by the stream and modeled the possibilities. If the beam was linking two objects in powered flight, prediction was impossible. If receiver and transmitter were mostly in free-fall, though, and only made corrections occasionally, the past and present data combined gave her a plausible forecast for the beam's future orientation.

Jasim looked into her simulation, a thought-bubble of stars and equations hovering above the water. "The whole path will lie out of bounds," he said.

"No kidding." The Aloof's territory was more or less spherical, which made it a convex set: you couldn't get between any two points that lay inside it without entering the territory itself. "But look how much the beam spreads out. From the fluorine data, I'd say it could be tens of kilometers wide by the time it reaches the receiver."

"So they might not catch it all? They might let some of the beam escape into the disk?" He sounded unpersuaded.

Leila said, "Look, if they really were doing everything possible to hide this, we would never have seen these blips in the first place."

"Gas clouds with this much fluorine are extremely rare. They obviously picked a frequency that wouldn't be scattered under ordinary circumstances."

"Yes, but that's just a matter of getting the signal through the local environment. We choose frequencies ourselves that won't interact with any substance that's likely to be present along the route, but no choice is perfect, and we just live with that. It seems to me that they've done the same thing. If they were fanatical purists, they'd communicate by completely different methods."

"All right." Jasim reached into the model. "So where can we go that's in the line of sight?"

The short answer was: nowhere. If the beam was not blocked completely by its intended target it would spread out considerably as it made its way through the galactic disk, but it would not grow so wide that it would sweep across a single point where the Amalgam had any kind of outpost.

Leila said, "This is too good to miss. We need to get a decent observatory into its path."

Jasim agreed. "And we need to do it before these nodes decide they've drifted too close to something dangerous, and switch on their engines for a course correction."

They crunched through the possibilities. Wherever the Amalgam had an established presence, the infrastructure already on the ground could convert data into any kind of material object. Transmitting yourself to such a place, along with whatever you needed, was simplicity itself:

lightspeed was the only real constraint. Excessive demands on the local resources might be denied, but modest requests were rarely rejected.

Far more difficult was building something new at a site with raw materials but no existing receiver; in that case, instead of pure data, you needed to send an engineering spore of some kind. If you were in a hurry, not only did you need to spend energy boosting the spore to relativistic velocities—a cost that snowballed due to the mass of protective shielding—you then had to waste much of the time you gained on a lengthy braking phase, or the spore would hit its target with enough energy to turn it into plasma. Interactions with the interstellar medium could be used to slow down the spore, avoiding the need to carry yet more mass to act as a propellant for braking, but the whole business was disgustingly inefficient.

Harder still was getting anything substantial to a given point in the vast empty space between the stars. With no raw materials to hand at the destination, everything had to be moved from somewhere else. The best starting point was usually to send an engineering spore into a cometary cloud, loosely bound gravitationally to its associated star, but not every such cloud was open to plunder, and everything took time, and obscene amounts of energy.

To arrange for an observatory to be delivered to the most accessible point along the beam's line of sight, traveling at the correct velocity, would take about fifteen thousand years all told. That assumed that the local cultures who owned the nearest facilities, and who had a right to veto the use of the raw materials, acceded immediately to their request.

"How long between course corrections?" Leila wondered. If the builders of this hypothetical network were efficient, the nodes could drift for a while in interstellar space without any problems, but in the bulge everything happened faster than in the disk, and the need to counter gravitational effects would come much sooner. There was no way to make a firm prediction, but they could easily have as little as eight or ten thousand years.

Leila struggled to reconcile herself to the reality. "We'll try at this location, and if we're lucky we might still catch something. If not, we'll try again after the beam shifts." Sending the first observatory chasing after the beam would be futile; even with the present free-fall motion of the nodes, the observation point would be moving at a substantial fraction of lightspeed relative to the local stars. Magnified by the enormous distances involved, a small change in direction down in the bulge could see the beam lurch thousands of light-years sideways by the time it reached the disk.

Jasim said, "Wait." He magnified the region around the projected path of the beam.

"What are you looking for?"

He asked the map. "Are there two outposts of the Amalgam lying on a straight line that intersects the beam?"

The map replied in a tone of mild incredulity. "No."

"That was too much to hope for. Are there three lying on a plane that intersects the beam?"

The map said, "There are about ten-to-the-eighteen triples that meet that condition."

Leila suddenly realized what it was he had in mind. She laughed and squeezed his arm. "You are completely insane!"

Jasim said, "Let me get the numbers right first, then you can mock me." He rephrased his question to the map. "For how many of those triples would the beam pass between them, intersecting the triangle whose vertices they lie on?"

"About ten-to-the-sixth."

"How close to us is the closest point of intersection of the beam with any of those triangles—if the distance in each case is measured via the worst of the three outposts, the one that makes the total path longest."

"Seven thousand four hundred and twenty-six light-years."

Leila said, "Collision braking. With three components?"

"Do you have a better idea?"

*Better than twice as fast as the fastest conventional method?* "Nothing comes to mind. Let me think about it."

Braking against the flimsy interstellar medium was a slow process. If you wanted to deliver a payload rapidly to a point that fortuitously lay somewhere on a straight line between two existing outposts, you could fire two separate packages from the two locations and let them "collide" when they met—or rather, let them brake against each other magnetically. If you arranged for the packages to have equal and opposite momenta, they would come to a halt without any need to throw away reaction mass or clutch at passing molecules, and some of their kinetic energy could be recovered as electricity and stored for later use.

The aim and the timing had to be perfect. Relativistic packages did not make inflight course corrections, and the data available at each launch site about the other's precise location was always a potentially imperfect prediction, not a rock-solid statement of fact. Even with the Amalgam's prodigious astrometric and computing resources, achieving millimeter alignments at thousand-light-year distances could not be guaranteed.

Now Jasim wanted to make three of these bullets meet, perform an elaborate electromagnetic dance, and end up with just the right velocity needed to keep tracking the moving target of the beam.

In the evening, back in the house, they sat together working through simulations. It was easy to find designs that would work if everything went perfectly, but they kept hunting for the most robust variation, the one that was most tolerant of small misalignments. With standard two-body collision braking, the usual solution was to have the first package, shaped like a cylinder, pass right through a hole in the second package. As it emerged from the other side and the two moved apart again, the magnetic fields were switched from repulsive to attractive. Several "bounces" followed, and in the process as much of the kinetic energy as possible was gradually converted into superconducting currents for storage, while the rest was dissipated as electromagnetic radiation. Having three objects meeting at an angle would not only make the timing and positioning more critical, it would destroy the simple, axial symmetry and introduce a greater risk of instability.

It was dawn before they settled on the optimal design, which effectively split the problem in two. First, package one, a sphere, would meet package two, a torus, threading the gap in the middle, then bouncing back and forth through it seventeen times. The plane of the torus would lie at an angle to its direction of flight, allowing the sphere to approach it head-on. When the two finally came to rest with respect to each other, they would still have a component of their velocity carrying them straight toward package three, a cylinder with an axial borehole.

Because the electromagnetic interactions were the same as the two-body case—self-centering, intrinsically stable—a small amount of misalignment at each of these encounters would not be fatal. The usual two-body case, though, didn't require the combined package, after all the bouncing and energy dissipation was completed, to be moving on a path so precisely determined that it could pass through yet another narrow hoop.

There were no guarantees, and in the end the result would be in other people's hands. They could send requests to the three outposts, asking for these objects to be launched at the necessary times on the necessary trajectories. The energy needs hovered on the edge of politeness, though, and it was possible that one or more of the requests would simply be refused.

Jasim waved the models away, and they stretched out on the carpet, side by side.

He said, "I never thought we'd get this far. Even if this is only a mirage, I never thought we'd find one worth chasing."

Leila said, "I don't know what I expected. Some kind of great folly: some long, exhausting, exhilarating struggle that felt like wandering through a jungle for years and ending up utterly lost."

"And then what?"

"Surrender."

Jasim was silent for a while. Leila could sense that he was brooding over something, but she didn't press him.

He said, "Should we travel to this observatory ourselves, or wait here for the results?"

"We should go. Definitely! I don't want to hang around here for fifteen thousand years, waiting. We can leave the Nazdeek observatories hunting for more beam fluorescence and broadcasting the results, so we'll hear about them wherever we end up."

"That makes sense." Jasim hesitated, then added, "When we go, I don't want to leave a back-up."

"Ah." They'd traveled from Najib leaving nothing of themselves behind: if their transmission had somehow failed to make it to Nazdeek, no stored copy of the data would ever have woken to resume their truncated lives. Travel within the Amalgam's established network carried negligible risks, though. If they flung themselves toward the hypothetical location of this yet-to-be-assembled station in the middle of nowhere, it was entirely possible that they'd sail off to infinity without ever being instantiated again.

Leila said, "Are you tired of what we're doing? Of what we've become?"

"It's not that."

"This one chance isn't the be-all and end-all. Now that we know how to hunt for the beams, I'm sure we'll find this one again after it shifts. We could find a thousand others, if we're persistent."

"I know that," he said. "I don't want to stop, I don't want to end this. But I want to *risk* ending it. Just once. While that still means something."

Leila sat up and rested her head on her knees. She could understand what he was feeling, but it still disturbed her.

Jasim said, "We've already achieved something extraordinary. No one's found a clue like this in a million years. If we leave that to posterity, it will be pursued to the end, we can be sure of that. But I desperately want to pursue it myself. With you."

"And because you want that so badly, you need to face the chance of losing it?"

"Yes."

It was one thing they had never tried. In their youth, they would never have knowingly risked death. They'd been too much in love, too eager for the life they'd yet to live; the stakes would have been unbearably high. In the twilight years, back on Najib, it would have been an easy thing to do, but an utterly insipid pleasure.

Jasim sat up and took her hand. "Have I hurt you with this?"

"No, no." She shook her head pensively, trying to gather her thoughts. She didn't want to hide her feelings, but she wanted to express them precisely, not blurt them out in a confusing rush. "I always thought we'd reach the end together, though. We'd come to some point in the jungle, look around, exchange a glance, and know that we'd arrived. Without even needing to say it aloud."

Jasim drew her to him and held her. "All right, I'm sorry. Forget everything I said."

Leila pushed him away, annoyed. "This isn't something you can take back. If it's the truth, it's the truth. Just give me some time to decide what I want."

They put it aside, and buried themselves in work: polishing the design for the new observatory, preparing the requests to send to the three outposts. One of the planets they would be petitioning belonged to the Snakes, so Leila and Jasim went to visit the nest for a second time, to seek advice on the best way to beg for this favor. Their neighbors seemed more excited just to see them again than they were at the news that a tiny rent had appeared in the Aloof's million-year-old cloak of discretion. When Leila gently pushed her on this point, Sarah said, "You're here, here and now, our guests in flesh and blood. I'm sure I'll be dead long before the Aloof are willing to do the same."

Leila thought: What kind of strange greed is it that I'm suffering from? I can be feted by creatures who rose up from the dust through a completely different molecule than my own ancestors. I can sit among them and discuss the philosophy of life and death. The Amalgam has already joined every willing participant in the galaxy into one vast conversation.

And I want to go and eavesdrop on the Aloof? Just because they've played hard-to-get for a million years?

They dispatched requests for the three modules to be built and launched by their three as-yet unwitting collaborators, specifying the final countdown to the nanosecond but providing a ten-year period for the project to be debated. Leila felt optimistic; however blasé the Nazdeek nest had been, she suspected that no space-faring culture really could resist the chance to peek behind the veil.

They had thirty-six years to wait before they followed in the wake of their petitions; on top of the ten-year delay, the new observatory's modules would be traveling at a fraction of a percent below lightspeed, so they needed a head start.

No more telltale gamma ray flashes appeared from the bulge, but Leila hadn't expected any so soon. They had sent the news of their discovery to other worlds close to the Aloof's territory, so eventually a thousand other groups with different vantage points would be searching for the same kind of evidence and finding their own ways to interpret and exploit it. It hurt a little, scattering their hard-won revelation to the wind for anyone to use—perhaps even to beat them to some far greater prize—but they'd relied on the generosity of their predecessors from the moment they'd arrived on Nazdeek, and the sheer scale of the overall problem made it utterly perverse to cling selfishly to their own small triumph.

As the day of their departure finally arrived, Leila came to a decision. She understood Jasim's need to put everything at risk, and in a sense she shared it. If she had always imagined the two of them ending this together—struggling on, side by side, until the way forward was lost and the undergrowth closed in on them—then *that* was what she'd risk. She would take the flip side to his own wager.

When the house took their minds apart and sent them off to chase the beam, Leila left a copy of herself frozen on Nazdeek. If no word of their safe arrival reached it by the expected time, it would wake and carry on the search.

Alone.

## VI

"Welcome to Trident. We're honored by the presence of our most distinguished guest."

Jasim stood beside the bed, waving a triangular flag. Red, green and blue in the corners merged to white in the center.

"How long have you been up?"

"About an hour," he said. Leila frowned, and he added apologetically, "You were sleeping very deeply, I didn't want to disturb you."

"I should be the one giving the welcome," she said. "You're the one who might never have woken."

The bedroom window looked out into a dazzling field of stars. It was not a view facing the bulge—by now Leila could recognize the distinctive spectra of the region's stars with ease—but even these disk stars were so crisp and bright that this was like no sky she had ever seen.

"Have you been downstairs?" she said.

"Not yet. I wanted us to decide on that together." The house had no physical wing here; the tiny observatory had no spare mass for such frivolities as embodying them, let alone constructing architectural follies in the middle of interstellar space. "Downstairs" would be nothing but a scape that they were free to design at will.

"Everything worked," she said, not quite believing it.

Jasim spread his arms. "We're here, aren't we?"

They watched a reconstruction of the first two modules coming together. The timing and the trajectories were as near to perfect as they could have hoped for, and the superconducting magnets had been constructed to a standard of purity and homogeneity that made the magnetic embrace look like an idealized simulation. By the time the two had locked together, the third module was just minutes away. Some untraceable discrepancy between reality and prediction in the transfer of momentum to radiation had the composite moving at a tiny angle away from its expected course, but when it met the third module the magnetic fields still meshed in a stable configuration, and there was energy to spare to nudge the final assembly precisely into step with the predicted swinging of the Aloof's beam.

The Amalgam had lived up to its promise: three worlds full of beings they had never met, who owed them nothing, who did not even share their molecular ancestry, had each diverted enough energy to light up all their cities for a decade, and followed the instructions of strangers down to the atom, down to the nanosecond, in order to make this work.

What happened now was entirely in the hands of the Aloof.

Trident had been functioning for about a month before its designers had arrived to take up occupancy. So far, it had not yet observed any gamma ray signals spilling out of the bulge. The particular pulse that Leila and Jasim had seen triggering fluorescence would be long gone, of course, but the usefulness of their present location was predicated on three assumptions: the Aloof would use the same route for many other bursts of data; some of the radiation carrying that data would slip past the intended receiver; and the two nodes of the network would have continued in free-fall long enough for the spilt data to be arriving here still, along the same predictable path.

Without those three extra components, delivered by their least reliable partners, Trident would be worthless.

"Downstairs," Leila said. "Maybe a kind of porch with glass walls?"

"Sounds fine to me."

She conjured up a plan of the house and sketched some ideas, then they went down to try them out at full scale.

They had been into orbit around Najib, and they had traveled embodied to its three beautiful, barren sibling worlds, but they had never been in interstellar space before. Or at least, they had never been conscious of it.

They were still not truly embodied, but you didn't need flesh and blood to feel the vacuum around you; to be awake and plugged-in to an honest depiction of your surroundings was enough. The nearest of Trident's contributor worlds was six hundred light-years away. The distance to Najib was unthinkable. Leila paced around the porch, looking out at the stars, vertiginous in her virtual body, unsteady in the phoney gravity.

It had been twenty-eight thousand years since they'd left Najib. All her children and grandchildren had almost certainly chosen death long ago. No messages had been sent after them to Nazdeek; Leila had asked for that silence, fearing that it would be unbearably painful to hear news, day after day, to which she could give no meaningful reply, about events in which she could never participate. Now she regretted that. She wanted to read about the lives of her grandchildren, as she might the biography of an ancestor. She wanted to know how things had ended up, like the time traveler she was.

A second month of observation passed, with nothing. A data feed reaching them from Nazdeek was equally silent. For any new hint of the beam's location to reach Nazdeek, and then the report of that to reach Trident, would take thousands of years longer than the direct passage of the beam itself, so if Nazdeek saw evidence that the beam was "still" on course, that would be old news about a pulse they had not been here to intercept. However, if Nazdeek reported that the beam had shifted, at least that would put them out of their misery immediately, and tell them that Trident had been built too late.

Jasim made a vegetable garden on the porch and grew exotic food in the starlight. Leila played along, and ate beside him; it was a harmless game. They could have painted anything at all around the house: any planet they'd visited, drawn from their memories, any imaginary world. If this small pretense was enough to keep them sane and anchored to reality, so be it.

Now and then, Leila felt the strangest of the many pangs of isolation Trident induced: here, the knowledge of the galaxy was no longer at her fingertips. Their descriptions as travelers had encoded their vast personal memories, declarative and episodic, and their luggage had included prodigious libraries, but she was used to having so much more. Every civilized planet held a storehouse of information that was simply too bulky to fit into Trident, along with a constant feed of exabytes of news flooding in from other worlds. Wherever you were in the galaxy, some news was old news, some cherished theories long discredited, some facts hopelessly out of date. Here, though, Leila knew, there were billions of rigorously established truths—the results of hundreds of millennia of thought, experiment, and observation—that had slipped out of her reach. Questions that any other child of the Amalgam could expect to have answered instantly would take twelve hundred years to receive a reply.

No such questions actually came into her mind, but there were still moments when the mere fact of it was enough to make her feel unbearably rootless, cut adrift not only from her past and her people, but from civilization itself.

Trident shouted: "Data!"

Leila was halfway through recording a postcard to the Nazdeek Snakes. Jasim was on the porch watering his plants. Leila turned to see him walking through the wall, commanding the bricks to part like a gauze curtain.

They stood side by side, watching the analysis emerge.

A pulse of gamma rays of the expected frequency, from precisely the right location, had just washed over Trident. The beam was greatly attenuated by distance, not to mention having had most of its energy intercepted by its rightful owner, but more than enough had slipped past and reached them for Trident to make sense of the nature of the pulse.

It was, unmistakably, modulated with information. There were precisely repeated phase shifts in the radiation that were unimaginable in any natural gamma ray source, and which would have been pointless in any artificial beam produced for any purpose besides communication.

The pulse had been three seconds long, carrying about ten-to-the-twenty-fourth bits of data. The bulk of this appeared to be random, but that did not rule out meaningful content, it simply implied efficient encryption. The Amalgam's network sent encrypted data via robust classical channels like this, while sending the keys needed to decode it by a second, quantum channel. Leila had never expected to get hold of unencrypted data, laying bare the secrets of the Aloof in an instant. To have clear evidence that someone in the bulge was talking to someone else, and to have pinned down part of the pathway connecting them, was vindication enough.

There was more, though. Between the messages themselves, Trident had identified brief, orderly, unencrypted sequences. Everything was guesswork to a degree, but with such a huge slab of data statistical measures were powerful indicators. Part of the data looked like routing information, addresses for the messages as they were carried through the network. Another part looked like information about the nodes' current and future trajectories. If Trident really had cracked that, they could work out where to position its successor. In fact, if they placed the successor close enough to the bulge, they could probably keep that one observatory constantly inside the spill from the beam.

Jasim couldn't resist playing devil's advocate. "You know, this could just be one part of whatever throws the probes back in our faces, talking to another part. The Aloof themselves could still be dead, while their security system keeps humming with paranoid gossip."

Leila said blithely, "Hypothesize away. I'm not taking the bait."

She turned to embrace him, and they kissed. She said, "I've forgotten how to celebrate. What happens now?"

He moved his fingertips gently along her arm. Leila opened up the scape, creating a fourth spatial dimension. She took his hand, kissed it, and placed it against her beating heart. Their bodies reconfigured, nerve-endings crowding every surface, inside and out.

Jasim climbed inside her, and she inside him, the topology of the scape changing to wrap them together in a mutual embrace. Everything vanished from their lives but pleasure, triumph, and each other's presence, as close as it could ever be.

## VII

"Are you here for the Listening Party?"

The chitinous heptapod, who'd been wandering the crowded street with a food cart dispensing largesse at random, offered Leila a plate of snacks tailored to her and Jasim's preferences. She accepted it, then paused to let Tassef, the planet they'd just set foot on, brief her as to the meaning of this phrase. People, Tassef explained, had traveled to this world from throughout the region in order to witness a special event. Some fifteen thousand years before, a burst of data from the Aloof's network had been picked up by a nearby observatory. In isolation, these bursts meant very little; however, the locals were hopeful that at least one of several proposed observatories near Massa, on the opposite side of the bulge, would have seen spillage including many of the same data packets, forty thousand years before. If any such observations had in fact taken place, news of their precise contents should now, finally, be about to reach Tassef by the longer, disk-based routes of the Amalgam's own network. Once the two observations could be compared, it would become clear which messages from the earlier Eavesdropping session had made their way to the part of the Aloof's network that could be sampled from Tassef. The comparison would advance the project of mapping all the symbolic addresses seen in the data onto actual physical locations.

Leila said, "That's not why we came, but now we know, we're even more pleased to be here."

The heptapod emitted a chirp that Leila understood as a gracious welcome, then pushed its way back into the throng.

Jasim said, "Remember when you told me that everyone would get bored with the Aloof while we were still in transit?"

"I said that would happen eventually. If not this trip, the next one."

"Yes, but you said it five journeys ago."

Leila scowled, preparing to correct him, but then she checked and he was right.

They hadn't expected Tassef to be so crowded when they'd chosen it as their destination, some ten thousand years before. The planet had given them a small room in this city, Shalouf, and imposed a thousand-year limit on their presence if they wished to remain embodied without adopting local citizenship. More than a billion visitors had arrived over the last fifty years, anticipating the news of the observations from Massa, but unable to predict the precise time it would reach Tassef because the details of the observatories' trajectories had still been in transit.

She confessed, "I never thought a billion people would arrange their travel plans around this jigsaw puzzle."

"Travel plans?" Jasim laughed. "We chose to have our own deaths revolve around the very same thing."

"Yes, but we're just weird."

Jasim gestured at the crowded street. "I don't think we can compete on that score."

They wandered through the city, drinking in the decades-long-carnival atmosphere. There were people of every phenotype Leila had encountered before, and more: bipeds, quadrupeds, hexapods, heptapods, walking, shuffling, crawling, scuttling, or soaring high above the street on feathered, scaled, or membranous wings. Some were encased in their preferred atmospheres; others, like Leila and Jasim, had chosen instead to be embodied in ersatz flesh that didn't follow every ancestral chemical dictate. Physics and geometry tied evolution's hands, and many attempts to solve the same problems had converged on similar answers, but the galaxy's different replicators still managed their idiosyncratic twists. When Leila let her translator sample the cacophony of voices and signals at random, she felt as if the whole disk, the whole Amalgam, had converged on this tiny metropolis.

In fact, most of the travelers had come just a few hundred light-years to be here. She and Jasim had chosen to keep their role in the history of Eavesdropping out of their précis, and Leila caught herself with a rather smug sense of walking among the crowd like some unacknowledged sage, bemused by the late-blooming, and no doubt superficial, interest of the masses. On reflection, though, any sense of superior knowledge was hard to justify, when most of these people would have grown up steeped in developments that she was only belatedly catching up with. A new generation of observatories had been designed while she and Jasim were in transit, based on "strong bullets": specially designed femtomachines, clusters of protons and neutrons stable only for trillionths of a second, launched at ultra-relativistic speeds so great that time dilation enabled them to survive long enough to collide with other components and merge into tiny, short-lived gamma-ray observatories. The basic trick that had built Trident had gone from a one-off gamble into a miniaturized, mass-produced phenomenon, with literally billions of strong bullets being fired continuously from thousands of planets around the inner disk.

Femtomachines themselves were old hat, but it had taken the technical challenges of Eavesdropping to motivate someone into squeezing a few more tricks out of them. Historians had always understood that in the long run, technological progress was a horizontal asymptote: once people had more or less everything they wanted that was physically possible, every incremental change would take exponentially longer to achieve, with diminishing returns and ever less reason to bother. The Amalgam would probably spend an eon inching its way closer to the flatline, but this was proof that shifts of circumstance alone could still trigger a modest renaissance or two, without the need for any radical scientific discovery or even a genuinely new technology.

They stopped to rest in a square, beside a small fountain gushing aromatic hydrocarbons. The Tassef locals, quadrupeds with slick, rubbery hides, played in the sticky black spray then licked each other clean.

Jasim shaded his eyes from the sun. He said, "We've had our autumn child, and we've seen its grandchildren prosper. I'm not sure what's left."

"No." Leila was in no rush to die, but they'd sampled fifty thousand years of their discovery's consequences. They'd followed in the wake of the news of the gamma ray signals as it circled the inner disk, spending less than a century conscious as they sped from world to world. At first they'd been hunting for some vital new role to play, but they'd slowly come to accept that the avalanche they'd triggered had out-raced them. Physical and logical maps of the Aloof's network were being constructed, as fast as the laws of physics allowed. Billions of people on thousands of planets, scattered around the inner rim of the Amalgam's territory, were sharing their observations to help piece together the living skeleton of their elusive neighbors. When that project was complete it would not be the end of anything, but it could mark the start of a long hiatus. The encrypted, classical data would never yield anything more than traffic routes; no amount of ingenuity could extract its content. The quantum keys that could unlock it, assuming the Aloof even used such things, would be absolutely immune to theft, duplication, or surreptitious sampling. One day, there would be another breakthrough, and everything would change again, but did they want to wait a hundred thousand years, a million, just to see what came next?

The solicitous heptapods—not locals, but visitors from a world thirty light-years away who had nonetheless taken on some kind of innate duty of hospitality—seemed to show up whenever anyone was hungry. Leila tried to draw this second one into conversation, but it politely excused itself to rush off and feed someone else.

Leila said, "Maybe this is it. We'll wait for the news from Massa, then celebrate for a while, then finish it."

Jasim took her hand. "That feels right to me. I'm not certain, but I don't think I'll ever be."

"Are you tired?" she said. "Bored?"

"Not at all," he replied. "I feel *satisfied*. With what we've done, what we've seen. And I don't want to dilute that. I don't want to hang around forever, watching it fade, until we start to feel the way we did on Najib all over again."

"No."

They sat in the square until dusk, and watched the stars of the bulge come out. They'd seen this dazzling jewelled hub from every possible angle now, but Leila never grew tired of the sight.

Jasim gave an amused, exasperated sigh. "That beautiful, maddening, unreachable place. I think the whole Amalgam will be dead and gone without anyone setting foot inside it."

Leila felt a sudden surge of irritation, which deepened into a sense of revulsion. "It's a place, like any other place! Stars, gas, dust, planets. It's not some metaphysical realm. It's not even far away. Our own home world is twenty times more distant."

"Our own home world doesn't have an impregnable fence around it. If we really wanted to, we could go back there."

Leila was defiant. "If we really wanted to, we could enter the bulge."

Jasim laughed. "Have you read something in those messages that you didn't tell me about? How to say 'open sesame' to the gatekeepers?"

Leila stood, and summoned a map of the Aloof's network to superimpose across their vision, crisscrossing the sky with slender cones of violet light. One cone appeared head-on, as a tiny circle: the beam whose spillage came close to Tassef. She put her hand on Jasim's shoulder, and zoomed in on that circle. It opened up before them like a beckoning tunnel.

She said, "We know where this beam is coming from. We don't know for certain that the traffic between these particular nodes runs in both directions, but we've found plenty of examples where it does. If we aim a signal from here, back along the path of the spillage, and we make it wide enough, then we won't just hit the sending node. We'll hit the receiver as well."

Jasim was silent.

"We know the data format," she continued. "We know the routing information. We can address the data packets to a node on the other side of the bulge, one where the spillage comes out at Massa."

Jasim said, "What makes you think they'll accept the packets?"

"There's nothing in the format we don't understand, nothing we can't write for ourselves."

"Nothing in the unencrypted part. If there's an authorization, even a checksum, in the encrypted part, then any packet without that will be tossed away as noise."

"That's true," she conceded.

"Do you really want to do this?" he said. Her hand was still on his shoulder, she could feel his body growing tense.

"Absolutely."

"We mail ourselves from here to Massa, as unencrypted, classical data that anyone can read, anyone can copy, anyone can alter or corrupt?"

"A moment ago you said they'd throw us away as noise."

"That's the least of our worries."

"Maybe."

Jasim shuddered, his body almost convulsing. He let out a string of obscenities, then made a choking sound. "What's wrong with you? Is this some kind of test? If I call your bluff, will you admit that you're joking."

Leila shook her head. "And no, it's not revenge for what you did on the way to Trident. This is our chance. *This* is what we were waiting to do—not the Eavesdropping, that's nothing! The bulge is right here in front of us. The Aloof are in there, somewhere. We can't force them to engage with us, but we can get closer to them than anyone has ever been before."

"If we go in this way, they could do anything to us."

"They're not barbarians. They haven't made war on us. Even the engineering spores come back unharmed."

"If we infest their network, that's worse than an engineering spore."

"'Infest'! None of these routes are crowded. A few exabytes passing through is nothing."

"You have no idea how they'll react."

"No," she confessed. "I don't. But I'm ready to find out."

Jasim stood. "We could send a test message first. Then go to Massa and see if it arrived safely."

"We could do that," Leila conceded. "That would be a sensible plan."

"So you agree?" Jasim gave her a wary, frozen smile. "We'll send a test message. Send an encyclopedia. Send greetings in some universal language."

"Fine. We'll send all of those things first. But I'm not waiting more than one day after that. I'm not going to Massa the long way. I'm taking the shortcut, I'm going through the bulge."

## VIII

The Amalgam had been so generous to Leila, and local interest in the Aloof so intense, that she had almost forgotten that she was not, in fact, entitled to a limitless and unconditional flow of resources, to be employed to any end that involved her obsession.

When she asked Tassef for the means to build a high-powered gamma-ray transmitter to aim into the bulge, it interrogated her for an hour, then replied that the matter would require a prolonged and extensive consultation. It was, she realized, no use protesting that compared to hosting a billion guests for a couple of centuries, the cost of this was nothing. The sticking point was not the energy use, or any other equally microscopic consequence for the comfort and amenity of the Tassef locals. The issue was whether her proposed actions might be seen as unwelcome and offensive by the Aloof, and whether that affront might in turn provoke some kind of retribution.

Countless probes and spores had been gently and patiently returned from the bulge unharmed, but they'd come blundering in at less than lightspeed. A flash of gamma rays could not be intercepted and returned before it struck its chosen target. Though it seemed to Leila that it would be a trivial matter for the network to choose to reject the data, it was not unreasonable to suppose that the Aloof's sensibilities might differ on this point from her own.

Jasim had left Shalouf for a city on the other side of the planet. Leila's feelings about this were mixed; it was always painful when they separated, but the reminder that they were not irrevocably welded together also brought an undeniable sense of space and freedom. She loved him beyond measure, but that was not the final word on every question. She was not certain that she would not relent in the end, and die quietly beside him when the news came through from Massa; there were moments when it seemed utterly perverse, masochistic, and self-aggrandising to flee from that calm, dignified end for the sake of trying to cap their modest revolution with a new and spectacularly dangerous folly. Nor, though, was she certain that Jasim would not change his own mind, and take her hand while they plunged off this cliff together.

When the months dragged on with no decision on her request, no news from Massa, and no overtures from her husband, Leila became an orator, traveling from city to city promoting her scheme to blaze a trail through the heart of the bulge. Her words and image were conveyed into virtual fora, but her physical presence was a way to draw attention to her cause, and Listening Party pilgrims and Tassefi alike packed the meeting places when she came. She mastered the locals' language and style, but left it inflected with some suitably alien mannerisms. The fact that a rumor had arisen that she was one of the First Eavesdroppers did no harm to her attendance figures.

When she reached the city of Jasim's self-imposed exile, she searched the audience for him in vain. As she walked out into the night a sense of panic gripped her. She felt no fear for herself, but the thought of him dying here alone was unbearable.

She sat in the street, weeping. How had it come to this? They had been prepared for a glorious failure, prepared to be broken by the Aloof's unyielding silence, and instead the fruits of their labor had swept through the disk, reinvigorating a thousand cultures. How could the taste of success be so bitter?

Leila imagined calling out to Jasim, finding him, holding him again, repairing their wounds.

A splinter of steel remained inside her, though. She looked up into the blazing sky. The Aloof were there, waiting, daring her to stand before them. To come this far, then step back from the edge for the comfort of a familiar embrace, would diminish her. She would not retreat.

The news arrived from Massa: forty thousand years before, the spillage from the far side of the bulge had been caught in time. Vast swathes of the data matched the observations that Tassef had been holding in anticipation of this moment, for the last fifteen thousand years.

There was more: reports of other correlations from other observatories followed within minutes. As the message from Massa had been relayed around the inner disk, a cascade of similar matches with other stores of data had been found.

By seeing where packets dropped out of the stream, their abstract addresses became concrete, physical locations within the bulge. As

Leila stood in Shalouf's main square in the dusk, absorbing the reports, the Aloof's network was growing more solid, less ethereal, by the minute.

The streets around her were erupting with signs of elation: polyglot shouts, chirps and buzzes, celebratory scents, and vivid pigmentation changes. Bursts of luminescence spread across the square. Even the relentlessly sober heptapods had abandoned their food carts to lie on their backs, spinning with delight. Leila wheeled around, drinking it in, commanding her translator to punch the meaning of every disparate gesture and sound deep into her brain, unifying the kaleidoscope into a single emotional charge.

As the stars of the bulge came out, Tassef offered an overlay for everyone to share, with the newly mapped routes shining like golden highways. From all around her, Leila picked up the signals of those who were joining the view: people of every civilization, every species, every replicator were seeing the Aloof's secret roads painted across the sky.

Leila walked through the streets of Shalouf, feeling Jasim's absence sharply, but too familiar with that pain to be overcome by it. If the joy of this moment was muted, every celebration would be blighted in the same way, now. She could not expect anything else. She would grow inured to it.

Tassef spoke to her.

"The citizens have reached a decision. They will grant your request."

"I'm grateful."

"There is a condition. The transmitter must be built at least twenty light-years away, either in interstellar space, or in the circumstellar region of an uninhabited system."

"I understand." This way, in the event that the Aloof felt threatened to the point of provoking destructive retribution, Tassef would survive an act of violence, at least on a stellar scale, directed against the transmitter itself.

"We advise you to prepare your final plans for the hardware, and submit them when you're sure they will fulfill your purpose."

"Of course."

Leila went back to her room, and reviewed the plans she had already drafted. She had anticipated the Tassefi wanting a considerable safety margin, so she had worked out the energy budgets for detailed scenarios involving engineering spores and forty-seven different cometary clouds that fell within Tassef's jurisdiction. It took just seconds to identify the best one that met the required conditions, and she lodged it without hesitation.

Out on the streets, the Listening Party continued. For the billion pilgrims, this was enough: they would go home, return to their grandchildren, and die happy in the knowledge that they had finally seen something new in the world. Leila envied them; there'd been a time when that would have been enough for her, too.

She left her room and rejoined the celebration, talking, laughing, dancing with strangers, letting herself grow giddy with the moment. When the sun came up, she made her way home, stepping lightly over the sleeping bodies that filled the street.

The engineering spores were the latest generation: strong bullets launched at close to lightspeed that shed their momentum by diving through the heart of a star, and then rebuilding themselves at atomic density as they decayed in the stellar atmosphere. In effect, the dying femtomachines constructed nanomachines bearing the same blueprints as they'd carried within themselves at nuclear densities, and which then continued out to the cometary cloud to replicate and commence the real work of mining raw materials and building the gamma ray transmitter.

Leila contemplated following in their wake, sending herself as a signal to be picked up by the as-yet-unbuilt transmitter. It would not have been as big a gamble as Jasim's with Trident; the strong bullets had already been used successfully this way in hundreds of similar stars.

In the end, she chose to wait on Tassef for a signal that the transmitter had been successfully constructed, and had tested, aligned, and calibrated itself. If she was going to march blindly into the bulge, it would be absurd to stumble and fall prematurely, before she even reached the precipice.

When the day came, some ten thousand people gathered in the center of Shalouf to bid the traveler a safe journey. Leila would have preferred to slip away quietly, but after all her lobbying she had surrendered her privacy, and the Tassefi seemed to feel that she owed them this last splash of color and ceremony.

Forty-six years after the Listening Party, most of the pilgrims had returned to their homes, but of the few hundred who had lingered in Shalouf nearly all had shown up for this curious footnote to the main event. Leila wasn't sure that anyone here believed the Aloof's network would do more than bounce her straight back into the disk, but the affection these well-wishers expressed seemed genuine. Someone had even gone to the trouble of digging up a phrase in the oldest known surviving language of her ancestral species: *safar bekheyr*, may your journey be blessed. They had written it across the sky in an ancient script that she'd last seen eighty thousand years before, and it had been spread among the crowd phonetically so that everyone she met could offer her this hopeful farewell as she passed.

Tassef, the insentient delegate of all the planet's citizens, addressed the crowd with some somber ceremonial blather. Leila's mind wandered, settling on the observation that she was probably partaking in a public execution. No matter. She had said good-bye to her friends and family long ago. When she stepped through the ceremonial gate, which had been smeared with a tarry mess that the Tassefi considered the height of beauty, she would close her eyes and recall her last night on Najib, letting the intervening millennia collapse into a dream. Everyone chose death in the end, and no one's exit was perfect. Better to rely on your own flawed judgments, better to make your own ungainly mess of it, than live in the days when nature would simply take you at random.

As Tassef fell silent, a familiar voice rose up from the crowd.

"Are you still resolved to do this foolish thing?"

Leila glared down at her husband. "Yes, I am."

"You won't reconsider?"

"No."

"Then I'm coming with you."

Jasim pushed his way through the startled audience, and climbed onto the stage.

Leila spoke to him privately. "You're embarrassing us both."

He replied the same way. "Don't be petty. I know I've hurt you, but the blame lies with both of us."

"Why are you doing this? You've made your own wishes very plain."

"Do you think I can watch you walk into danger, and not walk beside you?"

"You were ready to die if Trident failed. You were ready to leave me behind then."

"Once I spoke my mind on that you gave me no choice. You insisted." He took her hand. "You know I only stayed away from you all this time because I hoped it would dissuade you. I failed. So now I'm here."

Leila's heart softened. "You're serious? You'll come with me?"

Jasim said, "Whatever they do to you, let them do it to us both."

Leila had no argument to make against this, no residue of anger, no false solicitousness. She had always wanted him beside her at the end, and she would not refuse him now.

She spoke to Tassef. "One more passenger. Is that acceptable?" The energy budget allowed for a thousand years of test transmissions to follow in her wake; Jasim would just be a minor blip of extra data.

"It's acceptable." Tassef proceeded to explain the change to the assembled crowd, and to the onlookers scattered across the planet.

Jasim said, "We'll interweave the data from both of us into a single packet. I don't want to end up at Massa and find they've sent you to Jahnom by mistake."

"All right." Leila arranged the necessary changes. None of the Eavesdroppers yet knew that they were coming, and no message sent the long way could warn them in time, but the data they sent into the bulge would be prefaced by instructions that anyone in the Amalgam would find clear and unambiguous, asking that their descriptions only be embodied if they were picked up at Massa. If they were found in other spillage along the way, they didn't want to be embodied multiple times. And if they did not emerge at Massa at all, so be it.

Tassef's second speech came to an end. Leila looked down at the crowd one last time, and let her irritation with the whole bombastic ceremony dissipate into amusement. If she had been among the sane, she might easily have turned up herself to watch a couple of ancient fools try to step onto the imaginary road in the sky, and wish them *safar bekheyr*.

She squeezed Jasim's hand, and they walked toward the gate.

## IX

Leila's fingers came together, her hand empty. She felt as if she was falling, but nothing in sight appeared to be moving. Then again, all she could see was a distant backdrop, its scale and proximity impossible to judge: thousands of fierce blue stars against the blackness of space.

She looked around for Jasim, but she was utterly alone. She could see no vehicle or other machine that might have disgorged her into this emptiness. There was not even a planet below her, or a single brightest star to which she might be bound. Absurdly, she was breathing. Every other cue told her that she was drifting through vacuum, probably through interstellar space. Her lungs kept filling and emptying, though. The air, and her skin, felt neither hot nor cold.

Someone or something had embodied her, or was running her as software. She was not on Massa, she was sure of that; she had never visited that world, but nowhere in the Amalgam would a guest be treated like this. Not even one who arrived unannounced in data spilling out from the bulge.

Leila said, "Are you listening to me? Do you understand me?" She could hear her own voice, flat and without resonance. The acoustics made perfect sense in a vast, empty, windless place, if not an airless one.

Anywhere in the Amalgam, you *knew* whether you were embodied or not; it was the nature of all bodies, real or virtual, that declarative knowledge of every detail was there for the asking. Here, when Leila tried to summon the same information, her mind remained blank. It was like the strange absence she'd felt on Trident, when she'd been cut off from the repositories of civilization, but here the amputation had reached all the way inside her.

She inhaled deeply, but there was no noticeable scent at all, not even the whiff of her own body odor that she would have expected, whether she was wearing her ancestral phenotype or any of the forms of ersatz flesh that she adopted when the environment demanded it. She pinched the skin of her forearm; it felt more like her original skin than any of the substitutes she'd ever worn. They might have fashioned this body out of something both remarkably lifelike and chemically inert, and placed her in a vast, transparent container of air, but she was beginning to pick up a strong stench of ersatz physics. Air and skin alike, she suspected, were made of bits, not atoms.

*So where was Jasim?* Were they running him too, in a separate scape? She called out his name, trying not to make the exploratory cry sound plaintive. She understood all too well now why he'd tried so hard to keep her from this place, and why he'd been unable to face staying behind: the thought that the Aloof might be doing something unspeakable to his defenseless consciousness, in some place she couldn't hope to reach or see, was like a white hot blade pressed to her heart. All she could do was try to shut off the panic and talk down the possibility. *All right, he's alone here, but so am I, and it's not that bad.* She would put her faith in symmetry; if they had not abused her, why would they have harmed Jasim?

She forced herself to be calm. The Aloof had taken the trouble to grant her consciousness, but she couldn't expect the level of amenity she was accustomed to. For a start, it would be perfectly reasonable if her hosts were unable or unwilling to plug her into any data source equivalent to the Amalgam's libraries, and perhaps the absence of somatic knowledge was not much different. Rather than deliberately fooling her about her body, maybe they had looked at the relevant data channels and decided that *anything* they fed into them would be misleading. Understanding her transmitted description well enough to bring her to consciousness was one thing, but it didn't guarantee that they knew how to translate the technical details of their instantiation of her into her own language.

And if this ignorance-plus-honesty excuse was too sanguine to swallow, it wasn't hard to think of the Aloof as being pathologically secretive without actually being malicious. If they wanted to keep quiet about the way they'd brought her to life lest it reveal something about themselves, that too was understandable. They need not be doing it for the sake of tormenting her.

Leila surveyed the sky around her, and felt a jolt of recognition. She'd memorized the positions of the nearest stars to the target node where her transmission would first be sent, and now a matching pattern stood out against the background in a collection of distinctive constellations. She was being shown the sky from that node. This didn't prove anything about her actual location, but the simplest explanation was that the Aloof had instantiated her here, rather than sending her on through the network. The stars were in the positions she'd predicted for her time of arrival, so if this was the reality, there had been little delay in choosing how to deal with the intruder. No thousand-year-long deliberations, no passing of the news to a distant decision-maker. Either the Aloof themselves were present here, or the machinery of the node was so sophisticated that they might as well have been. She could not have been woken by accident; it had to have been a deliberate act. It made her wonder if the Aloof had been expecting something like this for millennia.

"What now?" she asked. Her hosts remained silent. "Toss me back to Tassef?" The probes with their reversed trajectories bore no record of their experience; perhaps the Aloof wouldn't incorporate these new memories into her description before returning her. She spread her arms imploringly. "If you're going to erase this memory, why not speak to me first? I'm in your hands completely, you can send me to the grave with your secrets. Why wake me at all, if you don't want to talk?"

In the silence that followed, Leila had no trouble imagining one answer: to study her. It was a mathematical certainty that some questions about her behavior could never be answered simply by examining her static description; the only reliable way to predict what she'd do in any given scenario was to wake her and confront her with it. They might, of course, have chosen to wake her any number of times before, without granting her memories of the previous instantiations. She experienced a moment of sheer existential vertigo: this could be the thousandth, the billionth, in a vast series of experiments, as her captors permuted dozens of variables to catalog her responses.

The vertigo passed. Anything was possible, but she preferred to entertain more pleasant hypotheses.

"I came here to talk," she said. "I understand that you don't want us sending in machinery, but there must be something we can discuss, something we can learn from each other. In the disk, every time two space-faring civilizations met, they found they had something in common. Some mutual interests, some mutual benefits."

At the sound of her own earnest speech dissipating into the virtual air around her, Leila started laughing. The arguments she'd been putting for centuries to Jasim, to her friends on Najib, to the Snakes on Nazdeek, seemed ridiculous now, embarrassing. How could she face the Aloof and claim that she had anything to offer them that they had not considered, and rejected, hundreds of thousands of years before? The Amalgam had never tried to keep its nature hidden. The Aloof would have watched them, studied them from afar, and consciously chosen isolation. To come here and list the advantages of contact as if they'd never crossed her hosts' minds was simply insulting.

Leila fell silent. If she had lost faith in her role as cultural envoy, at least she'd proven to her own satisfaction that there was something in her smarter than the slingshot fence the probes had encountered. The Aloof had not embraced her, but the whole endeavor had not been in vain. To wake in the bulge, even to silence, was far more than she'd ever had the right to hope for.

She said, "Please, just bring me my husband now, then we'll leave you in peace."

This entreaty was met in the same way as all the others. Leila resisted speculating again about experimental variables. She did not believe that a million-year-old civilization was interested in testing her tolerance to isolation, robbing her of her companion and seeing how long she took to attempt suicide. The Aloof did not take orders from her; fine. If she was neither an experimental subject to be robbed of her sanity, nor a valued guest whose every wish was granted, there had to be some other relationship between them that she had yet to fathom. She had to be conscious for a reason.

She searched the sky for a hint of the node itself, or any other feature she might have missed, but she might as well have been living inside a star map, albeit one shorn of the usual annotations. The Milky Way, the plane of stars that bisected the sky, was hidden by the thicker clouds of gas and dust here, but Leila had her bearings; she knew which way led deeper into the bulge, and which way led back out to the disk.

She contemplated Tassef's distant sun with mixed emotions, as a sailor might look back on the last sight of land. As the yearning for that familiar place welled up, a cylinder of violet light appeared around her, encircling the direction of her gaze. For the first time, Leila felt her weightlessness interrupted: a gentle acceleration was carrying her forward along the imaginary beam.

"No! Wait!" She closed her eyes and curled into a ball. The acceleration halted, and when she opened her eyes the tunnel of light was gone.

She let herself float limply, paying no attention to anything in the sky, waiting to see what happened if she kept her mind free of any desire for travel.

After an hour like this, the phenomenon had not recurred. Leila turned her gaze in the opposite direction, into the bulge. She cleared her mind of all timidity and nostalgia, and imagined the thrill of rushing deeper into this violent, spectacular, alien territory. At first there was no response from the scape, but then she focused her attention sharply in the direction of a second node, the one she'd hoped her transmission would be forwarded to from the first, on its way through the galactic core.

The same violet light, the same motion. This time, Leila waited a few heartbeats longer before she broke the spell.

Unless this was some pointlessly sadistic game, the Aloof were offering her a clear choice. She could return to Tassef, return to the Amalgam. She could announce that she'd put a toe in these mysterious waters, and lived to tell the tale. Or she could dive into the bulge, as deep as she'd ever imagined, and see where the network took her.

"No promises?" she asked. "No guarantee I'll come out the other side? No intimations of contact, to tempt me further?" She was thinking aloud, she did not expect answers. Her hosts, she was beginning to conclude, viewed strangers through the prism of a strong, but very sharply delineated, sense of obligation. They sent back the insentient probes to their owners, scrupulously intact. They had woken this intruder to give her the choice: Did she really want to go where her transmission suggested, or had she wandered in here like a lost child who just needed to find the way home? They would do her no harm, and send her on no journey without her consent, but those were the limits of their duty of care. They did not owe her any account of themselves. She would get no greeting, no hospitality, no conversation.

"What about Jasim? Will you give me a chance to consult with him?" She waited, picturing his face, willing his presence, hoping they might read her mind if her words were beyond them. If they could decode a yearning toward a point in the sky, surely this wish for companionship was not too difficult to comprehend? She tried variations, dwelling on the abstract structure of their intertwined data in the transmission, hoping this might clarify the object of her desire if his physical appearance meant nothing to them.

She remained alone.

The stars that surrounded her spelt out the only choices on offer. If she wanted to be with Jasim once more before she died, she had to make the same decision as he did.

Symmetry demanded that he faced the same dilemma.

*How would he be thinking?* He might be tempted to retreat back to the safety of Tassef, but he'd reconciled with her in Shalouf for the sole purpose of following her into danger. He would understand that she'd want to go deeper, would want to push all the way through to Massa, opening up the shortcut through the core, proving it safe for future travelers.

Would he understand, too, that she'd feel a pang of guilt at this presumptuous line of thought, and that she'd contemplate making a sacrifice of her own? He had braved the unknown for her, and they had reaped the reward already: they had come closer to the Aloof than anyone in history. Why couldn't that be enough? For all Leila knew, her hosts might not even wake her again before Massa. What would she be giving up if she turned back now?

More to the point, what would Jasim expect of her? That she'd march on relentlessly, following her obsession to the end, or that she'd put her love for him first?

The possibilities multiplied in an infinite regress. They knew each other as well as two people could, but they didn't carry each other's minds inside them.

Leila drifted through the limbo of stars, wondering if Jasim had already made his decision. Having seen that the Aloof were not the torturers he'd feared, had he already set out for Tassef, satisfied that she faced no real peril at their hands? Or had he reasoned that their experience at this single node meant nothing? This was not the Amalgam, the culture could be a thousand times more fractured.

This cycle of guesses and doubts led nowhere. If she tried to pursue it to the end she'd be paralyzed. There were no guarantees; she could only choose the least worst case. If she returned to Tassef, only to find that Jasim had gone on alone through the bulge, it would be unbearable: she would have lost him for nothing. If that happened, she could try to follow him, returning to the bulge immediately, but she would already be centuries behind him.

If she went on to Massa, and it was Jasim who retreated, at least she'd know that he'd ended up in safety. She'd know, too, that he had not been desperately afraid for her, that the Aloof's benign indifference at this first node had been enough to persuade him that they'd do her no harm.

That was her answer: she had to continue, all the way to Massa. With the hope, but no promise, that Jasim would have thought the same way.

The decision made, she lingered in the scape. Not from any second thoughts, but from a reluctance to give up lightly the opportunity she'd fought so hard to attain. She didn't know if any member of the Aloof was watching and listening to her, reading her thoughts, examining her desires. Perhaps they were so indifferent and incurious that they'd delegated everything to insentient software, and merely instructed their machines to babysit her while she made up her mind where she wanted to go. She still had to make one last attempt to reach them, or she would never die in peace.

"Maybe you're right," she said. "Maybe you've watched us for the last million years, and seen that we have nothing to offer you. Maybe our technology is backward, our philosophy naive, our customs bizarre, our manners appalling. If that's true, though, if we're so far beneath you, you could at least point us in the right direction. Offer us some kind of argument as to why we should change."

Silence.

Leila said, "All right. Forgive my impertinence. I have to tell you honestly, though, that we won't be the last to bother you. The Amalgam is full of people who will keep trying to find ways to reach you. This is going to go on for another million years, until we believe that we understand you. If that offends you, don't judge us too harshly. We can't help it. It's who we are."

She closed her eyes, trying to assure herself that there was nothing she'd regret having left unsaid.

"Thank you for granting us safe passage," she added, "if that's what you're offering. I hope my people can return the favor one day, if there's anywhere you want to go."

She opened her eyes and sought out her destination: deeper into the network, on toward the core.

X

The mountains outside the town of Astraahat started with a gentle slope that promised an easy journey, but gradually grew steeper. Similarly, the vegetation was low and sparse in the foothills, but became steadily thicker and taller the higher up the slope you went.

Jasim said, "Enough." He stopped and leaned on his climbing stick.

"One more hour?" Leila pleaded.

He considered this. "Half an hour resting, then half an hour walking?"

"One hour resting, then one hour walking."

He laughed wearily. "All right. One of each."

The two of them hacked away at the undergrowth until there was a place to sit.

Jasim poured water from the canteen into her hands, and she splashed her face clean.

They sat in silence for a while, listening to the sounds of the unfamiliar wildlife. Under the forest canopy it was almost twilight, and when Leila looked up into the small patch of sky above them she could see the stars of the bulge, like tiny, pale, translucent beads.

At times it felt like a dream, but the experience never really left her. The Aloof had woken her at every node, shown her the view, given her a choice. She had seen a thousand spectacles, from one side of the core to the other: cannibalistic novas, dazzling clusters of newborn stars, twin white dwarfs on the verge of collision. She had seen the black hole at the galaxy's center, its accretion disk glowing with X-rays, slowly tearing stars apart.

It might have been an elaborate lie, a plausible simulation, but every detail accessible from disk-based observatories confirmed what she had witnessed. If anything had been changed, or hidden from her, it must have been small. Perhaps the artifacts of the Aloof themselves had been painted out of the view, though Leila thought it was just as likely that the marks they'd left on their territory were so subtle, anyway, that there'd been nothing to conceal.

Jasim said sharply, "Where are you?"

She lowered her gaze and replied mildly, "I'm here, with you. I'm just remembering."

When they'd woken on Massa, surrounded by delirious, cheering Eavesdroppers, they'd been asked: *What happened in there? What did you see?* Leila didn't know why she'd kept her mouth shut and turned to her husband before replying, instead of letting every detail come tumbling out immediately. Perhaps she just hadn't known where to begin.

For whatever reason, it was Jasim who had answered first. "Nothing. We stepped through the gate on Tassef, and now here we are. On the other side of the bulge."

For almost a month, she'd flatly refused to believe him. *Nothing? You saw nothing?* It had to be a lie, a joke. It had to be some kind of revenge.

That was not in his nature, and she knew it. Still, she'd clung to that explanation for as long as she could, until it became impossible to believe any longer, and she'd asked for his forgiveness.

Six months later, another traveler had spilt out of the bulge. One of the die-hard Listening Party pilgrims had followed in their wake and taken the shortcut. Like Jasim, this heptapod had seen nothing, experienced nothing.

Leila had struggled to imagine why she might have been singled out. So much for her theory that the Aloof felt morally obliged to check that each passenger on their network knew what they were doing, unless they'd decided that her actions were enough to demonstrate that intruders from the disk, considered generically, were making an informed choice. Could just one sample of a working, conscious version of their neighbors really be enough for them to conclude that they understood everything they needed to know? Could this capriciousness, instead, have been part of a strategy to lure in more visitors, with the enticing possibility that each one might, with luck, witness something far beyond all those who'd preceded them? Or had it been part of a scheme to discourage intruders by clouding the experience with uncertainty? The simplest act of discouragement would have been to discard all unwelcome transmissions, and the most effective incentive would have been to offer a few plain words of welcome, but then, the Aloof would not have been the Aloof if they'd followed such reasonable dictates.

Jasim said, "You know what I think. You wanted to wake so badly, they couldn't refuse you. They could tell I didn't care as much. It was as simple as that."

"What about the heptapod? It went in alone. It wasn't just tagging along to watch over someone else."

He shrugged. "Maybe it acted on the spur of the moment. They all seem unhealthily keen to me, whatever they're doing. Maybe the Aloof could discern its mood more clearly."

Leila said, "I don't believe a word of that."

Jasim spread his hands in a gesture of acceptance. "I'm sure you could change my mind in five minutes, if I let you. But if we walked back down this hill and waited for the next traveler from the bulge, and the next, until the reason some of them received the grand tour and some didn't finally became plain, there would still be another question, and another. Even if I wanted to live for ten thousand years more, I'd rather move on to something else. And in this last hour . . . " He trailed off.

Leila said, "I know. You're right."

She sat, listening to the strange chirps and buzzes emitted by creatures she knew nothing about. She could have absorbed every recorded fact about them in an instant, but she didn't care, she didn't need to know.

Someone else would come after them, to understand the Aloof, or advance that great, unruly, frustrating endeavor by the next increment. She and Jasim had made a start; that was enough. What they'd done was more than she could ever have imagined, back on Najib. Now, though, was the time to stop, while they were still themselves: enlarged by the experience, but not disfigured beyond recognition.

They finished their water, drinking the last drops. They left the canteen behind. Jasim took her hand and they climbed together, struggling up the slope side by side.

John Barnes has commercially published dozens of volumes of fiction, including science fiction, men's action adventure, two collaborations with astronaut Buzz Aldrin, a collection of short stories and essays, one fantasy and one mainstream YA novel, plus two self-published novels, and around forty short stories. His recent books include *Losers in Space*, *Raise the Gipper!*, and *The Last President*. His personal blog is thatjohnbarnes.blogspot.com and he contributes frequent articles about analytics and metrics in business to AllAnalytics.com. He has done a rather large number of occasionally peculiar things for money, mainly in business consulting, academic teaching, and show business, fields which overlap more than you'd think. Since 2001, he has lived in Denver, Colorado, where he has a wonderful spouse, an average income, and a bad attitude, which he feels is actually the best permutation.

# THE LOST PRINCESS MAN

## *John Barnes*

What are the people like in the Krevpiceaux country?" An aristocrat stood over Aurigar's table.

Careful not to spill the carafe of wine or knock the remains of his noodles-and-mussels to the floor, Aurigar staggered up from his chair and bowed. "Lord Leader Sir?"

"You heard the question the first time."

The lord bulged with stimumuscle. His face had been fashionably planed-and-pitched and geneted gun-steel blue; it looked like the entrance to the villain's fortress in a dwellgame.

*He will be extremely fast, too, they optimize the nervous system at the same time they grow stimumuscle, and he's legal to carry any weapon and I don't even have a resident alien carry permit and Oh! Samwal defend me, I can't run, I can't fight, probably he's even smarter than I am,* Aurigar thought.

"I have never been to the Creffenho country, Lord Leader Sir," Aurigar said, "but it is said that—"

"You're telling the truth." Lenses and mirrors flickered in Lord Leader Sir's eye socket, briefly spoiling the illusion of an empty black pit. "But it is disturbing that you are pretending to have misheard the question." The lord extended his hand, palm up, and his fingers flowed forward, splitting into myriad filaments. Through Aurigar's shirt, they stung like jellyfish tentacles and gripped like screws. They moved Aurigar's skin out of the way, then his flesh, flowed around his ribs, and stopped his heart.

Terror restarted his heart; the neural connection from the aristocrat's fingers stopped it again, restarted it, and then made it flutter, before restoring a steady, deep beat.

"When I pull my fingers back out," the blue-faced man asked, eye sockets glittering and whirling silver and glass, "shall I leave you with your heart operating, or not operating?" He raced Aurigar's heart into painful thunder, then slowed it to the low throb of deep meditation. "I will choose *not* operating if you do not make a choice. Operating, or not operating?"

"Operating, if it pleases you, Lord Leader Sir."

"Oh, *whatever* I do will please *me*. Never fear that." The filaments slid back and out, resolving into fingers just above Aurigar's chest; the fingers reacquired nails and ridges, and presently looked like anyone else's. No blood leaked, but Aurigar's chest tingled where nerves did not quite like how they had been re-meshed. "Thank you, I *will* have a seat, and from here on we'll drink on my tab." Gesturing to Aurigar to resume his seat, the stimumuscled lord sat in the folding chair opposite like a mountain poised upon a dandelion. "What are the people like in the Krevpiceaux country?"

"Well, Lord Leader Sir, I'd have to say . . . well, stolid. Quiet, hard-working, eat-what's-in-front-of-you types. You'll never hear any of them saying that any work is degrading. Tell 'em to shovel shit with a manual shovel, or even their hands—they do it, and no complaints."

"Stupid, do you think?"

Before Aurigar could answer, the carafes of better wine arrived, and the blue man poured a generous glass and pushed it across the table to him. "I don't care if you get drunk, but stay honest. Would you like some appetizers for the table? I know a man who lives your sort of life often finds great pleasure in eating until he is ill."

"Yes, Lord Leader Sir." A lifetime of not being sure when there would be more again had trained Aurigar never to turn down any good thing, even in a surprisingly pleasant nightmare.

When the lord had tasted his wine and Aurigar had finished a glass—and with the promise of a great heap of food on the way—the blue-faced man leaned forward and smiled quite pleasantly. "Now, I already know that you are, by profession, a lost princess man, and that at the moment you are celebrating a successful season. Your bank account in Nue Swuis-she is number AFBX-1453–1962–3554–7889. You booked passage under the name Bifred Prohelo on the *Tambourlaine* tomorrow, stateroom sixteen. I know how Baldor the Nose met his well-deserved end and why your alibi held up—excellent job, by the way. You are allergic to asparagus, the dog you had as a boy was named Magrat, and you are susceptible to sore feet. Will you accept that it is impossible to lie to me?"

"Yes, Lord Leader Sir."

"Good answer."

The naneurs in the wine were adjusting Aurigar's taste and smell to appreciate it; it was the wine most exactly to his taste he'd ever had. He tried an experiment—he thought *Rats are bigger than whales*—and instantly the wine tasted like vinegar, his stomach rolled over, and his head hurt. He thought *I will tell my lord anything he wants*; the wine tasted of sunshine on a meadow just after a cool rain.

"Now," the aristocrat said. "Back to the question. Would you say the Krevpiceauxi are stupid?"

"They are pigheadedly proud to be ignorant of anything they find in books, but *not* stupid. They value shrewdness, deception, facing facts, and even verbal quickness, as long as it serves some larger purpose like making a sale or evading police questioning. In fact, they are smart in a way that makes my con easier to work."

"Interesting. Have more wine—oh, and here are the appetizers—and do go on, taking a bit of time between to chew and savor, eh? What you just said interests me very much."

Like anyone whose fortunes have suddenly, inexplicably, improved, Aurigar was becoming more comfortable. For just a moment, after the first delightful fish roll, he thought, *I can tell him that*—and his tongue tasted as if he had been chewing brass. He reminded himself that truth was good and took a sip of excruciatingly delicious wine. "Well, then, Lord Leader Sir, very few people know this about the lost princess business: the girl knows the truth and comes along willingly with the connivance of her family."

"*Really?* I had not heard that."

"Well, you know, Lord Leader Sir, lost princesses are all the rage in dwellgames. Everyone has played a dozen dwellgames in which the smooth talking stranger—that would be me—"

The lord smiled warmly. "You amuse me. My sources say you are very good at it."

"Yes, I suppose I am good at it. I have stayed away from brilliance, which is hazardous."

"And that in itself is brilliant in its own way. So, then, you—the smooth talker—show up in some remote location where there is an unhappy beautiful girl—"

"Rarely beautiful. Genetion is cheap, and a necessity anyway to put off the insurance-company detectives. The 'lost princess' can be, honestly, plain-faced, with a body that looks like it was piled up at random, and an absolutely lunar complexion. My clients will genete her until she looks better than most real princesses, begging the Lord Leader Sir's pardon if he is related to any."

"Pardon readily granted." The lord knocked back half a glass at a gulp, with a visible shudder. "I am related to thousands of them. So you wander among these stolid farm-folk, and you find some girl to convince that she is a lost princess—usually *the* lost princess?"

"Another myth, Lord Leader Sir. I never tell anyone that she is the Princess Ululara, because she has certainly been warned about strangers who tell her that story. Indeed, I dismiss any such idea; I say, 'Look, sweetie, there's about a billion settled planets under the Imperium, the Emperor's family had *one* baby disappear, so out of maybe four quadrillion humans in the galaxy, *you're* the princess?' Besides, usually their age on their fostindenture papers is wrong for Ululara. I show them that. I say, 'Forget it. If somebody really did snatch Princess Ululara just before the bomb went off, they dropped her down the stairs and killed her, or drowned her in the bathtub, the first day. Then they tossed the little thing into the nearest instant composter and she was potting-soil five minutes later. More likely, it's all just a phantom of the security system and she vaporized with everyone else in the palace. Either way, she's been dead twenty-nine marqs—and you are not she.' Actually, usually I say 'you ain't her,' to fit in better."

"And how do the girls respond to that?"

"They're disappointed—they were harboring the hope, as most unhappy fostindented girls of that generation do. Then I say, 'You seem upset. Perhaps you were hoping that you weren't just another fostindent. You want to know why you don't get along with your family, they don't understand you and worry about ridiculous things—oh, I can see that you're not really one of *them*, it's obvious.' They are, of course, astonished at how well I know them." He flapped a hand to dismiss a lifetime of hard-earned skill. "And so forth, you know. Eventually, I reveal that I am searching for quite a different princess, of a quite minor house, though perfectly verifiable."

"Verifiable?"

"Well, for example, this year I told two girls of sixteen marqs that they might be Princess Pegasa Whon, who would be sixteen, and was kidnapped at about the right date. It's a big galaxy. In four quadrillion people, there are about one hundred million princesses, and, oddly enough, perhaps ten thousand lost ones. At a rough approximation, that's a hundred lost princesses of any particular age, though I don't do much business above forty marqs. One little data search to match age and physical type, and you're in business. Or I am, begging Lord Leader Sir's pardon."

"I do enjoy pardoning you," the lord said. He took a sip and held it in his mouth before swallowing; you were supposed to do that to train the naneurs, Aurigar remembered, and did it himself. The extraordinary wine hastened to surpass itself. The lord asked, "But you say most of them go willingly and knowingly?"

"Well, yes. Only about half the money comes from brothel-owners; the rest is the kickbacks I get in insurance fraud collected by the family. Anyone who buys a fostindent takes out kidnap insurance, and it pays the whole estimated value over the forty-marq indenture and then some. So not only is the girl getting herself a better life, but the family gets a big shot of insurance money, just after one of my false-front companies purchases their outstanding debt at a very deep discount. Then they pay that debt back, to me, at full value. Everyone wins—me, the girl, the family, the family's creditors, the brothel-owners—well, everyone except the insurance companies."

"Given the appeal of the idea, I don't see why these things are not more widely known."

"Honestly, it is in the interests of lost princess men to maintain the horror stories, Lord Leader Sir. It needs to look like a real kidnapping or the insurance company will not pay. Thus, I need to tell the girl a plausible story and make sure she repeats it to several trustworthy blabbermouths—I even coach them to tell it well." He put on a falsetto that he thought was much more girlish than it really was. 'We told her he was a con man and that the lost princess was the oldest con in the book, but she had stars in her eyes, poor thing.' Add a bit of the theatrical to the actual departure—perhaps the girl screaming and her sponsor-parents taking a few wild shots in my direction—and it looks much less like fraud to the detectives."

"And the Krevpiceauxi, who are cunning but not intellectual, are good for this con . . . because?"

"They're blunt, not easily fooled, and hate authority. After listening for a while, the girl says, 'I think you are working the lost princess con, and the minute you have me off planet, you will pump me full of drugs, and I will wake up chained to a bed with a large number of Imperial troops lined up and waiting to have a turn on me.' At which point, I say, 'Well, of course.'"

"You *admit* it?"

"Absolutely, Lord Leader Sir. I then explain that it is better for me if she comes along willingly—fewer clues for the insurance detectives—and that her first stop will be a luxury hospital where she will be geneted into stunning beauty, and tweaked to make her depression-proof, nymphomaniacal, multiorgasmic, and extremely self-confident. Good conversation is highly prized as well, and many men have fetishes for talents like singing or drawing, so the girls also get a year or two developing their most developable talents and receiving a good broad education. The worst is only that during the marq or so it takes to heal into her new form, she will itch a great deal, since her old flesh feels like scar tissue being sloughed off as the new grows in.

"As for Imperial troops, she will encounter them one at a time if at all—and if she's lucky. They are themselves heavily geneted, well educated, highly paid specialists, like herself, and more likely to hire her to come along as a companion on a five-solar-system exotic tour than as fun for a night.

"Besides, under the sumptuary laws, she will be a luxury good. She can't legally be sold to poor or even middle class people unless she is so badly behaved that her owners do so as punishment. As for being owned, we are all theoretically owned by His Supreme Might—"

"His Late Supreme Might," the lord said. "Or had you not heard?"

"I'm a very focused professional; I dwell the crime, investment, and lifestyle instrucks, but not politics, sports, or entertainment." Aurigar hoped that he sounded dignified, but since wayward sauce had spotted his shirt, probably not.

The aristocrat nodded. "Well, then. I am High Supreme Lord Cetuso, which you may know is a junior branch of the Imperial House itself—no, get up, protocol would call for you to get onto the floor entirely facedown, and in this place that would make an utter mess of you, much worse than that little blob on your shirt you keep daubing at. Would you happen to know, since you are concerned with high-ranking lineages, just what the hereditary function of the Cetusos is?"

Aurigar realized. "Samwal defend us!"

"He may have to. Yes. We are the authenticators of the Imperial line. It is well known that the late Emperor was quite mad and could not be geneted into anything that should be allowed to breed, so he died without issue. The Galactic Imperium should now pass to his sister, the lost princess Ululara. If she is alive, we must find her and restore her. If she is dead, there are other, more distant, heirs. But if she is neither proved dead nor found alive . . . well, the fourth Civil War, a thousand years ago, left us with ten thousand vitrified worlds and more than a hundred exploded suns."

"And you think that one of my lost princesses—"

"Seven marqs ago. We have her trail right up to where she talked to you. The insurance-company detectives—a strikingly incompetent lot, by the way—"

"They ought to be incompetent. I pay them enough." Aurigar drained his glass. "Then here's to the new Empress. The only Krevpiceauxi—that's why you asked about that benighted continent on that armpit of a planet, yes?—well, the Krevpiceauxi of exactly that age would be Miriette Phodway. I am pleased to inform you, Lord Leader Cetuso Sir, that I can take you straight to her. I think you will get along very well with her."

"Is she—forgive the question—at all mad?"

"Not at all insane, Lord Leader Cetuso Sir. And since she did so well and I did not deceive her in any way, not furious either—in fact she's risen far from that start; nowadays she's one of my best customers, buying a girl or two every marq from me."

"Then you will introduce me. Afterward, I will of course cover the cost of your unused ticket and then put you on a much better liner to wherever you wish to go, with ten lost princesses worth of profit added to your kick—at a minimum, more if I need you longer. Is she far off?"

"At Waystonn, and in two days, there's a liner departing—"

"A *liner*? If you can bear to let us pack this food and wine to go, you can resume drinking and dining on my yacht in about twenty minutes, and we can be on our way. Unless you have some matter to settle?"

"I had, but let him live, Lord Leader Sir. Good fortune should be shared."

Aurigar could not think of Miriette as Ululara, though he supposed eventually he would have to. "Right this way," she said, taking his arm, and beckoning Lord Leader Cetuso Sir to follow them. "Where'd you hire the geneted goon?"

"Actually, I work for the Lord Leader," Aurigar said. A glance back told him that Cetuso was mercifully amused at being called a geneted goon—or, considering who had said it, perhaps obsequiously amused.

Waystonn was about the hundredth busiest port in the Galactic Empire—but since there were just over forty-one billion, one hundred nineteen million ports, that was hardly a small distinction. It occupied the entire surface of a conveniently far-out moon of a conveniently close-in gas giant around a conveniently small star, and the only other occupied orbit of the star, below the gas giant, held a stable Lagrange hex of superheavies. Thus for the port of Waystonn, near the galactic center and with several arm-to-arm trajectories running through it, the total escape velocity was low and the slingshot effect tremendous, so that getting out to jump distance was easy and cheap. Waystonn also had a dense inert-organics atmosphere with a high Reynolds number and a large scale height, and thus aerobraking to the surface was cheap.

Whatever all that meant. Cetuso had assigned him to know it, but had never asked him to repeat it.

Anyway, all that really mattered was that the lost Ululara had progressed from being a hayakawite miner's indentured fosterling to being one of the hundred most important procurers in the Galactic Empire in less than eight marqs.

The Empress-to-be beamed at him like a favorite uncle. "Well, so, you now have an employer, and therefore this must be about his business rather than yours. So . . . ?"

Telling the truth was beginning to come naturally. "Well," he said. "This is Lord Leader Cetuso Sir, keeper of the Imperial bloodline, and it seems I made a mistake when I talked to you."

Cetuso launched into the story. She listened intently through the whole thing and then burst into great, glad, uproarious laughter. "Wow, wow, wow, Aurigar. We have *both* really moved up in the world. So now instead of purported kidnappings of farmers' daughters, you've moved up to capturing successful businesswomen, and you're doing so well that you can afford a geneted actor to make your story plausible. Well, then, let's have a tissue sample from each of you," she said, "and since it will take four hours to run a high-end search, in memory of how much good you did me, Aurigar, and of how much you have both made me laugh, I shall send you up to private rooms where you will each have, so to speak, one on the house."

In Miriette's office, Aurigar sat quietly, occasionally dozing and exhausted, reverently converting the last two hours into perpetual happy memory. Cetuso entered, moving as ever like a dancer half his age and a third of his size, and slipped into the larger chair, appropriating the hassock. A serving robot glided in and set out two glasses for the men. Silently, they toasted and drank.

After a long and equally reverent silence from Cetuso, and a second glass served and begun, Aurigar ventured, "It probably reflects my lack of sophistication, but this was without question the best time I've ever had in a house."

"Whether or not you lack sophistication," the Lord Leader Sir responded, "your experience in no way reflects that, because this was also *my* favorite experience of all time, which is to say, given my resources, appetites, and time devoted to exploration, it might be the finest available anywhere, ever."

Miriette looked into the office. "Well," she said. "That was a very interesting investigation. I trust the accommodations were suitable, Aurigar?"

"Very."

"And Lord Leader Cetuso Sir," she said, dropping a very impressive curtsy. "Also satisfactory?"

"Beyond words," he said, rising to his feet and bowing very low. "Then I take it you have confirmed my identity."

"Oh, yes," she said. "And I am more impressed with Aurigar than ever. To make whatever con he is running plausible, he has actually corrupted a very highly placed public official. I know I want into this deal now, whatever it is, but of course you'll have to tell me what you are actually up to, and cut me in as a partner. Whatever is behind all this must be simply astonishing. I know you'll have to confer with whoever your hidden partners are, but as soon as you can tell me what's really going on, come right back, and we'll see what sort of deal we can do." Her eyes sparkled and she kissed Aurigar on both cheeks. "And Aurigar, even if your partners won't let you tell me, don't be a stranger anyway. You have no idea how much you impress me."

•

"Really, it's almost to be expected," Lord Leader Cetuso said. "*All* Imperials get extensive genetion. Heirs and near-heirs get even more, beginning right at the embryo stage. Even our late, mad Emperor was a polymathic genius; the madness was due to a botched assassination attempt by his mother, and some unfortunate abuse at the hands of his older brother of equally revered memory. So, naturally, Ululara, or Miriette, is beautiful, competent, cold-blooded, pragmatic, charismatic, all the things she needs to be. She was literally born to rule the galaxy. Climbing up from high-end prostitute to mistress of a hundred brothels in a few short years might have been a challenge for other people, but it was well within her capabilities." He told the robot, "Standard setup for Aurigar."

"I'm not hungry, Lord Leader Sir."

"Have something to eat anyway. It always reduces your worrying and mellows your mood, and that helps you to be the splendid companion you usually are. And it's your clear, calm thought I need now."

The robot brought the platter, and Aurigar munched, forlornly at first, but then resolutely, as if it might be taken away from him, and finally with that certain calm decision that generally preceded his best ideas. He looked up to see Cetuso smiling, and thought he detected a twinkle in one of the mirrors of his eye sockets.

"I do hate being predictable," Aurigar said.

"We all do, but it's part of what makes us useful." Cetuso smiled at him. Aurigar felt cold fear that the Lord Leader Sir might be genuinely fond of him. "Now, if you need to eat all of that and then nap," Cetuso said, "you have plenty of time; considering the distances and numbers involved, we probably have the better part of a marq to get the Empress onto the throne, and loyal client members of my family will make sure no one does anything rash. So rest, eat, and think of what we should do next."

A thought bothered Aurigar, but refused to come to the surface, so he spoke without it. "Just supposing we *do* find a way to persuade her that she is who she actually is, and assuming she wants the job, is there going to be a problem with any of a billion worlds or so realizing that they are being ruled from afar by—pardon the expression, but a former—"

Cetuso laughed. "Oh, there will be a predictable number of uprisings. So long as it's just a planet by itself, the Imperial forces will do the usual—the multiple decimation for which they are famous."

Aurigar shuddered. "I heard stories about that, growing up."

"Notice the durability of the effect. The last time your homeworld · rebelled, and had to be set straight, was more than eight thousand marqs ago. There is something about the 'ten tenths' concept that stays in the mind."

Aurigar remembered a vast stone desert stretching out before him, some time before his father left, because he remembered he was holding Magrat's collar and listening to his father explain: "It's simple, Aurie, they 'delete ten tenths,' as they call it. One-tenth of all those of noble blood. One-tenth of all commoners. One-tenth of all slaves. One of the ten largest cities. Ten of the hundred largest cities. One hundred of the thousand largest cities. One-tenth of all livestock. One-tenth of all growing crops. One-tenth of all the forests. All the soil down to rock from one-tenth of the habitable surface. You see, everyone knows the formula, and everyone knows not to rebel, or not to let rebels get control of the planet. And the Emperor is always merciful; overlaps count. By slicing off the piece in front of us, he met not just the soil requirement, but half a dozen of the others as well. Nearly all the cities needed to make up the quota were located there, for example."

Aurigar remembered how much he had hated his father, how sad he had always felt when looking at the decimated parts of worlds from spaceship windows, and how pathetic it seemed to him that he had never once had to coerce or trick a girl into the lost princess routine; every one of them had come willingly, because it was so much better than what she had.

He forced his attention back to the present, but couldn't help asking, "But why does the Emperor care?"

"Empress, as soon as we can make it clear to her that that's what she is."

"I meant in general, Lord Leader Sir," Aurigar said, skirting the edge of the great lord's dislike for lectures not delivered by himself, "but all right, why does the *Empress* care if she has a planet fewer, here and there, out of a billion? She could just seal them off for a while, just a loose blockade to raise prices, and then wait for trade pressure and apathy to bring them back into line."

To Aurigar's surprise, Cetuso sat back, rubbed his bare blue scalp thoughtfully, and said, "Why does anyone do anything, dear fellow? We have the technology to make every one of four quadrillion human beings as rich and comfortable as that person could reasonably consume, and to sustain that forever; between dwell, jump, and nano, there's no reason why anyone would ever need to leave home except for fun, and no reason why there needs to be a charge on anything. So why do you suppose we have people in dreadful and dangerous jobs such as mining, ranching, and prostitution? Why don't we just synthesize materials from lifeless planets, jump it to where the people are, grow perfect food in tanks for everyone, and indulge everyone's sensual whims eternally in dwellspace? We could do that, you know, for everyone, and still have plenty left over for the people who wanted to travel or go camping or whatever."

Aurigar stared at him. "I've never thought of that. I just thought there were a lot of shitty jobs someone had to do. Do you have an answer?"

"Of course, dear fellow. We aristocrats are born with all the answers, you know, it's just a matter of getting them loaded into our heads. And the answer is: there's only one real pleasure; everything else is just satisfactions of urges. And the one real pleasure is getting one's way over and against resistance. The only thing human beings really enjoy is making *other* people do what they don't want to. Simple as that. Why do you think there are waiters, shop clerks, and prostitutes? In this age—and for the past thirty kilomarqs at least—everything they actually do or provide could be done better and cheaper by nano or dwell, and everyone could have as much of that as they want. We *need* poor people, and other gender and biological and spiritual underclasses, so that there will be people who—ideally hating it, or submissively fawning over it—must do what rich people tell them, because otherwise there's no point to being *rich*. That's all. Simple, isn't it, dear fellow—now that you're about to be rich?"

*Ninety-four, Aurigar thought, counting the number of times Cetuso called him "dear fellow." He wasn't sure yet why he was counting; he had only started to count them in the last day or so, but now his mind always watched that little register, the "dear fellow" count. And why am I able to keep it so accurately? For that matter, he thought, I knew so much about Waystonn that I would never need to know, and Cetuso prefers my advice to all others, even though I'm just a tenth-rate con man and procurer. And now my father, who was barely there when I was a child, surfaces in a critical memory—*

Aurigar realized. There was no better word—it was the first and only realization of his life.

"Well," he said. "I know how to make this work." He was unsurprised to recall that Geepo owed him a large favor. "I know a man I can get, the best in the Empire in multimapping dwellfaces."

"Why would you know such a person and what would we want with him?"

"Geepo is profoundly useful in salvage operations. Every so often, genetion goes wrong, or a girl decides to balk or try to escape, or for some reason her buyer simply cannot sell her physically, so we put her into dwell, and interface her into a simulation that generates decisions and behavior for some *other* simulation that *is* salable. A girl may dwell the life of a beautiful princess madly in love with a gallant knight, and behave accordingly in dwell, while dozens or hundreds of men assume the role of the traveling salesman—she experiences them as the knight, they experience her as the bored housewife. Not as good as real, but salable in the cheap markets."

"And this Geepo is good at dwellfaces?"

"The very best in the human trades. The three times I've used him, he has been phenomenally expensive, and utterly worth it. He is difficult to work with, like every real artist, but certainly fond of money—"

"Like every real artist. I believe I see your point."

Miriette beamed. "Three of you this time." She smiled particularly at Geepo. "Do you prefer to explain the actual deal yourself, or are you one of those that always wants the lackeys to do the talking?"

"Er, actually," Geepo said, rubbing his upper lip in a way that made Aurigar think of rabbits, "I'm a lackey here myself."

"Oh," she said, fixing him with the "you are fascinating" stare. "We'll *have* to talk. Now, Aurigar, are you going to tell me what all this is about?"

"Well," he said, "I have convinced my principals that you could not be easily tricked into a dwelltank."

"From which I would never emerge?"

"Exactly."

She nodded. "Then let me tell you what I guessed. Your principals, who are probably the owners of a certain very large chain of brothels based in the 11/6 arm of the galaxy—"

"I have not named them," Aurigar said.

"Nor have I. At any rate, these principals of yours estimated that my managerial and business skills were considerably in excess of theirs, true?"

"Actually they believe that left to yourself you would have a galactic monopoly within nineteen marqs."

"I was planning for eleven," she said.

"There is little doubt you know better than they," Cetuso put in.

"There is *no* doubt, Lord Leader Sir. Now, if they could get me to run their enterprise, that monopoly could be theirs, and soon. So you would have taken me to your palace in Jinkhangy, Lord Leader Sir, where all preparation would be under way for my 'coronation.' I would have gone into dwell for an 'extensive briefing' or 'protocol training' or whatever, and never have awakened in reality—but in dwell I would have gone through the coronation, appointed my cabinet, begun the process of ruling the galaxy. Back in reality, I would have been running all the brothels in the galaxy, through a multimapping interface."

"You have discerned the entire thing," Cetuso said gravely. "I hope you are not offended. You must admit it was rather a good scheme."

"It was," she admitted. "And their commitment to it is demonstrated by the sheer enormity of the bribe they must have offered you to take part. Tell me, Aurigar, how many of your other lost princesses are now 'ruling the galaxy' while actually doing accounts receivables for a discount clothing chain?"

Aurigar shrugged, inwardly pleased that he had anticipated the question. "Being able to fake being a great lay is very common," he said. "First-rate administrative talent is much rarer, and most businesses are not large or complex enough to need it. You are rather in the nature of a unique case."

"Of course I am; I should have realized. All right, then, let me propose an alternative. Your principals will hire me to run their entire operation for them, via dwell. For one-fifth of every day, time to be set by me, I will unhook, run my own operation, and do just as I please. My operation will not be absorbed into theirs. I expect generous compensation and a sizable piece of the overall operation. I will take a long list of precautions to make sure that I return from my first dwell, and I will be fully empowered while in dwellspace, so that I can arrange matters such that you will never dare to think of trying to hold me in dwellspace. Does that sound fair?"

"I was carefully instructed," Aurigar said, "not to argue about any issues regarding safeguards, or the definitions of words such as 'generous' or 'sizable.' Our principals are aware of the great need to rebuild the trust that they admittedly squandered. I think you may consider that we have a deal."

"Aurigar, my only remaining question is, why an honest pimp, con man, fraud, and kidnapper like yourself would get involved in something as nasty as large-scale corporate activity?"

"The money was good."

"Oh, but if *that's* your excuse, what will be next? Politics? Well, suit yourself, but I hate to see your talent squandered so squalidly."

"Can you see what she has been doing in there?" Cetuso asked, for the fifth time.

Geepo shrugged, pulled his visor down, and spread his sensegloved fingers into the plextank before him. His fingers danced and wriggled over myriad pseudosurfaces. "Lord Leader Cetuso Sir, she has been through all the business records, penetrated all the locked files, and outcopied everything. She has also set up a remarkably complex and probably unanalyzable system of bombs, traps, alarms, triggers, and poisons so no one can ever hold her in dwellspace against her will."

"Of course," Cetuso said, "you are keeping track of those and can enable us to keep her inside—"

"That is *not* what was agreed to! It would be *extremely* unethical. Even the beginnings of an attempt would make detection certain by a person of ordinary skill, and the princess is building the cleverest protection I've ever seen. We are dealing with no mean or small mind here, Lord Leader Cetuso Sir, and I should be terrified to try to step in contrary to her wishes."

Cetuso's tone was dark and the silver flashes in his eye sockets were ominous. "So there is no way to control her—all we can do is try to stay on her good side?"

Remembering that the lord was three times Geepo's weight in superfast, superstrong muscle—and could not be prosecuted for killing a commoner—Geepo could barely nod.

Cetuso sighed. "Well, Aurigar, from what you know of madams, would *you* want one running the galaxy?"

"Well, yes and no, Lord Leader Sir. No, in that most of them are cruel and petty. Yes, in that they tend to be decisive, knowledgeable about human nature, and focused on the main chance."

"And from what I know of princesses, they have generally been pressured into some semblance of grace and largeness of spirit, but they are obsessed with improving people, prone to vacillating, and disdainful of the most practical and effective way of doing anything. Probably we are about to acquire an Empress with the personal ethics of a pimp and the broad vision of a spoiled aristocrat, about like any other political leadership of the last few kilomarqs. Hard on ordinary people I suppose, but what isn't? And we have no reason to care about them. Time to pursue preferment, eh, dear fellow?"

*Four hundred thirty-two, and now it will turn out I already have preferment.*

"Already taken care of," Geepo said. "I cast each of us, in the princess's dwellspace, as particularly proficient branch managers, with dwellspace abilities mapped to our real talents on the outside. Your diplomatic ability, Lord Leader Cetuso Sir, for example, maps to a gift for motivating exotic women and attracting discerning customers—"

"You mean I've been cast as a particularly classy pimp for jaded, kinky aristocrats?"

"Exactly, Lord Leader Sir. I would say you are certain to gain a post in the Inner Cabinet. Of course, interacting with you through her interface and yours, she will think you are that pimp, but when she communicates with you, her avatar on the screen will call you by your right name and cabinet rank. After a while, you will barely notice that anything is different."

"This mapping, between pimp and cabinet post—was it easy?"

"Exceedingly so, Lord Leader Sir."

"I guessed as much." The mirrors in his dark eye sockets flashed brightly a few times, and his blue face was still, except for the hint of a satisfied smile.

Aurigar looked around from his command station. There were at least a thousand screenminders within sight, most of them directly over his head, and if it were not for the semicircle of plextanks in which he stood, each showing an aspect of the situation surrounding the six worlds remaining in rebellion, he might have been in any large orbiting office complex around any inhabited planet.

But he was the commander of the Galactic Expeditionary Force, and he could confirm it by looking at the plextank showing six suns, all that remained of the Cleanlist Rebellion against the Empress; she had refused their surrender for the sake of example. At his touch, the plextank display rearranged to show up-close images of each system, no longer to scale, but with all six stars and seventeen inhabited worlds visible as spheres, the systems arranged in a hex around a central data console.

*It's not even new, now, but it's still strange,* he thought, and idly plucked at the sleeve of the silly getup he had to wear in public.

At his side, Cetuso said, "You've really done well for yourself, dear fellow."

"I suppose so, Lor—er, Cetuso." *Seventeen thousand four hundred twenty-seven.*

The blue man smiled. "Still not used to your peerage?"

"I doubt I ever will be. To judge by the—"

The image in the central tank vanished; Ululara, in full Imperial regalia, appeared. "Supremor Aurigar, are we ready?"

He felt in the plextank once more, for form's sake. "We are."

"Then proceed at once. We have a victory celebration to start."

Aurigar shrugged and spoke the order. More than a thousand screenminders watched for errors or to countermand as thousands of robots, each prepositioned on a sizable asteroid, sprayed the surface with trillions of nanobots. In a matter of a few hundred nanomarqs, well before any remote sensor could hope to detect them, the nanobots had spread their conducting filament-nets of conductors; an instant later, an antimatter fizzle bomb popped up from the main robot and burst, feeding energy into the nanobots' vast antennae, supplying the energy for the transformation.

"Only four not responding, sir," Cetuso said; for this operation he was the Assistant Supremor.

*I like "sir" better than "dear fellow."* Aurigar nodded. "We expected fifteen to twenty intercepts. This is good." Modern warfare, Aurigar reflected, was now all espionage, remote sensing, and cryptography; with nanobots, quantum computation, and jump tech, you would be hit by every weapon that you didn't detect before it was fired. The four lost weapons had been found and mined by the enemy, killed perhaps three nanomarqs after activation, before they could even deploy their nanobots. Right now, light was spreading out from the antimatter fizzles that powered the conversion, and as the light reached them, a hundred thousand sensors in each of the uninhabited systems would be relaying it through jump transmitters to the enemy. They would know the attack was under way within seventeen micromarqs—but the enemy would not exist within one micromarq.

Still, the enemy backlash must have started by now, their jumpweapons forming and leaping to revenge. Aurigar wondered whether the Imperial forces would take any hits at all; the last time, they had not, but intel estimated a 10 percent chance that the enemy had determined the location of Jinkhangy. To the Empress's image in the plextank before him, he said, "Word on the enemy counterattack?"

Geepo said, "Consider yourself congratulated, sir. Crypto, intel, and search found twenty-six enemy weapon seeds and mined them; they detonated simultaneously with our attack."

"Detonate" was not quite the right word; Aurigar's silent mines had opened wormholes into the cores of blue-white giant stars, and the enemy weapons-to-be had vanished as planet-sized masses of stellar core had burst into existence within the asteroids on which they sat.

"Any jumpspace interceptions?"

"The usual. We sprayed the jumpspace approaches to Jinkhangy with interceptors. Thirteen hits, most of which were probably smugglers or ships that didn't stick to the flight plan, which will certainly teach them a lesson. Our best estimate is that not more than three of them were enemy weapons. All in all, not just a successful operation but a cheap one, and—"

"Silence, please, from everyone," Aurigar said.

They all fell quiet; his peculiar passion for dead silence at the moment of truth was legendary, and the legend was known to be accurate—as were the legends about what happened when he did not get that dread, respectful silence.

Ululara's image ghosted over the hex arrangement of the six Cleanlist systems, arranged to show stars and inhabited planets as spheres and the major stations as points. The countdown in the center of the plextank reached zero.

Thirty-some stations flashed and were gone; an asteroid-mass of vacuum-energy receivers had popped out of jumpspace inside each one, converting instantaneously to relativistic nucleons. *About forty million people,* Aurigar thought, *gone in less time than it takes a signal to cross a synapse.*

The view, with Ululara still ghosted over it, switched to just-activated sleeper satellites over the seventeen planets. Aurigar had just time to think of all the continents and oceans, cities, mountains, deserts, glaciers, temples to a thousand gods, dew-scented mornings, and glorious stormy sunsets in progress, kisses never to be finished, and hands reaching for each other that would never touch, eighty billion people, and a trillion works of art.

The jumpweapons entering the cores of the seventeen worlds opened wormholes to the great black hole at the galaxy's core. Within the space of one breath, planetary surfaces sagged and fell like a deflating balloon. Each place where a planet had been flashed white-hot as the energy just outside the event horizon escaped from the ripping apart and the brutal collisions of the last bits of matter. Then the spy satellites, too, plunged into the black hole.

The view switched briefly to more distant cameras; the black holes swelling from each wormhole were dark spheres, bending starlight weirdly around themselves, swelling for just a moment until the wormholes destabilized and the black ball of the event horizon contracted back to starry void.

There was no point in sending the stars into nova, except as examples. That was all the point the Empress required. The six stars flared brilliantly; over the next few days they would briefly reach far out beyond their former habitable zones, and then gradually recede. Nothing would ever live in those systems again. In a few dekamarqs, the inhabitants of neighboring systems would throw carefully orchestrated festivals to celebrate the brief flarings in their night sky—and be reminded that though she was called "the merciful and mighty," she remained Her Supreme Might.

Aurigar sighed. He wondered how many of the eighty billion had been standing close to someone they loved, so that as that awful fall began, they had been able to clutch a hand or hug close to each other.

*Total forever: 17,427. Good enough.* Aurigar drew a breath and waited.

Geepo screamed.

Cetuso made a strangled sound.

Aurigar smiled. "That would be Jinkhangy," he said. "Just a start; the provincial capital worlds are going even as we speak, and the galaxy is now swarming with self-replicating robots seeking out and blasting every instrument of Imperial authority into nucleons."

Geepo's and Cetuso's slack expressions were amusing, but Aurigar took no time to relish them. "Oh, the Cleanlists had to go, of course—evil as the Imperium, and ten times madder. Now, for my next act of public service, I eliminate the Imperium. The homeworlds of the high aristocracy are vanishing at this moment, and billions of ships hurrying around on Imperial business are turning to plasma in real space, or unresolvability in jumpspace. The people of each individual planet will work out their own destinies. All the stars are free."

The whole speech rang curiously flat, considering that Aurigar had been mentally rehearsing it since the "dear fellow" count was less than one thousand. *Well, no doubt it is neither the first nor the last line well-composed in advance to be spoiled when it is delivered.*

Cetuso moaned, his jaw hanging open, and the mirrors and lenses in his eye sockets turned slowly and out of coordination; probably he had not yet understood. Aurigar considered taunting him—*your favorite lackey, my dear fellow! was not what you thought. You and your adored Empress and the whole aristocracy and system of domination perish now! and I shall piss upon your steaming remains.* But whereas the thought was swift as light itself, the words would have been far too slow, so before Cetuso's moan of uncomprehending despair acquired even a hint of comprehension, Aurigar slashed the cutting laser vertically from the blue man's head to his feet, so that he fell into two pieces with steam pouring from his flash-cooked guts in the middle.

Aurigar stepped forward, looked down into the red gap between the blue half-faces, and smelled the roasted reek of the man's entrails. The mirrors and lenses now flashed and turned with the last of their momentum. He holstered his weapon, opened his trousers, and urinated, filling the eye sockets. "For every time you fed me, for every time you said I amused you, and for seventeen thousand four hundred twenty-seven times you called me 'dear fellow.'"

Geepo was sobbing.

Ululara said, "He was my kinsman and you are far too flippant with his body."

*I sent four weapons after her physical location on Waystonn! The plextank displayed nothing.*

Aurigar whirled. She stood behind him, rather disarming in pink pajamas, but quite well-armed with a cutting laser pointed at his face. He was acutely aware that he had holstered his own, and then modesty made him reach for his open fly.

"No," she said. "Keep your hands away from your body." She smiled, then, the genuine warm smile she'd had as Miriette, so long ago. "Poor Aurigar, we both had secrets we couldn't tell. I actually knew that I really *was* the Empress after my fourth trip into the multimapped dwellspace you had Geepo build for me. A kidnapper and pimp like you, Aurigar, might not choose to pay attention to politics, but a businessperson with interstellar interests like me has no choice. Once I had confirmed that whatever I did as madam and CEO in my dwellspace had an exact analogy in the actions of the new-crowned Empress, I knew the truth, and shortly I found my way out of the world Geepo built and into the real one. I have been ruling the galaxy directly ever since, just leaving a shell up to fool you, Cetuso, and Geepo."

Geepo moaned, "I am stupid."

"No," Empress Ululara said, "I am competent."

"You cannot stop the robots and replicators already at work," Aurigar said. "You remain alive, and you may kill me, but you can no longer rule your empire; you are an Empress only in name."

"That is exactly right," she said.

And now Aurigar was certain, as he had been for so many marqs, since well before they put her on the throne, and he smiled broadly. "I am tired of this game," he said, "and curious about what I have forgotten and will wake to. You may press that trigger at any time."

"Of course I may," she said. "An Empress does what she likes, always." And she pushed the button down.

For Aurigar, the world ceased. If he had existed to feel it, he would have been startled beyond all words to find that he did not wake into any other existence.

Miriette lifted the dwellcap from her head and shook her damp hair. The clock showed she had been in the simulation for just under two micromarqs. She had a few more micromarqs till old Phodway would come home; the kitchen and the kids were already clean and dinner-ready.

The image of Lord Leader Cetuso Sir appeared at the corner of her screen. "Any luck?"

"Another one who got a bad case of conscience and went radical—very cleverly, too. I've sent you the file. Quite ingenious and well worth study. He assassinated you, by the way, and it seemed rather personal. Generally a bad boy all around. How many more lost princess men do we have left to try?"

"More than a hundred to go, and this was only the twelfth one we've examined, Princess. We'll find you the right one to get you out of the Krevpiceaux country, don't worry. Never fear. At one or two per your day, it won't even take very long."

She felt like pouting, but she did not feel like it nearly enough to do so and spoil her dignity. "I'm getting *very* tired of caring for all Phodway's fostindents, and having to keep him sober, and all that. I really want to start working my way out of hiding."

"Oh, you'll have to hide somewhere till your brother dies, in any case. I've told you that. And we're working on that too, of course. Just remember that until your memplant woke up and told you to contact me, you had no idea you even *were* in hiding, or that you were anything other than a purchased orphan. Let alone who you actually are." The mirrors in his eye sockets flashed and twinkled. "We *will* find a lost princess man who will stay loyal. And then we *will* get you out of the Krevpiceaux, but not out of hiding. I barely got you out of your mother's palace ahead of the explosion, and your brother's disposition, you may trust me, has not improved in the intervening twenty-nine marqs. *Patience*, Your Supreme Might-to-Be, *patience*."

"I know. I know. It's just I'm facing feeding four kids, sobering up a drunk, cleaning the shack as far as it can be cleaned, and sharing a bed with two of the other fostindents. But I can manage patience. I did have one question to raise—this was the third lost princess man in a row to figure out that he was in a simulation. Like the other ones, he thought it was his and he was the center of it."

"Naturally. What man doesn't think he's the center of the universe?" Cetuso's image on the screen paused for not more than a hundred nano-marqs, then shrugged, the immense blue muscles of his shoulders rising and falling like waves on the sea. "I've scanned his moments of recog-nition, and I don't think we can change policy; our lost princess man will have to be smart enough to do what we need, simulations cannot be perfect, and many of them will see through it. At least none of them so far has figured out where or how we read and recorded him, or why we're doing it, so there's no danger that one of them will leave behind any warning for the others, and as long as they don't, it doesn't complicate the task, really." He smiled warmly. "And everything really is on course, Princess. Regrettable as it is, just put in another—"

"Miriette!" Henredd was calling from the kitchen. "Miriette, the water is boiling!"

"Drop the noodles in and I'll be there in a moment," she said. Cetu-so's image looked disgustingly pitying, so she stuck her tongue out at him before she blanked the screen.

Through the kitchen viewwall, she watched the Krevpiceauxi mistral wail and shriek its way up into a full-blown black-dust storm, the kind that was equally likely to strand them inside for days or blow over before bedtime. Phodway would appreciate a hot meal and a clean bed after mak-ing his way home through *that*, anyway. At least he was not unkind and he thanked her often.

Henredd stood beside her, his bony shoulder pressing against her lower ribs, arm around her unself-consciously, and said, "I like being here when you cook." They'd gotten Henredd from an illegal dealer, and the first year they'd had him, he'd barely spoken, mostly just cried; a little kind attention and some efficient care had brought him around, and Miri-ette had to admit she'd learned how to do that from Phodway's treatment of her when she was young, back before he'd fallen into the bottle. She turned the fish cakes over and rubbed Henredd's head; he snuggled more closely against her.

*Once I'm on the throne, I will have Cetuso take care of these people, very, very generously. An empress does not have much need for love, but it is good to know about it, and an empress must show gratitude.*

The boy under her arm squirmed and ran off to play; she contemplated her skill in the kitchen with proud dismay. *Patience, patience, patience.*

Cetuso could feel nothing from his extended hand; to get the maximum bandwidth for accessing Aurigar's mind and memories, he'd had to turn every available nerve to the purpose. The lost princess man's facial expression showed that the filaments rushing through Aurigar's body to his heart and brain were painful and distressing; it could and would all be erased at need, if the man lived. The plate of mussels and noodles lay inverted and broken on the floor. Aurigar's boot touched it and slipped slightly, and Cetuso made that foot move to a secure spot on the dry floor behind.

Cetuso had no fear of being disturbed, knowing as he did that everyone in the place feared to disturb him, or even to look at him to see what he was doing. He relayed the copy of Aurigar to the princess's computer, waited through the micromarqs while she played Aurigar out in simulation, and talked her through the usual disappointment. He might have pointed out that they needed a man of extraordinary abilities to accomplish what was needed, and also one who would not resent how he was used, one who would understand the Imperium as well as the Empress herself and yet feel only deep loyalty. There would be such a man, he was confident, but this was not he.

A few micromarqs later, when he knew she was feeling better, and she had been called off to cook supper for the miner's brats, he turned his attention back to Aurigar. A few people had gotten up and left quietly, not wanting to be witnesses; the rest looked at their drinks, their plates, or the wall.

Cetuso proceeded systematically. First he erased the simulation data from Aurigar's brain, then the memory of their conversation, then all the memories, and finally the instincts, the sensory processing, and the autonomic processes, before his filaments slashed Aurigar's brains into wet chopped meat beyond any possibility of neurodissection or nanoreconstruction.

Cetuso's filaments withdrew, merging into thin tentacles between the corpse's ribs, then broad thick strands outside the chest. As the tips popped free, they reshaped into fingers splayed on the man's chest. Cetuso pushed lightly.

Aurigar's corpse crashed to the floor. No one looked up, but a number of people winced; Cetuso recorded their reaction and relayed it to the political police. Probably they just had weak stomachs (you never could tell what would bother even the most normal, practical, hardened heart), but better safe than sorry.

He flashed the main mirror in his left eye to draw the bartender's gaze. Cetuso pointed to the accounting screen behind the bar, using his mind-link to add a few month's revenues to the bar's receipts. The bartender looked down, saw the numbers, looked up, and was mindful enough not to do anything but look away. Cetuso smiled; silence, like all good things, was at its best and costliest when absolutely pure, and it never paid to skimp on it.

He would have nodded nicely enough at anyone who looked up as he left, but as usual, no one did. Out on the street, where everyone could see him and what he was, he walked as if invisible.

Aliette de Bodard lives and works in Paris, where she has a day job as a System Engineer. She studied Computer Science and Applied Mathematics, but moonlights as a writer of speculative fiction. She is the author of the critically acclaimed Obsidian and Blood trilogy of Aztec noir fantasies, as well as numerous short stories, which garnered her two Nebula Awards, a Locus Award and a British Science Fiction Association Award. Works include *The House of Shattered Wings* (Roc/Gollancz, 2015 British Science Fiction Association Award), a novel set in a turn-of-the-century Paris devastated by a magical war, and its upcoming sequel *The House of Binding Thorns* (April 2017, Roc/Gollancz). She also published *The Citadel of Weeping Pearls* (*Asimov's* Oct/Nov 2015), a novella set in the same universe as her Vietnamese space opera *On a Red Station Drifting*. She lives in Paris with her family, in a flat with more computers than warm bodies, and a set of Lovecraftian tentacled plants intent on taking over the place.

# THE WAITING STARS

## *Aliette de Bodard*

The derelict ship ward was in an isolated section of Outsider space, one of the numerous spots left blank on interstellar maps, no more or no less tantalizing than its neighbouring quadrants. To most people, it would be just that: a boring part of a long journey to be avoided—skipped over by Mind-ships as they cut through deep space, passed around at low speeds by Outsider ships while their passengers slept in their hibernation cradles.

Only if anyone got closer would they see the hulking masses of ships: the glint of starlight on metal, the sharp, pristine beauty of their hulls, even though they all lay quiescent and crippled, forever unable to move—living corpses kept as a reminder of how far they had fallen; the Outsiders' brash statement of their military might, a reminder that their weapons held the means to fell any Mind-ships they chose to hound.

On the sensors of *The Cinnabar Mansions*, the ships all appeared small and diminished, like toy models or avatars—things Lan Nhen could have held in the palm of her hand and just as easily crushed. As the sensors' line of sight moved—catching ship after ship in their field of view, wreck after wreck, indistinct masses of burnt and twisted metal, of ripped-out engines, of shattered life pods and crushed shuttles—Lan Nhen felt as if an icy fist were squeezing her heart into shards. To think of the Minds within—dead or crippled, forever unable to move . . .

"She's not there," she said, as more and more ships appeared on the screen in front of her, a mass of corpses that all threatened to overwhelm her with sorrow and grief and anger.

"Be patient, child," *The Cinnabar Mansions* said. The Mind's voice was amused, as it always was—after all, she'd lived for five centuries, and would outlive Lan Nhen and Lan Nhen's own children by so many years that the pronoun "child" seemed small and inappropriate to express the vast gulf of generations between them. "We already knew it was going to take time."

"She was supposed to be on the outskirts of the wards," Lan Nhen said, biting her lip. She had to be, or the rescue mission was going to be infinitely more complicated. "According to Cuc . . . "

"Your cousin knows what she's talking about," *The Cinnabar Mansions* said.

"I guess." Lan Nhen wished Cuc was there with them, and not sleeping in her cabin as peacefully as a baby—but *The Cinnabar Mansions* had pointed out Cuc needed to be rested for what lay ahead; and Lan Nhen had given in, vastly outranked. Still, Cuc was reliable, for narrow definitions of the term—as long as anything didn't involve social skills, or deft negotiation. For technical information, though, she didn't have an equal within the family; and her network of contacts extended deep within Outsider space. That was how they'd found out about the ward in the first place . . .

"There." The sensors beeped, and the view on the screen pulled into enhanced mode on a ship on the edge of the yard which seemed even smaller than the hulking masses of her companions. *The Turtle's Citadel* had been from the newer generation of ships, its body more compact and more agile than its predecessors': designed for flight and maneuvers rather than for transport, more elegant and refined than anything to come out of the Imperial Workshops—unlike the other ships, its prow and hull were decorated, painted with numerous designs from old legends and myths, all the way to the Dai Viet of Old Earth. A single gunshot marred the outside of its hull—a burn mark that had transfixed the painted citadel through one of its towers, going all the way into the heartroom and crippling the Mind that animated the ship.

"That's her," Lan Nhen said. "I would know her anywhere."

*The Cinnabar Mansions* had the grace not to say anything, though of course she could have matched the design to her vast databases in an eyeblink. "It's time, then. Shall I extrude a pod?"

Lan Nhen found that her hands had gone slippery with sweat all of a sudden; and her heart was beating a frantic rhythm within her chest, like temple gongs gone mad. "I guess it's time, yes." By any standards, what they were planning was madness. To infiltrate Outsider space, no matter how isolated—to repair a ship, no matter how lightly damaged . . .

Lan Nhen watched *The Turtle's Citadel* for a while—watched the curve of the hull, the graceful tilt of the engines, away from the living quarters; the burn mark through the hull like a gunshot through a human chest. On the prow was a smaller painting, all but invisible unless one had good eyes: a single sprig of apricot flowers, signifying the New Year's good luck—calligraphied on the ship more than thirty years ago by Lan Nhen's own mother, a parting gift to her great-aunt before the ship left for her last, doomed mission.

Of course, Lan Nhen already knew every detail of that shape by heart, every single bend of the corridors within, every little nook and cranny available outside—from the blueprints, and even before that, before the rescue plan had even been the seed of a thought in her mind—when she'd stood before her ancestral altar, watching the rotating holo of a ship who was also her great-aunt, and wondering how a Mind could ever be brought down, or given up for lost.

Now she was older; old enough to have seen enough things to freeze her blood; old enough to plot her own foolishness, and drag her cousin and her great-great-aunt into it.

Older, certainly. Wiser, perhaps; if they were blessed enough to survive.

There were tales, at the Institution, of what they were—and, in any case, one only had to look at them, at their squatter, darker shapes, at the way their eyes crinkled when they laughed. There were other clues, too: the memories that made Catherine wake up breathless and disoriented, staring at the white walls of the dormitory until the pulsing, writhing images of something she couldn't quite identify had gone, and the breath of dozens of her dorm-mates had lulled her back to sleep. The craving for odd food like fish sauce and fermented meat. The dim, distant feeling of not fitting in, of being compressed on all sides by a society that made little sense to her.

It should have, though. She'd been taken as a child, like all her schoolmates—saved from the squalor and danger among the savages and brought forward into the light of civilization—of white sterile rooms and bland food, of awkward embraces that always felt too informal. Rescued, Matron always said, her entire face transfigured, the bones of her cheeks made sharply visible through the pallor of her skin. Made safe.

Catherine had asked what she was safe from. They all did, in the beginning—all the girls in the Institution, Johanna and Catherine being the most vehement amongst them.

That was until Matron showed them the vid.

They all sat at their tables, watching the screen in the center of the amphitheatre—silent, for once, not jostling or joking among themselves. Even Johanna, who was always first with a biting remark, had said nothing—had sat, transfixed, watching it.

The first picture was a woman who looked like them—smaller and darker-skinned than the Galactics—except that her belly protruded in front of her, huge and swollen like a tumor from some disaster movie. There was a man next to her, his unfocused eyes suggesting that he was checking something on the network through his implants—until the woman grimaced, putting a hand to her belly and calling out to him. His eyes focused in a heartbeat, and fear replaced the blank expression on his face.

There was a split second before the language overlays kicked in—a moment, frozen in time, when the words, the sounds of the syllables put together, sounded achingly familiar to Catherine, like a memory of the childhood she never could quite manage to piece together—there was a brief flash, of New Year's Eve firecrackers going off in a confined space, of her fear that they would burn her, damage her body's ability to heal . . . And then the moment was gone like a popped bubble, because the vid changed in the most horrific manner.

The camera was wobbling, rushing along a pulsing corridor—they could all hear the heavy breath of the woman, the whimpering sounds she made like an animal in pain; the soft, encouraging patter of the physician's words to her.

"She's coming," the woman whispered, over and over, and the physician nodded—keeping one hand on her shoulder, squeezing it so hard his own knuckles had turned the color of a muddy moon.

"You have to be strong," he said. "Hanh, please. Be strong for me. It's all for the good of the Empire, may it live ten thousand years. Be strong."

The vid cut away, then—and it was wobbling more and more crazily, its field of view showing erratic bits of a cramped room with scrolling letters on the wall, the host of other attendants with similar expressions of fear on their faces; the woman, lying on a flat surface, crying out in pain—blood splattering out of her with every thrust of her hips—the camera moving, shifting between her legs, the physician's hands reaching into the darker opening—easing out a sleek, glinting shape, even as the woman screamed again—and blood, more blood running out, rivers of blood she couldn't possibly have in her body, even as the *thing* within her pulled free, and it became all too clear that, though it had the bare shape of a baby with an oversized head, it had too many cables and sharp angles to be human . . .

Then a quiet fade-to-black, and the same woman being cleaned up by the physician—the thing—the baby being nowhere to be seen. She stared up at the camera; but her gaze was unfocused, and drool was pearling at the corner of her lips, even as her hands spasmed uncontrollably.

Fade to black again; and the lights came up again, on a room that seemed to have grown infinitely colder.

"This," Matron said in the growing silence, "is how the Dai Viet birth Minds for their spaceships: by incubating them within the wombs of their women. This is the fate that would have been reserved for all of you. For each of you within this room." Her gaze raked them all, stopping longer than usual on Catherine and Johanna, the known troublemakers in the class. "This is why we had to take you away, so that you wouldn't become broodmares for abominations."

"We," of course, meant the Board—the religious nuts, as Johanna liked to call them, a redemptionist church with a fortune to throw around, financing the children's rescues and their education—and who thought every life from humans to insects was sacred (they'd all wondered, of course, where they fitted into the scheme).

After the class had dispersed like a flock of sparrows, Johanna held court in the yard, her eyes bright and feverish. "They faked it. They had to. They came up with some stupid explanation on how to keep us cooped here. I mean, why would anyone still use natural births and not artificial wombs?"

Catherine, still seeing the splatters of blood on the floor, shivered. "Matron said that they wouldn't. That they thought the birth created a special bond between the Mind and its mother—but that they had to be there, to be awake during the birth."

"Rubbish." Johanna shook her head. "As if that's even remotely plausible. I'm telling you, it has to be fake."

"It looked real." Catherine remembered the woman's screams; the wet sound as the Mind wriggled free from her womb; the fear in the face of all the physicians. "Artificial vids aren't this . . . messy." They'd seen the artificial vids: slick, smooth things where the actors were tall and muscular, the actresses pretty and graceful, with only a thin veneer of artificially generated defects to make the entire thing believable. They'd learnt to tell them apart from the rest; because it was a survival skill in the Institution, to sort out the lies from the truth.

"I bet they can fake that, too," Johanna said. "They can fake everything if they feel like it." But her face belied her words; even she had been shocked. Even she didn't believe they would have gone that far.

"I don't think it's a lie," Catherine said, finally. "Not this time."

And she didn't need to look at the other girls' faces to know that they believed the same thing as her—even Johanna, for all her belligerence— and to feel in her gut that this changed everything.

Cuc came online when the shuttle pod launched from *The Cinnabar Mansions*—in the heart-wrenching moment when the gravity of the ship fell away from Lan Nhen, and the cozy darkness of the pod's cradle was replaced with the distant forms of the derelict ships. "Hey, cousin. Missed me?" Cuc asked.

"As much as I missed a raging fire." Lan Nhen checked her equipment a last time—the pod was basic and functional, with barely enough space for her to squeeze into the cockpit, and she'd had to stash her various cables and terminals into the nooks and crannies of a structure that hadn't been meant for more than emergency evacuation. She could have asked *The Cinnabar Mansions* for a regular transport shuttle, but the pod was smaller and more controllable; and it stood more chances of evading the derelict ward's defenses.

"Hahaha," Cuc said, though she didn't sound amused. "The family found out what we were doing, by the way."

"And?" It would have devastated Lan Nhen, a few years ago; now she didn't much care. She *knew* she was doing the right thing. No filial daughter would let a member of the family rust away in a foreign cemetery—if she couldn't rescue her great-aunt, she'd at least bring the body back for a proper funeral.

"They think we're following one of Great-great-aunt's crazy plans."

"Ha," Lan Nhen snorted. Her hands were dancing on the controls, plotting a trajectory that would get her to *The Turtle's Citadel* while leaving her the maximum thrust reserve in case of unexpected maneuvers.

"I'm not the one coming up with crazy plans," *The Cinnabar Mansions* pointed out on the comms channel, distractedly. "I leave that to the young. Hang on—" she dropped out of sight. "I have incoming drones, child."

Of course. It was unlikely the Outsiders would leave their precious war trophies unprotected. "Where?"

A translucent overlay gradually fell over her field of vision through the pod's windshield; and points lit up all over its surface—a host of fast-moving, small crafts with contextual arrows showing basic kinematics information as well as projected trajectory cones. Lan Nhen repressed a curse. "That many? They really like their wrecked spaceships, don't they."

It wasn't a question, and neither Cuc nor *The Cinnabar Mansions* bothered to answer. "They're defense drones patrolling the perimeter. We'll walk you through," Cuc said. "Give me just a few moments to link up with Great-great-aunt's systems . . . "

Lan Nhen could imagine her cousin, lying half-prone on her bed in the lower decks of *The Cinnabar Mansions*, her face furrowed in that half-puzzled, half-focused expression that was typical of her thought processes—she'd remain that way for entire minutes, or as long as it took to find a solution. On her windshield, the squad of drones was spreading—coming straight at her from all directions, a dazzling ballet of movement meant to overwhelm her. And they would, if she didn't move fast enough.

Her fingers hovered over the pod's controls before she made her decision and launched into a barrel maneuver away from the nearest incoming cluster. "Cousin, how about hurrying up?"

There was no answer from Cuc. Demons take her, this wasn't the moment to overthink the problem! Lan Nhen banked sharply, narrowly avoiding a squad of drones, who bypassed her—and then turned around, much quicker than she'd anticipated. Ancestors, they moved fast, much too fast for ion-thrust motors. Cuc was going to have to rethink her trajectory. "Cousin, did you see this?"

"I saw." Cuc's voice was distant. "Already taken into account. Given the size of the craft, it was likely they were going to use helicoidal thrusters on those."

"This is all fascinating—" Lan Nhen wove her way through two more waves of drones, cursing wildly as shots made the pod rock around her—as long as her speed held, she'd be fine . . . She'd be fine . . . "—but you'll have noticed I don't really much care about technology, especially not now!"

A thin thread of red appeared on her screen—a trajectory that wove and banked like a frightened fish's trail—all the way to *The Turtle's Citadel* and its clusters of pod-cradles. It looked as though it was headed straight into the heart of the cloud of drones, though that wasn't the most worrying aspect of it. "Cousin," Lan Nhen said. "I can't possibly do this—" The margin of error was null—if she slipped in one of the curves, she'd never regain the kinematics necessary to take the next.

"Only way." Cuc's voice was emotionless. "I'll update as we go, if Great-great-aunt sees an opening. But for the moment . . . "

Lan Nhen closed her eyes, for a brief moment—turned them towards Heaven, though Heaven was all around her—and whispered a prayer to her ancestors, begging them to watch over her. Then she turned her gaze to the screen, and launched into flight—her hands flying and shifting over the controls, automatically adjusting the pod's path—dancing into the heart of the drones' swarm—into them, away from them, weaving an erratic path across the section of space that separated her from *The Turtle's Citadel*. Her eyes, all the while, remained on the overlay—her fingers speeding across the controls, matching the slightest deviation of her course to the set trajectory—inflecting curves a fraction of a second before the error on her course became perceptible.

"Almost there," Cuc said—with a hint of encouragement in her voice. "Come on, cousin, you can do it—"

Ahead of her, a few measures away, was *The Turtle's Citadel*: its pod cradles had shrivelled from long atrophy, but the hangar for docking the external shuttles and pods remained, its entrance a thin line of grey across the metallic surface of the ship's lower half.

"It's closed," Lan Nhen said, breathing hard—she was coming fast, much too fast, scattering drones out of her way like scared mice, and if the hangar wasn't opened . . . "Cousin!"

Cuc's voice seemed to come from very far away; distant and muted somehow on the comms system. "We've discussed this. Normally, the ship went into emergency standby when it was hit, and it should open—"

"But what if it doesn't?" Lan Nhen asked—the ship was looming over her, spreading to cover her entire windshield, close enough so she could count the pod cradles, could see their pockmarked surfaces—could imagine how much of a messy impact she'd make, if her own pod crashed on an unyielding surface.

Cuc didn't answer. She didn't need to; they both knew what would happen if that turned out to be true. *Ancestors, watch over me*, Lan Nhen thought, over and over, as the hangar doors rushed towards her, still closed—*ancestors watch over me . . .*

She was close enough to see the fine layers of engravings on the doors when they opened—the expanse of metal flowing away from the center, to reveal a gaping hole just large enough to let a small craft through. Her own pod squeezed into the available space: darkness fell over her cockpit as the doors flowed shut, and the pod skidded to a halt, jerking her body like a disarticulated doll.

It was awhile before she could stop shaking for long enough to unstrap herself from the pod; and to take her first, tentative steps on the ship.

The small lamp in her suit lit nothing but a vast, roiling mass of shadows: the hangar was huge enough to hold much larger ships. Thirty years ago, it had no doubt been full, but the Outsiders must have removed them all as they dragged the wreck out there.

"I'm in," she whispered; and set out through the darkness, to find the heartroom and the Mind that was her great-aunt.

"I'm sorry," Jason said to Catherine. "Your first choice of posting was declined by the Board."

Catherine sat very straight in her chair, trying to ignore how uncomfortable she felt in her suit—it gaped too large over her chest, flared too much at her hips, and she'd had to hastily readjust the trouser-legs after she and Johanna discovered the seamstress had got the length wrong. "I see," she said, because there was nothing else she could say, really.

Jason looked at his desk, his gaze boring into the metal as if he could summon an assignment out of nothing—she knew he meant well, that he had probably volunteered to tell her this himself, instead of leaving it for some stranger who wouldn't care a jot for her—but in that moment, she didn't want to be reminded that he worked for the Board for the Protection of Dai Viet Refugees; that he'd had a hand, no matter how small, in denying her wishes for the future.

At length Jason said, slowly, carefully, reciting a speech he'd no doubt given a dozen times that day, "The government puts the greatest care into choosing postings for the refugees. It was felt that putting you onboard a space station would be—unproductive."

Unproductive. Catherine kept smiling; kept her mask plastered on, even though it hurt to turn the corners of her mouth upwards, to crinkle her eyes as if she were pleased. "I see," she said, again, knowing anything else was useless. "Thanks, Jason."

Jason colored. "I tried arguing your case, but . . . "

"I know," Catherine said. He was a clerk; that was all; a young civil servant at the bottom of the Board's hierarchy, and he couldn't possibly get her what she wanted, even if he'd been willing to favor her. And it hadn't been such a surprise, anyway. After Mary and Olivia and Johanna . . .

"Look," Jason said. "Let's see each other tonight, right? I'll take you someplace you can forget all about this."

"You know it's not that simple," Catherine said. As if a restaurant, or a wild waterfall ride, or whatever delight Jason had in mind, could make her forget this.

"No, but I can't do anything about the Board." Jason's voice was firm. "I can, however, make sure that you have a good time tonight."

Catherine forced a smile she didn't feel. "I'll keep it in mind. Thanks."

As she exited the building, passing under the wide arches, the sun sparkled on the glass windows—and for a brief moment she wasn't herself—she was staring at starlight reflected in a glass panel, watching an older woman running hands on a wall and smiling at her with gut-wrenching sadness . . . She blinked, and the moment was gone; though the sense of sadness, of unease, remained, as if she were missing something essential.

Johanna was waiting for her on the steps, her arms crossed in front of her, and a gaze that looked as though it would bore holes into the lawn.

"What did they tell you?"

Catherine shrugged, wondering how a simple gesture could cost so much. "The same they told you, I'd imagine. Unproductive."

They'd all applied to the same postings—all asked for something related to space, whether it was one of the observatories, a space station; or, in Johanna's case, outright asking to board a slow-ship as crew. They'd all been denied, for variations of the same reason.

"What did you get?" Johanna asked. Her own rumpled slip of paper had already been recycled at the nearest terminal; she was heading north, to Steele, where she'd join an archaeological dig.

Catherine shrugged, with a casualness she didn't feel. They'd always felt at ease under the stars—had always yearned to take to space, felt the same craving to be closer to their home planets—to hang, weightless and without ties, in a place where they wouldn't be weighed, wouldn't be judged for falling short of values that ultimately didn't belong to them. "I got newswriter."

"At least you're not moving very far, " Johanna said, a tad resentfully.

"No." The offices of the network company were a mere two streets away from the Institution.

"I bet Jason had a hand in your posting," Johanna said.

"He didn't say anything about that—"

"Of course he wouldn't." Johanna snorted, gently. She didn't much care for Jason; but she knew how much his company meant to Catherine—how much more it would come to mean, if the weight of an entire continent separated Catherine and her. "Jason broadcasts his failures because they bother him; you'll hardly ever hear him talk of his successes. He'd feel too much like he was boasting." Her face changed, softened. "He cares for you, you know—truly. You have the best luck in the world."

"I know," Catherine said—thinking of the touch of his lips on hers; of his arms, holding her close until she felt whole, fulfilled. "I know."

The best luck in the world—she and Jason and her new flat, and her old haunts, not far away from the Institution—though she wasn't sure, really, if that last was a blessing—if she wanted to remember the years Matron had spent hammering proper behavior into them: the deprivations whenever they spoke anything less than perfect Galactic, the hours spent cleaning the dormitory's toilets for expressing mild revulsion at the food; or the night they'd spent shut outside, naked, in the growing cold, because they couldn't remember which Galactic president had colonized Longevity Station—how Matron had found them all huddled against each other, in an effort to keep warm and awake, and had sent them to Discipline for a further five hours, scolding them for behaving like wild animals.

Catherine dug her nails into the palms of her hands—letting the pain anchor her back to the present; to where she sat on the steps of the Board's central offices, away from the Institution and all it meant to them.

"We're free," she said, at last. "That's all that matters."

"We'll never be free." Johanna's tone was dark, intense. "Your records have a mark that says 'Institution'. And even if it didn't—do you honestly believe we would blend right in?"

There was no one quite like them on Prime, where Dai Viet were unwelcome; not with those eyes, not with that skin color—not with that demeanor, which even years of Institution hadn't been enough to erase.

"Do you ever wonder . . . " Johanna's voice trailed off into silence, as if she were contemplating something too large to put into words.

"Wonder what?" Catherine asked.

Johanna bit her lip. "Do you ever wonder what it would have been like, with our parents? Our real parents."

The parents they couldn't remember. They'd done the math, too—no children at the Institution could remember anything before coming there. Matron had said it was because they were really young when they were taken away—that it had been for the best. Johanna, of course, had blamed something more sinister, some fix-up done by the Institution to its wards to keep them docile.

Catherine thought, for a moment, of a life among the Dai Viet—an idyllic image of a harmonious family like in the holo-movies—a mirage that dashed itself to pieces against the inescapable reality of the birth vid. "They'd have used us like broodmares," Catherine said. "You saw—"

"I know what I saw," Johanna snapped. "But maybe . . . " Her face was pale. "Maybe it wouldn't have been so bad, in return for the rest."

For being loved; for being made worthy; for fitting in, being able to stare at the stars without wondering which was their home—without dreaming of when they might go back to their families.

Catherine rubbed her belly, thinking of the vid—and the *thing* crawling out of the woman's belly, all metal edges and shining crystal, coated in the blood of its mother—and, for a moment she felt as though she were the woman—floating above her body, detached from her cloak of flesh, watching herself give birth in pain. And then the sensation ended, but she was still feeling spread out, larger than she ought to have been—looking at herself from a distance and watching her own life pass her by, petty and meaningless, and utterly bounded from end to end.

Maybe Johanna was right. Maybe it wouldn't have been so bad, after all.

The ship was smaller than Lan Nhen had expected—she'd been going by her experience with *The Cinnabar Mansions*, which was an older generation, but *The Turtle's Citadel* was much smaller for the same functionalities.

Lan Nhen went up from the hangar to the living quarters, her equipment slung over her shoulders. She'd expected a sophisticated defense system like the drones, but there was nothing. Just the familiar slimy feeling of a quickened ship on the walls, a sign that the Mind that it hosted was still alive—albeit barely. The walls were bare, instead of the elaborate decoration Lan Nhen was used to from *The Cinnabar Mansions*—no scrolling calligraphy, no flowing paintings of starscapes or flowers; no ambient sound of zither or anything to enliven the silence.

She didn't have much time to waste—Cuc had said they had two hours between the moment the perimeter defenses kicked in and the moment more hefty safeguards were manually activated—but she couldn't help herself: she looked into one of the living quarters. It was empty as well, its walls scored with gunfire. The only color in the room was a few splatters of dried blood on a chair, a reminder of the tragedy of the ship's fall— the execution of its occupants, the dragging of its wreck to the derelict ward—dried blood, and a single holo of a woman on a table, a beloved mother or grandmother: a bare, abandoned picture with no offerings or incense, all that remained from a wrecked ancestral altar. Lan Nhen spat on the ground, to ward off evil ghosts, and went back to the corridors.

She truly felt as though she were within a mausoleum—like that one time her elder sister had dared her and Cuc to spend the night within the family's ancestral shrine, and they'd barely slept—not because of monsters or anything, but because of the vast silence that permeated the whole place amidst the smell of incense and funeral offerings, reminding them that they, too, were mortal.

That Minds, too, could die—that rescues were useless—no, she couldn't afford to think like that. She had Cuc with her, and together they would . . .

She hadn't heard Cuc for a while.

She stopped, when she realized—that it wasn't only the silence on the ship, but also the deathly quiet of her own comms system. Since—since she'd entered *The Turtle's Citadel*—that was the last time she'd heard her cousin, calmly pointing out about emergency standby and hangar doors and how everything was going to work out, in the end . . .

She checked her comms. There appeared to be nothing wrong; but whichever frequency she selected, she could hear nothing but static. At last, she managed to find one slot that seemed less crowded than others. "Cousin? Can you hear me?"

Noise on the line. "Very—badly." Cuc's voice was barely recognizable. "There—is—something—interference—"

"I know," Lan Nhen said. "Every channel is filled with noise."

Cuc didn't answer for a while; and when she did, her voice seemed to have become more distant—a problem had her interest again. "Not—noise. They're broadcasting—data. Need—to . . . " And then the comms cut. Lan Nhen tried all frequencies, trying to find one that would be less noisy; but there was nothing. She bit down a curse—she had no doubt Cuc would find a way around whatever blockage the Outsiders had put on the ship, but this was downright bizarre. Why broadcast data? Cutting down the comms of prospective attackers somehow didn't seem significant enough—at least not compared to defense drones or similar mechanisms.

She walked through the corridors, following the spiral path to the heartroom—nothing but the static in her ears, a throbbing song that erased every coherent thought from her mind—at least it was better than the silence, than that feeling of moving underwater in an abandoned city—that feeling that she was too late, that her great-aunt was already dead and past recovery, that all she could do here was kill her once and for all, end her misery . . .

She thought, incongruously, of a vid she'd seen, which showed her great-grandmother ensconced in the heartroom—in the first few years of *The Turtle's Citadel*'s life, those crucial moments of childhood when the ship's mother remained onboard to guide the Mind to adulthood. Great-grandmother was telling stories to the ship—and *The Turtle's Citadel* was struggling to mimic the spoken words in scrolling texts on her walls, laughing delightedly whenever she succeeded—all sweet and young, unaware of what her existence would come to, in the end.

Unlike the rest of the ship, the heartroom was crowded—packed with Outsider equipment that crawled over the Mind's resting place in the center, covering her from end to end until Lan Nhen could barely see the glint of metal underneath. She gave the entire contraption a wide berth—the spikes and protrusions from the original ship poked at odd angles, glistening with a dark liquid she couldn't quite identify—and the Outsider equipment piled atop the Mind, a mass of cables and unfamiliar machines, looked as though it was going to take awhile to sort out.

There were screens all around, showing dozens of graphs and diagrams, shifting as they tracked variables that Lan Nhen couldn't guess at—vital signs, it looked like, though she wouldn't have been able to tell what.

Lan Nhen bowed in the direction of the Mind, from younger to elder—perfunctorily, since she was unsure whether the Mind could see her at all. There was no acknowledgement, either verbal or otherwise.

Her great-aunt was in there. She had to be.

"Cousin." Cuc's voice was back in her ears—crisp and clear and uncommonly worried.

"How come I can hear you?" Lan Nhen asked. "Because I'm in the heartroom?"

Cuc snorted. "Hardly. The heartroom is where all the data is streaming from. I've merely found a way to filter the transmissions on both ends. Fascinating problem . . . "

"Is this really the moment?" Lan Nhen asked. "I need you to walk me through the reanimation—"

"No you don't," Cuc said. "First you need to hear what I have to say."

The call came during the night: a man in the uniform of the Board asked for Catherine George—as if he couldn't tell that it was her, that she was standing dishevelled and pale in front of her screen at three in the morning. "Yes, it's me," Catherine said. She fought off the weight of nightmares—more and more, she was waking in the night with memories of blood splattered across her entire body; of stars collapsing while she watched, powerless—of a crunch, and a moment where she hung alone in darkness, knowing that she had been struck a death blow—

The man's voice was quiet, emotionless. There had been an accident in Steele; a regrettable occurrence that hadn't been meant to happen, and the Board would have liked to extend its condolences to her—they apologized for calling so late, but they thought she should know . . .

"I see," Catherine said. She kept herself uncomfortably straight—aware of the last time she'd faced the board—when Jason had told her her desire for space would have been unproductive. When they'd told Johanna . . .

Johanna.

After a while, the man's words slid past her like water on glass—hollow reassurances, empty condolences, whereas she stood as if her heart had been torn away from her, fighting a desire to weep, to retch—she wanted to turn back time, to go back to the previous week and the sprigs of apricot flowers Jason had given her with a shy smile—to breathe in the sharp, tangy flavor of the lemon cake he'd baked for her, see again the carefully blank expression on his face as he waited to see if she'd like it—she wanted to be held tight in his arms and told that it was fine, that everything was going to be fine, that Johanna was going to be fine.

"We're calling her other friends," the man was saying, "but since you were close to each other . . . "

"I see," Catherine said—of course he didn't understand the irony, that it was the answer she'd given the Board—Jason—the last time.

The man cut off the communication; and she was left alone, standing in her living room and fighting back the feeling that threatened to overwhelm her—a not-entirely unfamiliar sensation of dislocation in her belly, the awareness that she didn't belong here among the Galactics; that she wasn't there by choice, and couldn't leave; that her own life should have been larger, more fulfilling than this slow death by inches, writing copy for feeds without any acknowledgement of her contributions—that Johanna's life should have been larger . . .

Her screen was still blinking—an earlier message from the Board that she hadn't seen? But why—

Her hands, fumbling away in the darkness, made the command to retrieve the message—the screen faded briefly to black while the message was decompressed, and then she was staring at Johanna's face.

For a moment—a timeless, painful moment—Catherine thought with relief that it had been a mistake, that Johanna was alive after all; and then she realized how foolish she'd been—that it wasn't a call, but merely a message from beyond the grave.

Johanna's face was pale, so pale Catherine wanted to hug her, to tell her the old lie that things were going to be fine—but she'd never get to say those words now, not ever.

"I'm sorry, Catherine," she said. Her voice was shaking; and the circles under her eyes took up half of her face, turning her into some pale nightmare from horror movies—a ghost, a restless soul, a ghoul hungry for human flesh. "I can't do this, not anymore. The Institution was fine; but it's got worse. I wake up at night, and feel sick—as if everything good has been leached from the world—as if the food had no taste, as if I drifted like a ghost through my days, as if my entire life held no meaning or truth. Whatever they did to our memories in the Institution—it's breaking down now. It's tearing me apart. I'm sorry, but I can't take any more of this. I—" she looked away from the camera for a brief moment, and then back at Catherine. "I have to go."

"No," Catherine whispered, but she couldn't change it. She couldn't do anything.

"You were always the strongest of us," Johanna said. "Please remember this. Please. Catherine." And then the camera cut, and silence spread through the room, heavy and unbearable, and Catherine felt like weeping, though she had no tears left.

"Catherine?" Jason called in a sleepy voice from the bedroom. "It's too early to check your work inbox . . . "

Work. Love. *Meaningless*, Johanna had said. Catherine walked to the huge window pane, and stared at the city spread out below her—the mighty Prime, center of the Galactic Federation, its buildings shrouded in light, its streets crisscrossed by floaters; with the bulky shape of the Parliament at the center, a proud statement that the Galactic Federation still controlled most of their home galaxy.

Too many lights to see the stars; but she could still guess; could still feel their pull—could still remember that one of them was her home.

*A lie, Johanna had said. A construction to keep us here.*

"Catherine?" Jason stood behind her, one hand wrapped around her shoulder—awkwardly tender as always, like that day when he'd offered to share a flat, standing balanced on one foot and not looking at her.

"Johanna is dead. She killed herself."

She felt rather than saw him freeze—and, after a while, he said in a changed voice, "I'm so sorry. I know how much she meant . . . " His voice trailed off, and he too, fell silent, watching the city underneath.

There was a feeling—the same feeling she'd had when waking up as a child, a diffuse sense that something was not quite right with the world; that the shadows held men watching, waiting for the best time to snatch her; that she was not wholly back in her body—that Jason's hand on her shoulder was just the touch of a ghost, that even his love wasn't enough to keep her safe. That the world was fracturing around her, time and time again—she breathed in, hoping to dispel the sensation. Surely it was nothing more than grief, than fatigue—but the sensation wouldn't go away, leaving her on the verge of nausea.

"You should have killed us," Catherine said. "It would have been kinder."

"Killed you?" Jason sounded genuinely shocked.

"When you took us from our parents."

Jason was silent for a while. Then: "We don't kill. What do you think we are, monsters from the fairy tales, killing and burning everyone who looks different? Of course we're not like that." Jason no longer sounded uncertain or awkward; it was as if she'd touched some wellspring, scratched some skin to find only primal reflexes underneath.

"You erased our memories." She didn't make any effort to keep the bitterness from her voice.

"We had to." Jason shook his head. "They'd have killed you, otherwise. You know this."

*"How can I trust you?" Look at Johanna, she wanted to say. Look at me. How can you say it was all worth it?*

"Catherine . . . " Jason's voice was weary. "We've been over this before. You've seen the vids from the early days. We didn't set out to steal your childhood, or anyone's childhood. But when you were left—intact . . . accidents happened. Carelessness. Like Johanna."

"Like Johanna." Her voice was shaking now; but he didn't move, didn't do anything to comfort her or hold her close. She turned at last, to stare into his face; and saw him transfixed by light, by faith, his gaze turned away from her and every pore of his being permeated by the utter conviction that he was right, that they were all right and that a stolen childhood was a small price to pay to be a Galactic.

"Anything would do." Jason's voice was slow, quiet—explaining life to a child, a script they'd gone over and over in their years together, always coming back to the same enormous, inexcusable choice that had been made for them. "Scissors, knives, broken bottles. You sliced your veins, hanged yourselves, pumped yourselves full of drugs . . . We had to . . . we had to block your memories, to make you blank slates."

"Had to." She was shaking now; and still he didn't see. Still she couldn't make him see.

"I swear to you, Catherine. It was the only way."

And she knew, she'd always known he was telling the truth—not because he was right, but because he genuinely could not envision any other future for them.

"I see," she said. The nausea, the sense of dislocation, wouldn't leave her—disgust for him, for this life that trapped her, for everything she'd turned into or been turned into. "I see."

"Do you think I like it?" His voice was bitter. "Do you think it makes me sleep better at night? Every day I hate that choice, even though I wasn't the one who made it. Every day I wonder if there was something else the Board could have done, some other solution that wouldn't have robbed you of everything you were."

"Not everything," Catherine said—slowly, carefully. "We still look Dai Viet."

Jason grimaced, looking ill at ease. "That's your *body*, Catherine. Of course they weren't going to steal that."

Of course; and suddenly, seeing how uneasy he was, it occurred to Catherine that they could have changed that, too, just as easily as they'd tampered with her memories; made her skin clearer, her eyes less distinctive; could have helped her fit into Galactic society. But they hadn't. *Holding the strings to the last*, Johanna would have said. "You draw the line at my body, but stealing my memories is fine?"

Jason sighed; he turned towards the window, looking at the streets. "No, it's not, and I'm sorry. But how else were we supposed to keep you alive?"

"Perhaps we didn't want to be alive."

"Don't say that, please." His voice had changed, had become fearful, protective. "Catherine. Everyone deserves to live. You especially."

*Perhaps I don't*, she thought, but he was holding her close to him, not letting her go—her anchor to the flat—to the living room, to life. "You're not Johanna," he said. "You know that."

*The strongest of us*, Johanna had said. She didn't feel strong; just frail and adrift. "No," she said, at last. "Of course I'm not."

"Come on," Jason said. "Let me make you a tisane. We'll talk in the kitchen—you look as though you need it."

"No." And she looked up—sought out his lips in the darkness, drinking in his breath and his warmth to fill the emptiness within her. "That's not what I need."

"Are you sure?" Jason looked uncertain—sweet and innocent and naïve, everything that had drawn her to him. "You're not in a state to—"

"Ssh," she said, and laid a hand on his lips, where she'd kissed him. "Ssh."

Later, after they'd made love, she lay her head in the hollow of his arm, listening to the slow beat of his heart like a lifeline; and wondered how long she'd be able to keep the emptiness at bay.

"It goes to Prime," Cuc said. "All the data is beamed to Prime, and it's coming from almost every ship in the ward."

"I don't understand," Lan Nhen said. She'd plugged her own equipment into the ship, carefully shifting the terminals she couldn't make sense of—hadn't dared to go closer to the center, where Outsider technology had crawled all over her great-aunt's resting place, obscuring the Mind and the mass of connectors that linked her to the ship.

On one of the screens, a screensaver had launched: night on a planet Lan Nhen couldn't recognize—an Outsider one, with their sleek floaters and their swarms of helper bots, their wide, impersonal streets planted with trees that were too tall and too perfect to be anything but the product of years of breeding.

"She's not here," Cuc said.

"I—" Lan Nhen was about to say she didn't understand, and then the true import of Cuc's words hit her. "Not here? She's alive, Cuc. I can see the ship; I can hear her all around me . . . "

"Yes, yes," Cuc said, a tad impatiently. "But that's . . . the equivalent of unconscious processes, like breathing in your sleep."

"She's dreaming?"

"No," Cuc said. A pause, then, very carefully: "I think she's on Prime, Cousin. The data that's being broadcast—it looks like Mind thought-processes, compressed with a high rate and all mixed together. There's probably something on the other end that decompresses the data and sends it to . . . Arg, I don't know! Wherever they think is appropriate."

Lan Nhen bit back another admission of ignorance, and fell back on the commonplace. "On Prime." The enormity of the thing; that you could take a Mind—a beloved ship with a family of her own—that you could put her to sleep and cause her to wake up somewhere else, on an unfamiliar planet and an alien culture—that you could just transplant her like a flower or a tree . . . "She's on Prime."

"In a terminal or as the power source for something," Cuc said, darkly.

"Why would they bother?" Lan Nhen asked. "It's a lot of power expenditure just to get an extra computer."

"Do I look as though I have insight into Outsiders?" Lan Nhen could imagine Cuc throwing her hands up in the air, in that oft-practiced gesture. "I'm just telling you what I have, Cousin."

Outsiders—the Galactic Federation of United Planets—were barely comprehensible in any case. They were the descendants of an Exodus fleet that had hit an isolated galaxy: left to themselves and isolated for decades, they had turned on each other in huge ethnic cleansings before emerging from their home planets as relentless competitors for resources and inhabitable planets.

"Fine. Fine." Lan Nhen breathed in, slowly; tried to focus at the problem at hand. "Can you walk me through cutting the radio broadcast?"

Cuc snorted. "I'd fix the ship, first, if I were you."

Lan Nhen knelt by the equipment, and stared at a cable that had curled around one of the ship's spines. "Fine, let's start with what we came for. Can you see?"

Silence; and then a life-sized holo of Cuc hovered in front of her—even though the avatar was little more than broad strokes, Great-great-aunt had still managed to render it in enough details to make it unmistakably Cuc. "Cute," Lan Nhen said.

"Hahaha," Cuc said. "No bandwidth for trivialities—gotta save for detail on your end." She raised a hand, pointed to one of the outermost screens on the edge of the room. "Disconnect this one first."

It was slow, and painful. Cuc pointed; and Lan Nhen checked before disconnecting and moving. Twice, she jammed her fingers very close to a cable, and felt electricity crackle near her—entirely too close for comfort.

They moved from the outskirts of the room to the center—tackling the huge mount of equipment last. Cuc's first attempts resulted in a cable coming loose with an ominous sound; they waited, but nothing happened. "We might have fried something," Lan Nhen said.

"Too bad. There's no time for being cautious, as you well know. There's . . . maybe half an hour left before the other defenses go live." Cuc moved again, pointed to another squat terminal. "This goes off."

When they were finished, Lan Nhen stepped back, to look at their handiwork.

The heartroom was back to its former glory: instead of Outsider equipment, the familiar protrusions and sharp organic needles of the Mind's resting place; and they could see the Mind herself—resting snug in her cradle, wrapped around the controls of the ship—her myriad arms each seizing one rack of connectors; her huge head glinting in the light—a vague globe shape covered with glistening cables and veins. The burn mark from the Outsider attack was clearly visible, a dark, elongated shape on the edge of her head that had bruised a couple of veins—it had hit one of the connectors as well, burnt it right down to the color of ink.

Lan Nhen let out a breath she hadn't been aware of holding. "It scrambled the connector."

"And scarred her, but didn't kill her," Cuc said. "Just like you said."

"Yes, but—" But it was one thing to run simulations of the attack over and over, always getting the same prognosis; and quite another to see that the simulations held true, and that the damage was repairable.

"There should be another connector rack in your bag," Cuc said. "I'll walk you through slotting it in."

After she was done, Lan Nhen took a step back; and stared at her great-aunt—feeling, in some odd way, as though she were violating the Mind's privacy. A Mind's heartroom was their stronghold, a place where they could twist reality as they wished, and appear as they wished to. To see her great-aunt like this, without any kind of appearance change or pretence, was . . . more disturbing than she'd thought.

"And now?" she asked Cuc.

Even without details, Lan Nhen knew her cousin was smiling. "Now we pray to our ancestors that cutting the broadcast is going to be enough to get her back."

Another night on Prime, and Catherine wakes up breathless, in the grip of another nightmare—images of red lights, and scrolling texts, and a feeling of growing cold in her bones, a cold so deep she cannot believe she will ever feel warm no matter how many layers she's put on.

Johanna is not there; beside her, Jason sleeps, snoring softly; and she's suddenly seized by nausea, remembering what he said to her—how casually he spoke of blocking her memories, of giving a home to her after stealing her original one from her. She waits for it to pass; waits to settle into her old life as usual. But it doesn't.

Instead, she rises, walks towards the window, and stands watching Prime—the clean wide streets, the perfect trees, the ballet of floaters at night—the myriad dances that make up the society that constrains her from dawn to dusk and beyond—she wonders what Johanna would say, but of course Johanna won't ever say anything anymore. Johanna has gone ahead, into the dark.

The feeling of nausea in her belly will not go away: instead it spreads, until her body feels like a cage—at first, she thinks the sensation is in her belly, but it moves upwards, until her limbs, too, feel too heavy and too small—until it's an effort to move any part of her. She raises her hands, struggling against a feeling of moving appendages that don't belong to her—and traces the contours of her face, looking for familiar shapes, for anything that will anchor her to reality. The heaviness spreads, compresses her chest until she can hardly breathe—cracks her ribs and pins her legs to the ground. Her head spins, as if she were about to faint; but the mercy of blackness does not come to her.

"Catherine," she whispers. "My name is Catherine."

Another name, unbidden, rises to her lips. *Mi Chau.* A name she gave to herself in the Viet language—in the split instant before the lasers took her apart, before she sank into darkness: Mi Chau, the princess who unwittingly betrayed her father and her people, and whose blood became the pearls at the bottom of the sea. She tastes it on her tongue, and it's the only thing that seems to belong to her anymore.

She remembers that first time—waking up on Prime in a strange body, struggling to breathe, struggling to make sense of being so small, so far away from the stars that had guided her through space—remembers walking like a ghost through the corridors of the Institution, until the knowledge of what the Galactics had done broke her, and she cut her veins in a bathroom, watching blood lazily pool at her feet and thinking only of escape. She remembers the second time she woke up; the second, oblivious life as Catherine.

Johanna. Johanna didn't survive her second life; and even now is starting her third, somewhere in the bowels of the Institution—a dark-skinned child indistinguishable from other dark-skinned children, with no memories of anything beyond a confused jumble . . .

Outside, the lights haven't dimmed, but there are stars—brash and alien, hovering above Prime, in configurations that look *wrong*; and she remembers, suddenly, how they lay around her, how they showed her the way from planet to planet—how the cold of the deep spaces seized her just as she entered them to travel faster, just like it's holding her now, seizing her bones—remembers how much larger, how much wider she ought to be . . .

There are stars everywhere; and superimposed on them, the faces of two Dai Viet women, calling her over and over. Calling her back, into the body that belonged to her all along; into the arms of her family.

"Come on, come on," the women whisper, and their voices are stronger than any other noise; than Jason's breath in the bedroom; than the motors of the floaters or the vague smell of garlic from the kitchen. "Come on, Great-aunt!"

She is more than this body; more than this constrained life—her thoughts spread out, encompassing hangars and living quarters; and the liquid weight of pods held in their cradles—she remembers family reunions, entire generations of children putting their hands on her corridors, remembers the touch of their skin on her metal walls; the sound of their laughter as they raced each other; the quiet chatter of their mothers in the heartroom, keeping her company as the New Year began; and the touch of a brush on her outer hull, drawing the shape of an apricot flower, for good luck  . . .

"Catherine?" Jason calls behind her.

She turns, through sheer effort of will; finding, somehow, the strength to maintain her consciousness in a small and crammed body alongside her other, vaster one. He's standing with one hand on the doorjamb, staring at her—his face pale, leached of colors in the starlight.

"I remember," she whispers.

His hands stretch, beseeching. "Catherine, please. Don't leave."

He means well, she knows. All the things that he hid from her, he hid out of love; to keep her alive and happy, to hold her close in spite of all that should have separated them; and even now, the thought of his love is a barb in her heart, a last lingering regret, slight and pitiful against the flood of her memories—but not wholly insignificant.

Where she goes, she'll never be alone—not in the way she was with Jason, feeling that nothing else but her mattered in the entire world. She'll have a family; a gaggle of children and aunts and uncles waiting on her, but nothing like the sweet, unspoiled privacy where Jason and she could share anything and everything. She won't have another lover like him—naïve and frank and so terribly sure of what he wants and what he's ready to do to get it. Dai Viet society has no place for people like Jason— who do not know their place, who do not know how to be humble, how to accept failure or how to bow down to expediency.

Where she goes, she'll never be alone; and yet she'll be so terribly lonely.

"Please," Jason says.

"I'm sorry," she says. "I'll come back—" a promise made to him; to Johanna, who cannot hear or recognize her anymore. Her entire being spreads out, thins like water thrown on the fire—and, in that last moment, she finds herself reaching out for him, trying to touch him one last time, to catch one last glimpse of his face, even as a heart she didn't know she had breaks.

"Catherine."

He whispers her name, weeping, over and over; and it's that name, that lie that still clings to her with its bittersweet memories, that she takes with her as her entire being unfolds—as she flies away, towards the waiting stars.

# ALIEN ARCHEOLOGY

## *Neal Asher*

The sifting machine had been working nonstop for twenty years. The technique, first introduced by the xeno-archaeologist Alexion Smith and frowned on by others in his profession as being too blunt an instrument, was in use here by a private concern. An Atheter artifact had been discovered on this desert planetoid: a species of plant that used a deep extended root system to mop up platinum grains from the green sands, which it accumulated in its seeds to drop on the surface. Comparative analysis of the plant's genome—a short trihelical strand—proved it was a product of Atheter technology. The planet had been deep-scanned for other artifacts, then the whole project abandoned when nothing else major was found. The owners of the sifting machine came here afterward in the hope of picking up something the previous searchers had missed. They had managed to scrape up a few minor finds, but reading between the lines of their most recent public reports, Jael knew they were concealing something and, breaking into the private reports from the man on the ground here, learned of a second big find.

Perched on a boulder, she stepped down the magnification of her eyes to human normal so that all she could see was the machine's dust plume from the flat green plain. The Kobashi rested in the boulder's shade behind her. The planetary base was some ten kilometers away and occupied by a sandapt called Rho. He had detected the U-space signature of her ship's arrival and sent a terse query as to her reason for being here. She expressed her curiosity about what he was doing, to which he had replied that this was no tourist spot before shutting down communication. Obviously he was the kind who relished solitude, which was why he was suited for this assignment and was perfect for Jael's purposes. She could have taken her ship directly to his base, but had brought it in low below the base's horizon to land it. She was going to surprise the sandapt, and rather suspected he wouldn't consider it a pleasant surprise.

This planet was hot enough to kill an unadapted human and the air too thin and noxious for her to breathe, but she wore a hotsuit with its own air supply, and, in the one-half gravity, could cover the intervening distance very quickly. She leapt down the five meters to the ground, bounced in a cloud of dust, and set out in a long lope—her every stride covering three meters.

Glimmering beads of metal caught Jael's attention before she reached the base. She halted and turned to study something like a morel fungus—its wrinkled head an open skin of cubic holes. Small seeds glimmered in those holes, and as she drew closer some of them were ejected. Tracking their path she saw that when they struck the loose dusty ground they sank out of sight. She pushed her hand into the ground and scooped up dust in which small objects glittered. She increased the sensitivity of her optic nerves and ramped up the magnification of her eyes. Each seed consisted of a teardrop of organic matter attached at its widest end to a dodecahedral crystal of platinum. Jael supposed the Atheter had used something like the sifting machine far to her left to collect the precious metal; separating it from the seeds and leaving them behind to germinate into more of these useful little plants. She pocketed the seeds—she knew people who would pay good money for them—though her aim here was to make a bigger killing than that.

She had expected Rho's base to be the usual inflated dome with resin-bonded sand layered over it, but some other building technique had been employed here. Nestled below an escarpment that marked the edge of the dust bowl and the start of a deeply cracked plain of sun-baked clay, the building was a white-painted cone with a peaked roof. It looked something like an ancient windmill without vanes, but then there were three wind generators positioned along the top of the escarpment—their vanes wide to take into account the thin air down here. Low structures spread out from either side of the building like wings, glimmering in the harsh white sun glare. Jael guessed these were greenhouses to protect growing food plants. A figure was making its way along the edge of these towing a gravsled. She squatted down and focused in.

Rho's adaptation had given him skin of a deep reddish gold, a ridged bald head, and a nose that melded into his top lip. She glimpsed his eyes, which were sky blue and without pupils. He wore no mask—his only clothing being boots, shorts, and a sun visor. Jael leapt upright and broke into a run for the nearest end of the escarpment, where it was little more than a mound. Glancing back she noticed the dust trail she'd left and hoped he wouldn't see it. Eventually she arrived at the foot of one of the wind generators and from her belt pouch removed a skinjector and loaded it with a selection of drugs. The escarpment here dropped ten meters in a curve from which projected rough reddish slates. She used these as stepping-stones to bring her down to the level of the base then sprinted in toward the back wall. She could hear him now—he was whistling some ancient melody. A brief comparison search in the music library in her left-hand aug revealed the name: "Greensleeves." She walked around the building as he approached.

"Who the hell are you?" he exclaimed.

She strode up to him. "I've seen your sifting machine; have you had any luck?"

He paused for a moment, then, in a tired voice, said, "Bugger off."

But by then she was on him. Before he could react, she swung the skinjector round from behind her back and pressed it against his chest, triggered it.

"What the . . . !" His hand swung out and he caught her hard across the side of the face. She spun, her feet coming up off the ground, and fell in ridiculous slow motion in the low gravity. Error messages flashed up in her visual cortex—broken nanoconnections—but they faded quickly. Then she received a message from her body monitor telling her he had cracked her cheekbone—this before it actually began to hurt. Scrambling to her feet again she watched him rubbing his chest. Foam appeared around his lips, then slowly, like a tree, he toppled. Jael walked over to him thinking, You're so going to regret that, sandapt. Though maybe most of that anger was at herself—for she had been warned about him.

Getting him onto the gravsled in the low gravity was surprisingly difficult. He must have weighed twice as much as a normal human. Luckily the door to the base was open and designed wide enough to allow the sled inside. After dumping him, she explored, finding the laboratory sited on the lower floor, living quarters on the second, the U-space communicator and computer systems on the top. With a thought, she summoned the Kobashi to her present location, then returned her attention to the computer system. It was sub-AI and the usual optic interfaces were available. Finding a suitable network cable, she plugged one end into the computer and the other into the socket in her right-hand aug, then began mentally checking through Rho's files. He was not due to send a report for another two weeks, and the next supply drop was not for three months. However, there was nothing about his most recent find, and recordings of the exchanges she had listened to had been erased. Obviously, assessing his find, he had belatedly increased security.

Jael went back downstairs to study Rho, who was breathing raggedly on the sled. She hoped not to have overdone it with the narcotic. Outside, the whoosh of thrusters announced the arrival of the Kobashi, so Jael headed out.

The ship, bearing some resemblance to a thirty-yard-long abdomen and thorax of a praying mantis, settled in a cloud of hot sand in which platinum seeds glinted. Via her twinned augs she sent a signal to it and it folded down a wing section of its hull into a ramp onto which she stepped while it was still settling. At the head of the ramp the outer airlock door irised open and she ducked inside to grab up the pack she had deposited there earlier, then stepped back out and down, returning to the base.

Rho's breathing had eased, so it was with care that she secured his hands and feet in manacles connected by four braided cables to a winder positioned behind him. His eyelids fluttering, he muttered something obscure, but did not wake. Jael now took from the pack a bag that looked a little like a nineteenth-century doctor's case, and, four paces from Rho, placed it on the floor. An instruction from her augs caused the bag to open and evert, converting itself into a tiered display of diagnostic and surgical equipment, a small drugs manufactory, and various vials and chainglass tubes containing an esoteric selection of some quite alien oddities. Jael squatted beside the display, took up a diagnosticer, and pressed it against her cheekbone, let it make its diagnosis, then plugged it into the drug manufactory. Information downloaded, the manufactory stuck out a drug patch like a thin tongue. She took this up, peeled off the backing, and stuck it over her injury, which rapidly numbed. While doing this she sensed Rho surfacing into consciousness, and awaited the expected.

Rho flung himself from the sled at her, very fast. She noted he didn't even waste energy on a bellow, but was spinning straight into a kick that would have taken her head off if it had connected. He never got a chance to straighten his leg as the winder rapidly drew in the braided cables, bringing the four manacles together. He crashed to the floor in front of her, a little closer than she had expected, his wrists and ankles locked behind him—twenty years of digging in the dirt had not entirely slowed him down

"Bitch," he said.

Jael removed a scalpel from the display, held it before his face for a moment, then cut his sun visor strap, before trailing it gently down his body to start cutting through the material of his shorts. He tried to drag himself away from her.

"Careful," she warned, "this is chainglass and very, very sharp, and life is a very fragile thing."

"Fuck you," he said without heat, but ceased to struggle. She noted that he had yet to ask what she wanted. Obviously he knew. Next she cut away his boots, before replacing the scalpel in the display and standing.

"Now, Rho, you've been sifting sand here for two decades and discovered what, a handful of fragmentary Atheter artifacts? So, after all that time, finding something new was quite exciting. You made the mistake of toning down your public report to a level somewhere below dry boredom, which was a giveaway to me. Consequently I listened in to your private communications with Charles Cymbeline." She leaned down, her face close to his. "Now I want you to tell me where you've hidden the Atheter artifact you found two weeks ago."

He just stared up at her with those bland blue eyes, so she shrugged, stood up, and began kicking him. He struggled to protect himself, but she took her time, walking round him and driving her boot in repeatedly. He grunted and sweated and started to bleed on the floor.

"All right," he eventually managed. "Arcosect sent a ship a week ago—it's gone."

Panting, Jael stepped back. "There've been no ships here since your discovery." Walking back around to the instrument display she began to make her selection. While she employed her glittering instruments, his grunts soon turned to screams, but he bluntly refused to tell her anything even when she peeled strips of skin from his stomach and crushed his testicles in a set of forceps. But all that was really only repayment for her broken cheekbone. He told her everything when she began using her esoteric selection of drugs, could not do otherwise.

She left him on the floor and crossed the room to where a table lay strewn with rock samples and from there picked up a geological hammer. Back on the top floor she located the U-space coms—the unit was inset into one wall. Her first blow shattered the console, which she tore away.

She then began smashing the control components surrounding the sealed flask-sized vessels ostensibly containing small singularity generators and Calabri-yau frames. After a moment she rapped her knuckles against each flask to detect which was the false one, and pulled it out. The top unscrewed and from inside she withdrew a small brushed aluminum box with a keypad inset in the lid. The code he had given her popped the box open to reveal—resting in shaped foam—a chunk of green metal with short thorny outgrowths from one end.

Movement behind . . .

Jael whirled. Rho, catching his breath against the doorjamb, preparing to rush her. Her gaze strayed down to one of the manacles, a frayed stub of wire protruding from it. In his right hand he held what he had used to escape: a chainglass scalpel.

Careless.

Now she had seen him he hurled himself forward.

She could not afford to let him come to grips with her. He was obviously many times stronger than her. As he groped toward her she brought the hammer round in a tight arc against the side of his face, where it connected with a sickening crack. He staggered sideways, clutching his face, his mouth hanging open. She stepped in closer and brought the hammer down as hard as she could on the top of his head. He dropped, dragging her arm down. She released the hammer and saw it had punched a neat square hole straight into his skull and lodged there, then the hole brimmed with blood, and overflowed.

Gazing down at him, Jael said, "Oops." She pushed him with her foot but he was leaden, unmoving. "Oh, well." She pocketed the box containing the Atheter memstore. "One dies and another is destined for resurrection after half a million years. Call it serendipity." She relished the words for a moment, then headed away.

I woke, flat on my back, my face cold and my body one big ache from the sharpest pain at the crown of my skull, to my aching face, and on down to the throbbing from the bones in my right foot. I was breathing shallowly—the air in the room obviously thick to my lungs. Opening bleary eyes I lifted my head slightly and peered down at myself. I wore a quilted warming suit, that obviously accounted for why only my face felt cold. I realized I was in my own bedroom, and that my house had been sealed and the environment controls set to Earth-normal.

"You look like shit, Rho."

The whiff of cigarette smoke told me who was speaking before I iden-tified the voice.

"I guess I do," I said, "though who are you to talk?" I carefully heaved myself upright, then back so I was resting against the bed's headboard, then looked aside at Charles Cymbeline, my boss and the director of Arco-sect—a company with a total of about fifty employees. He too looked like shit, always did. He was blond, thin, wore expensive suits that required a great deal of meticulous cleaning, smoked unfiltered cigarettes though what pleasure he derived from them I couldn't fathom, and was very, very dead. He was a reification—a corpse with chemical preservative running in his veins, skin like old leather, with bone and the metal of some of the cyber mechanisms that moved him showing through at his finger joints. His mind was stored to a crystal inside the mulch that had been his brain. Why he retained his old dead body when he could easily afford a golem chassis or a tank-grown living vessel I wasn't entirely sure about either. He said it stopped people bothering him. It did.

"So we lost the memstore," he ventured, then took another pull on his cigarette. Smoke coiled from the gaps in his shirt, obviously making its way out of holes eaten through his chest. He sat in my favorite chair. I would probably have had to clean it, if I'd any intention of staying here.

"I reckon," I replied.

"So she tortured you and you gave it to her," he said. "I thought you were tougher than that."

"She tortured me for fun, and I thought maybe I could draw it out until you arrived, then she used the kind of drugs you normally don't find anywhere outside a Batian interrogation facility. And anyway, it would have come to a choice between me dying or giving up the memstore, and you just don't pay me enough to take the first option."

"Ah." He nodded, his neck creaking, and flicked ash on my carpet.

I carefully swung my legs to one side and sat on the edge of the bed. In one corner a pedestal mounted autodoc stood like a chrome insectile monk. Charles had obviously used it to repair much of the torture damage.

"You said 'she,'" I noted.

"Jael Feogril—my crew here obtained identification from DNA from the handle of that rock hammer we found embedded in your head. You're lucky to be alive. Had we arrived a day later you wouldn't have been."

"She's on record?" I inquired, as if I'd never heard of her.

"Yes—Earth Central Security supplied the details: born on Masada when it was an out-Polity world and made a fortune smuggling weapons to the Separatists. Well connected, augmented with twinned augs as you no doubt saw, and, it would appear, lately branching out into stealing alien artifacts. She's under a death sentence for an impressive list of crimes. I've got it all on crystal if you want it."

"I want it." It would give me detail.

He stared at me expressionlessly, wasn't really capable of doing otherwise.

"What have you got here?" I asked.

"My ship and five of the guys," he said, which accounted for the setting of the environmental controls since he certainly didn't need Earth-normal. "What are your plans?"

"I intend to get that memstore back."

"How, precisely? You don't know where she's gone."

"I have contacts, Charles."

"Who I'm presuming you haven't contacted in twenty years."

"They'll remember me."

He tilted his head slightly. "You never really told me what you used to do before you joined my little outfit. And I have never been able to find out, despite some quite intensive inquiries."

I shrugged, then said, "I'll require a little assistance in other departments."

He didn't answer for a while. His cigarette had burned right down to his fingers and now there was a slight bacony smell in the air. Then he asked, "What do you require?"

"A company ship—the Ulriss Fire since it's fast—some other items I'll list, and enough credit for the required bribes."

"Agreed, Rho," he said. "I'll also pay you a substantial bounty for that memstore."

"Good," I replied, thinking the real bounty for me would be getting my hands around Jael Feogril's neck.

From what we can tell, the Polity occupies an area of the galaxy once occupied by three other races. They're called, by us, the Jain, Csorians, and the Atheter. We thought, until only a few years ago, that they were all extinct—wiped out by an aggressive organic technology created by the Jain, which destroyed them and then burgeoned twice more to destroy the other two races—Jain technology. I think we encountered it, too, but information about that is heavily restricted. I think the events surrounding that encounter have something to do with certain Line worlds being under quarantine. I don't know the details. I won't know the details until the AIs lift the restrictions, but I do know something I perhaps shouldn't have been told.

I found the first five years of my new profession as an xeno-archaeologist something of a trial, so Jonas Clyde's arrival on the dust ball I called home came as a welcome relief. He was there direct from Masada—one of those quarantine worlds. He'd come to do some research on the platinum-producing plants, though I rather think he was taking a bit of a rest cure. He shared my home and on plenty of occasions he shared my whisky. The guy was nonstop—physically and mentally adapted to go without sleep—I reckon the alcohol gave him something he was missing.

One evening, I was speculating about what the Atheter might have looked like when I think something snapped in his head and he started laughing hysterically. He auged into my entertainment unit and showed me some recordings. The first was obviously the view from a gravcar taking off from the roof port of a runcible complex. I recognized the planet Masada at once, for beyond the complex stretched a checkerboard of dikes and ponds that reflected a gas giant hanging low in the aubergine sky.

"Here the Masadans raised squirms and other unpleasant life-forms for their religious masters," Jonas told me. "The people on the surface needed an oxygenating parasite attached to their chests to keep them alive. The parasite also shortened their life span."

I guessed it was understandable that they rebelled and shouted for help from the Polity. On the recording I saw people down below, but they wore envirosuits and few of them were working the ponds. Here and there I saw aquatic agrobots standing in the water like stilt-legged steel beetles.

The recording took us beyond the ponds to a wilderness of flute grasses and quagmires. Big fences separated the two. "The best discouragement to some of the nasties out there is that humans aren't very nutritious for them," Jonas told me. "Hooders, heroynes, and gabbleducks prefer their fatter natural prey out in the grasses or up in the mountains." He glanced at me, a little crazily I thought. "Now those monsters have been planted with transponders so everyone knows if something dangerous is getting close, and which direction to run to avoid it."

The landscape in view shaded from white to a dark brown with black earth gullies cutting between islands of this vegetation. It wasn't long before I saw something galumphing through the grasses with the gait of a bear, though on Earth you don't get bears weighing in at about a thousand kilos. Of course I recognized it, who hasn't seen a recording of these things and the other weird and wonderful creatures of that world? The gravcar view drew lower and kept circling above the creature. Eventually it seemed to get bored with running, halted, then slumped back on its rump to sit like some immense pyramidal Buddha. It opened its composite forelimbs into their two sets of three "sublimbs" for the sum purpose of scratching its stomach. It yawned, opening its big duck bill to expose thorny teeth inside. It gazed up at the gravcar with seeming disinterest, some of the tiara of green eyes arcing across its domed head blinking as if it was so bored it just wanted to sleep.

"A gabbleduck," I said to Jonas.

He shook his head and I saw that there were tears in his eyes. "No," he told me, "that's one of the Atheter."

Lubricated on its way by a pint of whisky the story came out piece by piece thereafter. During his research on Masada he had discovered something amazing and quite horrible. That research had later been confirmed by an artifact recovered from a world called Shayden's Find. Jain technology had destroyed the Jain and the Csorians. It apparently destroyed technical civilizations—that was its very purpose. The Atheter had ducked the blow, forgoing civilization, intelligence, reducing themselves to animals, to gabbleducks. Tricone mollusks in the soil of Masada crunched up anything that remained of their technology, monstrous creatures like giant millipedes ate every last scrap of each gabbleduck when it died. It was an appalling and utterly alien nihilism.

The information inside the Atheter memstore Jael had stolen was worth millions. But who was prepared to pay those millions? Polity AIs would, but her chances of selling it to them without ECS coming down on her like a hammer were remote. Also, from what Jonas told me, the Polity had obtained something substantially more useful than a mere memstore, for the artifact from Shayden's Find held an Atheter AI. So who else? Well, I knew about her, though until she'd stuck a narcotic needle in my chest, I had never met her, and I knew that she had dealings with the Prador, that she sold them stuff, sometimes living stuff, sometimes human captives—for there was a black market for such in the Prador Third Kingdom. It was why the Polity AIs were so ticked off about her.

Another thing about Jael was that she was the kind of person who found things out, secret things. She was a Masadan by birth so probably had a lot of contacts on her home world. I wasn't so arrogant as to assume that what Jonas Clyde had blabbed to me had not been blabbed elsewhere.

I felt certain she knew about the gabbleducks. And I felt certain she was out for the big killing. The Prador would pay billions to someone who delivered into their claws a living, breathing, thinking Atheter.

A tenuous logic chain? No, not really. Even as my consciousness had faded, I'd hear her last comment.

The place stank like a sea cave in which dead fish were decaying. Jael brought her foot down hard, but the ship louse tried to crawl out from under it. She put all her weight down on it and twisted, and her foot sank down with a satisfying crunch, spattering glutinous ichor across the crusted filthy floor. Almost as if this were some kind of signal, the wide made-for-something-other-than-human door split diagonally, the two halves revolving up into the wall with a grinding shriek.

The tunnel beyond was dank and dark, weedy growths sprouting like dead man's fingers from the uneven walls. With a chitinous clattering, a flattened-pear carapace scuttling on too many legs appeared and came charging out. It headed straight toward her but she didn't allow herself to react. At the last moment it skidded to a halt then clattered sideways. Prador second-child, one eye-palp missing and a crack healing in its carapace, a rail-gun clutched in one of its underhands, with power cables and a projectile belt-feed trailing back to a box mounted underneath it. While she eyed it, it fed some scrap of flesh held in one of its foreclaws into its mandibles and chomped away enthusiastically.

Next a bigger shape loomed in the tunnel and advanced at a more leisurely pace, its sharp feet hitting the floor with a sound like hydraulic chisels. The first-child was big—the size of a small gravcar—its carapace wider and flatter and looking as hard as iron. The upper turret of its carapace sported a collection of ruby eyes and sprouting above them it retained both of its palp-eyes, all of which gave it superb vision—the eyesight of a carnivore, a predator. Underneath its grating mandibles and the nightmare mouth they exposed, mechanisms had been shell-welded to its carapace. Jael hoped one of these was a translator.

"I didn't want to speak to you at a distance, since, even using your codes, an AI might have been listening in," she said.

After a brief pause to grate its mandibles together, one of the hexagonal boxes attached underneath it spoke, for some reason in a thick Marsman accent. "Our codes are unbreakable."

Jael sighed to herself. Despite having fought the Polity for forty years, some Prador were no closer to understanding that to AIs, no code was unbreakable. Of course all Prador weren't so dumb—the clever ones now ruled the Third Kingdom. This first-child was just aping its father, who was a Prador down at the bottom of the hierarchy and scrabbling to find some advantage to climb higher. However, that father had acquired enough wealth to be able to send its first-child off in a cruiser like this, and would probably be able to acquire more by cutting deals with its competitors—all Prador were competitors. The first-child would need to make those deals, for what Jael hoped to sell the father of this creature it might not be able to afford by itself.

"I will soon be acquiring something that could be of great value to you," she said. Mentioning the Atheter memstore aboard Kobashi would have been suicide—Prador only made deals for things they could not take by force.

"Continue," said the first-child.

"I can, for the sum of ten billion New Carth Shillings or the equivalent in any stable currency, including Prador diamond slate, provide you with a living, breathing Atheter."

The Prador dipped its carapace—perhaps the equivalent of a man tilting his head to listen to a private aug communication. Its father must be talking to it. Finally it straightened up again and replied, "The Atheter are without mind."

Jael instinctively concealed her surprise, though that was a pointless exercise since this Prador could no more read her expression than she could read its. How had it acquired that knowledge? She only picked it up by running some very complicated search programs through all the reports coming from the taxonomic and genetic research station on Masada. Whatever—she would have to deal with it.

"True, they are, but I have a mind to give to one of them," she replied. "I have acquired an Atheter memstore."

The first-child advanced a little. "That is very interesting," said the Marsman voice—utterly without inflection.

"Which I of course have not been so foolish as to bring here—it is securely stored in a Polity bank vault."

"That is also interesting." The first-child stepped back again and Jael rather suspected something had been lost in translation. It tilted its carapace forward again and just froze in place, even its mandibles ceasing their constant motion.

Jael considered returning to her ship for the duration. The first-child's father would now be making its negotiations, striking deals, planning betrayals—the whole complex and vicious rigmarole of Prador politics and economics. She began a slow pacing, spotted another ship louse making its way toward her boots and went over to step on that. She could return to Kobashi, but would only pace there. She played some games in her twinned augs, sketching out fight scenarios in this very room, between her and the two Prador, and solving them. She stepped on four more ship lice, then accessed a downloaded catalog and studied the numerous items she would like to buy. Eventually the first-child heaved itself back upright.

"We will provide payment in the form of one half diamond slate, one quarter a cargo of armor scales, and the remainder in Polity currencies," it said.

Jael balked a little at the armor scales. Prador exotic metal armor was a valuable commodity, but bulky. She decided to accept, reckoning she could cache the scales somewhere in the Graveyard and make a remote sale by giving the coordinates to the buyer.

"That's acceptable," she said.

"Now we must discuss the details of the sale."

Jael nodded to herself. This was where it got rather difficult. Organizing a sale of something to the Prador was like working out how to hand-feed white sharks while in the water with them.

I gazed out through the screen at a world swathed in cloud, encircled by a glittering ring shepherded by a sulphurous moon, which itself trailed a cometary tail resulting from impacts on its surface a hundred and twenty years old—less than an eye blink in interstellar terms. The first settlers, leaving just before the Quiet War in the Solar System, had called the world Paris—probably because of a strong French contingent amid them and probably because Paradise had been overused. Their civilization was hardly out of the cradle when the Polity arrived in a big way and subsumed them. After a further hundred years the population of this place surpassed a billion. It thrived, great satellite space stations were built, and huge high-tech industries sprang up in them and in the arid equatorial deserts down below. This place was rich in every resource—surrounding space also swarming with asteroids that were heavy in rare metals. Then, a hundred and twenty years ago, the Prador came. It took them less than a day to depopulate the planet and turn it into the hell I saw before me, and to turn the stations into that glittering ring.

"Ship on approach," said a voice over com. "Follow the vector I give you and do not deviate. At the pick-up point shut down to minimal life support and a grabship will bring you in. Do otherwise and you're smeared. Understood?"

"I understand perfectly," I replied.

Holofiction producers called this borderland between Prador and human space the Badlands. The people who haunted this region, hunting for salvage, called it the Graveyard and knew themselves to be grave robbers. Polity AIs had not tried to civilize the area. All the habitable worlds were still smoking, and why populate any space that acted as a buffer zone between them and a bunch of nasty clawed fuckers who might decide at any moment on a further attempt to exterminate the human race?

"You got the vector, Ulriss?" I asked.

"Yeah," replied my ship's AI. It wasn't being very talkative since I'd refused its suggestion that we approach using the chameleonware recently installed aboard. I eyed the new instruments to my left on the console, remembering that Earth Central Security did not look kindly on anyone but them using their stealth technology. Despite ECS being thin on the ground out here, I had no intention of putting this ship into "stealth mode" unless really necessary. Way back, when I wasn't a xeno-archaeologist, I'd heard rumors about those using inadequate chameleonware ending up on the bad end of an ECS rail-gun test firing. "Sorry, we just didn't see you," was the usual epitaph.

My destination rose over Paris's horizon, cast into silhouette by the bile-yellow sun beyond it. Adjusting the main screen display to give me the best view, I soon discerned the massive conglomeration of station bubble units and docked ships that made up the "Free Republic of Montmartre"—the kind of place that in Earth's past would have been described as a banana republic, though perhaps not so nice. Soon we reached the place designated, and, main power shut down, the emergency lights flickered on. The main screen powered down too, going fully transparent with a photoreactive smear of blackness blotting out the sun's glare and most of the space station. I briefly glimpsed the grabship approaching—basically a one-man vessel with a massive engine to the rear and a hydraulically operated triclaw extending from the nose—before it disappeared back into the smear. They used such ships here since a large-enough proportion of their visitors weren't to be trusted to get simple docking maneuvers right, and wrong moves in that respect could demolish the relatively fragile bubble units and kill those inside.

A clanging against the hull followed by a lurch told me the grabship now had hold of Ulriss Fire and was taking us in. It would have been nice to check all this with exterior cameras—throwing up images on the row of subscreens below the main one—but I had to be very careful about power usage on approach. The Free Republic had been fired on before now, and any ship that showed energy usage above the level-enabling weapons, usually ended up on the mincing end of the infamous rail-gun.

Experience told me that in about twenty minutes the ship would be docked, so I unstrapped and propelled myself into the rear cabin where, in zero-g, I began pulling on my gear. Like many visitors here I took the precaution of putting on a light spacesuit of the kind that didn't constrict movement, but would keep me alive if there was a blowout. I'd scanned through their rules file, but found nothing much different from when I'd last read it: basically you brought nothing aboard that could cause a breach—this mainly concerned weaponry—nor any dangerous biologicals. You paid a docking tax and a departure tax. And anything you did in the intervening time was your own business so long as it didn't harm station personnel or the station itself. I strapped a heavy carbide knife to my boot, and at my waist holstered a pepper-pot stun gun. It could get rough in there sometimes.

Back in the cockpit I saw Ulriss Fire was now drawing into the station shadow. Structural members jutted out all around and ahead I could see an old-style carrier shell, like a huge hexagonal nut, trailing umbilicals and docking tunnel connected to the curve of one bubble unit. Unseen, the grabship inserted my vessel into place and various clangs and crashes ensued.

"Okay, you can power up your airlock now—nothing else, mind."

I did as instructed, watching the display as the airlock connected up to an exterior universal lock, then I headed back to scramble out through the Ulriss Fire's airlock. The cramped interior of the carrier shell smelled of mold. I waited there, holding onto the knurled rods of something that looked like a piece of zero-g exercise equipment, eyeing brownish splashes on the walls while a saucer-shaped scanning drone dropped down on a column and gave me the once-over, then I proceeded to the docking tunnel, which smelled of urine. Beside the final lock into the bubble unit was a payment console, into which I inserted the required amount in New Carth Shillings. The lock opened to admit me and now I was of no further interest to station personnel. Others had come in like this. Some of their ships still remained docked. Some had been seized by those who owned the station to be broken for parts or sold on.

Clad in a coldsuit, Jael trudged through a thin layer of $CO_2$ snow toward the gates of the Arena. Glancing to either side, she eyed the numerous ships 2 down on the granite plain. Other figures were trudging in from them too and a lucky few were flying toward the place in gravcars. She'd considered pulling her trike out of storage, but it would have taken time to assemble and she didn't intend staying here any longer than necessary.

The entry arches—constructed of blocks of water ice as hard as iron at this temperature—were filled with the glimmering menisci of shimmer-shields, probably scavenged from the wreckage of ships floating about in the Graveyard, or maybe from the surface of one of the depopulated worlds. Reaching one of the arches, she pushed through a shield into a long anteroom into which all the arches debouched. The floor was flat granite cut with square spiral patterns for grip and a line of airlock doors punctuated the inner wall. This whole setup was provided for large crowds, which this place had never seen. Beside the airlock she approached was a teller machine of modern manufacture. She accessed it through her right-hand aug and made her payment electronically. The thick insulated lock door thumped open, belching vapor into the frigid air, freezing about her and falling as ice dust. Inside the lock, the temperature rose rapidly. $CO_2$ ice ablated from her boots and clothing, and after checking the atmosphere reading down in the corner of her visor she retracted visor and hood back down into the collar of her suit.

Beyond the next door was a pillared hall containing a market. Strolling between the stalls she observed the usual tourist tat sold in such places in the Polity, and much else besides. There, under a plasmel dome, someone was selling weapons, and beyond his stall she could hear the hiss and crack of his wares being tested in a thick-walled shooting gallery. There a row of food vendors were serving everything from burgers to alien arthropods you ate while they were still alive and that apparently gave some kind of high. The smell of coffee wafted across, along with tobacco, cannabis, and other more esoteric smokes.

All around the walls of the hall, stairs wound up to other levels, some connecting above to the tunnels leading to the arena itself, others to the pens and others to private concerns. She knew where to go, but had some other business to conduct first with a dealer in biologicals. Anyway, she didn't want the man she had specifically come here to see to think she was in a hurry, or anxious to buy the item he had on offer.

The dealer's emporium was built between four pillars, three floors tall and reaching the ceiling. The lower floor was a display area with four entrances around the perimeter. She entered and looked around. Aisles cut to a central spiral stair between tanks, terrariums, cages, display cases, and stock-search screens. She spotted a tank full of Spatterjay leeches, "Immortality in a bite! Guaranteed!," a cage in which big scorpionlike insects were tearing into a mass of purple and green bones and meat, and a display containing little tubes of seeds below pictures of the plants they would produce. Mounting the stairs, she climbed to the next floor where two catadapts were studying something displayed on the screens of a nanoscope. They looked like customers, as did the thin woman who was peering into a cylindrical tank containing living Dracocorp augs. On the top floor, Jael found who she was looking for.

The office was small, the rest of the floor obviously used for living accommodation. The woman with a severe skin complaint, baggy, layered clothing, and a tricorn hat, sat back with heavy snow boots up on her desk, crusted fingers up against her aug while she peered at screens showing views of those on the floors below. She was nodding—obviously conducting some transaction or conversation by aug. Jael stepped into the room, plumped herself down in one of the form chairs opposite, and waited. The woman glanced at her, smiled to expose a carnivore's teeth, and held up one finger. Wait one moment.

Her business done, the woman took her feet off the desk and turned her chair so she was facing Jael.

"Well, what can I do for you?" she asked, utterly focused. "Anything under any sun is our motto. We're also an agent for Dracocorp and are now branching out into cosmetics."

"Forgive me," said Jael, "if I note that you're not the best advert for the cosmetics."

The woman leant an elbow on the table, reached up, and peeled a thick dry flake of skin from her cheek. "That's because you don't know what you're seeing. Once the change is complete my skin will be resistant to numerous acids and even to vacuum."

"I'm here to sell," said Jael.

The woman sat back, not quite so focused now. "I see. Well, we're always prepared to take a look at what . . . people have to offer."

Jael removed a small sample tube from her belt cache, placed it on the desk edge and rolled it across. The woman took it up, peered inside, a powerful lens clicking down from her hat to cover her eye.

"Interesting. What are they?"

Jael tapped a finger against her right-hand aug. "This would be quicker."

A message flashed across to her, giving her a secure loading address. She transmitted the file she had compiled about the seeds gathered on that dusty little planet where she had obtained her real prize. The woman went blank for a few minutes while she ran through the data. Jael scanned around the room, wondering what security there was here.

"I think we can do business—once I've confirmed all this."

"Please confirm away."

The woman took the tube over to a combined nanoscope and multi-spectrum scanner and inserted it inside.

Jael continued, "But I don't want money, Desorla."

Desorla froze, staring at the scope's display. After a moment she said, "This all seems in order." She paused, head bowed. "I haven't heard that name in a long while."

"I find things out," said Jael.

Desorla turned and eyed the gun Jael now held. "What do you want?"

"I want you to tell me where Penny Royal is hiding."

Desorla chuckled unconvincingly. "Looking for legends? You can't seriously—"

Jael aimed and fired three times. Two explosions blew cavities in the walls, a third explosion flung paper fragments from a shelf of books, and a metallic tongue bleeding smoke slumped out from behind. Two cameras and the security drone—Jael had detected nothing else.

"I'm very serious," said Jael. "Please don't make me go get my doctor's bag."

Broeven took one look at me and turned white, well, as pale as a Krodorman can get. He must have sent some sort of warning signal, because suddenly two heavies appeared out of the fug from behind him—one a boosted woman with the face of an angel and a large grey military aug affixed behind her ear, the other an ophidapt man who was making a point of extruding the carbide claws from his fingertips. The thin guy sitting opposite Broeven glanced round, then quickly drained his schooner of beer, took up a wallet from the table, nodded to Broeven, and departed. I sauntered over, turned the abandoned chair round, and sat astride it.

"You've moved up in the world," I said, nodding to Broeven's protection.

"So what do I call you now?" he asked, the whorls in the thick skin of his face flushing red.

"Rho, which is actually my real name."

"That's nice—we didn't get properly acquainted last time we met." He held up a finger. "Gene, get Rho a drink. Malt whisky do you?"

I nodded. The woman frowned in annoyance and departed. Perhaps she thought the chore beneath her.

"So what can I do for you, Rho?" he inquired.

"Information."

"Which costs."

"Of course." I peered down at the object the guy here before me had left on the table. It was a small chainglass case containing a strip of chameleoncloth with three crab-shaped and, if they were real, gold buttons pinned to it. "Are those real?"

"They are. People know better than to try cheating me now."

I looked up. "I never cheated you."

"No, you promised not to open the outer airlock door if I told you what you wanted to know. My life in exchange for information and you stuck to your side of the deal. I can't say that makes me feel any better about it."

"But you're a businessman," I supplied.

"But I'm a businessman."

The boosted woman returned carrying a bottle of ersatz malt and a tumbler that she slammed down on the table before me, before stepping back. I can't say I liked having her behind me. I reached down and carefully opened a belt pouch, feeling the tension notch up a bit. The ophidapt partially unfolded his arms and fully extended his claws. I took out a single blue stone and placed it next to the glass case. Broeven eyed the stone for a moment then picked it up between gnarled forefinger and thumb. He produced a reader and placed the etched sapphire inside.

"Ten thousand," he said. "For what?"

"That's for services rendered—twenty-three years ago—and if you don't want to do further business with me, you keep it and I leave."

He slipped the sapphire, and the glass case, into the inner pocket of his heavy coat, then sat upright, contemplating me. I thought for a moment he was going to get up and leave. Trying to remain casual, I scanned around the interior of the bar and noticed it wasn't so full as I'd remembered it being and everyone seemed a bit subdued, conversations whispered and more furtive, no one getting shit-faced.

"Very well," he said. "What information do you require?"

"Two things: first I want everything you can track down about gab-bleducks possibly in or near the Graveyard." That got me a rather quizzical expression. "And second I want everything you can give me about Jael Feogril's dealings over the last year or so."

"A further ten thousand," he said, and I read something spooked in his expression. I took out another sapphire and slid it across to him. He checked it with his reader and pocketed it before uttering another word.

"I'll give you two things." He made a circular gesture with one finger. "Jael Feogril might be dealing out of her league."

"Go on."

"Them . . . a light destroyer . . . Jael's ship docked with it briefly only a month ago, before departing. They're still out there."

I realized then why it seemed so quiet in the bar and elsewhere in the station. The people here were those who hadn't run for cover, and were perhaps wishing they had. It was never the healthy option to remain in the vicinity of the Prador.

"And the second thing?"

"The location of the only gabbleduck in the Graveyard, which I can give you without even doing any checking, since I've already given it to Jael Feogril."

After he'd provided the information I headed away—I had enough to be going on with, and maybe, if I moved fast . . . I paused on my way back to my ship, seeing that Broeven's female heavy was walking along behind me, and turned to face her. She walked straight past me, saying, "I'm not a fucking waitress."

She seemed in an awful hurry.

On the stone floor two opponents faced off. Both were men, both were boosted. Jael wondered if people like them ever considered treatment for excessive testosterone production. The bald-headed thug was unarmed and resting his hands on his knees as he caught his breath, twin-pupil eyes fixed on his opponent. The guy with the long queue of hair was also unarmed, though the platelike lumps all over his overly muscled body were evidence of subcutaneous armor. After a moment they closed and began hammering at each other again, fists impacting with meaty snaps against flesh, blows blocked and diverted, the occasional kick slamming home, though neither of them was really built for that kind of athleticism.

Inevitably, one of them was called Tank—the one with the queue. The other was called Norris. These two had been hammering away at each other for twenty minutes to the growing racket from the audience, but whether that noise arose from the spectators' enjoyment of the show or because they wanted to get to the next event was debatable.

Eventually, after many scrappy encounters, Tank managed to deliver an axe kick to the side of Norris's head and laid him out. Tank, though the winner, needed to be helped from the arena too, obviously having overextended himself with that last kick. Once the area was clear, the next event was announced and a gate opened somewhere below Jael. She observed a great furry muscular back and wide head as a giant mongoose shot out. The creature came to an abrupt stop in the middle of the arena and stood up to the height of a man on its hindquarters. Jael discarded her beer tube and stood, heading over toward the pens. The crowd was now shouting for one of the giant cobras the mongoose dispatched with utterly unamazing regularity. She wasn't really all that interested.

The doors down into the pens were guarded by a thug little different to those who had been in the ring below. He was there because previous security systems had often been breached and some of the fighters, animal, human, or machine, had been knobbled.

"I'm here to see Koober," said Jael.

The man eyed her for a moment. "Jael Feogril," he said, reaching back to open the door. "Of course you are."

Jael stepped warily past then descended the darkened stair.

Koober was operating a small electric forklift on the tines of which rested the corpse of a seal. He raised a hand to her then motored forward to drop the load down into one of the pens. Jael stepped over and peered down at the ratty-looking polar bear that took hold of the corpse and dragged it back across the ice to one corner, leaving a gory trail.

Koober, a thin hermaphrodite in much-repaired mesh inlaid overalls, leapt off the forklift and gestured. "This way." He led her down a stair into moist rancid corridors then finally to an armored door that he opened with a press of his hand against a palm lock. At the back of the circular chamber within, squatting in its own excrement, was the animal she had come to see—thick chains leading from a steel collar to secure it to the back wall.

A poor-looking specimen, about the size of a Terran black bear, its head was bowed low, the tip of its bill resting against the ground. Lying on the filthy stone beside it were the dismembered remains of something obviously grown hastily in a vat—weak, splintered bones and watery flesh, tumors exposed like bunches of grapes. While Jael watched, the gabbleduck abruptly hissed and heaved its head upright. Its green eyes ran in an arc across its domed head, there were twelve or so of them: two large egg-shaped ones toward the center, two narrow ones below these like underscores, two rows of small round ones arcing out to terminate against two triangular ones. They all had lids—the outer two blinking open and closed alternately. Its conjoined forelimbs were folded mummy-like across the raised crosshatch ribbing of its chest, its gut was baggy and veined, and purple sores seeped in its brown-green skin.

"And precisely how much did you want for this?" inquired Jael disbelievingly.

"It's very rare," said Koober. "There's a restriction on export now and that's pushed prices up. You won't find any others inside the Graveyard, and those running wild on Polity worlds have mostly been tagged and are watched."

"Why then are you selling it?"

Koober looked shifty—something he seemed better at doing than looking after the animals he provided for the arena. "It's not suitable."

"You mean it won't fight," said Jael.

"Shunder-club froob," said the gabbleduck, but its heart did not seem to be in it.

"All it does is sit there and do that. We put it up against the lion"—he pointed at some healing claw marks in its lower stomach—"and it just sat there and starting muttering to itself. The lion tried to jump out of the arena."

Jael nodded to herself, then turned away. "Not interested."

"Wait!" Koober grabbed her arm. She caught his hand, turned it into a wrist lock, forcing him down to his knees.

"Don't touch me." She released him.

"If it's a matter of the price—"

"It's a matter of whether it will even survive long enough for you to get it aboard my ship, and even then I wonder how long it will survive afterward."

"Look, I'll be taking a loss, but I'm sure we can work something out . . . ." Inside, Jael smiled. When the deal was finally struck she allowed that smile out, for even if the creature died she might well net a profit just selling its corpse. She had no intention of letting it die. The medical equipment, and related gabbleduck physiology files aboard

Kobashi should see to that, along with her small cargo of frozen Masadan grazers—the gabbleduck's favored food.

I was feeling slightly pissed off when, after the interminable departure from Paris station, the grabship finally released Ulriss Fire. Even as the grabship carried my ship out I'd seen another ship departing the station under its own power. It seemed that there were those for whom the rules did not apply, or those who knew who to bribe.

"Run system checks," I instructed.

"Ooh, I never thought of that," replied Ulriss.

"And there was me thinking AIs were beyond sarcasm."

"It's a necessary tool used for communicating with a lower species," the ship's AI replied. I still think it was annoyed that I wouldn't let it use the chameleonware.

"Take us under," I said, ignoring the jibe.

Sudden acceleration pushed me back into my chair, and I felt, at some point deep inside my skull, the U-space engine come online. My perception distorted, the stars in the cockpit screen faded, and the screen greyed out. It lasted maybe a few seconds, then Ulriss Fire shuddered like a ground car rolling over a mass of deep potholes, and a starry view flicked back into place.

"What the fuck happened?"

"Checking," said Ulriss.

I began checking as well, noting that we'd traveled only about eighty million miles and had surfaced in the real in deep space. However, I was getting mass readings out there.

"We hit USER output," Ulriss informed me.

I just sat there for a moment, wracking my brains to try and figure out what a "user" was. I finally admitted defeat. "I've no idea what you're talking about."

"I see," said Ulriss, in an irritatingly superior manner. "The USER acronym stands for Underspace Inference Emitter—"

"Shouldn't that be UIE, then?"

"Do you want to know what a USER is, or would you rather I began using my sarcasm tool again?"

"Sorry, do carry on."

"A USER is a device that shifts a singularity in and out of U-space via a runcible gate, thus creating a disturbance that knocks any ships that are within range out of that continuum. The USER here is a small one aboard the Polity dreadnought currently three thousand miles away from us. I don't think we were the target. I think that was the cruiser now coming up to port."

With the skin crawling on my back, I took up the joystick and asserted positional control, nudging the ship round with a spurt of air from its attitude jets. Stars swung across the screen, then a large ugly-looking vessel swung into view. It looked like a flattened pear, but one stretched from a point on its circumference. It was battered, its brassy exotic armor showing dents and burns that its memform and s-con grids had been unable to deal with, and that hadn't been repaired since. Missile ports and the mouths of rail-guns and beam weapons dotted that hull, but they looked perfectly serviceable. Ulriss had neglected to mention the word Prador before the word cruiser. This is what had everyone checking their online wills and talking in whispers back in Paris.

"Stealth mode?" suggested Ulriss with a degree of smugness.

"Fucking right," I replied.

The additional instruments came alight and a luminescent ribbing began to track across the screen before me. I wondered how good the chameleonware was, since maybe bad chameleonware would put us in even greater danger—the Prador suspecting some sort of attack if they detected us.

"And now if you could ease us away from that thing?"

The fusion drive stuttered randomly—a low power note and firing format that wouldn't put out too regular ionization. We fell away, the Prador cruiser thankfully receding, but now, coming into view, a Polity dreadnought. At one time, the Prador vessel would have outclassed a larger Polity ship. It was an advantage the nasty aliens maintained throughout their initial attack during the war: exotic metal armor that could take a ridiculously intense pounding. Now Polity ships were armored in a similar manner, and carried weapons and EM warfare techniques that could penetrate to the core of Prador ships.

"What the hell is happening here?" I wondered.

"There is some communication occurring, but I cannot penetrate it."

"Best guess?"

"Well, ECS does venture into the Graveyard, and it is still considered Polity territory. Maybe the Prador have been getting a little bit too pushy."

I nodded to myself. Confrontations like these weren't that uncommon in the Graveyard, but this one was bloody inconvenient. While I waited, something briefly blanked the screen. When it came back on again I observed a ball of light a few hundred miles out from the cruiser, shrinking rather than expanding, then winking out.

"CTD imploder," Ulriss informed me.

I was obviously behind the times. I knew a CTD was an antimatter bomb, but an "imploder"? I didn't ask.

After a little while the Prador ship's steering thrusters stabbed out into vacuum and ponderously turned it over, then its fusion engines flared to life and began taking it away.

"Is that USER still on?" I asked.

"It is."

"Why? I don't see the point."

"Maybe ECS is just trying to make a point."

The USER continued functioning for a further five hours while the Prador ship departed. I almost got the feeling that those in the Polity dreadnought knew I was there and were deliberately delaying me. When it finally stopped, it took another hour before U-space had settled down enough for us to enter it without being flung out again. It had all been very frustrating.

People knew that if a ship was capable of traveling through U-space it required an AI to control its engines. Mawkishly they equated artificial intelligence with the godlike creations that controlled the Polity, somehow forgetting that colony ships with U-space engines were leaving the Solar System before the Quiet War, and before anyone saw anything like the silicon intelligences that were about now. The supposedly primitive Prador, who had nearly smashed the Polity, failed because they did not have AI, apparently. How then did they run the U-space engines in their ships? It came down, in the end, to the definition of AI—something that had been undergoing constant revision for centuries. The thing that controlled the engines in the Kobashi, Jael did not call an AI. She called it a "control system" or sometimes, a "Prador control system."

Kobashi surfaced from U-space on the edge of the Graveyard far from any sun. The coordinates Desorla had reluctantly supplied were constantly changing in relation to nearby stellar bodies, but, checking her scanners, Jael saw that they were correct, if this black planetoid—a wanderer between stars—was truly the location of Penny Royal. The planetoid was not much bigger than Earth's Moon, was frigid, without atmosphere, and had not seen any volcanic activity quite possibly for billions of years. However, her scans did reveal a cannibalized ship resting on the surface and bonded-regolith tunnels winding away from it like worm casts to eventually disappear into the ground. She also measured EM output—energy usage—for signs of life. Positioning Kobashi geostationary above the other ship, she began sending signals.

"Penny Royal, I am Jael Feogril and I have come to buy your services. I know that the things you value are not the same as those valued by . . . others. If you assist me, you will gain access to an Atheter memstore, from which you may retain a recording."

She did not repeat the message. Penny Royal would have seen her approach and been monitoring her constantly ever since. The thing called Penny Royal missed very little.

Eventually she got something back: landing coordinates—nothing else. She took Kobashi down, settling between two of those tunnels with the nose of her ship only fifty yards from the other ship's hull. Studying the other vessel she recognized a Polity destroyer, its sleek lines distorted, parts of it missing as if it had been slowly been draining into the surrounding tunnels. After a moment she saw an irised airlock open. No message—the invitation was in front of her. Heading back into her quarters she donned an armored spacesuit, took up her heavy pulse-rifle with its underslung minilauncher, her sidearm, and a selection of grenades. Likely the weapons would not be enough if Penny Royal launched some determined attack, but they might and that was enough of a reason. She resisted the impulse to go and check on the gabbleduck, but it was fine, its sores healed and flesh building up on its bones, its nonsensical statements much more emphatic.

Beyond Kobashi her boots crunched on a scree surface. Her suit's visor set to maximum light amplification, she peered down at a surface that seemed to consist entirely of loose flat hexagonal crystals, like coins. They were a natural formation and nothing to do with this planetoid's resident. However, the thing that stabbed up through this layer nearby—like an eyeball impaled on a thin curved thorn of metal—certainly belonged to Penny Royal.

Jael finally stepped into the airlock, and noticed that the inner door was open too, so she would not be shedding her spacesuit. For no apparent reason other than to unnerve her, the first lock door swiftly closed once she was through. Within the ship she necessarily turned on her suit lights to complement the light amplification. The interior had been stripped right down to the hull members. All that Penny Royal had found no use for elsewhere, lay in a heap to one side of the lock, perhaps ready to be thrown outside. The twenty or so crew members had been desiccated—hard vacuum freeze-drying and preserving them. They rested in a tangled pile like some nightmare monument. Jael noticed the pile consisted only of woody flesh and frangible bone. No clothing there, no augs, no jewelry. It occurred to her that Penny Royal had not thrown these corpses outside because the entity might yet find a use for them.

She scanned about herself, not quite sure where to go now. Across the body of the ship from her was the mouth of one of those tunnels, curving down into darkness. There? No, to her right the mouth of another tunnel emitted heat a little above the ambient. Stepping over hull beams she began to make her way toward it, then silvery tentacular fingers eased out around the lip of the tunnel and heaved out an object two yards across and seemingly formed by computer junk from the ship compressed into a sphere. Lights glimmered inside the tangle and it extruded antennas, and eyes like the one she had seen outside. Settling down it seemed to unravel slightly, whereupon a fleshless golem unpeeled from its surface, stood upright, and advanced a couple of paces, a thick ribbed umbilicus still keeping it connected.

During the Prador-Human war it had been necessary to quickly manufacture the artificial intelligences occupying stations, ships, and drones, for casualties were high. Quality control suffered and these intelligences, which in peacetime would have needed substantial adjustments, were sent to the front. As a matter of expediency, flawed crystal got used rather than discarded. Personality fragments were copied, sometimes not very well, successful fighters or tacticians recopied. The traits constructed or duplicated were not necessarily those evincing morality. Some of these entities went rogue and became what were described as black AIs.

Like Penny Royal.

Standing at his shoulder, the boosted woman, Gene, gave Koober the confidence to defy me. I'd already told him that I knew Jael had bought the gabbleduck from him, I just wanted to know if he knew anything else: who else she might have seen here, where she was going . . . anything really. I was equally curious to know how Broeven's ex-employee had ended up here. It struck me that this went beyond the bounds of coincidence.

"I don't have to tell you nothing, Sandman," he said, using my old name with its double meaning.

"True, you don't," I replied. I really hated how the scum I'd known twenty years ago all seemed to have floated to the top. "Which is why I'm prepared to pay for what you can tell me."

He glanced back at his protection, then crossed his arms. "You were the big man once, but that ain't so now. I got my place here at the Arena and I got a good income. I don't even have to speak to you." He unfolded his arms and waved a finger imperiously. "Now piss off."

Not only was he defiant, but stupid. The woman, no matter how vigilant, could not protect him from a seeker bullet or a pin, coated with bone-eating nanite, glued to a door handle. But I didn't do that sort of stuff now. I was retired. I carefully reached into my belt pouch and took out one of my remaining etched sapphires. I would throw it, and while the gem arced through the air toward Koober and the woman, I reckoned on getting the drop on them. My pepper-pot stun gun was lodged in the back of my belt. Of course I'd take her down first. I tossed the gem and began to reach.

She moved. Koober went over her foot and was heading for the ground. The sapphire glimmered in the air still as the barrel of the pulse-gun centered on my forehead. I guess I was rusty, because I didn't even consider throwing myself aside. For a moment I just thought, That's it, but no field-accelerated pulse of aluminum dust blew my head apart. She caught the gem in her other hand and flipped it straight back at me. With my free hand I caught it, my other hand relaxing its grip on my gun and carefully easing out to one side, fingers spread.

"I believe my boss just told you to leave," she said.

Koober was lying on the floor swearing, then he looked up and paused—only now realizing what had happened.

I nodded an acknowledgment to Gene, turned, and quickly headed for the stair leading up from the pens, briefly glimpsed an oversized mongoose chewing on the remains of a huge snake on the arena floor, then headed back toward the market where I might pick up more information. What the hell was a woman like her doing with a lowlife like Koober? It made no sense, and the coincidence of her being here just stretched things too far. I wondered if Broeven had sent her to try to cash in—guessing I was probably after something valuable. Such thoughts concerned me—that's my excuse. She came at me from a narrow side-tunnel. I only managed to turn a little before she grabbed me, spun me round, and slammed me against the wall of the exit tunnel. I turned, and again found myself looking down the barrel of that pulse-gun. People around us quickly made themselves scarce.

"Koober had second thoughts about letting you go," she said.

"Really?" I managed.

"He is a little slow, sometimes," she opined. "It occurred to him, once you were out of sight, that you might resent his treatment of you and come back to slip cyanide in his next soy burger."

"He's a vegetarian?"

"It's working with the animals—put him off meat."

I watched her carefully, wondering why I was still alive. "Are you going to kill me?"

"I haven't decided yet."

"Have you ever killed anyone?"

"Many people, but in most cases the choice was theirs."

"That's very moral of you."

"So it would seem," she agreed. "Koober is shit-scared of you. Apparently you're a multiple murderer?"

"Hit man."

"Murderer."

Ah, I thought I knew what she was now.

"I think you know precisely who I am and what I was," I said. "Now I'm a xeno-archaeologist trying to track down stolen goods."

"I stayed here too long," she said distractedly, shaking her head. "It was going to be my pleasure to shut Koober down." She paused for a moment, considering. "You should stay out of this, Rho. This has gone beyond you."

"If you say so," I said. "You've got the gun."

She lowered her weapon, then abruptly holstered it. "If you don't believe me, then I suggest you go and see a dealer in biologicals called Desorla. Apparently Jael visited her before coming to see Koober, and their dealings involved Jael shooting out the cameras and security drones in Desorla's office."

"Just biologicals?"

"Desorla has  . . . connections."

She moved away and right then I felt no inclination to go after her. Maybe she was feeding me a line of bullshit or maybe she was giving me the lead I needed. If not, I'd come back to the pen well prepared.

In the market, one of the stall holders quickly directed me toward Desorla's emporium. I entered through one of the floor-level doors and found no activity inside. A spiral staircase led up, but a gate had been drawn across it and locked. I recognized the kind of lock immediately and set to work on it with the tools about my person. Like I said, I was rusty, it took me nearly thirty seconds to break the programs. I climbed up, scanned the next floor, then climbed higher still to the top floor.

The office was clean and empty, so I kicked in the flimsy door into the living accommodation. Nothing particularly unusual here . . . then I saw the blood on the floor and the big glass bottle on her coffee table. Stepping round the spatters I peered into the bottle, and, in the crumpled and somewhat scabby pink mass inside, a nightmare eyeless face peered out at me. Then something dripped on top of my head. I looked up . . . .

Over by the window I caught my breath, but no one was giving me time for that. Arena security thugs were running toward the emporium and beyond them I could see Gene striding off toward the exit. I opened the window just as the thugs entered the building below me, did a combination of scramble and fall down the outside of the building and hit the stone flat on my back. I had to catch my breath then. After a moment I heaved myself upright and headed for the exit, closing up the visor and hood of my envirosuit and keeping Gene just in sight. I went fast through an airlock far to the left of her, and some paces ahead of her, and was soon running down counting arches. I drew my carbide knife and dropped down beside one arch, hoping I'd counted correctly.

She stepped out to my left. I knew I could not give her the slightest chance or she would take me down yet again. I drove the knife in to the side, cut down, grabbed and pulled. In a gout of icy fog her visor skittered across the stone. Choking, she staggered away from me, even then drawing her pulse-gun, which must have been cold-adapted. I drove a foot into her sternum, knocked the last of her air out. Pulse-gun shots tracked along the frigid stone past me and I brought the edge of my hand down on her wrist, cracking bone, and knocking the weapon away. Her fist slammed into my ribs and her foot came up to nearly take my head off. Blind and suffocating, she was the hardest opponent I'd faced hand-to-hand . . . or maybe it was that rustiness again. But she went down, eventually, and I dragged her to Ulriss Fire before anoxia killed her.

"Okay," I said as she regained consciousness. "What the fuck killed her?"

After a moment of peering at the webbing straps binding her into the chair, she said, "You broke my wrist."

"Talk to me and I'll let my autodoc work on it. You set me up, Gene. Is that your real name?"

She nodded absently, though whether that was in answer to my question I couldn't tell. "I noticed you said 'what' rather than 'who.'"

"A human who takes the trouble to skin someone alive and nail them to the ceiling without making a great deal more mess than that shouldn't be classified as a who. It's a thing." I watched her carefully—trying to read her. "So maybe it was a thing . . . rogue golem?"

"Rho Var Olssen, employed by ECS for wet ops outside the Line, a sort of one-man vengeance machine for the Polity, who maybe started to like his job just a little too much. Who are you to righteously talk about classifications?"

"So you know about me. I had you typed when you insisted on calling me a murderer. Nothing quite so moralistic as an ECS agent working outside of her remit—helps to justify it all."

"Fuck you."

"Hit a nerve did I?" I paused, thinking that perhaps I was being a little naïve. She was baiting me to lead me away from the point. "So it was a golem that killed Desorla?"

"In a sense," she admitted grudgingly. "She was watched and she said too much—to Jael, specifically."

"Tell me more about Jael."

Staring at me woodenly she said, "What's to tell? We knew her interest in ancient technology and we knew she kept a careful eye on people like you. We put something in the way of your sifter and made sure she found out about it."

I felt hollow. "The memstore . . . it's a fake?"

"No, it's the real thing, Rho. It had to be."

I thought about me lying on the floor of my home with a rock hammer embedded in my skull. "I could have died."

"An acceptable level of collateral damage in an operation like this," she said flatly.

I thought about that for one brief horrible moment. Really, there were many people on many worlds trying to find Atheter artifacts, but how many of them were like me? How many of them were so inconvenient? I imagined this was why some AI had chosen my life as an "acceptable level of collateral damage."

"And what is this operation?" I finally asked. "Are you out to nail Prador?" She laughed.

"I guess not," I said.

"You worked out what Jael was doing yourself. I don't know how . . . " She gazed at me for a moment, but I wasn't going to help her out. She continued, "If she can restore the mind to a gabbleduck, she has an item to sell to the Prador that will net her more wealth than even she would know how to spend. But there's a problem: you don't just feed the memstore to the gabbleduck, you're not even going to be able to jury-rig some kind of linkup using aug technology. That memstore is complex alien tech loaded in a language few can understand."

"She needs an AI . . . or something close . . . "

"On the button, but though some AIs might venture outside Polity law as we see it, there are certain lines even they won't cross. Handing over a living Atheter to the Prador is well over those lines."

"A Prador AI, then."

"The only ones they have are in their ships—their purpose utterly fixed. They don't have the flexibility."

"So what the fuck—"

"Ever heard of Penny Royal?" she interrupted.

I felt a surge of almost superstitious dread. "You have got to be shitting me."

"No shit, Rho. You can see this is out of your league. We're done here."

"You put some kind of tracer in the memstore."

She gave me a patronizing smile. "Too small. We needed U-tech."

Suddenly I got the idea. "You put it in the gabbleduck."

"We did." She stared at me for a long moment, then continued resignedly, "The signal remains constant, giving a Polity ship in the Graveyard the creature's location from moment to moment. The moment the gabbleduck is connected to the memstore, the signal shuts down, then we'll know that Penny Royal has control of both creature and store, and then the big guns move in. This is over, Rho. Can't you see that? You've played your part and now the game has moved as far beyond you as it has moved beyond me. It's time for us both to go home."

"No," I said. I guessed she didn't understand how being tortured, then nearly killed, had really ticked me off. "It's time for you to tell me how to find Jael. I've still got a score to settle with her."

Jael did not like being this close to a golem. Either they were highly moral creatures who served the Polity and would not look kindly on her actions, and who were thoroughly capable of doing something about them, or they were the rare amoralimmoral kind, and quite capable of doing something really nasty. No question here—the thing crammed in beside her in the airlock was a killer, or, rather, it was a remote probe, a submind that was part of a killer. As she understood it, Penny Royal had these submind golem scattered throughout the Graveyard, often contributing to the title of the place.

After the lock pressurized, the inner door opened to admit them into the Kobashi. While Jael removed her spacesuit the golem just stood to one side—a static silver skeleton with hardware in its rib cage, cybermotors at its joints and interlinked down its spine, and blue-irised eyeballs in the sockets of its skull. She wondered if it had willingly subjected itself to Penny Royal's will or been taken over. Probably the latter.

"This way," she said to it once she was ready, and led the way back toward the ship's hold. Behind her the golem followed with a clatter of metallic feet. Why did it no longer wear syntheflesh and skin? Just to make it more menacing? She wasn't sure Penny Royal was that interested in interacting with people. Maybe the usual golem coverings just didn't last in this environment.

At her aug command a bulkhead door thumped open and she paused beside it to don a breather mask before stepping through into an area caged off from the rest of the hold. The air within was low in oxygen and would slowly suffocate a human, but it mixing with the rest of the air in the ship while this door was open wasn't a problem since the pressure differential pushed the ship air into this space. The briefly higher oxygen levels would not harm the hold's occupant since its body was rugged enough to survive a range of environments—probably its kind was engineered that way long ago. Beyond the caged area in which they stood, the floor was layered a foot deep with flute grass rhizomes—as soggy underfoot as sphagnum. The walls displayed Masadan scenery overlaid with bars so the occupant didn't make the mistake of trying to run off through them. Masadan wildlife sounds filled the air and there were even empty tricone shells on the rhizome mat for further authenticity.

The gabbleduck looked a great deal more alert and a lot healthier than when Koober had owned it. As always, when she came in here, it was squatting in one corner. Other than via the cameras in here, she had seen it do nothing else. It was as if, every time she approached, it heard her and moved to that corner, which should not have been possible since the bulkhead door was thoroughly insulated.

"Subject appears adequate," said the golem. "It will be necessary to move it into the complex for installation."

"Gruvver fleeg purnok," said the gabbleduck dismissively.

"The phonetic similarity of the gabble to human language has always been puzzling," said the golem.

"Right," said Jael. "The memstore?" She gestured to the door and the golem obligingly moved out ahead of her.

She overtook the golem in the annex to the main airlock, opened another bulkhead door, and led the way into her living area. Here she paused. "Before I show you this next item, there are one or two things we need to agree on." She turned and faced the golem. "The gabbleduck and the memstore must go no deeper into your complex than half a mile."

The golem just stared at her, waiting, not asking the question a human would have asked. It annoyed Jael that Penny Royal probably understood her reasoning and it annoyed her further that she still felt the need to explain. "That keeps it within the effective blast radius of my ship. If I die, or if you try to take from me the gabbleduck or the memstore, I can aug a signal back here to start up the U-space engine, the field inverted and ten degrees out of phase. The detonation would excise a fair chunk of this planetoid."

The golem just said, "The AI here is of Prador manufacture."

"It is."

"My payment will be a recording of the Atheter memstore, and a recording of the Prador AI."

"That seems . . . reasonable, though you'll receive the recording of the Prador AI just before I'm about to leave." She didn't want Penny Royal to have time to work out how to crack her ship's security.

At that moment, the same Prador AI—without speaking—alerted her to activity outside the ship. Using her augs she inspected an external view from the ship's cameras. One of the tunnel tubes, its mouth filled with some grublike machine, was advancing toward Kobashi.

"What's going on outside?" she inquired politely.

"I presume you have no spacesuit for the gabbleduck?"

"Ah."

Despite her threat, Jael knew she wasn't fully in control here. She stepped up to one wall, via her aug commanding a safe to open. A steel bung a foot across eased out then hinged to one side. She reached in, picked up the memstore, then held it out to the golem. The test would come, she felt certain, when Penny Royal authenticated that small item.

The golem took the memstore between its finger and thumb and she noticed it had retained the syntheflesh pads of its fingers. It paused, frozen in place, then abruptly its rib cage split down the center and one half of it hinged aside. Within lay optics, the grey lump of a power supply, and various interconnected units like steel organs. There were also dark masses spread like multiarmed starfish that Jael suspected had not been there when this golem was originally constructed. It pressed the memstore into the center of one of these masses, which writhed as if in pain and closed over it.

"Unrecognized programming format," said the golem.

No shit, thought Jael.

The golem continued, "Estimate at one hundred and twenty gigabytes, synaptic mapping and chronology of implantation . . . ."

Jael felt a sudden foreboding. Though measuring a human mind in bytes wasn't particularly accurate, the best guestimate actually lay in the range of a few hundred megabytes, so this memstore was an order of magnitude larger. But then her assumption, and that of those who had found it, was that the memstore encompassed the life of one Atheter. This was not necessarily the case. Maybe the memories and mind maps of a thousand Atheter were stored in that little chunk of technology.

Finally the golem straightened up, reached inside its chest, and removed the memplant, passing it back to Jael. "We will begin when the tunnel connects," it said. "How will you move the gabbleduck?"

"Easy enough," said Jael, and went to find her tranquilizer gun.

Ulriss woke me with a "Rise and shine, the game is afoot . . . well, in a couple of hours—the signal is no longer Dopplering so Jael's ship is back in the real."

I lay there blinking at the ceiling as the lights gradually came up, then pushed back the heat sheet, heaved myself over the edge of the bunk, and dropped to the floor. I staggered, feeling slightly dizzy, my limbs leaden. It always takes me a little while to get functional after sleep, hence the two-hour warning from Ulriss. After a moment, I turned to peer at Gene, who lay slumbering in the lower bunk.

"Integrity of the collar?" I inquired.

"She hasn't touched it," the ship AI replied, "though she did try to persuade me to release her by appealing to my sense of loyalty to the organization that brought me into being."

"And your reply?"

"Whilst no right-thinking AI wants the Prador to get their hands on a living Atheter or one of their memstores, your intent to retrieve that store and by proxy carry out a sentence already passed on Jael Feogril should prevent rather than facilitate that. Polity plans will be hampered should you succeed, but, beside moral obligations, I am a free agent and Penny Royal's survival or otherwise is a matter of indifference to me. Should you fail, however, your death will not hamper Polity plans."

"Hey thanks—it's nice to know you care."

Sleepily, from the lower bunk, Gene said, "You're rather sensitive for someone who was once described as a walking abattoir."

"Ah," I said, "so you're frightened of me. That's why you gave me the coding of that U-space signal?"

She pushed back her blanket and sat up. She'd stripped down to a thin singlet and I found the sight rather distracting, as I suspect was the intention. Reaching up, she fingered the metal collar around her neck. "Of course I'm frightened—you've got control of this collar."

"Which will inject you with a short duration paralytic, not blow your head off as I earlier suggested," I replied.

She nodded. "You also suggested that if I didn't tell you what you wanted to know you would demonstrate on me the kind of things Jael did to you."

"I've never tortured anyone," I said, before remembering that she'd read my ECS record. "Well . . . not anyone that didn't deserve it."

"You would have used drugs, and the other techniques Jael used on you."

"True"—I nodded—"but I didn't need to." I gazed at her. "I think you've been involved in this operation for a while and rather resent not being in at the kill. I was your opportunity to change that. I understand—in the past I ended up in similar situations myself."

"Yes, you liked to be in at the kill," she said, and stooped down to pick up her clothing from where she had abandoned it on the floor—she'd sacked out after me, which had been okay as soon as I put the collar on her since Ulriss had been watching her constantly.

I grunted and went off to find a triple espresso.

After a breakfast of bacon, eggs, mushroom steak, beans, a liter of grapenut juice, and more coffee, I reached the stage of being able to walk through doors without bouncing off the doorjamb. Gene ate a megaprawn steak, drank a similar quantity of the juice, and copious quantities of white tea. I thought I might try her breakfast the next time I used stores or the synthesizer. Supposing there would be a next time—only a few minutes remained before we surfaced from U-space. Gene followed me into the cockpit and sat in the copilot's chair, which was about as redundant as the pilot's chair I sat in with the AI Ulriss running the ship.

We surfaced. The screen briefly showed stars, then banding began to travel across it. I glanced at the additional controls for chameleonware and saw that they had been activated.

"Ulriss—"

"Jael's ship is down on the surface of a free-roaming planetoid next to an old vessel that seems to have been stripped and from which bonded-regolith tunnels have spread."

"So Penny Royal is there and might see us," I supplied.

"True," Ulriss replied, but that was not my first concern. The view on the screen swung across, magnified, and switched to light amplification, bringing to the fore the planetoid itself and the Prador cruiser in orbit around it.

"Oh, shit," I opined.

We watched the cruiser as, using that stuttering burn of the fusion engine, Ulriss took us closer to the planetoid. Luckily there had been no reaction from the Prador ship to our arrival, and as we drew closer I saw a shuttle detach and head down.

"I wonder if this is part of Jael's plan," I said. "I would have thought she'd get the memstore loaded, then meet the Prador in some less vulnerable situation."

"Agreed," said Gene through gritted teeth. She glanced across at me. "What do you intend to do?"

"I intend to land." I adjusted to screen controls to give me a view of Jael's ship, the one next to it, and the surrounding spread of pipelike tunnels. "She's probably in there somewhere with the memstore and the gabbleduck. Shouldn't be a problem getting inside."

We watched the shuttle continue its descent and the subsequent flare of its thrusters as it decelerated over the network of tunnels.

"It could get . . . somewhat fraught down there. Do you have weapons?" Gene asked.

"I have weapons."

The Prador shuttle was now landing next to Jael's vessel.

"Let me come in with you," said Gene.

I didn't answer for a while. I just watched. Five Prador clad in armored spacesuits and obviously armed to the mandibles departed the shuttle. They went over to one of the tunnels and gathered there. I focused in closer in time to see them move back to get clear of an explosion. It seemed apparent that they weren't there at either Jael's or Penny Royal's invitation.

"Of course you can come," I said eventually.

Jael frowned at the distant sound of the explosion and the roar of atmosphere being sucked out—the latter sound was abruptly truncated as some emergency door closed. There seemed only one explanation: the Prador had placed a tracker on the Kobashi when she had gone to meet them.

"Can you deal with them?" she asked.

"I can deal with them," Penny Royal replied through its submind golem.

The AI itself continued working. Before Jael, the gabbleduck was stretched upright, steel bands around its body, and a framework clamping its head immovable. It kept reaching up with one of its foreclaws to probe and tug at the framework, but, heavily tranquilized, it soon lost interest, lowered its limb, and began muttering to itself.

From this point, equipment—control systems, an atmosphere plant and heaters, stacked processing racks, transformers, and other items obviously taken from the ship above—spread in every direction and seemed chaotically connected by optics and heavy-duty superconducting cables. Some of these snaked into one of the surrounding tunnels where she guessed the ship's fusion reactor lay. Lighting squares inset in the ceiling illuminated the whole scene. She wondered if Penny Royal had put this all together after her arrival. It seemed possible, for the AI, working amid all this like an iron squid, moved at a speed almost difficult to follow. Finally the AI moved closer to the gabbleduck, fitting into one side of the clamping framework a silver beetle of a ship's autodoc, which trailed optics to the surrounding equipment.

"The memstore," said Penny Royal, a ribbed tentacle with a spatulate end snapping out to hover just before Jael's chest.

"What about the Prador?" she asked. "Shouldn't we deal with them first?"

Two of the numerous eyes protruding on stalks from the AI's body flicked toward the golem, which abruptly stepped forward, grabbed a hold in that main body, then merged. In that moment Jael saw that it was one of many clinging there.

"They have entered my tunnels and approach," the AI replied.

It occurred to her then that Penny Royal's previous answer of "I can deal with them" was open to numerous interpretations.

"Are you going to stop them coming here?" she asked.

"No."

"They will try to take the memstore and the gabbleduck."

"That is not proven."

"They'll attack you."

"That is not proven."

Jael's frustration grew. "Very well." She unslung her combined pulse-rifle and launcher. "You are not unintelligent, but you seem to have forgotten about the instructions I left for the Kobashi on departing. Those Prador will try to take what is mine without paying for it, and I will try to stop them. If I die, the Kobashi detonates and we all die."

"Your ship will not detonate."

"What?"

"I broke your codes two point five seconds after you departed your ship. Your ship AI is of Prador construction, its basis the frozen brain tissue of a Prador first-child. The Prador have never understood that no code is unbreakable and your ship AI is no different. It would appear that you are no different."

Another boom and the thunderous roar of atmosphere departing reached them. Penny Royal quivered, a number of its eyes turning toward one tunnel mouth.

"However," it said with a heavy resignation, "these Prador are showing a marked lack of concern for my property, and I do not want them interrupting this interesting commission." Abruptly the golem began to peel themselves from Penny Royal's core, five in all, until what was left was a spiny skeletal thing. Dropping to the floor, they detached their umbilici and scuttled away. Jael shuddered—they moved without any emulation of humanity, sometimes on all fours, but fast, horribly fast. They also carried devices she could not clearly identify. She did not suppose their purpose to be anything pleasant.

"Now," said Penny Royal, snapping the spatulate end of its tentacle open and closed, "the memstore."

Jael reached into her belt cache, took out the memstore, and handed it over. The tentacle retracted and she lost it in a blur of movement. Items of equipment shifted and a transformer began humming. The autodoc pressed its underside against the gabbleduck's domed head and closed its gleaming metallic limbs around it. She heard a snickering, swiftly followed by the sound of a bone drill. The gabbleduck jerked and reached up. Tentacles sped in and snaked around its limbs, clamping them in place.

"Wharfle klummer," said the gabbleduck with an almost frightening clarity.

Jael scanned around the chamber. Over to her right, across the chamber from the tunnel mouth where Penny Royal had earlier glanced at—the one it seemed likely the Prador would be coming from if they made it this far—was a stack of internal walling and structural members from the cannibalized ship. She headed over, ready to duck for cover, and from there watched the AI carry out its commission.

How long would it take? She had no idea, but it seemed likely that it wouldn't be long. Now the autodoc would be making nanotube synaptic connections in line with a program the AI had constructed from the cerebral schematic in the memstore, it would be firing off electrical impulses and feeding in precise mixes of neurochemicals—all the stuff of memory, thought, mind. Already the gabbleduck seemed straighter, its pose more serious, its eyes taking on a cold metallic glitter. Or was she just seeing what she hoped for?

"Klummer wharfle," it said. Wasn't that one of those frustrating things for the linguists who studied the gabble, that no single gabbleduck had ever repeated its meaningless words? "Klummer klummer," it continued. "Wharfle."

"Base synaptic network established," said Penny Royal. "Loading at one quarter—layered format."

Jael wasn't entirely sure what that meant, but it sounded like the AI was succeeding. Then, abruptly, the gabbleduck made a chittering, whistling, clicking sound, some of the whistles so intense they seemed to stab straight in behind Jael's eyes. Something else happened: a couple of optic cables started smoking, then abruptly shriveled, a processing rack slumped, something like molten glass pouring out and hissing on the cold stone. After a moment, Penny Royal released its grip upon the creature's claws.

"Loading complete."

After a two-tone buzzing Jael recognized as the sound of bone and cell welders working together, the autodoc retracted. The gabbleduck reached up and scratched its head. It made that sound again, and, after a moment, Penny Royal replied in kind. The creature shrugged and all its bonds folded away. It dropped to the floor and squatted like some evil Buddha. It did not look in the least bit foolish.

"They chose insentience," said Penny Royal, "and put in place the means of retaining that state, in U-space, constructed there before they sacrificed their minds."

"And what does that mean?" Jael asked.

Three stalked eyes swiveled toward her. "It means, human, that in resurrecting me you fucked up big-time—now, go away."

She wondered how it had happened: when Penny Royal copied the memstore, or through some leakage during the loading process. There must have been a hidden virus or worm in the store.

Suddenly, both the gabbleduck and Penny Royal were enclosed in some kind of bubble. It shifted slightly, and, where it intersected any of the surrounding equipment, sheared clean through. Within, something protruded out of nothingness like the peak of a mountain—hints of vastness beyond. Ripples, like those in sunlit water, traveled down to the tip, where they ignited a dull glow that grew brighter with each succeeding ripple.

Jael, always prepared to grab the main chance, also possessed a sharply honed instinct for survival. She turned and ran for the nearest tunnel mouth.

"Something serious happened in there," I said, looking at the readings Ulriss had transmitted to me on my helmet display.

"Something?" Gene inquired.

"All sorts of energy surges and various U-space signatures." I read the text Ulriss had also transmitted—text since a vocal message, either real time or in a package, would have extended the transmission time and given Penny Royal more of a chance of intercepting it and breaking the code. "It seems that just before those surges and signatures the U-signal from the gabbleduck changed. They've installed the contents of the memstore . . . how long before the Polity dreadnought gets here?"

"It isn't far away—it should be able to jump here in a matter of minutes."

"Then what happens?"

"They either bomb this place from orbit or send down an assault team."

"You can't be more precise than that?"

"I would guess the latter. ECS will want to retrieve the gabbleduck."

"Why? It's just an animal!"

I could see her shaking her head within her suit's helmet. "Gabbleducks are Atheter even though they've forgone intelligence. Apparently, now that Masada is part of the Polity, they are to receive the same protections as Polity citizens."

"Right." I began tramping through the curiously shaped shale toward the hole the Prador had blown in one of Penny Royal's pipes. The protections Polity citizens received were on the basis of the greatest good for the greatest number. If a citizen needed to die so ECS could take out a black AI, I rather suspected that citizen would die. A sensible course would have been to retreat to Ulriss Fire and then retreat from this planetoid, however human Polity citizens numbered in the trillions and the gabbleduck population was just in the millions. I rather suspected Polity AIs would be quite prepared to expend a few human lives to retrieve the creature.

"Convert to text packet for ship AI," I said. "Ulriss, when that dreadnought gets here, tell it that we're down here and that Penny Royal doesn't look likely to be escaping, so maybe it can hold off on the planet busters."

After a moment, I received an acknowledgment from the Ulriss, then I stepped into the gloom of the pipe and looked around. To my right the tunnel led back toward the cannibalized ship. According to the energy readings, the party was to my left and down below. I upped light amplification then said, "Weapons online"—a phrase shortly repeated by Gene.

My multigun suddenly became light as air as suit assister motors kicked in. Crosshairs appeared on my visor, shifted from side to side as I swung the gun across. A menu down one side gave me a selection of firing modes: laser, particle beam, and a list of projectiles ranging from inert to high explosive. "Laser," I told the gun, because I thought we might have to cut our way in at some point, and it obliged by showing me a bar graph of energy available. I could alter numerous other settings to the beam itself, but the preset had always been the best. Then I added, "Autoresponse to attack." Now, if anyone started shooting at me, the gun would take control of my suit motors to aim and fire itself at the aggressor. I imagined Gene was setting her weapon up to operate in the same manner, though with whatever other settings she happened to be accustomed to.

The tunnel curved round and then began to slope down. In a little while we reached an area where debris was scattered across the floor, this including an almost intact hermetically sealed cargo door. Ahead were the remains of the wall out of which it had been blown. I guess the Prador had found the cargo door too small for them, either that or had started blowing things up to attract attention. The Prador were never ones to tap gently and ask if anyone was in. We stepped through the rubble and moved on.

The pipe began to slope down even more steeply and we both had to turn on the gecko function of our boot soles. Obviously this was not a tunnel made for humans. Noting the scars in the walls I wondered just precisely what it had been made for. What did Penny Royal look like anyway? Slowly, out of the darkness ahead, resolved another wall with a large airlock in it. No damage here. Either the Prador felt they had made their point or this lock had simply been big enough to admit them. I went over and gazed at the controls—they were dead, but there was a manual handle available. I hauled on it, but got nowhere until upping the power of my suit motors. I crunched the handle over and pulled the door open. Gene and I stepped inside, vapor fogged around us from a leak through the interior door. I pulled the outer closed then opened the inner, and we stepped through into the aftermath of a battle that seemed to have moved on, because distantly I could hear explosions, the thunderous racket of rail-guns, and the sawing sound of a particle cannon.

The place beyond was expanded like a section of intestine and curved off to our right. A web of support beams laced all the way around, even across the floor. Items of machinery were positioned here and there in this network, connected by s-con cables and optics. I recognized two fusion reactors of the kind I knew did not come from the stripped vessel above and wondered if it was just one in a series so treated. In a gap in the web of floor beams, an armored Prador second-child seemed to have been forced sideways halfway into the stone, its legs and claw on the visible side sticking upward. It was only when I saw the glistening green spread around it that I realized I was seeing half a Prador lying on the stone on its point of division. Tracking a trail of green ichor across, I saw the other half jammed between the wall beams.

"Interesting," said Gene.

It certainly was. If something down here had a weapon that could slice through Prador armor like that—there was no sign of burning—then our armored suits would be no defense at all. We moved out, boots back to gecko function as, like tightrope walkers, we balanced on beams. With us being in so precarious a position, this was a perfect time for another Prador second-child to come hurtling round the corner ahead.

The moment I saw the creature, my multigun took command of my suit motors and tracked. I squatted to retain balance, said, "Off auto, off gecko," then jumped down to the floor. Gene was already there before me. Yeah—rusty. The first-child was emitting an ululating squeal and moving fast, its multiple legs clattering down on the beams so it careened along like gravcar flown by a maniac. I noticed that a few of its legs were missing, along with one claw, and that only a single palp-eye stood erect, directed back toward whatever pursued it. On its underside it gripped in its manipulator hands a nasty rail-gun. It slammed to a halt, gripping beams, then fired, the smashing clattering racket almost painful to hear as the gun sprayed out an almost solid line of projectiles. I looked beyond the creature and saw the sparks and flying metal tracking along the ceiling and down one wall, but never quite intersecting with the path of something silvery. That silvery thing closed in, its course weaving. It disappeared behind one of the reactors and I winced as rail-gun missiles spanged off of the housing, leaving a deep trail of dents. The thing shot out from under the reactor, zigged and zagged, was upon the Prador in a second, then past.

The firing ceased.

The Prador's eye swiveled round then dipped. The creature reached tentatively with its claw to its underside. It shuddered, then with a pulsing spray of green ichor, ponderously slid into two halves.

I began scanning round for whatever had done this.

"Over there," said Gene quietly, over suit com. I looked where she was pointing and saw a skeletal golem clinging to a beam with its legs. It was swaying back and forth, one hand rubbing over its bare ceramal skull, the other hanging down with some gourd-shaped metallic object enclosing it. Easing up my multigun I centered the crosshairs over it and told the gun, "Acquire. Particle beam, continuous fire, full power," and wondered if that would be enough.

The golem heard me, or it detected us by some other means. Its head snapped round a full hundred-and-eighty degrees and it stared at us. After a moment, its head revolved slowly back as if it were disinterested. It hauled itself up and set off back the way it had come. My heart continued hammering even as it moved out of sight.

"Penny Royal?" I wondered.

"Part of Penny Royal," Gene supplied. "It was probably one like that who nailed Desorla to her ceiling."

"Charming."

We began to move on, but suddenly everything shuddered. On some unstable worlds I'd experienced earthquakes, and this felt much the same. I'd also been on worlds that had undergone orbital bombardment.

"Convert to text packet for ship AI," I said. "Ulriss, what the fuck was that?"

Ulriss replied almost instantly, "Some kind of gravity phenomena centered on the gabbleduck's location."

At least the Polity hadn't arrived and started bombing us. We moved on toward the sound of battle, pausing for a moment before going round a tangled mass of beams in which lay the remains of another second-child and a scattering of silvery disconnected bones. I counted two golem skulls and was glad this was a fight I'd missed. Puffs of dust began lifting from the structures around us, along with curls of a light metal swarf. I realized a breeze had started and was growing stronger, which likely meant that somewhere there was an atmosphere breach. Now, ahead, arc-light was flaring in accompaniment to the sound of the particle cannon. The wide tunnel ended against a huge space—some chamber beyond. The brief glimpse of a second-child firing upward with its railgun, and the purple flash of the particle weapon told us this was where it was all happening.

Bad choice, thought Jael as she ducked down behind a yard-wide pipe through which some sort of fluid was gurgling. A wind was tugging at her cropped hair, blowing into the chamber ahead where the action seemed to be centered. She unhooked her spacesuit helmet from her belt and put it on, dogged it down, then ducked under the pipe, and crawled forward beside the wall.

The first-child had backed into a recess in the chamber wall to her right, a second-child crouched before it. The three golem were playing hide-and-seek amid the scattered machinery and webworks of beams. Ceiling beams had been severed, some still glowing and dripping molten metal. There was a chainglass observatory dome above, some kind of optical telescope hanging in gimbals below it. An oxygen fire was burning behind an atmosphere plant—an eight-foot pillar wrapped in pipes and topped with scrubber intakes and air output funnels. The smoke from this blaze rose up into a spiral swirl then stabbed straight to a point in the ceiling just below the observatory dome, where it was being sucked out. Around this breach beetlebots scurried like spit bugs in a growing mass of foamstone.

The other second-child, emitting a siren squeal as it scurried here and there blasting away at the golem, had obviously been sent out as a decoy—a ploy that worked when, sacrificing two of its legs and a chunk of its carapace, it lured out one of the golem. The second-child's right claw snapped out and Jael saw that the tip of one jaw was missing. From this an instantly recognizable turquoise beam stabbed across the chamber and nailed the golem center-on. Its body vaporized, arms, legs, and skull clattering down. One arm with the hand enclosed by some sort of weapon fell quite close to Jael and near its point of impact a beam parted on a diagonal slice. Some kind of atomic shear, she supposed.

Watching this action, Jael was not entirely sure which side she wanted to win. If the Prador took out the two remaining golem they would go after the Atheter in the chamber behind her. Maybe they would just ignore her, maybe they would kill her out of hand. If the golem finished off the Prador they might turn their attention on her. And she really did not know what to expect from whatever now controlled them. Retreating and finding some other way out was not an option—she had already scanned Penny Royal's network of tunnels and knew that any other route back to Kobashi would require a diversion of some miles, and she rather suspected that thing back there would not give her the time.

The decoy second-child lucked out with the next golem, or rather it lucked out with its elder kin. Firing its rail-gun into the gap between a spherical electric furnace and the wall, where one of the golem was crouching, the second-child advanced. The golem shot out underneath the furnace toward the Prador child. A turquoise bar stabbed out, nailing the golem, but it passed through the second-child on the way. An oily explosion centered on a mass of legs collapsed out of sight. The first-child used its other claw to nudge out its final sibling into play. The remaining golem, however, which Jael had earlier seen on the far side of the room, dropped down from above to land between them.

It happened almost too fast to follow. The golem spun, and in a spray of green the second-child slid in half along a diagonal cut straight through its body. The first-child's claw and half its armored visual turret and enclosing visor fell away. Its fluids fountained out as it fell forward, swung in its remaining claw, and bore down. The golem collapsed, pinned to the floor under the claw containing the particle weapon. A turquoise explosion followed underneath the collapsing Prador, then oily flames belched out.

Jael remained where she was, watching carefully. She scanned around the chamber, but there seemed no sign of any more of those horrible golem. The Prador just lay there, its legs sprawled, its weaponized claw trapped underneath it, its now exposed mandibles grinding, ichor still flowing from the huge incision from its visual turret. Jael realized she couldn't have hoped for a better outcome. After a moment she stepped out, her weapon trained on the Prador.

"Jael Feogril," its translator intoned, and it began scrabbling to try and get some purchase on the slick floor.

"That's me," said Jael, and fired two explosive rounds straight into its mouth. The two detonations weren't enough to break open the Prador's enclosing artificial armor, but their force escaped. Torn flesh, organs, ichor, and shattered carapace gushed from the hole the golem had cut. Jael stood there for a moment, hardly able to see through the green sludge on her visor. She peered down at something like a chunk of liver hanging over her arm, and pulled it away. Yes, a satisfactory outcome, apart from the mess.

"Jael Feogril," said a different voice. "Drop the gun, or I cut off your legs."

I was telling myself at the time that I needed detail on the location of the memstore. Rubbish, of course. The energy readings had located it in the chamber beyond—somewhere near to the gabbleduck. I should have just fried her on the spot then gone on to search. Twenty years earlier I would have, but now I was less tuned-in to the exigencies of surviving this sort of game. Okay, I was rusty. She froze, seemed about to turn, then thought better of it and dropped the weapon she'd just used to splash that Prador.

With Gene walking out to my left, I moved forward, crosshairs centered on Jael's torso. What did I want? Some grandstanding, some satisfaction in seeing her shock at meeting someone she'd left for dead, a moment or two to gloat before I did to her what she had done to the first-child? Yeah, sure I did.

With her hands held out from her body, she turned. It annoyed me that I couldn't see her face. Glancing up I saw that the beetlebots had about closed off the hole, because the earlier wind had now diminished to a breeze.

"Take off your helmet," I ordered.

She reached up and undogged the manual outer clips, lifted the helmet carefully, then lowered it to clip it to her belt. Pointless move—she wouldn't be needing it again. Glancing aside I saw that Gene had moved in closer to me. No need to cover me now, I guessed.

"Well, hello, Rho," said Jael, showing absolutely no surprise on seeing me at all. She smiled. It was that smile, the same smile I had seen from her while she had peeled strips of skin from my torso.

"Goodbye, Jael," I said.

The flicker of a high-intensity laser punched smoke, something slapped my multigun, and molten metal sprayed, leaving white trails written across the air.

"Total malfunction. Safe mode—power down," my helmet display informed me. I pulled the trigger anyway, then gazed down in bewilderment at the slagged hole through the weapon.

"Mine, I think," said Jael, stooping in one to pick up her weapon and fire. Same explosive shell she'd used against the Prador. It thumped into my chest, hurling me back, then detonated as it ricocheted away. The blast flung me up, trailing flame and smoke, then I crashed down feeling as if I'd been stepped on by some irate giant. My chainglass visor was gone and something was sizzling ominously inside my suit. Armored plates were peeled up from my arm, which I could see stretched out ahead of me, and my gauntlet was missing.

"What the fuck are you doing here with him?" Jael inquired angrily.

"He turned up on Arena before I left," Gene replied. "Just to be on the safe side I was keeping to the Pens until Penny Royal's golem left."

"And you consider that an adequate explanation?"

"I put Arena Security onto him, but he somehow escaped them and ambushed me outside." Gene sounded somewhat chagrined. "I let him persuade me to give him the U-signal code from the gabbleduck."

I turned my head slightly but only got a view of tangled metal and a few silver golem bones. "Ulriss," I whispered, but received only a slight buzzing in response.

"So much for your wonderful ECS training."

"It was enough to convince him that I still worked for them."

So, no ECS action here, no Polity dreadnought on the way. I thought about that encounter I'd seen between the Prador cruiser and the dreadnought. I'd told Gene about it and she'd used the information against me, convincing me that the Polity was involved. Of course, what I'd seen was the kind of saber-rattling confrontation between Prador and Polity that had been going on in the Graveyard for years.

"What's the situation here?" Gene asked.

"Fucked," Jael replied. "Something's intervened. We have to get out of here now."

I heard the sounds of movement. They were going away, so I might survive this. Then the sounds ceased too abruptly.

"You used an explosive shell," Gene noted from close by.

"What?"

"He's still alive."

"Well," said Jael, "that's a problem soon solved."

Her boots crunched on the floor as she approached, and gave me her location. I reached out with my bare hand and slid it into slick silvery metal. Finger controls there. I clamped down on them and saw something shimmering deep into twisted metal.

"Collar!" I said, more in hope than expectation, before heaving myself upright. Jael stood over me, and beyond her I saw Gene reach up toward her neck, then abruptly drop to the floor. I swung my arm across as Jael began to bring her multigun up to her shoulder. A slight tug—that was all. She stood there a moment longer, still aiming at me, then her head lifted and fell back, attached still at the back of her neck by skin only, and a red stream shot upward. Air hissing from her severed trachea, she toppled.

I carefully lifted my fingers from the controls of the golem weapon, then caught my breath, only now feeling as if someone had worked me over from head to foot with a baseball bat. Slowly climbing to my feet I expected to feel the pain of a broken bone somewhere, but there was nothing like that. No need to check on Jael's condition, so I walked over to Gene. She was unconscious and would be for some time. I stooped over her and unplugged the power cable and control optics of her weapon from her suit, then plugged them into mine. No response and of course no visor readout. I set the weapon to manual and turned away. I decided that once I'd retrieved the memstore—if that was possible—I would come back in here and take her suit, because mine certainly would not get me to Ulriss Fire.

The hum of power and the feeling of distorted perception associated with U-jumping greeted me. I don't know what that thing was poised over the gabbleduck, nor did I know what kind of force-field surrounded it and that other entity that seemed the bastard offspring of a sea urchin and an octopus. But the poised thing was fading, and as it finally disappeared, the field winked out and numerous objects crashed to the floor.

I moved forward, used the snout of my weapon to lift one tentacle, and then watched it flop back. Penny Royal, I guessed. It was slumped across the floor beams and other machinery here. The gabbleduck turned its head as if noticing me for the first time, but it showed no particular signs of hostility, nor did it seem to show any signs of it containing some formidable alien intelligence. I felt sure the experiment here had failed, or rather, had been curtailed in some way. Something's intervened, Jael had said. Nevertheless, I kept my attention focused on the creature as I searched for and finally found the memstore. It was fried but I pocketed it anyway, for it was my find, not something ECS had put in the path of my sifting machine.

Returning to the other chamber, I there stripped Gene of her space-suit and donned it myself.

"Ulriss, we can talk now."

"Ah, you are still alive," the AI replied. "I was already composing your obituary."

"You're just a bundle of laughs. You know that?"

"I am bursting with curiosity and try to hide that in levity."

I explained the situation to which Ulriss replied, "I have put out a call to the Polity dreadnought we sighted and given it this location."

"Should we hang around?"

"There will be questions ECS will want to ask, but I don't see why we should put ourselves at their disposal. Let their agents find us."

"Quite right," I replied.

I bagged up a few items, like that golem weapon, and was about to head back to my ship when I glanced back and saw the gabbleduck crouching in the tunnel behind.

"Sherber grodge," it informed me.

Heading back the way I'd come into this hellhole, I kept checking back on the thing. Gabbleducks don't eat people apparently—they just chew them up and spit them out. This one followed me like a lost puppy and every time I stopped it stopped too and sat on its hindquarters, occasionally issuing some nonsensical statement. I got the real weird feeling, which went against all my training and experience, that this creature was harmless to me. I shook my head. Ridiculous. Anyway, I'd lose it at the airlock.

When I did finally reach the airlock and began closing that inner door, one big black claw closed around the edge and pulled it open again. I raised my gun, crosshairs targeting that array of eyes, but I just could not pull the trigger. The gabbleduck entered the airlock and sat there, close enough to touch and close enough for me to fry if it went for me. What now? If I opened the outer airlock door the creature would die. Before I could think of what to do, a multijointed arm reached back and heaved the inner door closed, while the other arm hauled up the manual handle of the outer door, and the lock air pressure blew us staggering into the pipe beyond.

I discovered that gabbleducks can survive in vacuum . . . or at least this one can.

Later, when I ordered Ulriss to open the door to the small hold of my ship, the gabbleduck waddled meekly inside. I thought then that perhaps something from the memstore had stuck. I wasn't sure—certainly this gabbleduck was not behaving like its kind on Masada.

I also discovered that gabbleducks will eat raw recon bacon.

I hold the fried memstore and think about what it might have contained, and what the fact of its existence means. A memstore for an Atheter mind goes contrary to the supposed nihilism of that race. A race so nihilistic could never have created a space-faring civilization, so that darkness must have spread amid them in their last days. The Atheter recorded in the memstore could not have been one of the kind that wanted to destroy itself, surely?

I'm taking the gabbleduck back to Masada—I feel utterly certain now that it wants me to do this. I also feel certain that to do otherwise might not be a good idea.

Paul M. Berger has been a Japanese bureaucrat, an M.I.T. program manager, an Internet entrepreneur, a butterfly wrangler, a museum administrator and (God help him) a Wall Street recruiter, all of which, in the aggregate, may have prepared him for nothing except the creation of speculative fiction. His work has appeared in publications including *The Magazine of Fantasy & Science Fiction*, Rich Horton's *The Year's Best Science Fiction and Fantasy 2011*, *Strange Horizons*, *Interzone*, *Podcastle*, and *Escape Pod*. The story of his battle against giant Japanese spiders was the first true-life memoir published in *Weird Tales*. He is a graduate of the 2008 Clarion workshop, and a founding member of the stunningly talented New York-based writers's group Altered Fluid.

# THE MUSE OF EMPIRES LOST

## *Paul Berger*

A ship had come in, and now everything would change. Jemmi had recently become adept at crouching under windows and listening around corners, so when the village went abuzz with the news, she heard all the excitement. She was hungry and lonely, and she thought of Port-Town and the opportunities that would be found there now, and she left the village before light. She went with only the briefest pang of homesickness, and she went by the marsh trail rather than the main road, because if she had met any of her neighbors along the way, they would have stoned her.

The path was swallowed up by the murky water sooner than she expected, and the gray silt sucked at Jemmi's worn straw zori with each step. Poor old Sarasvati, always laboring to bestow ease and prosperity upon her people, and always falling a bit more behind. These were supposed to be fields, but the marshes stretched closer to their houses each year. She couldn't even get any decent fish to breed there. In the village they clucked their tongues and said that was old Sara's nanos going, as if anyone knew what that meant or could do anything about it. But sometimes you could melt handfuls of this silt down and chip it into very sharp little blades that would hold their edge for a shave or two and could be bartered for a bite to eat. Sometimes you could see it slowly writhe in your hand.

Now that the village had turned against her, Sara was Jemmi's closest and only chum. When Jemmi was at her most alone she would sit quietly and concentrate on a tiny still spot deep in her center and maybe think a few words in her heart, and a spark would answer, and a huge warm and beloved feeling would spread through her. She knew that was Sara speaking to her. Everyone wanted Sara to listen to them, but Sara barely ever spoke back to anyone.

By midday Jemmi struck a road, and the next morning she reached Port-Town. Her parents had taken her there once when she was little, so she already knew to expect the tumult and smells and narrow streets packed with new faces, but the sheer activity spun her around as she tried to track everything that moved through her line of sight. Jewel-green quetzals squabbled and huddled together under the eaves of high-peaked shingled roofs, and peacocks dodged rickshaw wheels and pecked at the dust and refuse in the streets. There was plenty of food here if she could get it, and fine things to own, stacked in stalls and displayed in shop windows.

She was drawn most of all, though, to the mass of humanity that surrounded her—she could practically taste their thoughts and needs as they swirled by. The townsfolk were thronging towards the old wharf, and she let herself be swept up with them. Sometimes men or women brushed against her or jostled her without a glance or a second thought, and she grinned to herself at the rare physical contact.

An ambitious vendor had piled bread and fruit into a wooden cart at the edge of the street to catch the passers-by, and Jemmi stopped in front of him.

"Neh, what ship is it?" she asked above the din.

"Haven't you heard, then?" he replied. "It's Albiorix!"

Jemmi thought he was mocking her until she caught the man's exultant smile. *Albiorix*—no ship had stopped here for more than a generation, and now this! Albiorix was the stuff of legend, a proud giant among ships, braver and broader-ranging than any other. If Sarasvati was on Albiorix's route now, they would all be rich again.

"Who was on board, then?"

"No one's seen them yet. Looks like they'll be debarking any minute."

Jemmi checked her urge to race off towards the wharf. She put her hand on the vendor's forearm and smiled her warmest smile, and as he stood distracted and fuddled she swept an apple and two rolls into her pockets. She turned and ran before the man's head cleared.

The crowds along the quay were packed tight and jostling viciously, but Jemmi plunged in and no one noticed or resisted as she slipped right up to the barrier. A boy was standing near her. He was clear-eyed and honey-skinned and probably about two years older than she was. Judging from his clothes and the rich dagger that hung at his belt—the hilt bound with real wire—his family was quite well-to-do. With visions of regular meals and a roof over her head, she sidled towards him. The boy looked over her rags and begrimed face and straightaway disregarded her. Jemmi held firm and let the motion of the crowd press him close to her. The back of his hand brushed against her bare wrist, and he unconsciously jerked it away. She shifted her weight so that she was a fraction closer to him. The next time he moved he touched her again, and she imagined that he was not quite so quick to pull back.

The third time they touched she kept her hand against his, and the boy did not pull away. He turned shyly to Jemmi.

"Hello," he said. "My name's Roycer."

At that moment, the entire length of Sarasvati trembled with a gentle impact, and the crowd's cheer was deafening.

Outside, languid in the vacuum of space, Albiorix stroked Sarasvati's stony mantle with the fluid tip of a miles-long tentacle—an overture and an offering. Sarasvati recalled Albiorix of old, and his strength and boldness were more than she could have hoped for. She extended a multitude of soft arms from deep within the moonlet that served as her shelter and her home, and entwined them with his. She dwarfed him as she embraced him. Her tentacles brushed the length of his nacreous spiral shell, and in the silence dizzying patterns of light flashed across both their surfaces. The colors matched and melded, until they raced along his arms and up hers and back again. Sarasvati was receptive, and eager to welcome Albiorix after his lonely journey across the vastness. He disentangled himself and drifted down to the tip of her long axis, and they both spread their arms wide as he clasped his head to the orifice there. She released her great outer valve for him, and he gently discharged his passengers and all their cargo. Sarasvati accepted them gracefully, and in return, flooded his interior with fresh atmosphere from her reserves. Now duty and foreplay had been dispensed with, and they embraced again in earnest, spinning in the void.

The sphincter on Sarasvati's inner surface dilated open, and the passengers off Albiorix stepped through into Port-Town, armed and alert.

The arrivals were well aware that half the inhabitants of any orbital would tear newcomers apart just to see what they carried in their packs, and they hustled down the quay in tight phalanxes that bristled with weapons. They no doubt came from richer lands—Jemmi noticed the glint of steel in the trappings of their spears and crossbows as they passed. One group brandished old-style plasma rifles, but Jemmi assumed that was a bluff; everyone knew the smart electronics hadn't worked since the day the Cosmopolis fell. The crowds parted grudgingly around this threat, and Roycer was pushed closer to Jemmi, his gaze never leaving her face.

The rest of the townsfolk watched the arrivals' every move as they sought shelter in the winding streets. Those that could strike deals with families or inns to harbor them were likely to survive. This must have been an especially long voyage, Jemmi thought, or else star travel must be harder than anyone remembered. These arrivals all looked sunken-cheeked and worn down as if drained, or haunted by something they could not name.

One last traveler stepped through into Sarasvati, alone. He was the oddest thing Jemmi had ever seen. He was tall and slightly stooped and unnaturally pale—both his skin and his sparse hair were the same shade of thin gruel—and although at a distance Jemmi assumed he was very old, as he approached Jemmi realized she could not guess his age at all. His only luggage was a canister that hung from his shoulder on a strap. He walked unarmed along the barrier and Jemmi was certain he would be snatched up, yet no one in the throng made a move towards him or particularly noted his presence. He took his time, scanning the faces and garments as if looking for something. He stopped in front of Jemmi and her boy, and smiled. His teeth were the same color as his skin, and were all broad and very large in his gums.

"You'll do," he told the boy. "Shouldn't we be getting home now?"

Wordlessly, the boy nodded and released Jemmi's hand. He slipped under the barrier and joined the traveler, and led him down the quay into town.

Jemmi, stunned with amazement and impotent wrath, stood there slack-jawed until long after they left her sight.

With the excitement over, the crowd melted away, and Jemmi saw no chances to get close to anyone else. She spent the rest of the day sidestepping traffic and looking into windows, and she was able to grab a bit more to eat in the same manner she had acquired breakfast. After dusk one or two men on the darkened streets spoke to her, but they didn't look useful and she didn't like what their voices implied, so after that she took to helping people ignore her. That meant she couldn't get indoors to sleep, but luckily Sara was still too distracted with her beau to make a proper rain. Jemmi spent the night curled at the foot of a weather-beaten neighborhood shrine at the end of a narrow alley. It was certainly not what she had hoped for when she had decided to make the journey to town, but it was not too different from what she had left behind. Amongst the incense ash and candle-stubs and tentacled figurines, some housewife had left a rag doll dressed in a new set of toddler's clothes, a supplication to Sara for an easy birth and a healthy baby. The offering of a portion of a family meal that sat alongside it had barely gone cold, but some things were sacred, and Jemmi was not tempted to take it.

She fell asleep thinking how happy she was for old Sara, and she dreamed a wondrously clear vision of the two lovers floating clasped together with countless arms, surrounded by stars, auroras chasing along their skins. Jemmi accepted the image without question, notwithstanding she had never seen a sky before.

She awoke when she felt that Sara was about to make dawn, and she stood in her alley to watch it. Directly overhead, the coil of viscera that stretched along Sarasvati's axis sparked and sputtered with flashes of bioluminescence, and then kindled down its entire length. As the light phased from gold to yellow to white, Jemmi was able to pick out the fields and woods and streets of her own village hanging high above and upside down along Sarasvati's great inner vault. It was significant to her only as a starting point; she had come to town now, and her home would be here. She set out walking again, looking for breakfast and Opportunity.

Before she found either, she found the traveler. He was sitting on the veranda of a home in a wealthy neighborhood, drinking tea and reading. The street was busy with passers-by, but none of them seemed to take any notice of his odd looks, or his book, or the fact that he seemed to actually know how to read it. Jemmi stopped in the street in front of him and stared.

The pale man stirred in his seat and looked up from his book. Jemmi's thoughts immediately shifted to other things—the kerchief on that woman walking past and how she would wear it if she had it, what plans the tradesman across the way might have for the bound lamb he carried, and wouldn't a single gutter down the middle of the street make it easier to clean than one down each side?—as if there were a broad, gentle pressure in the center of her mind. This, the thought struck her, must be what she made the people in crowds around her feel. She held her ground and pushed back.

The man met her gaze with a small, amused smirk. "What can I do for you, daughter?" he called down.

The pressure in Jemmi's mind immediately grew focused and became an urge to comply, practically dragging an answer from her. She refused, and met the force head-on. The compulsion increased, and she resisted.

She stood there frozen by the exertion, and suddenly the frontal assault on her mind dissipated, replaced by the barest sideways push that took her completely off balance.

"I had a boy," she called back, and heard the anger in her voice in spite of herself. "A boy and a dry place to sleep."

"Indeed?" the pale man answered. "Now, what would make you think—Oh my . . . " His little smirk wavered, and he said, mainly to himself, "Here, in this forsaken backwater? Can it be?" He considered his closed book for a moment, then put it aside and stepped to the veranda railing. "I think perhaps we should get to know each other. Won't you come up?"

If there was any coercion now, it was too subtle for Jemmi to feel, and she was intrigued by his bearing, and warily flattered. She joined him, and he sat her beside him like a lady of substance.

"My name," he said, "is Yee."

"Neh, that's a funny name, isn't it?"

His half-smirk returned. "Possibly. It was originally much longer, and there was a string of titles that went after it at one time, but these days Yee is sufficient for my needs." He had an old-fashioned accent that made her think of fancy dances attended by the lords of planets, and a way of speaking as if every word counted.

"I'm Jemmi, then."

"Jemmi, it is an unexpected pleasure to meet you. You are what, eleven, twelve years old?" Up close, Yee's eyes were nearly colorless, but Jemmi got the impression that if he looked too long at something, it would start to smolder—or maybe Yee would.

"Fourteen."

"Fourteen? Ah, yes, of course. Puberty would have begun. And I don't suppose you eat particularly well. Forgive me—I've been a neglectful host. Would you join me in breakfast?"

She nodded.

"I suspected as much. Roycer!" Yee called, barely raising his voice.

The boy from the crowd at the quay stepped out of the door as if he had been waiting beside it. He had the look of someone who had been working feverishly all night.

"I believe our guest could do with a bit to eat," said Yee.

"Breakfast! Of course!" said the boy, as if it were a stroke of genius. He disappeared back into the house.

"Tell me, Jemmi," continued Yee. "Do you have any family?"

She shook her head.

"So I conjectured. They didn't, by any chance, die under mysterious circumstances within the past few months, did they?"

The glance she shot him was all the answer he needed.

"I believe we have much in common, you and I . . . and I honestly can't recall ever saying that to anyone else."

Roycer hurried out of the house with a tray piled with a random assortment of cold meats and vegetables and cups and loaves and cheeses. He set it down before them and stepped away. Yee made a graceful gesture with an open palm, and Jemmi tore into it.

"Perhaps you could also prepare a bath for our guest," Yee suggested while she ate.

"Hot water!" the boy muttered to himself. "Cool water! And soap!" and raced back inside.

Yee watched Jemmi bolt down the food. "You would not be reduced to this if you were on a true world," he reflected. "A planet holds more riches than one person could ever grasp, and you would just be discovering you could take anything you desired right now. How ironic that you and I should both be trapped out in space, at the mercy of the vagaries of a forgotten fad."

Jemmi looked up. "What's that, then?"

"A fad?" said Yee. "A trend of fashion. A novelty. I'm sure you must take it for granted, but please believe me when I tell you that it is not at all an intuitive choice for a human to live in the belly of a mollusk adrift in the ether. When I commissioned the first orbitals, they were intended merely as pleasure palaces to keep my associates content and distracted. We gave the males mobility only to ensure that the species bred strong and true, not because we planned to ride them."

"You did? Like Sara? Like Albiorix?"

"Yes. Your Sarasvati is one of the oldest, one of my first. Through a twist of fate, I happened to be visiting one of her sisters the day the

Cosmopolis fell. There wasn't time to return groundside before the machines stopped working of course, and not even a big ship like Albiorix is strong enough to make planetfall.

"Without the smart machines, you and I may ride ships from one impoverished orbital to the next, while the planets are rich and savage, but utterly isolated. The resources to rebuild civilization are there, but always just beyond my reach."

Jemmi had no clear idea of how long ago the Cosmopolis had fallen, but if Yee had been there her original impression was correct, and he was quite old. She was still hungry, but she was smart enough to stop eating before she got sick or sleepy. She pushed the tray away from her, half its contents untouched. Yee seemed to note this with the barest hint of an approving nod. Jemmi thought back to Sara's joy at the unexpected arrival of a suitor, and connected it to this unexpected man.

"Neh, why did Albiorix come back to Sara?"

"Ah, truth be told, it was not his intention at all. Albiorix prefers his route through his regular harem, and he likely planned to call on Demeter, and then Freya. It was time for me, however, to move rimward. It was a considerable struggle to make him accept my lead."

No one had ever taken such pains to answer Jemmi's questions before. She composed another one. "Why rimward, then?"

His smirk this time was a bit indulgent. "I have been to the galactic core, and I no longer believe I will find what I seek there. I am a man on a quest, you see."

The boy appeared in the doorway. "The bath is ready," he announced to the veranda in general.

"Roycer serves with excellent enthusiasm," Yee confided with a lowered voice. "Do you find everyone in Sarasvati so?"

Jemmi shrugged, nonplussed. "No one ever serves me," she admitted.

"Indeed? Well that must change. That must change immediately." He stood and offered his hand. "Would you care to join us inside?"

Roycer and Yee led her into the house, which was very old. Parts of it must have been built before the Fall, because they were made of textureless materials Jemmi had no words for, while other rooms were made of wood and stone. They passed through a side parlor, where the rest of Roycer's family lolled in chairs or sprawled across the rug. Jemmi counted two parents, a brother, and three sisters, all with sunken, husk-like faces. They were all dead. She was very surprised—her parents had looked the same way when they died.

"A pity, I know," said Yee, gesturing towards the corpses with an upraised chin, "but I needed to simplify the household, and the boy is strong enough for my needs for the time being." Roycer didn't seem to see them at all.

Roycer's family was so rich they had a room just for baths, at the back of the house. It was floored with rough flagstones and had a hearth for heating the water, and a high-backed earthenware tub right in the middle. Jemmi thought it was very odd to take a bath in someone else's house in the middle of the day, and momentarily froze with the apprehension that she was being entrapped, but Yee dismissed it with a shake of his head.

"If you want to pass as townsfolk," he told her, "you really shouldn't be noticeably filthier than they are. Besides, I am too old to take advantage of you, and I promise Roycer will be a perfect gentleman. He will scrub your back if you like."

Yee graciously turned to face the wall, and on her other side, Roycer did the same. Perhaps this was what the high-born did during morning visits. Jemmi let her ragged tunic and leggings fall to the floor, and stepped in. The water was hotter than any water she had ever touched, but she was committed, so she gasped and puffed and slid herself down the side of the tub in tender increments. Her knees immediately disappeared behind swirls of brown. It was scalding, but she discovered that if she kept her legs pressed together and moved only when absolutely necessary, it was nearly relaxing. When she was settled, Yee sat himself on a stool in a corner, looking for all the world like a pale long-legged spider. Roycer remained where he was.

Jemmi picked up a cloth and swiped experimentally at dark patches on her skin. Yee suggested she try the soap, and she had more luck that way. Underneath, she was rather fair, and turning pink in the hot water.

"Neh, Yee," she said, comparing a pink-scrubbed arm to a besmudged one. "Where are you from?"

"Ah," he said. "I was born in the chief city of the greatest dominion the world had ever known."

"The Cosmopolis Core?"

He shook his head. "Long before that. This was so long ago that it was little more than a legend to the builders of the Cosmopolis. In those days our god walked apart from us as a formless creature of faith and awe, quite unlike the beings who have given us their bodies to be our homes and our worlds in this age. He failed us in the end, I suppose, because that empire fell. It was not the first empire to fall, and it certainly was not the last, but it fell badly when it went. And I was a young boy, trapped on a narrow and crowded island of towers when the chaos descended."

Jemmi was silent. Anyone raised among the half-buried reminders of the abrupt and terrible failure of the Cosmopolis had a visceral understanding of that type of chaos.

"This was all so far back that I can recall only the memories of recalling it centuries later. But I know the instrument of our downfall was a plague, that our enemies brought among us. Death tore through us so quickly that we who considered ourselves the capital of the world and the heart of its hope were no longer a city, but brutal pockets of marauders running through a steel-and-glass wasteland. I was thirteen then, and the sickness seized me suddenly. It was clear that I would die, but I did not. When I fought to live, I was somehow able to reach out and find strength in the people closest to me. When I recovered, I found they had wasted away in proportion to the vigor I gained. My parents and siblings were dead and empty around me, and I was utterly alone.

"Then the savages who had been our neighbors found our home and ransacked it. I cowered and sought to make myself invisible to their eyes, and they walked past me without seeing me, though I could have put out a hand and touched them. At that point I realized I was now something different, but there was no one to explain it to me."

Jemmi knew exactly what he meant.

"Many dark years followed, but I survived, and my people worked diligently to rebuild something of their society, and I always amassed the best of everything. Gradually I realized this industriousness was my own doing—I could not force a man to do a thing he did not wish to do, but I could place an idea in that man's head and give him the drive to realize it at any cost. The same way, I believe, that you are now learning to do, Jemmi. I felt your mind as you stood out on the street. A power has begun to emerge in you, though you do not know how to use it. This is a rare and precious gift. In all the history of the world, it may be only we two who have had it. And you are the first I have ever told.

"While the rest of our planet squabbled in the dust, my people strove in lockstep and regained their learning and power. They had been close to the secret of star travel when I was a child, though this knowledge was lost for generations during the dark ages. Eventually, though, I saw that mankind's future lay in its ability to spread across worlds, and I gave them the urge to create that technology. When they finally left to cross space in the first great wormhole-drive craft, I went with them, always as a counselor, never as a ruler. That is the proper role for you and me."

Jemmi nodded, wide-eyed.

"I have kept mankind focused on its own advancement and prosperity and culled the weak and the distractions, and I accept relatively little in return—I take no more from my people than the barest life force necessary to remain alive and continue in my role. I have shepherded humanity through eons of history, and ensured that each new empire was built according to my design. The Cosmopolis was my greatest work. Only when it fell and the worlds were sundered from one another did humanity lose my guidance. And look what has become of you."

Jemmi had never had a clear picture of life under the Cosmopolis, but she suddenly sensed that it must have been unimaginably finer than the way people lived now, and she felt ashamed.

"So you see, that is why I am here. To rescue mankind. I must rebuild the Cosmopolis."

To Jemmi sitting in her tub that sounded so grand it was absurd. "From Sarasvati? She's old and poor. How would she help, then?"

"As I told you, I am a man on a quest. I need only to reach an inhabited planet to raise humanity up again. But for that, I need a shuttle—one of the old machines. I have searched since the Great Fall, and none remain intact in any of the orbitals between here and the center. Perhaps there is one left in Sarasvati."

"But, neh, the old machines don't work."

Yee smiled his half-smirk again. "I believe that if I can find a shuttle, I can render it operable." His tone became more urgent. "Join with me, Jemmi. I will have need of your support in the days ahead. Add your power to mine, and there will be nothing we cannot do. We will save mankind from itself and bring order to the stars and lead an empire that spans the galaxy and can never be overthrown!"

"Okay."

He stopped short as if he had prepared more to say. "Excellent," he said.

"But I don't know what help I can be."

"People want to help *you*, Jemmi," said Yee. "It's in your nature. Roycer?"

Roycer stepped up behind her with a long-handled brush, and began to rub warm suds along her spine. Jemmi decided she enjoyed the sensation, and leaned forward to give him more surface to work with. He ran the brush up and down the same route, mechanically focused on the center of her back.

"If you'd like him to do something else, you may direct him," said Yee. "I hand the reins over to you. Simply feel his mind and put the idea into it. You'll find he will be avid to put it into action."

"Don't I need to touch him, then?"

"You shouldn't—I don't," Yee told her.

Jemmi thought back to her earlier struggle with Yee, and reached out with her mind the way she imagined he had. She sensed nothing, so she pressed stronger and further. Suddenly she connected—and she was immense and floating in space, lost and engrossed in animal passion, tangled with Albiorix and straining mightily against his thrusts to receive him deeper and deeper within her. She had gone too far, and was now in Sarasvati's mind.

Overwhelmed by the sensation and shocked by her transgression, Jemmi recoiled and shook herself free of Sara. As she went, she caught a final flash of Sara's sight—stars wheeling around her, and much closer, a blue disk half covered with a whorl of white. Then she was back in the tub.

"Nothing, eh?" Yee said gently from his corner. "Well, try again. You'll do it."

She took a deep breath and reached out again, this time barely past her own skin. She felt Yee in the room with her—he nearly filled it—so she turned the other way and touched Roycer. She hesitated, then decided that people like Yee and herself were beyond bashfulness, and gave the boy the idea of her right shoulder.

The brush moved from her spine and made gentle circles around her right shoulder blade. This was nothing at all like how she was used to confounding minds. It was subtle and focused and efficient. She immediately saw it as a thing of beauty, as if she had been born to it.

"Excellent!" It sounded a little strained when Yee said it. "It seems you learn more quickly than I did. But always be aware that his enthusiasm may be diverted to other ideas."

The brush was now circling her left shoulder.

Jemmi gently reminded Roycer of her right side, and the brush returned to make its circles there. Yee moved him away again—and it was more challenge than test. Jemmi pictured her right shoulder in detail and pressed the image into Roycer's mind, and then pressed even harder in response to Yee's redoubled pressure. Roycer stood frozen, torn between the two equal demands. After nearly a minute, the long-handled brush began to shudder silently.

"Well, there's no point in breaking him," Yee said a bit too lightly. "I still have some plans for the boy."

Behind her Roycer emitted a sigh, and the brush resumed its gentle circles on her right shoulder blade.

Afterwards, when Yee suggested that the bath had done as much for her as could reasonably be expected, she stood up into a large towel Roycer held for her. She pressed the water out of her hair, and tossed the towel over her shoulder like a gown.

"Neh, am I beautiful now?" she asked.

Yee looked her over with an eye that had appraised queens.

"Why would you ask such a thing?" he said at last. "For you, that will never matter."

So Jemmi moved in with Yee and Roycer, and got her warm dry bed and a boy to serve her after all. The bedroom was filled with magnificent girl-things that had been Roycer's sisters' and Yee said were now all hers. She dressed herself in a frock of a crisp, shiny fabric that would be ruined forever if it were even in the same room with a speck of grease, and put ribbon after ribbon into her hair until the whole mass could practically stand on its own. Yee saw it and muttered a vague comment that restraint was often the better part of elegance, so she kicked the dress into a corner and changed into a more practical working skirt.

The next day, as they finished breakfast and sat looking over the jumbled heap of everything Roycer had pulled out of the larder, Yee slid his chair back and observed, "We seem to have exhausted this house's stores. Come—it's time we went to the market." Jemmi and Roycer followed him out.

Jemmi loved crowds, and to her mind the market was the best part of Port-Town. Yee led them to the busiest, most densely-packed street, where folk shoved to get by them and hawkers vied to drown out each others' voices. He turned to Jemmi, and his voice carried perfectly without raising at all. "Roycer and I have some business to attend to and will leave you to do the shopping," he told her coolly. "Please do not return until you have acquired everything you think the household needs. And do try not to get yourself killed while you're about it. I have noticed subtlety is not your strong suit."

He steered Roycer into the crowd, and they disappeared in a few steps. Jemmi didn't even have a basket. Was Yee kicking her out already? Had she failed somehow? Or did it just mean he wanted her to practice putting ideas in peoples' heads? She couldn't tell, and she felt alone again, and very exposed. She fought to stay in one place for a long while until the buffeting from the shoppers became unbearable, and then, near tears, she fled to a quiet corner at the edge of the square.

She forced herself to breathe deeply until she was nearly calm again, and then reached out for the comfort of feeling Sara.

There was a brief, dizzying sensation of stretching through free-fall and then she was back in Sara's mind, gargantuan but still less than a mote in the immeasurable space that surrounded her. The Herculean coupling with Albiorix showed no sign of slowing, but those sensations were too strong for Jemmi and she turned to other aspects of Sara's awareness.

Sara, she saw, floated in a barren void but carried her ecosystem entire within her, as if someone had taken an empty house set in a garden, then turned all of it inside-out. She gloried in the living beings she harbored, both because they were the foundation of her own survival, and because they had sprung from her own body. Designed into the core of her awareness was the drive to shore up that precarious balance by any means possible. She could win over allies and choose favorites, and smite the enemies growing inside her as if they were incipient contagions.

Jemmi saw the spindle-shaped world inside Sara through Sara's own mind, and she felt the angst and darkness that had been taking hold as her facility to orchestrate that environment slipped away. Sara was old and proud and secretly ashamed to be failing in her duty. Her wordless hopes were focused on the great egg she had prepared for Albiorix. If it quickened, she would have a glorious new life within her for a time, and then the lives she sheltered would have a new home.

Jemmi showed herself to Sara and guilelessly let the fact of her budding talent flow through. For a moment she felt Sara freeze the link between them, as if assessing the best way to react to some startling threat. But when Sara came back, her response was to engulf Jemmi with the sensation that she knew her and cherished her and reveled in her. It overwhelmed Jemmi and flooded through her, and she was powerless against it. Sara had unlimited reserves of love to draw on, and she used them mercilessly.

Jemmi was pinned there like an enraptured butterfly for a long, timeless instant. She was unable to move or think, and she wouldn't have given it up for anything. Finally, when the effect was deep enough, Sara bid her farewell and gently withdrew.

Finding herself squatting by herself on muck-covered cobblestones, Jemmi hugged herself and sobbed quietly. She would have clawed her way back into Sara's mind, but the connection had ended with a note of finality that she would not overstep. Gradually, she realized she was not empty, but filled with warmth and strength, and she could think of nothing but the great heart that had given her that. She now knew down through her bones that she would never have any use for Yee's old empires or for planets where there was nothing at the other side of the sky but more sky, because Sarasvati was her world. Jemmi belonged here, where she could reach out with her hand or mind and touch her god, and if there was anything beyond Sara, it did not interest her.

But for the time being at least, Yee was helping her learn her own strength. She remembered the task he had given her and half-heartedly stepped to the edge of the crowd. She extended her mind just the slightest bit beyond her own skin, and the maelstrom of thoughts and words and desires that hit her was like ducking her head under a waterfall. She drew back and focused on the thoughts of the woman closest to her.

The invasion of privacy was thrilling. The woman was picking vegetables from big baskets, and Jemmi found herself swimming through twisting currents of intentions and half-ignored impressions and the occasional diamond-clear string of words. She wondered if she might become lost in the woman's mind if she got any closer.

Ever so gently—not at all like guiding Roycer's hand—she tossed in the notion that a vendor across the square might be willing to negotiate his price, and watched the ripples spread out across the woman's other thoughts. Her eyes lit, and she hurried away from the table.

*Start at the beginning,* Jemmi decided. She strode up to the vegetable seller, and graciously allowed him to place his hastily emptied wicker basket on her arm. Then she moved on to a baker, who placed two loaves into it with a flourish as if it was the wittiest thing in the world, and strolled on into the heart of the square.

Jemmi returned home at the head of a small, heavily-laden parade. She directed the string of young men carrying her parcels to line them up along the veranda, and then sent them off. Yee stepped out of the house to observe this, then turned back inside with an audible sniff. Jemmi ran up after him.

"Neh, I can do it!" she told him. "I did it!"

"I daresay you did," he said. "And made quite a scene, by the looks of it. It's a wonder they didn't have you burned at the stake. Have Roycer move your booty inside." He turned away again.

Jemmi was crestfallen.

"Neh, Yee," she blurted. He stopped. "How come Sara—Why don't things work like they did in the olden days?" she asked.

That must have been the right question to ask him, because he immediately warmed to her again. "Ah," he said. "It was the machines. Few people remember that it was the destruction of the machines that caused the fall of the Cosmopolis, and not the other way around. In the days of its greatest strength, the Cosmopolis had enemies who preferred utter anarchy to the order and prosperity it gave them. They were fools and fanatics. They introduced a machine pandemic that spread from one end of inhabited space to the other."

"And all the machines got sick?"

"Not at first. It slept quietly for years, and then at a pre-ordained signal it struck everywhere, simultaneously. All the smart electronics died at that moment, and the Cosmopolis was shattered. To re-create the technology that humans or Sarasvati relied on, we will have to build from the beginning again: steam and iron. It is a long road, but I have walked it before."

Jemmi did not trust Yee, and she didn't think she liked him, but she would follow him anywhere if it would save Sara.

"In fact, Roycer and I were able to uncover some information towards that end while you were out," he told her. "We learned that Sarasvati originally had a shuttle port at either extremity. These were large and busy, so they likely contained several shuttles at the time of the Fall, but they were quite prominent and I expect they were plundered generations ago. There were also several emergency evacuation portals scattered throughout her. These have been lost, and there is a chance that one may be untouched. They will have to be searched out."

That seemed like a lot of work to Jemmi. "Why don't you just ask Sara?"

Yee scoffed. "And what would the question be? The ships and orbitals are very simple beasts, and even if they understood, they couldn't form an answer. But come, I will show you how it's done." He stepped over her groceries and led her back down into the street.

"What we need is people who seem persistent and resourceful, and whose absence will not be noted overly much," said Yee. "People like you and me—but expendable, of course."

Yee approached a laborer in a floppy, grease-stained cap pulling a heavy cart, and smiling and clasping his long pale hands together, asked him if he knew anything about the old-days shuttle port at the end of Sarasvati's long axis. The man, obviously annoyed, shook his head and looked at Yee as if he were cracked. Yee appeared disappointed, and observed it was a pity, since it wouldn't do to go spreading this around, but he was eager for news of any undamaged shuttles, and was more than willing to reimburse the man who brought that news quite handsomely. A fortune, really. At any rate, if he heard of anything, Yee lived right over there—the house with the veranda, can you see?—and would be delighted to receive any news. The man moved on as if he was glad to be rid of Yee. His steps became increasingly more hesitant though, as if something was unfolding in his mind. Finally, about a hundred paces down the street he abandoned his cart completely with a furtive look back, and sprinted away along the quickest route out of Port-Town.

The next man Yee spoke to developed a frantic urge to make the grueling trek to the ruins of the shuttle port at Sarasvati's far end and return to report on his findings. After that, four others became fascinated with the pressing need to locate one of the lost evacuation ports scattered along her length. It seemed to Jemmi that before they hurried off, each of them had been struck by the sudden inspiration for a scheme that simultaneously delighted them and tortured them.

"If a man sees it as a struggle to express an idea from within, he'll exhaust everything he has to bring it to fruition," Yee explained, as the last one began to run. "Well, after your success in the market this morning, I believe I can leave the rest to you. You'll need to send out about another dozen or so." He turned to go.

"Neh, why so many?"

"One of the first things you must learn, Jemmi, is that one man acting alone will change nothing. To have progress, you must mobilize a society. Once we are on a world, you will see how quickly entire kingdoms move forward when they embrace the goals we give them."

Yee returned to the house and stepped over the groceries on the veranda as he went in. Jemmi stalked the street recruiting searchers for the rest of the afternoon, and the food sat out there until evening, when she reckoned she had snared enough.

There was no dawn the next morning. Jemmi jumped out of her big bed with a sense of foreboding and a gut feeling that it was later than it looked. She ran down the wooden stairs and out onto the road in her bare feet. Shock and woe were palpable in the air and the soil, and Sara was lamenting with all her heart. Then it hit Jemmi—Albiorix was dead. He had weakened and gone still and fallen slack in Sara's embrace, and she was nearly paralyzed by loneliness and the weight of this new failure.

People in the villages high overhead began to wake and light lamps and fires as they tentatively started their day. The scattering of weak sparks in the darkness was a pale imitation of the stars Jemmi had seen through Sara's eyes. Yee stepped out onto the veranda and silently leaned over the rail to look upwards and sniff, as if he were tasting the weather.

"Yee—Do you know? Albiorix is dead," Jemmi said.

"I'm not surprised," answered Yee. "He was stubbornly fixed on his old route, and I had to relieve him of much of his strength before he would accept my course. We're lucky I made it this far."

Jemmi's hands were fists. "How could you do that?"

"I know what you're thinking—and it's not a problem. Albiorix has always been trailed by younger males as he makes his rounds. I'm sure Horus or Xolotl will be here by the time we are ready to move on."

"But she was going to have his baby!" Jemmi managed.

"Not likely. The orbitals and ships are improbable beings, so they must be part animal, part machine," Yee told her. "I'm certain you've noticed Sarasvati is no longer the paradise she was intended to be. Since the Fall, they have been unable to replenish the nanomachines that they need to grow and heal themselves. I doubt there would have been any offspring." He shrugged.

Jemmi tried to say something, but her grief and rage were like a solid mass that seared through her throat and chest. She had no words to express the depth of his sin and blasphemy. She knew that to strike at Yee would be suicide, so instead, she forced herself to turn from him and raced down the darkened street. When her legs tired, she walked through Port-Town as she had on her first night, staying to the shadows and peeking in windows.

It was hours before she got bored with wandering and returned home. Yee was out.

"Roycer!" Jemmi said. "Where's the jar, then?"

"Which jar, Jemmi?" he asked.

"The one he brought with him off Albiorix. Where does he hide it?"

He paused, and she flicked the boy's mind to give him just a bit of encouragement. "In the tub room. Underneath the floor stones."

"Show me."

Roycer led her to the room with the tub and lifted a flat stone away. In the space beneath was the gray canister Yee had carried when they had first seen him. Jemmi pulled it out. It was obviously very old, because it was made of a single piece of something very smooth and very strong. She grasped the cap, but it would not turn. It had an indentation the shape of a palm on top, but nothing happened when she pressed her hand against it. She handed it back to Roycer and told him to return it just as they found it. He could demonstrate astounding attention to detail when prompted.

As he moved the stone back into place, Sarasvati stirred herself to remember her duty, and her sky sullenly flickered and kindled with morning light, half a day late.

Jemmi and Yee and Roycer continued to live together over the next dozen or so days, but Jemmi saw Yee as little as possible. She also began to avoid looking directly at Roycer. The boy seemed brittle and stretched thin, and he was getting weak and clumsy. He was no longer pretty. Jemmi suspected he would be replaced shortly.

The laborer in the floppy hat returned after a few days, limping and exhausted as if he had run all the way up to the old shuttle port and back. It had been picked clean, he reported, and nothing bigger than a wagon-wheel was left. Several nights after that, the searcher that had been sent to the far end of Sarasvati crawled across the veranda and scratched weakly at the door. He could not speak, but he had just enough strength left to convey that he had also found nothing. Roycer dragged the body inside before the neighbors noticed.

Jemmi approached Yee the next morning. "Neh, Yee, how long will the other searchers be gone?"

Yee snorted. "Were you expecting them back? The task you gave them was to return only when they could report something of value, and to continue searching until then. I'd be surprised if many of them are still standing. Your old Sarasvati is worthless to us, as I expected." He seated himself and picked up his book.

"You and I should begin planning our departure. One of the younger orbitals further rimward is more likely to have what we need."

Jemmi slipped outside and sat in a corner of the veranda. She stretched her mind out across the emptiness, and touched Sara.

All of Sara that was not dedicated to the physics of regulating her inner environment was still in mourning for Albiorix, and she was in no mood to notice Jemmi.

*Please, Sara! I'm going to have to leave if you don't . . . We're all going to have to leave!* She visualized Sarasvati's interior deserted and bare, and prodded her with the image. Resentful, Sara turned part of her attention to Jemmi, and sluggishly recognized her as one marked as her own.

*You have to help us find a shuttle, or else he's going to take me far away.* There was no reaction to the words, of course. Jemmi tried to make an image of a shuttle, but she had no idea what a spacecraft would look like. Instead, she imagined people flying in and out of Sarasvati.

Sara responded with a picture of a flawless white fish, smoother than an egg and shaped like a teardrop, with stubby fins. The fish dove out of a hole in the side of Sarasvati's asteroid and swam across empty space.

*That must be it, then! Where?*

But Sara did not have a mind that could answer a question like that.

Jemmi leapt onto the veranda railing and caught hold of the edge of the roof, then scrambled on top of the house. From its peak she could look down along Sarasvati's entire inner length as it curved over her head in lieu of a sky.

*Is it there?* she asked, looking at a spot directly across, and kept the interrogative at the front of her mind as she moved her eyes across Sarasvati's interior. When Jemmi reached a point that was far off—90° around and two-thirds of the way towards her other end—Sara stirred, and Jemmi's vision of the spot came into clear focus. She had a sudden image of the white shuttle in a smooth white cavern, clasped by metal arms that held it suspended over the floor.

*Thank you, Sara! Thank you! Now I'll never have to leave you.*

Jemmi gently withdrew and left Sara to her grief. She remained on the veranda until she had collected herself, and went inside.

"Neh, Yee," she said as if she was discussing the weather. "I've found a shuttle."

Yee looked up from his book, as cold as ice. "Do not even think of toying with me, child—you would die before you hit the ground. Run along."

"It's smooth and white, in a big white room. One of my searchers made it back."

Yee was out of his seat and gripping her collar as if propelled by lightning. "Where?" he demanded. "Let me talk to him!"

She shook her head. "Can't. He's dead now. But I know where it is." She took him to the mullioned window and pointed out the spot to him.

"There? Where the river makes the bend around the tip of the cloud forest?" He calculated. "That's a three-day journey. Roycer—the packs!" Jemmi heard heavy footsteps running frenetically through the house, and Roycer burst into the room carrying two loaded rucksacks and an enormous backpack.

"We leave now," said Yee said to her. "Prepare anything you need to take."

He left the room. Jemmi could think of nothing, so she sat and waited. When Yee passed through again, he had the gray canister slung over his shoulder, and he didn't pause to see if they followed him.

Three days later, Jemmi was farther from home than she had ever been. They had had men pull them in carts day and night for most of the way, but the last one had dropped from exhaustion just as they decided to leave the road, and they had hiked through the brush on their own.

They stood in a clearing in a jungle. Humid air, blown erratically out of an obstructed duct from one of Sarasvati's lungs, met the cool currents overhead and sent a thick perpetual cloud rolling through the trees. Moisture dripped from the leaves like rain. In front of them was a symmetrical grassy mound, like a small hill standing alone.

"This is assuredly an evacuation portal," said Yee, pacing around it. "That's the entrance, and it is overgrown and partially buried, so the space beyond certainly could have remained intact. But how did your source know what was inside?"

He shot Jemmi a glance. She shrugged.

"No matter. We are very close, and our day is at hand." He removed two packets from his rucksack and tucked them in the tumbled stones that filled a door-shaped indentation. "Roycer, light this string here and here, please, then join me quickly." He strode away. "Jemmi, you might care to accompany me."

She followed Yee back into the trees. Roycer came running up, and then there was an explosion that sent earth and spinning shards of timber flying past them. The cloud amongst them jumped, and Sarasvati flinched violently under their feet.

A third of the mound was blasted away. The explosion had removed the layer of soil and stone covering it, and laid bare several yards of a deep purple-pink gash that oozed and glistened wetly. Jemmi wondered if the wound was as bad for Sara as it looked, or if on her miles-long body it was less than a scratch. Of the doorway only smoke and rubble remained, but beyond it was a steep shaft that led down through Sarasvati.

Yee tossed aside his pack and hurried in. Roycer and then Jemmi followed him down a long spiral staircase, smooth flowing steps formed by Sarasvati's living body. When daylight could no longer reach them, the steps above and below them glowed to light their way. They descended so far that Jemmi could feel herself becoming heavier.

A chitinous membrane blocked the passage and drew them up short. Yee placed his hand in its center, and it dilated open. They stepped through, and it silently closed behind them. Another blocked their way, and the air pressure changed and Jemmi's ears popped before it opened for them.

The stairs here were no longer alive. They were mathematically perfect, with precise lines and right angles that had never existed in Jemmi's world. They were a sterile white, against which Yee and Roycer seemed both more vivid and less whole. Jemmi had left Sarasvati, and was standing in the bare asteroid that protected her soft flesh from the harsh vacuum.

The white staircase was short, and it opened up into a cavernous chamber walled and floored in featureless white. The vaulted ceiling was a warm silky gray, chased with flickers of colored lights—Sarasvati's outer surface, pressed tight across the top of the space. At the center, as big as a house, a pristine fish-shaped shuttle was suspended over the floor by a set of jointed steel arms.

Yee rushed forward with a sound that was part gasp and part sob. He circled the shuttle, reaching out a hand and pulling it back to his mouth as if he were afraid to touch it. Jemmi ran her palm along its side. It was smoother than an egg, and cool.

"It's whole, and perfect!" Yee crowed. "At long last, I've done it!"

Jemmi nudged at it. "But, neh, Yee," she said. "It's dead. It doesn't go."

"Ah, but it will now." He caressed the canister he carried.

"What's in that thing, then?"

"Today, it is the greatest treasure in all the galaxy. I have carried it with me since before the Fall, when I first began to suspect that my enemies might take extreme measures to divest humanity of my direction."

"I thought you said they were the enemies of Cosmopolis."

"I may have—did you think there was any difference?"

Near the tail of the shuttle, Yee gingerly pried open a tiny drawer in the craft's skin and inspected its interior with one eye. Then he placed his palm on the lid of the canister and twisted. It came off with a chuff of air. He handed the lid to Roycer, and reverently held the container out towards Jemmi.

"Behold—one and a half liters of breeder nanos, sealed away long prior to the Fall." Inside was a gritty paste. It smelled like hot sand and rising bread dough. "This is quite possibly the last batch in existence untouched by the machine plague. Each speck can replicate thousands of the same nanomachines that built and ran the technology of the Cosmopolis. What I hold here is enough to raise an entire planet from the dark ages back to enlightenment. It is the key to our next empire."

He lifted the canister to the intake panel. "It would not do to waste it—would half a spoonful be too much?" He tilted a drop in. "The nanos will find the diagnostic system, and it will activate them to begin whatever repairs it needs."

He pushed the little drawer closed and bore those eyes of his into the surface of the spacecraft as if willing it to let him see its inner workings. Nothing happened for as long as Jemmi could hold her breath, and then a faint ticking and hissing sound emerged. Yee cackled with delight. "It will be no time at all now," he told Jemmi. "In a few hours you'll have had your first taste of fresh air. You will have seen your first sunset."

"But then we'll come back to Sara, neh?"

Still preoccupied, he answered, "What's that? Don't be absurd. Once you're on a real planet, you won't spare another thought for this rat-hole."

Jemmi turned her back on him. Near the entrance stood a heavy hand crank and a podium topped with switches and levers. She ran her hands over the alien textures and idly toyed with the switches to hear them click.

She closed a simple circuit that had remained alive across the centuries, and the floor beneath them disappeared, phasing into transparency. Her heart lurched and she groped for balance. She stood atop a star-spattered bottomless void, and looked between her feet far out into nothing. Suddenly, an edge of the emptiness was occluded by a shape that swung past her. For a moment, staring up into the chamber was a golden-green, slit-pupilled, lidless eye—flat, dead, and far broader than the entire launch bay. It was Albiorix.

Sara was unable to bring herself to release him, and he wafted like marsh-grass in her embrace.

Jemmi stood transfixed until he swept beyond her range of vision, and said carefully, "Neh, Yee. I don't think I want to go with you."

Yee faced her, and his voice was cold with threat. "That is unacceptable, Jemmi. You have a great responsibility to humanity, and I need you by my side for the great works I will do. You will be my empress. One way or another you will accompany me, and I assure you that you will rejoice in the opportunity."

Jemmi averted her eyes from his. She reached out and placed a thought in Roycer's mind: *Roycer, kill Yee. It's important.*

Roycer sized up Yee with a stony glance, and quietly shucked his heavy pack. He took a few wary steps, and then rushed him. Suddenly startled, Yee snapped his head around, and Roycer froze in mid-stride. His muscles shuddered horribly as Jemmi leaned the force of her mind against Yee's. Blood trickled down Roycer's chin from where his jaw had clenched on his tongue.

"Is this the best you can do, child?" Yee sneered. "Use the last gasp of an exhausted puppet against me? Countless others with real weapons have made the attempt, and they have all failed." His stoop disappeared, and he became a towering presence in the white chamber. "I am the immortal Andrew Constantin Fujiwara Borsanyi, founder of the Cosmopolis, eternal First Lord of the League of Man, and architect of all mankind's history. Who are you?"

Jemmi had no answer to that.

She released her pressure on Roycer, and he fell backwards towards her across the invisible floor. Instead, she reached out to Sara. She had to grope because she no longer knew where to find her, but at last they touched, and Jemmi's urgency roused Sara's attention. Jemmi concentrated all her awareness on the launch bay, dead Albiorix, and Yee standing next to the shuttle.

*He's the one!* She flung the rage and fear towards Sara. *He killed Albiorix! And now he'll do worse—*

The thought suddenly bloomed in Jemmi's mind that the most clever and crucial thing she could do was get down on her knees and bow her head. She welcomed the idea as an inspired stroke of brilliance, and rushed to kneel in submission. She heard Yee's footsteps snap against the crystal floor as he sauntered towards her, and it did not trouble her.

They felt the rumbling through the walls and the floor then. It started hushed and far off, a sustained roll of thunder that rushed up and overtook them.

Yee cocked his head and frowned, and then his eyes widened as he identified the sound: Sara had spasmed her entire boneless body in a long rolling wave, like a rope snapped across miles of ground. It was the roar of an earthquake, focused and aimed right at him.

Jemmi grabbed Roycer and spurred him with an intensity that sent him scrabbling maniacally past her into the cover of the stairwell. She dove in after him.

Yee dropped the canister and extended his arms overhead, not to fend off Sara's body, but to reach into her mind. He stood there for the space of a heartbeat, but there was no time to learn to contact her, and he abruptly broke and fled for the stairwell, all gangly arms and legs.

He snatched at Jemmi's ankle, and from somewhere she found the wherewithal to shout, "Your nanos!" throwing all the weight and urgency she could into the thought. Yee stared at her and hesitated a moment—perhaps it was the power of her suggestion, or perhaps it was the age-old habit of cherishing his burden—and then spun back into the launch bay.

At that moment the living ceiling of the chamber lurched high up with a great solid heave that pulled the air screaming past their ears and whip-lashed back down into the launch bay. It hammered against the invisible floor in a paroxysm of violence that obliterated Jemmi's scream. The shuttle and its equipment, which could bear the forces of vacuum, fire and ice and had stood unmarked for centuries, were instantly pulverized into a thin stratum of wreckage. Yee, standing among them, was mashed into nothing.

The wave rolled off again just as quickly, trailed by the sound of reced-ing thunder. A stunning silence stretched for several minutes, punctu-ated as bits of unrecognizable debris rained down towards the stars from where they were embedded in Sarasvati's side, clattering or splatting to a stop against the crystal.

Jemmi pressed her face hard against the stairwell wall and waited until the world had stopped reverberating. It took a long time before she judged it was safe to move.

"Let's go, then," she said to Roycer—no compulsion, just an order. "Ah, wait."

She threaded her way into the launch bay and picked through the ankle-high detritus until she found Yee's canister. It was dented and scraped, but almost none of the paste had been spilled. She took it.

"Now we can go." She led Roycer back into Sarasvati, and up the long stairs. She was careful not to touch his thoughts again. Near the top of the climb, he stumbled to his knees, and clear-minded for the first time in weeks, sobbed with horror and loss. Jemmi sat several steps above him with her arms wrapped around her shins and waited patiently, mindful of all the things Roycer had seen and done, allowed no feeling but solicitude for Yee's needs. He doubled over and retched. When he began glaring at her during his pauses for breath, Jemmi picked herself up and continued climbing. He hurried to follow.

Jemmi stepped out through the ragged hole at the surface and climbed to the top of the mound. The air tasted to her as if it were filled with pain and righteous fury. A raw pink line now ran from the end of Sarasvati, crossing over the stairwell, and continuing deep into her interior. A strip of ground more than a hundred paces wide had wrenched itself clear, exposing the bare flesh beneath it. Trees, stones, earth and bits of homes lay tossed and scattered to either side for as far as she could see. In the hazy distance, a series of aftershocks or convulsions raised dust clouds and sent ripples running back towards them. Jemmi's own body burned in aggrieved empathy. She would never let anyone hurt Sara again.

Roycer joined her on the rubble and surveyed the destruction.

"What *are* you?" he asked.

Jemmi blinked for a moment, and while she considered, he shifted his weight and raised his fists to strike her. She flicked his mind and he went still. And that gave Jemmi her answer.

"Bow down," she told Roycer. "Get on your knees and bow down before me. I am the priestess of Sarasvati. I have come, and everything will change now."

With that, as her boy knelt with earnest awe and reverence, Jemmi walked to the place where Sara's wound was the worst, and poured the contents of Yee's canister out into it.

Yoon Ha Lee's space opera novel *Ninefox Gambit* is forthcoming in June 2016 from Solaris Books, and his collection *Conservation of Shadows* came out from Prime Books in 2013. His short fiction has appeared in *Tor.com*, *The Magazine of Fantasy & Science Fiction*, *Clarkesworld*, *Lightspeed*, *Beneath Ceaseless Skies*, and other venues. He lives in Louisiana with his family and an extremely lazy cat, and has not yet been eaten by gators.

# GHOSTWEIGHT

## *Yoon Ha Lee*

It is not true that the dead cannot be folded. Square becomes kite becomes swan; history becomes rumor becomes song. Even the act of remembrance creases the truth.

What the paper-folding diagrams fail to mention is that each fold enacts itself upon the secret marrow of your ethics, the axioms of your thoughts.

Whether this is the most important thing the diagrams fail to mention is a matter of opinion.

"There's time for one more hand," Lisse's ghost said. It was composed of cinders of color, a cipher of blurred features, and it had a voice like entropy and smoke and sudden death. Quite possibly it was the last ghost on all of ruined Rhaion, conquered Rhaion, Rhaion with its devastated, shadowless cities and dead moons and dimming sun. Sometimes Lisse wondered if the ghost had a scar to match her own, a long, livid line down her arm. But she felt it was impolite to ask.

Around them, in a command spindle sized for fifty, the walls of the war-kite were hung with tatters of black and faded green, even now in the process of reknitting themselves into tapestry displays. Tangled reeds changed into ravens. One perched on a lightning-cloven tree. Another, taking shape amid twisted threads, peered out from a skull's eye socket.

Lisse didn't need any deep familiarity with mercenary symbology to understand the warning. Lisse's people had adopted a saying from the Imperium's mercenaries: In raven arithmetic, no death is enough.

Lisse had expected pursuit. She had deserted from Base 87 soon after hearing that scouts had found a mercenary war-kite in the ruins of a sacred maze, six years after all the mercenaries vanished: suspicious timing on her part, but she would have no better opportunity for revenge. The ghost had not tried too hard to dissuade her. It had always understood her ambitions.

For a hundred years, despite being frequently outnumbered, the mercenaries in their starfaring kites had cindered cities, destroyed flights of rebel starflyers, shattered stations in the void's hungry depths. What better weapon than one of their own kites?

What troubled her was how lightly the war-kite had been defended. It had made a strange, thorny silhouette against the lavender sky even from a long way off, like briars gone wild, and with the ghost as scout she had slipped past the few mechanized sentries. The kite's shadow had been human. She was not sure what to make of that.

The kite had opened to her like a flower. The card game had been the ghost's idea, a way to reassure the kite that she was its ally: Scorch had been invented by the mercenaries.

Lisse leaned forward and started to scoop the nearest column, the Candle Column, from the black-and-green gameplay rug. The ghost forestalled her with a hand that felt like the dregs of autumn, decay from the inside out. In spite of herself, she flinched from the ghostweight, which had troubled her all her life. Her hand jerked sideways; her fingers spasmed.

"Look," the ghost said.

Few cadets had played Scorch with Lisse even in the barracks. The ghost left its combinatorial fingerprints in the cards. People drew the unlucky Fallen General's Hand over and over again, or doubled on nothing but negative values, or inverted the Crown Flower at odds of thousands to one. So Lisse had learned to play the solitaire variant, with jerengjen as counters. You must learn your enemy's weapons, the ghost had told her, and so, even as a child in the reeducation facility, she had saved her chits for paper to practice folding into cranes, lilies, leaf-shaped boats.

Next to the Candle Column she had folded stormbird, greatfrog, lantern, drake. Where the ghost had interrupted her attempt to clear the pieces, they had landed amid the Sojourner and Mirror Columns, forming a skewed late-game configuration: a minor variant of the Needle Stratagem, missing only its pivot.

"Consider it an omen," the ghost said. "Even the smallest sliver can kill, as they say."

There were six ravens on the tapestries now. The latest one had outspread wings, as though it planned to blot out the shrouded sun. She wondered what it said about the mercenaries, that they couched their warnings in pictures rather than drums or gongs.

Lisse rose from her couch. "So they're coming for us. Where are they?"

She had spoken in the Imperium's administrative tongue, not one of the mercenaries' own languages. Nevertheless, a raven flew from one tapestry to join its fellows in the next. The vacant tapestry grayed, then displayed a new scene: a squad of six tanks caparisoned in Imperial blue and bronze, paced by two personnel carriers sheathed in metal mined from withered stars. They advanced upslope, pebbles skittering in their wake.

In the old days, the ghost had told her, no one would have advanced through a sacred maze by straight lines. But the ancient walls, curved and interlocking, were gone now. The ghost had drawn the old designs on her palm with its insubstantial fingers, and she had learned not to shudder at the untouch, had learned to thread the maze in her mind's eye: one more map to the things she must not forget.

"I'd rather avoid fighting them," Lisse said. She was looking at the command spindle's controls. Standard Imperial layout, all of them—it did not occur to her to wonder why the kite had configured itself thus—but she found nothing for the weapons.

"People don't bring tanks when they want to negotiate," the ghost said dryly. "And they'll have alerted their flyers for intercept. You have something they want badly."

"Then why didn't they guard it better?" she demanded.

Despite the tanks' approach, the ghost fell silent. After a while, it said, "Perhaps they didn't think anyone but a mercenary could fly a kite."

"They might be right," Lisse said darkly. She strapped herself into the commander's seat, then pressed three fingers against the controls and traced the commands she had been taught as a cadet. The kite shuddered, as though caught in a hell-wind from the sky's fissures. But it did not unfurl itself to fly.

She tried the command gestures again, forcing herself to slow down. A cold keening vibrated through the walls. The kite remained stubbornly landfast.

The squad rounded the bend in the road. All the ravens had gathered in a single tapestry, decorating a half-leafed tree like dire jewels. The rest of the tapestries displayed the squad from different angles: two aerial views and four from the ground.

Lisse studied one of the aerial views and caught sight of two scuttling figures, lean angles and glittering eyes and a balancing tail in black metal. She stiffened. They had the shadows of hounds, all graceful hunting curves. Two jerengjen, true ones, unlike the lifeless shapes that she folded out of paper. The kite must have deployed them when it sensed the tanks' approach.

Sweating now, despite the autumn temperature inside, she methodically tried every command she had ever learned. The kite remained obdurate. The tapestries' green threads faded until the ravens and their tree were bleak black splashes against a background of wintry gray.

It was a message. Perhaps a demand. But she did not understand.

The first two tanks slowed into view. Roses, blue with bronze hearts, were engraved to either side of the main guns. The lead tank's roses flared briefly.

The kite whispered to itself in a language that Lisse did not recognize. Then the largest tapestry cleared of trees and swirling leaves and rubble, and presented her with a commander's emblem, a pale blue rose pierced by three claws. A man's voice issued from the tapestry: "Cadet Fai Guen." This was her registry name. They had not reckoned that she would keep her true name alive in her heart like an ember. "You are in violation of Imperial interdict. Surrender the kite at once."

He did not offer mercy. The Imperium never did.

Lisse resisted the urge to pound her fists against the interface. She had not survived this long by being impatient. "That's it, then," she said to the ghost in defeat.

"Cadet Fai Guen," the voice said again, after another burst of light, "you have one minute to surrender the kite before we open fire."

"Lisse," the ghost said, "the kite's awake."

She bit back a retort and looked down. Where the control panel had once been featureless gray, it was now crisp white interrupted by five glyphs, perfectly spaced for her outspread fingers. She resisted the urge to snatch her hand away. "Very well," she said. "If we can't fly, at least we can fight."

She didn't know the kite's specific control codes. Triggering the wrong sequence might activate the kite's internal defenses. But taking tank fire at point-blank range would get her killed, too. She couldn't imagine that the kite's armor had improved in the years of its neglect.

On the other hand, it had jerengjen scouts, and the jerengjen looked perfectly functional.

She pressed her thumb to the first glyph. A shadow unfurled briefly but was gone before she could identify it. The second attempt revealed a two-headed dragon's twisting coils. Long-range missiles, then: thunder in the sky. Working quickly, she ran through the options. It would be ironic if she got the weapons systems to work only to incinerate herself.

"You have ten seconds, Cadet Fai Guen," said the voice with no particular emotion.

"Lisse," the ghost said, betraying impatience.

One of the glyphs had shown a wolf running. She remembered that at one point the wolf had been the mercenaries' emblem. Nevertheless, she felt a dangerous affinity to it. As she hesitated over it, the kite said, in a parched voice, "Soul strike."

She tapped the glyph, then pressed her palm flat to activate the weapon. The panel felt briefly hot, then cold.

For a second she thought that nothing had happened, that the kite had malfunctioned. The kite was eerily still.

The tanks and personnel carriers were still visible as gray outlines against darker gray, as were the nearby trees and their stifled fruits. She wasn't sure whether that was an effect of the unnamed weapons or a problem with the tapestries. Had ten seconds passed yet? She couldn't tell, and the clock of her pulse was unreliable.

Desperate to escape before the tanks spat forth the killing rounds, Lisse raked her hand sideways to dismiss the glyphs. They dispersed in unsettling fragmented shapes resembling half-chewed leaves and corroded handprints. She repeated the gesture for fly.

Lisse choked back a cry as the kite lofted. The tapestry views changed to sky on all sides except the ravens on their tree—birds no longer, but skeletons, price paid in coin of bone.

Only once they had gained some altitude did she instruct the kite to show her what had befallen her hunters. It responded by continuing to accelerate.

The problem was not the tapestries. Rather, the kite's wolf-strike had ripped all the shadows free of their owners, killing them. Below, across a great swathe of the continent once called Ishuel's Bridge, was a devastation of light, a hard, glittering splash against the surrounding snow-capped mountains and forests and winding rivers.

Lisse had been an excellent student, not out of academic conscientiousness but because it gave her an opportunity to study her enemy. One of her best subjects had been geography. She and the ghost had spent hours drawing maps in the air or shaping topographies in her blankets; paper would betray them, it had said. As she memorized the streets of the City of Fountains, it had sung her the ballads of its founding. It had told her about the feuding poets and philosophers that the thoroughfares of the City of Prisms had been named after. She knew which mines supplied which bases and how the roads spidered across Ishuel's Bridge. While the population figures of the bases and settlement camps weren't exactly announced to cadets, especially those recruited from the reeducation facilities, it didn't take much to make an educated guess.

The Imperium had built 114 bases on Ishuel's Bridge. Base complements averaged 20,000 people. Even allowing for the imprecision of her eye, the wolf-strike had taken out—

She shivered as she listed the affected bases, approximately sixty of them.

The settlement camps' populations were more difficult. The Imperium did not like to release those figures. Imperfectly, she based her estimate on the zone around Base 87, remembering the rows of identical shelters. The only reason they did not outnumber the bases' personnel was that the mercenaries had been coldly efficient on Jerengjen Day.

Needle Stratagem, Lisse thought blankly. The smallest sliver. She hadn't expected its manifestation to be quite so literal.

The ghost was looking at her, its dark eyes unusually distinct. "There's nothing to be done for it now," it said at last. "Tell the kite where to go before it decides for itself."

"Ashway 514," Lisse said, as they had decided before she fled base: scenario after scenario whispered to each other like bedtime stories. She was shaking. The straps did nothing to steady her.

She had one last glimpse of the dead region before they curved into the void: her handprint upon her own birthworld. She had only meant to destroy her hunters.

In her dreams, later, the blast pattern took on the outline of a running wolf.

In the mercenaries' dominant language, jerengjen originally referred to the art of folding paper. For her part, when Lisse first saw it, she thought of it as snow. She was four years old. It was a fair spring afternoon in the City of Tapestries, slightly humid. She was watching a bird try to catch a bright butterfly when improbable paper shapes began drifting from the sky, foxes and snakes and stormbirds.

Lisse called to her parents, laughing. Her parents knew better. Over her shrieks, they dragged her into the basement and switched off the lights. She tried to bite one of her fathers when he clamped his hand over her mouth. Jerengjen tracked primarily by shadows, not by sound, but you couldn't be too careful where the mercenaries' weapons were concerned.

In the streets, jerengjen unfolded prettily, expanding into artillery with dragon-shaped shadows and sleek four-legged assault robots with wolf-shaped shadows. In the skies, jerengjen unfolded into bombers with kestrel-shaped shadows.

This was not the only Rhaioni city where this happened. People crumpled like paper cutouts once their shadows were cut away by the onslaught. Approximately one-third of the world's population perished in the weeks that followed.

Of the casualty figures, the Imperium said, It is regrettable. And later, The stalled negotiations made the consolidation necessary.

Lisse carried a map of the voidways with her at all times, half in her head and half in the Scorch deck. The ghost had once been a traveler. It had shown her mnemonics for the dark passages and the deep perils that lay between stars. Growing up, she had laid out endless tableaux between her lessons, memorizing travel times and vortices and twists.

Ashway 514 lay in the interstices between two unstable stars and their cacophonous necklace of planets, comets, and asteroids. Lisse felt the kite tilting this way and that as it balanced itself against the stormy voidcurrent. The tapestries shone from one side with ruddy light from the nearer star, 514 Tsi. On the other side, a pale violet-blue planet with a serenade of rings occluded the view.

514 was a useful hiding place. It was off the major tradeways, and since the Battle of Fallen Sun—named after the rebel general's emblem,

a white sun outlined in red, rather than the nearby stars—it had been designated an ashway, where permanent habitation was forbidden.

More important to Lisse, however, was the fact that 514 was the ashway nearest the last mercenary sighting, some five years ago. As a student, she had learned the names and silhouettes of the most prominent war-kites, and set verses of praise in their honor to Imperial anthems. She had written essays on their tactics and memorized the names of their most famous commanders, although there were no statues or portraits, only the occasional unsmiling photograph. The Imperium was fond of statues and portraits.

For a hundred years (administrative calendar), the mercenaries had served their masters unflinchingly and unfailingly. Lisse had assumed that she would have as much time as she needed to plot against them. Instead, they had broken their service, for reasons the Imperium had never released—perhaps they didn't know, either—and none had been seen since.

"I'm not sure there's anything to find here," Lisse said. Surely the Imperium would have scoured the region for clues. The tapestries were empty of ravens. Instead, they diagrammed shifting voidcurrent flows. The approach of enemy starflyers would perturb the current and allow Lisse and the ghost to estimate their intent. Not trusting the kite's systems—although there was only so far that she could take her distrust, given the circumstances—she had been watching the tapestries for the past several hours. She had, after a brief argument with the ghost, switched on haptics so that the air currents would, however imperfectly, reflect the status of the void around them. Sometimes it was easier to feel a problem through your skin.

"There's no indication of derelict kites here," she added. "Or even kites in use, other than this one."

"It's a starting place, that's all," the ghost said.

"We're going to have to risk a station eventually. You might not need to eat, but I do." She had only been able to sneak a few rations out of base. It was tempting to nibble at one now.

"Perhaps there are stores on the kite."

"I can't help but think this place is a trap."

"You have to eat sooner or later," the ghost said reasonably. "It's worth a look, and I don't want to see you go hungry." At her hesitation, it added, "I'll stand watch here. I'm only a breath away."

This didn't reassure her as much as it should have, but she was no longer a child in a bunk precisely aligned with the walls, clutching the covers while the ghost told her her people's stories. She reminded herself of her favorite story, in which a single sentinel kept away the world's last morning by burning out her eyes, and set out.

Lisse felt the ghostweight's pull the farther away she walked, but that was old pain, and easily endured. Lights flicked on to accompany her, diffuse despite her unnaturally sharp shadow, then started illuminating passages ahead of her, guiding her footsteps. She wondered what the kite didn't want her to see.

Rations were in an unmarked storage room. She wouldn't have been certain about the rations, except that they were, if the packaging was to be believed, field category 72: better than what she had eaten on training exercises, but not by much. No surprise, now that she thought about it: from all accounts, the mercenaries had relied on their masters' production capacity.

Feeling ridiculous, she grabbed two rations and retraced her steps. The fact that the kite lit her exact path only made her more nervous.

"Anything new?" she asked the ghost. She tapped the ration. "It's a pity that you can't taste poison."

The ghost laughed dryly. "If the kite were going to kill you, it wouldn't be that subtle. Food is food, Lisse."

The food was as exactingly mediocre as she had come to expect from military food. At least it was not any worse. She found a receptacle for disposal afterward, then laid out a Scorch tableau, Candle Column to Bone, right to left. Cards rather than jerengjen, because she remembered the scuttling hound-jerengjen with creeping distaste.

From the moment she left Base 87, one timer had started running down. The devastation of Ishuel's Bridge had begun another, the important one. She wasn't gambling her survival; she had already sold it. The question was, how many Imperial bases could she extinguish on her way out? And could she hunt down any of the mercenaries that had been the Imperium's killing sword?

Lisse sorted rapidly through possible targets. For instance, Base 226 Mheng, the Petaled Fortress. She would certainly perish in the attempt, but the only way she could better that accomplishment would be to raze the Imperial firstworld, and she wasn't that ambitious. There was Bridgepoint 663 Tsi-Kes, with its celebrated Pallid Sentinels, or Aerie 8 Yeneq, which built the Imperium's greatest flyers, or—

She set the cards down, closed her eyes, and pressed her palms against her face. She was no tactician supreme. Would it make much difference if she picked a card at random?

But of course nothing was truly random in the ghost's presence.

She laid out the Candle Column again. "Not 8 Yeneq," she said. "Let's start with a softer target. Aerie 586 Chiu."

Lisse looked at the ghost: the habit of seeking its approval had not left her. It nodded. "The safest approach is via the Capillary Ashways. It will test your piloting skills."

Privately, Lisse thought that the kite would be happy to guide itself. They didn't dare allow it to, however.

The Capillaries were among the worst of the ashways. Even starlight moved in unnerving ways when faced with ancient networks of voidcurrent gates, unmaintained for generations, or vortices whose behavior changed day by day.

They were fortunate with the first several capillaries. Under other circumstances, Lisse would have gawked at the splendor of lensed galaxies and the jewel-fire of distant clusters. She was starting to manipulate the control interface without hesitating, or flinching as though a wolf's shadow might cross hers.

At the ninth—

"Patrol," the ghost said, leaning close.

She nodded jerkily, trying not to show that its proximity pained her. Its mouth crimped in apology.

"It would have been worse if we'd made it all the way to 586 Chiu without a run-in," Lisse said. That kind of luck always had a price. If she was unready, best to find out now, while there was a chance of fleeing to prepare for a later strike.

The patrol consisted of sixteen flyers: eight Lance 82s and eight Scout 73s. She had flown similar Scouts in simulation.

The flyers did not hesitate. A spread of missiles streaked toward her. Lisse launched antimissile fire.

It was impossible to tell whether they had gone on the attack because the Imperium and the mercenaries had parted on bad terms, or because the authorities had already learned of what had befallen Rhaion. She was certain couriers had gone out within moments of the devastation of Ishuel's Bridge.

As the missiles exploded, Lisse wrenched the kite toward the nearest vortex. The kite was a larger and sturdier craft. It would be better able to survive the voidcurrent stresses. The tapestries dimmed as they approached. She shut off haptics as wind eddied and swirled in the command spindle. It would only get worse.

One missile barely missed her. She would have to do better. And the vortex was a temporary terrain advantage; she could not lurk there forever.

The second barrage came. Lisse veered deeper into the current. The stars took on peculiar roseate shapes.

"They know the kite's capabilities," the ghost reminded her. "Use them. If they're smart, they'll already have sent a courier burst to local command."

The kite suggested jerengjen flyers, harrier class. Lisse conceded its expertise.

The harriers unfolded as they launched, sleek and savage. They maneuvered remarkably well in the turbulence. But there were only ten of them.

"If I fire into that, I'll hit them," Lisse said. Her reflexes were good, but not that good, and the harriers apparently liked to soar near their targets.

"You won't need to fire," the ghost said.

She glanced at him, disbelieving. Her hand hovered over the controls, playing through possibilities and finding them wanting. For instance, she wasn't certain that the firebird (explosives) didn't entail self-immolation, and she was baffled by the stag.

The patrol's pilots were not incapable. They scorched three of the harriers. They probably realized at the same time that Lisse did that the three had been sacrifices. The other seven flensed them silent.

Lisse edged the kite out of the vortex. She felt an uncomfortable sense of duty to the surviving harriers, but she knew they were one-use, crumpled paper, like all jerengjen. Indeed, they folded themselves flat as she passed them, reducing themselves to battledrift.

"I can't see how this is an efficient use of resources," Lisse told the ghost.

"It's an artifact of the mercenaries' methods," it said. "It works. Perhaps that's all that matters."

Lisse wanted to ask for details, but her attention was diverted by a crescendo of turbulence. By the time they reached gentler currents, she was too tired to bring it up.

They altered their approach to 586 Chiu twice, favoring stealth over confrontation. If she wanted to char every patrol in the Imperium by herself, she could live a thousand sleepless years and never be done.

For six days they lurked near 586 Chiu, developing a sense for local traffic and likely defenses. Terrain would not be much difficulty. Aeries were built near calm, steady currents.

"It would be easiest if you were willing to take out the associated city," the ghost said in a neutral voice. They had been discussing whether making a bombing pass on the aerie posed too much of a risk. Lisse had balked at the fact that 586 Chiu Second City was well within blast radius. The people who had furnished the kite's armaments seemed to have believed in surfeit. "They'd only have a moment to know what was happening."

"No."

"Lisse—"

She looked at it mutely, obdurate, although she hated to disappoint it. It hesitated, but did not press its case further.

"This, then," it said in defeat. "Next best odds: aim the voidcurrent disrupter at the manufactory's core while jerengjen occupy the defenses." Aeries held the surrounding current constant to facilitate the calibration of newly built flyers. Under ordinary circumstances, the counterbalancing vortex was leashed at the core. If they could disrupt the core, the vortex would tear at its surroundings.

"That's what we'll do, then," Lisse said. The disrupter had a short range. She did not like the idea of flying in close. But she had objected to the safer alternative.

Aerie 586 Chiu reminded Lisse not of a nest but of a pyre. Flyers and transports were always coming and going, like sparks. The kite swooped in sharp and fast. Falcon-jerengjen raced ahead of them, holding lattice formation for two seconds before scattering toward their chosen marks.

The aerie's commanders responded commendably. They knew the kite was by far the greater threat. But Lisse met the first flight they threw at her with missiles keen and terrible. The void lit up in a clamor of brilliant colors.

The kite screamed when a flyer salvo hit one of its secondary wings. It bucked briefly while the other wings changed their geometry to compensate. Lisse could not help but think that the scream had not sounded like pain. It had sounded like exultation.

The real test was the gauntlet of Banner 142 artillery emplacements. They were silver-bright and terrible. It seemed wrong that they did not roar like tigers. Lisse bit the inside of her mouth and concentrated on narrowing the parameters for the voidcurrent disrupter. Her hand was a fist on the control panel.

One tapestry depicted the currents: striations within striations of pale blue against black. Despite its shielding, the core was visible as a knot tangled out of all proportion to its size.

"Now," the ghost said, with inhuman timing.

She didn't wait to be told twice. She unfisted her hand.

Unlike the wolf-strike, the disrupter made the kite scream again. It lurched and twisted. Lisse wanted to clap her hands over her ears, but there was more incoming fire, and she was occupied with evasive maneuvers. The kite folded in on itself, minimizing its profile. It dizzied her to view it on the secondary tapestry. For a panicked moment, she thought the kite would close itself around her, press her like petals in a book. Then she remembered to breathe.

The disrupter was not visible to human sight, but the kite could read its effect on the current. Like lightning, the disrupter's blast forked and forked again, zigzagging inexorably toward the minute variations in flux that would lead it toward the core.

She was too busy whipping the kite around to an escape vector to see the moment of convergence between disrupter and core. But she felt the first lashing surge as the vortex spun free of its shielding, expanding into available space. Then she was too busy steadying the kite through the triggered subvortices to pay attention to anything but keeping them alive.

Only later did she remember how much debris there had been, flung in newly unpredictable ways: wings torn from flyers, struts, bulkheads, even an improbable crate with small reddish fruit tumbling from the hole in its side.

Later, too, it would trouble her that she had not been able to keep count of the people in the tumult. Most were dead already: sliced slantwise, bone and viscera exposed, trailing banners of blood; others twisted and torn, faces ripped off and cast aside like unwanted masks, fingers uselessly clutching the wrack of chairs, tables, door frames. A fracture in one wall revealed three people in dark green jackets. They turned their faces toward the widening crack, then clasped hands before a subvortex hurled them apart. The last Lisse saw of them was two hands, still clasped together and severed at the wrist.

Lisse found an escape. Took it.

She didn't know until later that she had destroyed 40% of the aerie's structure. Some people survived. They knew how to rebuild.

What she never found out was that the disrupter's effect was sufficiently long-lasting that some of the survivors died of thirst before supplies could safely be brought in.

In the old days, Lisse's people took on the ghostweight to comfort the dead and be comforted in return. After a year and a day, the dead unstitched themselves and accepted their rest.

After Jerengjen Day, Lisse's people struggled to share the sudden increase in ghostweight, to alleviate the flickering terror of the massacred.

Lisse's parents, unlike the others, stitched a ghost onto a child.

"They saw no choice," the ghost told her again and again. "You mustn't blame them."

The ghost had listened uncomplainingly to her troubles and taught her how to cry quietly so the teachers wouldn't hear her. It had soothed her to sleep with her people's legends and histories, described the gardens and promenades so vividly she imagined she could remember them herself. Some nights were more difficult than others, trying to sleep with that strange, stabbing, heartpulse ache. But blame was not what she felt, not usually.

The second target was Base 454 Qo, whose elite flyers were painted with elaborate knotwork, green with bronze-tipped thorns. For reasons that Lisse did not try to understand, the jerengjen dismembered the defensive flight but left the painted panels completely intact.

The third, the fourth, the fifth—she started using Scorch card values to tabulate the reported deaths, however unreliable the figures were in any unencrypted sources. For all its talents, the kite could not pierce military-grade encryption. She spent two days fidgeting over this inconvenience so she wouldn't have to think about the numbers.

When she did think about the numbers, she refused to round up. She refused to round down.

The nightmares started after the sixth, Bridgepoint 977 Ja-Esh. The station commander had kept silence, as she had come to expect. However, a merchant coalition had broken the interdict to plead for mercy in fourteen languages. She hadn't destroyed the coalition's outpost. The station had, in reprimand.

She reminded herself that the merchant would have perished anyway. She had learned to use the firebird to scathing effect. And she was under no illusions that she was only destroying Imperial soldiers and bureaucrats.

In her dreams she heard their pleas in her birth tongue, which the ghost had taught her. The ghost, for its part, started singing her to sleep, as it had when she was little.

The numbers marched higher. When they broke ten million, she plunged out of the command spindle and into the room she had claimed for her own. She pounded the wall until her fists bled. Triumph tasted like salt and venom. It wasn't supposed to be so easy. In the worst dreams, a wolf roved the tapestries, eating shadows—eating souls. And the void with its tinsel of worlds was nothing but one vast shadow.

Stores began running low after the seventeenth. Lisse and the ghost argued over whether it was worth attempting to resupply through black market traders. Lisse said they didn't have time to spare, and won. Besides, she had little appetite.

Intercepted communications suggested that someone was hunting them. Rumors and whispers. They kept Lisse awake when she was so tired she wanted to slam the world shut and hide. The Imperium certainly planned reprisal. Maybe others did, too.

If anyone else took advantage of the disruption to move against the Imperium for their own reasons, she didn't hear about it.

The names of the war-kites, recorded in the Imperium's administrative language, are varied: Fire Burns the Spider Black. The Siege of the City with Seventeen Faces. Sovereign Geometry. The Glove with Three Fingers.

The names are not, strictly speaking, Imperial. Rather, they are plundered from the greatest accomplishments of the cultures that the mercenaries have defeated on the Imperium's behalf. Fire Burns the Spider Black was a silk tapestry housed in the dark hall of Meu Danh, ancient of years. The Siege of the City with Seventeen Faces was a saga chanted by the historians of Kwaire. Sovereign Geometry discussed the varying nature of parallel lines. And more: plays, statues, games.

The Imperium's scholars and artists take great pleasure in reinterpreting these works. Such achievements are meant to be disseminated, they say.

•

They were three days' flight from the next target, Base 894 Sao, when the shadow winged across all the tapestries. The void was dark, pricked by starfire and the occasional searing burst of particles. The shadow singed everything darker as it soared to intercept them, as single-minded in its purpose as a bullet. For a second she almost thought it was a collage of wrecked flyers and rusty shrapnel.

The ghost cursed. Lisse startled, but when she looked at it, its face was composed again.

As Lisse pulled back the displays' focus to get a better sense of the scale, she thought of snowbirds and stormbirds, winter winds and cutting beaks. "I don't know what that is," she said, "but it can't be natural." None of the imperial defenses had manifested in such a fashion.

"It's not," the ghost said. "That's another war-kite."

Lisse cleared the control panel. She veered them into a chancy void-current eddy.

The ghost said, "Wait. You won't outrun it. As we see its shadow, it sees ours."

"How does a kite have a shadow in the void in the first place?" she asked. "And why haven't we ever seen our own shadow?"

"Who can see their own soul?" the ghost said. But it would not meet her eyes.

Lisse would have pressed for more, but the shadow overtook them. It folded itself back like a plumage of knives. She brought the kite about. The control panel suggested possibilities: a two-headed dragon, a falcon, a coiled snake. Next a wolf reared up, but she quickly pulled her hand back.

"Visual contact," the kite said crisply.

The stranger-kite was the color of a tarnished star. It had tucked all its projections away to present a minimal surface for targeting, but Lisse had no doubt that it could unfold itself faster than she could draw breath. The kite flew a widening helix, beautifully precise.

"A mercenary salute, equal to equal," the ghost said.

"Are we expected to return it?"

"Are you a mercenary?" the ghost countered.

"Communications incoming," the kite said before Lisse could make a retort.

"I'll hear it," Lisse said over the ghost's objection. It was the least courtesy she could offer, even to a mercenary.

To Lisse's surprise, the tapestry's raven vanished to reveal a woman's visage, not an emblem. The woman had brown skin, a scar trailing from one temple down to her cheekbone, and dark hair cropped short. She wore gray on gray, in no uniform that Lisse recognized, sharply tailored. Lisse had expected a killer's eyes, a hunter's eyes. Instead, the woman merely looked tired.

"Commander Kiriet Dzan of—" She had been speaking in administrative, but the last word was unfamiliar. "You would say Candle."

"Lisse of Rhaion," she said. There was no sense in hiding her name.

But the woman wasn't looking at her. She was looking at the ghost. She said something sharply in that unfamiliar language.

The ghost pressed its hand against Lisse's. She shuddered, not understanding. "Be strong," it murmured.

"I see," Kiriet said, once more speaking in administrative. Her mouth was unsmiling. "Lisse, do you know who you're traveling with?"

"I don't believe we're acquainted," the ghost said, coldly formal.

"Of course not," Kiriet said. "But I was the logistical coordinator for the scouring of Rhaion." She did not say consolidation. "I knew why we were there. Lisse, your ghost's name is Vron Arien."

Lisse said, after several seconds, "That's a mercenary name."

The ghost said, "So it is. Lisse—" Its hand fell away.

"Tell me what's going on."

Its mouth was taut. Then: "Lisse, I—"

"Tell me."

"He was a deserter, Lisse," the woman said, carefully, as if she thought the information might fracture her. "For years he eluded Wolf Command. Then we discovered he had gone to ground on Rhaion. Wolf Command determined that, for sheltering him, Rhaion must be brought to heel. The Imperium assented."

Throughout this Lisse looked at the ghost, silently begging it to deny any of it, all of it. But the ghost said nothing.

Lisse thought of long nights with the ghost leaning by her bedside, reminding her of the dancers, the tame birds, the tangle of frostfruit trees in the city square; things she did not remember herself because she had been too young when the jerengjen came. Even her parents only came to her in snatches: curling up in a mother's lap, helping a father peel plantains. Had any of the ghost's stories been real?

She thought, too, of the way the ghost had helped her plan her escape from Base 87, how it had led her cunningly through the maze and to the kite. At the time, it had not occurred to her to wonder at its confidence.

Lisse said, "Then the kite is yours."

"After a fashion, yes." The ghost's eyes were precisely the color of ash after the last ember's death.

"But my parents—"

Enunciating the words as if they cut it, the ghost said, "We made a bargain, your parents and I."

She could not help it; she made a stricken sound.

"I offered you my protection," the ghost said. "After years serving the Imperium, I knew its workings. And I offered your parents vengeance. Don't think that Rhaion wasn't my home, too."

Lisse was wrackingly aware of Kiriet's regard. "Did my parents truly die in the consolidation?" The euphemism was easier to use.

She could have asked whether Lisse was her real name. She had to assume that it wasn't.

"I don't know," it said. "After you were separated from them, I had no way of finding out. Lisse, I think you had better find out what Kiriet wants. She is not your friend."

I was the logistical coordinator, Kiriet had said. And her surprise at seeing the ghost—It has a name, Lisse reminded herself—struck Lisse as genuine. Which meant Kiriet had not come here in pursuit of Vron Arien. "Why are you here?" Lisse asked.

"You're not going to like it. I'm here to destroy your kite, whatever you've named it."

"It doesn't have a name." She had been unable to face the act of naming, of claiming ownership.

Kiriet looked at her sideways. "I see."

"Surely you could have accomplished your goal," Lisse said, "without talking to me first. I am inexperienced in the ways of kites. You are not." In truth, she should already have been running. But Kiriet's revelation meant that Lisse's purpose, once so clear, was no longer to be relied upon.

"I may not be your friend, but I am not your enemy, either," Kiriet said. "I have no common purpose with the Imperium, not anymore. But you cannot continue to use the kite."

Lisse's eyes narrowed. "It is the weapon I have," she said. "I would be a fool to relinquish it."

"I don't deny its efficacy," Kiriet said, "but you are Rhaioni. Doesn't the cost trouble you?"

Cost?

Kiriet said, "So no one told you." Her anger focused on the ghost.

"A weapon is a weapon," the ghost said. At Lisse's indrawn breath, it said, "The kites take their sustenance from the deaths they deal. It was necessary to strengthen ours by letting it feast on smaller targets first. This is the particular craft of my people, as ghostweight was the craft of yours, Lisse."

Sustenance. "So this is why you want to destroy the kite," Lisse said to Kiriet.

"Yes." The other woman's smile was bitter. "As you might imagine, the Imperium did not approve. It wanted to negotiate another hundred-year contract. I dissented."

"Were you in a position to dissent?" the ghost asked, in a way that made Lisse think that it was translating some idiom from its native language.

"I challenged my way up the chain of command and unseated the head of Wolf Command," Kiriet said. "It was not a popular move. I have been destroying kites ever since. If the Imperium is so keen on further conquest, let it dirty its own hands."

"Yet you wield a kite yourself," Lisse said.

"Candle is my home. But on the day that every kite is accounted for in words of ash and cinders, I will turn my own hand against it."

It appealed to Lisse's sense of irony. All the same, she did not trust Kiriet.

She heard a new voice. Kiriet's head turned. "Someone's followed you." She said a curt phrase in her own language, then: "You'll want my assistance—"

Lisse shook her head.

"It's a small flight, as these things go, but it represents a threat to you. Let me—"

"No," Lisse said, more abruptly than she had meant to. "I'll handle it myself."

"If you insist," Kiriet said, looking even more tired. "Don't say I didn't warn you." Then her face was replaced, for a flicker, with her emblem: a black candle crossed slantwise by an empty sheath.

"The Candle is headed for a vortex, probably for cover," the ghost said, very softly. "But it can return at any moment."

Lisse thought that she was all right, and then the reaction set in. She spent several irrecoverable breaths shaking, arms wrapped around herself, before she was able to concentrate on the tapestry data.

At one time, every war-kite displayed a calligraphy scroll in its command spindle. The words are, approximately:

I have only one candle

Even by the mercenaries' standards, it is not much of a poem. But the woman who wrote it was a soldier, not a poet.

The mercenaries no longer have a homeland. Even so, they keep certain traditions, and one of them is the Night of Vigils. Each mercenary honors the year's dead by lighting a candle. They used to do this on the winter solstice of an ancient calendar. Now the Night of Vigils is on the anniversary of the day the first war-kites were launched; the day the mercenaries slaughtered their own people to feed the kites.

The kites fly, the mercenaries' commandant said. But they do not know how to hunt.

When he was done, they knew how to hunt. Few of the mercenaries forgave him, but it was too late by then.

The poem says: So many people have died, yet I have only one candle for them all.

It is worth noting that "have" is expressed by a particular construction for alienable possession: not only is the having subject to change, it is additionally under threat of being taken away.

Kiriet's warning had been correct. An Imperial flight in perfect formation had advanced toward them, inhibiting their avenues of escape. They outnumbered her forty-eight to one. The numbers did not concern her, but the Imperium's resources meant that if she dealt with this flight, there would be twenty more waiting for her, and the numbers would only grow worse. That they had not opened fire already meant they had some trickery in mind.

One of the flyers peeled away, describing an elegant curve and exposing its most vulnerable surface, painted with a rose.

"That one's not armed," Lisse said, puzzled.

The ghost's expression was unreadable. "How very wise of them," it said.

The forward tapestry flickered. "Accept the communication," Lisse said.

The emblem that appeared was a trefoil flanked by two roses, one stem-up, one stem-down. Not for the first time, Lisse wondered why people from a culture that lavished attention on miniatures and sculptures were so intent on masking themselves in emblems.

"Commander Fai Guen, this is Envoy Nhai Bara." A woman's voice, deep and resonant, with an accent Lisse didn't recognize.

So I've been promoted? Lisse thought sardonically, feeling herself tense up. The Imperium never gave you anything, even a meaningless rank, without expecting something in return.

Softly, she said to the ghost, "They were bound to catch up to us sooner or later." Then, to the kite: "Communications to Envoy Nhai: I am Lisse of Rhaion. What words between us could possibly be worth exchanging? Your people are not known for mercy."

"If you will not listen to me," Nhai said, "perhaps you will listen to the envoy after me, or the one after that. We are patient and we are many. But I am not interested in discussing mercy: that's something we have in common."

"I'm listening," Lisse said, despite the ghost's chilly stiffness. All her life she had honed herself against the Imperium. It was unbearable to consider that she might have been mistaken. But she had to know what Nhai's purpose was.

"Commander Lisse," the envoy said, and it hurt like a stab to hear her name spoken by a voice other than the ghost's, a voice that was not Rhaioni. Even if she knew, now, that the ghost was not Rhaioni, either. "I have a proposal for you. You have proven your military effectiveness—"

Military effectiveness. She had tallied all the deaths, she had marked each massacre on the walls of her heart, and this faceless envoy collapsed them into two words empty of number.

"—quite thoroughly. We are in need of a strong sword. What is your price for hire, Commander Lisse?"

"What is my—" She stared at the trefoil emblem, and then her face went ashen.

It is not true that the dead cannot be folded. Square becomes kite becomes swan; history becomes rumor becomes song. Even the act of remembrance creases the truth.

But the same can be said of the living.

Tobias S. Buckell is a *New York Times*-bestselling author born in the Caribbean. He grew up in Grenada and spent time in the British and US Virgin Islands, which influence much of his work.

His novels and over fifty stories have been translated into eighteen different languages. His work has been nominated for awards like the Hugo, Nebula, Prometheus, and the John W. Campbell Award for Best New Science Fiction Author.

He currently lives in Bluffton, Ohio, with his wife, twin daughters, and a pair of dogs. He can be found online at www.TobiasBuckell.com

# A COLD HEART

## *Tobias S. Buckell*

In the mining facility's automated sickbay she'd put her metal hand on your chest and said, "I'm sorry." The starry glinting fragments of ice and debris bounced around the portholes. Twinkling like stars, but shaken loose of their spots in the dark vacuum.

They shot her hand, but she had pushed the raiders right back off her claim. The asteroid was still bagged and tagged as her own to prospect. You never told her they were all dead now, mere bloodstains on the corridors of Ceres, but one imagines she suspects as much.

"I have a cold hand, but you have a cold heart," she had said. "I can't love a cold heart."

And it's true.

Strange place to part ways, but she's been thinking about it for a while. Susan knows her path.

"You'll keep hunting for your memories?" she asks. "That corporate data fence?"

You nod. "I'll have more time on my hands."

It's a strange thing to image a whole brain down to the quantum level. Crack a person apart and bolt a stronger skeletal system into him. Refashion him into a machine, a weapon to be used for one's gain. Then burn the memories out. Use the lie of getting them back as a lure to make that human serve you. But stranger things had been done during the initial occupation of Earth.

Now you'll be having those back. You want to know who you were.

You want more than just the one they left you to whet your appetite.

Your first encounter with the *Xaymaca Pride*'s crew is an intense-looking engineer. Small scabs on her shaved head show she's sloppy with a blade, and there's irritation around the eye sockets, where a sad-looking metal eye has been welded into the skin somewhere in a cheap bodyshop.

"You're the mercenary," she says. "Pepper."

You're both hanging in the air inside the lock. The pressure differential slightly pushes at your ears. You crack your jaw, left, right, and the pressure ceases. The movement causes your dreadlocks to shift around you, tapping the side of your face.

"I'm not on a job," you tell her. "I don't work for anyone anymore."

But you used to. And there's a reputation. It's spread in front of you like a bow wave. Dopplering around, varying in intensity here and there.

Five years working with miners, stripping ore from asteroids enveloped in plastic bags and putting in sweat-work, and all anyone knows about is the old wetwork. Stuff that should have been left to the shadows. Secrets never meant for civilians.

But that shit didn't fly out in the tight tin cans floating around the outer solar system. Everyone had their noses in everyone else's business.

"The captain wants to see you before detach."

Probably having second thoughts, you think. Been hard to find a way to get out of the system, because the new rulers of the worlds here want you dead for past actions. You can skulk around the fringes, or even go back to Earth and hide in the packed masses and cities.

But to go interstellar: you eventually get noticed when you're one of the trickle of humanity leaving to the other forty-eight habitable worlds. Particularly if you're one of the few that's not a servant of the various alien species that are now the overlords of humanity.

The bridge crew all twist in place to get a good look at you when you float into the orb-shaped cockpit at the deep heart of the cylindrical starship. They're all lined up on one plane of the cockpit, the orb able to gimbal with the ship's orientation to orient them to the pressures of high acceleration.

Not common on an average container ship. Usually those were little more than a set of girders cargo could get slotted into with a living area on one end and engines on the other.

The captain hangs in the air, eyes drowned in shipboard internal information, but now he stirs and looks at you. His skin is brown, like yours. Like many of the crew's. From what you've heard, they all hail from the Caribbean. DeBrun has been smuggling people out of the solar system to points beyond for a whole year now.

"I'm John deBrun," he says. "You're Pepper."

You regard him neutrally.

DeBrun starts the conversation jovially. "In order to leave the solar system, I need anti-matter, Pepper. And no one makes it but the Satraps and they only sell to those they like. They own interstellar commerce, and most of the planets in the solar system. And according to the bastard aliens, you do not have interstellar travel privileges. I've let you aboard, to ask you a question, face to face."

You raise an eyebrow. It's a staged meeting. DeBrun is putting on a show for the bridge crew. "Yes?"

"Why should I smuggle you from here to Nova Terra's Orbital?"

A moment passes as you seem to consider that, letting deBrun's little moment stretch out. "It'll piss off the Satraps, and I'll wait long enough so that it's not obvious you're the ship that slipped me in."

DeBrun dramatically considers that, rubbing his chin. "How will you do that?"

"I'm going to steal something from a Satrap."

"Steal what?"

"My memories," you tell him.

DeBrun grins. "Okay. We'll take you."

"Just like that?"

"You know who we are, what we're planning to do?"

You nod. "An exodus. To find a new world, free of the Satrapy."

"Not to find," deBrun says. "We found it. We just need to get there again, with five ships. And having you distract the Satrap at our rally point . . . well, I like that. There are a lot of people hiding on that habitat, waiting to get loaded up while we fuel. The first people of a whole new world, a new society. You should join."

"The Satrap at your rally point has something I want."

"So I've heard. Okay. Jay, shut the locks, clear us out. Our last passenger is on board."

Jay and DeBrun could be brothers. Same smile. Though you're not sure. You don't look at people that much anymore. Not since Susan. You don't care anymore. You can explore the fleshy side of what remains of you after you get the memories back.

Because they will make you whole again.

The ship's cat adopts you. It hangs in the air just above the nape of your neck, and whenever the ship adjusts its flight patch claws dig into the nape of your neck.

Claws, it seems, are a benefit in zero gravity.

No matter how many times you toss the furball off down the corridor it finds its way back into your room.

How many wormholes between Earth and Nova Terra? You lose track of the stomach-lurching transits as the cylindrical ship burns its way upstream through the network.

You dream about the one memory you still have. The palm tree, sand in your toes.

It could have been a vacation, that beach. But the aquamarine colors just inside the reef feel like *home*. It's why, when you heard the shipboard accents, you followed the crew back to this ship and chose it. The oil-cooked johnny cakes, pate, curry, rice . . . muscle memory and habit leave you thinking you came from the islands.

You don't know them. But they are your people.

At Nova Terra, slipping out via an airlock and a liberated spacesuit, you look back at the pockmarked outer shell of the ship. It's nestled against the massive, goblet-shaped alien habitat orbiting Nova Terra's purplish atmosphere, itself circling the gas giant Medea. The few hundred free humans who live here call the glass and steel cup-shaped orbital Hope's End.

You're a long way from home now. Hundreds of wormholes away, each of them many lightyears of jumps. Each wormhole a transit point in a vast network that patch together the various worlds the Satrapy rules over.

Too far to stop now. You only were able to come one way. This wasn't a round-trip ticket. You'll have to figure out how to get back home later.

Once you have memories. Once you know exactly where that palm tree was, you'll have something to actually go back *for*.

The woman who sits at the table across from you a week later does so stiffly, and yet with such a sense of implied ownership that your back tenses. There's something puppet-like, and you know the strings are digital. Hardware buried into this one's neuro-cortex allow something else to ride shotgun.

Something.

She's in full thrall, eyes glinting with an alien intelligence behind them. The Satrap of Hope's End has noticed your arrival and walked one of his human ROVs out to have a chat. That it took it two days for it to notice you, when you've just been sitting out in the open all this time, demonstrates a level of amateurishness for its kind.

Then again, Hope's End is sort of the Satrapy's equivalent of a dead-end position. A small assignment on a small habitat in orbit. The real players live down the gravity well, on the juicy planets.

"I know who you are," the woman says. Around you free humans in gray paper suits stream to work in the distant crevices of the station. Life is hard on Hope's End, you can tell just by their posture. The guarded faces, the invisible heaviness on the shoulders.

You say nothing to the woman across from you.

"You are here without permission. Do you know I could have you killed for that?"

"You could try that," you say. "The cost would be high."

"Oh, I imagine." She leans back, and flails an arm in what must be some far-off alien physical expression badly translated. There is a pit, a cavern, somewhere deep in the bowels of Hope's End. Somewhere with three quarter's gravity, and a dirt pit, and a massive recreation pool. And slopping around is a giant wormy trilobite of an alien. "I know a lot about you. More than you know about yourself."

Indeed.

The thing you need is that cavern's location.

Until you get that, everything is a dance. A game. A series of feints and jabs. Your life is the price of a single misstep.

But what do you have to lose? You don't know. Because you can't remember. It was taken from you. The Satrap owns everything you would lose by dying. You're already dead, you think.

"So why haven't you killed me?" you ask the Satrap.

"The *Xaymaca Pride*," it says. "They're sneaking people around my habitat. As if I wouldn't notice. And they're hoping to leave . . . for a new world."

"You believe deBrun's propaganda?" you ask. Because even you don't half believe it. The man is slightly messianic. He's probably going to lead them all to their deaths, so far from Earth. Alone among uncaring, hard aliens the likes of which haven't even bothered to make it to Earth.

The Satrapy is vast. Hundreds of wormhole junctions between each habitable world, and dozens and dozens of those linked up. And the Satraps hold the navigation routes to themselves. The few individual ships out there blunder around and retrace their steps and are lucky they're not shot down by the Satrapy's gun banks in the process.

"DeBrun destroyed his own ship upon return from the Fringes," the woman says. "He has memorized the location in his head."

"Ah. So you believe it is true." A ship. There were corporations on Earth that couldn't afford an interstellar ship. Not a small act, destroying one.

"Many people raised funds to create this . . . Black Starliner Corporation's fleet," the Satrap's thrall says. "I believe the world he found is real. Unspoiled and real. And I want it for myself." That last bit is lashed out. There is hunger in that statement, and a hint of frustration.

This Satrap is trapped up here, while its siblings cavort on the surface of Nova Terra. They have thousands of humans and aliens in thrall at their disposal, chipped with neurotech that let them create an army of servants they can remote control around with mere thought.

"I am stuck in this boring, metal cage. But I have great plans. Would you like to know how you got that scar above your left inner thigh? The jagged one, that is faded because you've had it since you were a teenager?"

You stop breathing for a second. Unconsciously you run a hand down and trace the zig-zag pattern with your thumb.

"You were climbing a fence. Barbed wire curled around the top, and you were trying to get over it into a field. You slipped. You were so scared, for a split second, as it ripped open your leg. The blood was so bright in the sun, and the ground tumbled up toward you as fell, in shock."

When you break the stare, you've lost a little battle of the wills. "So you do have them."

"I love collecting the strangest things," the Satrap said through the woman. Now that you are paying attention, you see that her hair is unwashed, and that there are sores above her clavicle. "I have two thousand humans, in thrall to me. Many other species as well. And I've used these eyes to pry, sneak, and attempt my way on board. I want John deBrun. I'm tired of watching these free humans skulk about."

"So go pick him up," you say.

"Oh, yes. I want to sink my tendrils into deBrun's fleshy little mind and suck those coordinates out. But he remains on that damn ship, with guards ever at the airlocks. I've learned he has protocols for an attack, and anything I can do leaves me too high a risk of him dying in a large attack. So I want *you* to bring me John deBrun. It is the sort of thing, I'm told, you are good at."

"And in exchange you give me my memories back?"

"You're every bit as sharp as your memories indicate you ever were," the woman says, and stands up.

"What if I refuse? What if I go after the memories myself?" you smile.

"You are alone, on a station, where only a few hold their own freedom. Every other eye in here is in thrall to me. Most of the time, they are free to engage in their petty lives, but the moment I desire, I could command them all to rip you from limb to limb with their bare hands. I considered it. But I think instead, we will both be happier if you bring John deBrun to level A7. Portal fourteen. My security forces will be waiting."

And there is your way in.

You wait in the shadows.

You've often been something that goes bump in the night.

The Satraps consider themselves gods to the species they rule over. But sometimes, gods want other gods killed. In theory their reasons are arcane and unknowable. But as far as you can tell they are the usual: jealousy. Covetousness. A desire for more power.

Sometimes gods want other gods to die, and you decided you didn't just want to go bump in the night and scare people. You decided you could aim higher than being just a human assassin. And when the Satrap of Mars decided it wanted the blue jewel of Earth, you let it sharpen you into a weapon the likes of which few wished to imagine.

All that gooey alien nanotechnology that burrowed through your pores, all that power . . .

Behold the giant slayer, you once thought, looking in the mirror.

You weren't supposed to live, but even jealous alien eyes from the dusty red ruin of Mars couldn't imagine the hells you would face to continue feeding your quest. It had no idea the depths of your anger. The strength of your resolve.

It didn't know you had such a cold, cold heart, and that it had helped make it so much colder. You were already steel, and artificial sinew. It only furthered a transformation that had begun long ago.

•

The gun that John deBrun points at your head when he comes into his quarters is capable of doing much more than give you a headache. He's good. Knew you were in the room. Maybe considered flushing out this part of the ship, but instead comes in to talk.

He's keeping his distance though.

"You're here for the coordinates, aren't you?" he asks.

You nod. "I am."

You keep your hands in the air and sit down. You want John as comfortable as possible.

"If it's not me, someone else will come. They'll cut your head off and run it back to the Satrap. What I have in mind is a little different."

John shakes his head sadly. He lifts up his shirt to show several puckered scars. "You're not the first to try. We have systems in place to deal with this. Every possible variable. I have to assume that everyone is trying to stop me. Other humans, my own crew, people at Hope's End. I'm tougher than they realize."

"You'll want to do this my way," you say.

"And why is that?"

"Because it is happening, John. This right now is happening: I will take you to the Satrap. Because I have come too far, and done too many things, to not go there and get my memories back. Nothing else matters to me. Not you, your ships, your cause, the people in this habitat. There is nothing for me there. There is everything in the Satrap's den."

John shakes his head. "Do you know how much they've taken from us? You think your memories are the worst of it? Let me lay down some history on you: there's always been someone taking it away. They took it away from people like us when we were transported across an ocean. Taken away when aliens landed and ripped our countries away from us. Claimed our planets. There's a long, long list of things ripped away from people in history. You are not alone."

"Unlike them," you say, "what was taken from me is just within reach now."

"At a price," John says.

"Everything has a price," you say, moving toward him.

John blinks, surprised. He's been thinking we were having a dialogue, but you were waiting for the gun to dip slightly. For his attention to waver.

He's a good shot. Hits you right in the chest. A killing shot. One that would have stopped anyone else. The round penetrates, explodes. Shrapnel shreds the place a heart usually rests.

But that is just one small part. One bloodstream.

That faint hiccup of backup pumps dizzies you slightly as your blood pressure shifts and adapts. You cough blood, and grab John. You break his hand as you disarm him and knock him out.

For a while you sit next to him, the horrible feeling in your chest filling you with waves of pain.

Eventually that ebbs. You evaluate the damage, glyphs and messages ghosting across your eyeballs as your body, more alien machine than human, begins to process the damage and heal itself.

You won't be facing the Satrap in optimal fighting condition.

But you're so close. And if you delay, you invite the risk of the Satrap sending someone for John. That could be messy. And it won't give you the one thing you really want out of all this: an invitation into the Satrap's personal cavern, deep past its layers of defenses.

*Hello there you slimy alien shit,* you're thinking. *I've got a treat for you.*

*Just come a little closer, and don't mind the big teeth behind this smile.*

You snap the ammonia capsule apart under John's nose and he jerks awake. You're both in a loading bay near the rim of Hope's End. Water drips off in a corner, and the industrial grit on the walls is old and faded. A section of the habitat that has fallen into disuse.

"Don't do this. You should join us, Pepper. Leave all this behind. Start something fresh."

"That's not what's happening right now," you say. "The direction of this journey was set a long time ago." The door at the far end of the bay creaks open.

"You can't kill a Satrap," he says.

You lean next to him. "Your ships, they were never going to leave Hope's End. The Satrap here gave you enough fuel to bring those people here. But right now, you're being given dribs and drabs of antimatter. Enough to go back and forth to Earth. But not enough to make it back where you want to go with a whole fleet, right?"

John is silent.

You laugh. "The creature strings you along, until it can get what it wants. And then every single person who came here, well, they'll truly understand the name the few hundred free humans scraping by here gave it. Won't they? Hope's End. Because even if you're free, you're not free of the Satrap's long arm. And you'll be the one who lured them here with tales of a free world."

John lets out a deep breath, and slumps forward.

"But listen to me. Work with me, and I'll help you get what you need. Do you understand?"

"Neither of us will walk away alive from this," John says. "We are both dead men. We're talking, but we are dead men."

The empty-eyed vassals of the Satrap encircle you, a watchful, coordinated crowd that sighs happily as their eyes confirm that you have indeed delivered John deBrun.

"I want my memories, now," you say, holding tight to John.

"Come with us."

Somewhere deep inside, hope stirs. Anticipation builds.

Caution, you warn.


You're both herded deep into Hope's End by ten humans in thrall to the Satrap. Away from the green commons, below the corridors, below the subways and utility pipes, out of storage, and into the core ballast in the heart of the structure. The shadows are everywhere, and fluids drip slowly in the reduced gravity.

Muck oozes from grates, and biological mists hang in the air, thick on the lungs.

The Satrap's subterranean cavern is dim, and the wormy trilobite itself slouched in a dust pit at the center. The long tendrils around its maw socketed into machines, and from those machines, controlled anyone unfortunate enough to be in thrall.

A curious adaptation. You imagine the Satrap evolved somewhere deep underground, where it could lie in wait and plunge its neuro-tendrils into a prey's spine. And then what? It could use predators to grab prey, without harm to itself? Use prey as lures, dangling around that eager, gaping mouth.

"Finally," all ten voices around you say in unison.

John is shoved to the floor in front of you, and you move into the next section of your plan. You reach up to your back and use carbon-fibre fingernails to rip into the scars on your back.

This hurts.

But pain doesn't last forever. Not the pain of your skin ripping apart, or your fingers pulling. The pain of grabbing the handle just underneath as you pull the modified machete of your shoulder blade with a wet tearing and hiss.

Memory strata reforms the blade's handle to fit your grasp, and the black edge of the blade sucks the light into it. The molecular surface is hydrophobic, the viscera and blood on it slide off and splash to the floor.

The Satrap's thralls move toward you, but you put the edge of the short blade against the back of John's skull. "Don't."

As one, they all pull back.

You could have killed John with your bare hands, you don't need the sword. This is part statement. Theater to help the Satrap realize that you're far more dangerous than it has realized. Because, if it can get away with it, the Satrap will have both its prize and keep your memories.

And that isn't going to be happening.

"Give me my memories," you tell it.

"Let me have my new world," it replies in ten voices.

Ten. That's all it has surrounding you.

But you want those memories, so the standoff continues. You broadcast your implacability. You will not be moving until you are given those memories. And first.

"Tell it half the coordinates," you order John. You push the edge of the machete against his neck. Let's dangle the prize a little, you think.

"No," John says firmly.

"John," You kneel next to him. And you whisper, "it will die with those coordinates in its head. Trust me. Don't hold it to just yourself now, let it go. Let go of the burden. Let me help you. And then this will be all over."

But you notice something in his response.

He has been sharing the burden. Someone else knows the coordinates. Who? His first mate. Jay. There was a bond there, you remember.

John stumbles to his feet. "If you want the coordinates, you'll have to rip them out of my head yourself," he says to the Satrap.

And why would he do that?

His body is warm, near feverish. A Satrap wouldn't notice. Not a Satrap that had people under thrall to it with sores on their skin. But you notice.

You're not the only player in this game. John has a different plan. A plan to protect the coordinates. A plan to give his people time to grab what they need: fuel. He's got a bomb in him. Hidden, like your machete..

Well done, Mr. deBrun, you think.

Something moves from in the shadows. A large man with shaggy hair, seven and a half feet tall, muscle and fat and pistoned machine all stitched together like an art show gone wrong. A glimpse of what you could have been, if you'd been designed for strength and strength alone.

In the palm of his oversized hand, a brick that leaked superconducting fluid. ShinnCo logo on the outside and all. The last time you saw it . . . the last time you saw it, you'd woken up in a room and a man in a suit had sat with it in his lap. He'd explained to you that you were in that box. Everything that had once been you, at least. And now they owned it. And by extension, you.

"A copy of your memories," the Satrap says. "You'll hand deBrun over. I know you. I have tasted your memories. Partaken of you."

"You know who I was, know who I *am*," you say. "That was the me before, I'm the me after they took all that, sliced me apart, rebuilt me, and deployed me."

You grab John's head, and before anyone in the cavern can twitch, you slice his head off and hold it up into the air. John's body slumps forward, blood fountaining out over the rock at your feet.

"How long before the dying neurons are inaccessible in here?" you shout.

Everything in the room is flailing, responding to the movements of the Satrap's tendrils as they shake in anger.

You ignore all that. "Give me. My memories."

The Satrap calms. "You are too impertinent," the mouths around you chorus. "I am near immortal. I know the region the man was in. I will continue hunting for that world, and I will eventually have it. But you . . . "

The large man crushes the memory box. Hyperdense storage crumples easily under the carbon fiber fingers and steaming coolant bursts from between his knuckles.

Fragments drop to the ground.

You stare at them, lips tight.

"Ah," the Satrap sighs all around you. "Now those memories only live inside me. They are, once again, unique within flesh. So . . . if you kneel and behave from now on, I'll tell you all about your life. Every time you complete a task, you will return and bow before me right here, and I will tell you about your life. I will give you your past back. Just hand me the head, and kneel."

"You actually believe that I will hand you this head, and take a knee?" you ask.

"I do. From here, those are your only two choices. So the question is . . . "

You throw the head aside and hold the machete in both hands firmly.

As expected, half the men and women in thrall scrabble for the head. There's a twinge of regret. Maybe John would have been able to hide in his ship if you hadn't shown up. Maybe he would have been able to sneak enough fuel to his ragged fleet to make for that hidden world.

But you doubt it.

And here you are.

Killing the puppets who are in thrall to the Satrap is a thankless task. They are human. Many of them would not have asked for this life. They are people from the home world who fell on hard times, and were given a promise of future wealth in exchange for service. If they live long enough. Others were prepaid: a line of credit, a burst of wealth for a year, and then thrall. Others are criminals, or harvested from debtor's prison. Prisoners of war left over from various conflicts.

The Satrapy is "civilized." So it says. It doesn't raid for subjects. They have to, nominally, be beings that have lost their rights. Or agreed to lose them.

Doesn't mean most can't see what thralldom is.

But you kill anyway. Their blood, sliding down the hydrophobic blade to drench your sleeves. The three nearest, beheaded quickly and cleanly. There's no reason to make them suffer.

You walk through a mist of their jugular blood settling ever so slowly to the ground in the lower gravity. The Satrap, realizing what's happening, pulls humans around itself. One of them holds deBrun's head in their arms covetously.

The big guy is the artillery.

He advances, legs thudding, even here. Dust stirs. You walk calmly at him. He swings, a mass-driver, extinction-level powered punch that grazes you. Because what you have is speed. Mechanical tendons that trigger and snap you deep into his reach.

Just the whiff of his punch catches you in the ribs, though. They all crack, and alloys underneath are bent out of shape.

Warning glyphs cascade down your field of sight.

You ignore it all to bury your blade deep into the giant's right eye socket, then yank up.

Even as the body falls to the ground, you're facing the Satrap once more.

"I've already called my brothers and sisters down on the ground to come for you," it says through the remaining puppets. "You are dead."

"People keep telling me that," you say.

And maybe they're right.

The puppets come at you in a wedge. All seven. It's trying to overwhelm you.

You use the machete to cut through the jungle of flesh, leaving arms and limbs on the ground. And when you stand in front of the Satrap, it wriggles back away from you in fear.

"Let me tell you a memory," it begs through speakers, using the machines now that it has been shorn of biological toy things.

"It's too late," you tell it. "I'm dead."

You drive the machete deep. And then you keep pushing until you have to use your fingers to rip it apart.

There's a sense throughout the habitat that something major has shifted. Free humans are bunched together in corners, and others are dazed and wandering around. The rumor is that the Satrap has suddenly disappeared, or died. But what if it comes back? What happens when other Satraps arrive?

You find the docks and a row of deBrun's crew with guns guarding the lock. They stare at you, and you realize you are still covered in blood and carrying a machete. Everyone on the station has given you a wide, wide berth.

"If you wanted to steal fuel, now's the time," you tell them. "The Satrap's not going to be able to stop you. Everyone out there doesn't know what to do."

There are some other alien races sprinkled in throughout the station. But they seem to have locked themselves away, sensing something has gone wrong.

Smart.

"Who did the captain leave in charge, if he died?" you ask. They don't answer, but take you back into the ship, and the first mate comes up.

"You're in charge?" you ask.

"Yes," he nods. "I'm John."

You frown. "He called you Jay on the bridge, when I came out."

The first mate smiles sadly. "John deBrun. The junior John deBrun. Jay because we don't need two Johns on the bridge. Though . . . I guess that won't happen anymore."

"He gave you the coordinates, in case he was taken."

John's son nods. "You were taken with him, by the Satrap? You were there?"

You pause for a moment, trying to find words that suddenly flee you. You change direction. "You have three hours to steal as much fuel as you can before forces from the planet below arrive. We should both be long gone by then. Understand?"

"Three hours isn't long enough."

You shrug. "Take what time you have been given."

"You don't understand, we're taking on extra people. People we didn't plan to take on. That adds to the mass we need to spin up. We have the other ships docking hard, and we're taking refugees from Hope's End. People, who if they stay, will be back in thrall at the end of those few hours. We won't have enough fuel to get where we need to go. Maybe, three quarters of the way?"

And out there in space, you were either there or not. There was no part way. No one was getting out on foot to push a ship. Those are cold calculations. They come with the job of captain. Air. Food. Water. Carbon filters. Fuel.

"Sounds like you need to shut your locks soon," you say. "Or you risk throwing away your father's sacrifice."

"I will not leave them," John says calmly. "He may have been able to. You may. But I will not. We are human beings. We should not leave other human beings behind."

"Then you'd better hope your men hurry on the fuel siphoning."

You have no use for goodbyes. You leave him in his cockpit. But you stand in the corridor by yourself in the quiet. Your legs buckle slightly. A wound? Overtired muscles sizzling from the performance earlier? You lean against the wall and take a deep breath.

When you let go, you stare at the bloody handprint.

You lost it all. So close, and you lost it all.

And now what? What are you?

You'll never have those memories. They aren't you anymore. You are you. What you have right now, is you. What you do next, will be you. What will that be?

A cold heart and a bloody hand. That's what you've been. What you are.

You turn and go back into the cockpit.

"Is the planet real?" you ask. And look at John's son for any hint, any sign of a lie. You can see pulse, heat, and micro-expressions. Things that help you fight, spot the move. And now, spot intent.

"It's real."

"There is another way," you say.

"And what is that?"

"Take me with you. Get as much fuel as you can, but leave early. Even if it means we only get halfway to where you are going. I killed the Satrap, and everything protecting him. And it wasn't the first. When we run out of fuel, we'll dock and I'll rip more fuel out of their alien hands for you. For you. Understand? I can train more like me. When your fleet passes through, those that stand against us will rue it. I will do this because there is a debt here, understand?"

John looks warily at you. "You were with my father. He didn't kill the Satrap?"

"There is a debt," you repeat.

"He helped you?"

"Give me weapons. The non-humans on the station, they enjoy a position of power. They have avoided mostly being in thrall, as we are the new species for that. So even though we have time, they will figure out what we are doing and act against us. You'll want me out there, buying you time."

John nods, and reaches out a hand to shake.

You don't take it. You can't take it. Not with his father's blood still on it.

"Weapons," you repeat. "Before your men start dying unnecessarily."

Cycled through the locks, deBrun's men behind you, you walk past the stream of frightened people heading for the ship.

You stand in the large docking bays and survey the battlefield.

This is who you are. This is who you will be. This is who you choose.

A cold heart and bloody hands.

When this is over, when you help deliver them to their new world and repay your debt, you can go home to Earth. Stalk for clues to your past. See if you wander until you find that palm tree on the island you remember.

But for now, you are right here.

Right now.

Waiting for the fight to come to you.

Robert Silverberg has been a professional writer since 1955, and has published more than a hundred books and close to a thousand short stories.
Among his best-known novels are *Lord Valentine's Castle, Dying Inside, Night-
wings, The World Inside,* and *Downward to the Earth.* He is a many-time winner
of the Hugo and Nebula awards, was Guest of Honor at the World Science
Fiction Convention in Heidelberg, Germany, in 1970, and in 2004 was named
a Grand Master by the Science Fiction Writers of America, of which he is a
past president.

Silverberg was born in New York City, but he and his wife Karen have
lived for many years in the San Francisco Bay Area. They and an assortment
of cats share a sprawling house of unusual architectural style, surrounded by
exotic plants.

# THE COLONEL RETURNS
# TO THE STARS

## *Robert Silverberg*

O n the day that the Colonel found himself seized by circumstances
and thrust back against his will into active service he had risen
early, as usual, he had bathed in the river of sparkling liquid gold
that ran behind his isolated villa in a remote corner of the Aureus Highlands, he had plucked a quick handful of dagger-shaped golden leaves
from the quezquez tree for the little explosive burst of energy that chewing them always provided, and he had gone for his morning stroll along
the glimmering crescent dunes of fine golden powder that ran off down
toward the carasar forest, where the slender trunks of the long-limbed
trees swayed in the mild breeze like the elongated necks of graceful lam-
mis-gazelles. And when the Colonel got back to the villa an hour later for
his breakfast the stranger was there, and everything began to change for
him in the life that he had designed to be changeless forever more.

The stranger was young—*seemed* young, anyway; one never could
really tell—and compactly built, with a tightly focused look about him.

His eyes had the cold intensity of a fast-flowing river of clear water; his lips were thin, with deep vertical lines at their sides; his thick, glossy black hair was swept backward against his head like the wings of a raven. The little silver badge of the Imperium was visible on the breast of his tunic.

He was standing on the open patio, arms folded, smiling a smile that was not really much of a smile. Plainly he had already been inside. There was nothing to prevent that. One did not lock one's doors here. The Colonel, looking past him, imagined that he could see the fiery track of the man's intrusive footsteps blazing up from the green flagstone floor. He had entered; he had seen; he had taken note. The Colonel kept about himself in his retirement the abundant memorabilia of a long life spent meddling in the destinies of worlds. In his sprawling house on golden Galgala he had set out on display, for his eyes alone, a vast array of things, none of them very large or very showy—bits of pottery, fossils, mineral specimens, gnarled pieces of wood, coins, quaint rusted weapons, all manner of ethnographic artifacts, and a great number of other tangible reminders of his precise and devastating interventions on those many worlds.

Most of these objects—a scrap of bone, a painted stone, a bit of tapestry, a blunted knife, a tattered banner that bore no emblem, a box of sullen-looking gray sand—had no obvious significance. They would have been baffling to any visitor to the Colonel's Galgala retreat, if ever a visitor were to come, although there had not been any in many years, until this morning. But to the Colonel each of these things had special meaning. They were talismans, touchstones that opened a century and a half of memories. From Eden, from Entrada, from Megalo Kastro, from Narajo of the Seven Pyramids, from snowy Mulano, from unhappy Tristessa, even, and Fenix and Phosphor and some two dozen others out of mankind's uncountable string of planets had they come, most of them collected by the Colonel himself but some by his pinch-faced limping father, the Old Captain, and even a few that had been brought back by his swaggering buccaneer of a grandfather, who had carved a path through the universe as though with a machete five hundred years before him.

The Colonel now was old, older than his father had lived to be and beginning to approach the remarkable longevity of his grandfather, and his days of adventure were over. Having outlived the last of his wives, he lived alone, quietly, seeking no contact with others. He did not even travel anymore. For the first two decades after his retirement he had, more from habit than any other motive, gone off, strictly as a tourist, on journeys to this world and that, planets like Jacynth and Macondo and Entropy and Duud Shabeel that he had never found occasion to visit during the course of his long professional career. But then he had stopped doing even that.

In his time he had seen enough, and more than enough. He had been everywhere, more or less, and he had done everything, more or less. He had overthrown governments. He had headed governments. He had survived a dozen assassination attempts. He had carried out assassinations himself. He had ordered executions. He had refused a kingship. He had lived through two poisonings and three marriages. And then, growing old, old beyond the hope of many further rejuvenations, he had put in for retirement and walked away from it all.

When he was young, restless and full of insatiable hungers, he had dreamed of striding from world to world until he had spanned the entire universe, and he had leaped with savage eagerness into the shining maw of each new Velde doorway, impatient to step forth onto the unknown world that awaited him. And no sooner had he arrived but he was dreaming of the next. Now, though, obsessive questing of that sort seemed pointless to him. He had decided, belatedly, that travel between the stars as facilitated by the Velde doorways or by the other and greater system of interstellar transport, the Magellanic one, was too easy, that the ease of it rendered all places identical, however different from one another they might actually be. Travel should involve travail, the Colonel had come to think. But modern travel, simple, instantaneous, unbounded by distance, was too much like magic. Matters had been different for the ancient explorers of ancient Earth, setting out on their arduous voyages of discovery across the dark unfriendly seas of their little planet with almost incomprehensible courage in the face of impossible odds. Those men of so many thousands of years ago, staking their lives to cross uncharted waters in tiny wooden ships for the sake of reaching alien and probably hostile shores on the very same world, had been true heroes. But now—now, when one could go almost anywhere in the galaxy in the twinkling of an eye, without effort or risk, did going anywhere at all matter? After the first fifty worlds, why not simply stay home?

The visitor said, "Your home is fascinating, Colonel." He offered no apology for trespassing. The Colonel did not expect one. With the smallest of gestures he invited the man inside. Asked him, in a perfunctory way, if he had had a good journey. Served him tea on the terrace overlooking the river. Awaited with formal politeness the explanation for the visit, for surely there had to be some explanation, though he did not yet know that it was ultimately going to break the atoms of his body apart once again, and scatter them once more across the cosmos, or he would have shut the man out of his house without hearing another word.

The man's surname was one that the Colonel recognized, one that had long been a distinguished one in the archives of the Imperium. The Colonel had worked with men of that name many years ago. So had his father. Men of that name had pursued his buccaneering grandfather across half the galaxy.

"Do you know of a world called Hermano?" the man asked. "In the Aguila sector, well out toward the Core?"

The Colonel searched his memory and came up with nothing. "No," he said. "Should I?"

"It's two systems over from Gran Chingada. The records show that you spent some time on Gran Chingada ninety years back."

"Yes, I did. But two systems over could be a dozen light-years away," said the Colonel. "I don't know your Hermano."

The stranger described it: an ordinary-sounding world, a reasonably pleasant world-shaped world, with deserts, forests, oceans, flora, fauna, climate. One of six planets, and the only habitable one, around a standard sort of star. Apparently it had been colonized by settlers from Gran Chingada some thirty or forty years before. Its exports were medicinal herbs, precious gems, desirable furs; various useful metals. Three years ago, said the stranger, it had ejected the Imperium commissioners and proclaimed itself independent.

The Colonel, listening in silence, said nothing. But for a moment, only a moment, he reacted as he might have reacted fifty years earlier, feeling the old reflexive stab of cold anger at that clanging troublesome word, *independent*.

The stranger said, "We have, of course, invoked the usual sanctions. They have not been effective." Gran Chingada, itself not the most docile of worlds, had chosen to people its colony-world by shipping it all the hard cases, its most bellicose and refractory citizens, a rancorous and uncongenial crowd who were told upon their departure that if they ever were seen on Gran Chingada again they would be taken to the nearest Velde doorway and shipped out again to some randomly chosen destination that might not prove to be a charming place to live, or even one that was suitable for human life at all. But the Hermano colonists, surly and contentious though they were, had found their new planet very much to their liking. They had made no attempt to return to their mother world, or to go anywhere else. And, once their settlement had reached the point of economic self-sufficiency, they had blithely announced their secession from the Imperium and ceased remitting taxes to the Central Authority. They had also halted all shipments of the medicinal herbs and useful metals to their trading partners throughout the Imperium, pending a favorable adjustment in the general structure of prices and tariffs.

A familiar image had been ablaze in the Colonel's mind since the first mention of Hermano's declaration of independence: the image of a beautiful globe of brilliantly polished silver, formerly flawless, now riven by a dark hideous crack. That was how he had always seen the Imperium, as a perfect polished globe. That was how he had always seen the attempts of one world or another to separate itself from the perfection that was the Imperium, as an ugly crevasse on the pure face of beauty. It had been his life's work to restore the perfection of that flawless silvery face whenever it was marred. But he had separated himself from that work many years ago. It was as though it had been done by another self.

Now, though, a little to his own surprise, a flicker of engagement leaped up in him: he felt questions surging within him, and potential courses of action, just as if he were still on active duty. Those medicinal herbs and useful metals, the Colonel began to realize, must be of considerably more than trifling significance to interstellar commerce. And, over and beyond that, there was the basic issue of maintaining the fundamental integrity of the Imperium. But all that was only a flicker, a momentarily renewed ticking of machinery that he had long since ceased to use. The maintenance of the fundamental integrity of the Imperium was no longer his problem. The thoughts that had for that flickering moment sprung up reflexively within him subsided as quickly as they arose. He had devoted the best part of his life to the Service, and had served loyally and well, and now he was done with all that. He had put his career behind him for good.

But it was clear to him that if he wanted to keep it that way he must be prepared to defend himself against the threat that this man posed, and that it might not be easy, for obviously this man wanted something from him, something that he was not prepared to give.

The stranger said, "You know where I'm heading with this story, Colonel."

"I think I can guess, yes."

The expected words came: "There is no one better able to handle the Hermano problem than you."

The Colonel closed his eyes a moment, nodded, sighed. Yes. What other reason would this man have for coming here? Quietly he said, "And just why do you think so?"

"Because you are uniquely fitted to deal with it."

Of course. Of course. They always said things like that. The Colonel felt a prickling sensation in his fingertips. It was clear now that he was in a duel with the Devil. Smiling, he said, making the expected response, "You say this despite knowing that I've been retired from the Service for forty years." He gestured broadly: the villa, the display of souvenirs of a long career, the garden, the river, the dunes beyond. "You see the sort of life I've constructed for myself here."

"Yes. The life of a man who has gone into hiding from himself, and who lives hunkered down and waiting for death. A man who dies a little more than one day's worth every day."

That was not so expected. It was a nasty thrust, sharp, brutal, intended to wound, even to maim. But the Colonel remained calm, as ever. His inner self was not so easily breached, and surely this man, if he had been briefed at all properly, knew that.

He let the brutality of the words pass unchallenged. "I'm old, now. Hunkering down is a natural enough thing, at my age. You'll see what I mean, in a hundred years or so."

"You're not *that* old, Colonel. Not too old for one last round of service, anyway, when the Imperium summons you."

"Can you understand," the Colonel said slowly, "that a time comes in one's life when one no longer feels an obligation to serve?"

"For some, yes," said the stranger. "But not for someone like you. A time comes when one *wishes* not to serve, yes. I can understand that. But the sense of obligation—no, that never dies. Which is why I've come to you. As I said, you are uniquely fitted for this, as you will understand when I tell you that the man who has made himself the leader of the Hermano rebellion is a certain Geryon Lanista."

*Lanista?*

It was decades since the Colonel had last heard that name spoken aloud. It crashed into him like a spear striking his breast. If he had not already been sitting, he would have wanted now to sink limply into a seat.

He controlled himself. "How curious. I knew a Geryon Lanista once," he said, after a moment. "He's long dead, that one."

"No," said the stranger. "He isn't. I'm quite sure of that."

"Are we talking about Geryon Lanista of Ultima Thule in the San Pedro Cluster?" The Colonel was struggling for his equilibrium, and struggling not to let the struggle show. "The Geryon Lanista who was formerly a member of our Service?"

"The very one."

"Well, he's been dead for decades. He killed himself after he bungled the Tristessa job. That was probably long before your time, but you could look it all up. He and I handled the Tristessa assignment together. Because of him, we failed in a terrible way."

"Yes. I know that."

"And then he killed himself, before the inquiries were even starting. To escape from the shame of what he had done."

"No. He *didn't* kill himself." Profoundly unsettling words, spoken with quiet conviction that left the Colonel a little dizzied.

"Reliable sources told me that he did."

Calm, the Colonel ordered himself. Stay calm.

"You were misinformed," the visitor said, in that same tone of deadly assurance. "He is very much alive and well and living on Hermano under the name of Martin Bauer, and he is the head of the provisional government there. The accuracy of our identification of him is beyond any doubt. I can show him to you, if you like. Shall I do that?"

Numbly the Colonel signalled acquiescence. His visitor drew a flat metal case from a pocket of his tunic and tapped it lightly. A solido figure of a man sprang instantly into being a short distance away: a stocky, powerfully built man, apparently of middle years, deep-chested and extraordinarily wide through the shoulders, a great massive block of a man, with a blunt-tipped nose, tight-clamped downturned lips, and soft, oddly seductive brown eyes that did not seem to be congruent with the bulkiness of his body or the harshness of his features. The face was not one that the Colonel remembered having seen before, but time and a little corrective surgery would account for that. The powerful frame, though, was something that no surgery, even now when surgery could achieve almost anything, could alter. And the eyes—those strange, haunted eyes—beyond any question they were the eyes of Geryon Lanista.

"What do you think?" the visitor asked.

Grudgingly the Colonel said, "There are some resemblances, yes. But it's impossible. He's dead. I know that he is."

"No doubt you want him to be, Colonel. I can understand that, yes. But this is the man. Believe me. You are looking at your old colleague Geryon Lanista."

How could he say no to that? Surely that was Lanista, here before him. Surely. Surely. An altered Lanista, yes, but Lanista all the same. What was the use of arguing otherwise? Those eyes—those freakishly wide shoulders—that barrel of a chest—

But there was no way that Lanista could be alive.

Clinging to a stubborn certainty that he was beginning not to feel was really solid the Colonel said, "Very well: the face is his. I'll concede that much. But the image? Something out of the files of fifty years ago, tarted up with a few little tweaks here and there to make him look as though he's tried recently to disguise himself? What's here to make me believe that this is a recent image of a living man?"

"We have other images, Colonel." The visitor tapped the metal case again, and there was the stocky man on the veranda of an imposing house set within a luxurious garden. Two small children, built to the same stocky proportions as he, stood beside him, and a smiling young woman. "At his home on Hermano," said the visitor, and tapped the case again. Now the stocky man appeared in a group of other men, evidently at a political meeting; he was declaiming something about the need for Hermano to throw off the shackles of the Imperium. He tapped the case again—

"No. Stop. You can fake whatever scene you want. I know how these things are done."

"Of course you do, Colonel. But why would we bother? Why try to drag you out of retirement with a bunch of faked images? Sooner or later a man of your ability would see through them. But we *know* that this man is Geryon Lanista. We have all the necessary proof, the incontrovertible genetic data. And so we've come to you, as someone who not only has the technical skills to deal with the problem that Lanista is creating, but the personal motivation to do so."

"Incontrovertible genetic data?"

"Yes. Incontrovertible. Shall I show you the genomics? Here: look. From the Service files, sixty years back, Geryon Lanista, his entire genome. And here, this one, from the Gran Chingada immigration records, approximately twenty years old, Martin Bauer. Do you see?"

The Colonel glanced at the images, side by side in the air and identical in every respect, shook his head, looked away. The pairing was convincing, yes. And, yes, they could fake anything they liked, even a pair of gene charts. There wasn't all that much difficulty in that. But to fake so *much*—to go to such preposterous lengths for the sake of bamboozling one tired old man—no, no, the logic that lay at the core of his soul cried out against the likelihood of that.

His last resistance crumbled. He yielded to the inescapable reality. Despite everything he had believed all these years, this man Martin Bauer *was* Geryon Lanista. Alive and well, as this stranger had said, and conspiring against the Imperium on a planet called Hermano. And the Service wanted him to do something about that.

For an instant, contemplating this sudden and disastrous turn of events, the Colonel felt something that wasn't quite fear and not quite dismay—both of them feelings that he scarcely understood, let alone had ever experienced—but was certainly a kind of discomfort. This had been a duel with the Devil, all right, and the Devil had played with predictably diabolical skill, and the Colonel saw that here, in the very first moments of the contest, he had already lost. He had not thought to be beaten so easily. He had lived his life, he had put in his years in the Service, he had met all dangers with bravery and all difficulties with triumphant ingenuity, and here, as the end of it all approached, he had come safely to rest in the harbor of his own invulnerability on this idyllic golden world; and in a moment, with just a few quick syllables, this cold-eyed stranger had ripped him loose from all of that and had tumbled him back into the remorseless torrents of history. He ached to refuse the challenge. It was within the range of possibility for him to refuse it. It was certainly his right to refuse it, at his age, after all that he had done. But—even so—even so—

"Geryon Lanista," the Colonel said, marveling. "Yes. Yes. Well, perhaps this really is him." There was a touch of hoarseness in his tone.— "You know the whole story, Lanista and me?"

"That goes without saying. Why else would we have come to you?"

The odd prickling in the Colonel's fingertips began to give way to an infuriating trembling. "Well, then—"

He looked across the table and it seemed to him that he saw a softening of those icy eyes, even a hint of moisture in them. An upwelling of compassion, was it, for the poor old man who had been so cruelly ensnared in the sanctity of his own home? But was that in any way likely, coming from *this* particular man, who had sprung from *those* ancestors. Compassion had never been a specialty of that tribe.

Perhaps they are making them softer nowadays, the Colonel thought, yet another example of the general decadence of modern times, and felt renewed pleasure in the awareness that he was no one's ancestor at all, that his line ended with him. And then he realized that he was wrong, that there was no compassion in this man at all, that those were simply the jubilant self-congratulatory tears of triumph in the other man's eyes.

"We can count on you?" the visitor asked.

"If you've been lying to me—"

"I haven't been lying," said the visitor, saying it in a flat offhanded way that conveyed more conviction than any number of passionate oaths might have done.

The Colonel nodded. "All right. I give in. You win. I'll do what I can do," he said, in a barely audible voice. He felt like a man who had been marched to the edge of a cliff and now was taking a few last breaths before jumping off. "Yes. Yes. There are, I hardly need to say, certain practical details that we need to discuss, first—"

There was something dreamlike about finding himself making ready for a new assignment after so many years. He wouldn't leave immediately, of course, nor would the journey to Hermano be anything like instantaneous. The maintenance of the villa during his absence had to be arranged for, and there was the background information of the Hermano situation to master, and certain potentially useful documents to excavate from the archives of his career, and then he would have to make the long overland journey to Elsinore, down on the coast, where the nearest Velde doorway was located. Even after that he still would have some traveling to do, because Gran Chingada and its unruly colony-world Hermano, both of them close to the central sector of the galaxy, were beyond the direct reach of Velde transmission. To complete his journey he would have to shift over to the galaxy's other and greater teleportation system, the ancient and unfathomable one that had been left behind by the people known as the Magellanics.

He had not expected ever to be jaunting across the universe again. The visit to Duud Shabeel, two decades before, had established itself in his mind as the last of all his travels. But plainly there was to be one more trip even so; and as he prepared for it, his mind went back to his first journey ever, the one his ferocious fiery-eyed grandfather had taken him on, in that inconceivably remote epoch when he was ten years old.

He had lived on Galgala even then, though not in the highlands but along the humid coast, where liquid gold came bubbling up out of the swamps. His grandfather had always had a special love for Galgala, the planet that had ruined the value of gold for the entire galaxy. Gold was everywhere there, in the leaves of the trees, in the sands of the desert, in the stones of the ground. Flecks of gold flowed in the veins of Galgala's native animals. Though it had been thousands of years since the yellow metal had passed as currency among humankind, the discovery of Galgala had finished it for all eternity as a commodity of value. But the old pirate who had engendered the Colonel's father was a medieval at heart, and he cherished Galgala for what its gold might have meant in the days when the whole of the human universe was just the little blue world that was Earth. He had made it his headquarters during his privateering career, and when he was old he had gone there to dwell until the end of his days. The Colonel's father, who in his parsimonious pinch-faced way claimed only the honorary title of Captain, was in the Service then, traveling constantly from world to world as need arose and only rarely coming to rest, and, not knowing what to do with the boy who would some day become the Colonel, had sent him to Galgala to live with his grandfather.

"It's time you learned what traveling is like," the old man said one day, when the boy who would become the Colonel was ten.

He was already tall and sturdy for his age, but he was still only ten, and his grandfather, even then centuries old—no one knew exactly how old he was, perhaps not even he himself—rose up and up beside him like a great tree, a shaggy-bearded tree with furious eyes and long black coils of piratical hair dangling to his shoulders and horrendous jutting cheekbones sharp as blades. The gaunt, bony old man had spent the many years of his life outside the law, the law that the Captain and later the Colonel would serve with such devotion, but no one in the family ever spoke openly of that. And although he had finally abandoned his marauding ways, he still affected the showy costume of his trade, the leather jerkin and the knee-high boots with the tapered tips and the broad-brimmed hat from which the eternally black coils of his long hair came tumbling superabundantly down.

They stood before the doorway, the future Colonel and his formidable grandfather, and the old man said, "When you step through it, you'll be scanned and surveyed, and then you'll be torn apart completely, down to the fragments of your atoms, altogether annihilated, and at the same moment an exact duplicate of you will be assembled at the other end, wherever that may be. How do you like that?"

The old man waited, then, searching for signs of fear or doubt on his grandson's face. But even then the boy understood that such feelings as fear or doubt ought not to be so much as felt, let alone displayed, in the presence of his grandfather.

"And where will we come out, then?" the boy who would be the Colonel asked.

"At our destination," said the old pirate, and casually shoved him toward the doorway. "You wait for me there, do you hear me, boy? I'll be coming along right behind."

The doorway on Galgala, like Velde doorways everywhere in the considerable sector of the galaxy where Velde-system terminals had been established, was a cubicle of black glass, four meters high, three meters wide, three meters deep. Along its inner walls a pair of black-light lenses stared at each other like enigmatic all-seeing eyes. On the rear wall of the cubicle were three jutting metal cones from which the Velde force emanated whenever a traveler crossed the threshold of the cubicle.

The theory of Velde transmission was something that everyone was taught when young, the way the law of gravity is taught, or the axioms of geometry; but one does not need to study Newton or Euclid very deeply in order to know how to descend a staircase or how to calculate the shortest way to get across a street, and one could make a fifty-light-year Velde hop without any real understanding of the concept that the universe is constructed of paired particles, equal masses of matter and antimatter, and that matter can decay spontaneously into antimatter at any time, but each such event must invariably be accompanied by the simultaneous conversion of an equivalent mass of antimatter into matter somewhere else—anywhere else—in the universe, so that the symmetry of matter is always conserved.

Velde's Theorem had demonstrated the truth of that, long ago, millennia ago, back in those almost unimaginable primeval days when Earth and Earth alone was mankind's home. Then Conrad Wilf, freebooting physicist, provided a practical use for Velde's equations by showing how it was possible to construct containment facilities that could prevent the normally inescapable mutual annihilation of matter and antimatter, thereby making feasible the controlled conversion of particles into their antiparticles. Matter that was held within a Wilf containment field could be transformed into antimatter and stored, without fear of instant annihilation, while at the same moment a corresponding quantity of anti-matter elsewhere in the universe was converted into matter and held in a corresponding Wilf field far away.

But Wilf conversions, contained though they were, still entailed a disconcerting randomness in the conservation of symmetry: when matter was destroyed here and a balancing quantity of antimatter was created elsewhere, *elsewhere* could be at any point at all in the universe, perhaps ten thousand kilometers away, perhaps ten billion light-years; everything was open-ended, without directionality or predictability. It remained for Simtow, the third of the three great pioneers of interstellar transport, to develop a device that tuned the Velde Effect so that the balancing transactions of Wilf conversions took place not randomly but within the confines of a specific closed system with Wilf containment fields at both ends. At the destination end, antimatter was stored in a Wilf containment vessel. At the transmission end, that which was to be transmitted would undergo a Velde transformation into antimatter, a transformation that was balanced, at the designated destination end, by the simultaneous and equivalent transformation of the stored antimatter into a quantity of matter identical to that which had been converted by the transmitter. The last step was the controlled annihilation of the antimatter that had been created at the transmission end, thereby recapturing the energy that had powered the original transmission. The effect was the simultaneous particle-by-particle duplication of the transmission matter at the receiving end.

The boy who would become the Colonel comprehended all this, more or less, at least to the extent of understanding that one was demolished *here* and reassembled instantaneously *there*. He knew, also, of the ancient experiments with inanimate objects, with small animals and plants, and finally with the very much living body of the infinitely courageous pio-neering voyager Haakon Christiansen, that showed that whatever went into a transmission doorway would emerge unharmed at its destination. All the same it was impossible for him to avoid a certain degree of uncer-tainty, even of something not very different from terror, in the moment when his grandfather's bony hand flung him toward the waiting doorway.

That uncertainty, that terror, if that is what it was, lasted only an instant's part of an instant. Then he was within the doorway and, because Velde transmission occurs in a realm where relativistic laws are irrele-vant, he found himself immediately outside it again, but he was some-where else, and it all looked so completely strange that there was no point in being frightened of it.

Where he found himself was a world with a golden-red sun that cast a hard metallic light altogether unlike the cheerful yellow light of Galgala's sun, which was the only sunlight he had ever seen. He was on a barren strip of flat sandy land with a lofty cliff at his back and what looked like a great oceanic expanse of pink mud in front of him. There were no living creatures in sight, no plants, no trees. He had never been in the presence of such utter emptiness before.

That sea of pink mud at whose border he stood stretched out as far as the horizon and, for all he knew, wrapped itself around it and kept going down the other side of the planet. It was indeed an ocean of mud: quivering, rippling mud, mud that seemed almost to be alive. Perhaps it *was* alive, a single living organism of colossal size. He could feel warmth radiating from it. He sensed a kind of sentience about it. Again and again some patch of its surface would begin throbbing spasmodically, and then it would send up odd projections and protuberances that slowly wriggled and writhed like questing tentacles before sinking down again into the huge sluggish mass from which it had arisen. He stared at it for a long while, fascinated by its eerie motions.

After a time he wondered where his grandfather was.

He should have followed instantly, should he not? But it didn't appear that he had. Instead the boy discovered himself alone in a way that was completely new to him, perhaps the only human being on a vast strange planet whose name he did not even know. At least twenty minutes had gone by. That was a long time to be alone in a place like this. He was supposed to wait here; but for how long? He wondered what he would do if, after another hour or two, his grandfather still had not arrived, and decided finally that he would simply step through the doorway in the hope that it would take him back to Galgala, or at least to some world where he could get help finding his way home.

Turning away from the sea, he looked backward and up, and then he understood where it was that his grandfather had sent him, for there on the edge of that towering cliff just in back of him he was able to make out the shape of a monumental stone fortress, low and long, outlined sharply against the glowering greenish sky like a crouching beast making ready to spring. Everyone in the galaxy knew what that fortress was. It was the ancient gigantic ruined building known as Megalo Kastro, from which this planet took its name—the only surviving work of some unknown extinct race that had lived here eight million years ago. There was nothing else like it in the universe.

"What do you say?" his grandfather said, stepping through the doorway with the broad self-congratulatory smile of someone arriving exactly on time. "Are you ready to climb up there and have a look around?"

It was an exhausting climb. The old man had long legs and a demon's unbounded vitality, and the boy had a ten-year-old's half-developed muscles. But he had no choice other than to follow along as closely as possible, scrambling frantically up the rough stone blocks of the staircase, too far apart for a boy's lesser stride, that had been carved in the face of the cliff. He was breathless by the time he reached the top, fifty paces to the rear of his grandfather. The old man had already entered the ruin and had begun to saunter through it with the proprietorial air of a guide leading a party of tourists.

It was too big to see in a single visit. They went on and on, and still there was no end to its vaulted chambers. "This is the Equinox Hall," his grandfather said, gesturing grandly. "You see the altar down at that end? And this—we call it the Emperor's Throne Room. And this—the Hall of Sacrifices. Our own names for them, you understand. Obviously we'll never know what they really were called." There were no orderly angles everywhere. Everything seemed unstable and oppressively strange. The walls seemed to waver and flow, and though the boy knew it was only an illusion, it was a profoundly troublesome one. His eyes ached. His stomach felt queasy. Yet his heart pounded with fierce excitement.

"Look here," said his grandfather. "The handprint of one of the builders, maybe. Or a prisoner's." They had reached the cellar level now. On the wall of one of the dungeon-like rooms was the white outline of a large hand, a hand with seven fingers and a pair of opposable thumbs, one on each side. An *alien* hand.

The boy who would become the Colonel shivered. No one knew who had built this place. Some extinct race, surely, because there was no known race of the galaxy today that could have done it except the human race—no others encountered thus far had evolved beyond the most primitive level—and mankind itself had not yet evolved when Megalo Kastro had been built. But it was not likely to have been the work of the great unknown race that humans called the Magellanics, either, because they had left their transporter doorways, immensely more efficient and useful than Velde doorways, on every world that had been part of their ancient empire, and there was no Magellanic doorway, nor any trace of one, on Megalo Kastro. So they had never been here. But *someone* had, some third great race that no one knew anything about, and had left this fortress behind, millions of years ago.

"Come," said his grandfather, and they descended and returned to the doorway, and went off to a world with an amber sky that had swirls of blue in it, and a dull reddish sun lying like a lump of coal along the horizon with a second star, brighter, high overhead. This was Cuchulain, said the old man, a moon of the subluminous star Gwydion, the dark companion of a star named Lalande 21185, and they were only eight light-years from Earth, which to the boy's mind seemed just a snap of the fingers away. That amazed him, to be this close to Earth, the almost legendary mother world of the whole Imperium. The air here was thick and soft, almost sticky, and everything in the vicinity of the doorway was wrapped in furry ropes of blue-green vegetation. In the distance a city of considerable size gleamed through the muzzy haze. The boy felt heavy here: Cuchulain's gravity nailed him to the ground.

"Can we go on from here to Earth?" the boy asked. "It's so near, after all!"

"Earth is forbidden," said the old man. "No one goes to Earth except when Earth does the summoning. It is the law."

"But you have always lived outside the law, haven't you?"

"Not this one," his grandfather said, and put an end to the discussion.

He was hurt by that, back then in his boyhood. It seemed unfair, a wanton shutting out of the whole universe by the planet that had set everything in motion for the human race. They should not close themselves off to their descendants this way, he told himself. But years later, looking back on that day with his grandfather, he would take a different view. They are right to keep us out, he would tell himself later. That is how it should be. Earth is long ago, Earth is far away. It should remain like that. We are the galactic people, the people born in the stars. We are the future. They are the past. They and we should not mingle. Our ways are not their ways, and any contact between them and us would be corrupting for both. For better or for worse they have turned us loose into the stars and we live a new kind of life out here in this infinite realm, nothing at all like theirs, and our path must forevermore be separate from theirs.

His grandfather had taken him to Cuchulain only because it was the contact point for a world called Moebius, where four suns danced in the sky, pearly-white triplets and a violet primary. The boy imagined that a world that had a name like Moebius would be a place of sliding dimensions and unexpected twisted vistas, but no, there was nothing unusual about it except the intricacy of the shadows cast by its quartet of suns. His grandfather had a friend on Moebius, a white-haired man as frail and worn as a length of burned rope, and they spent a day and a half visiting with him. The boy understood very little of what the two old men said: it was almost as if they were speaking some other language. Then they moved on, to a wintry world called Zima, and from there to Jackal, and from Jackal to Tycho, and from Tycho to Two Dogs, world after world, most of them worlds of the Rim where the sky was strangely empty, frighteningly black at night with only a few thousand widely spaced stars in view, not the bright, unendingly luminous curtain that eternally surrounded a Core world like Galgala, a wall of blazing light with no break in it anywhere; and then, just as the boy was starting to think that he and the old man were going to travel forever through the Imperium without ever settling down, they stepped through the doorway once more and emerged into the familiar warm sunlight and golden vegetation of Galgala.

"So now you know," his grandfather said. "Galgala is just one small world, out of many."

"How great the Imperium is!" cried the boy, dazzled by his journey. The vastness of it had stunned him, and the generosity of whatever creator it was that had made so many stars and fashioned so many beautiful worlds to whirl about them, and the farsightedness of those who had thought to organize those worlds into one Imperium, so that the citizens of that Imperium could rove freely from star to star, from world to world, without limits or bounds. For the first time in his life, but far from the last, he saw in his mind the image of that flawless silver globe, shining in his imagination like the brightest of all possible moons. His grandfather had worked hard to instill a love for anarchy in him, but the trip had had entirely the opposite effect. "How marvelous that all those different worlds should be bound together under a single government!" he cried.

He knew at once that it was the wrong thing to say. "The Imperium is the enemy, boy," said his grandfather, his voice rumbling deep down in his chest, his scowling face dark as the sky before a thunderstorm. "It strangles us. It is the chain around our throats." And went stalking away, leaving him to face his father, who had come back from a mission in the Outer Sector during his absence, and who, astonishingly, struck him across the cheek when the boy told him where he had been and what he had seen and what his grandfather had said.

"The enemy? A chain about our throats? Oh, no, boy. The Imperium is our only bulwark against chaos," his father told him. "Don't you ever forget that." And slapped him again, to reinforce the lesson. The boy hated his father in that moment as he had never hated him before. But in time the sting of the slaps was gone, and even the memory of the indignity of them had faded, and when the hour came for the boy to choose what his life would be, it was the Service that he chose, and not the buccaneering career of his demonic grandfather.

When the preparations for the start of his journey to rebellious Hermano were complete, the Colonel traveled by regular rail down to the coastal city of Elsinore, where, as he had done so many times in the distant past, he took a room in the Grand Terminus Hotel while the agents of the Imperium worked out his Velde pathway. He had not been in Elsinore for many years and had not thought ever to see it again. Nothing much had changed, he saw: wide streets, bustling traffic, cloudless skies, golden sunlight conjuring stunning brilliance out of the myriad golden flecks that bespeckled the paving-stones. He realized, contemplating now a new off-world journey when he had never expected to make any again, how weary he had become of the golden sameness of lovely Galgala, how eager—yes, actually eager—he was once more to be confronting a change of scene. They gave him a room on the third floor, looking down into a courtyard planted entirely with exotic chlorophyll-based plants, stunningly green against the ubiquitous golden hue of Galgala.

Three small purple dragons from some world in the Vendameron system lay twined in a cage at the center of the garden, as always. He wondered if these were the same dragons who had been in that cage the last time, years ago. The Colonel had stayed in this very room before, he was sure. He found it difficult to accept the fact that he was staying in it again, that he was here at the Terminus waiting to make one more Velde jump, after having put his time of traveling so thoroughly behind him. But the cold-eyed emissary from the Imperium had calculated his strategy quite carefully. Whatever vestigial sense of obligation to the Imperium that might still remain in the Colonel would probably not have been enough to break him loose from his retirement in order to deal with one more obstreperous colony. The fact that Geryon Lanista, his one-time protege, his comrade, his betrayer, was the architect of the Hermano rebellion was another matter entirely, though, one that could not be sidestepped. To allow himself to miss a chance to come face to face with Geryon Lanista after all these years would be to act as though not just his career in the Service but his life itself had come to its end.

The emissary who had come to him at his villa was gone. He had done his work and was on to his next task. Now, at the Grand Terminus Hotel, the Colonel's liaison man was one Nicanor Ternera, who had the gray-skinned, pudgy-faced look of one who has spent too much of his life in meetings and conferences, and who could not stop staring at the Colonel as though he were some statue of an ancient emperor of old Earth that had unaccountably come to life and walked out of the museum where he was on exhibit.

"These are your papers," Nicanor Ternera told him. "You'll hold formal ambassadorial accreditation as head of a trade legation that's based on Gavial, which as I think you know is a planet of the Cruzeiro system. You will not be going as a representative of the Imperium itself, but rather as a diplomat affiliated with the regional government of the Cruzeiro worlds. As you are already aware, the rebels won't at present allow officials of the Imperium to arrive on Hermano, but they're not otherwise closed to visitors from outside, even during the present period of trade embargo, which they describe as a temporary measure while they await recognition by the Imperium of their independent status."

"They'll wait a long time," said the Colonel. "Especially if they won't allow anyone from the Imperium to go in and explain the error of their ways to them." He glanced at the papers. "For the purpose of this mission my name is Petrus Haym?"

"Correct."

"Lanista will recognize me instantly for who I am. Or is this going to be the sort of mission I'll be doing in disguise?"

"You'll be disguised, to some degree, for the sake of being able to obtain entry. Once you've succeeded in getting access to Hermano as Petrus Haym of Gavial, you can decide for yourself when and how to reveal yourself to Lanista, which beyond any doubt you will at some point find necessary to do in order to bring the mission to a successful conclusion. From that point on you'll be functioning openly as an agent of the Imperium."

"And what leverage am I to have over them?" the Colonel asked.

"The ultimate," said Nicanor Ternera.

"Good," said the Colonel. He had expected no less. He would have accepted no less. Still, it was better to have it offered readily than to have to demand it.

Nicanor Ternera said, "You'll be accompanied on the trip by three genuine government people out of Gavial and another Imperium agent, a woman from Phosphor named Magda Cermak, who'll have the official rank of second secretary to the mission. She's been in the Service for a dozen years and has a good grasp of the entire situation, including your prior relationship with Geryon Lanista."

"You don't think I'd be better off handling this project entirely on my own?"

"It's altogether possible that you could. But we'd rather not take the risk. In any case it's essential to maintain the fiction of a trade delegation at least until you're safely on Hermano and have made contact with Lanista, and a properly plausible delegation involves five or six members, at least." Ternera looked to the Colonel for approval, which he reluctantly gave. "As these documents will show you, the crux of Gavial's issue is Hermano's termination of the export of a drug called cantaxion, the properties of which are beneficial to people suffering from a manganese deficiency, something that's chronic on Gavial. You'll find all the details in the attached documents. Gavial has already asked for an exception to the embargo, which you are now going to try to negotiate. Ostensibly the Hermanans are willing to discuss resumption of cantaxion exports in return for military weapons to be manufactured on Bacalhao, another of the Cruzeiro worlds."

"Which would be, of course, in complete violation of Imperium law, since the Imperium has placed an embargo of its own on doing business with Hermano. Am I supposed to conclude that Gavial is considering rebelling against the Imperium also?"

"Most definitely not. At our strong urging Gavial has indicated that it's at least open to the idea of entering into such transactions, provided they can be kept secret. That doesn't mean it actually would. How far you want to proceed with any of this once you make contact with Lanista himself is entirely up to you, naturally. I doubt that he'll find the idea that this is simply a trade mission very credible, once he realizes that it's you that he's dealing with, but of course that won't matter at that point."

"Of course," said the Colonel, who was already six moves ahead in the game that had to be played once he reached Hermano, and wished that Nicanor Ternera would hand over the rest of the briefing papers and disappear, which eventually he did, though not as swiftly as the Colonel would have preferred.

The first stop on his journey to Hermano was Entrada, where the Service's main operational center was located. Going to Entrada would be to make what could be thought of as a long jump in the wrong direction. Hermano, like Galgala, was a Core world, close to the center of the galaxy, whereas Entrada was one of what had once been called the Inner Worlds, and therefore was actually out on the Rim, because all distances had been measured from Earth in those early days. Earth itself was a Rim world, and Entrada, just a couple of dozen light-years distant from it, was off in the same obscure corner of the galaxy, far from the galactic core, as the original mother planet. But stellar distances had no significant meaning in Velde transmission and Entrada was where the Service had its most important base. Here the Colonel would undergo his transformation into Petrus Haym, diplomat from Gavial.

He had undergone so many transformations in his time that the Service had a better idea of what his baseline self looked like than he did himself. He knew that he was slightly above the median in height, that he was of mesomorphic build with longer-than-average limbs, and that the natural color of his eyes was olive-green. But his eyes had been blue and brown and violet and even scarlet on various occasions, his hair had been tinted every shade in the book and sometimes removed entirely, and his teeth and nose and ears and chin had been subjected to so much modification over the years that he no longer remembered their exact original configuration. When he had retired from the Service they had restored him, so they claimed, to baseline, but he was never entirely sure that the face he saw in the mirror each morning, the pleasant, thoughtful, agreeably nondescript face of a man who was certainly no longer young but nowhere near the end of his days, was really anything like the one that had looked back at him in the days before all the modifications had begun.

The concept of a baseline self was pretty much obsolete, anyway. Short of making fundamental rearrangements in a person's basic skeletal structure—and they were working on that one—it had, for many hundreds of years, been feasible to give anyone any appearance at all. Rebuilds were standard items for everyone, not just operatives of the Service. You could look young or old, benign or cruel, open-hearted or brooding, as you wished, and when you tired of one look you could trade it in for another, just as, up to a point, you could roll back the inroads of the aging process by fifty years or so every now and then. That sort of mutability had been available even in the Colonel's grandfather's day, and by now everyone took it for granted. It was only his sheer obstinate perversity of will that had led the Colonel's father to insist on retaining, for the last seventy years of his life, the limp that he had acquired while carrying out an assignment on one of the worlds of the Magnifico system and that he had proudly displayed forever after.

The Colonel hesitated only the tiniest part of a moment when finally he stood before the Elsinore doorway. Some fraction of him still did not want to do this, but it was, he knew, only an extremely small fraction. Then he stepped through and was annihilated instantly and just as instantly reconstituted at the corresponding doorway on Entrada.

It was close to a century since the Colonel had last been to the operations center on Entrada. Entrada was a place he had hoped never to see again. He remembered it as a tropical world, much too hot from pole to pole, humid and jungly everywhere, with two potent white suns that were set close together in the sky and went whirling around each other three or four times a day, giving the appearance of a single, weird, egg-shaped mass. Only Entrada's great distance from those two sizzling primaries made the planet habitable at all. The Colonel hated its steambath heat, its thick, almost liquid greenish-gold atmosphere, its lunatic profusion of vegetation, the merciless round-the-clock glare of those twin suns. And also it was a world severely afflicted by the presence of a strong lambda field, lambda being a force that had been unknown until the early days of Velde travel. In those days anyone making the transition from a low-lambda world to a high-lambda world found himself knocked flat on his back during a period of adaptation that might stretch across several months. The problem of lambda differential had been conquered over a thousand years ago, but even now some minor effects could be felt by new arrivals to a high-lambda world, a lingering malaise, a sense of spiritual heaviness, that took days or even weeks to shake off.

But the Colonel, having come once more to Entrada despite all expectation, found it easy enough to shrug off all its discomforts. This would be only a brief stop, and there would never be another, of that he was certain beyond all question. He went through it as one goes through a bad dream, waiting for the release that morning brings.

Obsequious Service officers met him at the transit station, greeting him in an almost terrified way, with a kind of heavy-handed stifling reverence, the way one might greet some frightful spectre returned from the tomb, and conveyed him to the operations center, which was ten times the size of the building the Colonel remembered. Once he was inside its windowless mass he might have been on any planet at all: Entrada and all its tropic hyperabundance had no presence within these well insulated halls.

"Colonel, this is how you are going to look," they told him, and a full-size image of Petrus Haym sprang into view in the air before him.

They had conceived Petrus Haym as a stolid burgher, round-cheeked, complacent, with heavy-lidded sleepy eyes, full lips, a short thick neck, a fleshy body, the very model and essence of what he was supposed to be, a man who had devoted his life to issues of tariff regulation and balances of trade. Indifferently the Colonel gave his approval, offering no suggestions whatever for revisions in the Haym format, though they seemed to be expecting them. He didn't care. The format they had conceived would do. To look like an animated stereotype of a trade commissioner would make it all the simpler for the Colonel to assume the identity he was supposed to take on.

That he would be able to operate convincingly as the accredited leader of a trade delegation from a planet he knew nothing about was not anything that he doubted. He was a quick study. In his time he had assumed all kinds of roles: he had been a priest of the Goddess, an itinerant collector of zoological specimens, an organizer of disenfranchised laborers, a traveling musician, a deeply compassionate counselor to the bereaved, and many other things, whatever was required to fit the task at hand, which was always, ultimately, the engineering of consent. Preserving the integrity of the Imperium had been his constant goal. The Imperium's scope verged on the infinite; so too, then, must his.

When they had done all that they needed to do with him at the operations center, and he had done all that he needed to do as well, he went on to the next stop on his journey, Phosphor, where the rest of his team was awaiting him.

Like many of the worlds of the Imperium, Phosphor was a planet of a multiple-sun system. The Colonel had visited it once before, early in his career, but all he remembered of the visit was that he had gone there to seek out and eliminate a veteran agitator who was living there in exile from his home world and laying plans to return home to engage in a fresh round of destabilizing activities. The Colonel recalled carrying out the job successfully, but the planet itself he had forgotten. Seeing it now, he still did not remember much about his earlier stay there. He had seen so many worlds, after all. Here, a huge cool red sun, old and dying, lay like an angry blemish in the east by day, and a hot blue one that was at least a couple of hundred units away blazed out of the west, bright as a beacon in the sky. Even at night—the unnerving, intensely black night of a Rim world that the Colonel had never learned to like—stray tendrils of light from one sun or the other streamed into view at the hemisphere's darkside edge.

The people of Phosphor did not seem to go in for somatic modification. The likeness they bore toward one another indicated that they seemed to cling almost defiantly to the somatotypes of the original handful of settlers of thousands of years ago, who must predominantly have been short, sinewy, broad-based folk, swarthy-skinned, beady-eyed. Magda Cermak, who was waiting for the Colonel at the Velde station, was the perfect exemplar of her people, a dark-haired, sharp-nosed woman who stood only chest-high to the Colonel but who was so solidly planted atop her thick, sturdy legs that a rolling boulder could not have knocked her down. She seemed about fifty, no more than that, and perhaps she actually was. She welcomed the Colonel in an efficient, uneffusive way, addressing him as Petrus Haym, inquiring without real curiosity about his journey, and introducing him to the three delegates from Gavial, two men and a woman, who stood diffidently to one side, a well-nigh invisible trio of pallid bureaucrats, fidgety, self-effacing, like the supernumeraries that in fact they were in the drama to come.

His point of arrival on Phosphor was its capital city, a sprawling, untidy place that bore the ancient historical name of Jerusalem. At the Imperium headquarters there, Magda Cermak provided the Colonel with an update on the activities of Geryon Lanista—Martin Bauer, as he was now—since their paths had last crossed on that ill-starred world, Tristessa, half a century before.

"The one part of the trail we don't have," Cermak said, "covers the period between his escape from Tristessa's companion planet and his arrival in the Aguila sector. The period in the immediate aftermath of the faked suicide, that is. We figure that he spent about twenty years as far out of sight as he could keep himself. Our best guess is that he may have been moving around in the Rim worlds during those years. One informant insists that he even spent a certain amount of time on Earth itself."

"Could that be so?" asked the Colonel.

Magda Cermak shrugged. "There's no way of knowing. He's probably capable of managing it, wouldn't you say? But if he did get to Earth, Earth doesn't know anything about it, and Lanista isn't going to tell us either."

"All right. That's twenty blank years. What about the next thirty?"

"He first turns up under the name of Paul Thurm as a grape farmer on Iriarte, but he doesn't last long there. A legal problem arises, Thurm vanishes, and at that point a couple of years are gone from the record. When we pick up the trail again we find him in one of the Aguila Sector systems as Heinrich Bauer, supposedly an expert on land reclamation. He spends four years on a planet called Thraka, teaching the locals how to drain swamps, and then he moves on to Alyatta, a world of an adjacent system, where he shows the people how to irrigate a desert."

"A highly versatile man," the Colonel said.

"Very. He's on Alyatta for six or seven years, apparently marrying and having a couple of children and acquiring substantial properties. Then once again he vanishes abruptly, leaving his family behind, and shows up on Gran Chingada, where his name now is *Martin* Bauer. We don't know the motive for the switch. Something to do with the abandonment of his family, perhaps, although why he didn't change the surname too is hard to understand. Possibly the 'Heinrich' entry was erroneous all along. Keeping detailed track of a whole galaxy full of people is only approximately possible, you know.—You have been to Gran Chingada, I understand."

"A long time ago. It's a rough place."

"It's quieter now. They got rid of their worst malcontents thirty years back."

"Shipping them off to Hermano, two star-systems away, I'm told."

"Correct."

"Was Martin Bauer among those who was sent into exile?"

"No. He emigrated voluntarily, a dozen years ago, after the settlement on Hermano was fairly well established. Supposedly he was brought in by the plantation owners who grow the herb from which cantaxion is made, on account of his old specialty, land reclamation. He became a plantation owner himself in a major way, and involved himself very quickly in politics there, and before long he had won election to the Council of Seven, the oligarchy that was the ruling body on Hermano before its declaration of independence from the Imperium."

"An oligarchy whose members are *elected*?" said the Colonel. "Isn't that a little unusual?"

Magda Cermak smiled. "'Politics' on Hermano doesn't mean that they have universal suffrage. The richest land-owners have run the place from the beginning. In the days of the Council of Seven, new members of the Council were chosen by the existing ones whenever a vacancy developed.

It appears that Bauer got very rich very fast and was able to buy his way onto the Council. From what I hear, he was always an extremely persuasive man."

"Quite," the Colonel said.

"The last report of the Imperium commissioners before their expulsion indicates that he quickly made himself the dominant figure on it. He was the one, as I expect you've already guessed, who maneuvered Hermano into breaking with the Imperium."

"And what is he now, King of Hermano? Emperor of Hermano?"

"First Secretary of the Provisional Government is his title. He and four other members of the old Council of Seven make up the provisional government."

"An oligarchy of five being more manageable than an oligarchy of seven, I suppose. The next phase in the process being the replacement of the provisional government with an even more manageable one-man dictatorship."

"No doubt," said Magda Cermak.

She had more to tell him, little details of Martin Bauer's life on Hermano—he had married again, it seemed, and had had another set of children, and lived in monarchical splendor on a great estate on the southern coast of Hermano's one settled continent. The Colonel paid no more attention to what she was saying than professional courtesy required. It came as no surprise to hear that Geryon Lanista was looking after himself well. That had always been a specialty of his.

What occupied the center of the Colonel's attention was the fact of the rebellion on Hermano itself. That the person formerly known as Geryon Lanista was the instrument by which that rebellion had come about concerned him only in an incidental way now; it was a purely personal datum that had succeeded nicely in entangling him, at a time when he had thought he had completely shed his identity as a functionary of the Service, in this enterprise. If he could settle the score with Geryon Lanista after all this time, so be it. That would not be a trivial thing, but it was nevertheless a peripheral one. It was the existence of the rebellion, rather than Lanista's involvement in it, that had in these recent days brought powerful old emotions up from the center of the Colonel's being, had reawakened in him that sense of the necessity of protecting the Imperium that had been the essential driving factor of his personality through his entire adult life.

A rebellion was an act of war, nothing else. And in a galaxy of many thousands of inhabited worlds, war could not be allowed to come back into existence.

There had been strife once, plenty of it, in the early years of the great galactic expansion. There had been trade wars and there had been religious wars and there had been real wars, in which whole worlds had been destroyed. The immensity of the spaces that separated one planet from another, one solar system from another, one stellar cluster from another, meant nothing at all in a civilization in which the far-flung Velde system and the even more expansive network of Magellanic gateways rendered travel over unthinkable distances a simpler and faster and safer process than a journey from one city to the next on the same continent had been in that era, many thousands of years in the past, when all of mankind had been confined to a single small world of the galaxy.

In those ancient days, war between cities, and then between states when states had evolved, had been commonplace events. Schoolchildren on a million worlds still studied the history and literature of Earth as if they themselves were citizens of that little planet. They would not be able to find Earth's sun on a chart of the skies if they searched for thirty centuries, but they could recite the names of a dozen or more of Earth's famous wars, going back even into dim prehistory to the oldest war of all, the great war between the Greeks and the Trojans, when men had fought with clanging swords.

That had been a small war fought by great men. Later, millennia later, when humanity had spilled forth into all the galaxy, had come great wars fought by small men, wars not between tiny cities but between worlds, and there had been raging chaos in the stars, terrible death, terrible destruction. And then the chaos had at last burned itself out and there had come peace, fragile at first, then more certain. The galaxy-spanning institution known as the Imperium maintained that peace with iron determination.

The Imperium would not allow war. The age of chaos was over forever. That was universally understood, understood by all—or nearly all.

"Well, then, shall we start out on our way to Hermano, and get on with the job?" said the Colonel, when Magda Cermak had finished her briefing at last.

The first segments of the Velde system had been constructed at a time when Earth was all there was to the human galaxy and no one seriously expected that the multitudinous stars of the galactic center would ever come within mankind's reach. Though Velde transmission itself was non-relativistic, the setting up of the original system had had to be carried out under the constraints of the old Einsteinian rules, in which the speed of light was the limiting velocity.

And so, piece by piece, the necessary receiving equipment was put in place by conventional methods of delivery on one after another of the so-called Inner Worlds, those that orbited stars lying within a sphere a hundred light-years in diameter with Earth at its center. Even though the equipment was shipped out aboard vessels traveling close to the Einsteinian limit, unmanned starships journeying outward with great sails unfurled to the photonic winds, finding potentially habitable worlds, releasing robots that would set the Velde receivers in position, then going on to the next world and the next, extending the highway of receiving stations from one star system to another, it took centuries to get the job done. And by then the Magellanics' transit system had been discovered, impinging—just barely—on the tiny segment of the galaxy where Earth had managed to set up its little network of Velde stations.

Nobody knew how old the Magellanic system was, nor who had built it, nor even how it worked. That their builders had originated in the nearby galaxy known as the Greater Magellanic Cloud was only a guess, which somehow everyone had embraced as though it were a proven fact. They might just as readily have come from the Andromeda galaxy, or the great spiral galaxy in Eridanus, or some other stellar cluster ten or twelve billion light-years away, whose component stars and all the inhabitants of its many worlds had perished back in the ungraspable remoteness of the distant past. No one knew; no one expected to find out. The only thing that was certain was that the so-called Magellanics had traveled freely through the galaxy that one day would be mankind's, roaming it some unknowable number of years ago, using a system of matter transmission to journey from world to world, and that among the artifacts they had left behind on those worlds were their matter-transmitters, still in working order, apparently designed to function through all of eternity to come.

They operated more or less as the Velde transmitters did—you stepped through *here* and came out *there*—but whether they worked on similar principles was also something that was unknowable. There was nothing to analyze. Their doorways had no moving parts and drew on no apparent power source. Certain brave souls, stumbling upon these doorways during the early days of exploration on the outer worlds of humanity's sphere of expansion, had stepped through them and emerged on other planets even farther out, and eventually some working knowledge of the network, which doorway led to what other world, had been attained. How many lives had been lost in the course of attaining that knowledge was another thing that could never be known, for only those explorers who had survived their trips through the doorways could report on what they had done. The others—instantly transported, perhaps, to some other galaxy, or to the heart of a star, or to a world of intolerable gravitational force, or one whose doorway had been surrounded, over the millennia, by a sea of molten lava—had not been able to send back useful information about their trips.

By now, though, humankind had been making use of the Magellanic doorways for upwards of ten thousand years. The usable routes had all been tested and charted and the doorways had played a determining role in mankind's expansion across immense galactic distances that otherwise might not have been crossed until some era unimaginably far off in the future. The little sphere of planets that once had been known as the Inner Worlds was now thought of as the Rim, out there on the edge of galactic civilization; Earth, the primordial world where everything had begun, had become almost a legend, unvisited and shrouded in myth, that had very little reality for most of the Imperium's trillions of citizens; the essential life of galactic mankind long ago had moved from the Rim to the close-packed worlds of the Core. Though Velde stations still were an important means of travel within local sectors of the galaxy, and new Velde links were being constructed all the time, most long-hop travel now was carried out via the Magellanic system, which required no input of energy and maintained itself free of cost to those who used its gateways. The Colonel's journey to Hermano would involve the use of both systems.

The first jump took him via Velde transmission from Phosphor to nearby Entropy, a world that the Colonel had visited as a tourist forty years before, in the early days of his retirement. He did not remember it as a particularly interesting place. He had gone there only to gain access to the Magellanic doorway on Trewen, fifty light-years away, where he could leap across the galaxy to lovely Jacynth, his intended destination back then.

Entropy was no more interesting now: a yellow-green sun, mild weather, a few small cities, three big moons dangling in a row across the daytime sky. Magda Cermak preceded him there, and his three Gavial associates followed along behind. When the whole group was assembled they did a Velde hop to Trewen, now as before a virtually uninhabited world, cool and dry and bleak, notable only because the Magellanics had chosen to plant one of their doorways on it. Transit agents from the Service were waiting there to conduct the Colonel and his party to the doorway, which was tucked away within a deep cave on a rocky plateau a few hundred meters from the Velde station.

It seemed like only the day before yesterday that the Colonel had made his previous visit to this place. There on the right side of the cave was the sleek three-sided doorway, tapering upward to a sharp point, framing within itself a darkness so intense that it made the darkness of a Rim-world night seem almost inconsequential. Along each of its three sides was a row of gleaming hieroglyphs, an incomprehensible message out of a vanished eon. The doorway was wide enough for several to go through at a time. The Colonel beckoned the three Gavial people through first, and then stepped through himself, with Magda Cermak at his side. There was no sensation of transition: he walked through the darkness and came out of another doorway on Jacynth, one of the most beautiful of all worlds, as beautiful, almost, as lost Tristessa: a place of emerald meadows and a ruby-red sky, where great trees with feathery silver leaves and scarlet trunks sprang up all about them and a milky waterfall went cascading down the side of an ebony mountain that rose in serried pinnacles just ahead. The Colonel would have been happy to end the journey at that point and simply remain on Jacynth, where even the most troubled soul could find contentment for a while, but there was no hope of that, for more Service personnel awaited him there to lead him on to the next doorway, and by day's end the Colonel had arrived on Gavial of the Cruzeiro system, halfway across the galaxy from that morning's starting point at the Grand Terminus Hotel on Galgala.

Not even a Colonel in the Service was able to know everything about every one of the worlds of the Imperium, or even very much about very many of them. The galaxy was simply too big. Before the dark-haired intruder had enmeshed him in this undertaking the Colonel had been aware of Cruzeiro only because it was that rare thing, a solar system that had more than one world—four, in fact—that was inhabitable by human beings without extensive modification. Of Gavial itself, or its neighbor Bacalhao, or the other two worlds of the Cruzeiro system, he knew nothing at all. But now he was going to be masquerading as a native of the place, no less, and so he needed to acquire some first-hand familiarity with it. He had carried out the usual sort of research in the days before leaving home, and that had given him all the background on Gavial that he needed, though not a fully three-dimensional sense of what sort of world it was. For that you had to spend a little time there. He did know how large Gavial was, though, its climatic and geographical details, the history of its colonization, its major products, and a host of other things that he was probably not going to need to draw upon during his stay on Hermano, but which, simply by being present in some substratum of his mind, would allow him to make a convincing pretense of being Gavialese. As part of that he had learned to speak in the thick-tongued Gavialese way, spitting and sputtering his words in a fashion that accurately mimicked the manner of speech of his three Gavialese companions.

At first Magda Cermak, who spoke Galactic with the sharp-edged precision that seemed to be typical of the natives of Phosphor, could be seen smothering laughter every time the Colonel began to speak.

"Is it so comic, then?" he asked her.

"You sound like a marthresant," she said, giggling.

"Remind me of what a marthresant is," said the Colonel.

It was, she explained, one of her world's marine mammals, a huge ungainly creature with a wild tangle of bristly whiskers and long flaring tusks, which made coarse whooping snorts that could be heard half a kilometer away when it came up for air. Saying that he sounded like a marthresant did not appear to be a compliment. But he thanked her gravely for the explanation and told her that he was happy that his accent provided her with a little reminder of home.

That seemed to amuse her. But perhaps she was wondering whether she had offended him, for she made a point of telling him that she found his own accent, the accent of Galgala, extremely elegant. Which obliged the Colonel to inform her that his accent was not Galgalan at all, that he had lived on Galgala only during his boyhood and in the years since his retirement, and that in the years between he had spent so much time on so many different worlds, counterfeiting so many different accents, that he had lost whatever his original manner of speech had been. What he normally spoke now was actually a kind of all-purpose pan-Galactic, a randomly assorted mixture of mannerisms that would baffle even the most expert student of linguistics.

"And will you have some Gavialese in the mix when this is all over?" she asked.

"Perhaps nothing worse than a little snorting and whooping around the edges of the consonants," he told her, and winked.

She appeared to be startled by his sudden playfulness. But it had emerged only in response to hers, when she had begun giggling over his accent. The Colonel had been aware from the first that she felt an almost paralyzing awe for him, which she had been attempting to conceal with great effort. Nothing unusual about that: he was a legendary figure in the Service, already famous throughout the galaxy long before she was born, the hero of a hundred extravagantly risky campaigns. Everyone he had come in contact with since taking on this assignment had regarded him in that same awe-stricken way, though some had been a little better at hiding it than others. There were times, looking back at all he had done, that he almost felt a twinge of awe himself. The only one who had seemed immune to the power of his fame was the cold-eyed man who had gone to him in the first place, someone, obviously, who was so highly placed in the modern Service that he was beyond all such emotion. All the others were overwhelmed by the accumulated grandeur of his reputation. But it would only make things more difficult all around as this project unfolded if Magda went on thinking of him as some sort of demigod who had condescended to step down from the heavens and move among mortals again this one last time. He was relieved that she was professional enough to shake some of that off.

They remained on Gavial for a week while he soaked up the atmosphere of the place, did a little further research, and endured a round of governmental banquets and tiresome speeches that were designed to help him believe that he really *was* a trade representative from this planet whose only purpose in visiting Hermano was to get the flow of a vitally needed medicine going again. By the time that week was nearing its end Magda's attitude toward him had loosened to the extent that she was able to say, "It must be strange to think that in a few days you're finally going to get a chance to come face to face with the man you hate more than anyone else in the universe."

"Lanista? I don't even know if that's really him, over there on Hermano."

"It is. There's no question that it is."

"The Service says he is, and says it has the proof, but I've had too much experience with the way the Service creates whatever evidence it needs to buy a hundred percent of anything the Service claims. But suppose that *is* Lanista on Hermano. Why do you think I would hate him? I don't even know what the word means, really."

"The man who was working against you behind your back on one of your most important projects, and who, when things were heading toward an explosion that he himself had set up, went off without giving you a word of warning that you were very likely to get killed? What do you call that, if not treachery?"

"Treachery is exactly what I would call it, indeed," said the Colonel.

"And yet you don't hate him for that?" She was floundering now.

"I told you," the Colonel said, trying to choose his words with great care, "that 'hate' isn't a word I understand very well. Hate seems so useless, anyway. My real concern here is that I could have misjudged that man so completely. I *loved* him, you know. I thought of him almost as a son. I brought him into the Service, I taught him the craft, I worked with him on a dozen jobs, I personally insisted on his taking part in the Tristessa thing. And then—then—then he—he—"

His throat went dry. He found himself unable to continue speaking. He was swept by feelings that he could only begin to comprehend.

Magda was staring at him in something close to horror. Perhaps she feared that she had pushed into territory that she had had no right to be exploring.

But then, as though trying to repair whatever damage she had caused, she pressed desperately onward.

"I didn't realize that you and Lanista were actually that—close. I thought he was just your partner on an assignment. Which would be bad enough, selling you out like that. But if in fact he was almost like—your—"

She faltered.

"My protege," the Colonel said. "Call him my protege." He went to the window and stood with his back to her, knotting his hands together behind him. He wished he had never let this conversation begin.

The sun, Cruzeiro, was starting to set, an unspectacular yellowish sun tinged with pale pink. A hard-edged crescent moon was edging upward in the sky. Behind it lay two sharp points of brilliant light, two neighboring worlds of this system. Bacalhao and Coracao, their names were. He thought that Bacalhao was the one on the left, but wasn't entirely sure which was which. You could usually see them both in the twilight sky here. The odd names, he supposed, were derived, as so many planetary names were, from one of the ancient languages of Earth, a world where, so it was said, they had had a hundred different languages all at once, and people from one place could scarcely understand what people from another place were saying. It was a wonder they had been able to accomplish anything, those Earthers, when they wouldn't even have been able to make themselves understood if they went as much as five hundred kilometers away from home. And yet they had managed to make the great leap out into space, somehow, and to spread their colonies over thousands of solar systems, and to leave their words behind as the names of planets, although no one remembered anymore what most of those words once meant.

"My protege," he said again, without turning to face her. "Who betrayed me, yes. That has always mystified me, that he would have done such a thing. But do I hate him for it? No."

*Yes*, he told himself. *Of course you do.*

Tristessa. A magical place, the Colonel had once thought. On Tristessa your eye encountered beauty wherever it came to rest. He remembered everything about it down to the finest detail: the sweet fragrance of its soft, moist atmosphere, the bright turquoise/emerald glory of its double sun, the throngs of magnificent winged reptiles soaring overhead, the glistening smoothness of the big, round white pebbles, like the eggs of some prehistoric monster, that formed the bed of the clear rushing stream that ran past his lodging. The pungent flavor of a triangular yellow fruit that dangled in immense quantities from nearby trees. The many-legged crab-like things, glossy black carapaces crisscrossed with jagged blood-red streaks, that roamed the misty forests searching in the dark rich loam for food, and looked up from their foraging to study you like solemn philosophers with a multitude of faceted amber eyes.

Its name, someone had told him once, was derived from a word of one of the languages of ancient Earth, a word that carried a connotation of "sadness," and certainly sadness was appropriate in thinking of Tristessa now. But how could they have known, when giving such a melancholy name to such a beautiful world, what sort of destiny was awaiting it five thousand years in the future?

For the Colonel, who was in the late prime of his career as an arch-manipulator of worlds, the Tristessa affair had begun as a routine political intervention, the sort of assignment he had dealt with on more occasions than he could count. He saw no special challenge in it. He expected that Geryon Lanista, whom he had been grooming for a decade or so to be his successor in the Service, would do much of the real work; the Colonel would merely supervise, observe, confirm in his own mind that Lanista was fully qualified to take things over from him.

Tristessa, lovely, underpopulated, economically undeveloped, had a companion world, Shannakha, less than thirty million kilometers away. Shannakha had been settled first. Its climate, temperate rather than tropical, wasn't as appealing as Tristessa's, nor was its predominantly sandy, rocky landscape anywhere near as beautiful. But it offered a wider range of natural resources—pretty little Tristessa had nothing much in the way of metals or fossil fuels—and it was on Shannakha that cities had been founded and an industrial economy established. Tristessa, colonized by Shannakha a few hundred years later, became the holiday planet for its neighbor in the skies. Shannakha's powerful merchant princes set up plantations where Tristessa's abundant fruits and vegetables could be raised and shipped to eager markets on the other world, and created great estates for themselves in the midst of those plantations; Shannakha's entrepreneurs built grand resort hotels for middle-class amusement on the beautiful island archipelagoes of Tristessa's tropical seas; and thousands of less fortunate Shannakhans settled on Tristessa to provide a labor force for all those estates, plantations, and hotels. It all worked very well for hundreds of years, though of course it worked rather better for the absentee owners on Shannakha than it did for their employees on Tristessa, since the Shannakhans prohibited any kind of ownership of Tristessan real estate or other property by Tristessans, kept payrolls as low as possible, and exported all profits to Shannakha.

But, as any student of history as well informed as the Colonel was would certainly know, the unilateral exploitation of one world by another does not work well forever, any more than the unilateral exploitation of one city or state by another had worked well in that long-ago era when all the human race was confined to that one little world called Earth. At some point a malcontent will arise who will argue that the assets of a place belong to the people who dwell in that place, and should not be tapped for the exclusive benefit of a patrician class living somewhere else, far away. And, if he is sufficiently persuasive and charismatic, that malcontent can succeed in finding followers, founding a movement, launching an insurrection, liberating his people from the colonial yoke.

Just that was in the process of happening when the Colonel was called in. Tristessa's charismatic malcontent had arisen. His name was Ilion Gabell; he came from a long line of farmers who raised and grew the agreeably narcotic zembani leaf that was the source of a recreational drug vastly popular on Shannakha; and because his natural abilities of leadership were so plainly manifest, he had been entrusted by a group of the plantation owners with the management of a group of adjacent zembani tracts that stretched nearly halfway across Tristessa's primary continent. That, unfortunately for the plantation owners, gave him access to clear knowledge of how profitable the Tristessa plantations really were. And now—so reliable informants had reported—he was on the verge of launching a rebellion that would break Tristessa free of the grasp of its Shannakhan owners. It was the Colonel's assignment to keep this from happening. He had chosen Geryon Lanista to assist him.

Lanista, who was fond of exploring both sides of an issue as an intellectual exercise, said, "And why, exactly, should this be any concern of the Imperium? Is it our job to protect the economic interests of one particular group of landowners against its own colonial employees? Are we really such conservatives that we have to be the policemen of the status quo all over the universe?"

"There would be wider ramifications to a Tristessa uprising," the Colonel said. "Consider: this Ilion Gabell gives the signal, and in a single night every Shannakhan who happens to be on Tristessa is slaughtered. Such things have occurred elsewhere, as you surely know. The Imperium quite rightly deplores wholesale murder, no matter what virtuous pretext is put forth for it. Next, a revolutionary government is proclaimed and transfers title to all Shannakhan-owned property on Tristessa to itself, to be held in the name of the citizenry of the Republic of Tristessa. What happens after that? Will Shannakha, peace-loving and enlightened, simply shrug and say that inasmuch as war between planets is illegal by decree of the Imperium, it therefore has no choice but to recognize the independence of Tristessa, and invites the Tristessans to enter into normal trade relationships with their old friends on the neighboring world?"

"Maybe so," said Lanista. "And that might even work."

"But the down side—"

"The down side, I suppose, is that it would send a signal to other planets in Tristessa's position that a rebellion against the established property interests can pay off. Which will create a lot of little Tristessa-style uprisings all over the galaxy, one of which might eventually explode into actual warfare between the mother world and its colony. Therefore a great deal of new toil for the Service will be required in order to keep those uprisings from breaking out, in which case it might be better to snuff out this one before it gets going."

"It might indeed," said the Colonel. "Now, the opposite scenario—"

"Yes. Shannakha, infuriated by the expropriation of its properties on Tristessa, retaliates by sending an armed expedition to Tristessa to get things under control. Thousands of Tristessans die in the
first burst of hostilities. Then a guerrilla war erupts as Gabell and
his insurrectionists are driven underground, and in the course of it
the plantations and resorts of Tristessa are destroyed, perhaps with
unusually ugly ecological consequences, and many additional casualties besides. Shannakha wrecks its own economy to pay for the war
and Tristessa is ruined for decades or centuries to come. And at the
end of it all we either wind up with something that's worse than the
status quo ante bellum, Shannakha still in charge of Tristessa but now
perhaps unable to meet the expense of rebuilding what was there
once, or else with two devastated planets, Tristessa independent but
useless and Shannakha bankrupt."

"And therefore—" the Colonel said, waiting for the answer that he
knew would be forthcoming.

Lanista provided it. "Therefore we try to calm Ilion Gabell down and
negotiate the peaceful separation of Tristessa and Shannakha by telling
Gabell that we will obtain better working conditions for his people, while
at the same time leading the Shannakhans to see that it's in their own
best interest to strike a deal before a revolution can break out. If we can't
manage that, I'd say that the interests of Tristessa, Shannakha, and the
Imperium would best be served by suppressing Ilion Gabell's little revolution out of hand, either by removing him permanently or by demon-
strating to him in a sufficiently persuasive way that he stands no chance
of success, and simultaneously indicating to the Shannakhans that they'd
better start treating the Tristessans a little more generously or they're
going to find themselves faced with the same problem again before long,
whether the revolution is led by Gabell or by someone else with the same
ideas. Yes?"

"Yes," said the Colonel.

So it was clear, then, what they had to try to achieve, and what they
were going to do to achieve it. All scenarios but one led to a violent outcome, and violence was a spreading sore that if not checked at its source
could consume an entire civilization, even a galactic one. The problems
on Tristessa, which were easily enough identified, needed to be corrected
peacefully before a worse kind of correction got under way. The Colonel
was as skillful an operative as there was and Geryon Lanista was nearly as

shrewd as he was, and he still had all the energy of youth, besides. Why, then, had it all gone so terribly wrong?

And then it was time at last to make the last jump in the sequence, the one from Gavial to Hermano, where, despite all that the Colonel had believed for the last fifty years, Geryon Lanista was very much alive and at the head of his own insurrectionist government.

Despite the general trade embargo, the Velde link between Hermano and certain worlds of the galaxy, such as Gavial, was still operational. Only the wildest of insurrectionists would take the rash step of cutting themselves completely off from interstellar transit, and Lanista was evidently not that wild. Velde connections required two sets of tuned equipment, one at each end of any link, and once a planet chose to separate itself from Velde travel it would need the cooperation of the Imperium to re-establish the linkage. Lanista hadn't cared to risk handing the Imperium a unilateral stranglehold over his planet's economy. There had been other rebellions, as he of all people would have known very well, in which the Imperium had picked a time of its own choosing to restore contact once it had been broken off by the rebels.

The Colonel was completely composed as they set out on this final hop of the long journey. He searched for anxiety within himself and found none. He realized that it must have been destined all along that before the end of his life he would once again come face to face with Geryon Lanista, so that there might be a settlement of that troublesome account at last.

And why, he asked himself, should there be any immediate cause for anxiety? For the moment he was Petrus Haym, emissary plenipotentiary from the Cruzeiro system to the provisional government of independent Hermano, and Lanista was Martin Bauer, the head of that provisional government. Whatever meeting there was to be between the two of them would be conducted, at least at first, behind those masks.

Hermano, the Colonel saw at once, was no Tristessa. Perhaps he had arrived in this hemisphere's winter: the air was cool, even sharp, with hardly any humidity at all. He detected a hint of impending snow in it. The sky had a grayish, gloomy, lowering look. There was an odd acrid flavor to the atmosphere that would require some getting used to. The gravity was a little above Standard Human, which was going to exacerbate the task of carrying the extra flesh of Petrus Haym.

Everything within immediate view had a thrown-together, improvised appearance. The area around the Velde station was one of drably utilitarian tin-roofed warehouses, with an unprepossessing medium-sized town of low, anonymous-looking buildings visible in the distance against a backdrop of bleak stony hills. Tufts of scruffy vegetation, angular and almost angry-looking, sprang up here and there out of the dry, sandy soil. There was nothing to charm the eye anywhere. The Colonel reminded himself that this planet had been settled only about forty years before by a population of exiles and outcasts. Its people probably hadn't found time yet for much in the way of architectural niceties. Perhaps they had little interest in such things.

Somber-faced port officials greeted him in no very congenial way, addressing him as Commissioner Haym, checking through his papers and those of his companions, and unsmilingly waving him and his four companions aboard a convoy of antiquated lorries that took them down a ragged, potholed highway into town. Alto Hermano, the place was called. A signpost at the edge of town identified it grandiosely as the planetary capital, though its population couldn't have been much over twenty or thirty thousand. The vehicles halted in a stark open square bordered on all four sides by identical five-story buildings with undecorated mud-colored brick facades. An official who introduced himself as Municipal Procurator Tambern Collian met them there. He was a gray-eyed unsmiling man, just as dour of affect as everyone else the Colonel had encountered thus far here. He did not offer the expectable conventional wishes that Commissioner Haym had had an easy journey to Hermano nor did he provide pleasantries of any other sort, but simply escorted the delegation from Cruzeiro into one of the buildings on the square, which turned out to be a hotel, grimly functionalist in nature, that the government maintained for the use of official visitors. It was low-ceilinged and dim, with the look of a third-class commercial hotel on a backwater world. Municipal Procurator Collian showed the Colonel to his quite modest suite without apologies, indifferently wished him a good evening, and left, saying he would call again in the morning to begin their discussions.

Magda Cermak's room was adjacent to his. She came by to visit, rolling her eyes, when the Municipal Procurator was gone. The coolness of their welcome plainly hadn't been any cause of surprise to her, but she was irritated all the same. A dining room on the ground floor of the hotel provided them with a joyless dinner, choice of three sorts of unknown meat, no wine available of any kind. Neither of them had much to say. Their hosts were all making it very clear that Hermano was a planet that had declared war on the entire universe. They were willing to allow the delegation from the Cruzeiro system to come here to try to work out some sort of trade agreement, since they appeared to see some benefit to themselves in that, but evidently they were damned if they were going to offer the visitors much in the way of a welcome.

Municipal Procurator Collian, it developed, was to be Commissioner Haym's primary liaison with the provisional government. Precisely what Collian's own role was in that government was unclear. There were times when he seemed to be just the mayor of this starkly functional little city, and others when he appeared to speak as a high functionary of the planetary government. Perhaps he was both; perhaps there was no clear definition of official roles here at the moment. This was, after all, a provisional government, one that had seized power only a few years before from a previous government that had itself been mostly an improvisation.

It was clear, at any rate, that First Secretary Bauer himself did not plan to make himself a party to the trade talks, at least not in their initial stages. The Colonel did not see that as a problem. He wanted a little time to take the measure of this place before entering into what promised to be a complex and perhaps dangerous confrontation.

Each morning, then, the Colonel, Magda, and the three Gavialese would cross the plaza to a building on the far side that was the headquarters of the Ministry of Trade. There, around a squarish conference table of the sort of inelegant dreary design that seemed especially favored by the Hermanan esthetic, they would meet with Municipal Procurator Collian and a constantly shifting but consistently unconvivial assortment of other Hermanan officials to discuss the problem of Hermano's embargo on all foreign trade, and specifically its discontinuation of pharmaceutical exports to Gavial that Gavial regarded as vital to the health of its citizens.

The factor behind the unconviviality soon became clear. The Hermanans, a prickly bunch inexperienced in galactic diplomacy, apparently were convinced that Commissioner Haym and his companions were here to accomplish some sort of trickery. But the Hermanans had no way of knowing that and had been given no reason to suspect it. And the faintly concealed animosity with which they were treating the visitors from Gavial would surely get in the way of reaching any agreement on the treaty that the Gavialese had ostensibly come here to negotiate, a treaty that would be just as beneficial to Hermano as it would to Gavial.

So it became the Colonel's immediate job—in the role of Petrus Haym, envoy from the Cruzeiro system, not as a functionary of the Imperium—to show the Hermanans that their own frosty attitude was counterproductive. For that he needed to make himself seem to be the opposite of deceitful: a good-hearted, willingly transparent man, open and friendly, a little on the innocent side, maybe, not in any way a fool but so eager to have his mission end in a mutually advantageous agreement that the Hermanans would think he might allow himself to be swayed into becoming an advocate for the primary interests of Hermano. Therefore, no matter the provocation, he was the soul of amiability. The technicians of the Service had designed him to look stout and sleepy and unthreatening, and he spoke with a comic-opera Gavialese accent, which was helpful in enabling him to play the part of an easy mark. He spoke of how much he longed to be back on Gavial with his wife and children, and he let it be perceived without explicitly saying so that for the sake of an earlier family reunion he might well be willing to entertain almost any proposal for a quick settlement of the negotiations. He made little mild jokes about the discomforts of his lodgings here and the inadequacies of the food to underscore his desire to be done with this job and on his way. When one of the authentic Gavialese betrayed some impatience with the seeming one-sidedness of the talks in their early stage, Commissioner Haym rebuked him good-naturedly in front of the Hermanans, pointing out that Hermano was a planet that had chosen an exceedingly difficult road for itself, and needed to be given the benefit of every doubt. And gradually the Hermanans began to thaw a bit.

The sticking point in the discussions was Hermano's request that the Cruzeiro worlds serve as Hermano's advocate before the Imperium in its quest for independence. What the Cruzeiro people knew, and Hermano probably knew it as well, was that the Imperium was never going to permit any world to secede. The only way that Gavial was going to get the pharmaceuticals that it wanted from Hermano, and for Hermano to get the weapons it wanted from the Cruzeiro worlds, was for the two groups to cook up a secret and completely illegal deal between them, in utter disregard not just of the wishes of the Imperium but of its laws.

Gavial had already signaled, disingenuously, that it was willing to do this—urged on by the Imperium, which had pledged that it would provide them with a continued supply of cantaxion in return for its cooperation. But Hermano, perhaps because it quite rightly was mistrustful of Gavial's willingness to enter into a secret illegal deal or perhaps because of the obstinate naivete of its leaders, was continuing to hold out for official recognition by Gavial and the other Cruzeiro worlds of Hermanan independence.

By prearrangement the Colonel and Magda Cermak took opposite positions on this issue. Magda—stolid, brusque, rigid, unsmiling—bluntly told the Hermanan negotiators the self-evident truth of the situation, which was that Gavial was not going to align itself with the Hermanan independence movement because nobody's requests for independence from the Imperium were ever going to get anywhere, that the Imperium would never countenance any kind of official recognition of any member world's independence. Such a thing would set a wholly unacceptable precedent. It was out of the question; it was scarcely worth even discussing. If Gavialese recognition of Hermanan independence was the price of reopening trade relations between Gavial and Hermano, she said coldly, then the Gavialese trade delegation might as well go home right now.

Meanwhile her associate, Commissioner Haym—genial, placid, undogmatic, a trifle lacking in backbone, maybe, and therefore readily manipulable—sadly agreed that getting the Imperium to allow a member world, no matter how obscure, to pull out of the confederation would be a very difficult matter to arrange, perhaps impossible. But he did point out that it was the belief of the rulers of Gavial that the current philosophy of the Imperium was strongly nonbelligerent, that the Central Authority was quite eager to avoid having to launch military action against unruly members. For that reason, Commissioner Haym suggested, certain highly influential officials in the government of Gavial felt that the Imperium might be willing, under the right circumstances, to forget about Hermano entirely and look the other way while Hermano went right on regarding itself as independent. "I am not, you realize, speaking on behalf of the Imperium," Commissioner Haym said. "How could I? I have no right to do that. But we of Gavial have been given to understand that the Imperium is inclined toward leniency in this instance." The essential thing was that Hermano would have to keep quiet about its claim to independence, though it could go on behaving as though it were independent all the same. That is, in return for that silence, Commissioner Haym indicated, the Central Authority might be willing to overlook Hermano's refusal to pay taxes to it, considering that those taxes were a pittance anyway. And Hermano would be free to strike whatever private deals with whatever Imperium worlds it liked, so long as it kept quiet about those too—such as, he said, the proposed weapons-for-drugs arrangement that would get a supply of cantaxion flowing to Gavial once again and allow Hermano to feel capable of protecting itself against possible Imperium aggression.

Commissioner Haym communicated these thoughts to Procurator Collian at a time when Magda Cermak was elsewhere. Demanding immediate independence, he reiterated, was probably going to achieve nothing. But independence for Hermano might just be achievable in stages. Accepting a kind of de facto independence now might well clear the way for full independence later on. And he offered—unofficially, of course—Gavial's cooperation in persuading the Imperium to leave Hermano alone while it went on along its present solitary way outside the confederation of worlds.

Collian looked doubtful. "Will it work? I wonder. And how can you assure me the cooperation of your planet's government when not even your own colleague Commissioner Cermak is in agreement with you on any of this?"

"Ah, Commissioner Cermak. Commissioner Cermak!" Commissioner Haym favored Procurator Collian with a conspiratorial smile. "A difficult woman, yes. But not an unreasonable one. She understands that our fundamental goal in coming here, after all, is to restore trade between Gavial and Hermano by any means possible. Which ultimately should be Hermano's goal, too." Commissioner Haym allowed a semblance of craftiness to glimmer in his heavy-lidded eyes. "This is, of course, a very ticklish business all around, because of the Imperium's involvement in our dealings. You and I understand how complicated it is, eh?" A wink, a nudge of complicity. "But I do believe that your planet and mine, working toward our mutual interests, can keep the Imperium out of our hair, and that Gavial will stand up for Hermano before the Imperium if we commissioners bring back a unanimous report. And do you know how I think I can swing her over to the position that you and I favor?" he asked. "If I could show her that we have the full backing of First Secretary Bauer—that he sees the plan's advantages for both our worlds, that he wholeheartedly supports it—I think we can work out a deal."

Municipal Procurator Collian seemed to think that that was an interesting possibility. He proposed that Commissioner Haym quickly prepare a memorandum setting forth all that they had discussed between themselves, which he could place before the First Secretary for his consideration. Commissioner Haym, though, replied mildly that Municipal Procurator Collian did not seem to have fully understood his point. Commissioner Haym was of the opinion that he could most effectively make his thoughts clear to the First Secretary during the course of a personal meeting. Collian was a bit taken aback by that. The evasive look that flitted across his chilly features indicated that very likely one was not supposed to consume the time of the First Secretary in such low-level things as meetings with trade commissioners. But then—the Colonel watched the wheels turning within the man—Collian began, so it seemed, to appreciate the merits of letting First Secretary Bauer have a go at molding with his own hands this extremely malleable envoy from Gavial. "I'll see what I can do," he said.

Not all of Hermano was as bleak as the area around the capital city, the Colonel quickly discovered. The climate grew moister and more tropical as he headed southward, scraggy grasslands giving way to forests and forests to lush jungles in the southernmost region of the continent, the one continent that the Hermanans had managed to penetrate thus far. The view from the air revealed little sign of development in the southern zone, only widely scattered plantations, little isolated jungle domains, separated from one another by great roadless swaths of dense green vegetation. He did not see anything amounting to continuous settlement until he was nearly at the shores of the ocean that occupied the entire southern hemisphere of this world, stretching all the way to the pole. Here, along a narrow coastal strip between the jungle and the sea, the elite of Hermano had taken up residence.

First Secretary Bauer's estate was situated at the midpoint of that strip, on a headland looking out toward the green, peaceful waters of that southern sea. It was expectably grand. The only surprising thing about it was that it was undefended by walls or gates or even any visible guard force: the road from the airstrip led straight into the First Secretary's compound, and the estatehouse itself, a long, low stone building rising commandingly on the headland in a way that reminded the Colonel of the fortress at Megalo Kastro, seemed accessible to anyone who cared to walk up to its door.

But the Colonel was taken instead to one of the many outbuildings, a good distance down the coastal road from the First Secretary's villa itself, and there he was left in comfortable seclusion for three long days. He had a five-room cottage to himself, with a pretty garden of flowering shrubs and a pleasant view of the sea. No one kept watch over him, but even so it seemed inappropriate and perhaps unwise to wander any great distance from his lodgings. His meals were brought to him punctually by silent servants: seafood of various kinds, mainly, prepared with skill and subtlety, and accompanied by pale wines that were interestingly tangy and tart. A small library had been provided for him, mostly familiar classics, the sort of books that Geryon Lanista had favored during their years of working together. He inspected the garden, he strolled along the beach, he ventured a short way into the dense forest of scrubby little red-leaved trees with aromatic bark on the inland side of the compound. The air here was soft and had a mildly spicy flavor, not at all bitter like the air up at Alto Hermano. The water of the sea, into which he ventured ankle-deep one morning, was warm and clear, lapping gently at the pink sands. Even the strong pull of this world's gravity was less oppressive here, though the Colonel knew that that was only illusion.

On the fourth day the summons to the presence of the First Secretary came to him.

The dispassionate tranquility that had marked the Colonel's demeanor since his departure from Gavial remained with him now. He had brought himself to his goal and whatever was fated to happen next would happen; he faced all possibilities with equanimity. He was taken into the great villa, conveyed down long silent hallways floored with gleaming panels of dark polished wood, led past huge rooms whose windows looked toward the sea, and delivered, finally, into a much smaller room, simply furnished with a desk and a few chairs, at the far end of the building. A man who unquestionably was Geryon Lanista waited for him there, standing behind the desk.

He was greatly altered, of course. The Colonel was prepared for that. The face of the man who stood before him now was the one he had seen in the solido that the dark-haired visitor had shown him in his villa on Galgala, that day that now seemed so long ago: that blunt-tipped nose, those downturned lips, the flaring cheekbones, the harsh jutting jaw, all of them nothing like the features of the Geryon Lanista he once had known. This man looked only to be sixty or so, and that too was unsurprising, though actually Lanista had to be close to twice that age; but no one ever looked much more than sixty any more, except those few who preferred to let a few signs of something approaching their true age show through to the surface. Lanista had had every reason to transform himself beyond all recognition since the debacle on Tristessa. The surprising thing, the thing that forced the Colonel for an instant to fight against allowing an uncontrolled reaction to make itself visible, was how easy it was for him to see beyond the cosmetic transformations to the real identity behind them.

Was it the hulking frame that gave him away, or the expression of the eyes? Those things had to be part of it, naturally. Very few men were built on such a massive scale as Lanista, and not even the canniest of cosmetic surgeons could have done anything about the breadth of those tremendous shoulders and that huge vault of a chest. His stance was Lanista's stance, the rock-solid stance of a man of enormous strength and physical poise: one's habitual way of holding one's body could not be unlearned, it seemed. And the eyes, though they were brown now and the Colonel remembered Lanista to have had piercingly blue ones, still had that eerie, almost feminine softness that had given such an odd cast to the old Lanista's otherwise formidably masculine face. Surely a surgeon could have done something about that. But perhaps one had tried, and even succeeded, and then the new eyes had come to reveal the innate expression of Lanista's soul even so, shining through inexorably despite everything: for there were the veritable eyes of Geryon Lanista looking out at him from this unfamiliar face.

The eyes—the stance—and something else, the Colonel thought, the mere intangible presence of the man—the inescapable, unconcealable essence of him—

While the Colonel was studying Martin Bauer and finding Geryon Lanista behind the facade, Martin Bauer was studying Commissioner Petrus Haym, giving him the sort of close scrutiny that any head of state trying to evaluate a visiting diplomat of whom he intended to make use could be expected to give. Plainly he was reading Petrus Haym's bland meaty face to assure himself that the Gavialese commissioner was just as obtuse and pliable as the advance word from Procurator Collian had indicated. The precise moment when Lanista made the intuitive leap by which he saw through the mask of Commissioner Petrus Haym to the hidden Colonel beneath was difficult for the Colonel to locate. Was it when the tiniest of muscular tremors flickered for an instant in his left cheek? When there was that barely perceptible fluttering of an eyelid? That momentary puckering at the corner of his mouth? The Colonel had had a lifetime's training in reading faces, and yet he wasn't sure. Perhaps it was all three of those little cues that signalled Lanista's sudden stunned realization that he was in the presence of the man he had looked to as his master and mentor, or perhaps it was none of them; but somewhere in the early minutes of this encounter Lanista had identified him. The Colonel was certain of that.

For a time neither man gave any overt indication of what he knew about the other. The conversation circled hazily about the ostensible theme of an exchange of arms for medicine and how that could be arranged in conjunction with Hermano's desire to break free from the political control of the Central Authority of the Imperium. The Colonel, as Haym, took pains to radiate an amiability just this side of buffoonery, while always drawing back from full surrender to the other man's wishes. Lanista, as Bauer, pressed Haym ever more strongly for a commitment to his cause, though never quite pouncing on him with a specific demand for acquiescence. Gradually it became clear to the Colonel that they were beginning to conduct these negotiations in the voices of Lanista and the Colonel, not in those of First Secretary Bauer and Commissioner Haym. Gradually, too, it became clear to him that Lanista was just as aware of this as he was.

In the end it was Lanista who was the one who decided to abandon the pretense. He had never been good at biding his time. It had been his besetting flaw in the old days that a moment would always come when he could no longer contain his impatience, and the Colonel saw now that no surgery could alter that, either. Commissioner Haym had been moving through the old circular path once more, asking the First Secretary to consider the problems that Gavial faced in weighing its need for cantaxion against the political risks involved in defying the decrees of the Central Authority, when Lanista said abruptly, in a tone of voice far more sharply focused and forceful than the woolly diplomatic one he had been using up until then, "Gavial doesn't have the slightest intention of speaking up for us before the Imperium, does it, Colonel? This whole mission has been trumped up purely for the sake of inserting you into the situation so you can carry out the Imperium's dirty work here, whatever that may be. Am I not right about that?"

"Colonel?" the Colonel said, in the Haym voice.

"Colonel, yes." Lanista was quivering, now, with the effort to maintain his composure. "I can see who you are. I saw it right away.—I thought you had retired a long time ago."

"I thought so too, but I was wrong about that. And I thought you were dead. I seem to have been wrong about that too."

For half a century the Colonel had lived, day in, day out, with the memories of his last two weeks on the paradise-world that Tristessa once had been. Like most bad memories, those recollections of the Tristessan tragedy, and his own narrow escape from destruction, had receded into the everyday background of his existence, nothing more now than the dull, quiet throbbing of a wound long healed, easily enough ignored much of the time. But in fact the wound had never healed at all. It had merely been bandaged over, sealed away by an act of sheer will. From time to time it would remind him of its existence in the most agonizing way. Now the pain of it came bursting upward once again out of that buried part of his consciousness in wave upon wave.

He was back on Tristessa again, waiting for Lanista to return from his mission to Shannakha. Lanista had gone to the companion world ten days before, intending to see the minister who had jurisdiction over Tristessan affairs and make one last effort to head off the conflict between the two planets that had begun to seem inevitable. He was carrying with him documents indicating that the Tristessa colonists were ready to launch their rebellion, and that only the promulgation by Shannakha of a radical program of economic reform could now avoid a costly and destructive struggle. Recent developments on Shannakha had given rise to hope that at least one powerful faction of the government was willing to offer some significant concessions to the Tristessan colonists. The Colonel, meanwhile, was holding talks with Ilion Gabell, the rebel leader, in an attempt to get him to hold his uprising off a little while longer while Lanista worked out the details of whatever concessions Shannakha might offer.

Gabell's headquarters were on the floating island of Petra Hodesta, five hundred hectares of grasses thick as hawsers that had woven themselves tightly together long ago and broken free of the mainland. The island, its grassy foundation covered now with an accretion of soil out of which a forest of slender blue-fronded palms had sprouted, circled in a slow current-driven migration through the sparkling topaz waters of Tristessa's Triple Sea, and Gabell's camp was a ring of bamboo huts along the island's shore. The Colonel had arrived five days earlier. He had a good working relationship with Gabell, who was a man of commanding presence and keen intelligence with a natural gift for leadership, forty or fifty years old and still in the first strength and flourish of his early manhood. The Colonel had laid out in great detail and more than customary forthrightness everything that Lanista had gone to the mother world to request; and Gabell had agreed to wait at least until he saw what portion of the things Lanista was asking for would be granted. He was not a rash or hasty man, was Gabell. But he warned that any kind of treachery on Shannakha's part would be met with immediate and terrible reprisals.

"There will be no treachery," the Colonel promised.

Petra Hodesta's wandering route now was taking it toward the northernmost of Triple Sea's three lobes, the one adjacent to Gespinord, the

Tristessan capital province. Since Lanista was due back from Shannakha in a few more days, it was the Colonel's plan to go ashore on the coast of Gespinord and make his way by airtrain to the main Velde terminal, two hundred kilometers inland at the capital city, to await his return. But he was less than halfway there when the train came spiraling down to its track with the sighing, whistling sound of an emergency disconnect and someone in uniform came rushing through the cars, ordering everyone outside.

Tristessa was under attack. Without warning Shannakhan troops had come pouring through every Velde doorway on the planet. Gespinord City, the capital, had already been taken. All transit lines had been cut. The Colonel heard distant explosions, and saw a thick column of black smoke rising in the north, and another, much closer, to the east. They were hideous blotches against the flawless emerald-green of the Tristessan sky; and there in the west the Colonel saw a different sort of blemish, the harsh dark face of stark stony Shannakha, low and swollen and menacing on the horizon. What had gone wrong up there? What—even while they were in the midst of delicate negotiations—had led the Shannakhans to break the fragile peace?

The train had halted at some provincial station bordered on both sides by rolling crimson meadows. Somehow the Colonel found a communications terminal. Reaching Lanista on Shannakha proved impossible: no outgoing contact with other worlds was being allowed. But against all probability he did manage to get a call through to the rebel headquarters on Petra Hodesta, and, what was even less probable than that, Ilion Gabell himself came to the screen. His handsome features now had taken on a wild, almost bestial look: the curling golden mane was greasy and disheveled, the luminous, meditative eyes had a frenzied glaze, his lips were drawn back in a toothy grimace. He gave the Colonel a look of searing contempt. "No treachery, you said. What do you call this? They've invaded us everywhere at once. Without warning, without any declaration of hostilities. They must have been planning it for years."

"I assure you—"

"I know what your assurance is worth," Gabell said. "Well, mine is worth more. The reprisals have already begun, Colonel. And as for you—"

A blare of visual static sliced across the screen and it went black. "Hello?" the Colonel shouted. "Hello? Hello?"

The stationmaster, bald and plump and nearly as wild-eyed as Gabell had looked, appeared from a back room. The Colonel identified himself to him. He gaped at the Colonel in amazement and blurted, "There's an order out for your arrest. You and that other Imperium agent, both. You're supposed to be seized by anyone who finds you and turned over to the nearest officers of the republic."

"What republic is that?"

"Republic of Tristessa. Proclaimed three hours ago by Ilion Gabell. All enemies of the republic are supposed to be rounded up and—"

"Enemies of the republic?" the Colonel said, astonished. He wondered if he was going to have to kill him. But the plump stationmaster clearly had no appetite for playing policeman. He let his eye wander vaguely toward the open door to his left and shrugged, and made an ostentatious show of turning his attention away from the Colonel, busying himself with important-looking papers on his desk instead. The Colonel was out through the door in a moment.

He saw no option but to make his way to the capital and find whatever was left of the diplomatic community, which no doubt was attempting to get off Tristessa as quickly as possible, and get himself off with them. Something apocalytic was going on here. The sky was black with smoke in every direction, now, and the drumroll of explosions came without a break, and frightful tongues of flame were leaping up from a town just beyond the field on his left. Was the whole planet under Shannakhan attack? But that made no sense. This place was Shannakha's property; destroying it by way of bringing it back under control was foolishness.

Gabell had spoken of reprisals. Was *he* the one behind the explosions?

It took the Colonel a week and a half to cover the hundred kilometers from the train station to the capital, a week and a half of little sleep and less food while he traversed a zigzag route through the devastated beauty of Gespinord Province, dodging anyone who might be affiliated with the rebels. That could be almost anybody, and was likely to be nearly everybody. A woman who gave him shelter one night told him of what the rebels were doing, the broken dams and torched granaries and poisoned fields, a war of Tristessa against itself that would leave the planet scarred for decades and worse than useless to its Shannakhan masters. At dawn she came to him and told him to go; he saw men wearing black rebel armbands entering the house on one side as he slipped away from it on the other.

He had three more such narrow escapes in the next four days. After the last of them he stayed away from inhabited areas entirely. He hurt his leg badly, slogging across a muddy lake. He cut his hand on a sharp palm frond and it became infected. He ate some unknown succulent-look-ing fruit and vomited for a day and a half. Skulking northward through swamps and over fresh ashheaps still warm from the torching, he started to experience the breaking down of his innate unquenchable vitality. The eternal self-restoring capacity of his many-times-rejuvenated body was no longer in evidence. A great weariness came over him, a sense of fatigue that approached a willingness to cease all striving and lie down forever. That was a new experience for him, and one that shocked him. He began to feel his true age and then to feel older than his true age, a thousand years older, a million. He was ragged and dirty and lame and his throat was perpetually parched and there was a pounding against the right side of his skull in back that would not stop; and as he grew weaker and weaker with the passing days he began to think that he was going to die before much longer, not from some rebel's shot but only from the rigors of this journey, the fever and the chill and the hunger. He cursed Geryon Lanista a thousand times. Whatever Lanista had been up to on Shannakha, could he not have taken a moment to send his partner on Tristessa some warn-ing that everything was on the verge of blowing up? Evidently not.

And then, at last, he stumbled into Gespinord City, where uniformed soldiers of Shannakha patrolled every street. He identified himself to one of them as a representative of the Imperium, and was taken to a makeshift dormitory in a school gymnasium where members of the diplomatic corps were being given refuge. There were about a dozen of them from five or six worlds, consular officials, mainly, who in ordinary times looked after the interests of tourists from their sectors of the galaxy that were holi-daying on Tristessa. All the tourists were long gone, and the few officials who remained had stayed behind only to supervise the final stages of the evacuation of the planet. One of them, a woman from Thanda Ban-danareen, saw to it that the Colonel was washed and fed and medicated, and afterward, when he had rested awhile, explained that the Tristessan Authority, which was the name under which the invaders from Shanna-kha were going, had ordered all outworlders to leave Tristessa at once. "I've been shippping people out for five days straight," she said, and the Colonel perceived for the first time that she was not much farther from exhaustion than he was himself. "There's no time to set coordinates. You go to the doorway and you step through and you work things out for yourself on the other side. Are you ready to go?"

"Now?"

"The sooner I get the last few stragglers out of here, the sooner I can go myself."

She led him to the doorway and, offering a word or two of thanks for her help, he entered its Velde field, a blind leap to anywhere, and came out, to his relief, on that glorious planet, Nabomba Zom, identifiable instantly by the astounding scarlet sea before him, which was shimmering with a violet glow as the first blue rays of morning struck its surface. There, in a guest lodge of the Imperium at the base of pale green mountains soft as velvet, the Colonel learned from a fellow member of the Service what had taken place on Shannakha.

It seemed that Geryon Lanista had badly overplayed his hand. For the sake of persuading the Shannakhans to adopt a more lenient Tristessa policy, Lanista had shown them forged documents indicating that Ilion Gabell's revolutionary army would not simply launch a rebellion on Tristessa if concessions weren't granted but would invade Shannakha itself. The Shannakhans had taken this fantasy seriously, much *too* seriously. Lanista had meant to worry them with it, but instead he terrified them; and in a frantic preemptive overreaction they hurriedly shipped an invading army to Tristessa to bring the troublesome colonists to heel. The worst-case scenario that Lanista had foreseen as a theoretical possibility, but did not seem to believe could happen, was going to occur.

The Colonel shook his head in disbelief. That Lanista—his own protege—would have done anything so stupid was next to impossible to accept; that he would have done so without telling him that he had any such crazy tactic in mind was an unpardonable breach of Service methodology. That he had not sent word to the fellow officer whom he had left behind in harm's way on Tristessa that events in this planetary system had begun to slide toward a ghastly cataclysm as a result of his bizarrely clumsy maneuver was unforgivable for a different reason.

It seemed Gabell had been anticipating an invasion from Shannakha and had had a plan all ready for it: a scorched-earth program by which everything on Tristessa that was of value to Shannakha would be destroyed within hours after the arrival of Shannakhan invaders. One overreaction had led to another; by the end of the first week of war Tristessa was utterly ruined. Between the furious destructiveness of the rebels and the brutal repression of the rebellion by the invaders that had followed, nothing was left of Tristessa's plantations, its great estates, its hotels, its towns and cities, but ashes.

"And Lanista?" the Colonel asked leadenly. "Where is he?"

"Dead. By his own hand, it would seem, though that isn't a hundred percent certain. Either he was trying to get away from Shannakha in a tremendous hurry and accidentally made a mess out of his Velde coordinates, or else he deliberately scrambled up the coding so that he wouldn't be reassembled alive at his destination. Whichever it was, there wasn't very much left of him when he got there."

"You really believed I was dead?" Lanista asked.

"I *hoped* you were dead. I *wanted* you to be dead. But yes, yes, I believed you were dead, too. Why wouldn't I? They said you had gone into a doorway and come out in pieces someplace far away. Considering what you had managed to achieve on Shannakha, that was a completely appropriate thing to have done. So I accepted what they told me and I went on believing it for the next fifty years, until some bastard from the Imperium showed up at my house with proof that you were still alive."

"Believe me, I thought of killing myself. I imagined fifty different ways of doing it. Fifty *thousand*. But it wasn't in me to do a thing like that."

"A great pity, that," the Colonel said. "You allowed yourself to stay alive and you lived happily ever after."

"Not happily, no," said Lanista.

He had fled from Shannakha in a desperate delirious vertigo, he told the Colonel: aware of how badly awry it all had gone, frantic with shame and grief. There had been no attempt at a feigned suicide, he insisted. Whatever evidence the Service had found of such a thing was its own misinterpretation of something that had nothing to do with him. Fearing that the truth about the supposed Tristessan invasion would emerge, that the Shannakhans would discover that he had flagrantly misled them, he had taken advantage of the confusion of the moment to escape to the nearest world that had a Magellanic doorway and in a series of virtually unprogrammed hops had taken himself into some shadowy sector of the Rim where he had hidden himself away until at last he had felt ready to emerge, first under the Heinrich Bauer name, and then, as a result of some kind of clerical error, as *Martin* Bauer.

In the feverish final hours before the Shannakhan invasion began he had, he maintained, made several attempts to contact the Colonel on Tristessa and urge him to get away. But all communications lines between Shannakha and its colony-world had already been severed, and even the Imperium's own private communications channels failed him. He asked the Colonel to believe that that was true. He *begged* the Colonel to believe it. The Colonel had never seen Geryon Lanista begging for anything, before. Something about the haggard, insistent look that came into his eyes made his plea almost believable. He himself had been unable to get any calls through to Lanista on Shannakha; perhaps the systems were blocked in the other direction too. That was not something that needed to be resolved just at this moment. The Colonel put the question aside for later consideration. For fifty years the Colonel had believed that Lanista had deliberately left him to die in the midst of the Tristessa uprising, because he could not face the anger of the Colonel's rebuke for the clumsiness of what he had done on Shannakha. Perhaps he didn't need to believe that any longer. He would prefer not to believe it any longer; but it was too soon to tell whether he was capable of that.

"Tell me this," he said, when Lanista at last had fallen silent. "What possessed you to invent that business about a Tristessan invasion of Shannakha in the first place? How could you ever have imagined it would lead to anything constructive? And above all else, why didn't you try the idea out on me before you went off to Shannakha?"

Lanista was a long while in replying. At length he said, in a flat, low, dead voice, the voice of a headstrong child who is bringing himself to confess that he has done something shameful, "I wanted to surprise you."

"What?"

"To surprise you and to impress you. I wanted to out-Colonel the Colonel with a tremendous dramatic move that would solve the whole crisis in one quick shot. I would come back to Tristessa with a treaty that would pacify the rebels and keep the Shannakhans happy too, and everything would be sweetness and light again, and you would ask me how I had done it, and I would tell you and you would tell me what a genius I was." Lanista was looking directly at the Colonel with an unwavering gaze. "That was all there was to it. An idiotic young subaltern was fishing for praise from his superior officer and came up with a brilliant idea that backfired in the most appalling way. The rest of my life has been spent in an attempt to atone for what I did on Shannakha."

"Ah," the Colonel said. "That spoils it, that last little maudlin bit at the end of the confession. 'An attempt to atone'? Come off it, Geryon. Atoning by starting up a rebellion of your own? Against the Imperium, which you once had sworn to defend with your life?"

Icy fury instantly replaced the look of intense supplication in Lanista's eyes. "We all have our own notions of atonement, Colonel. I destroyed a world, or maybe two worlds, and since then I've been trying to build them. As for the Imperium, and whatever I may have sworn to it—"

"Yes?"

"The Imperium. The Imperium. The universal foe, the great force for galactic stagnation. I don't owe the Imperium a thing." He shook his head angrily. "Let it pass. You can't begin to see what I mean.—The Imperium has sent you here, I gather. For what purpose? To work your old hocus-pocus on our little independence movement and bring me to heel the way you were trying to do with Ilion Gabell on Tristessa?"

"Essentially, yes."

"And how will you do it, exactly?" Lanista's face was suddenly bright with expectation. "Come on, Colonel, you can tell me! Consider it the old pro laying out his strategy one more time for the bumptious novice. Tell me. Tell me. The plan for neutralizing the revolution and restoring order."

The Colonel nodded. It would make no real difference, after all. "I can do two things. The evidence that you are Geryon Lanista and that you were responsible for the catastrophic outcome of the Tristessa rebellion is all fully archived and can quickly be distributed to all your fellow citizens here on Hermano. They might have a different view about your capability as a master schemer once they find out what a botch you made out of the Tristessa operation."

"They might. I doubt it very much, but they might.—What's the other thing you can do to us?"

"I can cut Hermano off from the Velde system. I have that power. The ultimate sanction: you may recall the term from your own Service days. I pass through the doorway and lock the door behind me, and Hermano is forever isolated from the rest of the galaxy. Or isolated until it begs to be allowed back in, and provides the Imperium with proof that it deserves to be."

"Will that please you, to cut us off like that?"

"What would please me is irrelevant. What would have pleased me would have been never to have had to come here in the first place. But here I am.—Of course, now that I've said all this, you can always prevent me from carrying any of it out. By killing me, for example."

Lanista smiled. "Why would I want to kill you? I've already got enough sins against you on my conscience, don't I? And I know as well as you do that the Imperium could cut us off from the Velde system from the outside any time it likes, and would surely do so if its clandestine operative fails to return safely from this mission. I'd wind up in the same position but with additional guilt to burden me. No, Colonel, I wouldn't kill you. But I do have a better idea."

The Colonel waited without replying.

"Cut us off from the Imperium, all right," Lanista said. "Lock the door, throw away the key. But stay here on the inside with us. There's no reason for you to go back to the Imperium, really. You've given the Imperium more than enough of your life as it is. And for what? Has serving the Imperium done anything for you except twisting your life out of shape? Certainly it twisted mine. It's twisted everybody's, but especially those of the people of the Service. All that meddling in interstellar politics—all that cynical tinkering with other people's governments—ah, no, no, Colonel, here at the end it's time for you to give all that up. Start your life over here on Hermano."

The Colonel was staring incredulously, wonderingly, bemusedly.

Lanista went on, "Your friends from Gavial can go home, but you stay here. You live out the rest of your days on Hermano. You can have a villa just like mine, twenty kilometers down the coast. The perfect retirement home, eh? Hermano's not the worst place in the universe to live. You'll have the servants you need. The finest food and wine. And an absolute guarantee that the Imperium will never bother you again. If you don't feel like retiring, you can have a post in the government here, a very high post, in fact. You and I could share the top place. I'd gladly make room for you. Who could know better than I do what a shrewd old bird you are? You'd be a vital asset for us, and we'd reward you accordingly.—What do you say, Colonel? Think it over. It's the best offer you'll ever get, I promise you that."

It was easiest to interpret what Lanista had said as a grotesque joke, but when the Colonel tried to shrug it away Lanista repeated it, more earnestly even than before. He realized that the man was serious. But, as though aware now that this conversation had gone on too long, Lanista suggested that the Colonel return to his own lodgings and rest for a time. They could talk again of these matters later. Until then he was always free to resume the identity of Petrus Haym of the Gavialese trade mission, and to go back to his four companions and continue to hatch out whatever schemes they liked involving commerce between Gavial and the Free Republic of Hermano.

He was unable to sleep for much of that night. So many revelations, so many possibilities. He hadn't been prepared for that much. None of the usual adjustments would work; but toward dawn sleep came, though only for a little while, and then he awoke suddenly, drenched in sweat, with sunlight pouring through his windows. Lanista's words still resounded in his mind. *The Imperium has twisted your life out of shape*, Lanista had said. Was that so? He remembered his grandfather saying, hundreds of years ago—thousands, it felt like—*The Imperium is the enemy, boy. It strangles us. It is the chain around our throats.* The boy who would become the Colonel had never understood what he meant by that, and when he came to adulthood he followed his father, who had said always that the Imperium was civilization's one bulwark against chaos, into the Service.

Well, perhaps his father had been right, and his grandfather as well. He had strapped on the armor of the Service of the Imperium and he had gone forth to do battle in its name, and done his duty unquestioningly throughout a long life, a very long life. And perhaps he had done enough, and it was time to let that armor drop away from him now. What had Lanista said of the Imperium? *The universal foe, the great force for galactic stagnation.* An angry man. Angry words. But there was some truth to them. His grandfather had said almost the same thing. An absentee government, enforcing conformity on an entire galaxy—

On that strange morning the Colonel felt something within him breaking up that had been frozen in place for a long time.

"What do you say?" Lanista asked, when the Colonel had returned to the small office with the desk and the chairs. "Will you stay here with us?"

"I have a home that I love on Galgala. I've lived there ever since my retirement."

"And will they let you live in peace, when you get back there to Galgala?"

"Who?"

"The people who sent you to find me and crush me," Lanista said. "The ones who came to you and said, *Go to a place called Hermano, Colonel. Put aside your retirement and do one more job for us.* They told you that a man you hate was making problems for them here and that you were the best one to deal with him, am I not right? And so you went, thinking you could help the good old Imperium out yet again and also come to grips with a little private business of your own. And they can send you out again, wherever else they feel like sending you, whenever they think you're the best one to deal with whatever needs dealing with."

"No," the Colonel said. "I'm an old man. I can't do anything more for them, and they won't ask. After all, I've failed them here. I was supposed to destroy this rebellion, and that won't happen now."

"Won't it?"

"You know that it won't," the Colonel said. He wondered whether he had ever intended to take any sort of action against the Hermano rebels. It was clear to him now that he had come here only for the sake of seeing Lanista once again and hearing his explanation of what had happened on Shannakha. Well, now he had heard it, and had managed to persuade himself that what Lanista had done on Shannakha had been merely to commit an error of judgment, which anyone can do, rather than to have sought to contrive the death of his senior officer for the sake of convering up his own terrible blunder. And now there was that strange sensation he was beginning to feel, that something that had been frozen for fifty years, or maybe for two hundred, was breaking up within him. He said, "Proclaim your damned independence, if you like. Cut yourselves off from the Imperium. It makes no difference to me. They should have sent someone else to do this job."

"Yes. They should have.—Will you stay?"

"I don't know."

"We're no longer of the Imperium and neither are you."

Lanista spoke once again of the villa by the sea, the servants, the wines, the place beside him in the high administration of the independent world of Hermano. The Colonel was barely listening. It would be easy enough to go home, he was thinking. Lanista wouldn't interfere with that. Hop, hop, hop, and Galgala again. His lovely house beside that golden river. His collection of memorabilia. The souvenirs of a life spent in the service of the Imperium, which is a chain about our throats. Home, yes, home to Galgala, to live alone within the security of the Imperium. The Imperium is the enemy of chaos, but chaos is the force that drives evolutionary growth.

"This is all real, what you're offering me?" he asked. "The villa, the servants, the government post?"

"All real, yes. Whatever you want."

"What about Magda Cermak and the other three?"

"What do you want done with them?"

"Send them home. Tell them that the talks are broken off and they have to go back to Gavial."

"Yes. I will."

"And what will you do about the doorways?"

"I'll seal them," Lanista said. "We don't need to be part of the Imperium. There was a time, you know, when Earth was the only world in the galaxy, when there was no Imperium at all, no Velde doorways either, and somehow Earth managed to get along for a few billion years without needing anything more than itself in the universe. We can do that too. The doorways will be sealed and the Imperium will forget all about Hermano."

"And all about me, too?" the Colonel asked.

"And all about you, yes."

The Colonel laughed. Then he walked to the window and saw that night had fallen, the radiant, fiery night of the Core, with a million million stars blazing in every direction he looked. The doorways would be sealed, but the galaxy still would be out there, filling the sky, and whenever he needed to see its multitude of stars he needed only to look upward. That seemed sufficient. He had traveled far and wide and the time was at hand, was more than at hand, for him to bring an end to his journeying. Well, so be it. So be it. No one would ever come looking for him here. No one would look for him anywhere; or, if looking, would never find him. At the Service's behest he had returned to the stars one last time; and now, at no one's behest but his own, he had at last lost himself among them forever.

# THE IMPOSSIBLES

## *Kristine Kathryn Rusch*

Alarm, six a.m. Earth time—the whole damn starbase ran on Earth time. Barely a moment to rub the sleep from her eyes, roll out of her bed, and bang her knees against the wall, just like she had every morning since she graduated from law school. Not quite the top of her class. Okay, twenty-fifth. Not the middle either, not last. Near the top, close to the top. Not in the top ten or even the top twenty—not in the area where she could've gotten *recruited* by some firm, somewhere.

Didn't matter that she went to Alliance Law, best school in the Earth Alliance, harder to get into than any school on the Moon or on Earth, harder than Harvard or Oxford or Armstrong Legal Academy. Only two hundred students qualified for Alliance Law every year, and only one hundred graduated three years later.

Those statistics meant nothing. All that mattered, apparently, was the top twenty. And Kerrie had been just five spots away from a guaranteed recruitment.

That was what she thought about every morning when her knees smacked into that wall. Then she would debate with herself: Was it the ninety on her second-year contracts exam? Or the essay she had to redo five times for her Earth Alliance Agreements class? Or the party she went to that last week first year that caused her to get up late for her Torts final, making Old Man Scott dock her two points for tardiness?

Or had she failed some indefinable thing—not volunteering for Fair Housing duty or failing to participate in Moot Court every single semester?

She didn't know—and she cared. She had had such high expectations for herself, and she hadn't achieved them.

Her family was happy—she was a lawyer in the prestigious Multicultural Tribunal system. But it wasn't as glamorous as all that. It wasn't glamorous at all—not that people outside the base, this single base dedicated almost entirely to InterSpecies Court for the First District, knew about the ugliness of the place. She had been shocked when she arrived nearly two years ago.

All newly minted lawyers arriving here for the first time were shocked. And all of them wondered what exactly led them here. Something they had done? Or something they hadn't?

It wasn't just the student loans. It couldn't just be the loans, with their lovely little check-off option: *Loan will be paid in full if student volunteers for public service internship post-graduation.*

Everyone checked that box, and the law firms that recruited, they paid off the loan so the student didn't have to.

Only she didn't get recruited. No one told her that only twenty students from every class get recruited when she applied to Alliance Law. They implied—as they handed her the damn loan forms—that *all* students of Alliance Law got recruited.

And she supposed that was probably true if looked at in a purely legalistic sense.

She would most likely be recruited when her stint was up, two months from now. After two years here, she had more experience in InterSpecies Law than half the professors who taught the courses at law schools all over the sector.

Horrible, awful experience, but experience nonetheless.

She rubbed her knee as she grabbed the outfit she chose for today—black skirt, black suit jacket, black blouse. No need to stand out, no need to dress well. She was as interchangeable as the shuttles constantly moving between here and Helena base.

She downloaded the morning's files through her links as she grabbed coffee from the tiny communal kitchen. The base provided almost everything: food, housing, clothing, if necessary. Food and caffeine were the most important because otherwise (the base had learned) too many of the baby lawyers passed out in court. They were so busy they forgot to eat, something else Kerrie didn't believe until she got here.

Too much work, not enough time to eat, let alone think. She thought law school was bad. Law school—the best law school in the Earth Alliance—was a cakewalk compared to Earth Alliance InterSpecies Court for the First District. The Court also known as The Impossibles.

Here everything was impossible from the caseload to the odds of winning. No one won, not really. The reality of the system was uglier than anyone ever imagined.

From the counter, she took a banana, which was a little longer and a little more orange than she liked. Fifteen thousand varieties of bananas alone were grown in the base's hydroponic gardens. The gardens stretched all along one tier of the base, providing fresh fruits and vegetables for the residents and the guests, if they could afford it. Guests who couldn't afford fresh got the same indefinable food served to the prisoners—all of whom were on their way somewhere else, all of whom were scared, confused, and, in their minds, completely innocent.

As she hurried out the door, she nearly rammed into one of the night court lawyers coming in (What was his name? Sam? She couldn't remember and she should have, since they shared a lease). He grunted at her, so exhausted he could hardly move, and she nodded back, a little refreshed after a real night's sleep.

Refreshed but preoccupied. As she scurried to the elevator, she sorted the twenty-five cases she had to deal with today into four categories—morning, afternoon, evening, and Please-God-Never. The Please-God-Nevers she hoped to pass up the food chain to the lifers who knew how the system worked. The lifers, who had arrived as loan lawyers like she did, and stayed because they claimed they liked it here. The lifers, who look five times older than they were, and who—somehow—still had just a whisper of idealism in their voices.

The idealism left her Day Three, when she had to send a toddler to the Wygnin for a crime his father committed six months before the kid was born. She couldn't stop it. Hell, she didn't even have time to review the file. She just had to plead and take the best deal—and in Earth Alliance InterSpecies Court there was no best deal, only a less egregious one.

The elevator took her to the main hallway for Courthouse Number One, which housed most of the InterSpecies courtrooms. There was no court "house," of course—that was just a linguistic formality from Earth. There were a lot of linguistic formalities because this place had no buildings, just floors and sections; more floors and sections than she thought possible. Floors and sections and rings—how could she forget rings?

Especially when she might have to go to the jail ring later in the day, although she hoped not.

The only thing she'd scored on since she arrived here was the apartment. Hers was close to work. Some of her colleagues rode on the tram from the outer rings of the starbase, losing two hours of sleep per day because they didn't dare doze for fear of missing their stop.

She didn't go down the main hallway. Instead, she took a short half flight of stairs because it was easier than waiting for another elevator. The half flight took her to the public defenders office, which had been her home away from home since she got out of law school.

After twenty-two months of actual survival—of not saying fuck it and letting Daddy or a rich cousin pay off her loan, of not prostituting herself, or telling the loan agency to stick it and take it out of her pay for the rest of her life—she actually rated a desk in the defenders office. Granted, it was in the back of the bullpen and barely as wide as the chair she got with it, but it was still a desk. Some days she saw it as a medal of honor.

Today she saw it as one stop too many in a day already overcrowded with too many stops.

She tossed the banana peel in the recycler near the door, a bit surprised she'd managed to eat at all. She had no memory of consuming that banana—and she should have. She didn't like the long orange variety; she thought they were too bitter and citrusy to be real bananas.

Apparently she was so hungry she didn't even notice, and besides, she was still shuffling case files in her head—trying to find the best order, one that sent her from courtroom to courtroom in a logical fashion and gave her the most possible time with clients.

She'd learned through hard experience that nothing mattered more than the schedule. Not reading the file, not figuring out which judge she faced. Finding time to meet the client, who often had a wish or an idea or a scintilla of information that might get the sentence reduced or lightened or—in a perfect universe—tossed out, although that had never happened to her or one of her clients or even to a client of anyone she had worked with.

She had heard rumors, of course. Gayle Giolotti had saved the lives of three kids on a technicality, and Sheri Hampstead actually got an acquittal by proving that the government bringing the case (Wygnin? Disty? Kerrie couldn't remember) didn't have the proper DNA identification of the accused.

She'd always planned to check on those rumors, but of course she didn't have time, and now her stint was nearly up, and once she left this godforsaken place, she would have no reason to look, no reason to check, no reason to think about it ever again.

A steaming mug of coffee sat on her desk along with a pair of shoes she thought she'd lost. Her boss, Maise Blum, rested one hip on the desk's corner, as if she planned to be there all day.

Maise was tall and thin. Forty, maybe fifty, maybe sixty, she was one of the lifers, and it showed in the frown lines etched alongside her mouth. Her long black hair, which she wore up, had a sprinkling of silver, but Kerrie couldn't tell if that was vanity, an attempt at gravitas, or an actual hereditary detail.

"Got a case for you," Maise said.

"Sorry," Kerrie said. "I'm here to check in and then I'm off to Judge Weiss's court to begin today's sprint."

"One case in exchange for ten of yours. I don't even care if it's ten of the toughies."

That caught Kerrie's attention. In her first month, she would have agreed without looking up. In her first year, she would have agreed without questions.

But she'd been here too long to trust a sweet deal.

"What the hell's wrong with it?" she asked.

"It's work," Maise said.

"They're all work," Kerrie said, taking the shoes and locking them into the bottom desk drawer. She'd actually written them off more than a year ago. She had forgotten that she had loaned them to Maise for some ritzy Bar Association dinner.

"Work you should do," Maise said. "This is your acquittal."

Kerrie froze, mid lock. She stood up slowly and even—for a half second—stopped multitasking her schedule. She shut down all but her emergency links, leaving only the appointment clock running along the bottom of the vision in her right eye.

"How come you don't want it?" Kerrie asked. "You've never had an acquittal."

"How do you know?" Maise asked, without a smile. Her dark eyes were so serious that Kerrie tilted her head.

"You have?"

"Not all of us talk about our successes." Maise's tone held bitterness, and Kerrie understood. Successes here weren't always one-hundred-percent positive. Most of them were bittersweet.

"So why not have another one?" Kerrie asked.

"I told you. It's work. Real work. Research work."

Kerrie hadn't done research work since she got here. She hadn't had time.

"They're all research work and none of it gets done," she said, realizing as she spoke she sounded like a lifer. "What makes this one different?"

"The client is pregnant."

Kerrie closed her eyes. She hated pregnancy cases. She had one a month, maybe more, and they were all heartbreaking and sad and horrible. One client asked if she should abort the fetus rather than lose the court case; another wanted to find out if Kerrie would adopt the baby herself so that the child wouldn't be considered a firstborn.

"No," Kerrie said. "No pregnancy cases."

"And the client says she's a member of the Black Fleet."

That sent a wave of interest through Kerrie, so intense it felt like a live thing. She hadn't had a feeling like that since law school. "She's willing to admit that she's part of a criminal organization to get out of an InterSpecies case?"

"Yep," Maise said. "You want it?"

"I still don't know why you're not taking it."

Maise crossed her arms. "She has her own lawyer. Peyti."

She spit the word. The Peyti had the best legal minds in the Earth Alliance, but they could be difficult to work with. It wasn't just their appearance, which was sticklike and gray. Their breathing masks made conversation difficult, and their insistence on following procedure to the letter usually offended the judges in the InterSpecies Courts.

The judges here had to get through as many cases as possible on a single day or backlog would overwhelm everything. And preventing backlog was as important—maybe more important—than delivering justice.

There was only so much room in the starbase's jails and prisons, there were only so many courts, and there was only so much time. Everyone in the First District who ran afoul with the laws of another culture brought the cases here to the special courts set up to reconcile one species' law with another.

Technically, the cases were supposed to go through the offended culture's courts, but everyone waived that part of the procedure so that the case could be tried in the InterSpecies courts. It wasn't an appeals court—that was on a different starbase in a different part of the First District—but it might as well have been, given the nature of the arguments here.

They were always based on procedure and technicalities, not on the facts of the case or the finer points of the law.

There was no way Kerrie could learn the case law from twenty-five different cultures for her twenty-five different cases that she had today alone. She had to wing it, and the judges knew she was winging it, and the prosecutors knew she was winging it. The formalities helped, and the commonalities helped as well. And she did try to bone up. Most of the cases involved familiar cultures—Disty, Wygnin, Rev—although occasionally she got something weird like the Gyonnese or the Ssachuss.

"Now the truth will out," Kerrie said. "Your Peyti prejudice could get you in trouble, you know."

"It's not a prejudice. I just don't have the patience to deal with them," Maise said.

Which was as good an excuse as any, Kerrie thought but did not say. "When's it on the docket?" Kerrie asked.

"Noon."

"Noon?" Kerrie's eyebrows went up. "Whose court?"

"Judge Langer."

Kerrie rolled her eyes. "Not the easiest judge in the universe."

"But one who will listen."

Kerrie knew that to be true. "I take this, you take all of my cases for today."

"No can do," Maise said. "I have seven I can't rearrange."

"All right; twenty cases, my choosing."

"I said ten."

"I was going to say no. I still can," Kerrie said.

"You're intrigued."

"Not enough to handle a tough case at noon and keep everything on my docket. Twenty cases, my choosing."

"Fifteen," Maise said.

"Done," Kerrie said, and proceeded to shuffle through files. Four this morning that she hadn't even looked at, keeping one. Three in the afternoon, and all of her evening docket—which was five. Plus three Please-God-Nevers that no one had been willing to take off her desk in more than two months.

She removed her own name as defense counsel and added Maise's before she sent the files to Maise, just so that there was no screw-up in the court listings.

Maise sent one file so fat through Kerrie's links that she actually got an overload warning. She had to switch the file to a different node, something she hadn't had to do since law school.

"You didn't tell me she was a convicted felon," Kerrie said.

"I did too," Maise said. "Black Fleet, remember? It'll work out."

"It better," Kerrie said, but Maise had already left.

Kerrie had to mentally shuffle files and rearrange her entire schedule. It now seemed deceptively simple: one case at nine a.m. in Courtroom 61 and another at noon in Courtroom 495. Never mind that Courtroom 495 was about as far from the public defender's office as possible. Never mind that Courtroom 61 was close.

Kerrie had to review the new file—she couldn't scan this one nor could she trust the Peyti lawyer who might have more years of experience, but who had probably never ever appeared in InterSpecies Court.

And that was always a recipe for disaster.

Not to mention the client. A pregnant felon, willing to move to criminal court rather than face whatever the hell she did somewhere inside the Earth Alliance.

But Kerrie was intrigued. She wasn't sure if that was good or bad.

Intrigued meant she'd pay attention, but intrigued also meant she could get emotionally involved.

And emotionally involved here meant heartbreak of the worst kind.

She set the thick file on AutoLearn, which would send the information directly to her brain. She hated AutoLearn, but she used it almost every day. AutoLearn didn't give her any real understanding of the file. It didn't even give her a good grasp of the facts. What it did was give her a sense of the file, a cursory knowledge of all of the details, which she would be able to find if she needed them during court.

The biggest problem with AutoLearn, however, was that the learning was actually time-stamped, and it would expire in two weeks if not reinforced. She usually didn't reinforce what she AutoLearned with real learning—the cases vanished that fast—but she had a hunch she might have to do so here.

While that program fed information to her brain, she headed to holding for a moment with her other client. She let his file run in front of her left eye: Fabian Fiske, which had to be some kind of made-up name. If she had time, she'd search the file to see if he legally changed his name somewhere along the way. But she didn't have time.

She barely had time to glance at the facts:

Fabian Fiske worked for Efierno Corporation as a construction day worker. That fact alone made her cringe. Most of the defendants she got here were construction day workers. They signed up because they needed the work and waived the right to company protection should anything go wrong.

Since construction workers usually went into strange areas before the bulk of the business itself, construction workers were more likely to break intercultural laws. And the least likely to have a good lawyer to defend them or have access to the corporation's Disappearance services.

Here was the problem, the fact of Kerrie's everyday life since she graduated from law school and ended up in this godforsaken place: Everyone believed that someone accused of breaking the law of another culture ended up in front of one of thirty Multicultural Tribunals—and technically that was true. Technically, Earth Alliance InterSpecies Court was a branch of the Multicultural Tribunal for the First District. In practice, there was nothing multicultural about the courts Kerrie stood before. No panel of judges from different cultures heard these cases. It wasn't practical.

Instead, a single judge from a rotating group of judges from different Earth Alliance cultures handled cases like Fiske's, usually with two or three questions, and a pound of the gavel. If a judge didn't act quickly, the court system would get jammed, because contrary to popular belief, people got accused of breaking other culture's laws all the time.

That wouldn't be a problem if the cultures weren't so vastly different. Over its history, the Earth Alliance made treaties with a wide variety of alien cultures. Those treaties facilitated trade within the sector, making the Earth Alliance the most powerful governing body in the known universe.

But the price of those treaties was steep—at least from the human perspective. The treaties all stated that the violator of a law got punished by the culture whose law was broken. It sounded straightforward, but the differences in cultures made for punishments humans—and many aliens—did not like.

The most famous early case, and one every law school student studied, was of a man who accidentally stepped on a flower—a crime in the community where he was temporarily assigned for work—and he was sentenced to death.

That sentence was carried out.

As were thousands—millions—of others. Humans didn't like that and refused over time to work for the large corporations. So the corporations developed a way of skirting the law; first by hiring the best lawyers for their people, and then when that didn't work, by setting up Disappearance services, allowing the employees accused of the most egregious crimes to get a new identity, leave their lives, and slip away.

Of course, those employees either paid for the service themselves or were high up enough in the corporate structure to qualify for a free Disappearance.

Independent Disappearance services also existed, but they were so expensive that someone who worked as a construction day worker couldn't afford the consultation fee, let alone the price of a full Disappearance.

On her way to the holding section of the courthouse, Kerrie had to go through security—a small machine that scanned her entire body. Then she had to go through another scan as she walked through the double doors.

The scans disrupted her file review, and she had to scan backward, missing—of course—the most important part: what, exactly, Fiske was accused of.

She didn't have trouble finding him. He was older than the image in his file by at least two decades, but he looked like a dried-out version of the man pictured. His hair was gray, his face lined, and his hands gnarled. The poorest of the poor. He couldn't even get his hands enhanced so that he could do his job properly.

"Fabian?" she asked.

He stood, politely, and nodded at her. A man who followed rules. He wore a rumpled blue work shirt and muddy pants that he brushed off as she walked toward him.

A trickle of compassion washed through her and she tamped it down. She couldn't afford it any more than he could afford to have a real defense.

"Do you have a suit?" she asked.

"No, miss," he said, inadvertently accenting their age difference and the fact that he had no idea who she was.

"I'm sorry," she said. "My name is Kerrie Steinmetz. I'm your lawyer. In court, you have to call me Ms. Steinmetz."

If she let him speak at all, which she doubted she would.

"All right," he said softly, bowing his head.

She sent a message across her links to Miguel, one of the paralegals. *Need a suit from the closet, size—*

She glanced at him, unable to measure, visually. She wasn't used to seeing men with such broad torsos and such slender legs. "What size do you wear?"

"What?" Fiske blinked at her.

"Suit. And shoes. What size do you wear?"

He shrugged. He had never owned a suit.

"Clothes, then," she said. "Shirt, pants, shoes."

She repeated the shoes in case he was overwhelmed, and softly, he answered her, color rising in his cheeks. The kind of man who didn't like revealing personal information. The kind of man who tried hard not to be noticed.

What the hell had he done?

She sent the information to the paralegal, then led Fiske to the chairs.

"I need you to go over this with me," she said. "Who is accusing you again?"

"The Baharn," he said.

She actually felt a second of hope, and tamped that down. Unlike many of the cultures she dealt with, the Baharn accepted financial fines in lieu of an actual sentence.

"And you . . . ?" She let her voice trail off.

"Got drunk." Fiske's voice wobbled. "I don't even remember it."

"But there's a visual, right?" she asked, not because she knew, but because that was how these things worked.

"I just passed out," he said. "They said I touched one of their—I don't know what they're called. The kid of someone important."

"Kid?" Kerrie asked before going farther. There were no fines when someone tampered with a Baharn child, no matter what caste the child belonged to.

"Teenager. Adult really, by our standards. Twenty-something. Full grown."

She nodded, feeling a bit of relief.

"I brushed him when I passed out. What was some religious kid doing in a human bar?" His voice went up. "No one will tell me that."

The kid had been trolling for trouble. Or a percentage of a fine. But she wasn't going to tell Fiske that, either.

"Did someone ask your companions for money to make it all go away?" she asked.

"They ran," he said. "They left me."

Smart people. And he had passed out.

The paralegal came in with a suit on a hanger, shoes dangling off it. "I need you to put this on for court," Kerrie said to Fiske.

He looked at it.

"You have to dress properly for court or they won't listen to you."

He took the clothes. "Where do I—?"

There were no private areas. She nodded toward a back corner. "Over there," she said. "We won't look."

She thanked the paralegal and told him to wait for a second, then turned her back as Fiske changed, using that moment to review the visual. It went down exactly as he said, except that the "kid"—a long-horned tentacled creature so wide that he didn't fit into a human chair—had hovered near the bar, clearly trolling.

She couldn't use that as an argument—that was an appeals argument or something that actually would have to go in front of a real Multicultural Tribunal with an expensive defense attorney arguing the case. Fiske didn't have the money for that and she didn't have the time.

Then she looked at the fine and frowned.

Fiske came back, shuffling in the shoes. They didn't quite fit him. He looked lost. He *was* lost, although not as lost as he had been before.

"You need to pay the fine," she said to him.

He shook his head. "I can't afford it."

She didn't insult him by telling him it was a small fine. To her, it was a small fine. To him, it probably was a fortune.

"You can't afford not to," she said. "If you go in front of the judge and you don't pay the fine, he'll send you to Baharn lock-up. Then someone will brush against you and the fine will go up. By the time you leave that place, you will have accidentally touched half a dozen Baharn, and each time, you'll receive a brand new fine."

"They can't do that," he said.

"Of course they can. You're already considered guilty of the crime. You've just compounded it. You get five years for every unpaid fine. After two weeks, you'll probably have forty years to serve. And after a month . . ." She shook her head, then softened her voice. "It's a death sentence, Fabian. You have to pay the fine."

"I can't," he said. "I don't have work. I don't have the money. My family will be destitute."

"What will happen to them if you are in prison for the rest of your life?" she asked.

He lowered his head.

In a gentler tone, she said, "The court will put you on a payment plan. You can pay as little as you like, and you can stretch the payments out for the rest of your life, but that'll keep you out of a Baharn prison."

He raised his head, his eyes wide. "I thought you could get me out of this. I was drunk. Can't we go to the judge and say it was an accident?"

"We can," she said. "He won't listen. And honestly, can you prove it?"

"What?" Fiske asked, clearly shocked.

"Can you prove that you didn't brush against that Baharn on purpose?"

"I was drunk," he said. "I passed out."

"Can you prove that?" she asked. "Were tests conducted at the scene?"

"I don't know," he said. "But my friends—"

"Ran. And they're not on this starbase, and you don't have the money to send for them. It'll cost more to bring them here than the entire fine with penalties and interest. Pay the fine, Fabian."

He swallowed.

"Or spend the rest of your life in a Baharn prison. Those are your choices."

He shook his head.

"Decide now, Fabian," she said, glad he had an unusual name, because she could remember it. She used to give her clients time to make a decision, but then she realized it wasn't worth it. That took time away from other clients. "This is your last chance."

"If you were me," he started, "what would you—"

"I'd pay the fine," she said. Then she put a hand on his back and shoved him toward the paralegal. "Miguel will take you to the court. I'm sending the filing ahead. You'll have to sign and set the payment schedule."

Then she sent the filing before Fiske had a chance to say anything else.

Her gaze met the paralegal's. "He's due in Judge Weiss's court at nine a.m. Take him to the clerk, fill out the last few details, and for godsake, make sure he's off the docket. If you fail to take him off the docket, I'll fire you myself, is that clear?"

The paralegal nodded, looking scared. She'd made that same threat last week to a different paralegal who was now no longer employed with the Public Defenders office. Unlike some of the other attorneys, she carried out her threats. There was no room for error here—and she had learned that the hard way.

She extended her hand. Fiske took it hesitantly.

"Stay on Earth or the Moon from now on, Fabian," she said. "Don't go near unfamiliar cultures, and I promise things will get better from here."

Then she let go, gave him a half smile, and left holding, feeling jubilant. She didn't let Fiske see her face because he wouldn't understand. The paralegal probably didn't either, but this was what passed for a win in Earth Alliance InterSpecies Court—and she had learned early to celebrate these wins, because they were all she had.

Of course, if she were the superstitious type, she would have wondered if this win boded ill for the morning's other big case.

But she wasn't superstitious. She wasn't going to let one tiny victory color the rest of her day.

Since she didn't have to go to court at nine a.m., she was free to see her new client. Prisoners didn't get transferred to the holding area until an hour before trial, so she had to go to the jail. As she left, she sent a message down her links to have her client moved to the interview room.

Two tram rides, jam-packed with lawyers and paralegals and law clerks, all heading to the jail to do something at the last minute before someone's court appearance. Had she taken two more trams, heading to the prison part of the base, she would have also encountered family, friends and hangers-on, but fortunately she wasn't going there. She didn't need to see any of that anyway.

The trams went through tunnels drilled deep in the base, far away from the outer rings. Transportation on the outer rings belonged to the shuttles to Helena Base. From Helena, people could go anywhere in the sector.

But security learned early on that running the shuttles and the trams on similar tracks facilitated jail breaks. So the tram system got moved to the deepest part of the base.

Since there was nothing to look at, Kerrie reviewed the case as best she could. But she had barely looked at any of the files by the time she reached the jail. She used the lawyer's entrance, pressing her hand against the door all the way in. Her identification opened those doors, but didn't stop the full-body scans, searching her for a weapon.

She'd learned to ignore that, even when the scans got invasive. Instead, she simply went deep inside her own mind, studying the cases, preparing for the next court session.

She stepped into the interview area, walled off from the rest of the jail by thick walls and soundproof barriers. A guard met her, called her by name, and took her down a corridor she had never seen before.

She expected to be in the large communal interview room, with privacy shields lowered over the table where she would sit with her client. She would have been able to see all the other lawyers talking to their clients, but not hear them.

Instead, the guard led her to a tiny room, made of the same clear material as the privacy shield. But a long table was bolted to the floor here, along with four chairs and a very visible panic button, in case she needed out. The door to the prisoner's wing was reinforced with shields and warnings, and the door on her side had some kind of prod attached that would zap the prisoner if he even tried to get out.

As she let herself in, she saw that the Peyti lawyer had already arrived, even though she hadn't asked for him. Her only indication of the Peyti's gender was his clothing, suit, tie, pants, even though Peyti culture didn't require those things at all. It showed the Peyti was sensitive to human conventions, and thought it important that humans know about him.

He was sticklike; so thin that he looked like he was about to break. His breathing mask covered the lower half of his face, and the three long, thin fingers on his right hand tapped the tabletop rhythmically.

He had no patience, which was unusual in a Peyti. And he was not as tall as the average Peyti.

She felt her heart sink. He was young—hence the clothing, the worries about what someone else would think, and the impatience.

She opened the door.

"I'm Kerrie Steinmetz," she said. "I'm the public defender your client requested."

He stood and extended his right hand.

"Uzvik," he said, voice so soft she could barely hear him. She understood why Maise hated working with the Peyti. They were hard to hear, for one thing, and for another, their names were confusing. Most Peyti she'd met had "Uz" in their names somewhere. She would have to be careful not to use the wrong suffix when she spoke to him.

She took the fingers gently in her own. They felt like bendable chopsticks. She had learned not to shake them or even grip them too hard. She didn't want to cause him pain.

She held the fingers for the requisite fifteen seconds, then let go. "I'm a bit confused, Uzvik. Public defenders get assigned for clients who can't pay. Yet you're here."

He tilted his head, a sign of sadness among the Peyti. "I am not being paid. It is a courtesy."

"For whom?" she asked.

"My client," he said.

"If you are not being paid, how is she your client?" Kerrie asked.

"Someone must stand by her," he said softly.

Crap. A loyal companion. She hated those. "Do you belong to the Multicultural Tribunal Bar?"

"No," he said so softly she could barely hear him.

"What's your specialty, then?"

"Criminal law," he said.

"With a specialty in what?" she asked.

"Piracy," he said, and if he had been human, his tone of voice would have made her think he was embarrassed by that.

"Then you're completely out of your jurisdiction and your presence here compromises my attorney-client confidentiality. You're going to have to leave."

He nodded and stood. "She is not guilty of this."

Kerrie would be rich if she got paid for every time someone said that to her. "You know as well as I do that it doesn't matter here."

He tilted his head, his big eyes sad. "I thought it does matter. There are stories—"

"From the Multicultural Tribunal," she said. "Not from Earth Alliance InterSpecies Court. Here you're guilty unless there's a technicality."

"She is not a citizen of the Earth Alliance," he said.

"I know that," Kerrie said. "I thought that was a point in her favor until I saw her sheet. She's a convicted criminal."

"Ah," he said, his eyes narrowing in a Peyti equivalent of a smile. "But she is not."

"Not what?"

"Convicted. You have not looked closely at the file, have you?"

"I just got it this morning," Kerrie said.

His brow wrinkled. "She has been here for two weeks. We put in the request before the prison ship brought her here."

Kerrie shrugged. She'd heard that complaint before too. "The wheels of justice turn slowly."

He looked alarmed. He extended those strange fingers just as the announcement came through her links. She had to sit down, hands on the table, because her client was coming into the room.

"I need you out of here," Kerrie said.

"I can be of assistance. Co-counsel."

"You're not certified to practice in this court," she said. "And because I know you're not certified, that won't invalidate her pleadings. So no more tricks. Get the hell out."

He didn't wait for her to repeat herself. He scurried past her and pulled open the main door.

"And don't stand in the corridor where she can see you," Kerrie said. "I'll file a complaint with the authorities of the jail and you'll lose all visiting privileges."

He bowed his head, then let himself out. She turned slightly so that she could see him disappear down the hall.

Then the warning echoed through her links again. She sat straight, regulation position, as the door opened and her client entered.

She was smaller than Kerrie expected, heartbreakingly thin in the manner of those raised in zero gravity. She moved slowly, clearly unused to and uncomfortable in Earth-normal gravity.

The pregnancy didn't help. She was in her third trimester, but how far along was hard to determine given her thinness. Her belly would look huge at six months let alone nine.

"Where's Uzvik?" she asked.

"He can't be here," Kerrie said. "He's not certified for this court."

The girl sat down heavily, one hand on her belly. She looked disappointed.

"If that was a strategy, it was a stupid one," Kerrie said. "I could be disbarred for letting him second chair."

"You could pretend you didn't know."

Kerrie wondered how many times this girl had asked someone to "pretend" they didn't know something for a court case.

"Is that how he's gotten you acquitted in all those other cases?"

The girl shrugged, unwilling to answer. Smart. Because Kerrie would have to file amended petitions, stating she had knowledge of actions contrary to the legal ethics.

"I don't know how things work in the Frontier," Kerrie said, referring to the part of the section where the Black Fleet had almost free range. "But here, following the rules matters."

It was all they had, really, even though she felt like a hypocrite saying so. The rules didn't work for almost everyone coming through the system—particularly when cases like Fiske's had to be considered victories.

"I'm not exactly sure what you thought you'd gain by bringing him along," Kerrie said in a tone harsher than she would usually use with a client so early in their discussion. "Your problem is with the Ziyit. They punish theft pretty simply. All you'll lose is a hand, one I'm sure your people in the Black Fleet can afford to replace. Your baby isn't at threat, and you're probably not going to go to prison. The Ziyit don't believe in incarceration."

"I can't afford replacement," she said. "I can't afford medical treatment at all."

Kerrie sighed and leaned back. She hated clients who lied to her. "The Black Fleet can afford anything it wants. It also has—from everything I've heard—some of the best medical facilities in the known universe. You can get the hand replaced. It'll be so perfect, your kid won't know what happened."

The girl shook her head. "I can't. Don't you know how this works? The Ziyit will cut off my hand, and then they won't tend to me. They won't even let me bring in a doctor to treat. Then they'll send me away for treatment. The blood loss alone could kill me. It'll probably kill my baby."

"So use an AutoBandage and make sure someone from the Fleet is nearby. One ship won't matter," Kerrie said. "The Ziyit don't care. They want the hand as a trophy. They'll display it as a deterrent. As interspecies punishments go, it's a relatively light one. They don't even care if your ship waits for you. They won't do anything to stop you from going there to get medical treatment. They'll just deny you treatment in their facilities which, I have to tell you, is a good thing."

"You don't understand," the girl said, rubbing her belly. "I can't go to the Fleet. They've tossed me out."

Kerrie stared at her and resisted the urge to shake her head. That changed everything. It explained why the Peyti lawyer wasn't getting paid. It explained the strange tactic as well.

Because the girl was in legal limbo. She wasn't a member of the Earth Alliance, so she had no access to Earth Alliance medical facilities unless she could pay for them. And her presence here meant that she couldn't pay for them.

She was right; even with AutoBandages, she'd bleed out before she got to a site that would allow someone impoverished access. That might take days, maybe weeks. Shipboard methods might keep her alive, but they wouldn't keep both her and the baby alive.

"I suppose you're guilty," Kerrie said.

The girl shrugged again, and Kerrie mentally cursed Maise. An acquittal. Yeah, that was going to happen. Instead, Maise had used her known prejudice against Peyti to pass off a nightmare case, one that would haunt Kerrie's dreams for the rest of her life. She'd lose, not just the girl, but the baby too.

"Why did the Fleet abandon you?" Kerrie asked.

The girl looked down. "Because I got caught," she said.

The story went like this:

The girl—whose name was Donnatella Waltarie—got a job working as human consultant to a Ziyit family that would be traveling into the Earth Alliance in a diplomatic role. The female head of the household (there were multiple females with multiple roles in Ziyit families) had received an appointment as the Ziyit ambassador to Messner at the far end of the sector.

It was a political appointment, given as patronage, not because the Ziyit female had any particular knowledge of the Earth Alliance or human culture. Donnatella was to tutor the younger females in human customs—and she did, for nearly two months.

Two months gave her time to find the Blueglass Stone, a famous piece of Ziyit jewelry that had an outsized value on the black market because of its rarity. Donnatella didn't say, but implied, that the Fleet had a buyer for the Stone.

On her last day with the Ziyit family—as they packed for their trip—she slipped the Stone into one of her pockets. She received her pay from the Ziyit family, took a shuttle to an outlying space station, and then rejoined the Fleet. The Stone left with her.

"But you said you got caught," Kerrie said.

The girl's lips twisted, as if she didn't want to discuss that moment. Kerrie would have to push her. Instead, she mentally scanned the file she had absorbed and got her answer.

The theft—caught on surveillance equipment—happened four years before the arrest.

Add to that the abandonment by the Black Fleet, and Kerrie had an inkling as to what was going on behind the scenes.

"Whose baby are you carrying?" Kerrie asked.

"It's not important," the girl said.

"I think it is. It's the reason all of this is happening to you. The Black Fleet abandoned you because its leaders had to choose sides—and you lost."

The girl shrugged. "That won't get me out of this mess. Even I know enough about the legal system here to know that."

"Won't the baby's father send a ship to help you with the medical part of your sentence?" Kerrie asked.

The girl's lips thinned. "No."

"And your parents—?"

"Dead," she said.

Kerrie frowned. "The Ziyit have images of you stealing the Stone. Then you got dumped so that you would be arrested here."

The girl nodded.

"If the punishment is carried out properly, you'll die or the baby will."

The girl leaned back, pretending calm, although she wasn't calm.

"Which will solve someone's problem with you in the Black Fleet, is that correct?"

The girl nodded once, as if she didn't want to.

Kerrie didn't want her to. She didn't want to know any of this because this girl, Donnatella, was right. It made no difference to Kerrie's job or the case before her.

The loss of a hand was a light sentence in InterSpecies Court because hands could be replaced. It was more traumatic to humans than it was to Ziyits who had twenty-six different appendages that could be considered hands. But humans—generally—survived the loss.

If Kerrie argued the case properly, she might get some consideration for Donnatella's condition—extra bandages, the presence of the Peyti when the sentence was carried out.

But that didn't solve the underlying problem. The girl had no money, and no way to get medical treatment inside the Alliance. She would get none on Ziyit, where the sentence would get carried out. And she couldn't afford transportation off the planet. The Alliance couldn't provide the transportation.

Donnatella—and her baby—would die there.

"You don't deny that you stole the Stone," Kerrie said.

The girl shrugged. "I am a thief for the Black Fleet. Or I was. I am good at what I do."

So was the Peyti, because he got her acquitted time and time again.

"You were born on one of the Black Fleet's ships," Kerrie said. "Outside of the Earth Alliance."

"On the ship, yes," the girl said. "Where, I don't know. The ships never keep track of where the children are born."

So she truly was not a member of the Earth Alliance, although Kerrie couldn't prove that. The Black Fleet also didn't issue birth certificates.

Kerrie leaned back, frowning, wondering if that lack of proof would help her get Donnatella to a medical facility.

Probably not. Because judges in InterSpecies Court always wanted proof, particularly when an attorney tried something original.

Which Kerrie would be doing here.

She had no proof—none—of Donnatella's citizenship. Or did she? She had files to check.

She stood. "You need to be in court at noon. Clean up. Dress well and say nothing."

"You're going to send me to the Ziyit, aren't you?" the girl asked.

For the first time, she seemed scared.

Kerrie knew better than to soothe her. Anything could happen in court, no matter how much an attorney planned. And when the deck was stacked against her, the way it was in InterSpecies Court, only a fool made promises.

"I won't send you to them," Kerrie said. "The judge will."

And then she left.

She had cleared her schedule of court appearances but not of cases. She was still buried, just not as momentarily busy. Still, there was always more to do.

Before she took the tram back, she saw two more of her clients stuck in jail. Normally, she wouldn't have had a chance to see them before they arrived in holding. This time, however, she was able to take their measure—not just of their appearances, but their willingness to plead. Of course, they both thought she could get them off and when she told them she couldn't, they asked if she could find a Disappearance service for them.

*Technically, she said piously, because she always had to say this piously, Disappearance services for people in your situation break the law. I can't break the law or I would lose my law license.*

As she rode back, she wondered if losing her license would be a bad thing. What was she doing, after all? Just processing people for various governments, sending them away. Getting them through the system so that they could receive punishment for crimes many of them didn't even understand.

She forced herself to review Donnatella's files instead of think. She searched and as she searched, she found what she was looking for. Her stomach knotted.

In nearly two years, she had never tried anything like this. But it was, as Maise said, her one chance at an acquittal.

She had to try.

Courtroom 495 was Kerrie's least favorite courtroom in the entire Inter-Species Court system. Despite its number, it was one of the older court-rooms, small and cramped, with a low ceiling, dark faux wood walls, and benches that hadn't been upgraded since the courtroom was built. A small dock separated the prosecution and defense table from the benches and from the jury box.

But there hadn't been a jury seated in this courtroom in decades. Jury trials were so rare here they had become a spectator sport and as such had moved to the larger courtrooms in the center of the so-called courthouse.

No one sat in those seats, however, making the courtroom oddly packed in all areas except one. The chairs even looked new there, which Kerrie always thought somewhat sad. She found it a commentary on the system eating everyone alive.

She arrived ten minutes early. Ten minutes early and she had even managed lunch. Lunch on the tram—cold sandwiches made of mystery food—but still more than she got on many afternoons.

As the court clerk called her case, Kerrie moved to the defense table. The bailiff went to holding to get Donnatella Waltarie. The Peyti, Uzvik, had a seat in the front row. He must have been there since Kerrie made him leave the jail.

The bailiff brought Donnatella into the courtroom. She looked well scrubbed, but tired. Her face was pale, with deep shadows under her eyes. Kerrie wondered if she had been crying.

She stopped at the defense table, but didn't sit down, hands clasped protectively over her belly. She had been to court before. She knew this wouldn't take long enough to make it worth her time to struggle into a chair, and then struggle out of it again.

Judge Langer glowered from the bench. She was fifty something, with hopes of moving up to real Multicultural Tribunal cases, not these quick gavel-pounders. Kerrie had stood before her twice before and learned that Langer tolerated no delays, no nonsense. But she did treat the lawyers equally, which was something most judges didn't do. Most judges favored the prosecution, because the law did.

The prosecutor, Peir Hroth, had graduated from law school at the same time as Kerrie. He too had loans to pay off. He too was doing his time here. He had opted for prosecution because he hoped to become a judge one day—and defense attorneys rarely (never) made it into important judgeships.

He had lost weight since he got here, and he looked even more tired than he had on the shuttle from Helena Base.

He glanced at Kerrie and nodded, one of the few prosecutors she had known before coming to InterSpecies Court who still remained cordial to her.

The court clerk called out the case number, and read the charges. Then the judge asked Kerrie, "Do you dispute?"

"We do, Your Honor," Kerrie said, stepping forward. "We ask that the charges get dropped."

A dispute never caught anyone's attention. Attorneys disputed the nature of the charges all the time, trying to lower the punishment. But when Kerrie asked that the charges get dropped, the murmur of conversation behind her—something she was so used to that she hadn't noticed it—ceased.

Everyone was staring at her, from Peir to the bailiff to her client.

And the judge, of course.

"Did I hear you correctly, Counselor?" the judge asked.

"Yes, Your Honor."

The judge leaned forward, her eyes glazed like people's often were when they reviewed something through their links. Kerrie knew the judge was scanning the file.

"I see nothing to dispute here, Counselor. The prosecution has a video of the crime."

Peir stepped forward, probably to argue that they had overwhelming evidence against Donnatella. But Kerrie didn't want him to get a word in.

"Yes, Your Honor," Kerrie said. "We do not dispute that the crime happened."

She heard a squeak of protest to her left. Donnatella didn't like that argument. But Kerrie didn't consult with her. Kerrie didn't have to, not on this.

"We dispute that the charges apply," Kerrie said.

"It's a theft, Your Honor," Peir said. "Of course they apply."

The judge waved her hand at him, silencing him. She looked intrigued, which relieved Kerrie—until she heard the judge's next words. "I hope you have a good reason to use the court's time on this, Counselor."

"I do, Your Honor," Kerrie said. "Donnatella Waltarie is not a member of the Earth Alliance. Our treaties with the Ziyit do not apply to her. We cannot send her into their justice system because we have no right to do so."

"She's a member of the Black Fleet," Peir said, giving Kerrie a sideways glance filled with disbelief. "Just because she's part of the Black Fleet doesn't mean she's *not* a member of the Earth Alliance. She could have joined them at any point in her life. Besides, Your Honor, her undisputed affiliation with the Black Fleet proves that she is a criminal and that she is willing to lie to achieve her own ends. Defense counsel is a nice person; she has probably decided this is the best way to help a pregnant client avoid a criminal prosecution."

Kerrie's eyebrows went up. Did he just call her a nice person? In front of the judge? The argument diminished Kerrie's standing as an attorney by questioning her judgment. Her cheeks flushed. The comment made her angry, as it was probably designed to do.

Instead of lashing back at Peir, she said, "I am honored that the prosecutor believes I am a nice person. I hope the court clerk will keep that in the record—"

Chuckles rose behind her. Others had caught the slight.

"—because it is court records that we are relying upon here," she said. "My client has been accused of many crimes. She has faced a judge or a jury on twelve separate occasions, and in each case, she has been acquitted."

"That's lovely for her, Your Honor," Peir said, "but those cases have no relevance—"

"If you would let me finish, Counselor," Kerrie said. She paused so the judge could weigh in. Peir's behavior was unorthodox in open court, but so was hers. The judge had probably forgotten what it was like to have an argument placed before her, with its rules and structures. All of her other cases on this day, in this week—hell, in this year—would be *pro forma* gavel-down cases: Two speeches, one by each attorney, a ruling, followed by a curt *next*. Nothing this elaborate had happened in this court in a long time.

The judge did not speak up. She was watching Kerrie closely, clearly waiting.

"In all twelve of those cases, Your Honor," Kerrie said, "my client stated that she was not a member of the Earth Alliance, that she had been born on a ship of the Black Fleet outside Earth Alliance territory. All twelve cases have been adjudicated in Earth Alliance courts. All twelve have court records, and judgments were made based upon the facts presented in those cases. In short, Your Honor, we have twelve different courts, scattered throughout the sector and the Earth Alliance itself, that have ruled that my client is not a subject of the Earth Alliance."

The courtroom was quiet now. Everyone stared at Kerrie, including Peir. He had a look of panic in his eyes. He had no idea how to argue this, or what to even say.

"Those twelve cases were human-on-human crime cases, Your Honor, which fall under Earth Alliance jurisdiction no matter whether the accused is part of the Alliance or not," Kerrie said. "This is the first case in which my client has been accused of theft against a nonhuman member of the Earth Alliance. Different laws apply. These laws are based on treaties between the Earth Alliance and the Ziyit. My client is not subject to those treaties since she belongs to neither culture. I can cite case law, Your Honor, if you would like. Jurisdictional issues were argued in the first years of the Multicultural Tribunals and they found—"

"I'm familiar with the law, Counselor." The judge looked bemused. "I have looked at the court cases, and you are right. Your client is not a member of the Earth Alliance. We have no choice but to drop the charges against Donnatella Waltarie. You are—"

"Your Honor!" Peir took an extra step forward, his voice filled with panic. "We ask that Ms. Waltarie be detained, so that we can ship her to the Ziyit so that they may prosecute her for these crimes."

"Have the Ziyit made an extradition request?" the judge asked.

"Um, no, Your Honor. But once they hear of this, they will—"

"I cannot rule on what someone will do, Counselor. I can only rule upon the cases in front of me. That's covered in the first week of law school. Are you in need of a refresher course?"

"No, Your Honor." Peir stepped back. "I'm sorry, Your Honor. But—"

"If you can figure out a reason to hold her, do so, Counselor," the judge said. "But I won't rule on it. This case is dismissed."

She brought her gavel down and the courtroom erupted. People began talking, laughing, shouting. Even the bailiff looked bemused.

Kerrie turned to Donnatella. "We have to get you out of here before they have a chance to contact someone on Ziyit."

Donnatella blinked at her, looking confused. "I'm free?"

"You are, unless they can get an extradition order. So let's go."

"How do I get out off the base?" Donnatella asked. "They brought me by shuttle."

"The shuttles are free and run every hour." Kerrie took Donnatella's arm and shepherded her toward the aisle. People were grabbing at them, asking questions and trying to talk. No one had had an acquittal this year—and technically, this wasn't one either. It was a dismissal. But the result was the same.

Donnatella wouldn't be punished for her crime.

"The shuttle will take me where?" Donnatella asked.

"Helena base," Kerrie said. "It's the nearest stop and large enough for you to get lost in. Come on."

She looked for the Peyti, but didn't see him. He would probably meet them at the shuttle station. She hurried Donnatella out of the courtroom and to the lawyers' elevator. As she got in, Kerrie ordered the doors closed so no one could follow them.

She didn't stop at the usual courthouse shuttle station stop. Instead, she went down to the public defender level, crossed the hall, and took another elevator. Donnatella had to struggle to keep up.

"Where are we going?" she asked.

"Somewhere they won't look for you." Kerrie took one flight of stairs down and walked through two doors. The second door opened to a small shuttle station. The red numbers above the door said the next shuttle was due to arrive in five minutes.

Donnatella stopped beside her, red-faced and breathing hard, her hand protectively over that stomach. She didn't say anything, though, about troubles, so Kerrie didn't ask.

She needed to get Donnatella on that shuttle.

"You will talk to no one once you board," Kerrie said. "If someone asks your name, you pretend not to hear the question. Move away. Do not identify yourself. There are no conductors or bots to take tickets. Don't let anyone trick you. If you don't identify yourself, they can't serve you with an extradition order. You don't need to identify yourself at the other end either. When you get there, just mingle with the crowd. Do you understand?"

"Yes." Donnatella's expression had lightened. She was almost smiling.

"Do you have money?" Kerrie asked, silently cursing herself for even thinking of the question.

"I can get it," Donnatella said.

"That's what I'm afraid of." The last thing Kerrie needed was for Donnatella to steal money on Helena base and get caught. Then she'd be served that extradition order. Kerrie needed Donnatella to get as far away from here, as quickly and easily as possible. "Do you have access to your own money?"

Donnatella smiled. "I don't have any money of my own."

Kerrie extended a hand. Donnatella looked down.

"Take my hand," Kerrie said.

Donnatella did. Kerrie pressed the unlinked money chip in her thumb. The unlinked account had no personal information on Kerrie at all. Just funds. It transferred its entire reserve into Donnatella's account. The entire reserve sounded like a lot, but Kerrie only used that account for incidentals. It had maybe one hundred credits.

"Now you have your own money," Kerrie said, letting go of Donnatella's hand.

"That was yours?" Donnatella asked.

"Yes," Kerrie said. The red numbers on the wall were counting down. The shuttle was only one station away. "Now it's yours."

"But you didn't have to do that." Donnatella's smile had faded. She looked shocked.

"Yes, I did," Kerrie said. The shuttle pulled up, doors slid open. The nearest car only had two passengers, both of whom looked exhausted. Family members of people on trial, probably.

"But—"

"Stop arguing and board," Kerrie said. "Remember what I told you."

"I owe you," Donnatella said as she climbed through the doors, using one hand to brace herself.

"No, you don't," Kerrie said.

"I do," Donnatella said with great emphasis. "And my people always repay our debts."

The doors swished closed. Donnatella stood by the window. She waved as the shuttle pulled out.

Kerrie watched it disappear. It had one more stop before it detached from the base and flew the short hop to Helena base. One hundred credits wouldn't get Donnatella far on Helena. It had two segments—the rich resort side and the cheap side that connected to the InterSpecies Court starbase. Donnatella couldn't afford an upscale hotel room there, but she could get herself a meal and maybe a low-rent place to stay. There were also good medical facilities on Helena that wouldn't turn away a woman about to give birth.

Kerrie let out a small sigh, then put a hand to her forehead.

She hadn't ever sent a client back on a shuttle. Just sobbing family members and disappointed friends.

She staggered back up the stairs, feeling lightheaded. She had won the morning, but she still had the afternoon and the evening to suffer the usual defeats.

As she walked to the public defenders office, she sorted the afternoon and evening cases, surprised at how light her workload was. She had forgotten that she had traded most of it for Donnatella's case.

Kerrie actually had time to get some real coffee before her next client meeting.

Maise stopped her before she reached her desk. Maise was smiling. "Come with me. You know the rules, right?"

Of course Kerrie knew the rules. Her job was about the rules. But she couldn't think about what applied at the moment.

Maise led her into the main conference room. It was stacked with empty coffee cups and discarded clothes that needed cleaning. The room smelled faintly of sweat and old food.

Maise closed the door.

"When you win a case," Maise said, "your debt is forgiven. You're free to go if you want, Kerrie."

Kerrie frowned. She had forgotten that rule, or maybe she never really believed it. Or she thought it wouldn't apply, because no one ever won.

"But I would stay at least another week if I were you," Maise said. "You're about to be recruited like no one gets recruited. Not even the number one graduate of Alliance Law gets pursued like you're about to. Someone is first in their class every year, but almost no one wins on the defense side in InterSpecies Court unless they're already a lifer. You've hit the jackpot, Kerrie."

Kerrie sat down. She had just sent a pregnant girl with no prospects to a resort she couldn't pay for, and that was a win? Kerrie made herself breathe.

"I'm going to be the first to recruit you," Maise said. "We need people like you to stay here, to fight the good fight. Most of the good attorneys go on to private practice, but the people who need us cycle through every day. And if you win a case—"

"You said I would win," Kerrie said. "That's why you gave me that case."

"I hoped," Maise said. "We get cases like that every now and then. But not everyone pulls out the win. You did."

Kerrie looked at her. A lifer? Here? Always behind, always scrambling, watching people who really didn't deserve their punishments shuffle away, never to be seen again.

"Thanks for the offer," Kerrie said. "I'll consider it."

She lied, of course. She couldn't do it. But she didn't want to say any more, not when Maise had orchestrated this.

"I can move someone to your afternoon cases," Maise said. "You can take the rest of the day off."

Kerrie shook her head. "You said I could leave if I wanted to."

"You can," Maise said. "But as I said, if you stay one week—"

"I will," Kerrie said. "I'll stay that week."

Because it was easier to stay and think than it was to flee just like Donnatella did.

Besides, Kerrie hadn't given life after this job much thought. She hadn't had time, for one thing, and for another, she had no idea who would recruit her, and if they didn't, what she wanted to do. Apparently, she was going to get recruited now. And that alone made her a little shaky.

"I'll take my cases for the day," Kerrie said. "But ease me out of the rest of the week."

"Done," Maise said.

Kerrie nodded, stood, and stopped. "Thanks," she said.

"Don't thank me," Maise said, and somehow that didn't sound like a perfunctory statement. Maise really didn't want credit. Probably because of her bigotry against the Peyti. Or maybe because she hadn't known · exactly how to approach the case herself.

Kerrie let herself out of the room. She'd buy herself a coffee somewhere else. She had time for once.

She murmured thanks to her colleagues as they congratulated her, a number of them touching her arm as if her good luck could rub off on them.

As she stepped outside of the office, a movement beside the door caught her eye.

The Peyti, Uzvik, straightened. He had been sitting there, and apparently he had been waiting for her.

"I already put Donnatella on the shuttle," Kerrie said. "She's probably in Helena now. I'm sure you can find her there."

"I did not come to see her," he said in his soft voice. It sounded hollow because of the breathing mask. "I came to see you."

Kerrie frowned. "Me?"

Uzvik nodded. "I have come to offer you work."

She stopped in the middle of the hallway. "Work?"

"The Black Fleet needs lawyers," Uzvik said.

"I'm sure they do," Kerrie said. "But I know nothing of Black Fleet law. I'm not even sure there is any."

"For their interactions with the Earth Alliance," Uzvik said.

She tilted her head, uncertain what he was saying. "You're recruiting me to work for the Black Fleet?"

"We pay our lawyers more than any other group. You cannot even make this much in private practice. You wouldn't even work that hard."

"I don't understand," Kerrie said. "What do you want with me?"

"You have proven yourself to be creative and flexible, two things the Black Fleet needs in its attorneys. Most lawyers cannot find the loophole that you discovered in this case. You are gifted, Counselor."

Gifted. Most lawyers. It took her a moment to process what he was saying.

"You were never here for Donnatella, were you?" Kerrie asked. "This was some kind of test, wasn't it?"

"Yes," Uzvik said.

"And if I failed, what then?" Kerrie asked. "Would Donnatella have gone to the Ziyit?"

"Yes," Uzvik said.

"You were willing to sacrifice her for a test?" Kerrie asked, her voice rising. "Did she know that?"

"Her case was legitimate," Uzvik said.

"So she didn't know," Kerrie said. "Would you have told me if I had let you second chair?"

"That would have defeated the test," Uzvik said.

"She could have died," Kerrie said.

"But she did not."

"Did you get her kicked out of the Black Fleet, then?" Kerrie asked. "Did you turn her in to the Earth Alliance?"

"No," Uzvik said. "The circumstances were of her own making."

"They were simply there for you to exploit," Kerrie said.

"Just so." Uzvik folded his long thin fingers.

"And you think that I would work for you after this?"

"It is easy work," he said. "You would make money and you would have maybe two cases per year."

"All I would have to do is sell my soul," Kerrie said.

"The matter of the human 'soul' has never been proven," Uzvik said.

Kerrie stared at him. He was Peyti, literal, difficult, brilliant.

"The Peyti are known for their ethics," she said.

"We are known for rigorously defending our clients to the fullest extent of Earth Alliance law," he said.

He was right; she had simply taken that as ethics.

"Get away from me," she said.

"I am authorized to make a generous offer—"

"No," she snapped. "Get the hell away from me."

"You would be perfect—"

"No." She walked toward the coffee nook, so fast she was nearly running. Just when she thought she had seen everything, every kind of permutation of Earth Alliance law, every type of victim, someone came up with something even more venal.

A test, one that would have sacrificed Donnatella for no reason at all.

"The result would have been the same." The Peyti had kept up with her. She could hear his labored breathing as he struggled to remain beside her. "She would have gone to Ziyit without my interference."

"But you could have prevented it." Kerrie said. Then she stopped again. The Peyti nearly walked into her. "Did Maise know about this?"

"We asked that the best be assigned this case," Uzvik said.

She did. She knew. And she had manipulated Kerrie into taking the case.

Kerrie's stomach turned. "I told you to get away from me," she said. "And I mean it. I'll call base security if I have to."

She turned around and headed back to the public defender's office. Uzvik remained where he was, looking small.

She went through the doors. Maise was talking to one of the associates. Kerrie was so angry, she almost couldn't speak.

She wondered if Maise's prejudice against Peyti was a ruse, one she used whenever she was working with the Black Fleet.

"Do you get a cut?" Kerrie asked.

Maise looked up.

"A recruitment cut?" Kerrie asked. "From the Black Fleet? Do they pay you to bring them the best and brightest?"

"Let's go to the conference room," Maise said.

"Let's not," Kerrie said. "Everyone can hear this. I quit. I'm done. And you guys, if Maise offers you a case, watch out. It might be poisoned."

"You should stay," Maise said. "The recruiters—"

"I know," Kerrie said. "I don't really care. I'm going to find a job. And it won't be one that requires a high-end recruiter. Because I'm done here. Right now."

Then she slammed her way out of the office. Messages ran along her links from the various lawyers in the PD's office. Some messages were automated, telling her how to wrap up her career with the InterSpecies Court. Others were filled with questions, questions she wasn't going to answer.

She went back to her apartment. Except for the night court lawyer who was asleep, the apartment was empty.

She went to her room and gathered her belongings. She would head to Helena. And there, she would figure out what to do.

At the moment, she saw only two options: She could contact independent Disappearance Services. They needed lawyers too. Of course, she would be crossing all kinds of lines, legal and ethical.

Although she would be doing it for a good cause.

Or she could ally herself with some of the legal groups that took big cases, cases that got appealed to the Multicultural Tribunals, cases that might lead to overturning treaties, and modifying laws.

All she knew was that she couldn't stay here. And she knew she couldn't work for an organization like the Black Fleet. An organization willing to sacrifice its own people as a test.

The Earth Alliance sacrificed its people to satisfy treaties, to facilitate trade.

She had been a blind participant to it all.

But she was blind no longer.

And she knew how she felt.

She hated all of it.

And she would never be part of it again.

# Utriusque Cosmi

## *Robert Charles Wilson*

Diving back into the universe (now that the universe is a finished object, boxed and ribboned from bang to bounce), Carlotta calculates ever-finer loci on the frozen ordinates of spacetime until at last she reaches a trailer park outside the town of Commanche Drop, Arizona. Bodiless, no more than a breath of imprecision in the Feynman geometry of certain virtual particles, thus powerless to affect the material world, she passes unimpeded through a sheet-aluminum wall and hovers over a mattress on which a young woman sleeps uneasily.

The young woman is her own ancient self, the primordial Carlotta Boudaine, dewed with sweat in the hot night air, her legs caught up in a spindled cotton sheet. The bedroom's small window is cranked open, and in the breezeless distance a coyote wails.

Well, look at me, Carlotta marvels: skinny girl in panties and a halter, sixteen years old—no older than a gnat's breath—taking shallow little sleep-breaths in the moonlit dark. Poor child can't even see her own ghost. Ah, but she will, Carlotta thinks—she *must*.

The familiar words echo in her mind as she inspects her dreaming body, buried in its tomb of years, eons, kalpas. *When it's time to leave, leave. Don't be afraid. Don't wait. Don't get caught. Just go. Go fast.*

Her ancient beloved poem. Her perennial mantra. The words, in fact, that saved her life.

She needs to share those words with herself, to make the circle complete. Everything she knows about the nature of the physical universe suggests that the task is impossible. Maybe so . . . but it won't be for lack of trying.

Patiently, slowly, soundlessly, Carlotta begins to speak.

Here's the story of the Fleet, girl, and how I got raptured up into it. It's all about the future—a bigger one than you believe in—so brace yourself.

It has a thousand names and more, but we'll just call it the Fleet. When I first encountered it, the Fleet was scattered from the core of the galaxy all through its spiraled tentacles of suns, and it had been there for millions of years, going about its business, though nobody on this planet knew anything about it. I guess every now and then a Fleet ship must have fallen to Earth, but it would have been indistinguishable from any common meteorite by the time it passed through the atmosphere: a chunk of carbonaceous chondrite smaller than a human fist, from which all evidence of ordered matter had been erased by fire—and such losses, which happened everywhere and often, made no discernible difference to the Fleet as a whole. All Fleet data (that is to say, all *mind*) was shared, distributed, fractal. Vessels were born and vessels were destroyed; but the Fleet persisted down countless eons, confident of its own immortality.

Oh, I know you don't understand the big words, child! It's not important for you to hear them—not *these* words—it's only important for me to *say* them. Why? Because a few billion years ago tomorrow, I carried your ignorance out of this very trailer, carried it down to the Interstate and hitched west with nothing in my backpack but a bottle of water, a half-dozen Tootsie Rolls, and a wad of twenty-dollar bills stolen out of Dan-O's old ditty bag. That night (tomorrow night: mark it) I slept under an overpass all by myself, woke up cold and hungry long before dawn, and looked up past a concrete arch crusted with bird shit into a sky so thick with falling stars it made me think of a dark skin bee-stung with fire. Some of the Fleet vectored too close to the atmosphere that night, no doubt, but I didn't understand that (any more than *you* do, girl)—I just thought it was a big flock of shooting stars, pretty but meaningless. And, after a while, I slept some more. And come sunrise, I waited for the morning traffic so I could catch another ride . . . but the only cars that came by were all weaving or speeding, as if the whole world was driving home from a drunken party.

"They won't stop," a voice behind me said. "Those folks already made their decisions, Carlotta. Whether they want to live or die, I mean. Same decision you have to make."

I whirled around, sick-startled, and that was when I first laid eyes on dear Erasmus.

Let me tell you right off that Erasmus wasn't a human being. Erasmus just then was a knot of shiny metal angles about the size of a microwave oven, hovering in mid-air, with a pair of eyes like the polished tourmaline they sell at those roadside souvenir shops. He didn't *have* to look that way—it was some old avatar he used because he figured that it would impress me. But I didn't know that then. I was only surprised, if that's not too mild a word, and too shocked to be truly frightened.

"The world won't last much longer," Erasmus said in a low and mournful voice. "You can stay here, or you can come with me. But choose quick, Carlotta, because the mantle's come unstable and the continents are starting to slip."

I half believed that I was still asleep and dreaming. I didn't know what that meant, about the mantle, though I guessed he was talking about the end of the world. Some quality of his voice (which reminded me of that actor Morgan Freeman) made me trust him despite how weird and impossible the whole conversation was. Plus, I had a confirming sense that *something* was going bad *somewhere*, partly because of the scant traffic (a Toyota zoomed past, clocking speeds it had never been built for, the driver a hunched blur behind the wheel), partly because of the ugly green cloud that just then billowed up over a row of rat-toothed mountains on the horizon. Also the sudden hot breeze. And the smell of distant burning. And the sound of what might have been thunder, or something worse.

"Go with you where?"

"To the stars, Carlotta! But you'll have to leave your body behind."

I didn't like the part about leaving my body behind. But what choice did I have, except the one he'd offered me? Stay or go. Simple as that.

It was a ride—just not the kind I'd been expecting.

There was a tremor in the earth, like the devil knocking at the soles of my shoes. "Okay," I said, "whatever," as white dust bloomed up from the desert and was taken by the frantic wind.

*Don't be afraid. Don't wait. Don't get caught. Just go. Go fast.*

Without those words in my head, I swear, girl, I would have died that day. Billions did.

She slows down the passage of time so she can fit this odd but somehow necessary monologue into the space between one or two of the younger Carlotta's breaths. Of course, she has no real voice in which to speak. The past is static, imperturbable in its endless sleep; molecules of air on their fixed trajectories can't be manipulated from the shadowy place where she now exists. Wake up with the dawn, girl, she says, steal the money you'll never spend—it doesn't matter; the important thing is to *leave*. It's time.

*When it's time to leave, leave.* Of all the memories she carried out of her earthly life, this is the most vivid: waking to discover a ghostly presence in her darkened room, a white-robed woman giving her the advice she needs at the moment she needs it. Suddenly Carlotta wants to scream the words: *When it's time to leave—*

But she can't vibrate even a single mote of the ancient air, and the younger Carlotta sleeps on.

Next to the bed is a thrift-shop night table scarred with cigarette burns. On the table is a child's night-light, faded cut-outs of Sponge-Bob Square-Pants pasted on the paper shade. Next to that, hidden under a splayed copy of *People* magazine, is the bottle of barbiturates Carlotta stole from Dan-O's ditty-bag this afternoon, the same khaki bag in which (she couldn't help but notice) Dan-O keeps his cash, a change of clothes, a fake driver's license, and a blue steel automatic pistol.

Young Carlotta detects no ghostly presence . . . nor is her sleep disturbed by the sound of Dan-O's angry voice and her mother's sudden gasp, two rooms away. Apparently, Dan-O is awake and sober. Apparently, Dan-O has discovered the theft. That's a complication.

But Carlotta won't allow herself to be hurried.

The hardest thing about joining the Fleet was giving up the idea that I had a body, that my body had a real place to be.

But that's what everybody believed at first, that we were still whole and normal—everybody rescued from Earth, I mean. Everybody who said "Yes" to Erasmus—and Erasmus, in one form or another, had appeared to every human being on the planet in the moments before the end of the world. Two and a half billion of us accepted the offer of rescue. The rest chose to stay put and died when the Earth's continents dissolved into molten magma.

Of course, that created problems for the survivors. Children without parents, parents without children, lovers separated for eternity. It was as sad and tragic as any other incomplete rescue, except on a planetary scale. When we left the Earth, we all just sort of re-appeared on a grassy plain as flat as Kansas and wider than the horizon, under a blue faux sky, each of us with an Erasmus at his shoulder and all of us wailing or sobbing or demanding explanations.

The plain wasn't "real," of course, not the way I was accustomed to things being real. It was a virtual place, and all of us were wearing virtual bodies, though we didn't understand that fact immediately. We kept on being what we expected ourselves to be—we even wore the clothes we'd worn when we were raptured up. I remember looking down at the pair of greasy second-hand Reeboks I'd found at the Commanche Drop Goodwill store, thinking: in Heaven? *Really?*

"Is there any place you'd rather be?" Erasmus asked with a maddening and clearly inhuman patience. "Anyone you need to find?"

"Yeah, I'd rather be in New Zealand," I said, which was really just a hysterical joke. All I knew about New Zealand was that I'd seen a show about it on PBS, the only channel we got since the cable company cut us off.

"Any particular part of New Zealand?"

"What? Well—okay, a beach, I guess."

I had never been to a real beach, a beach on the ocean.

"Alone, or in the company of others?"

"Seriously?" All around me people were sobbing or gibbering in (mostly) foreign languages. Pretty soon, fights would start to break out. You can't put a couple of billion human beings so close together under circumstances like that and expect any other result. But the crowd was already thinning, as people accepted similar offers from their own Fleet avatars.

"Alone," I said. "Except for *you.*"

And quick as that, there I was: Eve without Adam, standing on a lonesome stretch of white beach.

After a while, the astonishment faded to a tolerable dazzle. I took off my shoes and tested the sand. The sand was pleasantly sun-warm. Saltwater swirled up between my toes as a wave washed in from the coral-blue sea.

Then I felt dizzy and had to sit down.

"Would you like to sleep?" Erasmus asked, hovering over me like a gem-studded party balloon. "I can help you sleep, Carlotta, if you'd like. It might make the transition easier if you get some rest, to begin with."

"You can answer some fucking *questions,* is what you can *do!*" I said.

He settled down on the sand beside me, the mutant offspring of a dragonfly and a beach ball. "Okay, shoot," he said.

It's a read-only universe, Carlotta thinks. The Old Ones have said as much, so it must be true. And yet, she knows, she *remembers,* that the younger Carlotta will surely wake and find her here: a ghostly presence, speaking wisdom.

But how can she make herself perceptible to this sleeping child? The senses are so stubbornly material, electrochemical data cascading into vastly complex neural networks . . . is it possible she could intervene in some way at the borderland of quanta and perception? For a moment, Carlotta chooses to look at her younger self with different eyes, sampling the fine gradients of molecular magnetic fields. The child's skin and skull grow faint and then transparent as Carlotta shrinks her point of view and wanders briefly through the carnival of her own animal mind, the buzzing innerscape where skeins of dream merge and separate like fractal soap-bubbles. If she could manipulate even a single boson—influence the charge at some critical synaptic junction, say—

But she can't. The past simply doesn't have a handle on it. There's no uncertainty here anymore, no alternate outcomes. To influence the past would be to *change* the past, and, by definition, that's impossible.

The shouting from the next room grows suddenly louder and more vicious, and Carlotta senses her younger self moving from sleep toward an awakening, too soon.

Of course, I figured it out eventually, with Erasmus's help. Oh, girl, I won't bore you with the story of those first few years—they bored *me,* heaven knows.

Of course "heaven" is exactly where we weren't. Lots of folks were inclined to see it that way—assumed they must have died and been delivered to whatever afterlife they happened to believe in. Which was actually not *too* far off the mark: but, of course, God had nothing to do with it. The Fleet was a real-world business, and ours wasn't the first sentient species it had raptured up. Lots of planets got destroyed, Erasmus said, and the Fleet didn't always get to them in time to salvage the population, hard as they tried—we were *lucky,* sort of.

So I asked him what it was that caused all these planets to blow up.

"We don't know, Carlotta. We call it the Invisible Enemy. It doesn't leave a signature, whatever it is. But it systematically seeks out worlds with flourishing civilizations and marks them for destruction." He added, "It doesn't like the Fleet much, either. There are parts of the galaxy where we don't go—because if we *do* go there, we don't come back."

At the time, I wasn't even sure what a "galaxy" was, so I dropped the subject, except to ask him if I could see what it looked like—the destruction of the Earth, I meant. At first, Erasmus didn't want to show me; but after a lot of coaxing, he turned himself into a sort of floating TV screen and displayed a view "looking back from above the plane of the solar ecliptic," words which meant nothing to me.

What I saw was . . . well, no more little blue planet, basically.

More like a ball of boiling red snot.

"What about my mother? What about Dan-O?"

I didn't have to explain who these people were. The Fleet had sucked up all kinds of data about human civilization, I don't know how. Erasmus paused as if he was consulting some invisible Rolodex. Then he said, "They aren't with us."

"You mean they're dead?"

"Yes. Abby and Dan-O are dead."

But the news didn't surprise me. It was almost as if I'd known it all along, as if I had had a vision of their deaths, a dark vision to go along with that ghostly visit the night before, the woman in a white dress telling me *go fast*.

Abby Boudaine and Dan-O, dead. And me raptured up to robot heaven. Well, well.

"Are you sure you wouldn't like to sleep now?"

"Maybe for a while," I told him.

Dan-O's a big man, and he's working himself up to a major tantrum. Even now, Carlotta feels repugnance at the sound of his voice, that gnarl of angry consonants. Next, Dan-O throws something solid, maybe a clock, against the wall. The clock goes to pieces, noisily. Carlotta's mother cries out in response, and the sound of her wailing seems to last weeks.

"It's not good," Erasmus told me much later, "to be so much alone."

Well, I told him, I *wasn't* alone—he was with me, wasn't he? And he was pretty good company, for an alien machine. But that was a dodge. What he *meant* was that I ought to hook up with somebody human.

I told him I didn't care if ever set eyes on another human being ever again. What had the human race ever done for *me*?

He frowned—that is, he performed a particular contortion of his exposed surfaces that I had learned to interpret as disapproval. "That's entropic talk, Carlotta. Honestly, I'm worried about you."

"What could happen to me?" Here on this beach where nothing ever *really* happens, I did not add.

"You could go crazy. You could sink into despair. Worse, you could die."

"I could *die*? I thought I was immortal now."

"Who told you that? True, you're no longer *living*, in the strictly material sense. You're a metastable nested loop embedded in the Fleet's collective mentation. But everything's mortal, Carlotta. Anything can die."

I couldn't die of disease or falling off a cliff, he explained, but my "nested loop" was subject to a kind of slow erosion, and stewing in my own lonely juices for too long was liable to bring on the decay that much faster.

And, admittedly, after a month on this beach, swimming and sleeping too much and eating the food Erasmus conjured up whenever I was hungry (though I didn't really need to eat), watching recovered soap operas on his bellyvision screen or reading celebrity magazines (also embedded in the Fleet's collective memory) that would never get any fresher or produce another issue, and just being basically miserable as all hell, I thought maybe he was right.

"You cry out in your sleep," Erasmus said. "You have bad dreams."

"The world ended. Maybe I'm depressed. You think meeting people would help with that?"

"Actually," he said, "you have a remarkable talent for being alone. You're sturdier than most. But that won't save you, in the long run."

So I tried to take his advice. I scouted out some other survivors. Turned out, it was interesting what some people had done in their new incarnations as Fleet-data. The Erasmuses had made it easy for like-minded folks to find each other and to create environments to suit them. The most successful of these cliques, as they were sometimes called, were the least passive ones: the ones with a purpose. Purpose kept people lively. Passive cliques tended to fade into indifference pretty quickly, and the purely hedonistic ones soon collapsed into dense orgasmic singularities; but if you were curious about the world, and hung out with similarly curious friends, there was a lot to keep you thinking.

None of those cliques suited me in the long run, though. Oh, I made some friends, and I learned a few things. I learned how to access the Fleet's archival data, for instance—a trick you had to be careful with. If you did it right, you could think about a subject as if you were doing a Google search, all the relevant information popping up in your mind's eye just as if it had been there all along. Do it too often or too enthusiastically, though, and you ran the risk of getting lost in the overload—you might develop a "memory" so big and all-inclusive that it absorbed you into its own endless flow.

(It was an eerie thing to watch when it happened. For a while, I hung out with a clique that was exploring the history of the non-human civilizations that had been raptured up by the Fleet in eons past . . . until the leader of the group, a Jordanian college kid by the name of Nuri, dived down too far and literally fogged out. He got this look of intense concentration on his face, and, moments later, his body turned to wisps and eddies of fluid air and faded like fog in the sunlight. Made me shiver. And I had liked Nuri—I missed him when he was gone.)

But by sharing the effort, we managed to safely learn some interesting things. (Things the Erasmuses could have just *told* us, I suppose; but we didn't know the right questions to ask.) Here's a big for-instance: although every species was mortal after it was raptured up—every species eventually fogged out much the way poor Nuri had—there were actually a few very long-term survivors. By that, I mean individuals who had outlived their peers, who had found a way to preserve a sense of identity in the face of the Fleet's hypercomplex data torrent.

We asked our Erasmuses if we could meet one of these long-term survivors.

Erasmus said no, that was impossible. The Elders, as he called them, didn't live on our timescale. The way they had preserved themselves was by dropping out of realtime.

Apparently, it wasn't necessary to "exist" continuously from one moment to the next. You could ask the Fleet to turn you off for a day or a week, then turn you on again. Any moment of active perception was called a *saccade*, and you could space your saccades as far apart as you liked. Want to live a thousand years? Do it by living one second out of every million that passes. Of course, it wouldn't *feel* like a thousand years, subjectively; but a thousand years would flow by before you aged much. That's basically what the Elders were doing.

We could do the same, Erasmus said, if we wanted. But there was a price tag attached to it. "Timesliding" would carry us incomprehensibly far into a future nobody could predict. We were under continual attack by the Invisible Enemy, and it was possible that the Fleet might lose so much cohesion that we could no longer be sustained as stable virtualities. We wouldn't get a long life out of it, and we might well be committing a kind of unwitting suicide.

"You don't really go anywhere," Erasmus summed up. "In effect, you just go fast. I can't honestly recommend it."

"Did I ask for your advice? I mean, what *are* you, after all? Just some little fragment of the Fleet mind charged with looking after Carlotta Boudaine. A cybernetic babysitter."

I swear to you, he looked *hurt*. And I heard the injury in his voice.

"I'm the part of the Fleet that cares about you, Carlotta."

Most of my clique backed down at that point. Most people aren't cut out to be timesliders. But I was more tempted than ever. "You can't tell me what to do, Erasmus."

"I'll come with you, then," he said. "If you don't mind."

It hadn't occurred to me that he might *not* come along. It was a scary idea. But I didn't let that anxiety show.

"Sure, I guess that'd be all right," I said.

Enemies out there too, the elder Carlotta observes. A whole skyful of them. As above, so below. Just like in that old drawing—what was it called? *Utriusque cosmi.* Funny what a person remembers. Girl, do you hear your mother crying?

The young Carlotta stirs uneasily in her tangled sheet.

Both Carlottas know their mother's history. Only the elder Carlotta can think about it without embarrassment and rage. Oh, it's an old story. Her mother's name is Abby. Abby Boudaine dropped out of high school pregnant, left some dreary home in South Carolina to go west with a twenty-year-old boyfriend who abandoned her outside Albuquerque. She gave birth in a California emergency ward and nursed Carlotta in a basement room in the home of a retired couple, who sheltered her in exchange for housework until Carlotta's constant wailing got on their nerves. After that, Abby hooked up with a guy who worked for a utility company and grew weed in his attic for pin money. The hookup lasted a few years, and might have lasted longer, except that Abby had a weakness for what the law called "substances," and couldn't restrain herself in an environment where coke and methamphetamine circulated more or less freely. A couple of times, Carlotta was bounced around between foster homes while Abby Boudaine did court-mandated dry-outs or simply binged. Eventually, Abby picked up ten-year-old Carlotta from one of these periodic suburban exiles and drove her over the state border into Arizona, jumping bail. "We'll never be apart again," her mother told her, in the strained voice that meant she was a little bit high or hoping to be. "Never again!" Blessing or curse? Carlotta wasn't sure which. "You'll never leave me, baby. You're my one and only."

Not such an unusual story, the elder Carlotta thinks, though her younger self, she knows, feels uniquely singled out for persecution.

Well, child, Carlotta thinks, try living as a distributed entity on a Fleet that's being eaten by invisible monsters, *then* see what it feels like.

But she knows the answer to that. It feels much the same.

"Now you *steal* from me?" Dan-O's voice drills through the wall like a rusty auger. Young Carlotta stirs and whimpers. Any moment now, she'll open her eyes, and then what? Although this is the fixed past, it feels suddenly unpredictable, unfamiliar, dangerous.

Erasmus came with me when I went timesliding, and I appreciated that, even before I understood what a sacrifice it was for him.

Early on, I asked him about the Fleet and how it came to exist. The answer to that question was lost to entropy, he said. He had never known a time without a Fleet—he couldn't have, because Erasmus *was* the Fleet, or at least a sovereign fraction of it.

"As we understand it," he told me, "the Fleet evolved from networks of self-replicating data-collecting machine intelligences, no doubt originally created by some organic species, for the purpose of exploring interstellar space. Evidence suggests that we're only a little younger than the universe itself."

The Fleet had outlived its creators. "Biological intelligence is unstable over the long term," Erasmus said, a little smugly. "But out of that original compulsion to acquire and share data, we evolved and refined our own collective purpose."

"That's why you hoover up doomed civilizations? So you can catalogue and study them?"

"So they won't be *forgotten*, Carlotta. That's the greatest evil in the universe—the entropic decay of organized information. Forgetfulness. We despise it."

"Worse than the Invisible Enemy?"

"The Enemy is evil to the degree to which it abets entropic decay."

"Why does it want to do that?"

"We don't know. We don't even understand what the Enemy *is*, in physical terms. It seems to operate outside of the material universe. If it consists of matter, that matter is non-baryonic and impossible to detect. It pervades parts of the galaxy—though not *all* parts—like an insubstantial gas. When the Fleet passes through volumes of space heavily infested by the Enemy, our loss-rate soars. And as these infested volumes of space expand, they encompass and destroy life-bearing worlds."

"The Enemy's growing, though. And the Fleet isn't."

I had learned to recognize Erasmus's distress, not just because he was slowly adopting somewhat more human features. "The Fleet is my home, Carlotta. More than that. It's my body, my heart."

What he didn't say was that by joining me in the act of surfing time, he would be isolating himself from the realtime network that had birthed and sustained him. In realtime, Erasmus was a fraction of something reassuringly immense. But in slide-time, he'd be as alone as an Erasmus could get.

And yet, he came with me, when I made my decision. He was *my* Erasmus as much as he was the Fleet's, and he came with me. What would you call that, girl? Friendship? At least. I came to call it love.

The younger Carlotta has stolen those pills (the ones hidden under her smudged copy of *People*) for a reason. To help her sleep, was what she told herself. But she didn't really have trouble sleeping. No: if she was honest, she'd have to say the pills were an escape hatch. Swallow enough of them, and it's, hey, fuck you, world! Less work than the highway, an alternative she was also considering.

More shouting erupts in the next room. A real roust-up, bruises to come. Then, worse, Dan-O's voice goes all small and jagged. That's a truly bad omen, Carlotta knows. Like the smell of ozone that floods the air in advance of a lightning strike, just before the voltage ramps up and the current starts to flow.

Erasmus built a special virtuality for him and me to time-trip in. Basically, it was a big comfy room with a wall-sized window overlooking the Milky Way.

The billions of tiny dense components that made up the Fleet swarmed at velocities slower than the speed of light, but timesliding made it all seem faster—scarily so. Like running the whole universe in fast-forward, knowing you can't go back. During the first few months of our expanded Now, we soared a long way out of the spiral arm that contained the abandoned Sun. The particular sub-swarm of the Fleet that hosted my sense of self was on a long elliptical orbit around the supermassive black hole at the galaxy's core, and from this end of the ellipse, over the passing days, we watched the Milky Way drop out from under us like a cloud of luminous pearls.

When I wasn't in that room, I went off to visit other timesliders, and some of them visited me there. We were a self-selected group of radical roamers with a thing for risk, and we got to know one another pretty well. Oh, girl, I wish I could tell you all the friends I made among that tribe of self-selected exiles! Many of them human, not all: I met a few of the so-called Elders of other species, and managed to communicate with them on a friendly basis. Does that sound strange to you? I guess it is. Surpassing strange. I thought so too, at first. But these were people (mostly people) and things (but things can be people too) that I mostly liked and often loved, and they loved me back. Yes, they did. Whatever quirk of personality made us timesliders drew us together against all the speedy dark outside our virtual walls. Plus—well, we were survivors. It took not much more than a month to outlive all the remaining remnant of humanity. Even our ghosts were gone, in other words, unless you counted *us* as ghosts.

Erasmus was a little bit jealous of the friends I made. He had given up a lot for me, and maybe I ought to have appreciated him more for it. Unlike us formerly biological persons, though, Erasmus maintained a tentative link with realtime. He had crafted protocols to keep himself current on changes in the Fleet's symbol-sets and core mentation. That way, he could update us on what the Fleet was doing—new species raptured up from dying worlds and so forth. None of these newcomers lasted long, though, from our lofty perspective, and I once asked Erasmus why the Fleet even bothered with such ephemeral creatures as (for instance) human beings. He said that every species was doomed in the long run, but that didn't make it okay to kill people—or to abandon them when they might be rescued. That instinct was what made the Fleet a moral entity, something more than just a collection of self-replicating machines.

And it made *him* more than a nested loop of complex calculations. In the end, Carlotta, I came to love Erasmus best of all.

Meanwhile the years and stars scattered in our wake like dust—a thousand years, a hundred thousand, a million, more, and the galaxy turned like a great white wheel. We all made peace with the notion that we were the last of our kind, whatever "kind" we represented.

If you could hear me, girl, I guess you might ask what I found in that deep well of strangeness that made the water worth drinking. Well, I found friends, as I said—isn't that enough? And I found lovers. Even Erasmus began to adopt a human avatar, so we could touch each other in the human way.

I found, in plain words, a *home*, Carlotta, however peculiar in its nature—a *real* home, for the first time in my life.

Which is why I was so scared when it started to fall apart.

In the next room, Abby isn't taking Dan-O's anger lying down. It's nearly the perfect storm tonight—Dan-O's temper and Abby's sense of violated dignity both rising at the same ferocious pitch, rising toward some unthinkable crescendo.

But her mother's outrage is fragile, and Dan-O is frankly dangerous. The young Carlotta had known that about him from the get-go, from the first time her mother came home with this man on her arm: knew it from his indifferent eyes and his mechanical smile; knew it from the prison tattoos he didn't bother to disguise and the boastfulness with which he papered over some hole in his essential self. Knew it from the meth-lab stink that burned off him like a chemical perfume. Knew it from the company he kept, from the shitty little deals with furtive men arranged in Carlotta's mother's home because his own rental bungalow was littered with incriminating cans of industrial solvent. Knew it most of all by the way he fed Abby Boudaine crystal meth in measured doses, to keep her wanting it, and by the way Abby began to sign over her weekly Wal-Mart paycheck to him like a dutiful servant, back when she was working checkout.

Dan-O is tall, wiry, and strong despite his vices. The elder Carlotta can hear enough to understand that Dan-O is blaming Abby for the theft of the barbiturates—an intolerable sin, in Dan-O's book. Followed by Abby's heated denials and the sound of Dan-O's fists striking flesh. All this discovered, not remembered: the young Carlotta sleeps on, though she's obviously about to wake; the critical moment is coming fast. And Carlotta thinks of what she saw when she raided Dan-O's ditty bag, the blue metal barrel with a black gnurled grip, a thing she had stared at, hefted, but ultimately disdained.

We dropped back down the curve of that elliptic, girl, and suddenly the Fleet began to vanish like drops of water on a hot griddle. Erasmus saw it first, because of what he was, and he set up a display so I could see it too: Fleet-swarms set as ghostly dots against a schema of the galaxy, the ghost-dots dimming perilously and some of them blinking out altogether. It was a graph of a massacre. "Can't anyone stop it?" I asked.

"They would if they could," he said, putting an arm (now that he had grown a pair of arms) around me. "They will if they can, Carlotta."

"Can *we* help?"

"We are helping, in a way. Existing the way we do means they don't have to use much mentation to sustain us. To the Fleet, we're code that runs a calculation for a few seconds out of every year. Not a heavy burden to carry."

Which was important, because the Fleet could only sustain so much computation, the upper limit being set by the finite number of linked nodes. And that number was diminishing as Fleet vessels were devoured wholesale.

"Last I checked," Erasmus said (which would have been about a thousand years ago, realtime), "the Fleet theorized that the Enemy is made of dark matter." (Strange stuff that hovers around galaxies, invisibly—it doesn't matter, girl; take my word for it; you'll understand it one day.) "They're not material objects so much as *processes*—parasitical protocols played out in dark matter clouds. Apparently, they can manipulate quantum events we don't even see."

"So we can't defend ourselves against them?"

"Not yet. No. And you and I might have more company soon, Carlotta. As long-timers, I mean."

That was because the Fleet continued to rapture up dying civilizations, nearly more than their shrinking numbers could contain. One solution was to shunt survivors into the Long Now along with us, in order to free up computation for battlefield maneuvers and such.

"Could get crowded," he warned.

"If a lot of strangers need to go Long," I said . . .

He gave me a carefully neutral look. "Finish the thought."

"Well . . . can't we just . . . go Longer?"

Fire a pistol in a tin box like this ratty trailer and the sound is ridiculously loud. Like being spanked on the ear with a two-by-four. It's the pistol shot that finally wakes the young Carlotta. Her eyelids fly open like window shades on a haunted house.

This isn't how the elder Carlotta remembers it. *Gunshot?* No, there was no *gunshot*: she just came awake and saw the ghost—

And no ghost, either. Carlotta tries desperately to speak to her younger self, wills herself to succeed, and fails yet again. So who fired that shot, and where did the bullet go, and why can't she *remember* any of this?

The shouting in the next room has yielded up a silence. The silence becomes an eternity. Then Carlotta hears the sound of footsteps—she can't tell whose—approaching her bedroom door.

In the end, almost every conscious function of the Fleet went Long, just to survive the attrition of the war with the dark-matter beings. The next loop through the galactic core pared us down to a fraction of what we used to be. When I got raptured up, the Fleet was a distributed cloud of baseball-sized objects running quantum computations on the state of their own dense constituent atoms—*millions and millions* of such objects, all linked together in a nested hierarchy. By the time we orbited back up our ellipsis, you could have counted us in the thousands, and our remaining links were carefully narrowbanded to give us maximum stealth.

So us wild timesliders chose to go Longer.

Just like last time, Erasmus warned me that it might be a suicidal act. If the Fleet was lost, we would be lost along with it . . . our subjective lives could end within days or hours. If, on the other hand, the Fleet survived and got back to reproducing itself, well, we might live on indefinitely—even drop back into realtime if we chose to do so. "Can you accept the risk?" he asked.

"Can *you?*"

He had grown a face by then. I suppose he knew me well enough to calculate what features I'd find pleasing. But it wasn't his ridiculous fake humanity I loved. What I loved was what went on behind those still-gem-like tourmaline eyes—the person he had become by sharing my mortality. "I accepted that risk a long time ago," he said.

"You and me both, Erasmus."

So we held on to each other and just—*went fast.*

Hard to explain what made that time-dive so vertiginous, but imagine centuries flying past like so much dust in a windstorm! It messed up our sense of *place*, first of all. Used to be we had a point of view light-years wide and deep . . . now all those loops merged into one continuous cycle; we grew as large as the Milky Way itself, with Andromeda bearing down on us like a silver armada. I held Erasmus in my arms, watching wide-eyed while he updated himself on the progress of the war and whispered new discoveries into my ear.

The Fleet had worked up new defenses, he said, and the carnage had slowed; but our numbers were still dwindling.

I asked him if we were dying.

He said he didn't know. Then he looked alarmed and held me tighter. "Oh, Carlotta . . . "

"What?" I stared into his eyes, which had gone faraway and strange. *"What is it?* Erasmus, tell me!"

"The Enemy," he said in numbed amazement.

"What about them?"

*"I know what they are."*

The bedroom door opens.

The elder Carlotta doesn't remember the bedroom door opening. None of this is as she remembers it should be. The young Carlotta cringes against the backboard of the bed, so terrified she can barely draw breath. *Bless you, girl, I'd hold your hand if I could!*

What comes through the door is just Abby Boudaine. Abby in a cheap white nightgown. But Abby's eyes are yellow-rimmed and feral, and her nightgown is spattered with blood.

See, the thing is this. All communication is limited by the speed of light. But if you spread your saccades over time, that speed-limit kind of expands. Slow as we were, light seemed to cross galactic space in a matter of moments. Single thoughts consumed centuries. We felt the supermassive black hole at the center of the galaxy beating like a ponderous heart. We heard whispers from nearby galaxies, incomprehensibly faint but undeniably manufactured. Yes, girl, we were *that* slow.

But the Enemy was even slower.

"Long ago," Erasmus told me, channeling this information from the Fleet's own dying collectivity, "long ago, the Enemy learned to parasitize dark matter . . . to use it as a computational substrate . . . to evolve *within* it . . . "

*"How* long ago?"

His voice was full of awe. "Longer than you have words for, Carlotta. They're older than the universe itself."

Make any sense to you? I doubt it would. But here's the thing about our universe: it oscillates. It *breathes,* I mean, like a big old lung, expanding and shrinking and expanding again. When it shrinks, it wants to turn into a singularity, but it can't do that, because there's a limit to how much mass a quantum of volume can hold without busting. So it all bangs up again, until it can't accommodate any more emptiness. Back and forth, over and over. Perhaps, *ad infinitum.*

Trouble is, no information can get past those hot chaotic contractions. Every bang makes a fresh universe, blank as a chalkboard in an empty schoolhouse . . .

Or so we thought.

But dark matter has a peculiar relationship with gravity and mass, Erasmus said; so when the Enemy learned to colonize it, they found ways to propagate themselves from one universe to the next. They could survive *the end of all things material,* in other words, and they had already done so—many times!

The Enemy was genuinely immortal, if that word has any meaning. The Enemy conducted its affairs not just across galactic space, but across the voids that separate galaxies, clusters of galaxies, superclusters . . . slow as molasses, they were, but vast as all things, and as pervasive as gravity, and very powerful.

"So what have they got against the Fleet, if they're so big and almighty? Why are they killing us?"

Erasmus smiled then, and the smile was full of pain and melancholy and an awful understanding. "But they're not *killing* us, Carlotta. They're rapturing us up."

One time in school, when she was trying unsuccessfully to come to grips with *The Merchant of Venice,* Carlotta had opened a book about Elizabethan drama to a copy of an old drawing called *Utriusque Cosmi.* It was supposed to represent the whole cosmos, the way people thought of it back in Shakespeare's time, all layered and orderly: stars and angels on top, hell beneath, and a naked guy stretched foursquare between divinity and damnation. Made no sense to her at all. Some antique craziness. She thinks of that drawing now, for no accountable reason. *But it doesn't stop at the angels, girl. I learned that lesson. Even angels have angels, and devils dance on the backs of lesser devils.*

Her mother in her bloodstained nightgown hovers in the doorway of Carlotta's bedroom. Her unblinking gaze strafes the room until it fixes at last on her daughter. Abby Boudaine might be standing right here, Carlotta thinks, but those eyes are looking out from someplace deeper and more distant and far more frightening.

The blood fairly drenches her. But it isn't Abby's blood.

"Oh, Carlotta," Abby says. Then she clears her throat, the way she does when she has to make an important phone call or speak to someone she fears. "Carlotta . . . "

And Carlotta (the invisible Carlotta, the Carlotta who dropped down from that place where the angels dice with eternity) understands what Abby is about to say, recognizes at last the awesome circularity, not a paradox at all. She pronounces the words silently as Abby makes them real: "Carlotta. Listen to me, girl. I don't guess you understand any of this. I'm so sorry. I'm sorry for many things. But listen now. When it's time to leave, you leave. Don't be afraid, and don't get caught. Just go. Go *fast*."

Then she turns and leaves her daughter cowering in the darkened room.

Beyond the bedroom window, the coyotes are still complaining to the moon. The sound of their hooting fills up the young Carlotta's awareness until it seems to speak directly to the heart of her.

Then comes the second and final gunshot.

I have only seen the Enemy briefly, and by that time, I had stopped thinking of them as the Enemy.

Can't describe them too well. Words really do fail me. And by that time, might as well admit it, I was not myself a thing I would once have recognized as human. Just say that Erasmus and I and the remaining timesliders were taken up into the Enemy's embrace along with all the rest of the Fleet—all the memories we had deemed lost to entropy or warfare were preserved there. The virtualities the Enemies had developed across whole kalpas of time were labyrinthine, welcoming, strange beyond belief. Did I roam in those mysterious glades? Yes I did, girl, and Erasmus by my side, for many long (subjective) years, and we became— well, larger than I can say.

And the galaxies aged and flew away from one another until they were swallowed up in manifolds of cosmic emptiness, connected solely by the gentle and inexorable thread of gravity. Stars winked out, girl; galaxies merged and filled with dead and dying stars; atoms decayed to their last stable forms. But the fabric of space can tolerate just so much emptiness.

It isn't infinitely elastic. Even vacuum ages. After some trillions and trillions of years, therefore, the expansion became a contraction.

During that time, I occasionally sensed or saw the Enemy—but I have to call them something else: say, *the Great Old Ones,* pardon my pomposity—who had constructed the dark matter virtualities in which I now lived. They weren't people at all. Never were. They passed through our adopted worlds like storm clouds, black and majestic and full of subtle and inscrutable lightnings. I couldn't speak to them, even then; as large and old as I had become, I was only a fraction of what they were.

I wanted to ask them why they had destroyed the Earth, why so many people had to be wiped out of existence or salvaged by the evolved benevolence of the Fleet. But Erasmus, who delved into these questions more deeply than I was able to, said the Great Old Ones couldn't perceive anything as tiny or ephemeral as a rocky planet like the Earth. The Earth and all the many planets like her had been destroyed, not by any willful calculation, but by autonomic impulses evolved over the course of many cosmic conflations—impulses as imperceptible and involuntary to the Old Ones as the functioning of your liver is to *you,* girl.

The logic of it is this: Life-bearing worlds generate civilizations that eventually begin playing with dark matter, posing a potential threat to the continuity of the Old Ones. Some number of these intrusions can be tolerated and contained—like the Fleet, they were often an enriching presence—but too many of them would endanger the stability of the system. It's as if we were germs, girl, wiped out by a giant's immune system. They couldn't *see* us, except as a somatic threat. Simple as that.

But they could see the *Fleet.* The Fleet was just big enough and durable enough to register on the senses of the Old Ones. And the Old Ones weren't malevolent: they perceived the Fleet much the way the Fleet had once perceived *us,* as something primitive but alive and thinking and worth the trouble of salvation.

So they raptured up the Fleet (and similar Fleet-like entities in countless other galaxies), thus preserving us against the blind oscillations of cosmic entropy.

(Nice of them, I suppose. But if I ever grow large enough or live long enough to confront an Old One face to face, I mean to lodge a complaint. Hell *yes* we were small—people are some of the smallest thought-bearing creatures in the cosmos, and I think we all kind of knew that even before the end of the world . . . *you* did, surely. But pain is pain and grief is grief.

It might be inevitable, it might even be built into the nature of things; but it isn't *good*, and it ought not to be tolerated, if there's a choice.)

Which I guess is why I'm here watching you squinch your eyes shut while the sound of that second gunshot fades into the air.

Watching you process a nightmare into a vision.

Watching you build a pearl around a grain of bloody truth.

Watching you *go fast*.

The bodiless Carlotta hovers awhile longer in the fixed and changeless corridors of the past.

Eventually, the long night ends. Raw red sunlight finds the window.

Last dawn this small world will ever see, as it happens; but the young Carlotta doesn't know that yet.

Now that the universe has finished its current iteration, all its history is stored in transdimensional metaspace like a book on a shelf—it can't be changed. Truly so. I guess I know that now, girl. Memory plays tricks that history corrects.

And I guess that's why the Old Ones let me have access to these events, as we hover on the brink of a new creation.

I know some of the questions you'd ask me if you could. You might say, *Where are you really?* And I'd say, *I'm at the end of all things, which is really just another beginning.* I'm walking in a great garden of dark matter, while all things known and baryonic spiral up the ladder of unification energies to a fiery new dawn. I have grown so large, girl, that I can fly down history like a bird over a prairie field. But I cannot remake what has already been made. That is one power I do not possess.

I watch you get out of bed. I watch you dress. Blue jeans with tattered hems, a man's lumberjack shirt, those thrift-shop Reeboks. I watch you go to the kitchen and fill your vinyl Bratz backpack with bottled water and Tootsie Rolls, which is all the cuisine your meth-addled mother has left in the cupboards.

Then I watch you tiptoe into Abby's bedroom. I confess I don't remember this part, girl. I suppose it didn't fit my fantasy about a benevolent ghost. But here you are, your face fixed in a willed indifference, stepping over Dan-O's corpse. Dan-O bled a lot after Abby Boudaine blew a hole in his chest, and the carpet is a sticky rust-colored pond.

I watch you pull Dan-O's ditty bag from where it lies half under the bed. On the bed, Abby appears to sleep. The pistol is still in her hand. The hand with the pistol in it rests beside her head. Her head is damaged in ways the young Carlotta can't stand to look at. Eyes down, girl. That's it.

I watch you pull a roll of bills from the bag and stuff it into your pack. Won't need that money where you're going! But it's a wise move, taking it. Commendable forethought.

*Now go.*

I have to go too. I feel Erasmus waiting for me, feel the tug of his love and loyalty, gentle and inevitable as gravity. He used to be a machine older than the dirt under your feet, Carlotta Boudaine, but he became a man—*my* man, I'm proud to say. He needs me, because it's no easy thing crossing over from one universe to the next. There's always work to do, isn't that the truth?

But right now, you go. You leave those murderous pills on the night-stand, find that highway. Don't be afraid. Don't wait. Don't get caught. Just go. Go fast. And excuse me while I take my own advice.

Jack Campbell (John G. Hemry) is the author of the *New York Times* bestselling Lost Fleet series, the Lost Stars series, and the "steampunk with dragons" Pillars of Reality series. His most recent books are *The Lost Stars: Shattered Spear, The Lost Fleet: Beyond the Frontier: Leviathan,* and the Pillars of Reality novels *The Servants of the Storm* and *The Wrath of the Great Guilds.* Later this year, *Vanguard* will be published, the first in a new trilogy set centuries before the events in The Lost Fleet series. John's novels have been published in eleven languages. This year, Titan will begin bringing out a Lost Fleet comic series. His short fiction includes works covering time travel, alternate history, space opera, military SF, fantasy, and humor.

John is a retired US Navy officer who served in a wide variety of jobs, including surface warfare (the ship drivers of the Navy), amphibious warfare, anti-terrorism, intelligence, and some other things that he's not supposed to talk about. Being a sailor, he has been known to tell stories about Events Which He Says Really Happened (but which cannot be verified by any independent sources). This experience has served him well in writing fiction. He lives in Maryland with his indomitable wife "S" and three great kids (all three on the autism spectrum).

# SECTION SEVEN

## *John G. Hemry*

Valentia looked beautiful from orbit, but then most planets did. Foster gave the world a weary traveler's worth of attention as the lander glided down, reflecting that from a great distance you couldn't encounter temperature extremes or rough terrain or the bites of bugs that wanted to eat you even if they couldn't digest you. Not to mention encountering the people, who were always the source of the particular problems Foster dealt with.

The customs official barely glanced at Foster's standard ID before feeding it into his desk scanner. A moment later, the ID popped back out onto the counter where he could pick it up.

"HaveanicestayonValentiaMr.Oaks," the official mumbled before reaching for the ID offered by the next traveler.

Foster retrieved his ID, took two steps past the customs desk, and found himself facing a trio of individuals wearing dark uniforms and stern faces. One of the port police officers held out her hand. "May I examine your ID, sir?"

"Uh, of course." Foster let his own expression show an appropriate level of surprise and a hint of worry as he fished out the ID again. "Is something wrong?"

The officer took the ID and slid it into a portable reader before answering. "Just a random check, Mr. Oaks. Valentia wants to make sure all travelers have good stays here. What brings you to Valentia?"

Foster smiled with the practiced enthusiasm of a sales professional. "I represent Inner Systems Simulations. You've heard of ISS?"

The officer's responding smile was both polite and brief. "No. Sorry."

"We make some of the finest entertainment software. Just in the Inner Systems right now, but we want to expand our market. If you'd like, I can show you some of our—."

"That won't be necessary." The officer removed the ID from her scanner and returned it to Foster. "Have a nice visit to Valentia, Mr. Oaks."

Foster smiled back with the same degree of professional insincerity, though his smile could've been genuine. Posing as a sales professional had numerous advantages, not the least of which was the ability to drive away questioners by beginning to offer a sales pitch. It never hurt to cut short an interview, even though his false IDs couldn't be spotted by any scanner and his cover story was solid.

Outside of the port terminal Foster squinted against the brightness of Valentia's sun. He hailed a cab by raising one hand in a gesture understood everywhere humanity had gone, directing it to the short-term rental business apartment complex where Mr. Oaks had his reservation. Foster didn't bother looking around for anyone tailing his cab, since that would have been a tip-off he thought he might be followed. Instead, he watched the scenery roll by with every appearance of boredom.

Foster checked in, went up to an apartment whose interior decoration could've placed it on any of a score of worlds, and swiftly changed clothes. The Valentian styles in his bag hadn't aroused any suspicion at Customs, since many tourists didn't want to look like tourists. A few minutes later, he was leaving the apartment complex by a different way than that he'd entered through. A brisk walk took him to a restaurant, where he paused to examine the menu in the window while also checking the reflection for anyone following him. There weren't any apparent candidates, but Foster took the precaution of checking for tails in two other restaurant or shop windows before entering an establishment promising authentic Italian cuisine using the finest native Valentian ingredients.

Like all sit-down restaurants, it had restrooms. And like most restrooms, these were located near a service entrance. Foster had no trouble leaving via that entrance, then criss-crossing further into the city before finally entering a hotel and registering there as Juan Feres using another one of his IDs. Only after reaching his room there did Foster actually unpack.

His data pad linked to the local net with some difficulty, causing Foster to frown. Once linked, he located the local classified ads and searched for the one he wanted, one advertising antique Beta videotapes for sale at prices too high for anyone to be interested. Foster called up on his data pad an ecopy of a venerable novel entitled Dykstra's War and went to the page that correlated with the Standard Federation Julian Date. The prices and titles of the Beta tapes provided coded links to words on that page, giving Foster a phone number in the city.

The phone number was answered by a recording. Foster waited until the ancient sign of the beep sounded and spoke his message. "Juan here. I'm at the Grand Frontera Hotel, Room 354. I have a message from your sister Kelly on Innisfree."

Then Foster waited. After a bit, he began wishing he'd paused long enough to pick up some of the authentic Italian/Valentian food. Room Service provided an overpriced and overcooked plate of 'authentic nachos' which in addition to chips and cheese included some sort of small fish filets and what appeared to be a raw egg cracked into the center of the plate. Foster sighed, chewed some of the latest stomach calming medicines available in the inner systems, then ate carefully around the egg, or whatever it was. Dealing with local tastes in food was just one of the occupational hazards of his job.

A soft tone announced his room had received mail. He checked the message, ensuring its enthusiastic response included the counterphrase needed to confirm it'd come from his Valentian contact. Referring to Dykstra's War again, Foster decoded the information in the reply to find an address in the city.

The local mapping system balked at working with his data pad, causing Foster to frown again. He finally got the directions he needed, saw his destination was too far to walk, and headed for the public transit system, carrying his bag along. It didn't do to leave bags unattended in hotel rooms if you could help it. Especially bags whose shielded, wafer-thin concealed compartments contained a variety of false IDs as well as other useful materials.

Sitting on the subway gave Foster a decent excuse to idly glance around. None of the other passengers seemed to be suspicious, and none left at his stop. Foster nonetheless took a circuitous route to his destination, weaving back and forth along several blocks and checking unobtrusively for tails, before finally reaching the doorway of a private residence.

A nondescript man of medium size and build answered Foster's ring. "Hello. Are you Juan?"

"That's me. Wide and free from Innisfree." Foster winced internally at the code phrase. He didn't make them up, but he had to say them.

"I wasn't sure Kelly had left Barbadan. Is she still engaged to Collin?"

Foster nodded. "Now and forever."

Sign, countersign, and counter-countersign exchanged, the man let Foster in, closing the door carefully behind them, and led the way into the house, bringing Foster to a nicely laid-out library room and closing that door as well before speaking again. "I'm Kila. Jason Kila. Welcome to Valentia."

"Gordon Foster. This room's secure?"

"Tight as a drum. No one can see or hear us."

Foster sat in the nearest chair and leaned back, relaxing for the first time since he'd arrived on Valentia. "Can you bring me up to date?"

Kila sat down as well and shrugged. "Not much has changed since my last report. Just more of the same."

"I noticed compatibility problems with the local software."

"Oh, yeah. They've got this operating system they claim is easier to use and more reliable than Federation standard, and also fully compatible. Some of the stuff in it *is* easier to use, other's harder. I don't know about the reliable part. I do know it's less and less compatible every time they tweak it."

"We'll have to take care of that."

Kila grinned, his lips drawing back to expose his back teeth. "You've got authority to act?"

Foster nodded. "Once I've heard everything. What else?"

"Here." Kila fished in one pocket, then tossed a small object at Foster. "Local ammo."

"Hmm." Foster frowned down at the bullet. "It's too small for 9mm and seems too big for 5.6mm."

"Right. Good eye. It's 6.8mm."

"Six point eight?" Foster let exasperation show. "Why the hell are they producing ammunition incompatible with Federation small arms standards?"

Kila rolled his eyes disdainfully. "They wanted one round for pistols *and* rifles. So they picked something smaller than a 9mm pistol round and bigger than a 5.6mm rifle round. They call it universal ammo."

"Universal?" Foster laughed. "They create a new ammunition type incompatible with Federation standards and then label it universal? I guess I should give Valentia credit for sheer gall."

"Yeah. Between the operating system and the ammunition, we've got a slowly accelerating gap developing between Valentia and the rest of the Federation. There's already talk about altering the mass transit gauge 'to better suit local conditions.' It's all in my report."

"What about the Federation demarches to Valentia demanding conformity to standards? Has there been anything about those in the local press? Any public debate?"

"Nope." Kila shook his head for emphasis. "The government's sitting on the demarches. There's been a few questions raised about diverging standards, but they're very isolated. Most locals don't see it as anything to worry about."

"Okay. Valentia thinks they can sit in their own little corner of the Federation and do whatever they want." Foster flipped the bullet back to Kila.

Kila snagged the shiny object and eyed Foster. "Pretty much. What do we get to do about it?"

Foster turned up the corners of his mouth in a humorless smile. "We get to mess with a few things."

"Yee-hah. When do we start?"

"Right now. Have we got a software engineer on planet?"

Kila nodded. "Of course. Janeen Yule. She's very good."

"Give her this." Foster slid open the heel of his shoe, revealing another shielded compartment, and removed a data coin. "It contains a worm called Black Clown."

"Black Clown?" Kila took the coin gingerly, turning it over between two fingers. "What's it do?"

"It makes things harder. Have Yule make any necessary changes to match it to Valentia's new operating system. Once we introduce it onto the Valentian net it'll propagate like crazy."

"The Valentian firewalls won't stop it?"

"No."

Kila clearly wanted to ask more, but simply nodded. "I'll get it to Yule. Are you sure you don't want to hand it off personally? Yule might have some questions for you."

"If she does, you pass them to me. I want to maintain tight compartmentalization of this operation. I don't need to know what Yule's local cover is."

"You're the boss." The coin disappeared into Kila's clothing. "What about the ammunition?"

"I'll need access to the fabrication module controllers in the manufacturing facilities. For the ammunition, and for the firearms the Valentians are building to use that stuff."

Kila's brow furrowed for a moment. "You'll need to work directly with one of our on-planet people for that. Not Yule. Jane Smith."

"Jane Smith?"

"Yeah." Kila grinned. "Her real name sounds like a cover name. Jane's burrowed into the Valentian bureaucracy. She can get you that access and not leave any fingerprints."

"Cool. It's good to have a friend in the bureaucracy."

Kila smiled again, then looked at Foster questioningly. "Speaking of bureaucrats, I heard that rumor again. The one about our pensions and stuff not being honored because officially we don't exist as Federation employees."

"There's no truth in that. We're covered. Every one of us has an official and totally innocuous identity within the Federation government. I've personally confirmed that. Those identities have nothing to do with our real work, but they're accruing all the benefits we're entitled to."

"All of us? Everybody in Section Seven?"

Foster frowned and held up a warning hand. "That doesn't exist," he reminded Kila in a soft voice.

Kila looked like he was trying to eat his last words. "Damn. Sorry."

"Just don't say it again."

"I won't. I never say it. I don't know why I said—."

"Said what?"

"Why I said . . . " Kila finally got the idea. "Nothing. So, it's a go?"

"Yes. I'll stay at the Frontera a few more days and then shift hotels. Is the number from the classified ad good for contacting you routinely?"

"Now and then. Don't worry about coming by here. It's a mixed business and residential district, so there's always lots of foot traffic. You won't stand out."

"Good location. Nice work."

Foster met Jane Smith two days later at a public park. She wore nice but not flashy business attire which made her look more professional than attractive. "Tatya Ostov. Bureau of Inspections."

"Pleased to meet you." Foster felt a data coin slide into his palm as they shook hands.

"Yes. I understand you've come from the Genese Islands to help out in my branch. I appreciate your help, Mr. Danato."

"I'm glad to be here, Ms. Ostov."

"Your first inspection is set for tomorrow. Please report in to the Bureau front desk first thing in the morning. I'll go over your schedule then."

"Thank you." Smith/Ostov left, and Foster made his way to the next-closest library to pop the coin into his data pad. It contained all the information he needed to memorize about his role as Julio Danato, facilities inspector from the isolated Genese Island chain brought in temporarily to help eliminate an inspection backlog at the bureau.

Foster appeared at the Inspection Bureau the next morning, where the security guard scanned his ID, then handed it back with a bored nod. Security forces on every planet fought to ensure all identification data was compiled in a single place in order to assist their investigations. That also meant only a single place had to have false information inserted in order to mislead security forces. Naturally, security forces always insisted their ID sites where hack-proof. They were always wrong.

Smith greeted Foster with cool politeness. As Ostov and Danato, they went over an intensive inspection schedule, covering a wide range of manufacturing facilities. "You need to check to make sure all equipment is operating within proper tolerances and all safety requirements are being followed," she advised. "You have authority to access any equipment and systems necessary to do that."

Foster nodded, noting as he did so the small arms and ammunition manufacturing plants buried among the other facilities he'd have to inspect. "I won't have any trouble. This a pretty extensive list, though. I may have to work late a lot of nights to complete it in the time I have."

Ostov smiled with patent insincerity. "You're a salaried employee, Mr. Danato. It comes with the territory. If you have any questions or run into any difficulties, please give me a call."

Foster started work the next day. While analyzing the list of facilities closely, he'd discovered Jane Smith had arranged it so that he'd be hitting all the places associated with arms and ammunition late in the day. He'd have to put in a special mention about her foresight once this mission was over.

Most of the facilities he inspected had nothing to do with his real task, but provided cover for the ones he needed to reach. He plowed through the Bureau of Inspections checklist at each location, grateful that the Valentians hadn't yet diverged from Federation standards on manufacturing equipment and related software.

By the time he reached the first targeted facility, the week and that day were drawing to a close. Managers eager to get on with their weekend waved him onward as Foster assured them he could conduct his checks without their having to stay late.

His work would've been considerably more difficult in early industrial days when physical jigs and forms were used to guide manufacture of parts. Instead, Foster accessed the controllers which would direct computer-guided fabrication of the parts for the new 'universal standard Viper personal sidearm.' Tolerances were tricky things. If they were adjusted just a tiny bit, everything would still look fine, and initially any test weapons would work okay, but within a short time parts wouldn't work well together. It'd take awhile to figure out there was a problem, time during which manufacturers would inevitably claim operator error. If the controllers had a hidden worm cycling tolerance variances from part to part on a random basis, identifying the cause of the problem would be even more difficult.

Foster finished his work, closing it out without leaving any fingerprints within the controller software. He'd changed the master patterns and their backups, so the only way to eventually fix the Viper pistols would be to redesign them. By that time, they'd hopefully have as bad a reputation as Foster could hope for.

Another week went by, with another small arms facility and an ammunition plant included among Foster's bevy of inspection sites. His dry, routine reports were forwarded to the Bureau and buried within its data files, though not before Smith in her supervisor's job altered the identifiers on a few to make it look like someone else had inspected some of the arms facilities.

Foster was having a late lunch at a store cafeteria when he noticed an increasingly large and impatient crowd in the payment line. A heavy-set man at the front of the line was drumming his fingers on the counter as he stared at a flustered clerk trying to ring up his charge. "What's the problem? I haven't got all day."

The clerk mumbled what sounded like curses. "Excuse me, sir, I'm having trouble getting the system to accept your data."

The man glowered. "There's nothing wrong with my credit status."

"No, sir. It's just not accepting . . . good, there it . . . damn! Now it's balking at . . . "

He leaned over to look at her screen. "No wonder! You're using that crap the government's been pushing. Shift over to the old stuff."

"You mean the last edition of the Fed standard?" The clerk hit several buttons, waited a moment, then smiled. "It's working! Everything's fine, sir."

The customer shook his head and looked around at the others waiting in line. "That government stuff is developing more problems by the day. Didn't they bother testing it?"

Another customer nodded. "My entire office just went back to the Fed standard. It's not perfect, but at least it's not full of bugs."

A chorus of agreement sounded, but one man went against the tide. "The government's system is made in Valentia! Aren't any of you patriotic? Don't you want to support our government against the overbearing Federation?"

The woman who'd spoken earlier laughed. "The Federation isn't messing up my work. The government is, with its worthless, bug-addled, slow, and lock-up prone system. I need software that works. That's just common sense. Or do you want to stand in line forever while the government's system chokes on ringing up your charge?"

The Valentian patriot subsided with a scowl, making no protest when his charge went through on Federation standard software.

Foster watched the little drama blandly, not showing even the smallest trace of humor when the woman declared the Federation wasn't responsible for causing the system problems at her workplace. He'd seen more and more evidence that the Valentian software system was breaking down, displaying erratic and impossible to predict failures and slowdowns. As if it had never been properly tested. Or as if a Black Clown worm spread throughout everything using that software was mutating source codes in very subtle ways.

Another month passed. All of the facilities on Julio Danato's list had been inspected, and he officially returned to the Genese Islands with a brief parting thanks from supervisor Ostov. Now Juan Feres sat in his hotel room watching the local news.

A skeptical looking woman gestured toward a video window beyond her. "Reports continue to be received of problems with the new line of universal standard ammunition and the firearms produced to use it." The video window displayed a group of uniformed soldiers with angry faces, their hands slapping at their weapons. "Our sources tell us the rifles and pistols jam more often than they work. The ammunition is prone to misfires, and will sometimes jam the weapons as well. VelArms Manufacturing and Ares Ammunition, the primary suppliers of the universal standard weapons and ammunition, insist they have uncovered no problems in the factories and suggest users are failing to employ the new weapons properly."

The video window shifted, showing a figure distorted so that neither facial features nor sex could be determined. The figure's voice was also altered, hiding it as well. "We know how to use rifles! This stuff is junk. That's all there is to it. Half the time you can't even seat a magazine of ammo properly, and when you do you can't extract it. Give the stuff time, we were told. We've given it time. It's still junk. I don't want to risk my life on a weapon that don't work. What the hell was wrong with the Federation standard weapons?"

The skeptical newscaster spoke again. "Reports have also indicated that police forces in several cities which received universal standard firearms have abandoned them and gone back to Federation standard weapons. As one officer told us, 'I won't die with a jammed gun because some idiot bureaucrat decided to fix something that wasn't broken.' We will continue following this story and report on new developments."

Another two weeks passed. Foster waited with growing impatience, which was finally rewarded during a brief visit to Kila's safehouse.

Kila grinned. "Watch this."

Another newscaster, this time a smug young man, faced the screen. "The Senate today voted to convene a special investigation into the universal standard ammunition and weapons fiasco. Hours later, the government announced that what it now characterizes as the universal standards weapons 'experiment' would be discontinued due to adverse performance issues and cost overruns."

Kila shut off the screen. "Got 'em."

Foster smiled and nodded. "I believe the operating system issue has already been resolved."

Kila flopped into a chair. "That's my assessment, too. The Valentian system now has a solid reputation as a piece of junk. Even the government has shifted back to Federation standard, because the Valentian system has gotten too buggy." He eyed Foster. "That Black Clown is one mean little devil."

Foster sat as well, feeling satisfaction rise and fighting it down. He wasn't off planet yet. The mission wasn't concluded. "You have to know you have a problem, then you have to be able to identify the cause of that problem. We created problems for the Valentians, and let them reach the wrong conclusions as to the causes."

Kila's eyes narrowed as the front-door bell rang. He opened the door and leaned into the hallway to check the doorway monitor. "It's Jane."

Foster grimaced. Coincidence, but still a bit unnerving to have three of them together here. "That's all right."

Jane showed surprise at Foster's presence, then offered a bottle filled with amber liquid. "A toast to success?"

Glasses were filled and drunk. The liquor had a fiery, exotic tang that Foster enjoyed. Not all native foodstuffs were unpleasant.

Jane sank into her own chair and looked at Foster. "This is odd, isn't it? We've won, but no one'll ever know. We sabotaged an entire planet, and we, and our superiors, are the only ones who realize it."

Foster smiled. "Sabotage is a loaded term. I prefer saying we introduced inefficiencies into non-standard elements."

"And *I'm* supposed to be playing a bureaucrat! Why is this necessary? Why couldn't the Federation have just ordered Valentia to stick to Federation standard software and small arms?"

"The Federation did send demarches," Foster pointed out. "Which were ignored. Valentia realized the Federation could scarcely afford to force a member world to conform to standards. Not openly, anyway. What Valentia didn't count on was that there are other ways than brute force to increase the price and trouble of non-conformity to Federation standards."

Kila nodded. "Even I sometimes wonder why it matters so much. If the idiots want to diverge from Fed standards, let 'em. They're the ones who'll suffer."

Foster sighed. "Initially, yes. But they wouldn't be the only ones. Certainly, the initial effects of incompatible software and changes in manufacturing standards will be felt on the world which has more trouble and thus more expense in trade, as well as less market for its goods. Long-term, though, uniform standards are what hold political entities together. Humans love to innovate, to change. Once planets started diverging from uniform standards for software, manufacturing, and everything else, the process would just keep accelerating. That'd mean growing economic and social misalignment between worlds. Growing barriers to trade, exchange of ideas, travel, and so on. Eventually, that'd mean—."

"No more Federation," Jane finished. "You'd think people would know better. Just trying to introduce new standards here cost Valentia loads of money and effort, even if it had all worked."

Foster smiled again. "If people behaved rationally all the time, they wouldn't be people. And we wouldn't have the jobs we do."

"True. Never-ending jobs, from all I hear. Where are you going to next? Another assignment?"

Foster smiled with one corner of his mouth. "If it was, I couldn't tell you. But I've got some vacation time built up. I'm going home for a little while."

"Great. Where's that?"

Foster met the inquiry with another twist of his lip.

Jane looked embarrassed. "Sorry. I just meant to be polite."

"That's okay. You understand there's a lot of things we can't discuss, even among each other, just in case someone's cover gets blown."

Kila gave one of his fierce grins. "You mean things like, is Gordon Foster your real name?"

Foster smiled again. "Are you two really Jane Smith and Jason Kila?"

They all laughed, but none of them answered the question. Foster sometimes wondered if Section Seven was really the far-beyond top secret title of his organization, or if Section Seven was itself merely a code name for some more heavily classified designation kept even from him. Wheels within wheels, and it usually didn't make sense to try figuring out where if anywhere it all ended. If people knew Section Seven existed, what Section Seven did, it couldn't function anymore, and the Federation would slowly start coming apart. Foster didn't see any good reason not to accept things as they were.

Foster made his final goodbyes and left. He altered his way back to Juan Feres' latest temporary lodging, checked out, then returned as Mr.

Oaks to the short-term rental apartment. He plugged in his data port, watching as it seamlessly matched the Federation standard operating system now being employed by the rental agency. Foster completed checking out Mr. Oaks, then headed back down to the street to hail a cab back to the port terminal.

On the shuttle into space, he looked back at the globe floating in space. Foster had read of an early scientist who proclaimed he could move a world with a long enough lever. Foster's secretive levers weren't long, but thanks to their invisibility they moved worlds nonetheless. As Valentia fell away beneath the shuttle, Foster finally allowed himself a small smile of satisfaction.

Ken Scholes is the award-winning, critically-acclaimed author of five novels and three short story collections. His work has appeared in print for over fifteen years.

Ken's eclectic background includes time spent as a label gun repairman, a sailor who never sailed, a soldier who commanded a desk, a Baptist preacher, a nonprofit executive, a musician and a government procurement analyst. He has a degree in History from Western Washington University.

Ken is a native of the Pacific Northwest and makes his home in Saint Helens, Oregon, where he lives with his twin daughters and plays gigs at his local Village Inn Lounge. You can learn more about him by visiting www.kenscholes.com.

# INVISIBLE EMPIRE OF ASCENDING LIGHT

### Ken Scholes

Tana Berrique set down her satchel and ran a hand over the window plate in her guest quarters. The opaque, curved wall became clear, revealing the tropical garden below. She'd spent most of the past six years living in guest quarters from planet to planet, inspecting the shrines, examining the Mission's work, encouraging the Mission's servants. But the room here at the Imperial Palace on Pyrus came closest to being her home.

She sighed and a voice cleared behind her.

"Missionary General Berrique?"

She didn't turn immediately. Instead, she watched a sky-herd of chantis move against the speckled green carpet of vines, trees and underbrush. "Yes, Captain Vesper?" The birdlike creatures dropped back into the trees and she turned.

She'd heard of this one. Young but hardened in the last Dissent, Alda Vesper climbed the ranks fast to find himself commanding the best of the best, Red Morning Company of the Emperor's Brigade. He stood before her in the doorway, one hand absently toying with the pommel of his short sword, his face pale. "I bring word, Missionary General."

"So soon?" She glanced back at the window, ran her hand over the plate to fog out the garden's light. "By the look on your face, I must assume that he's now Announced himself?"

The captain nodded. "He has. Just a few minutes ago."

Sadness washed through her. She'd known he would Announce; she'd just hoped otherwise. And now Consideration must be given. Afterwards, the path to Declaration could follow. And along that road lay death and destruction unless he truly did Ascend. She'd overseen four Considerations since taking office six years earlier. All had led to Declarations; all had ended in bloodfeuds. She'd discouraged all from Declaring, had seen the obvious outcomes clearly despite their blind faith and inflated hopes. None had listened. Millions dead from men who would be gods.

"Then I will Consider him," she told the captain. "We must move before the others consolidate and shift their allegiances. Ask the Vice-Regent to petition his father for a lightbender to take us. Tell him I specifically requested Red Morning Company to assist the Consideration."

He bowed his head, his smile slight but pleased, fingertips touching the gold emblazoned sun on the breast of his scarlet uniform. "Yes, Missionary General."

He spun and left, ceremonial cloak billowing behind him.

I've only just arrived, Tana Berrique thought as she picked up her satchel, and yet once more I depart. She brushed out the lights to her guest quarters and exited the room and its heaven-like view.

The lightbender vessel *Gold of Dawning* took three days to reach Casillus. One day on each side to clear the demarcation lines under sunsail, one day to power up and bend.

The Missionary General boarded the Captain's yacht with Vesper and a squad of brigadiers. She'd exchanged her white habit for the plain gray of the Pilgrim Seeker and let her hair down out of respect for Casillian custom. She and Captain Vesper took the forward passenger cabin just behind the cockpit and forward from his squad.

*Gold of Dawning* spit them out into space. The vessel's executive officer piloted them planet-side himself. There were no viewscreens in the passenger cabin but Tana knew vessels under many family flags took up their positions around the planet. They waited for her to do her part as she had done before, and they waited for the Declaration.

She thumbed the privacy field and turned to Vesper. "Where is he, then?"

"They've taken him to the local Imperial Shrine for safekeeping. Once he Announced, word spread fast."

They'd watched this one for some time. The Mission had seen the potential in his humble birth, in the calloused hands of his lowborn parents, in the scraps of data they'd fed into the matrix. By age seven, they'd known he would match in the high ninetieth percentile. Now at fifteen, he was easily the youngest to score so near the ideal and the second youngest to Announce before reaching his majority. She'd seen some of his paintings, some of his poems. She'd heard a snippet from a song a year earlier. Now, she reviewed his results and charted them on the divine matrix.

"At the moment, he's only a ninety-eight three," she said out loud.

"Only?" Vesper asked. "Has there been higher?"

She nodded. "When I was an Initiate years ago we saw a ninety-eight six."

His surprised look and indrawn breath made her smile. "A ninety-eight six? I've never heard this."

"There are many things you've not heard," Tana told him. "And you have not heard this either . . . from me." She raised her eyebrows in gentle warning.

Vesper nodded to show agreement. "What happened to him?"

"Her," she said. "This one was a girl."

He scowled. "A girl?"

"Yes. A young woman. Quite rare, I know, considering our understanding of the matrix. And in answer to your question: she died."

"No surprise there," he said. "The disappointed can be quite unforgiving. And the unforgiving can be quite brutal."

Tana nodded. "True. But this one never Declared. She Announced and then took her own life shortly after her Consideration."

She wasn't sure why she told him this. By the letter of the law, it was a breach in the Mystery. But by the spirit, Tana felt drawn to the young man. Or perhaps, she thought, it's been too long since I've trusted anyone outside the Mission.

Vesper seemed surprised. "Took her own life without Declaring? That seems odd." He chuckled. "Why?"

"I think," Tana Berrique said, "she saw something the rest of us couldn't see at the time." Now she hinted at heresy and treason and backed away from the words carefully, studying the sudden firmness of the captain's jaw, the tightness around his eyes.

He looked around, shifting uncomfortably in his seat. The question hung out there like forbidden fruit and she knew he would not ask it.

She patted his leg in the way she thought a mother might. "Pay no mind to me, young Captain. I'm tired and eager to be done with this work."

He relaxed. Eventually, she closed her eyes and meditated to clear her mind for Consideration. The yacht sped on. Somewhere in her silence, she fell into a light sleep and woke up as the atmosphere gently shook her.

He waited in a vaulted chamber in the lower levels of the Imperial Shrine. Captain Vesper's men took up their positions around the shrine, supplementing the Shrine Guard. A duo of Initiates accompanying the shrine's Pilgrim Seeker escorted the Missionary General through room after room.

"We are honored to have you," the Pilgrim Seeker said.

"I am honored to attend," Tana said, following the proper form. "Though I face the day with dread and longing."

The Pilgrim Seeker nodded, her eyes red from crying. "Perhaps he will Ascend."

"Perhaps he will not," Tana Berrique said. "Either way, today will be marked by loss. For one to Ascend, another must Descend."

"In our hope, we grieve." The Pilgrim Seeker quoted from an obscure parameter of the matrix. "And we are here."

They stood in a small anteroom, watching the boy in the chamber through a one-way viewscreen. He sat quietly in a chair. A plain-clad couple stood near the door. The man had his arm around the woman. They looked hopeful and mournful at the same time.

"His parents," the Pilgrim Seeker said.

The Missionary General felt anger well up inside her. "He's very young," she told them. "Who encouraged him to Announce?"

"He did it himself, Mum," the father said.

"And how did he know?"

The mother spoke up. "We didn't even know ourselves. I swear it."

Tana frowned. "Very well. I will give him Consideration." She lowered her voice so that only the parents could hear. "I hope you know what price this all may come to."

The mother collapsed, sobbing against her husband. He patted her shoulder, pressing her to his chest. When his eyes locked with Tana Berrique's she saw fire in them. "We didn't know. Have done with it and let us be." Now tears extinguished their ferocity. "If we had known, don't you think we'd have fled with him years ago?"

The despair in his words stopped her. She felt their grief wash over her, capsizing her anger. She forced a gentle smile, too late. "Perhaps your son will Ascend."

"Perhaps," the father said.

She drew a palm-sized matrix counter from her pocket and thumbed it on. She felt it vibrating into her hand, ready to calculate his responses and add them into the equation as she gave Consideration. Tana Berrique nodded to the Pilgrim Seeker, who opened the door into the chamber. She walked into the room and stood above him. He sat, eyes closed, breathing lightly.

One of the Initiates brought a chair and set it before the boy, then left. She sat, placed the matrix counter on the floor between them, and waited for the door to whisper closed. When it did, she smiled.

"What is your name?" she asked.

The boy opened his eyes and looked up at her. "I would like a privacy field, please."

She flinched in surprise. The counter chirped softly, flashing green. Ninety-eight four, now. "A privacy field? It's not done that way."

His eyes narrowed. "It's done any way you say it is, Missionary General Tana Berrique. This is your Consideration."

Surprise became fear. The green light flashed him a solid ninety-eight six now as his words registered against the equation. She waved to the hidden viewscreen and a privacy field hummed to life around them. "You know a great deal for someone so young."

The boy laughed. It sounded like music and it washed her fear. He leaned forward. "Perhaps I'm not so very young," he said.

"That's what I'm here to Consider," she told him. "May I follow the form?"

He nodded.

"What is your name?"

"I am called H'ru in this incarnation."

She raised her eyebrows. "This incarnation?" she repeated.

"Yes."

She watched the counter. He was nearing ninety-nine. "And your other names?" she asked.

He shrugged. "Are they important?"

"They may be, H'ru. I don't know."

He shook his head. "They are not."

Tana changed the subject. "What led you to Announce?"

His young brow furrowed. "I was told to."

"By your parents?"

He chuckled, the brief laugh ending in a secret smile.

"By one of the Families?"

The smile faded. "By myself," he said.

She shook her head, not sure she heard correctly. The counter did not chirp or hum, no light flickered from it. "Could you say that again?"

"I told myself to Announce," he said.

She felt her stomach lurch. "That's not possible."

"Ask me. Return to Pyrus, wake me, and ask me yourself." His smile returned. "After you are finished with the Consideration, of course."

"The Regent would never allow it. And even if he did—" She suddenly realized she had lost focus, lost composure, spoken aloud. The counter still did nothing. She scooped down, picked it up to see if it still hummed. It did.

"I've stopped it," he said.

"How?" she asked.

"I willed it to stop and it stopped."

"What else can you will?" she asked.

He shook his head. "We'll not talk around circles, Tana Berrique. You do not need a counter to know who I am."

She let the air rush out of her. He was right. She didn't need it to know. The four before had been betrayed by either humility without strength or arrogance without power. Their equations had tested the matrix, to be sure, but they could not Ascend. After Declaring, the house-factions and bloodfeuds had undone them and they'd died on the run from followers turned vengeful from disappointment and fear. But this one was different and it shook her.

"You've not met me before," he said. "The others were near but false. Except for one."

She nodded. She blinked back tears, fought the growing knot in her throat.

"You're wondering why I took my life before," he asked. "It's what you told the Captain on your flight in. I saw something the rest of you could not see at the time. But you see it now, don't you?"

She nodded again and swallowed.

"Your god, your Emperor of Ascending Light, has lain near death for too long while the Regent and his kin hold power in wait for another god to rise. But they intend no new Ascendant be found. They use this trick of Announcement, Consideration and Declaration to extend both hope and fear. But in the end, no one Ascends. The Dissents tear out the heart of the Empire and only strengthen the aspect of a few."

Her hands shook. Her bladder threatened release. She shifted on the chair, then pitched forward onto her knees. "What is your will, Lord Emperor?"

He touched her hair and she looked up. He smiled down, his face limned in the room's dim light. "Take your seat, Tana Berrique."

Mindful to obey, she returned to her chair. "My Lord?"

"H'ru," he said with a gentle voice. "Just H'ru."

Tana felt confusion and conflict brewing behind her eyes. "But surely when you Declare, you shall Ascend unhindered? How could they prevent you?"

"They will not prevent me," he said. "*You* will." He paused, letting the words sink in to her. "And I shall neither Ascend nor Declare."

"But my role is Consideration. I take no part in—"

"I will tell you to," he said. "And because I am your Emperor, you will obey."

"I do not understand," she said.

"You will." He patted her hand. "When the Regent calls you out, say to him *S'andril bids you to recall your oath in the Yellowing Field*. He will admit you to me. And I will tell you what to do."

She sat there before him for a few minutes, letting the privacy field absorb the sound of her sobs as he held her hands in his and whispered comfort to her.

At long last, she stood, straightened her habit, and waved for the privacy field to be turned off. The counter stopped at ninety-nine three. She looked down at the boy. "This Consideration is closed," she said. "You may do what you will."

The boy nodded. "I understand."

Without a glance, without meeting the eyes of the Pilgrim Seeker or the parents, she strode from the chamber, passed through the anteroom and said nothing at all to anyone else.

Back at Pyrus, she spent her time gazing down on the garden while she waited for the Regent to call her out. No Declaration had swept up from

Casillus and the pockets of ships, loaded with troops, continued to deploy strategically around that world and others while everyone waited.

Captain Vesper finally came for her. She had not spoken to him since before the Consideration but she knew that he could see her unrest. He fell back into his official role though she saw his brow furrowing and his mouth twitching as unasked questions played out beneath his skin.

She followed as he led her into the throne room.

The Regent sat on a smaller throne to the left of the central dais and its massive, empty crystalline throne. To the right, his son, the Vice-Regent, sat. He waved the Imperial Brigade members away.

After they had gone, he motioned the Missionary General forward.

"Well?" he finally asked. "There has been no Declaration from Casillus. Then I learn that you made no report on this Consideration." He scowled, his heavy beard, woven with gems and strands of gold, dragging against his chest. "What do you say for yourself?"

"I say nothing for myself, Regent." She intentionally left off the word *Lord*.

"I find that highly unusual, Missionary General."

She shrugged. "I'm sorry you find it so."

"Can you speak about this child H'ru and his Announcement?"

"I can. He Announced and I Considered."

"And?"

Tana Berrique paused, not sure how to pick her way through this minefield. Lord help me, she thought, and I will simply be direct. She met the Regent's eyes. "What do you want me to say?"

"What I want," the Regent said in a cold voice, "is to know when the Family warships and armies will either stand down or take action. Something that will not happen until this boy makes up his mind. We do not need another Dissent. We do not need another false god Declaring and moving our worlds into civil war."

She continued to stare at him. "I find it interesting, Regent, that you did not at any point mention wanting a new god to Ascend and bring all this uncertainty to a close."

His face went red and he growled deep in his chest. "If you were not the Missionary General," he said in a low voice, his hands white-knuckling the sides of his chair, "I would have you killed for those words."

She smiled. "So you do want the new god to Ascend, for our Emperor of Ascending Light to sleep at long last, knowing his people are safe for a season?"

"Of course I do," he said. "We all do."

*Now she took her moment.* "Very well," she said. *"S'andril bids you to recall your oath in the Yellowing Field."*

His eyes popped, his face went white and his mouth dropped open. "What did you say?"

"You heard me quite well. And I assume that you know what it means."

Shaking, he stood up. "It can't be."

"It is."

His son looked pale, too, but clearly didn't understand what was happening. Tana Berrique wasn't sure herself, but she felt the power from her words and their hard impact.

"He told me this day would come. He told me those words would come." The large old man started to cry.

"Father?" The son stood as well. "What does this mean?"

"An old promise, son. Go gather your things."

Tana watched the son's face go red. "My things? What are you saying?"

"Our work is done," the Regent said. "We're going home now."

"But this *is* my home. You said so. You said—"

In a bound, the old man stood over his son, hand raised to slap him down. The son buckled and cowered on the floor as his father's voice roared out: "What I said doesn't matter. We leave now and hope for mercy later."

"I'll let myself in," Tana Berrique told him.

Behind the throne room, in his private bedchamber, the Emperor of Ascending Light lay beneath a stasis field, attended by scuttling jeweled spiders that preserved his life. Tana Berrique stood at the foot of the massive circular bed, her body trembling at the sight of him.

He'd been a big man once, muscled and broad-shouldered, but the years had withered him to kindling. His white hair ran down the sides of his head like streams of milk spilled onto a silk pillow. His hands were folded around his scepter. She stepped forward and dropped to her knees beside his bed, thumbing off the stasis field to awaken him from long sleep. The spiders clattered and scrambled, unsure of what to do with this un-programmed event. The paper-thin eyelids fluttered open and a light breath rattled out.

Tana Berrique bowed her head. "You summoned me, Lord."

"Yes." His voice rasped, paper rustling wood. "Are my people well?"

"They are not, Lord. They need you."

The tight mouth pulled, thin wisps of beard moving with the effort. "Not as such."

And she knew what was coming now. The reality of it settled in as she recalled the boy's words. They will not prevent me, he had said, *you* will. "What would you bid me, Lord?"

"Kill me," the Emperor of Ascending Light whispered. One hand released the scepter and thin, dry, brittle fingers sought her hand. "Let it all change." He coughed and a spider moved to wipe his mouth. "It is time for change."

"I don't think I can." She felt the tears again, hot and shameful, pushing at her eyes and spilling out. She wanted to drop his hand but could not. "I don't think I can. I can't."

He shushed her. "You can. Because I am your Emperor." His lips twitched into a gentle smile. "You will obey."

Tana Berrique stood and bent over her god. She felt the sweat from her sides trickle forward tracing the line of her breasts as she leaned. She felt the tears tracing similar paths down her cheeks. She shuddered, bent further, and kissed the dry, rattling lips. She placed her hands gently on the thin neck and squeezed, the soft hair of his beard tickling her wrists. The eyelids fluttered closed. She kept squeezing until her shoulders shook. She kept squeezing while the spiders panicked and climbed over one another to somehow complete their program and preserve a life. She kept squeezing until she knew that he had gone. Her hands were still on the throat when heavy boots pounded the hallway.

"Missionary General!" Captain Vesper's voice shouted from outside, "Is the Emperor okay? The Regent's retinue is packing for a rapid withdrawal and no one is telling me any—" She heard him clatter into the room. "What are you doing?" he screamed.

She turned quickly to face him. Panting, eyes wild, face drawn in agony, the young officer pulled his sword. "What are you doing?" he asked again, pointing its tip at her as he took a step forward.

"I'm doing what I'm told," she said. "And by the Ascending Light you'll do the same or watch all our Lord worked for crumble and decay."

He paused, uncertainty washing his face.

"You already know, Alda." She gestured to the bed. "He wanted more than this for his people."

The sword tip wavered. "I thought we were working for more," he spat.

"We are. He was." She waited. "I'm doing what he said."

"What proof have you?"

She shook her head. "None but his words to me and me alone. And something about the Yellowing Field. I don't know what—it meant something to the Regent, though."

Alda went paler. The sword dropped. "The Yellowing Field? Are you sure?"

"You know of it?"

His shoulders slumped. "I do. It's a Brigade story from the forging of the Empire."

"I've never heard this," she said.

He walked forward, looking down at the Emperor. "There are many things you've not heard," he told her. "When S'andril was young he saved a boy who swore he would repay him. 'I have saved your life today,' the Emperor told this boy, 'and one day I will bid you repay me by not saving mine.'" He looked up at her. "I am at your service."

She sat on the edge of the bed. "We're not finished yet," she told him. "There's more."

He nodded. "The boy?"

He understands, she thought. He truly understands. Her words came slowly. "It will be bloody. Many will die. But after this, we can rebuild. There will be no further Dissents. The Families will burn out their rage and then we can have peace." Because, she hoped, if the god is truly dead then the idea of that god can live on without harm.

His voice was firm. "His family, too?"

"No. Spare them but keep it quiet. Just him. He won't struggle. It's what he wants."

"And after?" Alda Vesper stood.

She played the words to herself, then said them carefully. "After, I will Declare the boy myself and give witness to his Ascent." An eternal emperor, she thought, on the throne of each heart. An invisible empire of Ascending Light.

"God help us," Vesper said. He spun on his heel and left.

She sat there for a while and wondered what her life had suddenly become. And she wondered what would come after the lie her god bid her tell?

She would return to her guest quarters. She would clear the window and sit in front of it and stare down into the garden, wondering what it would be like to breathe the hot air of Pyrus, swim the boiling rivers of its jungles, pluck the razor flowers by the water's edge. She would address the Council of Seekers and dismantle the Mission. She would write it all down, this new gospel, for the generations to come after and go into hiding from the wrath of the disappointed and unforgiving.

Finally, she stood to leave.

Vesper's words registered with her. God help us, he'd said.

She looked down at the Emperor of Ascending Light one final time.

"He already has," she whispered.

A thirty-year veteran of science fiction, Robert Reed is a prolific short story writer and winner of the 2007 Hugo Award for his novella, "A Billion Eves." His most recent book, *The Memory of Sky*, a Great Ship trilogy, was published by Prime Books in 2014. His next novel will be *The Trials of Quentin Maurus*—a self-published alternate history adventure of ordinary life. Reed's own ordinary life revolves around his wife and daughter in Lincoln, Nebraska.

# THE MAN WITH THE GOLDEN BALLOON

### Robert Reed

1

Quee Lee learned about the Vermiculate from an unlikely source—a painfully respectable gentleman who never took pleasure from adventuring or the unexpected. But their paths happened to cross during a feast given by mutual friends, and after the customary pleasantries, he gently pulled the ancient woman aside, remarking, "I have some news that might be of interest to you."

"Well, I have interest to spare," she said.

Then with a precise, mildly perturbed voice, he explained how one tiny portion of the Great Ship had never been adequately mapped.

"How can that be?" Quee Lee asked skeptically. "The captains' first priority was to locate every shipboard cavern and dead-end tunnel. Even the tiniest crevice wears some unique name."

"Oh, the captains were thorough," the man admitted, never one to openly doubt authority. "But the Ship has the mass and volume of Uranus, with engines bigger than moons and fuel tanks that can swallow oceans whole."

Yes, mapping the enigmatic body was a challenge. But the early captains were clever, stubborn souls. Their survey began with several million robots—small, elegantly designed machines bristling with sensors and curious limbs. Scrambling through the Ship's interior, the robots memorized every empty volume, and whenever a passageway split in two, the robots paused, feasting on the local rock and metal while building copies of their obsessive selves. As prolific as carpenter ants or harum-scarum fleas, those early scouts soon numbered in the trillions, and ruled by simple unyielding instructions, they moved ever deeper inside the Ship, eventually scurrying down every hole, fashioning a precise three-dimensional model of the Ship's vacant interior.

But the method had limitations. Doorless bubbles and pockets and finger-wide seams lay out of reach; more than a few long caverns were sealed beneath kilometers of iron and hyperfiber. Yet with sonic probes and neutrino knives, the Ship's engineers made even those buried places visible. The only unmapped region was the Ship's distant core. The Master Captain was being honest when she stood on the bridge, proclaiming that her fabulous machine had been mapped in full; and its crew and countless passengers had little reason but to believe every promise that this voyage would remain routine—a blissful journey that would eventually circumnavigate the bright heart of the Milky Way.

Quee Lee explained all of this, and her companion bristled.

"I understand how the Ship was mapped," he said. "What I'm telling you is that despite everyone's best efforts, a few empty spaces are lurking out there."

"And how do we know this?"

"Because the Master Captain owns a team of AI savants—brilliant machines designed to do nothing but ponder the Ship and its mysteries. One of those AIs recently made a fresh analysis of old data, and one glaring gap was discovered. One blank spot on the captains' map and nobody understands how this could have happened."

"And when did we learn this?"

"But we haven't learned anything," he countered, his voice breaking at the edges. "This is a very grave, very important business. Only the highest ranking captains know about the flaw."

"And you," she pointed out.

"Well, yes, I know portions of the story. But I can't tell how or why, and please don't ask me."

"And why are you telling me?"

"Because it occurred to me," he said, producing a hopeful smile. "You of all people would appreciate hearing this news."

Give a rich secret to the blandest soul, and he will turn into a fountain of knowledge. And Quee Lee was a charming presence as well as a very desirable audience: A wealthy woman from the Old Earth and one of a handful of humans onboard the Ship who could remember that precious moment when their species turned a sensitive ear to the sky, hearing intelligent sounds raining down from the stars. In that sense, she was a remarkable and very rare creature—a lady of genuine fame inside the human community. She was also beautiful and poised, socially gifted and universally liked. Given this kind of opportunity, any healthy, insecure heterosexual male would work hard to impress Quee Lee.

"Our captains are worried," her confidant said. "The Master Captain took the trouble of waking one of the old surveying robots and putting it down a promising hole. And do you know what happened?"

"You're going to tell me, I hope."

"The robot lost its way." The man shivered, bothered by this turn of events. "The machine fumbled around in the darkness, and then with nothing to say for itself, it climbed back out of the hole again."

"Fascinating," she said.

"I knew you would enjoy this," he whispered, offering a smile and quick wink. After millennia of traveling together, he had finally managed to engage the interest of this beautiful creature.

"Perri will want to hear this story," she mentioned.

"But I wish you wouldn't mention it," the man said. Then a worse possibility occurred to him. "I understood your husband is traveling now. He isn't here with us, is he?"

"Oh, but he is." For the last several weeks, Perri had been riding a saddle strapped to the back of a squid-like alien called the Gi-Gee, enjoying wild swims in a frigid river of ammonium hydrate. But by chance, he had just now slipped into the party. Of course her husband would want to learn of this news. A thousand souls were scattered across the room, human and otherwise. Most of the celebrants were dressed in gaudy, look-at-me costumes—which was only proper, since these were among the wealthiest, most powerful individuals to be found in the galaxy. But looking past the towering egos, Quee Lee waved at the only human male dressed in plain, practical clothes.

"I don't want this to be known," the man said. "Not outside our little circle, please."

The tone was the message: Perri was neither wealthy nor important, which made him unacceptable.

But Quee Lee laughed off the insult as well as the earnest pleas for silence. "Oh, I'm sure my husband's already heard about the Vermiculate," she said. "Perri knows the Ship as well as any captain does, and he knows everyone onboard who matters too." Then she winked, adding sweetly, "And he knows you, of course."

"Of course."

Yet for some reason Perri wasn't familiar with this rumor. He listened intently as Quee Lee related the mystery, and yes, he was familiar with the region called the Vermiculate. It was an intricate nest of dry caves, very few entrances leading to a million dead ends. But he never knew that some portion of those caverns had escaped mapping.

The other man rocked nervously side to side.

"Tell it again," Perri demanded, tugging at the fellow's elbow. "From the beginning, everything you know."

But there weren't many new details to share.

"I think I see what's happening," Perri said. "This is just an old rumor reborn. The first two passengers to come onboard the Great Ship started this story. Over drinks or in somebody's bed, they convinced themselves there had to be secret places and unmapped corners. It helped heighten the sense of adventure, don't you see? And every century or two, without fail, that same old legend puts on a new costume and takes its walk in public."

"But this is no rumor," the man said. "And I don't approve of legends. What I told you is the truth, I swear it."

"Yet you won't name your source," Perri pointed out.

"I cannot," the man said. "Frankly, I wish I hadn't said this much."

Unlike all of the well-moneyed souls in the room, Perri wore a boyish face and a pretty, almost juvenile smile. When it served his needs, he played the role of a smart child surrounded by very foolish adults. "It scares the hell out of you, doesn't it, sir? You hear about this puzzle, and you're the kind of creature who won't fall asleep unless every puzzle is solved, every question mark erased."

"And what is wrong with that?" asked the rumor's source.

"What's right about it?" Perri asked.

Quee Lee had expected that response, and when it came, she laughed softly.

The gentleman bristled, looking at her. "My dear, I thought you would be interested in this matter. But if you're going to tease me—"

"I didn't mean that," she began.

But the man had his excuse to turn and march away. No doubt he would avoid Quee Lee for the rest of the day, and if genuinely angry, she wouldn't see him for the next fifty years.

"I shouldn't have laughed," Quee Lee admitted.

"And he shouldn't forgive you," said Perri. "But he will."

True enough. Fifty years of chilled silence was nothing among immortals. All but the most malicious slights were eventually pardoned, or at least discarded as memories not worth carrying any farther. "It's too bad that the story isn't true," she said. "I wish there was an unmapped cave hiding out there."

"Oh, but there is," said Perri.

Quee Lee worked through the possibilities. "You lied to me," she complained. "You'd already heard about the Vermiculate."

"I didn't, and I haven't."

"Then how can you say—?"

"Easily," he interrupted. "Your friend might be a wonderful soul. He might be charitable and sweet—"

"Hardly."

"But the man has never once shown me the barest trace of imagination. I seriously doubt that he could dream up such a tale, and I know he wouldn't repeat some wild fable, unless it came from a reasonable, responsible source."

"Such as?"

"One of the captains," said Perri.

"But why would an officer take any passenger into his or her confidence?" She hesitated, and laughed. "I suppose our friend is rather wealthy."

"Wealthier even than you," Perri agreed.

"And if he happened to be sleeping with a captain . . . "

"That's my cynical guess."

Nothing about her husband's mind was unknown. "You already know which captain it is. Don't you?"

"I have a robust notion," he said.

"Tell"

"Not here." Stroking her arm with a fond hand, he said, "My candidate has rank and connections, and she's desperately fond of money. And if you mix those qualifications with the fact that she, like that prickly man sulking over there, doesn't appreciate mysteries . . . "

"Is the Vermiculate unmapped?" she asked.

"If any place is." With long fingers, he drew elaborate shapes in the air between them. "Join all of those empty caves together and straighten them out, and you'll have a single tunnel long enough to reach from your

Earth to Neptune and partway home again. So yes, it's easy to imagine that some AI expert could massage the old data, and one corner here and one little room there might have escaped notice and naming. And maybe after eighty thousand years of sleep, one of the original survey robots gets awakened and shoved down a hole, but because of its age, it malfunctions, which makes these events far more mysterious than they actually are."

On her own, Quee Lee had narrowed the list of suspect captains to three, perhaps four. With a quiet, conspiratorial voice, she asked, "Who's going to make our discreet inquires? You or me?"

"Neither of us," Perri said.

"Then you're not my husband," she teased. "The man I married would want to finish the mapping himself."

Perri shrugged and grinned. "We can make our own good guesses. Besides, if we get ourselves noticed, what began as a tiny anomaly mentioned on a pillow becomes much more: An area of potential embarrassment to the godly rulers of the Great Ship. Then our nameless captain will personally march into that empty corner, and keep me from having my little bit of fun."

"And me too," said Quee Lee.

"Or quite a lot of fun," Perri added, wrapping an arm around his wife's waist. "If you're in the mood for a little darkness, that is."

## 2

Yet nothing was simple about this simple-sounding quest. Finding holes inside the existing maps required months of detailed analysis by several experts paid well for their secrecy as well as their rare skills. Meanwhile, half a dozen of Perri's best friends heard about his newest interest, and by turning in past favors earned slots on the expedition roster. Then Quee Lee decided to invite two lady-friends who had been pressing for centuries to join her on a "safe adventure", which was what this would be. The Vermiculate might be imperfectly known, but there was no reason to expect danger. The dry caves were filled with the standard minimal atmosphere—nitrogen and oxygen and nothing else. There were no artificial suns or lights, and the only heat was thermal leakage from the nearby habitats and reactors. Even if the worst happened—if everyone lost their way and their supplies were exhausted—the result would be a bothersome thirst and gradual starvation. Bioceramic minds would sever all connections with their failing bodies, and when no choice was left, ten humans would sit down in the darkness and quietly turn into mummies, waiting for their absence to be noted and a rescue mission to track them down, waking them up and then teasing them endlessly.

But Perri didn't approve of losing his way. Meticulously recording their position on the new, modestly improved map, he earned gentle ribbing and then not-so-gentle ribbing from the others. Of course the Vermiculate was far too enormous to explore, even in a thousand years. But their flex-skin car took them to areas of interest, and before stepping away from each base camp, he made his team memorize the local tunnels and chambers. Everyone had to stay with at least one companion, he insisted. He begged for the others to carry several kinds of torches as well as locator tools, noisemakers and laser flares. But eighteen days of that kind of mothering caused one of Quee Lee's friends to break every rule. She picked a random passageway and ran for parts unknown, at least to her. Carrying nothing but one small torch and a half-filled water bottle, she invested ten hours into solitary adventuring, and then discovered that she had no worthwhile ideas where she was in the universe.

Perri and Quee Lee found the explorer sitting in a dead-end chamber, shivering inside her heated clothes—shivering out of anxiety and the first hunger experienced in ages. But it was a lesson that took, and from that moment on, everyone's wandering was done with at least the minimal precautions.

Boredom was what began defeating the explorers.

The Vermiculate's walls were stone buttressed with low-grade hyperfiber. No human eye had ever seen these tunnels, but the novelty was minimal. Some places were beautiful in their shape and proportions, but it was an accidental beauty. The Ship's builders might have had a purpose for each twist and turn, every sudden room and the little tubes that gave access to the next portion of the maze. But living eyes found nothing strange or interesting, and after two months of wandering, the novice adventurers were losing their interest.

One by one, the expedition shrank.

First to leave was the woman who hadn't gotten lost. Then Perri's friends complained about these dreary circumstances, each demanding a ride to the nearest exit point. The only ones left were identical twin brothers and that dear old friend of Quee Lee who had gotten lost and scared, and who since then, to the surprise of everyone, had discovered a genuine fondness for spelunking.

Or maybe it was the brothers who held her interest. One night, when the camp lights were dropping down to a nightly glow, Quee Lee spotted the twins slipping into her friend's little shelter—entering her home from opposite ends, and neither appearing again until morning.

Another month of roving brought few highlights. Half a dozen tunnels showed evidence of foot-traffic over the last few thousand years. The desiccated slime trail of a Snail-As-God was a modest surprise. Inside one cave was the broken scale from a harum-scarum shin, and a few meters farther along, a liter of petrified blood left behind by a human male. And then came that momentous afternoon when they discovered a graveyard of surveying robots—ten thousand machines that had pulled themselves into neat, officious piles before dropping into an eternal diagnostic sleep.

Two days later, Perri brought his team to the bottom of a deep, deep chimney. Mathematical wizards had labeled that location as "mildly interesting". The Vermiculate displayed patterns, sometimes predictable and occasionally repeatable, and according to sophisticated calculations, that very narrow hole should lead to a large "somewhere else". But the unknown refused to expose itself with a glance. Two little tunnels waited at the bottom of the chimney, yet every sonic pulse and cursory examination showed that they were long and exceptionally ordinary repositories of the same-old-shit.

The five humans broke into two groups.

Perri and Quee Lee slipped into the shorter tunnel. As always, they brought tracking equipment as well as the sniffers constantly searching for organic traces left by past visitors, and they carried heated clothes and survival rations and a variety of lights to offer feeble glows or sun-blazing fires. But the most effective sensor came in pairs, and it was the bluish-yellow eyes that noticed the sudden hole in the floor.

"Stop," said Perri.

Quee Lee paused, one gloved hand dropping, fingertips reaching to within a hair's width of the emptiness.

"Look," he advised.

"I see it," she said. But she didn't know what she saw. After days and weeks of staring at structural hyperfiber, she recognized that here was something different. The area surrounding the hole was peculiar. Holding a variable beam to the floor, she slipped through a series of settings. Hyperfiber was the strongest baryonic substance known—the bones of the Ship and the basis of every starfaring civilization—yet she had never seen light flickering against hyperfiber quite like this. It was as if the floor could feel their weight, and the photons were betraying the floor's tiny vibrations.

"Do you know what this is?" Perri asked.

"Do you?"

"The source," he said. "The source of our rumor."

She shone a second light up and down the tunnel. There was no sign of disabled robots or the detritus left by mapping crews. But the captains could have cleaned up their trash, since captains liked to keep their secrets secret, particularly when it came to curious passengers.

"This hole is fresh," Perri said. And when Quee Lee reached toward the edge, he said, "Don't. Unless you want to cut off a finger or two."

The floor was pure hyperfiber—a skin only a few atoms thick at its thickest. Because the stuff was so very thin, the light flickered. What they were trusting with their combined weight was close to nothing, like worn paint stretched across empty air, and the edge of the hole was keener than the most deadly sword.

"But a robot should have noticed," she guessed. "If we can see that the floor here is different . . . "

"Yeah, I've given that some thought too," said Perri. "We're about as deep into the Vermiculate as you can go, or so we thought. A few surveyors probably started working above us, and when they were overwhelmed, they stopped and ate the rock and replicated themselves."

"Imperfect copies," she said.

"Flawed but not badly, and nobody noticed." He shrugged, enjoying the game without taking anything too seriously. "Whatever the reason, the machine that first crawled into this tunnel wasn't paying close attention. It didn't notice what should have been obvious, and that's why the Ship's map was incomplete."

"Just like the rumor says," Quee Lee agreed. "Except there isn't much mystery, because if the captains found something remarkable—"

"We wouldn't get within ten kilometers," Perri agreed.

With every tool, including her warm brown eyes, Quee Lee examined the floor and the hole and the blackness below.

Perri did the same.

And then for the first time in perhaps a hundred years, one of them managed to surprise the other.

It wasn't the adventurous spouse who spoke first.

Pointing down, Quee Lee said, "That hole's just wide enough for me."

"If we string tethers to the ceiling," Perri mentioned. "And if there's another floor worth standing on below us."

"What about our friends?"

"I'll go gather them up," he began.

"No." Then for the second time, she surprised her husband. "We'll leave a note behind. We can tell them to follow, if they want."

Perri smiled at the ancient creature.

"This is our adventure," she concluded. "Yours, and mine."

3

What lay below was the same as everything above. The sole difference was that no public map showed these particular cavities and chimneys, and the long tunnels and little side vents always led to a wealth of new places devoid of names. Perri's navigational kit claimed that they had wandered twelve kilometers before beginning their hunt for a campsite. A series of electronic breadcrumbs led back to the original hole and their left-behind note, and speaking through the crumbs, Quee Lee discovered that her lady-friend and the twins hadn't bothered to look for them. She mentioned why that might be, and the two enjoyed a lewd laugh. Then following one promising passageway around its final bend, they entered the largest room they had seen in weeks.

The floor of the room was an undulating surface, like water stirred by deep currents. They selected a spacious bowl of cool gray hyperfiber, and with the camp light blazing beside them, they made love. Then they ate and drank their fill, and at a point with no obvious significance, Perri strolled over to his pack and bent down, intending to snatch some tiny item from one of the countless pockets.

That was the moment when every light went out.

Quee Lee was sitting on her memory-chair, immersed in sudden darkness. Her first instinct was to believe that she was to blame. Their camp light was in front of her. Had she given it some misleading command? But their other torches were extinguished, the night total, or perhaps for some peculiar reason her eyes had suddenly decided to go completely blind.

Then from a distance, with a moderately concerned voice, her husband asked, "Darling? Are you there?"

"I am." Perri was blind too, or every one of their lights had failed. Either way, something unlikely had just occurred. "What do you think?" she asked.

"That it's ridiculously dark in here," said Perri.

Perfectly, relentlessly black.

"Do you feel all right?" he asked.

"I feel fine," she said.

"I do too." He was disappointed, as if some little ache might help answer their questions. "Except for being worried, I suppose."

Perri's foot kicked the pack.

"Darling?"

"I'm hunting for the echo-catchers."

"Good."

Then he said, "Found one."

She listened for the high squeak of sonar.

But he said, "Nope. Not working either."

She rubbed her eyes.

"Sing to me," he said. "I'll follow your voice."

Softly, Quee Lee sang one of the first tunes that she had ever learned—a nursery rhyme too old to have an author, its beguiling lyrics about rowing and time wrapped around a long dead language.

Moments later, she heard Perri's soft steps and one deep breath as he settled on the ground directly to her right.

She stopped singing.

Then Perri called from off to her left, from some distance, telling her, "Don't quit singing now. I'm still trying to find you, darling."

A long moment brought nothing. The darkness remained silent and unknowable. And then from her right, from a place quite close, a voice that she did not recognize softly insisted, "Yes, please. Sing, please. I rather enjoy that wonderful little tune of yours."

4

Quee Lee began to jump up.

"No, no," the voice implored. "Remain seated, my dear. There is absolutely no reason to surrender your comfort."

She settled slowly, warily.

Perri called her name.

Clearing her throat, Quee Lee managed to say, "I'm here. Here."

"Are you all right?"

"Yes."

"But I thought I heard—"

"Yes."

"Is somebody with you?"

Inside the same moment, two voices said, "Yes."

Then the new voice continued. "I was hoping that your wife would sing a little more," it remarked. "But I suppose I have spoiled the mood, which is my fault. Please, Perri, will you join us? Sit beside Quee Lee, and I promise: Neither of you will come to any harm. A little conversation, a little taste of companionship . . . that's all I wish for now . . . "

Again, with urgency, Perri asked, "Are you all right?"

How could Quee Lee answer that question? "I'm fine, yes." Except she was startled, and for many rational reasons, she was scared, and with the darkness pressing down, she was feeling a thrilling lack of control.

Her husband's footsteps seemed louder than before. In the perfect blackness, he stepped by memory, and then perhaps sensing her presence, he stopped beside her and reached out with one hand, dry warm fingertips knowing just where her face would be waiting.

She clung to his hand with both of hers.

"Sit, please," the stranger insisted. "Unless you absolutely must stand."

Perri settled on one edge of her soft chair. His hand didn't leave her grip, and he patted that knot of fingers with his free hand. As well as she knew her own bones, Quee Lee knew his. And she leaned into that strong body, glad for his presence and confident that he was glad for hers.

"Who are you?" asked Perri.

Silence answered him.

"Did you disable our lights?" he asked.

Nothing.

"You must have," Perri decided. "And my infrared corneas and nexus-links too, I realized."

"All temporary measures," the stranger said.

"Why?"

Silence.

"Who are you?" asked Quee Lee asked. "And what's your name?"

Something here was funny. The laughter sounded genuine, weightless and smooth, gradually falling away into an amused silence. Then what might or might not have been a deep breath preceded the odd statement, "As I rule, I don't believe in names."

"No?" Quee asked.

"As a rule," the voice repeated.

Perri asked, "What species are you?"

"And I will warn you," the voice added. "I don't gladly embrace the concept of species either."

The lovers sat as close as possible, speaking to each other with the pressure of their hands.

Finally, Quee Lee took it upon herself to say, "We're human, if that matters to you."

There was no response.

"Do you know our species?" she asked.

And then Perri guessed, "You're a Vapor-track. Nocturnal to the point where they can't endure even the weakest light—"

"Yes, I know humans," the stranger responded. "And I know Vapor-tracks too. But I am neither. And I am not nocturnal, nor diurnal. The time of day and the strength of the ambient light are absolutely no concern to me."

"But why are you down here?" Quee Lee asked.

Their companion gave no response.

"This is a remote corner of the Ship," Perri said. "Why would any sentient organism seek out this place?"

"Why do you?" was the response.

"Curiosity," Perri confessed. "Is that your motivation?"

"Not in the least."

The voice was more male than female, and it sounded nearly as human as they did. But those qualities could be artifacts of any good translator. It occurred to Quee Lee that layers of deception were at play, and what they heard had no bearing at all on what, if anything, was beside them.

"I could imagine that I am a substantial puzzle for the two of you," the voice allowed.

The humans responded with their own silence.

"Fair enough," their companion said. "Tell me: Where were each of you born?"

"On the Great Ship," Perri volunteered.

"I come from the Earth," Quee Lee offered.

"Names," the stranger responded. "I ask, and you instantly offer me names."

"What else could we say?" asked Quee Lee.

"Nothing. For you, there are no other polite options. But as a rule, I prefer places that don't wear names. Cubbyholes and solar systems that have remained outside the catalogs, indifferent to whichever label that a passerby might try to hang on its slick invisible flesh."

Quee Lee listened to her husband's quick, interested breathing.

After reflection, Perri said, "And that's why you're here. This is one place inside the Great Ship that has gone unnoticed, until now."

"Perhaps that is my reason," the voice allowed.

"Is there a better answer?" Perri asked.

Silence.

"You have no name," Quee Lee pressed.

The silence continued, and then suddenly, an explanation was offered. "I don't wear any name worth repeating. But I do have an identity. A self. With my own history and limitations as well as a wealth of possibilities, most of which will never come to pass."

They waited.

The voice continued. "What I happen to be is a government official, one of the harmless and noble followers of rules. But when necessary, I can become a brazen, fearless warrior. Except when my best choice is to be a coward, in which case I can flee any threat with determination and remarkable skill. Yet in most circumstances, I am just an official: The loyal servant to any exceptionally fine cause."

"Which cause?" both humans asked.

"In service to the galactic union," the entity replied. "That is my defining role . . . a role which I have played successfully for the last three hundred and seven million years, by your arbitrary and self-centered count."

Human hands squeezed, relaxed.

Quee Lee took it upon herself to confess, "I'm sorry. But we don't entirely believe you."

"You claim you were born on the Earth. Is that true, my dear?"

She hesitated.

"'Earth.' Your home planet carries a simple utterance. Am I right?"

She said, "Yes."

"I happen to know your small world. But when I made my visit, the stars were completely unaware of that self-given name."

"And what do you know about the Earth?" Perri asked.

"Actually, quite a lot," their companion promised. Then once again, it fell into a long, long silence.

5

Separately, Quee Lee and Perri had come to identical conclusions: The voice was rhythmic and deep, not just easy to listen to but impossible to ignore. Every word was delivered with clarity, like the voice of a highly trained actor. But woven through that perfection were hints of breathing and little clicks of tongues or lips, and once in a great while, a nebulous sound that would leak from the mouth or nostrils . . . or some other orifice hiding in the darkness. Whatever was speaking to them was slightly taller than their ears, and their best guess was that the creature was sitting on a lump of hyperfiber less than three meters from them. There was mass behind the voice. Sometimes a limb moved, or maybe the body itself. Perhaps they heard the creak of its carapace or the complaining of stiff leathery clothes, or maybe a tendril was twisting back against itself. Unless there was no sound except what the two humans imagined they could hear out in the unfathomable blackness.

As far as they could determine, their nameless companion was alone. There wasn't any other presence, or a whisper of a second voice. Somehow the creature had slipped into their camp, perhaps even before the lights died, and neither one of them had perceived anything out of the ordinary.

Or maybe there was nothing but the voice.

Sound. Or a set of elaborate sounds, contrived for effect and existing only as so much noise produced by nothing but the unlit air or the fierce motions of individual atoms.

Somebody could be playing an elaborate joke on the two of them. Perri had many clever friends. A few of them might have worked together, going to the trouble to bring him and Quee Lee into this empty hole, snatching them up in some game that would continue until the fun was exhausted and the lights returned. Quee Lee could envision just that kind of trick: One moment, a mysterious voice. And then just as suddenly, a thousand good friends would be standing around them, congratulating the married pair for some minor anniversary.

"Is this a special occasion?" Quee Lee asked herself.

That route seemed lucrative. She smiled, and the nervousness in her body began to drain away. How many months and years of work had gone into this silly joke? But she had seen through all of the cleverness, and she even considered a preemptive shout and laugh, perhaps throwing out the names of the likely conspirators.

Meanwhile the creature continued to explain what might not be real. "My preferred method of travel is to move alone, and always by the most invisible means. This is standard behavior for officials in my station. We will finish one task in some portion of the Union, and that success brings another task to bear. Since news travels slowly across the galaxy, entities like ourselves are granted considerable freedom of action. No other organization is confident enough to tolerate such power in their agents."

"What kind of tasks?" Perri asked.

"Would you like an example?"

"Please."

"I am thinking of a warehouse that I had built and stocked—a hidden warehouse in an undisclosed location. And in the very next moment, I was dispatched to my next critical mission."

"A warehouse," said Perri.

"Not a romantic word, I grant you. But it was, and is, a vast, invisible facility full of rare and valuable items. I have never returned to the site, but it most likely remains locked and unseen today. Idle but always at the ready. Waiting for that critical, well-imagined age when its contents help with some great, good effort. But that is the Union's way: We have an elaborate structure, robust and overlapping, enduring and invincibly patient; which is only natural, since we are the oldest, most powerful political entity within this galaxy."

"The Union," Perri said dubiously.

"Yes."

"I thought you didn't approve of names."

"I offer it because you expect some kind of label. But like any contrivance, 'the Union' doesn't truly fit what is real." A smug, superior tone had taken hold, but it was difficult for the audience to take offense. After all, this was just a voice in the night, and who could say what was true and what was sane?

"Simply stated, my Union is a collection of entities and beliefs, memes and advanced tools, that have been joined together in a common cause. And what you call the Milky Way happens to be our most important possession—the central state inside a vast, ancient empire."

"No," Perri said. "No."

Silence.

Quee Lee felt her husband's tension. Leaning forward, she told their companion, "There are no empires."

A long black silence held sway, and then came a sound not unlike the creak of a joint needing oil.

"Many, many species have tried to build empires," she continued, naming a few candidates to prove her knowledge of the subject. "The galaxy's first five sentient races accomplished the most, but they didn't do much. The galaxy is enormous. Its planets are too diverse and far too numerous to be ruled by a thousand governments, and star travel has always been a slow, dangerous business. When one species rises, it gains control over only a very limited region. Measure the history of empires against the life stories of suns and worlds, and even the most enduring régime is temporary and tiny."

She concluded by saying, "No one authority has ever controlled any substantial portion of the galaxy."

"I applaud that generous sense of doubt," said the stranger. "May I ask, my dear? What are you?"

"What do you mean?"

"By blood, I think you must be Chinese. Am I right?"

"Mostly, yes," she said.

"And the city of your birth?"

"Hong Kong," she whispered.

"Hong Kong, yes. A place I know, yes. Of course you understand that your China was a great empire, and more than once. And as I recall from my studies of long-ago Earth, there was a period—a brief but not unimportant time—when the port of Hong Kong belonged to the greatest empire ever to exist on your little world. A minor green island sitting in a cold distant sea called itself Great Britain, and with its steam-driven fleets, it somehow managed to hang its flag above a fat fraction of the world's population."

"I know about Britain," she said.

"Now tell me this," their companion continued. "An old rickshaw driver plies his trade on the narrow Hong Kong streets. Does that lowly man care who happens to serve as governor of his home city? Does it matter to him if the fellow on top happens to have yellow hair, or is a Mongol born on the plains of Asia, or even a Han Chinese who is a third-cousin to him?"

"No," she said. "He probably doesn't think much about those matters."

"And what about the Hindu peasant who struggles to feed himself and his family from a patch of land downstream from Everest . . . the ruler of a farm that has never even once fallen under the indifferent gaze of the pale Northern man who works inside a distant government building? Does that farmer concern himself with the man who signs a long list of decrees and then dies quietly of malaria? And does he care at all about the gentleman who comes to replace that dead civil servant . . . another

Northern man who bravely signs more unread decrees before he dies of cholera?"

Quee Lee said nothing.

"Consider the Mayan lady nursing her daughter in Belize, or the Maori cattle herder in Kenya who happens to be the tall strong lord to his herd. Do they learn the English language? Can they even recognize their rulers' alphabet? And then there squats the Aboriginal hunter sucking the precious juice out of an emu egg. Is he even aware that fleets of enormous coal-fired ships are landing and then leaving from his coast each and every day?

"Each of these souls is busy, embroiled in rich and complex, if painfully brief lives. Within the British Empire, hundreds of millions of citizens go about their daily adventures. The flavor of each existence is nearly changeless. Taxes and small blessings come from on-high, but these trappings accomplish little, regardless which power happens to be flying the flags. A peasant's story is usually the same as his forefathers' stories, and if the peasant's children survive, they will inherit that same stubborn, almost ageless narrative."

Neither human spoke.

"Do these little people ever think of that distant green island?"

"I wouldn't be surprised if they didn't," Quee Lee allowed.

"But if they do think of Britain," the stranger began.

"What then?" Perri prompted.

"Would they love the Empire for its justice, order, and the rare peace that it brings to the human world?"

Neither of them responded.

"Of course they do not. What you do not know, you cannot love or despise. This is true for every life that has walked two moments of time. So long as the lives of these peasants remain small and steady, hating the British is not an option."

The voice paused, and what might have been a deep breath could be heard. "Make no mistake—I am not claiming that these are unsophisticated souls. They are far from simple, in fact. But their lives are confined. By necessity, the obvious and immediate are what matter to them. And the colors and shape of today's flag could not have less meaning."

"Suppose we agree," said Perri. "We accept your premise: For humans, empires tended to be big, distant machines."

"As it is for most species," was the reply.

In the dark, Quee Lee and her husband nodded.

"But I don't agree with that word 'big'," the stranger continued. "I believe that even the greatest empire, at the height of its powers, remains vanishingly small. To the brink of invisible, even."

"I don't understand," said Quee Lee.

"Let me remind you of this: Several million whales swam in your world's little ocean. They were great beasts possessing language and old cultures. But did even one species of cetaceans bow to the British flag? And what about the tiger eating venison on the Punjab? Did he dream of the homely human queen? And what role did the ants and beetles, termites and butterflies play in the world? They did nothing for Britannia, I would argue . . . and Britannia had no place in their relentless little minds."

Perri tried to laugh.

Quee Lee could think of nothing useful to say.

"The trouble," the voice began. Then it paused, perhaps reconsidering its choice of words. "Your mistake," it continued, "is both inevitable and comforting, and it is very difficult to escape. What you assume is that the names in history are important. Because you are smart, educated minds, you have taught yourselves much about your own past. But even the most famous name is lost among the trillions of nameless souls. And every empire that you think of when the subject arises . . . every political entity, no matter how impermanent and trivial . . . was visible only because it wasted its limited energies making certain that its name would outlive both its accomplishments and its crimes."

"Maybe so," Quee Lee allowed.

"Names," the voice repeated. "The worlds you know wear that unifying trait. The name brings with it a sense of purpose and a handle for its recorded history. Attached to one or a thousand words waits some center of trade, a nucleus of science, and you mistakenly believe that the most famous names mark the hubs of your great cosmopolitan galaxy."

Perri squeezed his wife's hand, fighting the temptation to speak.

"But the bulk of the galaxy . . . its asteroids and dust motes, sunless bodies and dark corners without number . . . those are the features that truly matter."

"Matter to whom?" Quee Lee asked.

"To the weaver ants and lowly fish, of course. The beetles and singing whales, and our rickshaw driver who knows the twisting streets of Hong Kong better than any Chinese emperor or British civil servant. Nameless citizens are those with substance, my dear." Something creaked, as if their companion shifted its weight, and the voice drifted slightly to one side. "I will confess that my empire is like all the others, only more so. The Union that I love and that I have served selflessly for eons is vast and ancient. But where England made maps and gave every corner its own label, my Union has wisely built itself upon places unknown."

Husband and wife contemplated that peculiar boast.

Then Quee Lee recalled an earlier thread. "You have visited the Earth, you claimed."

"I did once, yes."

"Was this before or after your invisible warehouse?"

"Afterwards, as it happens. Not long after."

"You mentioned receiving a new mission," Perri coaxed.

"Which leads indirectly to an interesting story." The next sound was soft, contented. "My orders arrived by a usual route. Whispered and deeply coded, the instructions from my superiors that were designed to resemble nothing but a smeared flicker of light thrown out from a distant laser array." The words were strung together with what felt like a grin. "Alone, I left my previous post. Alone, I rode inside a tiny vehicle meant to resemble a shard of old comet, using a simple ion motor to boost my velocity to where my voyage took slightly less than forty centuries—"

"By our arbitrary and self-centered count," said Perri.

"Which is not such a very long time." Those words were ordinary and matter-of-fact. Yet somehow the sound of them—their clarity and decidedly slow pace—conveyed long reaches of time and unbounded patience. "I traveled until I came to a nameless world. There was one ocean and several continents. The forests were green, the skies blue with white watery clouds. To fulfill the demands of my new mission, I selected an island not far from the world's largest continent: A young volcanic island where the local inhabitants built boats driven by oars and square sails, and they put up houses of wood and stone and planted half-wild crops in the fertile black soil. And their moments of free time were filled with the heartfelt worship of their moon and sun—the two bodies that ruled a sky that they would never truly understand."

"Was this the Earth?" asked Quee Lee.

There was a pause, and inside the darkness, motion.

And then the voice told them, "When these particular events occurred, my dear, there was no planet yet called 'the Earth'."

Quee Lee wrapped both hands around her husband's arm.

"Remember this," the voice continued. "The Union is the only power of consequence. And the Union holds its interest only in those dark realms that appear on no worthwhile map."

6

"A king happened to rule that warm, sun-washed island. He was simple and rather old, and I was tempted to kill him in some grand public fashion before taking his throne for myself. Yet my study of his species and its superstitions showed me a less bloody avenue. The king's youngest wife was pregnant, but the child would be stillborn. It was a simple matter to replace that failed infant and then bury what was Me inside healthy native flesh. Once born, I proved to the kingdom that their new prince was special. I was a lanky boy, physically beautiful, endowed with an unnatural strength and the gentle grace of wild birds. I didn't merely walk at an early age, I danced. And with a bold musical voice, I spoke endlessly on every possible subject, people fighting to kneel close to me, desperate to hear whatever marvel I offered next.

"The wise old women of my kingdom decided that I must be a god's child as much as a man's. Like a god's child, I predicted the weather and the little quakes that often rattled the island. I boasted that I could see far into the skies and over the horizon, and to prove my brave words, I promised that a boat full of strangers would soon drift past our island.

"My prediction was made in the morning, and by evening, I was proved right. The lost trireme was filled with traders or pirates. On a world such as that, what is the difference between those two professions? Whatever their intentions, my people were waiting for them, and after suitable introductions, I ordered the strangers murdered and their possessions divided equally among the general populace."

The voice paused.

In the dark, Quee Lee leaned hard against her husband.

And the story continued. "I was almost grown when that little old king stood before his people and named his heir. Two of my brothers were insulted, but I had anticipated their clumsy attempts at revenge. In a duel with bronze swords, I removed the head of the more popular son. Then I turned my back, allowing my second brother to run his spear through my chest—a moment used to prove that I was, as my people had always suspected, immortal.

"With my two hands, I yanked the spear from my heart.

"In anguish, my foe flung himself off one of our island's high cliffs.

"'Someday I will follow my brothers into the Afterlife,' I promised the citizens. 'But for the rest of your days, I will remain with you, and together we shall do the work of the gods.'

"And that was the moment, at long last, when the heart of my mission finally began."

Their companion paused.

"Are you going to explain your mission?" Perri asked.

"Hints and teases. I will share exactly what is necessary to explain myself, or at least I will give you the illusion of insights, placing you where your imaginations can fill in the unnamed reaches."

"About these natives," Quee Lee began. "Your people . . . what did they look like?"

Quietly and perhaps with a touch of affection, the voice explained, "They were bipedal, as you are. And they had your general height and mass, hands and glands. Like you, they presented hairless flesh to the world, except upon their faces and scalps and in their private corners. As a rule, most were dirty and drab, and on that particular island, their narrow culture reached back only a few generations. But their species had potential. Following ordinary pathways, natural selection had given them graceful fingers and an evolving language, busy minds and a compelling sense of tribe. In those following years, I showed my people how to increase the yields and quality of their crops. I taught them how to purify their water, how to carve and lift gigantic stones, and I helped them build superior ships that could chase the fat fish and slow leviathans that could never hide from my godly eyes. Then in the shadow of their smoldering volcano, I laid out a spacious palace surrounded by solid homes and wide avenues, and for three generations, my devoted followers built the finest city their species had ever known."

Once again, the voice ceased. But the silence was neither empty nor unimportant, accenting a sense of time crossed with clear purpose. Then a smooth laugh came, and their companion remarked, "If the two of you were dropped into similar circumstances, you would accomplish most if not all of my tricks. You are borderline immortals. Spears through your hearts would be nuisances at day's end. Armed with the knowledge common to your happy lives, you could visit some nameless world and convince its residents that you were divine, and in the next breath, you could call for whatever riches and little pleasures that your worshippers might scratch together for you.

"But what pleasures me is serving the Union.

"What I wanted . . . what my orders demanded from this one place, inside this single moment . . . was the construction of a significant machine, a device that would demand the full focus of a half-born civilization . . . "

"What machine?" asked Perri.

"If it proves important to know that, then I will tell you."

But Perri couldn't accept that evasive answer. "How many people lived in your city? Five thousand? Fifty thousand? I don't know what you were building, granted. But you're implying advanced technologies, and I'd have to guess that you'd need a lot more hands and minds than you would ever find on a tiny island in the middle of the sea . . . "

The first answer was prolonged silence.

Then the sharp creak of a limb or cold leather could be heard, and with quiet fury, the entity said, "You have listened carefully enough, sir. Pay strict attention to everything that I tell you."

"Remind me what you said," Perri said.

Another silence ended with what might have been a sigh. "I sat on my throne for seventy summers and several months," said the voice. "Then one day, I abruptly announced that my city was failing me. With a wave of my fist, I told my followers that they were not truly devoted, and they were not sufficiently thankful for my wise counsel, and I was contemplating the complete obliteration of their island-nation.

"With the next sunrise, the great volcano erupted. The rich rocky earth split wide. Ash was coughed into the blackened sky, and lava flowed into the boiling sea, and boulders as big as homes were dropped onto the cowering, inadequate heads around me. Then I pretended a sudden change of mind. I showed pity, even empathy. On the following day, after the dead were buried and the damage assessed, I dressed in a feathered robe and walked to the summit where I told the mountain to sleep again—which it would have done on its own, since the eruption had run its course. But a single moment of theatre erased the last shreds of doubt. Again, I had convinced my followers that I was supreme. You could not hear one muttered complaint about me, or doubts about my powers, or the slightest question concerning each of my past decisions.

"That seamless devotion was necessary.

"You see, the eruption was not a random event. And I didn't make the mountain tremble and belch just to scare the local souls.

"Even as I sat on my throne, I had been working. My assignment demanded the kinds of energy generated by top-grade fusion reactors. But reactors produce signatures visible at a great distance. Neutrinos are difficult to shield, and I didn't want prying eyes to notice my industrial plant. So instead of a reactor, I employed the lake of magma directly beneath our feet, creating an inefficient but enormous geothermal plant. When that plant awoke—when the first seawater poured down the pipes and into the reaction vessels—my island was shoved upwards like a balloon inflating. Watchful eyes noticed that every tide pool was suddenly baking in the sun. Our island was significantly taller, and a thousand hot springs flowed out of the high crevices, and the black ground was itself warm to the touch.

"On that good day, I ordered every woman of breeding age to come to the palace, to arrive with the evening bell, and I welcomed each of them individually, giving them a feast and plenty to drink, as well as jewelry and robes finer than anything they had known. Then to this nervous, worshipful gathering, I announced that each of them was carrying a child now.

"I promised my wives untroubled pregnancies and healthy, superior babies.

"Both promises came true.

"And you are correct, Perri. Sir. Fifty thousand followers would never have been enough. No natural species can bring the mental capacity demanded by this kind of delicate, highly technical work. So I enlarged the natives' craniums and restructured their neural networks, flinging them across fifty thousand generations of natural selection. Then I served as the children's only teacher. I taught them what they needed to know about the high sciences, and I made them experts in engineering, all while carefully preparing my kingdom for the next change."

Perri said, "Wait."

In the dark, Quee Lee felt her husband's body shifting. She recognized his excitement and interest, his emotions mirroring her own.

Again, he said, "Wait."

"Yes?"

"I've been thinking about what you've told us."

"Good."

"Where your logic leads . . . "

Silence.

"If you were willing to rewrite the biology of one species," Perri said, "you could just as well reshape others too."

"Ants?" Quee Lee blurted. "Were you a god to the island's ants?"

"Ants have no need for gods," the voice corrected. "They demand nothing but a queen blessed with spectacular fertility. But you've seen my logic, yes. You are paying attention. But then again, I knew that the two of you would prove a worthy audience."

Some small object clattered against hyperfiber—a clear, almost bell-like sound expanding and diminishing inside the gigantic room.

The voice returned. "By the time my first grandchildren were born, the ocean around my island was lit from below. Which was only reasonable, since the city above was just one portion of a much greater community—a nation numbering in the billions. My people supplied the genius, but to serve them, I had built a multitude of obedient minds trained for narrow, exceptionally difficult tasks. A full century of careful preparation had made me ready to begin the construction of a single mechanical wonder.

"Which was the moment, I should add, when all of my many troubles began . . . "

7

In the smothering blackness, Quee Lee held her husband by an arm, by his waist, and then she twisted her body in a particular way, inviting a groping hand, not caring in the least that the nameless entity might be able to perceive their timeless, much-cherished intimacies.

Perri started to ask the obvious question: "What troubles?"

But the voice interrupted. Louder than before, it said, "Human beings are an extraordinarily fortunate species. Wouldn't you agree?"

"I feel lucky," Quee Lee said.

But Perri guessed, "You're talking about something specific. Aren't you?"

"Tell me your opinion," the voice said. "Is this vessel a true blessing for you and yours?"

"You mean the Great Ship," she said.

"I mean the machine that surrounds us," it said. "The name itself has zero significance."

Perri laughed. "Well, I know at least a thousand other species that could have found it first. They were more powerful, more numerous, and far older than we are. All of them should have grabbed it up before we ever knew it existed."

"It is a magical machine," Quee Lee offered.

The entity made a few soft, agreeable noises. "Our galaxy has stubbornly refused to be dominated by any single species. But humans stumbled across this prize, claimed it first, and have held on to it since. A single possession has lifted the human animal into an exceptionally rare position. Your best captains have no choice but to thank the stars and Providence for this glorious honor. Today, your artisans and scientists are free to drink in the wisdom of the galaxy. Your wealthiest citizens can make this long journey in safety, sharing their air with the royalty of a hundred thousand worlds. But I think your greatest success rises from the hungriest, bravest souls among you.

"Each year, on average, seventeen-and-a-third colonial vessels push away from your ports. How many of your willing cousins are dropped to the surface of wild worlds and lucrative asteroids? How many homes and shops are being erected, new societies sprouting up in your wake? Now multiply those impressive numbers by the hundreds of thousands of years that you plan to invest in this circumnavigation of the galaxy. The totals are staggering. No society or species or even any compilation of cooperative souls has enjoyed the human advantage, and there is no reason to believe it will happen again.

"And consider this: How many species buy your berths? Thousands arrive each year, and in trade for a safe journey, they surrender every local map, cultural experiences and open-ended promises of help. That's why each of your new colonies has a respectable, enviable chance of survival. And that's why your species is hugging a small but respectable probability of dominating the richest portions of the galaxy.

"So now I ask you: When will this galaxy of ours become known everywhere and to every species as 'the Milky Way'?

"In other words, when will this wilderness become your possession?"

Considering that possibility, the humans couldn't help but smile.

But then Quee Lee sighed and shook her head, saying, "Never. Is that the answer you want?"

The voice turned quiet again, nearly whispering as it explained, "That kind of success shall never happen. No, never. Even in your blessed circumstances, this little whirlpool of creation remains too vast and far too complex for any species to dominate. Your makeshift empire is doomed at its birth. The best result that you might achieve—and even this is an unlikely future—is for this machine to complete its full circuit of the galaxy without being stolen from you, and for you to leave scattered in your wake twenty million human worlds. But what are twenty million names against those trillions of rocks big enough to be called planets? I promise that no matter its blessings, each one of your colonies will struggle. It is inevitable. Your species is relatively late on the scene. Easy rich worlds are scarce and typically walked by someone else. By the minute, your galaxy grows older. And with every breath, the sky grows more crowded. New species are evolving, and thinking machines are designing their next generations, and almost everything that lives strives hard to live forever, or nearly so."

The smiles had vanished.

For a long moment, neither human spoke.

Then Quee Lee suggested, "Maybe our empire should stop naming our worlds. If we emulated your Union  .  .  . if human beings decided to rule the dark and empty and the unmapped—"

"No," the voice interrupted.

Then with a palpable scorn, it added, "I will share with you one common principle known by every true empire. Whether you are British or Mongolian, Roman or American: You may never, ever allow a competing empire to sprout within your sacred borders.

"My Union stands alone.

"Never forget that.

"And when the inevitable future arrives  .  .  . when the final star burns out and the universe pulls itself into a great empty cold  .  .  . my Union will persist, and it will thrive, living happily on this galaxy's black bones: A force as near to Always as that word shall ever allow."

## 8

The humans felt chastened and a little angry, powerless to respond yet nonetheless intrigued by the stark implications. They held one another in ways that spoke—the touch of fingers, the pressure of a fat-clad knee, and the shared tastes of expelled air carrying odors that could only come from Perri, and only come from Quee Lee.

The voice returned, quietly mentioning, "My mission to the blue world had begun so easily, with much promise. Yet now its nature changed. In relatively quick succession, three problems emerged, each capable of threatening the project and my sterling reputation."

A thoughtful pause ended with a brief, disgusted sound.

"Remember the pirates mentioned before? The seafarers whom I let my people kill? They had floated out from the main continent, and with another hundred years of experience, their descendants were eager to return. That rocky green wilderness still lay over the horizon, but now it was speckled with dirty cities and fledging nations. Unlike my little island, those far places had always enjoyed culture and a deep history, every corner of their rich landscape adorned with some important little name.

"Bronze-and-brick technology was at work. Kings and educated minds were beginning to piece together the first, most obvious meanings of the universe. The largest triremes could wander far from land, and their captains knew how to navigate by the stars and moon. That those captains would try to visit my island was inevitable, which is why I took precautions. The leviathans patrolling my bright waters were instructed to scare off every explorer, and should fear not work, they were entitled to crush the wooden hulls and drown those stubborn crews.

"A few ships were sunk off our coast.

"The occasional corpse washed up on shore, swollen by rot and chewed upon by curious or vengeful mouths.

"One of the dead had been a scientist and scholar, and even as he drowned, he managed to grab hold of his life's work—a long roll of skin covered with dense writing and delicate sketches.

"The body was looted, and the book eventually found its way into the appreciative hands of one of my grandchildren.

"The island's original natives could never have understood the intense black scribbling, but my grandchild was more than intelligent and highly creative, he was also curious and unabashedly loyal to me. Using code-breaking algorithms, he taught himself the dead man's language. In his spare moments, he managed to translate the text in full. His purpose, it seems, was to make me proud of his genius. He was certainly thrilled of his own accomplishment, which was why he shared what he had learned with close friends and lovers. Then he walked to the palace and kneeled before my throne, presenting both the artifact and his translation for my honest appraisal.

"'They speak of us,' the young man reported. 'The rest of our world believes we are gods or the angels of gods or we have descended from the stars. They have convinced themselves that if they defeat the sea monsters and outsmart the currents, they can row themselves into our harbor and stand among us, and they will be heroes in the gods' eyes. And for their extraordinary bravery, we will award them with the secrets of All . . . '"

A brief pause.

"I'll ask this question again," said Perri. "This species . . . were they human . . . ?"

A sound came, soft but perhaps disgusted.

"Atlantis," Quee Lee whispered. "Is that this story?"

"My guess exactly," said Perri, hugging her until her ribs ached. Then he said the ancient name for himself, in the appropriate dead language.

"Once again, you have forgotten: The galaxy had no name for that world, much less for that long-ago island. But I won't stop you from imagining your Earth and its legendary lands, and I won't fight the labels that help you follow what I happen to say."

In the darkness, Perri squeezed his wife again, and she pushed her mouth into his ear, saying with relish, "It must be."

They had decided, together.

It was Atlantis.

"My grandchildren," the voice continued. "Several generations had passed since the first of them were born, and I should confess to one inevitable event. I have always taken lovers from the locals. A lover supplies information and oftentimes can be a tool for good methodical management. Bedding those who are most beautiful and intriguing is a natural consequence of my station. But one of those grandchildren proved more irresistible than usual. She was a young woman, as it happened. Though it just as likely could have been a man . . .

"By the standards of her species, she was physically small and exceptionally lovely.

"Among her gifted peers, she was considered brilliant and singularly blessed. The finest of the fine . . .

"That I took her into my bed was natural. That she retained her virginity until that night only enhanced her reputation with her people, and to a degree, with me. The bloodied sheet was hung from the palace wall for a full day, and when she appeared again in public, cheers made her stand tall as a queen—the center of attention smiling at her appreciative world.

"I was very fond of that little creature.

"As a lover, she was fearless and caring, bold and yet compliant too. And when we were not making love, she would ask me smart little questions about all matters of science and engineering. Her particular expertise involved the heart of the device that we were building together. There were puzzles to work through, matters that I didn't understand fully myself. I had never built such an object, you see. That's why the brilliant grandchildren were critical. But even though she understood many of the ideas behind our work, she always wanted to know more, and if possible, hold what she knew more deeply.

"Charming and crafty, she was, and I let myself be fooled. I confessed that there were subjects that could never, ever be discussed with her people. 'You will repeat none of this again,' I warned. 'Not even to the wind.'

"She promised to remain mute.

"Then I explained to her the true shape of the galaxy, and its great age, and I told the violent history of our glorious universe.

"And yes, there were moments when I mentioned the Union and my small, critical role within it.

"Then because she seemed so interested in the subject of Me, I confessed my age and gave a brief thorough accounting of past missions as well as some of the tricks that I was capable of."

The voice fell away.

In the blackness, a body stretched until the bones or carapace creaked, a sharp dry crack coming at the end.

"That lover was my second challenge," said the voice. "Although at that particular moment, I didn't appreciate the danger."

Quee Lee leaned away from Perri, begging her dark-adapted eyes to find any trace of wayward light. If she could just make out the creature that was sitting so close to them—

No. Nothing.

"One of our shared nights never seemed to end," said the voice. "Normal fatigues don't trouble me, but my lover, no matter how much improved genetically, needed sleep. She lived for dreams. Yet the girl somehow resisted every urge to close her lovely dark eyes. Twice in the dark, she managed to surprise me with tricks she had never shown before. I was appreciative. How could I not be? But then as the full moon set and the bright summer sun began to rise, she whispered, 'I was wondering my lord . . . about something else . . .'

"'What?' I asked.

"'But maybe I shouldn't,' she conceded.

"'Ask me anything,' I said, never voicing the obvious possibility that I wouldn't reply, or that I might simply lie.

"With a sleepy slow voice, my lover confessed, 'I am curious. When you speak of old missions, you usually seem to be out between the stars, or huddled beside some dying star, or cloaked inside a storm cloud of interstellar dust . . .'

"I nodded, and for a moment, she seemed to drop into sleep.

"But then she roused herself with a gasp, straightening her little body before asking, 'Why come here? Why visit our little world, my lord?'

"'It suits my present mission,' I conceded. 'Your volcano and the sea water are rich with rare elements and useful minerals—'

"'But you have told me this before . . . in other nights, you explained that in the baby days of any solar system, some if not most of the new worlds are flung out into the night. Their oceans freeze. Their atmospheres fall as snow. But radiation keeps their iron cores molten, and volcanoes still bubble up beneath the bitter ice, and a god like you could surely bring temporary life to those unnamed realms . . .'

"I listened to her, perhaps not quite believing just how bright she was.

"Then very quietly, I reminded her, 'Like those cold places, this world possesses no name. As far as the universe is concerned, your home is a random lump of dust and still-simple life forms.'

"For a long while, she stared at me.

"Those beautiful dark eyes . . . I cannot mention those eyes and not feel shame . . . a burning disgrace that keeps me from describing to you just how deep their hold was on me . . .

"But then the eyes closed, and my lover drifted into a rich, much deserved sleep. I thought the matter was finished. I didn't want to entertain any other possibility. And really, what reason did I have to believe that this worshipful little creature was a threat, or even if she was a threat that she could be ever present a genuine danger to the likes of me?

"I covered her with a fine linen sheet.

"Then for the following days and months, and years, nothing changed. No word or incident raised even the tiniest suspicion on my part. My lover was the same to me as she had always been, and I was as pleasant and giving to her and to all of my people.

"And then my third challenge arrived. This danger came from the sky, and even at a great distance, it brought the worst possible trouble. Out on the edge of the solar system was an automated probe. A harum-scarum probe was moving at a small fraction of light-speed. The harum-scarums have always been aggressive in their explorations and colonizations, and now one of their sharp-eyed robots was plunging out of the darkness, threatening to fly past my world while taking note of everything that might bear interest.

"I couldn't allow myself or my good work be seen.

"And sadly, the machines that I had left in orbit couldn't protect me. I needed to leave the island. Wisely, I didn't offer reasons or predict when I would return. As far as my people knew, I would be back among them before the next sunset or the coming full moon. But I begged them to continue our work—the delicate fabrication of a single machine that meant everything to me and to them."

In the dark, the voice dropped into a long airy sigh.

Then quietly, but with an unhealed pain, their companion said, "This was the moment when the rebellion began. And I think you can guess who stood on the silk cushions of my empty throne, whirling a titanium hammer above her head, shouting to the throng, 'It is time to save our world, my friends! To rescue our futures and gain control over our souls!'"

## 9

Emotions lay rich and fresh in the silence, born out of a sadness that could not be forgotten. Or maybe there was only silence, black and seamless, and the misery and burning sense of loss were supplied entirely by the human audience. It was impossible to tell which answer was correct, or if both were a little true. But then the humans heard a limb flex, the invisible body creaking as it shifted, not once but three times in quick succession. When the voice returned, it seemed slower. Each word was delivered alone, and between one word and the next laid a tiny silence, like a cold black mortar pushed between warm red bricks.

"I could have destroyed the automated probe at a distance. I could have used methods that would have made harum-scarum scientists believe that bad luck was responsible. Some random rock, a cosmic hazard that slipped past the machine's various armors. Nothing would seem too unusual about that. But erasing the danger was not the only problem. Harum-scarum probes are relatively common in our galaxy, and if I blithely obliterated them whenever our paths crossed, somebody would eventually see the pattern in my clumsiness.

"No, what I did was rise up into the sky to meet the danger directly.

"Like you, I am the loyal subject to a variety of laws concerning motion and energy. I had to race out into the solar system for a considerable distance, and then with methods that I cannot share, I invisibly changed my trajectory, racing back again, making certain that my momentum carried me close to the probe's vector.

"Together, that machine and I dove into the hot glare of the sun. I studied my opponent while it absorbed images of the two inner worlds. Then we climbed away from the sun, and at a moment when I would escape notice, I drifted closer and touched the machine with a thousand fingers, allowing its giant eyes to do their work even as I changed a small portion of what it could see.

"Together, we passed between the gray moon and my blue-green world.

"And then the danger was finished. The probe turned its attentions to the little red world coming next, and with my chore accomplished, I glanced backward, examining my home with my own considerable eyes.

"The rebellion was well underway.

"Twenty different security systems had been fooled, or by various means disabled. And now my clever little grandchildren had full control over their land and the ocean around them.

"Feigning loyalty, they had continued building the machine.

"Pretending subservience, most of them moved through their lives in the expected ways. But others openly prayed that I was dead, even while they planned my murder should I return. And still others pretended to die, their names removed from the city's rosters, freeing them to journey over to the mainland, taking with them tools and skills as well as a story that would inspire the primitive souls they would find waiting there.

"I was furious.

"In ways quite rare to me, I felt the powerful, consuming need for revenge.

"But motion and energy still held sway. I could not roar home in the next instant, and if I didn't wish to be noticed by the probe beside me, I would have to be patient enough to obey my original plan.

"Easing away from the probe consumed many days.

"I spent another month pushing against the universe, slowing myself to a near-halt before turning and plunging back into the brilliant sunshine.

"By then, the harum-scarum eyes were distant. But if the probe happened to glance back at my world, it might have noticed an island exploding before its time, a dark cloud spreading while a deep bubbling caldera defined the island's grave. But I resisted that instinctive violence.

Destroying my own work would have been an unacceptable cost, and worse, it would have been graceless.

"And of course I could have remotely shut down the entire operation, protecting my investment from malicious hands. But that meant new risks as well as long, embarrassing delays.

"Instead, I decided to dance with complete disaster, but aiming for total success."

After those words, a long pause seemed necessary.

Finally, Perri said, "You won't tell us. I know. But we would appreciate to know what the stakes were."

"I would like to know," Quee Lee said.

"What exactly you were building?" her husband pressed.

"Britannia," the voice replied. "Like any empire worth its salt . . . " A weak laugh washed over them. "How can you separate a true empire from all of the little pretenders? What did the British possess that their vanquished opponents lacked? Why were those Northern men superior to the tropical peasants in the field and the dogs in the street?

"Any good empire holds at least one skill that is its own.

"The Greeks had their highly-trained hoplites and several unique if contradictory forms of government. The Chinese had the most enduring civil services ever seen on your world. Romans were possessed by their engineering and brutal legions. And so long as British boats owned the seas, their power was accepted by a world that saw no option but bow in their mighty presence.

"An empire is always smarter than its competition.

"And my Union is far, far smarter than the human species. Or any other species you can name, for that matter.

"The device I was building . . . ? Well, I will tell you that it was a single component meant to be set inside a much larger machine. And that it was extremely rare and very valuable, embodying sciences that you have never mastered. Once assembled, the full apparatus can wield principles that your most brilliant minds might recognize as possible, but only that. The apparatus is magic. It is gorgeous. It was, and is, worth every cost."

A brief pause ended with Quee Lee's voice.

"So you returned to the Earth," she said. "To Thera, or Atlantis. Although it wore different names then, I suppose."

"Whatever the world, whatever the island," said the voice. "Yes, I returned, yes. To find my grandchildren engaged in an artful rebellion."

There was a long, contemplative pause.

Finally Perri asked, "And what happened then?"

"Worth every cost," the entity said once again. "I speak without doubts, telling you what I did that day. And for that matter, what I would do on this day, in an instant, if I saw any threat to my enduring Union.

"I would protect what I love."

## 10

Until that moment, the voice had been just so much noise. It was interesting and entertaining noise, the words intriguing if not completely believable. The narrative was compelling enough for the humans to feel empathy for the creatures that could well have been their own ancestors. Every portion of the disjointed tale deserved their attention as they tried to predict what would happen next and next after that; but there was no moment when they stopped wondering what kind of body was connected to the voice. Until then, that was the central question that kept begging to be answered.

Then they heard the words, "My enduring Union," and that simple utterance changed everything.

Wrapped around a bald statement was stiff, unyielding emotion. Quee Lee and Perri heard the threat, the promise, the conviction and purpose— and they instantly believed what they heard. Now both of them were considering what it would mean if this story, unlikely as it seemed, was in some fashion or another true. And that was when the formless entity beside them—mysterious and unknowable, bristly and proud—became markedly less interesting than the grim bit of history it was sharing with them now.

Human hands grabbed one another.

Each lover felt the other's body bracing for whatever came next.

Another silence was what the voice decided to offer. And then from the perfect darkness came a sound not unlike a tongue or two licking against lips threatening to grow dry.

Quee Lee and Perri had been married for tens of thousands of years. But as long as that might seem, marriage was infinitely older than their single relationship. And there were species that took intimacy to higher levels than humans could manage. The Janusians, for instance: Their little husbands rooted into the body of female hosts, literally joining into One. Yet among the human animals, Quee Lee and Perri were famous. Their relationship had evolved gradually into a complex and robust, enduring and very nearly impossible to define melange. There were a few humans who spent more time together than the two of them. Unlikely as it seemed, some married souls enjoyed their physical lives even more than these two managed. But no one could believe that any other human pair, on the Ship and perhaps anywhere else in the universe, was emotionally closer than that ancient Earth-born lady and her boyish life-mate.

At some point, everybody tried to tease them.

The happy couple generally welcomed good-natured barbs and admiring glances. But when asked to explain their success—when some friend of a friend insisted on advice for less-perfect relationships—they grew testy and impatient, even a little defensive. The truth was that they were helpless to define their relationship. A marriage was always larger than its participants, and what they possessed here was as mysterious and unlikely to them as it seemed to distant eyes. They couldn't understand why they had drawn so closely together. They didn't see why life had not yet found the means to yank them apart. But they were undeniably intimate and deeply dependent, up to the point where Quee Lee and Perri could never imagine being separated from one another in any lasting, hellish way.

"Can you read each other's thoughts?" people wanted to know.

Not at all, no.

"But it seems you can," some maintained. "The way you know what each other wants, what you're about to say and do—"

Did they do that?

"There's a trick at work," a few declared. "Dedicated nexuses let your minds share thoughts and feelings. Is that what you're doing right now . . . ?"

Not even a little. In fact, they made a point of avoiding mechanical shortcuts to authentic tongue-and-expression conversation.

Eventually somebody would ask, "When have you felt closest?"

What did that mean? Close how . . . ?

"What was the day—the incident—when you felt as if you were a single brain shared by two independent bodies . . . ?"

There were thousands of stories worthy of repetition, each able to satisfy the audience if not themselves. Several dozen favorites had become minor legends among the passengers. But the best answer was never offered, not even to the closest, dearest friends. It happened on that particular evening as they sat inside the perfect darkness, deep within the unmapped Vermiculate, immersed in the most isolated corner yet discovered within the Great Ship. That proud and stern and eternal voice promised them that it would do anything to protect what it loved, which was the Union; and for a singular moment, Quee Lee and Perri were one irreducible soul.

Now they finally believed the unlikely story.

Unseen tongues licked at dry lips, and the two lovers held each other with strong arms, sharing of flurry thoughts, speaking with nothing but the touch of fingers, the sound of breathing, the push of heavy breasts and the telltale flinch of a nervous penis.

"There is a Union," they decided together. "It is real."

And in the next moment, it occurred to them that the Union's loyal servant would never do anything that did not, in small ways or great, help its ageless cause.

Quee Lee pressed hard against her husband, and she shivered, and just before the voice spoke again, she whispered an obvious possibility into her husband's ear and skull:

"Our friend is on a mission! Now!"

And in the next instant, with thrilled horror, both of them thought, "It's telling us the story for a reason  .  .  . and we are the mission!"

## 11

With a sense of deeply buried pain, or at least an old, much-practiced anger, the voice continued.

"At last, I returned to the island. At last, I touched down in the Sunset Plaza, on an ellipse of crimson glass brick reserved for my shuttle and my immortal body. The plaza was flanked by tall apartment buildings buried beneath masses of vines—engineered greenery that thrived in the volcanic warmth, producing enough fruit and sweet nuts to feed the residents within. A thousand of my grandchildren quickly gathered around me, while thousands more sneaked looks from behind the curtains of their comfortable little homes. Every face made an effort to smile. Every head dipped in a show of respect—a gesture that I had never demanded from my subjects, that arose long ago on its natural own. Only one important face was missing, but the brave traitors anticipated my first question. Several knelt before me, palms to the sky, and they explained that I had been gone longer than anticipated, and my arrival had proved quite sudden, but yes, my mistress was as happy as anyone could be. In fact, she was waiting for me at the palace, rapidly making herself ready for my pleasures.

"The avenue was lined with pruned trees thriving inside big copper pots and rows of intricate geometric sculptures cut from the black native stone. The smallest citizens barely noticed my passing. They were the ants and fat beetles that I had reinvented for the purpose of little jobs, and unburdened by the demands of awe, they continued cutting down the weeds and disposing of trash. But a crew of enhanced crabs was pulling superconductive cables under the pavement, and when I passed near, they paused long enough to salute me with their elegant pincers—a signal learned from the grandchildren.

"Everybody was working hard to appear worshiping. Everybody wanted to shine with joy. And a few even managed to convince themselves that they were being honest. 'You were gone too long,' several complained, at different moments but always with the same worried, slightly put-upon tone. And then one or two remarked, 'We feared you were lost, that some horrid disaster had claimed you.'

"If that is what they wanted, those voices kept their thoughts hidden.

"Then at the mouth of an alleyway, I noticed a very young grandchild standing in the shadows, waiting for something. Not for me, it seemed . . . but in his stance and attitude, I could see anticipation.

"I paused and asked his name, even though I had already found his face in the public files. He introduced himself, and with a charming little smile mentioned that he had no memory of me. I had left for my errand among the stars while he was still just a toddler.

"He was barely more than that now. I smiled, telling him that it was my pleasure to meet him.

"He mentioned that I looked exactly as he expected, except I wasn't tall enough of course, and then his gaze drifted off toward the island's slumbering volcano.

"'What are you waiting for?' I inquired.

"'For you,' he replied. But before there was any misunderstanding, he added, 'I'm waiting for you to pass, and then I can go about my business.'

"'What is your business?'

"'To walk down to the Sunset Plaza and watch the night come,' he explained.

"'You like the setting sun, do you?'

"The young eyes smiled, and the mouth too. Then a smart little voice said, 'Yes,' and nothing else.

"The bodies surrounding us began to relax.

"With a fond hand, I stroked the boy's thick black hair and kissed him on the nose, and then continued with my triumphant stroll to the palace.

"No one was invited to follow me inside, and no one asked to join me. My shadow passed first through the iron gates and beneath the brass arches and into the grand hall. The air was scented with spice and smoke. The floor and walls and high ceiling were tiled in a fractal pattern, cultured sapphires and diamonds lending accents to an example of mathematical beauty that I have always appreciated. My throne stood at the end of the hall—the oldest object in the palace, gold flourishes and silk laid over my adoptive father's original chair.

"My shadow hesitated, and so did I.

"My grandchildren stood in a crowd outside, waiting for me to vanish.

"Suddenly a great damp shape emerged from a back door, walking on long mechanical legs. The creature was a leviathan whose ancestors had swum the local sea. I had made him smaller while changing his lungs and flesh to where he could thrive in indoors, adeptly serving me with whatever little duty that I might require.

"With a high-pitched warble, he welcomed me home.

"Whatever plots were lurking about, I sensed he was not involved and almost certainly unaware.

"I asked if I had been missed.

"'Always,' he replied with a quick series of clicks.

"'Where is she now?' I inquired.

"'In your quarters, lord.'

"'And has she been faithful to me?'

"'No,' the creature replied, without hesitation. 'I have seen her use her hands and several plastic devices. And once, the edge of a large pillow.'

"'Thank you for your honesty,' I said. 'And good evening to you.'

"No shadow led the way now. Alone, I climbed a long flight of dimly-lit steps and entered a narrow hallway that only seemed endless . . . an illusion lined with tall doors meant to impress and confuse the rare visitor. I walked a short distance and opened what seemed to be a random door. There was only one bedroom inside the palace, and it never occupied the same position twice. I entered through a random wall, and my lover flinched in surprise, starting to pull the sheets over her naked body before realizing it was me, only me.

"Together, we celebrated my return.

"I had been absent even longer than I had anticipated. The young creature that I had left in this bed was noticeably older. A few white hairs and a hundred little erosions marked the natural decline of a creature not born immortal and never told to expect such blessings. But she was just as fierce a lover as always, maybe more so. She insisted on satisfying herself by various means, and whenever my attentions seemed to waver, she would offer encouragements or measured complaints.

"'What kind of god are you?' she teased me once, in the dark. 'Are you going to let this old lady beat you at your game?'

"'I am tempted to lose, yes,' I confessed.

"Perhaps she heard more than one message in those words, because she paused and pulled away from me. Then like a hundred times before, she settled on my chest, legs spread, the smell of her thick and close.

"In a whisper, she mentioned, 'Your journey must have been considerable.'

"'My task was difficult,' I said.

"'We have continued with our work.' She said, 'Our work,' to make certain that I would hear the loyalty in those words. Then after a pause, she added, 'But of course you kept track of our progress.'"

"'Always,' I said.

"'Have we missed any goals?'

"'Never.'

"'Are you proud of us?'

"'Along the narrowest tangents, yes. Yes, I am very proud.'

"She refused to be surprised by my measured answer. And what worry she let show was small and easily controlled. The creature was exceptionally bright, after all. And she was wise in rare, precious ways. Extraordinary dangers were lurking, and she must have realized there was no way to keep me from seeing pieces of her scheme.

"Silently, she dropped her face to my face and kissed me.

"Then I placed my hand against her little throat, feeling her breath and the flinching of soft muscles, and I eased her back up into a sitting position. With a flat, cool tone, I said, 'It was reasonable, holding to the work schedule. And I was most impressed by how you managed to fool my security systems.'

"Perhaps her plan was to claim innocence. 'I didn't try to fool anything,' she might have said. 'I don't know what you're accusing me of.' Denial might have given the plotters precious time. But it also might have angered me, which would have brought my wrath down on them even sooner than they had planned.

"So instead of lying, my lover decided on poise. She shrugged her shoulders, asking, 'What do you know?'

"'That the good machine being built inside our mountain is almost finished. But your lieutenants have surreptitiously slipped other devices into its workings. You devised some very clever, extremely powerful bombs that you hope won't be noticed, and you will soon obliterate the purpose of my coming to this world.'

"Most souls would have tensed, hearing those words. Many would have panicked. But for my lover, that moment brought relief. Her duplicity was laid bare, and the simple fact that she was alive meant that perhaps she still retained some little chance of success here.

"I felt her throat relax against my hand.

"Then with great seriousness, I added, 'I also know you hope to murder me. Tonight, if possible. You have an array of weapons hiding here, and you have modified any piece of machinery that might injure me. I can even see dangers inside you, darling. Your body fat has been laced with acids that can be set free with a thought, turning you into a burning puddle that falls over my writhing, helpless body . . .'

"She stared down at me.

"In her gaze, I could see her asking herself if this was the moment for suicide. But why would I lie beneath her if I felt at all at risk?

"With a reasonable tone, she asked, 'Can we kill you?'

"'If I was foolish and a little blind, perhaps. But I am not, and I am not.'

"She nodded, accepting that verdict.

"And then she tensed through the shoulders and along her back, and with a small furious voice, she asked, 'But why shouldn't we try to kill you? When your work is finished, you intend to murder all of us. Isn't that so?'

"I didn't respond immediately.

"'You told me as much,' she claimed. 'When you sang about your secret Union and your need for nameless places . . . you practically confessed that when you were finished with this place, you wouldn't leave witnesses behind.'

"I waited for a moment. Then I warned her, 'You don't quite understand.'

"Then I dropped my hand, the fingers and broad palm stroking her body down to the point where her legs joined together. 'You are a special,

special soul,' I told her. 'My work would have been finished in another few years, and my plan was to take you with me. Out to the stars, out into the rich cold darkness.'

"The shock rolled across her features.

"Quietly, almost angrily, she said, 'No, you're lying.'

"But I was speaking the truth.

"With a fond, slightly paternal voice, I asked, 'How do you think I was brought into the Union? No one is born into this noble service. The rank and responsibilities are earned only on exceptionally rare occasions. In my case, another servant visited my home world and built several marvels before retreating back into the darkness with his treasures, and one of the treasures was the man lying beneath you now.'

"'No,' she whispered.

"And then, in pain, she said, 'Maybe. But this changes nothing. I wouldn't abandon my world, and I certainly won't let you blow up this volcano and make it as though this place never was.'

"'Is that what you think will happen?' I asked. 'That I would slaughter you and yours for no reason but my convenience?'

"She hesitated. Then with a figurative acid on her tongue, she asked, 'What do you mean?'

"'Unless provoked, I will not murder.'

"By the light of the moon, my lover looked into my face, and the beginnings of an explanation occurred to her. 'You won't murder, but you might take back all of your gifts. Our minds. The genetic manipulations. Wipe clean the ideas and concepts you brought down here to serve your damned Union.'

"I threw my palm across her mouth.

"Then I yanked her close, saying, 'Yes. That was my kind, responsible plan. You would come with me, and my magical device would come with us, and the other grandchildren would wake the following morning to discover . . . nothing. There would be a shared dream of a magical civilization, a public memory that would turn to legend in another day, and in another ten generations that would vanish into a muddled, impossible story.'

"She lay against me, her heart beating against what passed for my ribs.

"'I am sorry,' she told me.

"Into my ear, she said, 'Really, we haven't done anything wrong. Not yet. I can give commands, and every weapon will be put away, and you won't have to worry about any of us lifting so much as a lard-knife against you.'

"'That is not enough,' I said.

"'And you can kill me,' she promised. Then she repeated her offer, sounding as if she was begging. 'Kill me, and maybe the other adults. But leave our children. They don't know anything.'

"'Like the boy I spoke to? That child waiting between the plaza and the palace?'

"She hesitated.

"'At this moment,' I said, 'that tiny fellow is sitting beside the water, bare toes in the surf. And do you know what he is watching with all of his interest, every shred of passion? He watches the sky.'

"She did not move.

"'The sky,' I repeated. 'And in particular, he stares at this night's brightest stars.'

"The woman could not breathe.

"'You are a crafty soul, my dear. My darling.' I told her, 'I am extremely impressed by the thoroughness and audacity of your plan. Threatening the machine as well as my own immortal self . . . those are the tactics that anyone would expect. But you also dispatched a team of technicians to the mainland. You convinced the worshipful souls living there that they should help you. Since then, our people and theirs have been living in a distant valley, secretly fabricating an amazing machine of their own.

"'A radio beacon, as it happens.

"'To the best of your ability, you have been marking my passage across the heavens. You guessed that I was subverting a set of prying eyes, and you were correct. Your hope was to broadcast a huge, important signal. You wanted to be noticed. You wanted the probe to see you, perhaps. Or if you missed that mark, then at least one loud intelligent scream would race its way through the heart of our galaxy . . .

"'Your secret hope was to accomplish what I would never allow . . . you wanted to name your world, and to name it in exactly the manner that would make the universe take note of your presence.

"'And you were right, my sweet darling. That would have been your only hope of salvation.

"'But I visited that far valley and your secret beacon. Just this morning, I destroyed the dishes and power plant, and I slaughtered everyone in my reach, but I left the local communication system intact. During these last hours, every time you spoke to your fellow rebels, you were actually speaking to me.'"

Finally, the voice paused.

In the perfect darkness, a deep useless breath was taken.

Then the entity was talking again, quietly admitting, "I gave my lover one last freedom. She could be the last to die, or first. She chose to be first, and she did that herself, releasing the acids inside her body. But I was already standing at a safe distance from our bed, my back to the carnage. Hearing the screams and smelling the blistered flesh, I kept my eyes averted, reminding myself that the worst of this awful night was finally finished."

## 12

The two humans clung to one another.

In the same moment, in a rough chorus, they asked, "What happened? What did you do? What about the other people? What?"

A tight slow creak was audible, old leather or old bones moving.

From a point markedly closer than before, a mouth opened and breathed and then breathed again.

"I did precisely what I promised." The voice seemed to be within arm's reach. "However imperfectly, I have always strived to serve my cause, and that includes punishing those who dared rise up against me. I had no choice but to gather the worst of the offenders on the Sunset Plaza, and with the rest of the grandchildren watching, I removed them from the living world. Then I ordered the low-animals to clean the bricks of blood and pink tissues, and the dead bones were ground up and piled high on the nearest beach. And within five years, those who had survived my justice had managed to make up for lost time. Within ten years, my work was finished, and I carved away the gray summit of the volcano and pulled from the hot workroom a single machine encased in the finest hyperfiber—a wonder of genius and competence that made my stay on that world worth any cost."

The voice drifted even closer, and feeling the intrusion, Quee Lee instinctively leaned away.

Perri held her and spoke past her, asking, "When did the mountain erupt?"

Nothing.

"After you abandoned the world, did the island explode?"

A sound of amusement, weary and cool, ended with the simple pronouncement, "Never, no."

They waited.

"Your assumption has been that this was the Earth. And that is a reasonable, wrong assumption. But I let you believe what you wanted. As a rule, every species, no matter how open to odd notions and alien fancies, will find its own stories to be the most compelling.

"No, this wasn't your cradle world. And its people were perhaps not quite as human as I might have let on."

"What happened to them?" Quee Lee pressed.

"As I promised my lover, I undid my fancy tinkering. I made her citizens simple again, just as I pulled back the engineering of the other species. The population scattered. The palace was abandoned. Without trained hands to make repairs, the city fell into ruins. Within a few years of my departure, the island was a mystery already famous across half of that world. But its mountain would never erupt. My work had stolen away too much heat, and the magma lake below had cooled and turned to stone."

The voice paused.

Then with a matter-of-fact tone, it explained, "The Earth is blessed in many ways. It has a mature, very stable sun. Comets are rare beauties in the sky, not constant hazards. And it possesses a relatively thin crust, easily pierced and quick to bleed. But this world that I speak of is notably different. Its skin is much thicker than the Earth's, and much more resilient. As its core generates heat, oceans of magma build up slowly, millions of years required to reach that critical point when a thousand eruptions come at once.

"That harum-scarum probe surely recognized the inevitable—a world perched on the margins of a grand, yet thoroughly natural disaster.

"I left that world and placed my magical machine in a secret place. A new mission called to me from the sky, and I was en route when that nameless world suddenly and violently attacked itself. The sulfurous gases and blistering lava flows achieved everything that I had counted upon. Every convincing trace of my visit was erased. The continents were wracked by quakes. Ten thousand volcanoes spat ash and fire, and they exploded, flinging their poisons into the stratosphere. Every forest burned. Every breath brought blisters and misery. The ocean floors were wrenched upwards, forcing saltwater over the coastlands. My little island was washed clean beneath a quick succession of tsunamis, erasing even the palace. The human-like creatures were reduced to a few scattered populations, ignorant and desperate. And after another thousand years of geologic horror—when the skies finally cleared and the lava cooled to glass—not a single example of that very promising species could be found in Creation."

Those deadly words were absorbed in silence.

Then Quee Lee said, "How awful."

Softly, the voice asked, "In what way is this awful?"

"You allowed that to happen," she began.

"But the people were doomed," it said. "Long before I knew of their existence, they had a fate to face, and despite my considerable powers, there was little I could have done, except delaying the story's end by one day, or at the very best, maybe two."

The humans said nothing.

"If you need righteous anger," it continued, "direct your emotions toward the harum-scarums. Their probe saw the same future that I saw. Three of their colonies were near enough and powerful enough to launch rescue missions. Better than me, they could have saved a worthy sampling of those people before they passed out of existence. But no missions were launched. Their costs and the benefits were too much and too little, respectively. The battered world remained nameless until a starship eased its way into orbit. That particular ship was bringing colonists, I should mention—people who didn't care about the bones under their feet, people who wanted nothing but to start new lives on this rich empty place."

Quietly, Perri asked, "Is it a harum-scarum world?"

"No," the voice replied, "it is not."

"Then who has it?"

"Who else would be a likely suspect, my friend? Remembering all that we have discussed by now . . . "

Humans had claimed the empty world. The colonists might even be humans that had come from the Great Ship . . . people whom Quee Lee and Perri had met and even known well at one time or another . . .

Quee Lee was desperate to talk about anything else.

And Perri was too. With a scornful, demanding tone, he said, "I still don't believe in your Union."

"No? In what ways do you doubt it?"

"When you describe this organization, it sounds like an exclusive club or somebody's secret society. Not the imperial underpinnings of a powerful political machine."

A long pause ended when the voice said, "Power." It said the word four times, each utterance employing a different emotion. Amusement was followed by disgust, and then came contempt, and finally, a different species of amusement—a joyful, almost giddy rendering of the word, "Power." After that, there was a laugh that lingered until the voice decided to speak again.

"As you must have guessed by now," it told them, "I am embroiled in a new task in the service of my Union. A mission full of facets and difficult challenges, yes, and it is not something to be accomplished in an easy few centuries, either."

The humans held their breath.

The voice pushed even closer, less than an arm's length away, and from a mouth that they could only imagine came the reminder, "I did once visit your cradle world. Your Earth. Yes, I did."

Quee Lee nodded.

"Before it was named," Perri recalled.

"Moments before," the voice added. And then the bulk of an invisible body drifted even closer, hovering within a tongue's length of Quee Lee's ear, and an intimate whisper offered her a single date. A specific time. Then a place inside a city that she would never see again.

Quee Lee shivered.

Perri reached out with one arm, aiming for the face that had to be lurking in the blackness . . . but his hand closed on nothing, and nothing else came from the voice, and after a few moments more of clinging comfort with one another, their camp lights returned—a scorching white glare of photons that left them blinking, blinded in a new way altogether.


# 13

They didn't sleep that night, and they didn't miss sleep until the middle of the following morning. By then, Perri and Quee Lee had thoroughly explored the enormous room and most of the little tunnels leading out from it. But they didn't find any trace of visitors other than themselves. Their sniffers tasted surgically clean surfaces and cold air uncluttered by even a single flake of lost skin, and just as puzzling, none of their machines could explain why they had failed last night. Whatever the voice was, it had been careful. With its absence, it proved its great power . . . at least when it came to fooling a couple peasants who were ignorant of the real powers of a galaxy that they had barely begun to know.

There was talk about returning to the flex-car, or at least contacting their missing friends.

But one last tunnel needed a quick examination. And with Perri at the lead, they marched up into an increasingly narrow space that turned sharply, revealing a pair of security robots waiting for anyone who might wander where they didn't belong.

The robots were in slumber-mode, facing in the opposite direction.

Perri retreated, pulling his wife behind him. "They're the last in a string of sentries," he decided. "I bet if we found our way to the other side, we'd come across barricades and official warnings from the captains not to take one step farther."

"The captains don't know about our route?"

"Not yet," he said. Then with a soft conspiring voice, he added, "Maybe we should hurry home. Now. Before we get noticed."

They discovered their friends waiting at the flex-car. An argument had just ended, and one of the twin brothers refused to say anything to anyone. Apparently he had lost on the competition for the rich woman's affections, and his anger helped Quee Lee and Perri avoid the expected questions.

The tiny expedition abandoned the Vermiculate before evening.

Home again, the old married couple made love and ate enough for ten hungry people, and throughout the sex and the dinner, they discussed what they should do next, if anything. And then Quee Lee slept hard for three dream-laced hours. When she woke, Perri was standing over her. He was smiling. But it was a grim, concentrated smile—the look of a man who knew something enormous but unsatisfying.

"Want to hear a rumor?" he asked.

She sat up in bed, answering him with a look.

"Like we heard before, the captains did discover the hole in their maps, and they sent an old robot down into the hole. But it got lost and climbed out again, and it couldn't explain where it had gone wrong."

"That's the story I remember," she said.

"Engineers tore open the robot. Just to identify the malfunction. And that's when they found a message."

Quee Lee blinked, and waited.

"Addressed to the Master Captain," he continued, his smile warming by the moment. "After a thousand security checks, the invitation was delivered. Except for the Master Captain, and maybe a few Submasters, nobody knows what the message said. But a few days later, alone, the

Master Captain walked down that tunnel and vanished for nearly five hours. And when she emerged again, she looked sick. Shaken sick. The rumor claims that she actually cried in the presence of her security troops, which is why the whole story refuses to get wings and soar. It doesn't sound at all like the benign despot we know so well."

His wife agreed with a nod. "When did this happen?" she asked.

"Ten years ago, nearly."

"And since then?"

"Well," said Perri, "the Master Captain has quit weeping. If that's what you're curious about."

She lay back on her pillows.

"No," her husband said.

"What else?"

"I didn't wake you just to tell you something that might have happened. Or even to give you another mystery to chew on."

"Then why am I awake?"

"I know a man," Perri said. "And he's very good at pulling old memories out of very old skulls."

The magician was named Ash.

He was human, but he lived inside an alien habitat where the false sun never set. Sitting in a room full of elaborate machinery, Ash told his newest clients, "I can make promises, but they don't mean much. This date is a very big problem, madam. You were alive then, yes. But barely. This is a few years before bioceramic brains came into existence. You could have been the brightest young thing, but my tricks work best with the galactic-standard minds . . . brains that employ quantum many-world models to interface with a trillion sister minds . . . "

"Can you do anything?" Perri asked.

"I can take your money," Ash replied. "And I can also dig into the old data archives. You claim you have a place in mind?"

"Yes," Quee Lee said. Then she repeated the location just as the voice had given it to her.

"I assume you think you were there then," Ash said.

"I don't know if I was."

"And this is important?"

"We'll see," she said.

Ash began to work. He explained that on the Earth, for this very brief period of history, security systems as well as ordinary individuals tried to keep thorough digital records of everything that happened and that didn't happen. The trouble was that the machinery was very simple and unreliable, and the frequent upgrades as well as a few nasty electromagnetic pulses wiped clean a lot of records. Not to mention the malicious effects of the early AIs—entities who took great delight in creating fictions that they would bury inside whatever data banks would accept their artistic works.

"The chances of success," Ash began to say.

Then in the ancient records, he saw something entirely unexpected, and lifting his gaze, he mentioned to Quee Lee, "You were a pretty young lady."

"Did you find me?" she asked expectantly.

"Too easily," he allowed. Then he showed her a portion of the image—a girl who was nine or maybe eight years old, dressed in the uniform mandated by a good private school.

With a shrug, Ash allowed, "No need for paranoia. This does happen, on occasion." He gave commands to a brigade of invisible assistants, and then said, "If I can dig up a few more records, I think I can piece together what you and the man talked about."

"What man?" she asked.

Perri asked.

"The man standing beside you," Ash remarked. "The man with the golden balloon." Then he showed an image captured by a nearby security camera, adding, "I'm assuming he's your father, judging by his looks."

"He's not," she whispered.

"And now we have a second digital record," Ash said happily. "Hey, and now a third. See the adolescent boy down the path from you? Wearing the medallion on his chest? Well, that was a camera and a very good microphone. His video has been lost, but not the audio. I can't tell you how unlikely it is to have this kind of recording survive this long, in any usable form."

"What is the man saying to me?" Quee Lee asked nervously.

"Let me see if I can pull it up . . . "

And suddenly a voice that she hadn't thought about for eons returned. The young girl and the stranger were standing in Hong Kong Park, on the cobblestone path beside the lotus pond. A short white picket fence separated them from the water. Standing in the background were towers and a bright blue sky. With the noise of the city and other passersby erased, the voice began by saying, "Hello, Quee Lee."

"Hello," the young girl replied, nervous in very much the same fashion that the old woman was now. "Do I know you?"

"Hardly at all," the man replied.

The girl looked about, as if expecting somebody to come save her. Which there would have been: Quee Lee was the only child to a very wealthy couple who didn't let her travel anywhere without bodyguards and a personal servant. "Where are my people now?" she seemed to ask herself.

The voice said, "I will not hurt you, my dear."

Hearing that promise didn't help the girl relax.

"Ask me where I came from. Will you please?"

The youngster decided on silence.

But the strange man laughed, and pretending the question had been asked, he remarked, "I came from the stars. I am here on a great, important mission, and it involves your particular species."

The girl looked up at a face that carried a distinct resemblance to her face. Then she looked back down the path, hoping for rescue.

"In a little while," said the stranger, "my work here will be complete."

"Why?" the girl muttered.

"Because that is when one of your mechanical eyes will look at the most lucrative portion of the sky, at the perfect moment, and almost everything that you will need to know about the universe will be delivered to your doorstep."

The pretty black-haired girl hugged her laptop bag, saying nothing.

"When that day comes," said the man, "you must try and remember everything. Do you understand me, Quee Lee? That one day will be the most important moment in your species' history."

"How do you know my name?" she asked again.

"And this is not all that I am doing on your world." The man was handsome but quite ordinary, nothing about him hinting at anything that wasn't human. He was wearing a simple suit, rumpled at the edges. His right hand held the string that led up to a small balloon made from helium and gold Mylar. He smiled with fierce joy, telling her, "It has been decided. Your species has a great destiny in service of the Union."

In the present, two people gasped quietly.

"What's the Union?" the girl asked.

"Everything," was the reply. "And it is nothing."

The girl was prettiest when she was puzzled, like now.

"You won't remember any portion of our conversation," the man promised. "Ten minutes from now, you won't remember me or my words."

One hand smoothed her skirt, and she anxiously stared at her neat black shoes.

"But before I leave you, I wanted to tell you something else. Are you listening to me, Quee Lee?"

"No," she claimed.

The man laughed heartily. Then he bent down, placing their faces on the same level, and when he had her gaze, he said, "You were adopted, only your parents don't know that. The baby inside your mother had died, and I devised you out of things that are human, but also elements inspired by a wonderful old friend of mine."

The girl tried to step back but couldn't. Discovering that her feet were fixed to the pavement, she looked down and then up at the other adults walking past the long brown pond, and when she tried to scream, no sound came from her open mouth.

"I am not gracelessly cruel," the stranger told her. "You may think that of me one day. But even though I live to aid the workings of an enormous power, I make certain that I find routes to kindness, and when it offers itself, to love."

The little girl couldn't even make herself cry.

"Part of you," he said. Then he paused, and from two different perspectives, the audience watched as his free hand touched the girl's bright black hair. "The shape of your mind was born on another world, a world too distant to be seen today. And I once lied to that mind, Quee Lee. I told it that I could stand aside and watch it die forever."

She had no tears, but the man was crying, his face wet and sorry.

"I wish I could offer more of an apology," he said. And then he rose up again, pulling the balloon's string close to his chest while wiping at his wet face with a wrinkled sleeve. "But much is at stake . . . more than you might ever understand, Quee Lee . . . and this is as close to insubordination as this good servant can manage . . . "

Then he glanced at the security camera hidden in the trees and handed the string and balloon to the girl beside him. "Would you like this, Quee Lee? As a little gift from your grandfather?"

The girl discovered that she could move again.

"Take it," he advised.

She accepted the string with one little hand.

For a brief instant, they were posing, staring across the millennia in a stance that was strained but nonetheless sweet—the image of a little girl enjoying the park with some undefined adult relative.

"I will see you later," he mentioned.

Quee Lee released the string, watching the gold ball rise faster than she would have expected—shooting into the sky as if it weighed nothing at all.

When her eyes dropped, the stranger had stepped out of view.

And a few moments later, her father ran up the path to join her, asking, "Where did you go? I couldn't find you anywhere."

"I didn't go anywhere," the girl replied.

"Tell me the truth," the scared little man demanded. "Did you talk to somebody you shouldn't have talked to?"

She said, "No."

"Why are you lying?" he asked.

"But I'm not lying," she protested. Then with a wide, smart grin, the young Quee Lee added, "The sky is going to talk, Father. Did you know that? And he promised me, he did, that I am going to see him again later . . . !"

Since about the age six, Ruth Nestvold wanted to be a writer (or a singer, an actress, or President of the United States), but for many years she put practical pursuits first and writing fiction second. After completing a Ph.D. in literature, she took time off from academic pursuits to attend the Clarion West Writers Workshop, a six week "boot camp" for writers of science fiction and fantasy. She learned more there than she could have dreamed possible, changed her priorities, and gave up theory for imagination. Two years later, she sold her first short story to the acclaimed science fiction magazine *Asimov's*. Since then, she has sold over fifty pieces of short fiction to a variety of markets, including *Baen's Universe, Strange Horizons, Scifiction, F&SF, Realms of Fantasy*, and several year's best anthologies, and has been nominated for the Nebula, the Sturgeon, and the Tiptree awards. In 2007, the Italian translation of her novella "Looking Through Lace" won the "Premio Italia" for best international work. Her novel *Yseult* appeared in German translation as *Flamme und Harfe* with Random House Germany and has since been translated into Dutch and Italian. Other novels include *Shadow of Stone* and *Chameleon in a Mirror*. She is the founder of the Villa Diodati workshop for English-speaking writers of speculative fiction in Europe. She maintains a web site at www.ruthnestvold.com and blogs at ruthnestvold.wordpress.com.

# LOOKING THROUGH LACE

## *Ruth Nestvold*

### 1

Toni came out of the jump groggy and with a slight headache, wishing the Allied Interstellar Research Association could afford passage on Alcubierre drive ships—even if they did collapse an unconscionable amount of space in their wake. For a moment, she couldn't remember what the job was this time. She sat up and rubbed her eyes while the voice on the intercom announced that they would be arriving at the Sagittarius Transit Station in approximately one standard hour.

Sagittarius. Now she remembered. The women's language. Suddenly she felt much more awake. For the first time, she was on her way to join a first contact team, and she had work to do. She got up, washed her face in cold water at the basin in her compartment (at least AIRA could afford private compartments), and turned on the console again, calling up the files she had been sent when given her assignment to Christmas.

"List vids," she said. It was time she checked her theoretical knowledge against the real thing again. Just over three weeks she'd had to learn the Megan language, one week on Admetos after getting her new assignment and two weeks in transit. From the transit station, it would be another week before she finally set foot on the planet. Even with the latest memory enhancements, it was a daunting challenge. A month to learn a new language and its intricacies. A month to try to get a feel for a culture where women had their own language which they never spoke with men.

That had been her lucky break. Toni was the only female xenolinguist in this part of the galaxy with more than a year's experience. And suddenly she found herself promoted from grunt, compiling grammars and dictionaries, to first contact team.

She scrolled through the list of vids. This time, she noticed a title which hadn't caught her attention before.

"Play 'Unknown Mejan water ritual.'"

To judge by the AIC date, it had to be a video from one of the early, pre-contact-team probes. Not to mention the quality, which was only sporadically focused. The visuals were mostly of the bay of Edaru, and the audio was dominated by the sound of water lapping the shore.

But what she could see and hear was fascinating. A fearful young hominid male, tall and gracile, his head shaved and bowed, was being led out by two guards to the end of a pier. A small crowd followed solemnly. When they arrived at the end, another man stepped forward and, in the only words Toni could make out clearly, announced that Sentalai's shame would be purged. (Assuming, of course, that what had been deciphered of the men's language to this point was correct.)

The older man then motioned for the younger man to remove his clothes, fine leather garments such as those worn by the richer of the Edaru clans, and when he was naked, the two guards pushed him into the water.

Three women behind them conferred briefly. Then one of the three stepped forward and flung a length of lace after the young man.

Toni stared as the crowd on the pier walked back to shore. She could see no trace of the man who had been thrown in the water. According to her materials, the Mejan were excellent swimmers, growing up nearly as much in the water as out, and it should have been easy for him to swim back to the pier. But for some reason he hadn't.

It reminded her of nothing so much as an execution.

2

The entry bay of the small space station orbiting Christmas was empty and sterile, with none of the personal details that a place accumulated with time, the details that made it lived-in rather than just in use. Toni was glad she would soon be moving to the planet's surface. Blank walls were more daunting than an archaic culture and an unknown language anytime.

Two men were there to meet her, and neither one was the team xenolinguist.

The elder of the two stepped forward, his hand outstretched. "Welcome to the *Penthesilea*, Dr. Donato."

"Thank you, Captain Ainsworth. It's a pleasure to meet you. And please, call me Toni."

Ainsworth smiled but didn't offer his own first name in exchange. Hierarchies were being established quickly.

"Toni, this is Dr. Samuel Wu, the new xenoteam sociologist."

From their vid communications, Toni had expected to like Sam Wu, and now she was sure of it. His smile was slow and sincere and his handshake firm. Besides, he was in a similar position on the team, having been brought into the project late after the original sociologist, Landra Saleh, had developed a serious intolerance to something in the atmosphere of Christmas, despite the battery of tests they all went through before being assigned to a new planet.

"Nice to meet you in person, Toni," Sam said.

"Nice to meet you too." Toni looked from one to the other. "And Dr. Repnik? Was he unable to leave the planet?"

There was a short silence. "Uh, he thought Dr. Wu could brief you on anything that has come up since the last communication you received. Continued study of the language has precedence at this point."

Toni nodded. "Of course." But that didn't change the fact that another xenolinguist could brief her better than a sociologist—especially one who had only been on the planet a week himself.

As Ainsworth led her to her quarters aboard ship, she drew Sam aside. "Okay, what's all this about?"

"I was afraid you'd notice," he said, grimacing.

"And?"

"I guess it's only fair that you know what you'll be up against. Repnik didn't think a female linguist needed to be added to the team, but Ainsworth insisted on it."

Toni sighed. She had been looking forward to working with Repnik. Of the dozen inhabited worlds discovered in the last century, he'd been on the xenoteams of half of them and had been the initial xenolinguist on three. He had more experience in making sense of unknown languages than anyone alive. And the languages of Christmas were a fascinating puzzle, a puzzle she'd thought she would get a chance to work on with one of the greatest xenolinguists in the galaxy. Instead, she would be a grunt again—an unwanted grunt.

"Here we are," Ainsworth said, as the door to one of the cabins opened at his touch. "We'll have the entrance reprogrammed as soon as you settle in."

"Thank you."

"We'll be going planetside tomorrow. I hope that's enough time for you to recover from your journey."

It never was, but it was all she was going to get. "I'm sure I'll be fine."

"Good, then I will leave you with Dr. Wu so that he can brief you on anything you still need to know."

She set her bag down on the narrow bed and gazed out the viewport at the planet. It was a a striking sight. The discovery team that had done the first fly-by of the Sgr 132 solar system had given it the name Christmas. The vegetation was largely shades of red and the ocean had a greenish cast, while the narrow band of rings alternated shades of green and gold. There was only one major continent, looking from the viewport now like an inverted pine tree. The effect of the whole was like Christmas wrapping paper with the colors reversed.

One more day, and she'd finally be there.

Sam stepped up behind her. "Beautiful, isn't it?"

"And how." She gazed at the planet in silence for a moment and then turned to Sam. "So how did Repnik think he would be able to gather data on the women's language without a female xenolinguist?"

"He wanted to plant more probes and use the technicians and crew of the *Penthesilea*."

She shook her head. "But they're not trained in working with an alien language."

"That's what Ainsworth said." He raised one eyebrow and smiled. "Except he added that they were needed on the ship for the jobs they'd been hired to do."

Toni chuckled despite the ache in her gut. "I think I'm going to be very grateful you're on this team, Sam."

Sam grinned. "Ditto."

### 3

*From: The Allied Interstellar Community General Catalog. Entry for Sgr 132-3, also known as Christmas, or Kailazh (land) in the native tongue.*

The third planet in the system of Sgr 132 is 1.2 AU from its sun, has a diameter of 15,840 kilometers, a density of 3.9, and 0.92G. The day is 16.7 standard hours and the year 743 days (1.42 Earth years). It is iron poor but rich in light metals. Satellites: three shepherd moons within a thin ring of debris. Land mass consists largely of one supercontinent covering most of one pole and extending south past the equator. It is now known to be a seeded planet of hominid inhabitants with a number of plants and animals also related to Terran species. Date of original colonization of the planet is as yet unknown. Technological status: pre-automation, primitive machines, rudimentary scientific knowledge. There is no written language.

### 4

The first thing Toni noticed when she stepped off the shuttle was the scent of the air, tantalizing and slightly spicy, as if someone were baking cookies with cardamom and cinnamon.

The second thing she noticed was the gravity. Christmas had slightly lower gravity than Earth, but Toni had grown up on Mars, and it certainly felt more like home than Admetos had. Her joints still ached from the large planet's crushing gravity. Thank God she had been transferred.

The rings were only the third thing she noticed. They arched across the southern sky like some kind of odd cloud formation, pale but still visible in the daylight.

Sam saw the direction of her gaze. "Wait until you see them at sunset."

Toni nodded, smiling. "I wanted to say I can imagine, but I'm not sure I can."

Irving Moshofski, the xenoteam geologist, stepped forward to intro-duce himself and shook Toni's hand. "Nice to meet you, Dr. Donato. Gates and Repnik are waiting for us in town."

They followed Moshofski to their ground transportation, an open car-riage drawn by descendants of Terran horses, but taller and with lighter bone structure. This pair was a reddish-brown much deeper than the bays of Earth.

Toni took another deep breath of the air. "I swear, if they hadn't already named it Christmas for the colors, they would have changed the name to Christmas when they smelled the place."

"Everyone familiar with Terran Western culture says that," Moshofski said.

She climbed up into the open carriage behind Ainsworth and noted that it was well sprung, the workmanship of the wood smooth, and the leather seats soft. Their driver was a young Mejan man, tall and willowy, his skin a lovely copper color. As they settled into their seats, Toni greeted him in Alnar ag Ledar, "the language of the sea"—the universal language used by men and women on Christmas to communicate with each other.

Their driver lifted the back of his hand to his forehead in the Mejan gesture of greeting. "Sha bo sham, tajan."

She returned the gesture and turned to Ainsworth, suppressing a chuckle. "Why did he call me 'mother'?"

"That seems to be a term of respect for women here."

"At least that's something. But it looks like I still have a lot to learn."

Ainsworth nodded. "We all do. We strongly suspect the Mejan are withholding information from us. They're very reluctant to begin any kind of treaty negotiations with the Allied Interstellar Community."

"They don't trust us," Moshofski said.

Toni shrugged. "Is there any reason why they should?"

She leaned forward to address the driver, speaking rapidly in the men's language. "Moden varga esh zhamkaned med sherned?" *Do you trust the men from the sky?*

The driver looked over his shoulder at her and chuckled. "Roga desh varga an zhamnozhed, tajan." *Like I trust the stars.* Toni noticed that the laugh-ing eyes in his copper-brown face were an extraordinary smoky green color.

She raised one eyebrow. "Moshulan sham beli?" *Not to fall on you?*

He laughed out loud, and Toni leaned back in her seat, grinning.

The landing base was about ten kilometers outside of the biggest town, Edaru, and she studied the landscape avidly during the trip. She loved the sights and scents and sounds of strange worlds, the rhythms of a new language, the shape and color of plants she had never seen before. For someone from Earth, the red hues of the landscape on Christmas might have conjured associations of barrenness, although the rich shades from magenta to burnt umber were from the native vegetation itself, the wide, strangely-shaped leaves of the low-growing plants and the fronds of the trees. But it never would have occurred to Toni to associate reds and umbers with barrenness. For someone from Neubrandenburg on Mars, red was the color of homesickness.

Toni didn't notice Edaru until they were practically upon it. They came over a rise and suddenly the city, crowded around a large bay, was spread out before them. The buildings were low and close to the water. Despite occasional flooding, the Mejan were happiest as close to the sea as possible.

At the sight of their vehicle, people came out of their houses, standing in doorways or leaning on windowsills to watch them pass. A number lifted the backs of their hands to their foreheads in the Mejan gesture of greeting.

Christmas was one of the half-dozen seeded planets in the known universe, and as on other such planets, the human population had made some physical adjustments for life in the given environment, most obviously in their height and the prominent flaps of skin between their fingers. But to Toni, who had spent two years now on Admetos among what the human members of AIRA often referred to as the giant ants, they didn't appear alien at all, or at least only pleasantly so. The people she saw were tall, light-boned, dark-skinned and wide-chested, with long hair in various hues which they wore interlaced with thin braids enhanced by colorful yarn. She was surprised at how little difference there was in the styles worn by the men and the women—not what she would have expected from a world where the women spoke a separate, "secret" language.

Ships and boats of various sizes were docked at the wharves, and one large ship was sailing into port as they arrived. The materials sent to her had described them as primitive craft, but she found them graceful and beautiful. The long, low stone houses had rows of windows facing the sea and were ornamented with patterns of circles and waves in shades of red and purple and green and blue on a background of yellow. Some larger houses were built in a u-shape around a central courtyard. Toni stared and smiled and waved. It looked clean and peaceful, the children content and the women walking alone with their heads held high.

The common house—the main government building of Edaru—was located in the center of town near the wharves. Councilor Lanrhel himself waited for them, the back of his hand touching his forehead in greeting. She couldn't help thinking it looked like he was shading his eyes to see them better.

Lanrhel was a handsome man, even taller than the average Mejan, with streaks of gray in his reddish-brown hair, the gray looking almost like an extra shade in the colors of his braids. The pale, tooled leather of his short cape, the garment worn in the warm half of the year, was the same length as his tunic, reaching just past the tops of his thighs. He stood in the doorway, his open palm in front of his forehead, and Toni returned the gesture as she approached the building. When Lanrhel didn't relax, she glanced at Sam and Ainsworth, unsure what to do. Perhaps she had not made the gesture correctly. She repeated it and said in the best local dialect she could manage, "Negi eden an elamed elu mazhu velazh Edaru. An rushen eden sham." Which meant something like *I'm honored to be a guest in Edaru, thank you.* Except that the language of the Mejan had no verb for "to be" and tenses were expressed in auxiliary verbs which could go either before or after the main verb, depending on the emphasis.

The councilor smiled widely and lowered his arm, and Toni winced, realizing she had used the male first person pronoun. Her first official sentence on Christmas, and it was wrong. She was glad Repnik wasn't there. Sam and Ainsworth didn't seem to notice that she'd made a mistake, but when she glanced back at the driver with the smoky green eyes, she saw that he too had a grin on his wide lips.

"We are happy to have you visit our city," Lanrhel said and led them into the common house. They crossed a central hallway and entered a large room where about a dozen people were seated in a circle in comfortable chairs and sofas. Low tables were scattered in the center, and on them stood strange-looking fruits in glossy bowls made of the shells of large, native beetles. Decorative lace hangings graced the walls.

Lanrhel announced them, and the others rose. Toni was surprised to see almost as many women as men, all garbed in soft, finely tooled leather of different colors. Leather was the material of choice of the Mejan, and their tanning methods were highly advanced. Sam had speculated it was because they lived so much with water, and leather was more water-resistant than woven materials.

She recognized Repnik immediately. She knew his face from photos and vids and holos. He was thin and wiry, with deep wrinkles next to his mouth and lining his forehead. Despite age treatments, the famous linguist looked old, used-up even, more so than the images she'd seen had led her to believe. He was also shorter than she expected, barely topping her eyebrows.

He came forward slowly to shake her hand. "Ms. Donato?" he said, omitting her title.

Two could play that game. "Mr. Repnik. I'm honored to be able to work with you."

His eyes narrowed briefly. "It really is unfortunate that you were called to Christmas unnecessarily. I'm sure you will soon see that there is little contribution for you to make here. Despite the sex barrier, I've managed to collect enough material on my own to be able to study and analyze the women's dialect."

Sam had warned her on ship, but Repnik's unwelcoming attitude still stung. She did her best not to let it show, keeping her voice level. "A dialect? But it was my understanding that Alnar ag Eshmaled couldn't be understood by the men."

"Ms. Donato, surely you are aware that speakers of different dialects often cannot understand each other."

She bit her lip. If she was going to have a hand in deciphering the women's language, she had to get along with him. Instead of arguing, she shrugged and gave Repnik a forced smile. "Well, as they say, a language is a dialect with an army and a navy. And that's not what we have here, is it?"

Repnik gave her a pleased nod. "Precisely."

Jackson Gates, the team exobiologist, moved between them and introduced himself, earning Toni's gratitude. He was a soft-spoken, dark-skinned man with graying hair and beard, obviously the type who cared little about cosmetic age treatments. She judged his age at barely over fifty.

Lanrhel then introduced her to the other members of the Edaru council. The oldest woman, Anash, came forward and presented Toni with a strip of decorative lace, similar to the beautiful hangings on the walls. Toni lifted the back of her hand to her forehead again and thanked her.

The multitude of introductions completed, they sat down on the leather-covered chairs and couches, and Ainsworth asked in barely passable Mejan if anything had been decided regarding treaty negotiations with AIC. Lanrhel looked at Toni, and she repeated the request, adding the correct inclinations and stripping it of the captain's Anglicized word order. Why hadn't the councilor referred to Repnik? She'd been studying like a fiend for the last month, but surely his command of the language was better than hers.

Lanrhel leaned across the arm of his chair and murmured something to Anash. Toni caught mention of the treaty again, and the words for language, house, and her own name. Anash looked across the circle at her and smiled. She returned the smile, despite the headache she could feel coming on. The first day on a new planet was always difficult, and this time she'd had conflict brewing with her boss even before she got off the shuttle. But next to Anash, another woman had pulled out her crocheting (a far cry from the stiff formality of the official functions she'd had to endure on Admetos), a man with eyes the color of the sea on Christmas had joked with her, and she still had a sunset to look forward to.

And no one was going to toss her into the ocean just yet. She hoped.

## 5

*From: Preliminary Report on Alnar ag Ledar, primary language of Christmas. Compiled 29.09.157 (local AIC date) by Prof. Dr. Hartmut Repnik, h.c. Thaumos, Hino, Marat, and Polong, Allied Interstellar Research Association first contact team xenolinguist, Commander, Allied Interstellar Community Forces.*

The language of the Mejan people of Christmas is purely oral with both inflecting and agglutinating characteristics. Tense information seems to be given exclusively in an inflected auxiliary which takes the place of helping verbs and modals while also providing information on the addressee of the sentence. Nouns are gendered, masculine and feminine, but with some interesting anomalies compared to known languages. Adjectives are non-existent. The descriptive function is fulfilled by verbs (e.g. jeraz, "the state of being green").

## 6

The arc of the rings lit up like lacework in the last rays of the setting sun, while the sky behind it showed through purple and orange and pink. Toni took a deep breath and blinked away the tears that had started in her eyes at the shock of beauty. Beside her, Sam was silent, too wise to disturb her enjoyment of the moment.

They were sitting on the veranda of the house AIRA had rented for her and any other women from the ship who had occasion to come planetside. Together they watched as the colors faded and the sky grew dark. The small moons accompanying the rings appeared, while the brilliant lace became a dark band, starting in the east and spreading up and over.

"Maybe that's why they seem to set such a high store by lace," Toni finally said when the spectacle was over.

Sam nodded. "I've thought of that too."

She took a sip of the tea, sweet and hot with a flavor that reminded her subtly of ginger, and leaned back in her chair, pulling her sweater tighter around her. The night grew cold quickly, even though it was early fall and Edaru was in the temperate zone.

"What have you learned about the role of women since you've been here?" Toni asked.

"Well, since they will only talk to the men of Edaru, it's a bit difficult finding out anything. But they don't live in harems, that's for sure."

"Harems" was Repnik's term for the houses of women, although the residents could come and go as they pleased and the houses were off-limits for men completely, as far as the first contact team could determine.

She laughed, briefly and without humor. "I wonder what bit him."

Sam was quiet so long, she turned to look at him. In the flickering light of the oil lamp, his face was shadowed, his expression thoughtful. They had a generator and solar batteries for electricity in Contact House One and Two, but they tried to keep use of their own technology to a minimum.

"I don't think he ever had a life," Sam finally said. "Most people are retired by the time they reach the age of one hundred. But look at Repnik—what would he retire to? His reputation spans the known universe, but it's all he's got. There's no prestige in hanging out on a vacation planet, and I doubt if he knows how to have fun."

His generous interpretation of Repnik's behavior made her feel vaguely guilty. "True. But I still get the feeling he's got something against women."

"Could be. I heard he went through a messy divorce a few years back—his ex-wife was spreading nasty rumors about him. I'm glad I'm not the woman working under him."

"Bad choice of words, Sam."

He smiled. "Guilty as charged."

Mejan "music" from a house down the hill drifted up to them, an odd swooshing sound without melody which reminded Toni of nothing so much as the water lapping the shore. Some native insects punctuated the rhythm with a "zish-zish, zish-zish" percussion, but there were no evening bird sounds. According to Jackson Gates, the only native life forms of the planet were aquatic, amphibian, reptilian or arthropod. There were no flying creatures on Christmas at all—and thus no word for "fly" in the Mejan language. Since the arrival of the xenoteam, the term "elugay velazh naished" (*move in the air*) had come into use.

It was impossible for contact to leave a culture the way it was before. Leaving native culture untouched was an article of belief with AIRA, but it was also a myth.

Toni finished her tea and put down her mug. "It's occurred to me that Repnik is perhaps being led astray by the fact that Christmas is a seeded planet. Most of the other languages he worked on were of non-human species."

"Led astray how?"

"Well, when they look so much like us, you expect them to be like us too. Language, social structures, the whole bit."

"It's a possibility. Just don't tell him that."

"I'll try. But I have a problem with authority, especially when it's wrong."

Sam chuckled. "I don't think Repnik is serious about the harems, though. It's just his idea of a joke."

"Yeah, but there are also some odd things about the language which don't seem to go along with his analysis. Grammatical gender for example. Repnik refers to them as masculine and feminine, but they don't match up very well with biological sex. If he's right, then 'pirate' and even 'warrior' are both feminine nouns."

"I don't have any problem with that."

Toni pursed her lips, pretending to be offended. "But I do."

"I probably get them wrong all the time anyway."

"Don't you use your AI?" Like herself, Sam had a wrist unit. AI implants had been restricted decades ago because they led to such a high percentage of personality disorders.

He shrugged. "I don't always remember to consult it. Usually only when I don't know a word."

"And there's no guarantee the word will be in the dictionary yet or even that the AI will give you the right word for the context, even if it is."

"Exactly."

Toni gazed out at the night sky. Stars flickered above the horizon, but where the rings had been, the sky was black except for the shepherd moons. Below, the bay of Edaru was calm, the houses nestled close to the water, windows now lit by candlelight or oil lamps. She wondered where the green-eyed driver was, wondered what the Mejan executed people for, wondered if she would get a chance to work on the women's language.

She repressed the temptation to sigh and got up. "Come on, I'll walk you back to the contact house. I need to talk to Ainsworth before he returns to the ship."

## 7

*The legend of the little lace-maker*
*Recorded 30.09.157 (local AIC date) by Landra Saleh, sociologist, first contact*
*team, SGR 132-3 (Christmas / Kailazh).*

As long as she could remember, Zhaykair had only one dream—to become the greatest maker of lace the Mejan had ever known. All young girls are taught the basics of crocheting, but Zhaykair did not want to stop at that. She begged the women of her village to show her their techniques with knots, the patterns they created, and she quickly found the most talented lace-maker among them. Saymel did not belong to Zhaykair's house, but the families reached an agreement, and the little girl was allowed to learn from Saymel, although the job of Zhaykair's house was raising cattle.

But before she had seen nine summers (*note: approximately thirteen standard years—L.S.*), Zhaykair had learned all Saymel had to teach her. She begged her clan to allow her to go to the city of Edaru, where the greatest lace-makers of the Mejan lived. Her mothers and fathers did not want to send her away, but Saymel, who could best judge the talent of the young girl, persuaded them to inquire if the house of Mihkal would be willing to train her.

The elders sent a messenger to the Mihkal with samples of Zhaykair's work. They had feared being ridiculed for their presumption, but the messenger returned with an elder of the house of Mihkal to personally escort Zhaykair to the great city of Edaru.

Zhaykair soon learned all the Mihkal clan could teach her. Her lace was in such great demand, and there were so many who wanted to learn from her, that she could soon found her own house. Her works now grace the walls of all the greatest families of the Mejan.

8

"If Repnik refuses to allow you to work on the women's language, I'm not sure what I can do to help," Ainsworth said.

"Then why did you send for me?" Toni was only marginally aware of the cool night air against her skin as their open carriage headed for the AIC landing base. If she hadn't returned to the contact house with Sam, she would have missed Ainsworth completely. A deliberate move on his part, she suspected now.

"I thought I could bring him around," the Captain said now.

"Can't you order him?"

"I don't think that would be wise. With a little diplomacy, you can still persuade him. In the long run, he will have to see that he needs you to collect more data."

Toni rubbed her temples. The headache she'd first felt coming on during the introductions in the common house had returned with a vengeance. "He'll probably try to use remote probes."

"He already has. But since none of us are allowed in the women's houses, they can't be placed properly. We've tried three close to entrances and have lost them all."

"What happened to them?"

"One was painted over, one was stepped on and one was swept from a windowsill and ended in the trash."

Despite everything, she had to smile to herself.

They pulled up next to the temporary landing base, and the light from the stars and the moons was replaced by aggressive artificial light. Ainsworth patted her knee in a grandfatherly way. "Chin up, Donato. Do your work and do it well, and Repnik will recognize that you can be of use to him. We'll get that unknown language deciphered, and you will be a part of it. That's what you want, isn't it?"

"Yes." Maybe everyone was right and she was just overreacting to Repnik's reluctance to let her work on the women's language. It was certainly nothing new for AIRA researchers to feel threatened by others working in the same field and jealously defensive of their own area of expertise. Toni had seen it before, but that didn't mean she had to like it. Her first day on Christmas was not ending well.

At least she'd had the sunset.

The Captain got out of the carriage and waved at her as the driver turned it around and headed back into town.

When they were nearing the city again, Toni leaned forward, propping her arms on the leather-covered seat in front of her. The driver was the same one they'd had this morning. Strange that she'd been so fixated on Ainsworth and her own problems that she hadn't even noticed.

He glanced over his shoulder at her and smiled but said nothing.

Toni took the initiative. "Sha bo sham."

"Sha bo sham, tajan." The planes of his face were a mosaic of shadow and moonlight, beautiful and unfamiliar.

"Ona esh eden bonshani Toni rezh tajan, al?" *Me you call Toni not mother, yes?*

He laughed and shook his head in the gesture of affirmative, like a nod in Toni's native culture. "Bonlami desh an. Tay esh am eladesh bonshani Kislan." *Honored am I. And you me will call Kislan.*

She smiled and offered her hand as she would have in her own culture. He transferred the reins to one hand, then took her own hand gently and pressed it to his forehead. His skin was warm and dry. She couldn't see his smoky green eyes in the starlight, but she could imagine them. When he released her hand, she could have sworn it was with reluctance.

Perhaps the day was not ending so badly after all.

The women of Anash's family, the house of Ishel, were gentle but determined—they would not allow Toni to learn Alnar ag Eshmaled from them, "the language of the house," until she promised not to teach it to any men. Which of course was impossible. The point of research funded by AIRA was for it to be published and made accessible to everyone in the known galaxy. There were laws against restricting access to data on the basis of sex. Access to data could be restricted on the basis of security clearance perhaps, but not on the basis of sex.

"Bodesh fadani eshukan alnar ag eshmaled," Anash said, her expression sympathetic. *No man may speak the language of the house. Permission-particle-tense-marker-present for female addressee verb negative-marker-subject object*: with the mind of a linguist, Toni broke down the parts of the sentence, trying to figure out whether the women favored different sentence structures than the men.

So they weren't going to speak their language with her. She had spent her first two days setting up house and getting her bearings, and now that she finally had an appointment with some of the women of the planet, she learned that Repnik was right—she wouldn't be able to do the job she had come here to do.

But at least they had welcomed her into the women's house and were less careful with her than with the men of the contact team. With the camera in her AI, she had recorded Anash and Thuyene speaking in their own language several times. She felt a little bad about the duplicity—she'd never had to learn a language by stealth before—but if she was going to do the job she'd been hired for, she didn't have a choice. And when it came right down to it, AIRA never asked anyone's permission to send out the probes used in the first stages of deciphering a new language. Stealth always played a role.

But what a dilemma. The Allied Interstellar Research Association was required to make their knowledge of new worlds public. Not to mention that Toni would only be able to make her reputation as a xenolinguist if she could publish the results of her research. Perhaps they could work out some kind of compromise with AIRA that would make it possible for her to study the women's language anyway.

"May I still visit this house?" Toni asked in the men's language.

Anash smiled. "We are happy to welcome the woman from the sky. And perhaps you can teach us the language you speak, just as the men of the sky teach the men of the people."

"Why is it that you will speak with the men of Edaru and not with the men of the first contact team?"

The smile vanished from Anash's face. "They are offensive." In the Mejan language it was more like "exhibit a state of offensiveness," a verb used for descriptive purposes, but it was nonetheless different from the verb "to offend," which connoted an individual action.

"What have they done?" Toni asked.

The older woman's face seemed to close up. "They speak before they are spoken to."

Was that all it was? The men of the contact team had offended the Mejan sense of propriety? "So men of a strange house may not speak to a woman without permission?"

"They may not. That intimacy is only granted within families."

How simple it was after all: someone had merely made the mistake of not asking the right questions. She had read stories of contact teams that had suffered similar misunderstandings from just such a mistake. But how was anyone supposed to know which questions to ask when dealing with an utterly alien culture? It was no wonder the same mistakes were made over and over again.

Besides, their team had the excuse of having lost their sociologist early into the mission.

Toni rose and lifted the back of her hand to her forehead. "I will come again tomorrow at the same time, if that is convenient."

"I will send word."

Toni started to nod—and then caught herself and shook her head.

Visiting an unfamiliar world was exhausting business.

9

DG: *sci.lang.xeno.talk*
Subject: *We aren't redundant yet (was Why I do what I do)*
From: *A.Donato@aira.org*
Local AIC date: *21.10.157*

<insultingly uninformed garbage snipped>

Okay, I'll explain it again, even though I've been through this so many times on the DGs it makes my head spin.

No, we can't just analyze a couple of vids made by a drone and come up with a language. Even with all the sophisticated equipment for recording and analysis which we now possess, at some stage in deciphering an alien tongue we're still dependent on the old point and repeat method. The human element of interaction, of trial and error, remains a necessary part of xenolinguistics. IMNSHO, the main reason for this is that analyzing an alien language, figuring out the parts of speech and the rules at work (which is the really tough part, and *not* simple vocabulary), is more than just "deciphering"—a very unfortunate word choice, when it comes right down to it. "Deciphering" implies that language is like a code, that there is a one-to-one correspondence between words, a myth which supports the illusion that all you have to do is substitute one word for another to come up with meaning. Language imperialists are the worst sinners in this respect, folks with a native tongue with pretensions towards being a diplomatic language, like English, French or Xtoylegh.

People who have never learned a foreign language, who have always relied on the translation modules in their AIs to do a less-than-perfect job for them, often can't conceive how difficult this "deciphering" can be, with no dictionaries and no grammar books. An element you think at first is a noun could be a verb. Something interpreted as an indefinite article could very well be a case or time marking. You have no idea where the declensions go, no idea if the subject of the verb comes first or last or perhaps in the middle of the verb itself.

No linguistics AI ever built has been idiosyncratic enough to deal satisfactorily with the illogical aspects of language. Data analysis can tell you how often an element repeats itself and in which context, it can make educated guesses about what a particular linguistic element *might* mean, but the breakthroughs come from intuition and hunches.

AIs have been able to pass the Turing test for two centuries now, but they still can't pass the test of an unknown language.

10

As she left the women's house, Kislan was coming down the street in the direction of the docks.

"Sha bo sham, Kislan."

"Sha bo sham, Toni." He pronounced her name with a big grin and a curious emphasis on the second syllable. After three days planetside, she was beginning to see him with different eyes. She recognized now that the colors braided into his hair signified that by birth he was a member of the same family as Councilor Lanrhel himself, and he had "married" into the house of Ishel, one of the most important merchant clans in the city of Edaru. It seemed the council of Edaru had sent a very distinguished young man as transportation for their guests.

And he was part of some kind of big communal marriage.

"Where are you off to?" she asked in Mejan.

"The offices of Ishel near the wharves. A ship has returned after an attack by pirates and we must assess the damage."

"Are pirates a problem around here?"

Kislan shook his head in the affirmative. "It is especially bad in the east."

They stood in the street awkwardly for a moment, and then Kislan asked, "Where do you go now? May I walk with you?"

"Don't you have to get to work?"

He shrugged. That at least was the same gesture she was used to. "There is always time for conversation and company."

Toni grinned. "I'm on my way back to the contact house."

Kislan turned around and fell into step next to her. She asked him about his work and he asked her about hers, and it occurred to her how odd it was that this particular social interaction was so much like what she had grown up with and seen on four planets now.

Talking and laughing, they arrived at the contact house in much less subjective time than it had taken Toni to get to the house of Anash—and it was uphill. After they said their goodbyes, she watched Kislan stride down to the wharves, starting to worry about her own peace of mind.

But when she entered the main office of the contact house, she had other things to worry about.

"I hope you will remember to remain professional, Donato," Repnik said.

Toni resisted the urge to retort sharply and leaned against the edge of a table. There were no AIRA regulations forbidding personnel from taking a walk with one of the natives—or even sleeping with one, as long as the laws of the planet were not broken.

She ignored the implied criticism. "Kislan was telling me about how they lost a ship to pirates. What do we know about these pirates?"

"Not much," Sam said. "Ainsworth wants to do some additional surveillance of the eastern coast."

"How did your meeting with Anash go?" Repnik asked.

She took a deep breath. "They won't speak their language with me until I promise no men will ever learn it."

Repnik shrugged. "I told you your presence here was unnecessary."

Didn't he even have any intellectual curiosity left, any desire to figure out the puzzle? Whether he resented her presence or not, if he still had a scientific bone left in his body he would be taking advantage of having her here.

She stood and began to pace. "Wouldn't it be possible to work out a deal with AIRA? Something that would allow us to reach an agreement with the women about their language? If Alnar ag Eshmaled had a special status, then only certain researchers would have access to the information."

"You mean, *women* researchers."

Toni stopped pacing. "Well, yes."

"Which would mean I, the head of this contact team, would be barred from working on the women's language."

She barely registered the minor victory of Repnik now referring to Alnar ag Eshmaled as a language. She had painted herself into a very hazardous corner. "I was only thinking of how we could keep from offending the women of this planet."

"And how you could get all the credit for our findings."

"I didn't—"

Repnik stepped in front of her, his arms crossed in front of his chest. "I would suggest that you try to remember that you are an assistant in this team. Nothing more."

Toni didn't answer for a moment. Unfortunately, that wasn't the way she remembered the description of her assignment to Christmas. But it had named her "second" team xenolinguist. Which meant that if Repnik saw her as an assistant, she was an assistant, and there wasn't anything she could do about it. "Yes, sir. Anything else?"

"Tomorrow morning I would like you to work on compiling a more extensive dictionary with the material we have collected in the last several weeks."

"Certainly, sir." She picked her bag up off the floor and left Contact House One for the peace and safety of Contact House Two before she could say anything she would regret later.

How could she have been so stupid? In terms of her career, it would have been smarter to suggest using her visits to install surveillance devices, even if that would have been questionable within the framework of AIRA regulations. But of course Repnik would never agree to a strategy that would allow her to work on one of the languages of Kailazh exclusively.

When would she learn?

Toni pushed open the door of her house, slipped off her jacket and hung it over the back of a chair. Well, she was not about to break the laws of her host planet, Repnik or no Repnik, so before she hooked her mobile AI into her desk console, she set up a firewall to keep the men on the team from learning the women's language by accessing her notes.

Once her privacy was established, she told the unit to replay the women's conversation. The sounds of their voices echoed through the small house while she got herself something to eat.

"Index mark one," she said after the first short conversation was over, and her system skipped ahead to the next conversation. The first thing she noticed was that the women's language had a number of rounded vowel sounds which were absent in the men's, something like the German Umlaut or the Scandinavian "ø." At the same time, however, there were quite a few words which sounded familiar.

She finished the bread and cheese and tea and wiped her mouth on a napkin. "System, print a transcript of the replayed conversations using the spelling system developed by Repnik, and run a comparison with the material already collected on the men's language."

"Any desired emphasis?"

"Possible cognates, parallel grammatical structures, inflections."

While the computer worked, she laid out the printed sheet of paper on the desk in front of her. Sometimes she found it easier to work in hard copy than with a projection or on a screen. Doodling with a pencil or pen on paper between the lines could help her to see new connections, possibilities too far-fetched for the computer to take into consideration—but exactly what was needed for dealing with an arbitrary, illogical human system like language.

The transcript was little more than a jumble of letters. Before the initial analysis, the computer only added spaces at very obvious pauses between phonemes.

Pencil in hand, Toni gazed at the first two lines, the hodgepodge of consonants and vowels.

*Tün shudithunföslodi larasethal segumshuyethun rhünem kasem alandaryk.*
*Athneshalathun rhün semehfarkari zhamdentakh.*

The last recognized unit of meaning looked like a plural. Plural was formed in the men's language by adding the prefix "zham-" to the noun. There was no telling if those particular sounds were the same in the women's language, or even if the plural was built the same, but at least it gave her a place to start.

There was a faint warning beep, and the computer announced in its business-like male voice, "Initial analysis complete."

Toni looked up. "Give me the possible cognates. Output, screen." A series of word pairs replaced an image of the landscape of Neubrandenburg.

*Dentakh - tendag.*

But why would the women be discussing pirates in the middle of a conversation about languages? Was the cognate the computer had come up with correct? And if it was, what did it mean?

After she'd returned home from Contact House One, Toni had begun to feel another stress headache coming on—but now it had disappeared completely and without drugs.

She had a puzzle to solve.

"Print out the results of the analysis," she said, pulling her chair closer to the table holding the console.

Toni went to work with a smile.

## 11

*From: Preliminary Report on Alnar ag Eshmaled, secondary language of Kailazh (Christmas). Compiled 28.11.157 (local AIC date) by Dr. Antonia Donato, second xenolinguist, Allied Interstellar Research Association first contact team. (Draft)*

"The men's and women's languages of Kailazh (Christmas) are obviously related. While this does not completely rule out an artificially constructed secret language, as has been observed in various cultures among classes wanting to maintain independence from a ruling class, the consistency in the phonetic differences between the cognates discovered so far seems to indicate a natural linguistic development. A further argument against a constructed language could be seen in sounds used in the women's language which are nonexistent in the men's language.

Interestingly enough, the women's language appears to have the more formal grammar of the two, with at least two additional cases for articles (dative and genitive?), as well as a third form for the second person singular, all of which are unknown in Alnar ag Ledar. To confirm this, however, much more material will need to be collected.

## 12

She'd had approximately three hours of sleep, when her mobile unit buzzed the next morning. Toni burrowed out from under the pile of blankets and switched on audio. She didn't want anyone seeing her just yet.

"Yes?" she said and snuggled back into her warm nest of covers.

Repnik's voice drifted over to her, and she grimaced. "Donato, do you realize what time it is?"

"No. I still don't have the display set up," she replied, trying to keep the sleep out of her voice. "And I must have forgotten to set my unit to wake me last night. Sorry."

An impatient "hmpf" came from her system. "Jump lag or no jump lag, I'd like you over here, now."

The connection ended abruptly. Toni pushed the covers back and got up, rubbing her eyes. Nights were simply too short on Christmas—especially for someone who had forgotten to go to bed until the sun started coming up.

Leather togs on and coffee downed, she was soon back at Contact House One, keying in and correcting terms in the preliminary version of the dictionary. After giving her his instructions, Repnik had left with Sam for a tour of the tannery outside of town, where they would ask questions and collect data and make discoveries. Like usual, Gates and Moshofski were already out looking at boulders and bushes and beasts.

While she was left with drudgery.

It was funny how something she had done regularly for the last five years now seemed so much more tedious than it ever had before. Toni loved words enough that even constructing the necessary databases had always held a certain fascination for her—on her previous jobs. Besides, it was a means to an end, a preliminary step on the ladder to becoming a first contact xenolinguist working on her own language.

Now it was a step down.

She spent the morning checking and correcting new dictionary entries that the automatic analysis had made, consulting the central AI on her decisions, and creating links to grammatical variations, as well as audio and visual files, where available. And all that on only three hours of sleep.

"Fashar," the computer announced. "Lace, the lace. Feminine. Irregular noun. Indefinite form fasharu."

Toni did a search for "rodela," another word for lace in the Mejan language, and then added links between the words. Under the entry "fashar," she keyed in, "See also 'rodela' (lace) and 'rodeli' (to create lace or crochet)." She would have to ask Anash what precisely the difference was between "rodela" and "fashar," if any—as yet, nothing was noted in their materials.

Outside the door of the lab, she heard the sound of voices. Sam and Repnik returning from field work. Having fun.

"Fashela," the computer announced. "Celebrate. Verb, regular."

"That's the attitude," Toni muttered.

The door opened, and Repnik entered, followed by Sam, who looked a little sheepish. Getting chummy with the top of the totem pole.

Repnik sauntered over to her desk. "How is our dictionary coming along?" he asked in that perky voice bosses had when they were happy in the knowledge that they were surrounded by slaves. And were particularly pleased in the status of the slave before them.

"I'm up to the 'f's now in checking entries and adding cross references. Our material is a little thin on specific definitions, though."

The faint smile on his face thinned out and disappeared. "It is, is it?"

He looked offended for some reason. Toni had only been pointing out a minor weakness, common in early linguistic analysis of new languages, certainly not something to get irritated about. Man, was he touchy. She would have to tread even more carefully.

She drew a deep breath. "I've been tagging synonyms where we don't have any contextual information. We need to know more about the kinds of situations where one word or the other would be most appropriate. Would you like to ask the Mejan about the synonyms, or should I?"

"Make a note of it," Repnik said shortly.

"Certainly, sir."

"I have another meeting with Councilor Lanrhel. I'll see you both again tomorrow."

"But—"

"Tomorrow, Donato."

When he was gone, Toni joined Sam next to the small holo well set up in the lab, where he was viewing a scene of what looked like a festival.

She touched his elbow. "I learned something the other day in the women's house that you might find interesting."

"Bookmark and quit," Sam said to the holo projector before he swiveled around on his chair to face her. "That's right, I wanted to ask you about that meeting, but you left pretty abruptly yesterday."

Toni pulled over a chair and straddled it, leaning her forearms on the back. "I know. I should have stuck around, but our boss is really getting to me. Maybe I'm overreacting, but I'm starting to get the feeling that Repnik wants to make me quit."

Sam shook his head. "You *are* overreacting. Your suggestion yesterday, logical as it was, was practically calculated to make him feel threatened. Just give him some time to get used to you."

"I'll try."

"So, what did you find out for me?"

Toni chuckled. "Right. Anash told me yesterday that there's no specific taboo on women speaking with strange men. The reason they won't speak with the men of our team is because they offend them by speaking before they are spoken to."

Sam's eyes lit up. "Really?"

She nodded. "Do you know if you're guilty of offensive behavior yet?"

"I don't think so. When I got here, Repnik told me there was a taboo against strangers speaking with Mejan women *at all*, so I didn't even try. Wow. This changes everything."

"Yup. I wanted to get together with Anash and Thuyene again this afternoon. Since you're not one of the offensive ones, I could ask if we could meet outside of the women's house sometime, at a neutral location where you could join us."

"That would be great if you could organize it!" Sam said, his dark eyes alight with enthusiasm. "But maybe you can find out first how I *am* supposed to conduct myself."

"The young one with the hair of night and eyes like a *likish*?" Anash asked. A likish was one of the native amphibian creatures of Kailazh, with both legs and fins and a nostril/gill arrangement on its back which reminded Toni vaguely of whales. She had yet to see a likish, but she had seen pictures, and she could appreciate the simile.

Not having adjectives, Alnar ag Ledar could be quite colorful, if the speaker chose some other way to describe something than using the attribute verbs.

"*Al*," Toni said. *Yes*.

Anash gazed at her with a speculative expression—or at least what looked like it to Toni. Anash's eyes were slightly narrowed, her head tilted to one side, and her lips one step away from being pursed. "That one has not himself offended any of the women of Edaru," the older woman finally said. "You say he is a specialist in understanding the ways of a people?"

"Yes. He has replaced Landra Saleh, who I believe you met before she became ill."

"Then we will meet with him two days from now in the common house."

That would mean Toni would temporarily have to give up her surreptitious recordings in the women's house—but helping Sam would be worth it.

And when she told Sam the women had agreed to meet with him, his reaction more than made up for it. He was so enthusiastic, she felt as if she'd given him a present.

The day of their appointment, they walked together down the hill to the center of town, Toni sporting a new leather cape she'd purchased for a couple of ingots of iron from the string she wore around her neck. Iron was much more precious on Kailazh than gold.

As they wandered through the streets of the city, she examined the stands they passed. Most of the vendors they saw were men, but occasionally a lone woman sat next to bins of fruits and vegetables or shelves of polished plates and bowls made from the shells of oversized bugs. Such a female vendor would have to deal with male customers alone, some of whom would necessarily be strangers. Toni wondered what the protocols for such transactions might be. Perhaps now that they had started asking the right questions, they could discover something more about the rules governing relations between the sexes on Kailazh.

She did her best to act naturally on this alien world, but often she felt like a circus animal. People peered out of their windows at them as they passed, and children ran up to them, giggling and pointing and staring, or hid behind their mothers' or fathers' legs. It hadn't been any different on Admetos, but the beings staring after her there had looked like ants. As a result, it had been easier for her to ignore their behavior. But these were *people*, at least in a more visceral way for Toni, since she was a hominid herself.

It would take some time getting used to.

"From what you've learned since you arrived, do you know when one of those ceremonial gifts of lace is appropriate?" Toni asked Sam.

"No. But it seems to be something only given by women. We aren't on sure enough ground yet to start messing with symbolic gestures."

Toni gave a playful snort of disgust. "You've already been here two weeks! What have you been doing in all that time?"

Sam chuckled. "I may not trust myself with symbols, but I'm pretty sure we could bring Anash a bottle of that lovely dessert wine that Edaru is famous for. Have you tried it yet?"

"I'm still trying to stick mostly to foods I'm familiar with. I don't want to end up offworld like your predecessor."

"Well, once you feel daring enough, take my word for it, it's an experience you don't want to miss. And according to Jackson, the fruit *kithiu* which they use to make *denzhar* is descended from plain old Terran grapes."

"Okay, you've convinced me. Where's the nearest wine dealer?"

The merchant was a man, so Toni didn't have a chance to see what the interaction would be between Sam and a female merchant. They paid with a small bead each from the strings of precious metals they wore around their necks, and arrived at the common house just as Kislan was helping Anash and Thuyene out of an open carriage.

To her surprise, Toni felt a pang of something resembling jealousy. These two women both belonged to Kislan's family, and while Anash was probably old enough to be his mother, Thuyene wasn't much more than Toni's age; probably less biologically on this world without age treatments. Her glossy reddish-brown hair hung in a single thick braid to her waist, laced with threads the colors of her birth clan and her chosen clan. Her amber eyes were full of life and intelligence. And Kislan was in some kind of group marriage arrangement with her. Did he hold her hand a little longer than that of Anash? Or was her feverish, human-male-deprived imagination just taking her for a ride?

Anash waved. Toni gave herself an inner shake and returned the gesture.

"I am glad you did not have to wait," Anash said. "I was afraid business went longer than expected." She looked at Sam curiously, but he said nothing, just lifting the back of his hand to his forehead in the gesture of greeting.

Kislan said something rapidly to the women of his family in a low voice that Toni couldn't understand. She looked away, hoping her face wasn't as flushed as she felt.

The room Anash led them to in the common house was smaller than the one where they had met on Toni's arrival, but it was a comfortable, sunny room with large windows facing a central courtyard and lace hangings decorating the walls.

"My colleague Samuel Wu has brought you a gift in hopes that relations between you might begin in a spirit of harmony and trust," Toni said in the Mejan language as they took seats on upholstered brocade sofas. This was the first time on Christmas she'd seen furniture covered in anything besides leather, and she wondered if this room was usually reserved for special occasions.

Kislan sat down beside her, and Toni felt her pulse quicken and her cheeks grow hot. She really had been living too long among ants.

Anash addressed Sam directly. "Sha bo sham, Samuel. We thank you, both for the thoughtful gesture and the respect that goes with it. We will be happy to tell you of Mejan ways. We too are curious to hear about the ways of the people of the stars."

Sam got the bottle of *denzhar* out of his bag, while Toni checked the AI at her wrist to make sure she'd set it for record mode. Across from her, Thuyene pulled a crocheting project out of her own bag, and Toni suppressed a smile.

"Sha bo sham, tajan," Sam said, leaning across the table and presenting the wine to Anash. "I am honored to be able to speak with you and hope that my gift is welcome."

It appeared they had chosen well. A pleased smile touched Anash's lips as she accepted the bottle, and Toni almost sighed in relief.

Sam began by asking about the specific rules governing interaction between men and women. They soon learned that in addition to the disrespect shown if a man not of a woman's family spoke before being spoken to, there was a whole battery of taboos concerning what was appropriate when and with whom and at what age. It reminded Toni vaguely of what she had read long ago about Victorian England—except for the group marriages, of course.

While the conversation was fascinating, at least as far as Toni understood it, they never came anywhere near to the topic of sex proper, and the group marriages practiced on Christmas in particular. Sam was obviously doing his best to tread carefully, and open discussion of sexual practices was taboo in the majority of cultures in the galaxy.

"Boys move into the house of men when they are weaned, correct?" Sam asked.

Anash shook her head in the affirmative. "Yes." Toni felt the heat from Kislan's body next to her.

"Is there any kind of ritual associated with the move?"

"To leave the mother is to leave the sea, so there is a celebration on the beach called *mairheltan*."

Kislan spoke up. "It is the first memory I have, the *mairheltan*."

"What does the ritual consist of?" Sam asked.

"The boy who is to leave the house of women goes into the water with the mother and comes back out by himself," Thuyene explained. "Then there is a feast with fish and *dashik*, and the child receives a leather cape and a length of lace."

She used the term "roda ag *fashar*" not "rodel" when she spoke of lace. Toni remembered the dictionary entries she'd been working on the other day and couldn't help asking an off-topic question. "What exactly is the difference between 'fashar' and 'rodel'?"

Thuyene lifted up the crocheting she was working on. "This is 'rodela.'" She pointed to a wall hanging just past Kislan's shoulder. "This is 'fashar.'"

It was all lace to Toni, but she was beginning to see the difference. "So 'fashar' is the piece when it is finished?"

"Not always. The 'fashar' given to a boy when he joins the house of men only begins. The women of his house can add to the 'fashar' he is given as a boy."

Toni would have liked to find out more about the words, but Sam was asking another question himself. "If a boy has already begun to talk before he leaves the house of women, how is it he doesn't learn to speak the women's language?"

Anash chuckled. "His mother corrects him if he speaks the language that is wrong."

Sam laughed and looked at Kislan, who smiled and shrugged. Toni could see how that would be a very effective method to keep boys from learning the women's language.

The meeting continued until the light through the windows began to grow dim, and ended with a promise to show Sam around town the next day to see some of the places where women worked in Edaru. Anash couldn't accompany him herself, but she would see to it that one of the women of her house met him tomorrow morning at the Mejan equivalent of a café in the main square. Of course, he still was not allowed to visit any of the houses of women, but his enthusiasm at the sudden progress in his research was obvious in his voice and posture.

Toni had learned quite a bit herself that afternoon. It was surprising what you could discover if you only knew which questions to ask. Anash and Thuyene had been astonished at some of the things they told them about their native cultures as well, in particular the institution of marriage, which they only seemed to be able to understand in terms of property, of one partner "belonging" to the other.

She'd done her best to suppress her awareness of Kislan beside her, but the discussion of different forms of partnership unfortunately had quite the opposite effect. As a human male of Kailazh, Kislan was both familiar and exotic at the same time. A very desirable male, especially after she had spent all too long on a world full mostly of giant ants. All the senses in her body were screaming "potential partner" for some primordial reason, and she had the uncomfortable sensation that Kislan was aware of her in a similar way—even though he was part of some kind of group marriage with the women across from her.

He didn't speak much, and neither did she. Instead, they sat there, the lovely view of the red fern and coral-like vegetation visible through the window across from them.

On one level, Toni was relieved when Anash called an end to the meeting. On another, she wished they could continue to sit there and talk for hours, learn more about social arrangements on Christmas, find out how the Mejan viewed their own history. And on the primal level, she was humming. Feeling that kind of physical attraction again after so long, almost knee to knee and elbow to elbow, was mind- and body-racking.

She barely looked at Kislan as they took their leave, mentally kicking herself for the way she was responding to his physical presence.

"Their reaction to marriage forms in Terran culture was interesting, don't you think?" Sam said when they were out of earshot of the common house.

"You mean in terms of property?" Toni asked.

"Exactly. I wish we could find out more about their history. It makes me wonder if slavery might not be too far removed in the Mejan consciousness. Oh, and thank you."

"What for?"

Sam smiled that slow smile she had learned to like so much from the vids they had sent each other. "For giving me a crack at half a society."

## 13

*The Legend of the Three Moons*

Once, in the early days of the Mejan, after the Great War, there was a very attractive young man, more handsome than any other in all of the thirteen cities. When he came of age, Zhaykair, mother of the house of Sheli, asked if he would join their family, and he came willingly. The house had a good reputation for the fine lace it produced, and the women of the house were beautiful, their necks long, their shoulders wide, and their skin glossy.

A sister of the house looked on the man with desire and wished to have him for herself alone. The husband saw her beauty, her hair the color of night and her eyes like a dashik flower, and he swore to do anything for her; she made his blood run hotter than any woman he had ever seen. The sister went mad at the thought of him lying with other women, and she made him promise he would resist all others for her sake.

Zhaykair saw what her sister was doing and how it poisoned the atmosphere in the house. She went to the councilor to ask what he thought should be done with the young man.

"We will bring them before us and ask them what is more important, the peace of the house or their love."

So the sister and the husband were brought before the council. The mother gazed at the sister with sadness and said, "I cannot believe that you would disturb the peace of the house this way."

The sister began to cry. The husband jumped up, his hand raised against Zhaykair. When the sister saw what he intended to do, she threw herself upon him, but not before he had struck the mother.

By law, the husband had to be given back to the sea for striking a mother. The sister refused to let him go alone, and they returned to the sea together.

Zhaykair could not bear the thought of what had happened in her house and the sister's betrayal, and she followed them soon after. The sea in her wisdom wanted to make a lesson of them and gave the three lovers to the sky.

And now the sister, who never wanted to share the young man with another, must share him with Zhaykair every night. Sometimes it is the sister who is closer and sometimes the mother, but only for a short time does the sister ever have him to herself.

## 14

The next day, Toni met with the women on their own turf again. She was shown into the central courtyard by a beautiful young woman wearing the colors of Ishel and Railiu in the dark braids scattered through her heavy hair. The air was crisp and the sun bright, and they wandered among the houses, Anash and Thuyene pointing out more of the complex.

The first contact team referred to the residences of the families of Edaru as "houses" for the sake of simplicity—in actuality, they consisted of several buildings, with the young girls living in one, the mothers of the youngest children with their babies and toddlers in another, and the grown women with no children below the age of about three standard years in a third. There was also a smaller version of the Edaru common house, with a family refectory and rooms where all could gather and talk, play games, tell stories. Perhaps on the surface the setup did resemble a harem, but it obviously wasn't one.

"I hope you did not lose much in the pirate attack," Toni said during a lull in the conversation.

Anash looked grim. "Too much."

"This is the second ship attacked this summer," Thuyene added.

Suddenly, Toni realized how she might be able to get the Mejan to agree to the AIC treaty. Anash was obviously one of Lanrhel's main advisers, and he would listen to what she had to say. "So you also have a problem with pirates," she said casually.

"Why do you say 'also'?" Anash asked.

"There are many pirates among the stars too. That is the purpose of the Allied Interstellar Community—to form a common defense against the pirates of the sky."

Of course, that wasn't the only purpose: interstellar trade and research were at least equally important, with the emphasis on "trade." But Toni doubted she could interest anyone on Kailazh in trade with distant points of light that figured prominently in stories told in the evening to pass the time.

"But why should we fear them?" Thuyene asked. "We do not travel the stars, so they cannot attack the ships of the people."

"It's not that easy," Toni said, suppressing thoughts of how the other woman might be spending her nights—in the Ishel main house with Kislan. "They might come here."

Anash started. "Attack Edaru? From the sky?"

"Certainly from the sky."

In their surprise, Anash and Thuyene didn't think to lower their voices when they began discussing rapidly in the women's language, and Toni was able to capture a lengthy conversation on her wrist unit.

Finally they turned back to her. "How can that be?"

"As soon as Kailazh was discovered, the news of another culture was known to all the worlds with access to the network of the Allied Interstellar Community." But, of course, the word she used in the Mejan language wasn't actually "network": the term the first contact team used to approximate the interstellar exchange of information referred to the trade of professional couriers who traveled between the thirteen cities, dispensing messages and news.

"I see," Anash said. "And in this way, we become a part of this community before we even give permission." She used some kind of qualifier for "permission" which Toni was unfamiliar with, but she didn't deem it the right time to ask what it meant. Anash lifted the back of her hand to her forehead, and Toni's heart sank—she was being dismissed.

"Thuyene will see you out of the house," Anash said and turned on her heel.

Together they watched her stride back to the central building. "You should have told us sooner," Thuyene said quietly.

"I didn't know it was so important."

"I believe you. There is much we still do not know about each other."

*That* was certainly true.

When she returned to Contact House One, Toni found Sam sitting tensely in his desk chair and Repnik standing next to him, his arms folded in front of his chest.

Repnik turned, not relaxing his defensive posture. The stress lines between his eyes were even more pronounced than usual and his face was pale. "I'm glad you have finally arrived, Donato. I hear you took Sam to meet with the women yesterday without my authorization."

Toni blinked. Sam didn't *need* Repnik's authorization. Certainly, Repnik had seniority, but the experts of a first contact team were free to pursue their research however they saw fit. *She*, by contrast, was only second linguist, so it was a bit more logical for Repnik to boss her around.

"Uh, yes."

"I won't have it. I've already told Sam that he is not to meet with the women again unless I arrange it."

Which meant never. The women refused to negotiate with Repnik, that much was clear.

She looked at Sam, his lips pressed together and misery in his eyes.

Toni at least didn't have much to lose. She could put her neck out where Sam obviously wasn't willing to. "But he's chief sociologist."

"And I'm head of the first contact team."

She couldn't believe it. Either he was so fixated on maintaining complete control of the mission that he had lost it—or there was something he didn't want them to find out. She looked him in the eye, her hands on her hips. "Maybe we should see what Ainsworth has to say about that. Computer, open a channel to the *Penthesilea*."

"Access denied."

"What?!"

"Access denied," the computer repeated, logical as always.

"Why?"

"Prof. Dr. Hartmut Repnik has restricted access to communications channels. I am no longer authorized to initiate off-site communications without his permission."

The completely mundane thought darted through Toni's mind that she would no longer be able to participate in the AIC discussion groups. As if that mattered right now.

"I don't want you visiting any of the houses of women without my approval, either," Repnik continued, addressing Toni.

"But we're here to learn about these people."

"And the two of you have been conducting unauthorized research. Now if you'll excuse me, I have AIRA business to attend to."

When Repnik was out of the door, Toni turned to Sam. "Unauthorized research?"

Sam shrugged, looking wretched.

Toni dropped into the chair next to him. "So, you still think I'm over-reacting?"

Sam didn't respond to her attempt at a joke. "We're stuck, you know. He's going to tell Ainsworth some story about us now."

She propped her chin in her hand. "You must have done something to set him off. Can you think what it might be?"

He shook his head. "I just told him about the meeting with Anash and Thuyene yesterday."

"So he doesn't want either of us speaking directly with the women. But why?"

Sam shook his head, and Toni got up and began to pace. "Look, Sam, he can't get away with this. If Repnik really does contact Ainsworth about us with some fairy tale, then we'll also have our say, and it should be obvious that he's giving orders that hinder the mission."

"And what if he lies?"

"We have to tell Gates and Moshofski what's up."

"They won't be in until tonight."

They stared at each other in silence for a moment. "I think I need to take a walk."

Sam gave her a weak smile and waved her out the door. "Go. I'll hold down the fort."

Toni walked, long strides that ate up the stone-paved streets. She had devoted most of her adult life to AIRA, and she didn't know what she would do if they threw her out. Given the number of interstellar languages she could speak, there would always be jobs for her, but if she went into translating or interpreting, she would no longer be involved in the aspect of language she enjoyed most, the puzzle of an unknown discourse.

At least she wouldn't have to work with any more ants.

The weather was turning, appropriate to her mood, the gray-green sky heavy with the threat of rain. Toni made her way through narrow side streets to the sea wall at the south end of town. The green ocean below crashed against the wall, sending shots of spray up to the railing where she stood, and the wind tangled her hair around her face. She pulled her leather cape tighter around her body and gazed out to sea. The lacy rings of sunset probably would not be visible tonight, blocked out by the coming storm.

She heard a footstep behind her and turned. Kislan. He gazed at her with eyes that matched the sea, and she realized she had come out here close to the docks hoping they might run into each other.

He raised the back of his hand to his forehead, and she returned the gesture. "Sha bo sham, Kislan."

"Sha bo sham, Toni."

Her name in his language sounded slower, more formal, less messy, the "o" rounded and full, the syllables distinct and clear. She wondered what "Antonia" would sound like on his lips. She'd never liked the name, but she thought she might if he said it.

"How do you greet a friend in your language, someone you are close to?" Toni asked.

"Sha bo foda," he said. "Dum gozhung 'sha.'" *Or simply "sha."*

"Can we use 'fo' and 'foda' with each other?" she asked, offering her hand in the gesture of her homeworld.

He nodded, the negative on Kailazh, ignoring her hand. He didn't want to use the informal "you" form with her. He wouldn't take her hand anymore either, although he took Thuyene's when he was only leaving for an afternoon. But then, Thuyene was one of his wives, and she most certainly was not. She leaned her hip on the railing, gazing at the gray-green sea below the dark gray sky. There was no reason to feel hurt and every reason to feel relief. He was a part of the Ishel family, and she still didn't understand the way loyalty was regarded in these complex relationship webs. Definitely not something to get messed up with.

Tears began to collect at the corners of her eyes, and she wiped them away angrily. To her surprise, Kislan turned her to him and took her chin in one hand.

"Tell me," he said. The Mejan very rarely used the command form, and there was something shocking about it. It startled Toni into more honesty than she had intended.

"This is all so difficult."

He shook his head slowly and she gave a humorless laugh. Then her intellectual knowledge managed to seep through her emotional reaction. He *wasn't* disagreeing with her.

She twisted her face out of his hand and turned around to grip the railing at the top of the sea wall. A pair of arms encased in soft leather came around her and a pair of hands with their strange, wonderful webbing settled on hers. "You don't understand. It is not allowed for us to speak so with each other."

His chest was wide and hard against her back, welcome and strong. She had the unrelated, illogical thought that he probably had the high lung capacity of most of the Mejan, and wondered how long he could stay underwater comfortably.

"Al," Toni said, *yes*, unsure what exactly she was saying "yes" to.

Then there were a pair of lips, soft and warm, against the back of her neck, and it was too late to consider anything. She was in way over her head, infatuated with a man who had about a dozen official lovers.

His arm moved around her shoulders and he steered her away from the railing along the sea wall, away from the city. "It hurts me to see you weep. I would keep you from being alone."

To their left, the stone walls of the nearest buildings were painted in bright colors, colors to make the heart glad, shades of yellow and red and sea green.

She pulled herself together and dried her cheeks with the back of her hand. "It's no good. We barely understand each other."

"You speak our language very well."

"It's more than that. Our ways differ so much, when you say one thing, I understand another. We can't help but see each other through the patterns we know from the cultures we grew up with. Like looking through lace—the view isn't clear, the patterns get in the way."

Kislan shook his head—affirmation, she reminded herself. "Yes, I see. But I would never hurt you, Toni."

"Ah, but you do. I know it's not deliberate, but just by being a man who lives by the rules of the Mejan, you hurt me."

He shook his head again. "It has to do with the relationship between men and women in the culture where you come from?"

"Yes." Toni didn't trust herself with gestures.

They had nearly reached the end of the sea wall, and there were no buildings here anymore. Kislan took her hand in his own webbed one.

"You would want to have me for yourself?" Kislan asked. "Like the sister in the legend of how the moons got into the sky?"

"It is the way things are done in the world I come from," Toni said defensively.

He smiled at her. "That is a story that lives in my heart."

She stopped, surprised. "I thought it was meant to show the People how *not* to behave, a lesson."

Kislan laughed out loud. "Have you no stories in your culture that are meant to teach but tempt instead?"

Of course they did. Human nature was stubborn and contrary, and no matter what the culture, there would always be those who would rebel, who would see something different in the stories than what was intended. Even in a relatively peaceful, conformist society like that of the Mejan.

"Yes, there are some similarities."

They leaned against the railing and looked out at the harbor of Edaru, at the graceful, "primitive" ships swaying with the waves. The sea was unquiet, the sky still heavy.

Kislan let his shoulder rest against hers. "Although I know nothing about the worlds on the stars, I can understand a little how you cannot always make sense of our way of doing things. The People live all along the coast here, and the rule of the house is the same for all. But the pirates beyond the waters of the world and on the islands to the east live by rules hard for us to understand."

"What rules do they live by?"

"They have no houses and no loyalty. They buy and sell not only goods but also *zhamgodenta*."

That was a term Toni had not yet heard. "What does 'godenta' mean?"

"That is a word for a person who is bought and sold."

*Slavery.* Sam had been right.

## 15

*From: Mejan creation myth*
*Recorded 01.10.157 (local AIC date) by Landra Saleh, sociologist, first contact team, SGR 132-3 (Christmas / Kailazh).*

The war between the Kishudiu and the Tusalis lasted so many years and cost so many lives, there were no longer any women alive who had not known a life without war. Soon there were no longer any men left at all.

The women of the Kishudiu and the Tusalis looked around them at the destruction of their homes, saw that there was nothing left to save and no enemies left to fight. Together, they took the last ships and fled by sea.

After sailing for almost as many days as the war had years, they came to a beautiful bay on the other side of the world, a haven of peace, a jewel. Edaru.

## 16

Jackson Gates and Irving Moshofski were already there when Toni returned to Contact House One. Two pairs of dark eyes and one pair of gray turned to her in unison when she entered the lab.

"This is unprecedented," Jackson said.

"I hope so," Toni said. "But since this is the only first contact team I've ever been on, my experience is a bit limited."

The men smiled, and the atmosphere became a shade less heavy.

"One of us will have to be here in the lab at all times in case the *Penthesilea* makes contact," Moshofski said. "I checked the systems, and there doesn't seem to be a way for any of us to override Repnik's commands."

"So we have to wait until Ainsworth can do it," Toni said.

The other three nodded.

"I was beginning to wonder what Repnik was up to," Jackson said quietly. "He made a point of telling me you were having an affair with the young man who acted as your chauffeur from the landing base."

Toni swallowed. "I—no—I'm attracted to him, but, I—no." Then through her embarrassment she picked up on a detail of what he had said. "You mean Kislan wasn't your chauffeur when you first arrived?"

"No. We had a much older man driving us."

"Hm. Was he also a member of the ruling clans?"

"I don't remember offhand the colors he wore in his hair, but I don't think so."

"Interesting." So why had they sent her Kislan?

There was little else they could do without being able to contact the *Penthesilea*, so they said goodnight to each other and sought out their separate quarters.

With all of the day's upheavals, Toni had almost forgotten the recording she'd made in the morning, and she returned to the work she loved, relieved that she had something to take her mind off Repnik's irrational behavior.

The conversations she'd caught were a goldmine—or an iron mine, from the Mejan point of view. And it wasn't just the long exchange between Thuyene and Anash or the snippets from the other women in the Ishel family. The discoveries started when she began to study the unknown qualifier Anash had used when speaking to her. After analyzing the recordings of the women's language for similar occurrences of "kašem," she was almost certain it was a possessive pronoun.

Both the possessive and the genitive were unknown in the men's language—the linguistic forms for ownership.

Toni leaned back in her chair and regarded the notes she'd made in hard copy, the circles and question marks and lines and arrows. So what did she have? She had phonetic differences which seemed to indicate that the men's language had evolved out of the women's language and not the other way around. She had a gendered language in which the genders of the nouns didn't match up with gendered forms of address. She had warriors being named in one breath with pirates and pirates being named in one breath with language. She had a language spoken by men and named after the sea— and the sea was associated with the mother. She had grammatical cases that didn't exist in the men's language, a pairing which normally would lead her to conclude that the "secondary language" was the formalized, written language. If you looked at Vulgar Latin and Italian or any other of the common spoken languages in the European Middle Ages on Earth, it was the written language which had maintained the wealth of cases, while the romance languages which evolved out of it dispensed with much of that.

But the Mejan had no written language, because they had no system of writing.

She also had a boss who was doing his utmost to keep them from learning too much about the culture of the women.

And she had a man with eyes the color of a stormy green sea. A man who was married to about a dozen women at once.

Most of what she had were complications and questions. Where were the answers?

The next morning, Toni found Kislan on the docks, speaking with a captain of one of the ships belonging to his family. It probably would have been more logical to seek out Anash, but Toni didn't feel very logical.

Besides, her boss had pretty much forbidden her from speaking with the women of Christmas without his permission. Which she suspected meant never.

When he saw her striding his way, Kislan's eyes lit up, and her gut tightened in response. She touched her forehead with the back of her hand. "Sha bo dam," she said, using the plural second person. "I hope I'm not interrupting anything?"

Kislan nodded denial. "We are expecting a shipment of leather goods, and I merely wanted to see if it had arrived." He introduced Toni to the captain, Zhoran. She noted the threads braided into his hair, saw that he too wore the colors of both Lanrhel's family and the Ishel, and she looked at him more closely. His coloring was lighter than Kislan's, and he was obviously older, his golden-brown hair showing the first signs of gray at the temples. The bone structure of his face was very similar, though. She wondered if they were brothers.

Toni touched Kislan's elbow briefly. "May I speak with you alone?"

He shook his head. "Let us go to the office."

Toni followed him a short distance down a street leading away from the docks—away from the busy, noisy scene, much like that of any center for trade and travel. Despite the presence of horses and carriages, despite the color of the vegetation on the hills and the scent of the air, it reminded her a little of the many transit stations between wormhole tunnels that she had passed through on her travels between worlds. It looked nothing alike, but there was an energy level, an atmosphere, which was much the same, despite the different details.

Kislan had a small office in the rambling administration building of his family's trading business. On a table in the center of the room stood a counting machine similar to an abacus, and against one wall was a heavy door with a lock, the first lock Toni had even seen on Kailazh. But no desk. Without any system of writing, there was apparently no need for a desk.

When the door was closed behind her, Kislan pulled her into his arms and held her tightly. "Time has crawled by since you left me yesterday," he murmured into her hair.

The words and the arms felt incredibly good, but Toni couldn't allow herself to get involved with him—especially when she still didn't know whether fooling around outside the house was a sin or not. To judge by the legends she was familiar with, trying to monopolize a sexual partner was definitely a sin. Which was enough of a problem all by itself, seeing as she had no experience in sharing.

She slowly disentangled herself from Kislan's embrace. "I didn't seek you out for this. I wanted to ask you about something I don't understand, something that might help me understand more."

"Yes?"

"In your creation myth, all the men are killed in the war between the Kishudiu and the Tusalis. But how could the women have started a new society without men? Is there any explanation in the myth for that?"

Kislan shrugged. "What explanation is needed? Yes, all of the men died; the warriors, *zhamhainyanar*, but that is not everyone."

"'Hainyan'? I don't know that word yet. What does it mean?"

"'Hainyan' is the word for the man when a man and a woman are together as a family."

"But I thought that was 'maishal'?"

"No, no. 'Hainyan' is an old word. For the way it used to be. Much as you told us about the ways in the land you come from." He seemed to be both repelled and fascinated by the thought, and Toni remembered how he and Anash and Thuyene could only understand the marriages of Terran and Martian culture in terms of possession.

If Toni was right, and "yanaru" was the word for woman in Alnar ag Eshmaled, then the root of "hain-yan" could be "over-woman."

A husband—like on the world she came from.

"But that still doesn't explain how the Mejan came to be," she said.

"They made their slaves their husbands." This time he used the word "maishal."

Toni stared at him. The women had owned the men when they first came here. *Their* language had possessive cases, the men's language—the language which had evolved from the dialect of the slaves?—did not. And the pirates to the east, the men who kept slaves—was the word for pirate perhaps the original word for men in the women's language?

That would explain why Toni had thought they'd been discussing "pirates" when she asked if she could learn their language.

Suddenly things started coming together for her like a landslide. And she was almost certain Repnik had figured it out—which was why he was doing his best to hinder their research.

Because he couldn't be chief linguist on a planet where the chief language was a women's language.

Then the thought occurred to her: what had really happened to Landra Saleh?

She pushed away from Kislan. "I must speak with Repnik."

"Why?"

"I think I know now why he was trying to forbid me from talking to the women."

"He did that?"

"Yes."

"But how can he have the authority? Authority belongs to the mother." *Tandarish derdesh kanezha tajanar*. He used the attitude particle "der-" for "a fact that cannot be denied."

Toni stared at him, her mind racing. *Authority belongs to the mother*. Tandarish - tajanar. "Tan" and "tajan" could well have the same root, which would mean the authority of the mother was even embedded in the word itself.

She pulled a notebook and pen out of her shoulder bag, sat down on one of the chairs, and began jotting down the possible cognates with the women's language, along with the old word for husband. And slave. She was trying to come up with a cognate for the first half of the word "godent" when Kislan interrupted her.

"What are you doing?" he asked, sitting down in the chair next to her and peering over her shoulder.

She didn't have any words for writing in his language, so she tried to describe it. "I have an idea about the Language of the People, and I wanted to make the symbols for the words in my language before I forget."

"I have seen the men of the contact team do this before, but I thought it was something like painting." He laughed out loud. "I did not understand, none of us did. Among us, the men are not responsible for making *dalonesh*."

Toni wasn't familiar with the last word. "What does 'dalonesh' mean?"

Kislan shrugged. "Events, history, business—anything that should be passed on."

*Records*. He was speaking of records.

But in order to have records, you had to have a written language.

"Rodela," Toni murmured to herself. They had been even more dense than she'd suspected. The crocheting the women did during the meetings she'd attended was *writing*, making the records of important assemblies, and who knew what else.

"Yes," Kislan said, his voice thoughtful. "You mean, among the people from the sky both men and women learn *rodela*?"

*Both men and women learn crocheting*, Toni's brain translated for her stubbornly, and she had to laugh.

Kislan started away, and she laid a hand on his forearm. "I am sorry, I meant no offense. Repnik had translated 'rodela' with a word for a hobby practiced mostly by women on the world where he comes from. The answer to your question is: yes, on the worlds I know, Earth, Mars, Jyuruk and Admetos, we all learn writing, men and women both."

"I have often thought it would be good to know, but men are not regarded as masculine if they learn *rodela*. It is not taught to us."

*Men are not regarded as masculine if they learn crocheting.* Certainly not. That fit very well into the mindset the first contact team had brought with them to Christmas. But they were not talking about crocheting, they were talking about the power of passing on knowledge through the written word. In order for people of her cultural background to understand Kislan's statement, more than "rodela" would have to be changed. To get at the underlying attitude, the gender of the words would have to be changed as well: *Women are not regarded as feminine if they learn writing.*

*That* was the attitude that was behind what Kislan had said. He had not mentioned "rodela" like something he could easily do without, he had mentioned it with regret, like something denied to him. Even if the words were translated with their correct meanings, the sentence made no sense, at least not on any world in the Allied Interstellar Community. *Men are not regarded as masculine if they learn writing.*

"Is it forbidden?" Toni asked.

Kislan frowned, nodding. "It is not done. I know no man capable of *rodela*."

Toni took a deep breath. Suddenly everything about the Mejan looked completely different. The world had tilted and turned upside-down, and now the Christmas tree was right-side up. She couldn't believe how blind they had been, how blind *she* had been.

Except, perhaps, Repnik.

Of course, the first contact team had been plagued by bad luck from the start—or was it?—with no sociologist, no one to talk to the women, and a xenolinguist who was deliberately deceiving everyone. But that did not excuse the extent of the misunderstanding, and it certainly did not excuse her own mistakes. She'd felt that something was off, but she had allowed her own inherited attitudes to keep her from figuring out what it was.

"And the wall hangings?" she asked, beginning to pace. "What are those?"

He shrugged. "Genealogies, histories, famous stories. *Fashar.*"

Documents, books perhaps. Another word which would have to be changed. Translated as "lace" in the present dictionary. The books, the writing, it had been there right in front of their faces all this time. This had implications for their whole analysis of the language.

She stopped and turned to face him. "I have to speak with Repnik."

"Dai eden mashal." Which meant the same as "good" but was expressed in verb form. And if she had said the same thing to another woman, it would have been "dai desh mashal."

But after this, she would probably never trust her knowledge of another language again.


## 17

*The story of the young poet*
*Recorded 30.09.157 by Landra Saleh, retranslated 06.12.157 (local AIC date) by Antonia Donato.*

As long as she could remember, Zhaykair had only one dream—to become the greatest poet the Mejan had ever known. All young girls are taught the basics of writing, but Zhaykair would not stop at that. She begged the women of her village to teach her their way with words, the patterns they created, and she quickly found the most talented writer among them. Saymel did not belong to Zhaykair's house, but the families reached an agreement, and the little girl was allowed to learn from Saymel, although the job of Zhaykair's house was raising cattle.

But before she had seen nine summers, Zhaykair had learned all Saymel had to teach her. She begged her clan to allow her to go to the city of Edaru, where the greatest poets of the Mejan lived. Her mothers and fathers did not want to send her away, but Saymel, who could best judge the talent of the young girl, persuaded them to inquire if the house of Mihkal would be willing to take her on.

The elders sent a messenger to the Mihkal with some of Zhaykair's poems. They had feared being ridiculed for their presumption, but the messenger returned with an elder of the house of Mihkal to personally escort Zhaykair to the great city of Edaru.

Zhaykair soon learned all the Mihkal clan could teach her. Her poetry was in such great demand, and there were so many who wanted to learn from her, that she could soon found her own house. Her works now grace the walls of all the greatest families of the Mejan.


## 18

Toni found Repnik in the main square of Edaru, leaving the school of the house of Railiu, where boys memorized a wealth of Mejan legends and songs and were taught basic mathematics and biology and navigational skills.

But no crocheting.

"Sir!" Toni called out, rushing over to him. "I need to speak with you. Can we perhaps return to the contact house?"

"*You* can return to the contact house, Donato. I am going out to lunch with Sebair, the rector of the Railiu school."

Sebair strolled next to Repnik with his hand to his forehead, and Toni returned the gesture, greeting him less graciously than she should have.

"Sha bo sham, tajan," Sebair said in response, smiling despite her lack of manners.

"Mr. Repnik," Toni persisted. "I really need to speak with you. It's very important."

"I am sure you think it is. But you have a job to do, and what you have to tell me can wait until I get back to the lab."

Toni took a deep breath. "I know. What you've been trying to hide."

Repnik's stride faltered, but his confidence didn't, at least not as far she could tell. "I have no idea what you're talking about."

"I know that as far as the Mejan are concerned, I am the head of this contact team. And I know that they *do* have a system of writing."

Repnik stopped in his tracks. "You know *what?*"

So it seemed he hadn't gotten that far. He wasn't a good enough actor to fake that stare of surprise. He knew the women were the ones with the final say around here, but not what the crocheting really was. Toni felt a surge of satisfaction.

"And I also know that you've been trying to hinder the research of the first contact team."

An angry flush covered the chief linguist's face. "Ms. Donato, you are hallucinating."

"I don't think so. So don't you want to know what the system of writing is?"

Repnik snorted. "There is none. I knew before you came to Christmas that a woman dealing with a woman's language would lead to problems."

Finally, Toni could no longer control her temper. "Obviously not as many problems as a man dealing with a men's language," she spat out.

She saw his hand come up as if the moment were being replayed in slow motion. She knew it meant he was about to slap her, but she was too surprised to react. From that observing place in her mind, she saw Sebair start forward and try to stop Repnik, but then the flat of his palm met her cheek, the sting of pain sending tears to her eyes.

She lifted her own palm to cover the spot. Suddenly, utter silence reigned in the main square, everyone gaping at her and her boss. Then, just as suddenly, chaos broke out. The men who had been going about their business only minutes before converged upon Repnik and wrestled him to the ground.

Toni stood frozen, staring at the scene in front of her. Repnik had struck a mother.

The old man struggled beneath the three young men who held him down. "What is the meaning of this?" he yelled in Alnar ag Ledar.

Suddenly Lanrhel was there next to them. Toni wondered when he had joined the fray.

"Let him rise," the Councilor said.

The voluntary guards pulled Repnik to his feet, and Lanrhel faced him. "You know enough of our laws to know that to strike a mother means you must be returned to the sea."

Repnik wrenched one arm free and pointed at Toni. "*She* is no mother."

Lanrhel didn't even bother to answer, turning instead to Toni. "Tajan, do you need assistance?"

She was too confused to come up with the right gesture and shook her head. "No, it's nothing. Let him go, please."

A firm hand took her elbow. "Come." *Anash.*

"But Repnik . . . "

"Come. He must go with Lanrhel now."

Toni allowed herself to be led away to the common house and a small, private room. A basin of water was brought, and Anash pushed her into a chair and bathed her stinging cheek gently.

"You won't really throw him out to sea, will you?" Toni finally asked.

"I do not know yet what we will do. We have a dilemma."

They certainly did. Toni didn't even know if Repnik could swim. And if he could, he wouldn't be allowed to swim to shore. She didn't like him, but—a death sentence for a slap? "You can't give him back to the sea. He is not from this world. Where he's from, it's not a crime to slap a woman."

"Then it should be," Anash said grimly.

Anash was defending her, but it didn't feel like it. "Don't do this to him, please."

"How can you defend him after all the disrespect he has shown you?"

If Toni hadn't felt so horrible, she almost would have been tempted to laugh. That was the kind of reasoning shown by aristocracies and intolerant ruling powers throughout the histories of all the worlds she had ever visited. Disrespect as a capital crime.

Repnik hadn't been right to try to keep the truth from the first contact team, but he hardly deserved to walk the plank. Until this morning, she'd thought these women needed to be defended from the likes of Repnik. Now everything was on its head, everything.

As if to prove her point, Kislan entered the room, shutting the door gently behind him. He stared at her expectantly, and she finally remembered to greet him.

"Sha bo sham, Kislan."

"Sha bo sham, Toni." He approached and gave her a kiss, right in front of Anash.

His clan knew. They must have given him to her. *Like a present.* She was the visiting dignitary, and he was her whore. Had he thrown himself in her way willingly, or had he been forced to seek her out?

Toni pushed herself out of the chair, away from Kislan, and wandered over to the window. The central square of Edaru was unusually quiet for this time of day, just before the midday meal. People stood in small groups of two or three, speaking with earnest faces, spreading the news. By evening, the whole city would know that a man of the people from the sky had committed a grave crime against the sole woman of the contact team. If nothing was done, not only would Anash's authority be undermined, the first contact team would be seen as lawless and immoral.

She glanced up, above the rooftops of the buildings on the other side of the square, to the faint daytime hint of the lacy patterns in the sky, formed by the rings of Christmas.

The sky.

The old man wouldn't thank her, but she might have a way to save Repnik, keep him from being thrown into the ocean, and send him home safely.

"I have an idea," she breathed. "Criminals are returned to the sea, because that is where they are from, yes?"

Anash shook her head, watching Toni carefully.

"But the people of the first contact team do not come from the sea, they come from the sky."

"You are right," the older woman said. "This might be a solution."

Toni was the visiting dignitary, she had to remember that. "It is the only solution we can consider," she said in what she hoped was a voice of command.

Anash gazed at her as an equal. "Then we will give him back to the sky."

The ceremony took place on a sunny but cool afternoon three days later. Before arrangements could be made with the *Penthesilea*, they had to wait until the ship made contact itself. The taciturn Moshofski handled that end once Ainsworth overrode Repnik's commands, while Toni spent her time at the house of Ishel and in consultations with Lanrhel—aside from the one-sided shouting matches with Repnik, who was being kept under guard in the common house. Repnik had made it very clear that he intended to take Toni to interstellar court on charges of mutiny and conspiracy.

And if AIRA believed him, she was saving him to dig her own grave.

A construction resembling a pier was hastily built on a plain outside of town, between Edaru and the landing base. Although it was something of a trek for the town residents, several thousand people had made the trip to see Repnik returned to the sky.

With his head shaved, the old xenolinguist looked even older, gaunt and bare and bitter. Toni wished she didn't have to watch, let alone participate. The rest of the first contact team had elected to stay at home.

With a guard on either side, Repnik was accompanied down the waterless pier, Anash, Toni, and Thuyene a few paces behind. A shuttle from the *Penthesilea* waited at the end, Lanrhel and Ainsworth beside the door. Finally Repnik and his guards reached the councilor, and Lanrhel announced in his booming voice, "Mukhaired ag Repnik bonaashali der-ladesh." *Repnik's shame will now certainly be purged.* He then ordered the older man to strip. When Repnik refused, his guards stripped him forcibly.

Toni looked away. His humiliation was painful to see, his skinny, white flesh hanging loosely on his bones. He would hate her for the rest of his life, and she could hardly blame him.

Then Anash's hand on her elbow was urging her forward, pressing a bit of lace into her hand. A written record of Repnik's time on Christmas. Toni took a deep breath, looked up, and flung the *fashar* through the open doors of the shuttle.

Ainsworth nodded a curt goodbye, turned, and followed Repnik. The doors whisked shut, and the shuttle lifted off the ground.

After the ceremony, Anash led her to a small carriage to take her back to town. She was no longer surprised that the driver was Kislan again, and only a little surprised that Anash didn't join them.

Kislan was her present, after all.

If only Toni knew what to say, what to feel. He was still just as handsome, but she wasn't drawn to him in the same way as she had been only days before. She did not like what it said about herself, that she suddenly saw him so differently. Now he was a supplicant, whereas before he had been exotic and distant, a man of good standing in a powerful clan, nearly unattainable.

And she found that she didn't have the same feelings for someone who had been given to her as a welcoming gift.

"What is wrong, Toni?" Kislan asked gently after she hadn't spoken for minutes. His pronunciation of her name was a little like that of her Italian grandmother, and she had an odd impulse to cry.

"I don't know. I can't figure anything out."

"I thought you did not like Repnik?"

"No."

"Then why are you upset?"

"Things are so much stranger here than I thought. I'm confused. I need to think things out."

"And thinking things out includes me, yes?"

For a moment, Toni couldn't answer. "Yes."

Kislan looked away from her, concentrating on the road, and didn't speak again.

She arrived at Contact House One just as the lacy show of evening was beginning, her heart and mind a mess. The world was on its head and there were holes in the sky.

At the sound of hooves and wheels on the cobblestones, Sam, Jackson and Moshofski came out of the door to the courtyard, their expressions solemn.

Sam helped her down. "Ainsworth contacted us from the shuttle. They had to sedate Repnik."

Toni closed her eyes briefly. "I'm so sorry."

"No need, Donato," Jackson said. "Repnik was deliberately hindering AIRA work. And your plan kept him from being thrown into the sea."

"We've started to question what really happened to Landra," Moshofski added.

"I've been wondering about that too."

"We mentioned our suspicions to Ainsworth, and there will be an investigation," Jackson said.

She could only hope their suspicions were unfounded.

But Jackson wasn't done. "Given our new insights into the social structures on Christmas, you're to head the first contact team in future when dealing with the Mejan."

A smile touched Moshofski's serious features. "But in the lab, I'm to be the boss. Seniority, you know."

She could hardly believe it. "Certainly."

"Sam baked a cake to celebrate the two promotions," Jackson said. "Shall we test his talents?"

"I'll follow you in a minute."

The three men filed back into the contact house, and she came around the carriage to Kislan's side. "I never wanted to hurt you."

He gazed at her, not answering.

Toni looked away, at the sky above, the fabulous sunset over Edaru. "I'm sorry. I do not know what to think now. I will come see you again soon, and we can talk. Perhaps I can teach you our way of writing."

His eyes lit up. "Yes." He placed his free hand on her shoulder and nodded at the sky. "It's beautiful, isn't it?" *It is-in-a-state-of-beauty, yes?*

Toni shook her head. "Yes."

Steve Rasnic Tem's last novel, *Blood Kin* (Solaris, 2014), won the Bram Stoker Award. His latest novel, *UBO* (Solaris, January 2017), is a dark science fictional tale about violence and its origins, featuring such viewpoint characters as Jack the Ripper, Stalin, and Heinrich Himmler. He is also a past winner of the World Fantasy and British Fantasy Awards. A handbook on writing, *Yours To Tell: Dialogues on the Art & Practice of Fiction*, written with his late wife Melanie, recently appeared from Apex Books.

# A Letter from the Emperor

## *Steve Rasnic Tem*

A mishap occurred four sleeps from landfall. Jacob had been logging observations when he heard the alarm, so by the time he got down to the cargo bay it was all over. The bay door was breached. He stared at the switch through the window—it had been opened from inside the bay. Whatever had been inside the bay had been swept out into space.

"Anders?" he called through com. He waited. There was no answer. Ship command buzzed in his ear. *There are indications that Anders Nils . . .* Jacob shut the communication off. He didn't want to hear what command had to say. He went looking for Anders.

The forward crew cabin was empty. As were the toilets, the shower, records, navigation, engineering, recreation, general stores. Jacob had been in the recording room when the alarm went off. He systematically tried every compartment, passage, pipe, even the output trays of the garbage grinders. There was no place left to look. "Anders, please report your whereabouts," he called through com. Again no answer.

He waited. He turned the link to ship command back on. "Please report the whereabouts of Anders Nils," he said aloud.

*Anders Nils is not on board, a woman's voice spoke softly into his ear. Procedure is to query ship command first when there is an unscheduled breach of the cargo bay. Why did you fail to query ship command? Why did you shut off initial communications from ship command?*

Jacob didn't answer. He didn't know why he hadn't followed procedure. Maybe he already knew Anders was gone, but didn't want to hear command's confirmation. Was that it? It made very little sense—despite their long service together on messaging and data collection ships he and Anders weren't even friends, as far as he understood. Suddenly he wasn't sure. Was that possible?

How had they not become friends, enemies, something? Somehow he had avoided entanglement. He'd spent his long hours listening, the job they'd been trained to do, snatching the words out of space and trying to understand, and whenever possible delivering these stray messages to their intended destinations.

*Please respond to official queries.* Command's voice had lost some of its warmth, its naturalness. *You have a duty to respond to these questions.* Command was beginning to show its mechanical roots.

He was a professional, a sensor for the emperor, or for who- or whatever passed for the emperor these days, capturing the nuances machinery was still incapable of. "You record every stray fart," was the usual, vulgar summation of their duties. Such attention to detail discouraged both amity and enmity, as far as he was concerned.

He would be finishing the assignment alone. Perhaps even the entire tour of duty. The realization left him cold, furious. How was he supposed to manage it? Besides recording local observations and handling messaging, the ship delivered statements of regulation, and proclamations to the outlying settlements. But a quick replacement was impossible, out here on the farthest reaches of the empire, where the dividing line between empire and not-empire wasn't all that clear.

*Did Anders Nils speak to you before going to the cargo bay?*

Jacob gathered Anders's spare clothing into a bag. He catalogued his former crewmate's personal effects, his toiletries, his player, various small art objects.

*Please respond. Did Anders Nils speak to you of his intentions?*

Jacob ignored command's transmissions. He separated out all written notes and recordings, checking the storage on Anders's personal devices for data files and images. Anders's diary files were extensive and detailed, and he only had time to go through a sampling. The entries surprised him, but he had no time or inclination to be surprised.

*Did Anders Nils show observable signs of depression?*

He'd never liked talking to ship command. The fact that it appeared to possess more charisma and compassion than he did . . . grated.

He caught his first yawn while carefully placing Anders's personal documents into a sealed container. Over the next brief interval the yawns multiplied rapidly. There was no way to fight ship command's enforced sleep—he barely made it back to his bunk before oblivion wiped him away.

After sleep, command brought him up to dialogue regarding the incident. The temperature in the recording room had dropped noticeably into the discomfort zone.

"Please change your uniform to the appropriate formality." The voice out of the speaker was soft again, lush. He considered how brittle his own voice was in comparison. He brushed two fingers over his cuff until the correct dark blue color swam beneath them. "Correct." Pause. "The Emperor expresses his condolences for the loss of crewman reporter Anders Nils." The voice sounded achingly sincere. It made Jacob ashamed of his own underdeveloped powers of empathy. Another, awkwardly long pause. "How long did you serve with Anders Nils?"

"It would have been four years in a few sleeps."

"More precise, please."

"You have this information." He didn't bother to mask his annoyance,

"Answer please. We understand this may be a difficult time." Command rarely said "we." Suddenly Jacob felt quite unsure whom he was talking to.

Jacob ran his fingers over the table, accessing his personal diary. "Three years. Eleven months. Three weeks. Seventy-three hours. And four minutes, at least until the time of the hatch alarm."

Another long pause. Jacob knew this wasn't processing inefficiency. Com could formulate appropriate questions instantly. It was giving him time to think and remember, and it was measuring and analyzing that process. But as far as he knew, he had nothing to remember. So he waited.

"Did you know Anders had been depressed?"

"Was he?"

"Do you know why Anders would commit suicide?"

"Is that what he did? What is your percentage of certitude on that?"

"Forty-three percent."

"Then you don't know to a certainty."

Quite a long pause, then, "We do not know to a certainty."

"Then you don't know what you're talking about."

A red light glowed unsteadily on the panel. Jacob thought about Anders, concluded they'd never really been friends.

"You have heard the personal diaries of Anders Nils."

It wasn't a question. Wasn't command supposed to be asking questions? He answered anyway, thinking that at least he was doing *his* part. "I listened to some of it. There wasn't time for a full examination."

"What was your impression of the personal diaries of Anders Nils?"

"I . . . well, that's hard to say. He recorded a great deal. I suppose that surprised me. And they were well-composed, I think. Somewhat poetic, I suppose."

"Did any of the events described in the diaries of Anders Nils actually occur?"

"No, none that I heard. They were pretty outlandish."

"Please define 'outlandish,' as you understand it."

"Oh, unusual. Crazy. Impossible. We never went to the locations he describes. You know that very well. We did not visit those places, or have those adventures."

"You did not have the kind of relationship with Anders Nils he describes?"

"Well, no. No, I did not. I didn't know him all that well, actually."

"You were not friends?"

"Well, not close, not like that. We were acquaintances. We worked together. We had a working relationship."

"Why were you not friends?"

Jacob never would have expected command to ask such a thing. "I really don't know how to answer that," he finally replied.

"Why did you not know Anders was thinking of committing suicide?"

Jacob would not answer. He sat there silently, staring into the red eye lens mounted in the panel, until the countdown for landing preparations began.

The planet's surface was that light-trapping coating they'd used for official installations and supporting structures back before his grandfather was born. The fact that here and there it glistened and flowed with bits of color only emphasized how basically drab it all was. But it was durable and resistant to the attempts of most planetary ecologies to reclaim it.

"Welcome to Joy," the officer said, with what appeared to be a genuinely warm smile.

Jacob blinked. This wasn't the official designation. "From the looks of things, someone had a sense of humor."

"It would appear so," she said, still smiling. "Nine six oh gee four dash thirty-two."

"Then I'm in the correct place."

The com link in his ear murmured, *You may inform her that her uniform color has shifted out of sequence,* but he ignored that. True, her outfit appeared slightly on the purplish side, but it was probably the best she could do. It was no doubt decades old and difficult to calibrate.

"I'm pleased. We don't get many visitors."

Protocols were loose here, he observed. Not that he really cared. "I'm only scheduled for two sleeps," he said, not really wanting to discourage her friendly manner, although he was sure it came across that way.

"Well, we'll see what we can show you during that time. I know that the reporter ships like to record as much as possible during their limited visits."

*Com buzzed his ear. There are currently 432 undelivered regulatory messages due for 960G4-32. Too many for practical application. Please select at your discretion.* He had no intention of passing along any of these messages. In any case, how could they be enforced?

He nodded, thinking she probably hadn't even been born yet when the last such ship arrived. She'd probably briefed herself from some aging manual. The truth was the system didn't care that much about the outlying bases—just some basic facts on population and armaments for the statistical grids. He'd heard that the assumption had always been that such far-flung installations would fade in and out of participation in the empire over time. Otherwise their construction would have been made more pleasing.

"Anya, you should have called me." The man's voice was somewhat frail, but commanding as he trotted into the room. He raised a palm. Jacob returned the gesture tentatively, no longer accustomed to the act.

"I believe I did, Colonel," she said softly, stepping back from her post as the man stepped onto the platform.

"Terrible bother, this scan business," he said, face slightly red. "But required. Looking for tentacles, I suppose."

It was an old joke. Jacob waited for the inefficient sensors to grind to a halt. "Have you ever turned up any?"

"Certainly not with this device. There were Strangers about in the old days, and I might have run into a few during the sweeps. But hard to say. Back then they had these tag lines attached to every communication, 'If they're not a Friend, they might be a Stranger.' Remember those? Of course not—you're far too young. In any case, we were told they were all about. Problem is they were, are, so hard to identify. Has the process gotten any easier? Surely, with all the advances."

Jacob wondered what advances the old man could have been talking about. People could be so gullible out on the reaches. "Not that I know of. I've never seen a Stranger myself. Friends all, I suppose."

The aging officer stared at him. "You shouldn't make light of such things. I'm surprised that you haven't seen one of the enemy, as much as you travel. Do you have word, official of course, on the progress of the war?"

Jacob had the uneasy feeling that the man might keep him quarantined and under scan if he didn't provide a satisfactory answer. He wished he had Anders's ability at complete fabrication. His ear buzzed. *The war ebbs and flows, but remains constant. The empire continues to maintain.* Ashamed of himself, Jacob repeated command's answer word for word.

"Very well then." The officer motioned and Jacob was propelled forward up the ramp. The man's hand thrust forward, gripping his arm. "Welcome to our humble landing. Anya—Officer Bolduan—is preparing the statistical feed. Any specific observations you'd like to make?"

"Not really, as I was explaining to the other officer I'm only here two sleeps."

"Very well. You do realize your sleep regulation isn't enforced here. If you'd like to continue your accustomed sleep cycle you can return to your vessel at the appropriate intervals—"

"I'd like to give it a try."

"Certainly. Some have a difficult time transitioning." The officer looked down suddenly, as if intent on something on the instrument panel. "Do you have messages to deliver?" he asked without looking up.

Buzz. *432 undelivered regulatory messages.* Jacob shook his head in annoyance. "There are a few, probably obsolete, regulatory messages."

The officer laughed to himself. "Well, we hardly need more of those." He wetted his lips. "Anything for specific persons?"

Buzz. *Specific name is required for an adequate search. Misdirects now at over 62% due to addressing and time-delimiting malfunctions.*

"I'm not sure. I will certainly—"

"My father is retiring tomorrow," Anya spoke up, entering from the hall. "He's been waiting for his letter from the emperor."

●

They skittered across the dull-sealed surface of the world in a shallow vehicle looking somewhat like a huge sandal. An old geo-magnetic skimmer, as far as he could tell, although it had a home-made, jerry-built feel. Regulation replacement parts were unheard of out here (or in most of the empire, if the full truth were known). Now and then they'd pass over a deteriorated portion of the coating and the skimmer would fishtail with a twittering sound.

"It's really more stable than it seems." She was obviously amused by his discomfort. "I'm sorry about my father back there."

"He didn't do anything wrong. You embarrassed him."

She sighed. "Yes, I'm afraid I did. It's just that he's been waiting for that stupid letter for so long, and I knew he'd never ask about it directly."

"Well, yes, I surmised that. The way he began immediately apologizing for your uniform, and his, obviously to change the subject. 'My uniform is currently twenty-two points out of color phase. Officer Anya Bolduan's is currently thirty-six points out of color phase.' "

"The sad thing is he tracks those figures every day, and at the end of the month he graphs the progress. He worries about that sort of thing. It's like he expects my uniform will turn transparent in another year."

Jacob thought he might actually blush. The notion filled him with self-loathing. He couldn't look at her. "They're old uniforms. It can't be helped. I don't suppose it even matters."

"It matters very much to my father. And he only has another day for it to matter. So, is there a letter, Crewman Reporter Jacob Westman? Do you know anything, or is it all in that thing in your ear?"

She might not have seen his kind before, but she read manuals. "Patience, please. My ear is attempting to tell me what it knows."

*Letters from the emperor were given at one time to higher officers, including provisional officers in charge of outposts and settlements, upon the occasion of their retirement. The practice has been largely discontinued, declining rapidly as chains of command have become increasingly ambivalent. Rarely did such letters receive the emperor's personal attention. Last recorded incident of such a letter . . . records here are incomplete.*

"He knew the emperor at one time," she said. "They were friends. He served with him when they were both young. I think that's why he has his hopes so high."

*Monitoring this statement due to its high probability of fabrication. Positing truthfulness, such a relationship might possibly make a difference. Is it a friendship?*

*Please note the lower case "f." Probabilities difficult to determine, high inaccuracy due to questions as to whether a singular figure known as the "emperor" in fact now exists. Parameters classified.*

"Does your ear need more time?"

"Apparently. I'm sorry."

"So how does it feel, having that voice in your head all the time? I can't manage even the low volume of communications we deal with on Joy. Don't tell my father, but sometimes I unplug."

"Truthfully it becomes annoying at times. But it is," he stopped, watched her eyes, "company."

She nodded. "It does get lonely here, you know. Even after all this time, the older staff will be talking to you, and it feels like a genuine conversation, then suddenly they're treating you like you were a Stranger."

"From my observations in these outlying posts, that isn't unusual behavior."

"So are they still out there?"

*. . . speculations here are ill-advised . . .*

"Honestly, I really have no idea. Possibly."

"Is the emperor even still alive? We never hear anything out here."

*. . . lack of complete information is no excuse for misleading statements by crew-members acting in their official capacity . . .*

"I'm afraid I can't help you there, either. Some things work, I know that. We receive communications, including new regulations and orders. Although infrequently, supply ships arrive at destinations." Com buzzed his ear aggressively, but he ignored it. "Other military ships are encountered. The empire runs, although its borders apparently continue to change. And from my observation, most of the settlements appear to be running themselves. Maybe there's still an emperor, maybe there's a committee. People talk about the Strangers, but no one I know has ever seen one. Some people say there are no Strangers, and no emperor either."

"Well, there *was* an emperor. My father knew him. He says in the old days before he took command the emperor was expected to serve just like everyone else."

"He must have some interesting stories from that time."

The world's surface coating stopped abruptly, and the skimmer almost as quickly. The unsettled portion of Joy rolled out in front of them, its multicolored layers of stone swirling into cones, peaks, and shallow valleys. The late-afternoon light emphasized its strangeness, and its random highlighting of geologic features gave the landscape an appearance of constant movement.

"Very pretty," he said, feeling inadequate to the task of responding to such an exotic vision.

"Yes, but I'm afraid that ends the tour. Bad enough I go out there by myself without orders, but if you were to be injured—you can imagine, I'm sure. But it has such beauty and strangeness—I'm not sure I could handle so much Joy without it." She laughed. "That was a silly thing to say, I guess."

He wanted to tell her how much he enjoyed hearing her laughter, but of course did not. "You stay because of your father?"

"He retires tomorrow and I'm supposed to take over. Maybe then we can stretch things a bit, and I can find excuses to go out there more. Besides, he needs me for now. There are so many things he's unsure of."

"I can't promise any particular results, but I'll keep searching for some sort of message, at least some official recognition of his retirement."

"He *knew* the emperor, I'm sure of it. My father isn't the sort of person to fabricate things."

*. . . fabrication is always a potential hazard when inadequate information is present . . .*

"I believe you."

"But he doesn't have any *stories*. His memory stops after meeting the emperor, going out on those first tentative incursions. At some point his entire platoon came back with the emperor, and the powers that be must have suspected a Stranger was among them, because they were all examined, if that's even an adequate word for it. He's lost most of his memories of that period, and although his official record provides dates and locations, details are sparse."

*. . . possibilities of message retrieval using insufficient search parameters are questionable . . .*

"I hope a message comes through. I'll return to the ship, spend the rest of the day in queries."

"Even if you can't find anything, please come to the ceremony tomorrow? Having someone from outside in attendance, in official capacity or not—"

"Of course. Of course. I'll be there," he said, even though the idea of standing within a gathering of people he did not know made him cringe.

That evening he sat alone in the recording room in the hours before enforced sleep, as he would sit alone before many sleeps until the powers above (and there were thousands of layers, he thought, of powers above) chose someone to replace Anders. As he had sat alone time after time when Anders had still been alive and only a few meters away, simply another stranger listening for voices in the dark, recording what those voices had to say. Tonight there were a thousand such voices, most chronicling the minutiae of rulings and orders, specifications and principles, some calling out for contact from worlds not visited in generations, some pleading for assistance, remuneration, or the simple return of a greeting, and a few hesitant inquiries concerning Strangers, and fewer still wondering aloud if Strangers had at last taken over all that could be seen, heard, or imagined. The emperor himself, however, was conspicuously silent, as he had been silent, and invisible, all of Jacob's life. The possibility the sought-after letter might miraculously arrive seemed almost infinitely remote.

"Continue to parse and deliver all incoming and previously uncategorized communications," Jacob said aloud. "But please intersperse with entries from the diaries of Anders Nils."

Command remained silent, as it had all evening, but swiftly complied.

The hall where the ceremony was held was small, but so was the attendance. Official banners had been hung, each one a few points off in color as far as Jacob could determine, lending a not-entirely unpleasant but unmistakable disharmony to the proceedings.

The walls cycled images of the retiring colonel at various points in his career, but there were numerous, obvious gaps. A few of the images portrayed groups of officers and enlisted. Jacob wondered if any of the blurred, shadowed faces was that of their emperor.

People stood up one at a time and offered chronicles of their experiences serving with the colonel. Some talked about his skills as an administrator, a supervisor. One or two said he was a visionary, but provided no evidence for this claim. A man appearing older than the colonel told a semi-humorous story of their time serving together in the campaigns, but stopped abruptly and sat down. Jacob then realized the man must have also been part of the group suffering the examination which had scattered the colonel's memories.

Anya stood and told everyone what a good father he had been. She talked about his patience, and how much she respected him. When she sat down Jacob saw her warily eyeing the thin sheet of film Jacob held in his shaking hand.

"Is there anyone else?" a small man in a faded clerk's uniform asked.

Jacob stood and unsteadily made his way to the front of the room. When he turned around he looked for someone to focus on. He discovered he couldn't begin to look at the colonel, but watching Anya's face as he read was pleasant and barely possible. He held the sheet tightly to minimize the shaking.

"The vast spaces between us are filled with messages. In these scattered times few seem to find their intended destinations, or satisfy us with the things we've always wanted to hear. But sometimes you can stitch together a voice here, a voice there, until some clarity of feeling emerges. I cannot vouch for the complete accuracy of what I am about to read—it is difficult to verify the messages that come to us out of the vast unknown. But I intuit its general true feeling.

"To Colonel William Bolduan, officer in custody of Joy, from Joseph, once acquaintance and always friend, emperor of all he loves, hates, or imagines, on the occasion of the colonel's retirement from a lifetime of most meritorious service.

"Now, you may not remember because of measures taken both terrible and necessary, but when I hungered so long for sustenance, and courage, you made us a meal out of the wings of some glorious bird whose name was unfamiliar to all, whose face bore a map of the hard world we'd traveled, and while we ate, our eyes became like white jewels, and we paid each other out of laughter and song. For us there were no soldiers or emperors, no desperate orders or misguided honor to separate us, and we swore to each other the peace that comes with age. I would stand by you as your children were married, and we would tolerate no serious disagreement, and think nothing of the worlds that separated us, but praise the fineness of difference.

"When we woke I could see your embarrassment, the shame you felt for being so familiar, and you would not hear when I explained what all emperors know, that sometimes the heart must be lubricated if any truth is to be told.

"Still, we were no strangers to adventure. We were not strangers in our hearts. Without regret I followed you into the fires at Weilung, where the breath of the dying fliers erased our uniforms and then our hair. In agony you carried me to the fountains of that fading world, where those beautiful ghosts regretted our injuries, and we lay swaddled in their manes as the battles raged without us, until finally I could open my eyes without screaming, and you had that ship waiting, and past the eighty-two falls of those unfortunate worlds you transported me, until the rest of the fleet arrived, and there began our first separation.

"And you should know my people thought it improper. They called themselves my people but in truth I was irretrievably theirs. Some beings must remain separate, they told me, and a friendship of equals is a lie we tell children. So I had to content myself with reports of your exploits, your rescue mission between the two green seas, the time you brought the children (those oh-so-gullible children!) out of the mines at Debel 'Schian, and your long voyage out of the Cheylen clouds.

"If you could only remember our next meeting at the Hejen Temples! How broken I was over those jokes you told! I painted my cheeks like a little girl, and danced until you were too hoarse to sing. Later, when you were afraid your honor could not bear such frivolous and insane behavior, I somehow convinced you that sometimes insanity is the only reasonable response to atrocity, and the death of everything, and long voyages home, alone in the dark.

"But all this ends. And even I with such a grand, fully augmented memory, cannot remember the last time we laughed together, any more than you, my friend. It all has to end. And strangeness comes, and there is no science deep enough to explicate the secrets of the heart. An empire separates us, but still I think of you.

"Signed Joseph, your emperor."

Jacob returned immediately to his ship. His dialogue with command continued in the recording room, even as the vessel departed that atmosphere, trailing unanswered messages from the occupants of Joy.

"This is a continuation of queries related to the death of Anders Nils, crewman reporter third. Are you prepared to answer these queries?"

"Ask me anything. You may also repeat questions from our first session. Obviously, I have nothing better to do."

"Before proceeding to those queries we would like to ask you some possibly related questions concerning your stay on 960G4-32."

"Yes, I imagine you do."

"The letter you read from the Emperor Joseph—that was a complete fabrication, was it not?"

"Yes, a complete fabrication."

"The letter was fabricated from fabrications previously entered by Anders Nils in his diaries, concerning imaginary adventures you and he experienced while visiting a variety of worlds."

"Yes, that was the principal source—Ander's imaginary adventures and the imaginary friendship he invented for us. But I filled it in with a few details from the colonel's service record, some stray descriptive passages from this soup of transmissions I have travelled in these past nine years. The style came out of Li Po's *Exile's Letter*. Have you read it?"

"The poem is in the database."

"I admit I've hardly done it justice."

"So you admit the emperor's letter was a lie?"

Jacob waited, thinking, then said, "It is not a lie. It is an accurate depiction of the way Anders Nils felt about me, felt about the loneliness of the voyage. It is an accurate depiction of his yearnings. I also believe it is an accurate depiction of Colonel Bolduan's yearnings, and perhaps those of our maybe-living, maybe-not emperor as well. It is certainly an accurate depiction of my own feelings."

"But the events you've narrated, events which were supposedly experienced by Colonel Bolduan, are fictional."

"Those events, those memories are gone forever. They were taken from the colonel. If the colonel had lost a leg in combat, the service would have provided him with a prosthetic. The events I have narrated in the emperor's letter are a prosthetic for what he has lost."

"Do you know why Anders would commit suicide?"

"I cannot be sure. I will never be sure. But I believe the stories he had made up, or fabricated, to use your word, had ceased to work for him. He must have been terribly, terribly lonely."

"He should have spoken to you. He could have asked us for assistance."

"Some people are unable to ask, or tell. People do what they can do."

"Why did you not know Anders was thinking of committing suicide?"

"Because I failed at the one thing I have been so thoroughly trained to do. I failed to listen."

And there ended the interview. Jacob returned to his long nights listening, alone, waiting for Anders's replacement, wondering if there would even be a replacement. Now and then he would listen to Anders's diaries. Now and then he would make up diary entries of his own.

Command wrapped up its report and transmitted it into the empty space between its reported location and a vague approximation of the location called home, not knowing, or caring, if contact was made.

Melinda Snodgrass has written multiple novels and screenplays, and is best known for her work on *Star Trek: The Next Generation*. She has also worked on numerous other shows, including *The Profilers*, *Sliders*, and *Seaquest DSV*. She coedits the Wild Cards series with George R. R. Martin. Melinda is the author of The Edge series, which is published by Tor Books in the US and Titan Books in the UK. She lives in Santa Fe, New Mexico.

# The Wayfarer's Advice

## *Melinda Snodgrass*

We came out of Fold only twenty-three thousand kilometers from Kusatsu-Shirane. "Good job," I started to say, but was interrupted by blaring impact alarms.

"Shit, shit, shit," Melin at navigation chattered, and her fingers swept back and forth across the touch screen like a child finger painting. Our ship, the *Selkie*, obedient to Melin's sweeping commands, fired its ram jet. My stomach was left resting against the ceiling and my balls seemed to leap into my throat as we dropped relative to our previous position.

A massive piece of steel and composite resin, edges jagged and blackened by an explosion, tumbled slowly past our front viewport. It had been four years since I'd been cashiered from the Imperial Navy of the Solar League, but the knowledge gained during the preceding twenty years was still with me.

"That was an Imperial ship," I said. My eye caught writing on the hull. I had an impression of a name, and my gut closed down into an aching ball. It couldn't be . . . but if it *was* . . . I had to know. I added an order. "Match trajectory and image-capture."

Jax, the Tiponi Flute, piped through the breathing holes lining his sides, "Not good news for Kusatsu-Shirane if the League has found them." The alien had several of its leafy tendrils wrapped around handholds welded to the walls, and his elongated body swayed with the swoops and dives of the ship.

"I'd call that the understatement of the year," Baca grunted from his position at communication.

Three hundred years ago, humans had developed a faster-than-light drive and gone charging out into our arm of the Milky Way galaxy. There we had met up with a variety of alien races, kicked their butts, and subjugated them under human rule. But two hundred years before the human blitzkrieg began, there had been other ships that had headed to the stars. Long-view ships with humans in suspended animation, searching for new worlds.

Most of these pioneers were cranks and loons determined to set up their various ideas of utopia. Best guess was that probably eighty percent of them died either during the journey or shortly after locating on a planet. But some survived to create Reichart's World, and Nirvana, and Kusatsu-Shirane, and numerous others.

The League called them Hidden Worlds, and took a very dim view of human-settled planets that weren't part of the League. In fact, the League rectified that situation whenever they ran across one of these worlds. The technique was simple and brutal: The League arrived, used their superior firepower to force a surrender, then took away all the children under the age of sixteen and fostered them with families on League planets. They then brought in League settlers to swamp the colonists who remained behind.

But it hadn't worked this time, because there were pieces of Imperial ships orbiting Kusatsu-Shirane. Something had killed a whole battle group. Whatever it was, I didn't want it destroying my little trade vessel.

"Contact orbital control, and tell them we're friendlies," I ordered Baca.

"I've been trying, Tracy, but nobody's answering. Worse, the whole planet's gone silent. Nobody's talking to nobody."

"Some new Imperial weapon to knock out communications?" Melin asked.

"Are you picking up anything?" I asked.

"Music," Baca replied.

We all exchanged glances; then I said, "Let's hear it."

Baca switched from headphone to speaker, and flipped through the communication channels from the planet. Slow, mournful music filled the bridge. It wasn't all the same melody, but they all had one thing in common. Each melody was desperately sad.

Something terrible had happened on Kusatsu-Shirane, and judging by the debris, something equally terrible had happened in orbit. Periodically, Melin fired small maneuvering jets as she dodged through the ruins, but despite her best efforts the bridge echoed with pings and scrapes as debris impacted against the hull.

"Not the safest of neighborhoods, Captain," came my executive officer's voice in my left ear, and I jumped. Damn, the creature could move quietly! I gave a quick glance over my shoulder, and found myself looking directly into the Isanjo's sherry-colored eyes. Jahan had settled onto the back of my chair like Alice's Cheshire cat.

"We'll grab an identification and get out," I said.

Jahan wrapped her tail around my throat. I couldn't tell if the gesture was meant to convey comfort or a threat. An Isanjo's tail was powerful enough to snap a two-by-four. My neck would offer little challenge.

As if in answer to my statement, the screen on the arm of my jacket flared, adjusted contrast, and the name of the ship came into focus: *Nuestra Señora de la Concepción*. My impression had been correct. It had been *her* ship. I gave the bridge of my nose a hard squeeze, fighting to hold back tears.

"Holy crap, that's a flagship!" Baca yelped as he accessed the computer files.

"Under the command of Mercedes de Arango, the Infanta who would have held the lives of countless millions of humans and aliens in her hands once her father died," Jax recited in his piping tones. His encyclopedic memory baffled me. I had no idea how that much brain power could reside in something that looked like an oversized stalk of bamboo.

"Instead, she precedes him into oblivion," Jahan said.

The attention of my crew was like a pinprick, the unspoken question hung between us. "Yes, I was at the Academy with her," I said.

"So, did you *know* her?" Baca asked.

"I'm a tailor's son. What do you think?"

Baca reacted to my tone. "Just asking," he said sulkily.

A fur-covered hand swept lightly beneath my eyes. "You weep," Jahan said, and I was glad she had used her knuckle. An Isanjo's four-fingered hand is tipped with ferocious claws, capable of disemboweling another Isanjo or even a man. She leaned in closer and whispered, "And I note you did not actually answer the question."

"Twelve ships were destroyed here. Six thousand starmen died. If things had fallen out differently, I might have been among them," I said loudly. "Of course I'm upset."

"They came here to do violence to the people of Kusatsu-Shirane," Jax tweeted.

"It wasn't a duty they would have relished."

"But they would have done it," Jahan said. "The Infanta would have ordered it done."

I shrugged. "Orders are orders. I cleared a Hidden World once. When I was a newly minted lieutenant."

"And now you trade with them and keep them secret," Jahan said.

"Making me a traitor as well as a cashiered thief." I changed the subject. "We need to find out what happened down the gravity well."

"It will take a damn lot of fuel to set the ship down," Jax tweeted. Flutes were famous for their mathematical ability, and Jax was no exception. He was our purchasing agent, and I was pretty damn sure he was the reason the *Selkie* ran at a profit. He counted every Reales and squeezed it twice.

"I'll take the *Wasp*," I said, referring to the small League fighter craft we'd picked up at a salvage auction. The cannons had been removed, but it was still screamingly fast and relatively cheap to fly.

Melin had given us enough gravity that I could grip the sides of the access ladder, and slide down to the level that held the docking bay. Even so, Jahan, using her four hands and prehensile tail, reached the lower deck before me.

"I take it that you're coming along," I said as I hauled a spacesuit out of a locker.

"I will need to report to the Council."

"Chalking up another human atrocity," I said with black humor.

"It's what we do," the creature said shortly and she removed her suit from its locker. Isanjo suits always looked strange. They were equipped with a tail because the aliens used their tails for their high-steel construction work.

"And what happens when the ledger gets filled?" I asked as I stepped into the lower half of my suit.

"We will act," she said, and I knew that she was speaking of all the alien races. "There are a lot more of us than there are of you."

"Yeah, but none of you are as mean as us." I shrugged to settle the heavy oxygen pack onto my shoulders.

"But we're more patient."

"You've got me there."

I reflected that Isanjos now built our skyscrapers and our spaceships. Under human supervision, of course, but my God, there was so much opportunity for mischief if the aliens decided that it was time for them to act! I had a vision of skyscrapers collapsing and ships exploding.

I thought about the Hajin who worked as servants in our households. How easy it would be to poison a human family.

And the Tiponi Flutes did our accounting. They could crash the economy.

Humans were fucked. Good thing I worked on a ship crewed mostly by aliens. Maybe they liked me enough to keep me around.

We secured each other's helmets, and headed for the *Wasp*, which sat in the middle of the bay. Even sitting still, it looked like it was moving a million miles an hour. The needle nose and vertical tail screamed predator.

I took the front seat, and Jahan settled into the gunner's chair. The canopy dropped, I flipped on the engines, instruments, and radio, and called to the bridge. "We're ready."

For a few seconds, we could hear the air being sucked out of the bay and back into the rest of the ship. No sense wasting atmosphere. It cost money to make, as Jax frequently pointed out. Once the wind sounds died, the great outer doors swung slowly and ponderously open. Our view was dominated by the curving rim of the planet. Green seas and a small continent rolled past us. Beyond the bulk of the world, the stars glittered ice-bright. I sent us out into space, and immediately dodged a piece of broken ship.

"Do mind the trash," Jahan said.

Something was niggling at me. Something missing in the orbital mix—but I was too busy negotiating the floating debris to figure it out. Instead of heading directly to the planet, I took the time to explore the expanding circle of debris that had been the *Nuestra Señora de la Concepción*. We soon saw bits of floating detritus that had once been people. I studied each frozen face haloed with crystals of frozen blood.

"She's dead," Jahan said.

"I know," I said. But I couldn't accept it. She was the heir to the League. There may have been added protection for Mercedes. There had to have been. She could *not* be gone. Twenty minutes later, I admitted defeat, took us out of the debris field, and headed toward the planet.

We were passing relatively close to a small moon—Kusatsu-Shirane had five but the others weren't presently in view—when I heard it. A distress beacon, sending its cry into the void. We locked on and followed it. The life capsule had clamped itself limpetlike to the stony surface of the moon. The tiny computer brain that controlled the capsule had rightly figured that it was safer for the occupant not to be floating in a battle zone, and found refuge.

I landed the *Wasp*, popped the canopy, and pushed out with such force that I almost hit escape velocity from the tiny planetoid. Jahan's tail caught my ankle, and pulled me back.

Moving with a bit more caution, I approached the body-shaped container resting in a small crater. The black surface was etched with messages in every known League language, urging the finder to contact the navy headquarters on Hissilek. There was also a dire warning to any that might stumble upon the body that the DNA of the human inside was not to be harvested or touched in any way.

I brushed away the layer of fine dust and ice that covered the faceplate of the life capsule. It was Mercedes. Placed into a deep coma by drugs injected by the capsule. Her long dark brown hair, streaked now with silver at her temples, had been braided, and the braid lay across one shoulder. A few strands of hair had come loose, and caught in her lips at the moment that the capsule had slammed shut around her. I wanted to reach out and brush them away. I studied the long, patrician nose, the espresso-and-cream-colored skin. She was so beautiful—and she was alive.

"Hmm, I thought a princess would be prettier," Jahan said.

"She's beautiful!" I flared.

"Ah, I see now. You're in love with her."

We returned to the *Selkie*. There was no way to fit the capsule inside the *Wasp*. I reprogrammed the clamps and secured Mercedes to the hull. It made me uncomfortable treating her in such a disrespectful way, but I couldn't open the capsule in vacuum and I had no suit for her.

"That was a quick trip." Baca's voice filled my helmet.

"We found a survivor," I radioed back as I brought us in through the bay doors and dropped the *Wasp* onto the deck.

It was the work of minutes to unclamp the capsule from the side of the *Wasp*, and blow the seals. I eyed the tangle of IV tubes and the pinpricks of blood that stained her arms and legs where the needles had driven through her clothes and into her veins. While I was trying to figure out how to remove them without causing her pain, the capsule sensed warmth and atmosphere, and withdrew the needles that kept her in a deathlike coma.

I slid my arms beneath her and picked her up. I'd like to say that I swept her into my arms, but at five feet eight inches tall, she was not much shorter than me, and I had to work to carry her.

"You could have waited for a stretcher," Jahan said as she listened to my panting breaths, and noticed the way I braced myself against the wall of the lift. I shook my head, not wanting to waste the air. "And have you considered that you have put us all at grave risk by bringing her aboard? We were smuggling to a Hidden World. The League will not only imprison us for that, they will assume we know the location of other such worlds, and they won't be gentle in trying to elicit that information."

"I couldn't just leave her there."

"Because you're in love with her."

I summoned up a glare. I didn't have the breath for a response. We reached the fourth deck level, and I carried Mercedes into our small, but well-equipped, sick bay.

Dalea was waiting for us. I wasn't sure if Dalea had a medical license, but whatever her training was, she was very good. There had to be a story about why she'd signed aboard a ship, because she was Hajin, and the herbivores weren't common in space, but I hadn't managed to worm it out of her yet.

Her coat was white with streaks of red-brown, and a thick shock of chestnut hair curled across her skull and ran down her long neck and even longer spine to disappear beneath the waistband of her slacks. Somewhere along the evolutionary chain, a creature like a cross between a zebra and a giraffe had stood upright, the front legs had shortened to become arms, and the split hoof that passed for feet developed a third digit that served as a thumb.

I laid Mercedes on the bed, and Dalea began her examination. I was jiggling, shifting my weight from foot to foot, waiting. Finally, I couldn't contain my anxiety any longer.

"Is she hurt?"

"Bumps, bruises." Dalea filled a hypodermic. "She took a pretty good dose of radiation, probably when the flagship blew. This will help."

She gave Mercedes the injection. A few moments later there was a reaction. Mercedes stirred and moaned. I laid a hand on her forehead.

"She's in pain. What was in that shot?" I asked, suddenly suspicious of my alien shipmate.

"Nanobots that will repair her damaged DNA. That's not why she's moaning. She's coming out of a rapidly induced coma, and she's got that feeling of pins-and-needles in her extremities."

Dalea exchanged a glance with Jahan, who shrugged and said, "He's in love with her. What else can you expect?"

"Would you stop saying that," I said, exasperated.

"So stay with her," said Dalea. "I'm assuming that if you love her, you must know her, and she should wake up to a familiar face."

The two alien females left the sick bay. I broke the magnetic seal on a chair, pulled it over to the bedside, and sat down. I took Mercedes's limp hand where it hung over the side of the bed, and softly stroked it. It was her left hand, and the elaborate wedding set seemed to cut at my fingers.

*She should wake up to a familiar face.* What would that have been like? To sleep next to this woman? To have her scent in my nostrils? To have her long hair catch in my lips? Once, twenty-two years ago, I had experienced only the last of those fantasies. We had violated lights out at the Academy and met on the Star Deck. We had kissed, and her hair, floating in free fall, had caressed my face.

I was lost in a daydream, tending toward an actual dream, when Mercedes sighed and her fingers tightened on mine. My eyes jerked open, and I shot up out of the chair. She looked up at me, smiled, and murmured,

"Tracy. I dreamed I heard your voice. But you can't actually be here."

"But I am, your highness."

She frowned, and reached up. I leaned forward so she could touch my face. She looked around the tiny space, and she accepted the truth. "Once more you rescue me," she murmured.

Walking onto the bridge, I was met with three conversations all taking place simultaneously.

"Why are we still here? No trade, no money," from Jax.

"Are you going down?" from Baca.

"I think I know what killed the Imperials," from Melin.

I answered them in order of complexity. "Because I say so. Yes. What?"

Melin picked the question out of my surly and laconic reply. "Kusatsu-Shirane only has three moons now."

I sat down at my post. "They blew up two of their moons?"

"Yep. Apparently, the Imperials closed with the planet in their normal arrowhead formation. Given the regularity of the moons' orbits, the folks on Kusatsu-Shirane picked the two moons closest to the ships to destroy. The resulting debris went through the ships like shotgun pellets through cheese. *Boom!*" Melin accompanied the word with an expressive gesture.

"That would imply that the other three are booby trapped too."

"Most likely."

"*Madre de Dios!* I landed us on one of the remaining moons." I wiped away the sweat that had suddenly bloomed on my upper lip.

"I think it took a person with a finger on the trigger to set off the explosions," Melin offered. It was comfort, but not much.

"New plan. Let's stay away from the remaining moons," I said to our navigator.

"Good plan," she said, and turned back to her console.

Baca spoke up. "Then why the dirge from the planet? They won a mighty victory."

"But short term," Jahan said. I jumped. Damn it, she'd done it again. Her fur tickled my left ear.

I nodded. "What Jahan said. The battle group's course was filed with Central Command on Hissilek. When they neither call home nor come home, the League will come looking for them. Kusatsu-Shirane is going to be discovered."

"Tracy's right."

Mercedes's voice had always had this little catch in it. Very endearing and very sexy. I stood and turned around. She was on the platform lift, and she looked shaky. I hurried to her side, and assisted her into the chair Baca hastily vacated. He was staring like a pole-axed bull. I couldn't blame him. How often did an ordinary space tramp meet the heir to an empire?

"Uh . . . hello, ma'am, Luis Baca, communications. I'll get a message off to Hissilek."

"Where are you bound for next?" she asked me.

"Cuandru."

"A message won't reach League space faster than this ship. There will be military ships at Cuandru." She was right about that; Cuandru was the largest shipyard in the League. Mercedes smiled at me, but I noticed that the expression never reached her eyes. They were dark and haunted. "You're the captain."

"I am," I said.

"Congratulations. You finally made it."

"On a trading vessel." I hoped that the resentment didn't show too badly.

"Believe me, it's better than being an admiral," Mercedes said softly.

"I'll have to take your word for it."

"So why are you still in orbit?" she asked.

"We have no communication from the planet," Jax trilled. "We are uncertain if there is anyone to trade *with*."

"Tracy was on his way to the planet when he picked up your distress signal," Melin said.

"Did they evacuate?" Mercedes asked.

"It's possible, but not likely. There were close to a million people on Kusatsu-Shirane," I said.

Mercedes stood. "Then let us go and find out what has become of them."

"I'm not sure that's a good idea."

"I'm not asking. You're still my subject."

The final words came floating back over her shoulder. I followed her onto the lift.

The wind whispered down the deserted streets of Edogowa. There were no vehicles parked on the streets. It was all very tidy and orderly. It was near sunset, and to the west magnificent thunderheads formed a vibrant palette of blues, grays, reds, and golds. Two long but very narrow bands of rain extended from the clouds to the chaparral below. The bands looked like sweeping tendrils of gray hair, and where the rain hit the ground, the dust on this high desert plateau boiled into the air like milk froth.

"Where is everybody?" Baca asked. His eyes darted nervously from side to side.

Jahan came scrambling down the wall of a four-story office building. "Nobody's there. Lights are off. Computers shut down. It's like everybody's taken a holiday."

Mercedes shivered. I started to put my arm around her shoulders, but thought better of it and drew back. "Let's go to a house," she said.

"Why?" Jahan asked.

"When you think something terrible is about to happen, you want to be with your loved ones," Mercedes answered.

We had ended up landing the *Selkie* at the small spaceport. The *Wasp* could only comfortably carry two, and the melancholy music and the lack of human voices had me jumpy. I wanted backup. Jahan radioed our plan back to Melin, Jax, and Dalea.

Our footfalls echoed on the sidewalk and bounced off the sides of the buildings. I realized that something else was missing besides the people: the smell of cooking food. There were hundreds of restaurants in Edo-gowa. Most business was conducted over a meal, and deals were sealed with alcohol. Food was a ritual on Kusatsu-Shirane. But now all I smelled was that pungent mix of dust and rain and ozone as the storm approached.

The business district gave way to small wood houses with shoji screens on the windows, and graceful upturned edges on the roofs. Now we found vehicles, carefully parked at the houses. The clouds rolled in, dulling the color of the flowers in perfectly groomed beds. Overhead, thunder grumbled like a giant shifting in his sleep.

We picked a house at random and walked up to the front door. I knocked. Silence. I knocked again. Mercedes reached past me, grasped the knob, and opened the door.

"Trusting kind of place," Baca muttered.

"They want us to come in. To see," Mercedes said in a hollow tone.

No one asked the obvious *see what* question. It had taken me longer, but I had finally come to the same point as Mercedes in my analysis. Jap-anese-influenced culture, imminent loss of their children and their way of life—for the people of Kusatsu-Shirane there was only one possible solution.

The family was in the bedroom. The children lay in their mother's arms. Her lax hands were still over their eyes. She had a neat hole in her forehead. The children had been shot in the back of the head. The father slumped in a chair, chin resting on his chest. Blood formed a bib on the front of his shirt. The pistol had fallen from his hand.

Mercedes remained stone-faced as we toured more houses. It was the seventh house before she finally broke. A sob burst out, she turned toward me. My arms opened, and she buried her face against my chest. She was crying so hard that in a matter of moments, the front of my shirt was wet. It made me think of the father in the first house, his shirt wet with blood. I closed my arms tight around Mercedes, trying to hold back the horror.

"*Why?* They would have had a good life! Especially the children. Why would they do this? They're insane!"

"Because the life we offered wasn't the life they wanted," I said softly. "This was the last choice they could make for themselves, and they made it. I'm not saying it's a good choice, but I can understand it."

"They killed their *children*," Mercedes whispered. "Thousands of children." She broke out of my embrace, dragged frantic fingers through her hair. "Why? To keep them from us? We're not monsters!"

"That depends on where you're sitting in the pecking order," Jahan said in her dry way.

There was a silence for several long moments. Mercedes stood in the living room, surrounded by the dead. She looked lost and terribly frail. I stepped to her side and put my arm around her.

"Let's go," I said softly. "There's nothing here."

"Ghosts," she whispered. "They'll be here."

Melin plotted our course for Cuandru, the Isanjo home world. We boosted out of orbit, heading for open vacuum between the planets before we entered the Fold.

I left the bridge and went to visit Jax in his office/cabin. He was standing in a wading pool of water rehydrating his leaves, and holding a computer while he ran figures. Nervous whistling emerged from the sound valves that lined his sides. Each valve emitted a different, discordant tone. It was like a dentist drilling.

"How bad?" I asked.

"Bad. We didn't sell the low-tech farm equipment on Kusatsu-Shirane, which meant we didn't pick up loads of lacquer knickknacks to sell to your jaded ruling class on League worlds. We must hope for a big reward for rescuing the Infanta," Jax concluded.

"That's it? That's your only reaction to the death of a million people? We couldn't make the sale?"

The seven ocular organs around the alien's head swiveled to regard me. "What was it one of your ancient dictators said? One death is a tragedy; a million is a statistic. And, bluntly, they were not my kind, nor is it a choice I can condone."

*And that's why they call them alien*, I thought as I left. I decided not to ask the other alien members of the crew how they felt.

The bizarre philosophical discussion had meant that I hadn't voiced my real concern: that the League would decide we were somehow behind the destruction of the fleet and slap us in prison. It would be a black eye for the navy and the Infanta if the government had to admit that the citizens of a Hidden World had destroyed a battle group. Better to blame a slightly shady trading vessel commanded by a disgraced Imperial officer. I decided that it couldn't hurt to clear things up with Mercedes.

I had given her my cabin. It was slightly larger than the crew cabins, and the bed could actually hold two assuming they were friendly. Privacy on ships is the opposite of what one might expect. You'd think that people living in close confines inside a tin can would want the closed door and a private place. Instead I found that crews tended to live in a constant state of togetherness, like a group hug. We walked in and out of each other's cabins. When we weren't on duty we played games that involved lots of people. I think it's because space is so vast, so empty, and so cold that you want the comfort of contact with other living things.

Which is why I just walked in on Mercedes. She was kneeling in front of the small shrine I maintained to the Virgin, and she was saying the rosary. The click of the beads set a counterpoint to the bass throb of the engines, and I was startled when I realized she was using my rosary. But of course she would have to. Hers had been reduced to dust and atoms along with everything else aboard the *Nuestra*.

She gave me a brief nod, her lips continuing to move, and the familiar prayer just the barest of sound in the room. I sat down on the bed and waited. She wasn't that far from the end.

I closed my eyes and took the opportunity to offer up a prayer for my father, still laboring away in the tailor shop on Hissilek. A stroke—brought on, I was convinced, by my court-martial and subsequent conviction—had left him with a crippled right leg, but he still worked, making uniforms for the very men who had ruined me. Sometimes it felt like the most personal of betrayals, and I hated him for it, but in more rational moments, I realized that he had to eat, and that he had spent a lifetime outfitting the officers of the Imperial Navy. It wasn't like he could become a designer of ladies' fashion at age sixty-eight.

I jumped and my eyes flew open when I felt cool fingers touch my cheek. Mercedes was standing directly in front of me, and so close. She jerked back her hand at my startled reaction. I didn't want her to take my response as a rejection, so I reached out and grabbed her hand.

"It's all right; you just startled me," I said.

While at the same moment she was saying, "I'm sorry. You just had such a hurt and angry look on your face."

"Memories." I shrugged. "They're never a good thing."

"Really? I have some nice ones of you."

"Don't." I stood up and brushed past her. "All this proves is that the universe is a bitch and she has a nasty sense of humor."

"We were very good . . . friends once."

"Yes, but that was years ago, and a marriage ago." I couldn't help it. I looked back, hoping I'd hurt her, and was embarrassed when I realized I had.

But it was hard, so hard. She had married my greatest enemy from the Academy. Honorius Sinclair Cullen, Knight of the Arches and Shells, Duke de Argento, known to his friends and enemies as BoHo. He was an admiral now, too. I touched the scar at my left temple, a gift from BoHo, and his mocking tones seemed to whisper in the throb of the engines. *Lowborn scum.*

Mercedes sank down on the bed. "We all do what we must. That must be what the people on Kusatsu-Shirane thought." There was an ocean of grief in her dark brown eyes.

I walked back and sat down next to her. Sitting this close, I could see the web of crow's-feet around her eyes, and the two small frown lines between her brows. We were forty-four years old, and I wondered if either of us had ever known a day of unadulterated happiness.

"Has it been so bad?"

She looked down at her hand, twisted the wedding set, and finally pulled it off. It left a red indentation like a brand on her finger. "The palace makes sure his affairs are conducted discreetly, and they vet the women to make sure they aren't reporters or working for political opponents, and thank God there have been no bastards." She paused and gave me a rueful smile. "Unfortunately, no legitimate children either. If I don't whelp soon, my father may remove me from the succession."

There was a flare of heat in my chest. If she wasn't the Infanta, wasn't the heir, she could live as she pleased. Maybe even with a tailor's son. There was also a bitter pleasure in learning that BoHo was sterile.

"But look at you. *Captain* Belmanor. How did you come by this ship?"

"I won a share of it in a card game. It seemed great at first. Then I discovered how much was still owed on the damn thing. Sometimes I think Tregillis lost deliberately."

Mercedes laughed. She knew me too well. "Admit it. You love it. You're a captain, you go where you please, no orders from highborn twits with more braid than brains."

"Yes, but I wanted to stay in the navy. To prove that one of my kind could be an effective officer."

There was a silence; then she asked, "Were you guilty?"

"No."

"I thought not. But the evidence against you was—"

"Overwhelming. Yes. That should always be a clue that someone's being framed." I sat frowning, shifting through all the old hurts and injustices.

She hesitantly touched my shoulder. "I'm sorry. I thought about doing something."

"So why didn't you?" And I realized that I was less angry than honestly curious.

"I was afraid . . . "

"Of—?" She held up her hand, cutting off the rest of my question.

"There would have been whispers." We sat silent for a few minutes. The memory of the Star Deck returned. "Have you married?" she suddenly asked, pulling me back to the present.

"No. I never met anyone I wanted to marry."

"Liar." Her look challenged me. I realized that our thighs were touching, shoulders brushing. Her hair was tickling my ear and cheek. She smelled of sweat and faded perfume and woman.

"Mercedes, I'm . . . um . . . "

"You saved my life," she said softly, and she took my hand and laid it on her breast.

I jumped up and looked down at her. "No. Not because you're *grateful*. That would be worse than never having you."

"You loved me once."

"I still do." She had tricked me, and I had said it. I fell back on the only defense and the source of my greatest pain. "And you're another man's wife."

She stood. "Damn your middle-class morality! My life has been bound by expectations, rules, and protocol. I married a man I do not love. I became a military leader because of my father's frustration over his lack of a son. And now I've led my fleet to destruction, and the very thought of me and what I represent has driven the population of an entire planet to commit suicide! But I'm forced to live on with all the loss and regret. Can't I have one moment of happiness?" The agony in her voice nearly broke my resolve.

She turned away, hiding her tears. I gently took hold of her shoulders. "See if you still feel this way after a night's sleep. I don't want to add to those regrets."

I left before temptation overcame scruples.

We took the *Selkie* out to an area of open space, well away from any planetary bodies in the solar system, and folded. The ports now showed the strange gray filaments, like spiderweb or gray cotton candy, which was the hallmark of traveling past light-speed. I checked the watch implanted in the weave of my shirt. Midafternoon. I decided to check on Mercedes. There was no response to my gentle knock. Concerned, I slipped into the cabin and found her asleep, but there were traces of tears on her cheeks. She murmured disconsolately and her fingers plucked at the sheets. Feeling like a voyeur, I quietly left.

And was caught by Baca, who with unaccustomed seriousness said, "I was thinking about saying a Kaddish for the people, but I realized it was more Masada than Holocaust, and then I had to wonder if it was a righteous choice. To die rather than submit. Is that noble, or is it more noble to survive and persevere? What do you think?"

I looked at this stranger in Baca's body, and tried to compose an answer. We had stood at the edge of a massive graveyard, and I couldn't grasp it. All I knew was that this burden of guilt rested on the shoulders of the woman I loved. I couldn't do anything for the battle group or for Kusatsu-Shirane, but maybe I could do something for Mercedes.

She joined us that evening for supper. With Mercedes, it was a tight fit around the small table in the mess, but we all squeezed in. Jahan had prepared a slow-simmered stew of rehydrated vegetables and lamb for the omnivores, and there was a vegetarian dish for Dalea and Jax. Like all Isanjo food, it was highly spiced, so I drank more beer than normal. Perhaps it was due more to sitting so close to Mercedes.

Once the plates were cleared, Melin brought me a reader. I was embarrassed to display this silly ship custom in front of Mercedes. I hedged. "I don't remember where we were."

"The chapter entitled 'Wayfarers All,' page 159, second paragraph," Jax offered helpfully. I mentally cursed the creature for its perfect recall.

"What is this?" Mercedes asked.

"We read aloud after the final meal of the day," Jahan said. "Each one of us picks a book from our species. You never really know a culture until you've heard their poetry and read their great literature."

"An interesting way to spread understanding," Mercedes said thoughtfully.

"Yes, you don't allow it in your human schools and universities," Dalea said.

Mercedes blushed and I glared at the Hajin.

"And what human book did you select?" Mercedes hurriedly asked me, to cover the awkward moment.

*"The Wind in the Willows."*

Mercedes shifted her chair so she could better see me. "Please, do read."

I was embarrassed, and cleared my throat several times before starting, but after a few sentences, the soft magic of the story and the music of the words made me forget my special listener.

*"She will clothe herself with canvas; and then, once outside, the sounding slap of great green seas as she heels to the wind, pointing South! And you, you will come too, young brother; for the days pass, and never return, and the South still waits for you. Take the Adventure, heed the call, now ere the irrevocable moment passes!" My voice cracked on the final words. I coughed and reached for my beer and finished off the last sip.* "That's all the voice I have tonight," I said.

There were a few groans of disappointment, but the party broke up, some of the crew to return to the bridge, others to their cabins to sleep. I escorted Mercedes back to the cabin.

We stopped at the door, and an awkward silence fell over us both. "I've slept a night," she finally said quietly.

My collar suddenly grabbed my throat. I ran a finger around it. "Ah . . . yes, you have."

"I believe I'll take the wayfarer's advice," she murmured, and she kissed me.

I had enough wit, barely, to lock the door behind us.

Later, we lay in the narrow bed. I liked that it was narrow. It meant that she had to stay close. Her head was on my shoulder, and I twined a strand of her hair through my fingers. I was very aware of the scent of Mercedes: the deep musk of our sex mingling, the spice and pine smell of her hair— her breath, which seemed to hold a hint of vanilla. I kissed her long and deep, then pulled back and smacked my lips.

"What?"

"You taste like vanilla too," I answered. She blushed. It was adorable. She ran a hand through my dishwater blond hair. "I know, I'm shaggy. I'll get a haircut on Cuandru."

"I like it. It makes you look rakish. You were always so spit and polish."

"I had to be. Everyone was waiting for the 'lowborn scum' to disgrace the service."

She laid a hand across my mouth. "Don't. Forget about them. Forget the slights."

"Hard to do."

"Don't be a grievance collector," Mercedes said. She changed the subject. "Lot of silver in there."

I stroked the gray streaks at her temples. "Neither of us is as young as we used to be."

"Really? I would never have known that if you hadn't told me." She pulled my hair, and we laughed together.

I was on the verge of dozing off when she suddenly rested a hand on my chest and pushed herself up. Her hair hung around her like a mahogany-colored veil. My good mood gave way to alarm, because she looked so serious.

"Tracy, do something for me?"

"Of course."

"Don't report that you've found me. Not just yet. I want a little more time."

I did too. So I agreed.

Late in the sleep cycle, I was awakened by her cries. Tears slid from beneath her lashes and wet her cheeks though she was still asleep. She thrashed, fighting the covers. I caught her in my arms, and held her close.

"Mercedes, *mi amor*. Wake up. You're safe."

Her eyes opened and she blinked up at me in confusion. "They're dead." She gave a violent shiver, and covered her face with her hands, then looked in surprise at the tears clinging to her fingers. "I see those houses. The children. I killed them."

I rocked her. "Shhh, hush, you didn't." But it was only a half-truth and she knew it. And she was only mentioning half the dead. There was no word of the battle group. The men she'd commanded, and who had died no less surely than the people of Kusatsu-Shirane.

Eventually, she fell back to sleep. I lay awake, holding her close and wondering when the full trauma would hit.

Since there was an Imperial shipyard at Cuandru, I came out of Fold at the edge of the solar system. I didn't want the big point-to-point guns deciding that we were some kind of threat. I ordered Baca to tight beam our information—ship registry, previous ports of call (excluding the Hidden Worlds, of course), and cargo—to the planetary control. My radio man gave me a look.

"We're not mentioning the Infanta?"

"Not yet. Her orders," I answered, striving to sound casual. Melin and Baca exchanged glances, and Melin rolled her eyes. I felt the flush rising up my neck, into my face, until it culminated at the top of my ears. Not for the first time, I cursed my fair complexion.

"Then she better be a crew member," Jahan said. "Otherwise, they'll think we're white slavers and we kidnapped her."

"She's not young enough," I said.

"Oh, boy," Baca muttered.

"Better not let *her* hear you say that," Jahan said.

"What?" I demanded.

Melin said, "Captain, somebody's got to take you in hand and teach you how to be a boyfriend."

"I'm not her boyfriend. She's married. We're friends."

"Okay. Then you got a lot to learn about being a lover," Melin said.

At that moment, I hated my crew. I made an inarticulate sound and clutched at my hair. "Get her on the crew list." I stomped off the bridge.

I decided to take us in to dock at the station. I shooed Melin out of her post, and she proceeded to hover behind me like an overanxious mother. Through the horseshoe-shaped port, we could see the big cruisers under construction. Spacesuited figures, most of them Isanjos, clambered and darted around the massive skeletal forms. Against the black of space, the sparks off their welders were like newly born stars.

There was a light touch on my shoulder. I glanced up briefly. It was Mercedes, and sometime in the past few hours, she had cut her hair, dyed it red, and darkened her skin. Dalea loomed behind her.

"What's this?" I asked, hating the loss of that glorious mane.

"We had to do something to keep her from being recognized," Dalea said.

"I'm sure the port authorities will be expecting to find the Infanta aboard a tramp cargo ship," I said sarcastically, as I tweaked the maneuvering jets.

Jahan, seated at my command station, said "Tracy, her face is on the *money.*"

And so it was. She graced the twenty-Reales note. The picture was taken from an official portrait that had her wearing a tiara, long hair elaborately styled, and a diamond necklace at her throat. Now she wore a pair of my stained cargo pants, and one of Melin's shirts.

Jax came rustling onto the bridge. Now the entire crew and Mercedes were watching, but I wasn't nervous. I knew I was good. With brief bursts of fire from alternating jets, I took us through the maze of trading ships, station scooters, racing yachts, and military vessels. With a final burst of power from the starboard engines, I spun the ship ninety degrees and brought us to rest, like a butterfly landing on a flower, against a docking gantry at the main space station.

There was a brief outburst of applause. Mercedes leaned down and whispered, "You were the best pilot of our class." The touch of her lips and the puff of her breath against my ear sent a shiver through me.

She straightened, and addressed the crew. "So what now?"

"We try to find someone to buy the farm equipment, and we pick up another cargo," Jax fluted.

Melin stretched her arms over her head. "I want a martini and a massage. And maybe not in that order. Or maybe both at the same time."

Jahan uncoiled from the back of the captain's chair. "I'm going home to see my mates and kids."

"If the captain will give me money, I'll replenish our medical supplies," Dalea said.

Mercedes smiled at Baca. "And what about you?"

He blushed. "I'm gonna find a concert. Maybe go to the opera, depending on what's playing."

Mercedes tugged my hair. "And you need a haircut."

"I take it we're going planetside?" I asked.

"Oh, yes," Mercedes assured me.

Dalea's makeover worked. The guards glanced briefly at my ship papers, and waved us through and onto a shuttle to the planet.

It was foolish, crazy even. I planned to check us into an exclusive hotel, a place frequented by aristocrats and famous actors. It was going to take most of my savings, but I wanted . . . I wasn't sure exactly what I wanted. To make sure she was comfortable. To show her that I could be her equal. Fortunately, Mercedes was wiser than me. When I outlined my plan, she took my face between her hands and gently shook my head back and forth.

"No. First, you don't have to prove anything to me, and second, I'm likely to be recognized, red hair or no, and third, I've spent my life with these people. Let me have another life. A short time where I don't have to remember . . . " But she didn't finish the thought.

Jahan advised us, and we ended up in an Isanjo tree house hotel that sprawled through an old-growth forest on the outskirts of the capital city. To accommodate the occasional human visitor, there were swaying bridges between the trees, which Mercedes and I used with white-knuckled effort. As we crept across the swaying bridges, the Isanjo traveled branch to branch, and crossed the intervening spaces with great soaring leaps. The Isanjo were good enough to deliver meals to our aerie, so we spent our first day planetside in bed.

Wind whispered and then roared through the leaves as it brought down a storm from the mountains. It set our room to swaying. Lightning flashed through the wooden shutters, and thunder growled with a sound like a giant chewing on boulders. We clung to each other, torn between terror and delight. The rain came, hammering on the wooden roof, forcing its way through the shutters to spray lightly across our bodies. It broke the heat, and we shivered and snuggled close.

It would have been perfect except for her nightmares.

The next day, Mercedes took command. We went to explore the city, and to find a barber. Mercedes and the Hajin hairdresser discussed every cowlick, natural part, and the consistency of my hair before she would allow the alien to cut. Between them, they decided I should wear bangs. It felt strange, and I kept pushing them off my forehead, only to have my lady reach out and muss my hair each time I did.

We strolled through the Old Quarter, and I bought Mercedes a string of beads that she'd admired. We moved on, strolling along the river walk. Everyone seemed to be taking advantage of the good weather. Families spread blankets on the grass, children tussled like happy kittens, babies cried. Mercedes and I sat on a bench at the water's edge, listening to the water gurgle and chuckle while we shared an ice cream cone.

We ate dinner at an outdoor café. The Isanjo, being almost complete carnivores, know how to cook meat. Our steaks arrived running blood, tender, and subtly flavored by having been stuffed with cheese. We polished off a bottle of deep red wine between us, and talked about books and music and the wonderful things we'd seen during the day. She scrupulously avoided all talk of the empire, the navy, or Kusatsu-Shirane. We shared a dessert, a lighter-than-air concoction of mangos, some local fruit, cream, and pistachio nuts. I drained my coffee, and steeled myself for a conversation that had to happen.

"Mercedes."

"Yes?"

"You need to talk to someone. About what happened."

"I will. This policy can't stand. Not if it's going to lead to mass suicide," she said.

I shook my head. "Stop deflecting. You need to face what's happened, and figure out why you're identifying more with the people on Kusatsu-Shirane than you are with your own battle group."

"That's not fair."

"Tell me I'm wrong." She stayed silent. I left it there. "So, shall we go?"

"Yes."

I left money on the table, and we walked out onto the street. The air was soft after the tumultuous storms of the night before. The restaurants were still busy, and the many voices and many languages wove into something that was almost music. Then we heard real music. Dance music. Mercedes turned to me.

"Do you like to dance?"

"No," I said.

She grabbed my hand. "I love to dance." And I came along like the tail on her kite. There was a small band playing on a pier that thrust out into the river. Multicolored lanterns hung overhead. The Isanjo danced on the narrow wires that supported the lanterns. The humans, earthbound and awkward, danced on the wooden pier. I felt graceless and stupid. There had been no deportment and dance lessons in my youth, but Mercedes was gifted with grace and rhythm. She made me look good.

The dance ended, and we went off to the small bar to buy drinks. She took a long sip, and then kissed me. I tasted rum and basil.

"So, I'm forgiven for poking at you?"

"At least you notice when I'm crazy," she said.

"You're not crazy. The people on Kusatsu-Shirane were crazy."

"Were they? No one got to force them into a life—"

But she didn't get to finish the thought because there were murmurs from the crowd. Everyone was looking up. We followed suit and watched pinpricks of light appear and flash like brilliant diamonds in the night sky.

"That's a fleet coming in," I said.

Mercedes gripped me tightly. "Take me home."

It was a misnomer. We had no home, but I understood what she wanted. The comfort of bed, bodies pressed close, a roof to shut out the image of duty and responsibility now orbiting overhead.

We returned to the hotel and our lovemaking had a desperate quality. She clung to me, clawed at me as if she wanted to crawl inside my skin. Finally, I had nothing more to give. I lay gasping, body sweat-bathed, blood pounding in my ears.

Mercedes was curled up in a ball. I put an arm around her waist and spooned her. "Tracy." It was barely audible.

"Hmmm?"

"Let me stay. Really be a member of your crew." Tension and desperate longing etched every word, and her fingers clung like claws to my wrist. She turned over suddenly, her face inches from mine. "They think I'm dead. We can go away. Be together."

For an instant, I was giddy at the prospect. I thought of the worlds we'd visit together. Nights in my cabin. Listening to her read to the crew. But reality returned.

"No, love, they know you survived. Your capsule was beaming out continuous messages. When those signals stopped, they know you were found and the capsule opened. They would search for us, and they could never admit that you joined us voluntarily."

"And they would kill you," she said, her voice flat and dull.

"And beyond personal concerns, what happens if you don't take the throne? You know BoHo will try to rule in your place." She shuddered at the prospect. "We've had this moment. We couldn't expect it to last."

"It will last. At least until morning."

We didn't sleep. It would have wasted the time we still had together.

She wanted to say good-bye to everyone. I called them, and the crew assembled at a popular, if low-rent, diner. I ordered *huevos rancheros* because I could stir it together and no one would notice that I hadn't eaten. There was a brittle quality to our laughter, and only at the end did we discuss what lay between us.

Mercedes encompassed them all with a look. "Thank you all for your kindness. I'll never forget you and what you did for me. I also wanted you to know that there are going to be changes when I take the throne. There won't be another Kusatsu-Shirane, and I'll see that there's a review of the alien laws."

The parting took awhile because Dalea wanted to "make sure her patient was fit." Mercedes and the Hajin retreated to the bathroom. Jahan joined me and stretched out her claws.

"Will you survive?"

"I'll have to," I said with forced lightness.

Mercedes and Dalea returned. Mercedes had an indescribable expression on her face. I briefly took her hand. "All good?" I asked.

"Yes. Oh, yes," she said in a faraway voice.

Our next stop was the hair salon. My hairdresser from the day before stripped the red from Mercedes's hair, and restored it to its lustrous dark brown. Once he was finished, the Hajin studied her closely. Mercedes went imperious on him.

"All you've seen is a remarkable resemblance."

He stepped back, extended a front leg, and gave her a dignified bow. "Quite, ma'am."

We took a cab to the League Embassy. Barricades and guards surrounded the building. The driver cranked around to look at us. "They won't let me any closer than this," he said.

"That's fine," I said.

Mercedes and I looked at each other. Mercedes's eyes were awash with tears. I swallowed hard, trying to force down the painful lump that had settled in my throat.

"Good-bye," she said. She started to reach out a hand, then threw herself into my arms and pressed her lips to mine. She pulled away, opened the door, and got out.

I got out too, and watched as she walked quickly toward the elaborate gates of the embassy. She didn't look back. There was a flurry of reaction from the guards. The door of the embassy opened, and a flying wedge of men, led by BoHo, rushed out. Medals and ribbons glittered on the midnight blue of his uniform jacket, and the sunlight glinted off his jet-black hair. He was still handsome, though middle age had softened the lines of his jaw.

He went to kiss her, and Mercedes turned her face away.

My three alien crew members found me in a bar late that night.

"Go away."

Jax shuffled closer. "The ship's note's been paid off, so we own her free and clear. And we got a reward. A most generous reward. The Infanta meets her obligations. And I've procured a new cargo. We're ready to leave whenever you are."

Jahan curled up on the bar stool next to me. "The fleet has withdrawn. They're rushing back to Hissilek. Apparently, the emperor's had a stroke."

That pulled me out of my rapt contemplation of my scotch. I met those alien eyes, and I had that cold sensation of being surrounded by hidden forces that were plotting against humans.

"How . . . convenient," I managed.

"I think she'll be a good ruler," Jahan said. "Now the final bit of news." She gestured to Dalea.

"The Infanta is pregnant." I gaped at the Hajin. "Congratulations," Dalea added.

*I'm going to be a father. My child will be the heir to the Solar League. I will never know him or her.*

And I realized that maybe none of us ever gets to choose our lives. Our only choice is to live the life that comes to us, or go down into darkness.

I drained my scotch, and pushed back from the bar. "Let's go see what tomorrow holds."

Naomi Novik is the acclaimed and bestselling author of the Temeraire series, begun with *His Majesty's Dragon* and recently concluded with the ninth volume, *League of Dragons*. Her novel *Uprooted*, inspired by stories of Baba Yaga and the Polish fairy tales and folklore of her childhood, recently won the Nebula Award.

She co-founded the Organization for Transformative Works to support the work of fan creators and has been one of the primary developers of the open-source Archive of Our Own. She lives in New York City with her husband, Hard Case Crime founder Charles Ardai, and their daughter Evidence, surrounded by an excessive number of purring computers.

# Seven Years from Home

## *Naomi Novik*

### Preface

Seven days passed for me on my little raft of a ship as I fled Melida; seven years for the rest of the unaccelerated universe. I hoped to be forgotten, a dusty footnote left at the bottom of a page. Instead I came off to trumpets and medals and legal charges, equal doses of acclaim and venom, and I stumbled bewildered through the brassy noise, led first by one and then by another, while my last opportunity to enter any protest against myself escaped.

Now I desire only to correct the worst of the factual inaccuracies bandied about, so far as my imperfect memory will allow, and to make an offering of my own understanding to that smaller and more sophisticate audience who prefer to shape the world's opinion rather than be shaped by it.

I engage not to tire you with a recitation of dates and events and quotations. I do not recall them with any precision myself. But I must warn you that neither have I succumbed to that pathetic and otiose impulse to sanitize the events of the war, or to excuse sins either my own or belonging to others. To do so would be a lie, and on Melida, to tell a lie was an insult more profound than murder.

I will not see my sisters again, whom I loved. Here we say that one who takes the long midnight voyage has leaped ahead in time, but to me it seems it is they who have traveled on ahead. I can no longer hear their voices when I am awake. I hope this will silence them in the night.

Ruth Patrona

Reivaldt, Janvier 32, 4765

## THE FIRST ADJUSTMENT

I disembarked at the port of Landfall in the fifth month of 4753. There is such a port on every world where the Confederacy has set its foot but not yet its flag: crowded and dirty and charmless. It was on the Esperigan continent, as the Melidans would not tolerate the construction of a space-port in their own territory.

Ambassador Kostas, my superior, was a man of great authority and presence, two meters tall and solidly built, with a jovial handshake, high intelligence, and very little patience for fools; that I was likely to be relegated to this category was evident on our first meeting. He disliked my assignment to begin with. He thought well of the Esperigans; he moved in their society as easily as he did in our own, and would have called one or two of their senior ministers his personal friends, if only such a gesture were not highly unprofessional. He recognized his duty, and on an abstract intellectual level the potential value of the Melidans, but they revolted him, and he would have been glad to find me of like mind, ready to draw a line through their name and give them up as a bad cause.

A few moments' conversation was sufficient to disabuse him of this hope. I wish to attest that he did not allow the disappointment to in any way alter the performance of his duty, and he could not have objected with more vigor to my project of proceeding at once to the Melidan continent, to his mind a suicidal act.

In the end he chose not to stop me. I am sorry if he later regretted that, as seems likely. I took full advantage of the weight of my arrival. Five years had gone by on my homeworld of Terce since I had embarked, and there is a certain moral force to having sacrificed a former life for the one unknown. I had observed it often with new arrivals on Terce: their first requests were rarely refused even when foolish, as they often were. I was of course quite sure my own were eminently sensible.

"We will find you a guide," he said finally, yielding, and all the machinery of the Confederacy began to turn to my desire, a heady sensation.

Badea arrived at the embassy not two hours later. She wore a plain gray wrap around her shoulders, draped to the ground, and another wrap around her head. The alterations visible were only small ones: a smattering of green freckles across the bridge of her nose and cheeks, a greenish tinge to her lips and nails. Her wings were folded and hidden under the wrap, adding the bulk roughly of an overnight hiker's backpack. She smelled a little like the sourdough used on Terce to make roundbread, noticeable but not unpleasant. She might have walked through a spaceport without exciting comment.

She was brought to me in the shambles of my new office, where I had barely begun to lay out my things. I was wearing a conservative black suit, my best, tailored because you could not buy trousers for women readymade on Terce, and, thankfully, comfortable shoes, because elegant ones on Terce were not meant to be walked in. I remember my clothing particularly because I was in it for the next week without opportunity to change.

"Are you ready to go?" she asked me, as soon as we were introduced and the receptionist had left.

I was quite visibly *not* ready to go, but this was not a misunderstanding: she did not want to take me. She thought the request stupid, and feared my safety would be a burden on her. If Ambassador Kostas would not mind my failure to return, she could not know that, and to be just, he would certainly have reacted unpleasantly in any case, figuring it as his duty.

But when asked for a favor she does not want to grant, a Melidan will sometimes offer it anyway, only in an unacceptable or awkward way. Another Melidan will recognize this as a refusal, and withdraw the request. Badea did not expect this courtesy from me, she only expected that I would say I could not leave at once. This she could count to her satisfaction as a refusal, and she would not come back to offer again.

I was however informed enough to be dangerous, and I did recognize the custom. I said, "It is inconvenient, but I am prepared to leave immediately." She turned at once and walked out of my office, and I followed her. It is understood that a favor accepted despite the difficulty and constraints laid down by the giver must be necessary to the recipient, as indeed this was to me; but in such a case, the conditions must then be endured, even if artificial.

I did not risk a pause at all even to tell anyone I was going; we walked out past the embassy secretary and the guards, who did not do more than give us a cursory glance—we were going the wrong way, and my citizen's button would likely have saved us interruption in any case. Kostas would not know I had gone until my absence was noticed and the security logs examined.

## THE SECOND ADJUSTMENT

I was not unhappy as I followed Badea through the city. A little discomfort was nothing to me next to the intense satisfaction of, as I felt, having passed a first test: I had gotten past all resistance offered me, both by Kostas and Badea, and soon I would be in the heart of a people I already felt I knew. Though I would be an outsider among them, I had lived all my life to the present day in the self-same state, and I did not fear it, or for the moment anything else.

Badea walked quickly and with a freer stride than I was used to, loose-limbed. I was taller, but had to stretch to match her. Esperigans looked at her as she went by, and then looked at me, and the pressure of their gaze was suddenly hostile. "We might take a taxi," I offered. Many were passing by empty. "I can pay."

"No," she said, with a look of distaste at one of those conveyances, so we continued on foot.

After Melida, during my black-sea journey, my doctoral dissertation on the Canaan movement was published under the escrow clause, against my will. I have never used the funds, which continue to accumulate steadily. I do not like to inflict them on any cause I admire sufficiently to support, so they will go to my family when I have gone; my nephews will be glad of it, and of the passing of an embarrassment, and that is as much good as it can be expected to provide.

There is a great deal within that book which is wrong, and more which is wrongheaded, in particular any expression of opinion or analysis I interjected atop the scant collection of accurate facts I was able to accumulate in six years of over-enthusiastic graduate work. This little is true: the Canaan movement was an offshoot of conservation philosophy. Where the traditionalists of that movement sought to restrict humanity to dead worlds and closed enclaves on others, the Canaan splinter group wished instead to alter themselves while they altered their new worlds, meeting them halfway.

The philosophy had the benefit of a certain practicality, as genetic engineering and body modification was and remains considerably cheaper than terraforming, but we are a squeamish and a violent species, and nothing invites pogrom more surely than the neighbor who is different from us, yet still too close. In consequence, the Melidans were by our present day the last surviving Canaan society.

They had come to Melida and settled the larger of the two continents some eight hundred years before. The Esperigans came two hundred years later, refugees from the plagues on New Victoire, and took the smaller continent. The two had little contact for the first half-millennium; we of the Confederacy are given to think in worlds and solar systems, and to imagine that only a space voyage is long, but a hostile continent is vast enough to occupy a small and struggling band. But both prospered, each according to their lights, and by the time I landed, half the planet glittered in the night from space, and half was yet pristine.

In my dissertation, I described the ensuing conflict as natural, which is fair if slaughter and pillage are granted to be natural to our kind. The Esperigans had exhausted the limited raw resources of their share of the planet, and a short flight away was the untouched expanse of the larger continent, not a tenth as populated as their own. The Melidans controlled their birthrate, used only sustainable quantities, and built nothing which could not be eaten by the wilderness a year after they had abandoned it. Many Esperigan philosophers and politicians trumpeted their admiration of Melidan society, but this was only a sort of pleasant spiritual refreshment, as one admires a saint or a martyr without ever wishing to be one.

The invasion began informally, with adventurers and entrepreneurs, with the desperate, the poor, the violent. They began to land on the shores of the Melidan territory, to survey, to take away samples, to plant their own foreign roots. They soon had a village, then more than one. The Melidans told them to leave, which worked as well as it ever has in the annals of colonialism, and then attacked them. Most of the settlers were killed; enough survived and straggled back across the ocean to make a dramatic story of murder and cruelty out of it.

I expressed the conviction to the Ministry of State, in my pre-assignment report, that the details had been exaggerated, and that the attacks had been provoked more extensively. I was wrong, of course. But at the time I did not know it.

Badea took me to the low quarter of Landfall, so called because it faced on the side of the ocean downcurrent from the spaceport. Iridescent oil and a floating mat of discards glazed the edge of the surf. The houses were mean and crowded tightly upon one another, broken up mostly by liquor stores and bars. Docks stretched out into the ocean, extended long to reach out past the pollution, and just past the end of one of these floated a small boat, little more than a simple coracle: a hull of brown bark, a narrow brown mast, a grey-green sail slack and trembling in the wind.

We began walking out towards it, and those watching—there were some men loitering about the docks, fishing idly, or working on repairs to equipment or nets—began to realize then that I meant to go with her.

The Esperigans had already learned the lesson we like to teach as often as we can, that the Confederacy is a bad enemy and a good friend, and while no one is ever made to join us by force, we cannot be opposed directly. We had given them the spaceport already, an open door to the rest of the settled worlds, and they wanted more, the moth yearning. I relied on this for protection, and did not consider that however much they wanted from our outstretched hand, they still more wished to deny its gifts to their enemy.

Four men rose as we walked the length of the dock, and made a line across it. "You don't want to go with that one, ma'am," one of them said to me, a parody of respect. Badea said nothing. She moved a little aside, to see how I would answer them.

"I am on assignment for my government," I said, neatly offering a red flag to a bull, and moved towards them. It was not an attempt at bluffing: on Terce, even though I was immodestly unveiled, men would have at once moved out of the way to avoid any chance of the insult of physical contact. It was an act so automatic as to be invisible: precisely what we are taught to watch for in ourselves, but that proves infinitely easier in the instruction than in the practice. I did not *think* they would move; I knew they would.

Perhaps that certainty transmitted itself: the men did move a little, enough to satisfy my unconscious that they were cooperating with my expectations, so that it took me wholly by surprise and horror when one reached out and put his hand on my arm to stop me.

I screamed, in full voice, and struck him. His face is lost to my memory, but I still can see clearly the man behind him, his expression as full of appalled violation as my own. The four of them flinched from my scream, and then drew in around me, protesting and reaching out in turn.

I reacted with more violence. I had confidently considered myself a citizen of no world and of many, trained out of assumptions and unaffected by the parochial attitudes of the one where chance had seen me born, but in that moment I could with actual pleasure have killed all of them. That wish was unlikely to be gratified. I was taller, and the gravity of Terce is slightly higher than of Melida, so I was stronger than they expected me to be, but they were laborers and seamen, built generously and rough-hewn, and the male advantage in muscle mass tells quickly in a hand-to-hand fight.

They tried to immobilize me, which only panicked me further. The mind curls in on itself in such a moment; I remember palpably only the sensation of sweating copiously, and the way this caused the seam of my blouse to rub unpleasantly against my neck as I struggled.

Badea told me later that, at first, she had meant to let them hold me. She could then leave, with the added satisfaction of knowing the Esperigan fishermen and not she had provoked an incident with the Confederacy. It was not sympathy that moved her to action, precisely. The extremity of my distress was as alien to her as to them, but where they thought me mad, she read it in the context of my having accepted her original conditions and somewhat unwillingly decided that I truly did need to go with her, even if she did not know precisely why and saw no use in it herself.

I cannot tell you precisely how the subsequent moments unfolded. I remember the green gauze of her wings overhead perforated by the sun, like a linen curtain, and the blood spattering my face as she neatly lopped off the hands upon me. She used for the purpose a blade I later saw in use for many tasks, among them harvesting fruit off plants where the leaves or the bark may be poisonous. It is shaped like a sickle and strung upon a thick elastic cord, which a skilled wielder can cause to become rigid or to collapse.

I stood myself back on my feet panting, and she landed. The men were on their knees screaming, and others were running towards us down the docks. Badea swept the severed hands into the water with the side of her foot and said calmly, "We must go."

The little boat had drawn up directly beside us over the course of our encounter, drawn by some signal I had not seen her transmit. I stepped into it behind her. The coracle leapt forward like a springing bird, and left the shouting and the blood behind.

We did not speak over the course of that strange journey. What I had thought a sail did not catch the wind, but opened itself wide and stretched out over our heads, like an awning, and angled itself towards the sun. There were many small filaments upon the surface wriggling when I examined it more closely, and also upon the exterior of the hull.

Badea stretched herself out upon the floor of the craft, lying under the low deck, and I joined her in the small space: it was not uncomfortable nor rigid, but had the queer unsettled cushioning of a waterbed.

The ocean crossing took only the rest of the day. How our speed was generated I cannot tell you; we did not seem to sit deeply in the water and our craft threw up no spray. The world blurred as a window running with rain. I asked Badea for water, once, and she put her hands on the floor of the craft and pressed down: in the depression she made, a small clear pool gathered for me to cup out, with a taste like slices of cucumber with the skin still upon them.

This was how I came to Melida.

## THE THIRD ADJUSTMENT

Badea was vaguely embarrassed to have inflicted me on her fellows, and having deposited me in the center of her village made a point of leaving me there by leaping aloft into the canopy where I could not follow, as a way of saying she was done with me, and anything I did henceforth could not be laid at her door.

I was by now hungry and nearly sick with exhaustion. Those who have not flown between worlds like to imagine the journey a glamorous one, but at least for minor bureaucrats, it is no more pleasant than any form of transport, only elongated. I had spent a week a virtual prisoner in my berth, the bed folding up to give me room to walk four strides back and forth, or to unfold my writing-desk, not both at once, with a shared toilet the size of an ungenerous closet down the hall. Landfall had not arrested my forward motion, as that mean port had never been my destination. Now, however, I was arrived, and the dregs of adrenaline were consumed in anticlimax.

Others before me have stood in a Melidan village center and described it for an audience—Esperigans mostly, anthropologists and students of biology and a class of tourists either adventurous or stupid. There is usually a lyrical description of the natives coasting overhead among some sort of vines or tree branches knitted overhead for shelter, the particulars and adjectives determined by the village latitude, and the obligatory explanation of the typical plan of huts, organized as a spoked wheel around the central plaza.

If I had been less tired, perhaps I too would have looked with so analytical an air, and might now satisfy my readers with a similar report.

But to me the village only presented all the confusion of a wholly strange place, and I saw nothing that seemed to me deliberate. To call it a village gives a false air of comforting provinciality. Melidans, at least those with wings, move freely among a wide constellation of small settlements, so that all of these, in the public sphere, partake of the hectic pace of the city. I stood alone, and strangers moved past me with assurance, the confidence of their stride saying, "I care nothing for you or your fate. It is of no concern to me. How might you expect it to be otherwise?" In the end, I lay down on one side of the plaza and went to sleep.

I met Kitia the next morning. She woke me by prodding me with a twig, experimentally, having been selected for this task out of her group of schoolmates by some complicated interworking of personality and chance. They giggled from a few safe paces back as I opened my eyes and sat up.

"Why are you sleeping in the square?" Kitia asked me, to a burst of fresh giggles.

"Where should I sleep?" I asked her.

"In a house!" she said.

When I had explained to them, not without some art, that I had no house here, they offered the censorious suggestion that I should go back to wherever I did have a house. I made a good show of looking analytically up at the sky overhead and asking them what our latitude was, and then I pointed at a random location and said, "My house is five years that way."

Scorn, puzzlement, and at last delight. I was from the stars! None of their friends had ever met anyone from so far away. One girl who previously had held a point of pride for having once visited the smaller continent, with an Esperigan toy doll to prove it, was instantly dethroned. Kitia possessively took my arm and informed me that as my house was too far away, she would take me to another.

Children of virtually any society are an excellent resource for the diplomatic servant or the anthropologist, if contact with them can be made without giving offense. They enjoy the unfamiliar experience of answering real questions, particularly the stupidly obvious ones that allow them to feel a sense of superiority over the inquiring adult, and they are easily impressed with the unusual. Kitia was a treasure. She led me, at the head of a small pied-piper procession, to an empty house on a convenient lane. It had been lately abandoned, and was already being reclaimed: the walls and floor were swarming with tiny insects with glossy dark blue carapaces, munching so industriously the sound of their jaws hummed like a summer afternoon.

I with difficulty avoided recoiling. Kitia did not hesitate: she walked into the swarm, crushing beetles by the dozens underfoot, and went to a small spigot in the far wall. When she turned this on, a clear viscous liquid issued forth, and the beetles scattered from it. "Here, like this," she said, showing me how to cup my hands under the liquid and spread it upon the walls and the floor. The disgruntled beetles withdrew, and the brownish surfaces began to bloom back to pale green, repairing the holes.

Over the course of that next week, she also fed me, corrected my manners and my grammar, and eventually brought me a set of clothing, a tunic and leggings, which she proudly informed me she had made herself in class. I thanked her with real sincerity and asked where I might wash my old clothing. She looked very puzzled, and when she had looked more closely at my clothing and touched it, she said, "Your clothing is dead! I thought it was only ugly."

Her gift was not made of fabric but a thin tough mesh of plant filaments with the feathered surface of a moth's wings. It gripped my skin eagerly as soon as I had put it on, and I thought myself at first allergic, because it itched and tingled, but this was only the bacteria bred to live in the mesh assiduously eating away the sweat and dirt and dead epidermal cells built up on my skin. It took me several more days to overcome all my instinct and learn to trust the living cloth with the more voluntary eliminations of my body also. (Previously I had been going out back to defecate in the woods, having been unable to find anything resembling a toilet, and meeting too much confusion when I tried to approach the question to dare pursue it further, for fear of encountering a taboo.)

And this was the handiwork of a child, not thirteen years of age! She could not explain to me how she had done it in any way which made sense to me. Imagine if you had to explain how to perform a reference search to someone who had not only never seen a library, but did not understand electricity, and who perhaps knew there was such a thing as written text, but did not himself read more than the alphabet. She took me once to her classroom after hours and showed me her workstation, a large wooden tray full of grayish moss, with a double row of small jars along the back each holding liquids or powders which I could only distinguish by their differing colors. Her only tools were an assortment of syringes and eye-droppers and scoops and brushes.

I went back to my house and in the growing report I would not have a chance to send for another month I wrote, *These are a priceless people. We must have them.*

## THE FOURTH ADJUSTMENT

All these first weeks, I made no contact with any other adult. I saw them go by occasionally, and the houses around mine were occupied, but they never spoke to me or even looked at me directly. None of them objected to my squatting, but that was less implicit endorsement and more an unwillingness even to acknowledge my existence. I talked to Kitia and the other children, and tried to be patient. I hoped an opportunity would offer itself eventually for me to be of some visible use.

In the event, it was rather my lack of use which led to the break in the wall. A commotion arose in the early morning, while Kitia was showing me the plan of her wings, which she was at that age beginning to design. She would grow the parasite over the subsequent year, and was presently practicing with miniature versions, which rose from her worktable surface gossamer-thin and fluttering with an involuntary muscle-twitching. I was trying to conceal my revulsion.

Kitia looked up when the noise erupted. She casually tossed her example out of the window, to be pounced upon with a hasty scramble by several nearby birds, and went out the door. I followed her to the square: the children were gathered at the fringes, silent for once and watching. There were five women laid out on the ground, all bloody, one dead. Two of the others looked mortally wounded. They were all winged.

There were several working already on the injured, packing small brownish-white spongy masses into the open wounds and sewing them up. I would have liked to be of use, less from natural instinct than from the colder thought, which inflicted itself upon my mind, that any crisis opens social barriers. I am sorry to say I did not refrain from any noble self-censorship, but from the practical conviction that it was at once apparent my limited field-medical training could not in any valuable way be applied to the present circumstances.

I drew away, rather, to avoid being in the way as I could not turn the situation to my advantage, and in doing so ran up against Badea, who stood at the very edge of the square, observing.

She stood alone; there were no other adults nearby, and there was blood on her hands. "Are you hurt also?" I asked her.

"No," she returned, shortly.

I ventured on concern for her friends, and asked her if they had been hurt in fighting. "We have heard rumors," I added, "that the Esperigans have been encroaching on your territory." It was the first opportunity I had been given of hinting at even this much of our official sympathy, as the children only shrugged when I asked them if there were fighting going on.

She shrugged, too, with one shoulder, and the folded wing rose and fell with it. But then she said, "They leave their weapons in the forest for us, even where they cannot have gone."

The Esperigans had several kinds of land-mine technologies, including a clever mobile one which could be programmed with a target either as specific as an individual's genetic record or as general as a broadly defined body type—humanoid and winged, for instance—and set loose to wander until it found a match, then do the maximum damage it could. Only one side could carry explosive, as the other was devoted to the electronics. "The shrapnel, does it come only in one direction?" I asked, and made a fanned-out shape with my hands to illustrate. Badea looked at me sharply and nodded.

I explained the mine to her, and described their manufacture. "Some scanning devices can detect them," I added, meaning to continue into an offer, but I had not finished the litany of materials before she was striding away from the square, without another word.

I was not dissatisfied with the reaction, in which I correctly read intention to put my information to immediate use, and two days later my patience was rewarded. Badea came to my house in the mid-morning and said, "We have found one of them. Can you show us how to disarm them?"

"I am not sure," I told her, honestly. "The safest option would be to trigger it deliberately, from afar."

"The plastics they use poison the ground."

"Can you take me to its location?" I asked. She considered the question with enough seriousness that I realized there was either taboo or danger involved.

"Yes," she said finally, and took me with her to a house near the center of the village. It had steps up to the roof, and from there we could climb to that of the neighboring house, and so on until we were high enough to reach a large basket, woven not of ropes but of a kind of vine, sitting in a crook of a tree. We climbed into this, and she kicked us off from the tree.

The movement was not smooth. The nearest I can describe is the sensation of being on a child's swing, except at that highest point of weightlessness you do not go backwards, but instead go falling into another arc, but at tremendous speed, and with a pungent smell like rotten pineapple all around from the shattering of the leaves of the trees through which we were propelled. I was violently sick after some five minutes. To the comfort of my pride if not my stomach, Badea was also sick, though more efficiently and over the side, before our journey ended.

There were two other women waiting for us in the tree where we came to rest, both of them also winged: Renata and Paudi. "It's gone another three hundred meters, towards Ighlan," Renata told us—another nearby Melidan village, as they explained to me.

"If it comes near enough to pick up traces of organized habitation, it will not trigger until it is inside the settlement, among as many people as possible," I said. "It may also have a burrowing mode, if it is the more expensive kind."

They took me down through the canopy, carefully, and walked before and behind me when we came to the ground. Their wings were spread wide enough to brush against the hanging vines to either side, and they regularly leapt aloft for a brief survey. Several times they moved me with friendly hands into a slightly different path, although my untrained eyes could make no difference among the choices.

A narrow trail of large ants—the reader will forgive me for calling them ants, they were nearly indistinguishable from those efficient creatures—paced us over the forest floor, which I did not recognize as significant until we came near the mine, and I saw it covered with the ants, who did not impede its movement but milled around and over it with intense interest.

"We have adjusted them so they smell the plastic," Badea said, when I asked. "We can make them eat it," she added, "but we worried it would set off the device."

The word *adjusted* scratches at the back of my mind again as I write this, that unpleasant tinny sensation of a term that does not allow of real translation and which has been inadequately replaced. I cannot improve upon the work of the official Confederacy translators, however; to encompass the true concept would require three dry, dusty chapters more suited to a textbook on the subject of biological engineering, which I am ill-qualified to produce. I do hope that I have successfully captured the wholly casual way she spoke of this feat. Our own scientists might replicate this act of genetic sculpting in any of two dozen excellent laboratories across the Confederacy—given several years, and a suitably impressive grant. They had done it in less than two days, as a matter of course.

I did not at the time indulge in admiration. The mine was ignoring the inquisitive ants and scuttling along at a good pace, the head with its glassy eye occasionally rotating upon its spindly spider-legs, and we had half a day in which to divert it from the village ahead.

Renata followed the mine as it continued on, while I sketched what I knew of the internals in the dirt for Badea and Paudi. Any sensible mine-maker will design the device to simply explode at any interference with its working other than the disable code, so our options were not particularly satisfying. "The most likely choice," I suggested, "would be the transmitter. If it becomes unable to receive the disable code, there may be a failsafe which would deactivate it on a subsequent malfunction."

Paudi had on her back a case which, unfolded, looked very like a more elegant and compact version of little Kitia's worktable. She sat cross-legged with it on her lap and worked on it for some two hours' time, occasionally reaching down to pick up a handful of ants, which dropped into the green matrix of her table mostly curled up and died, save for a few survivors, which she herded carefully into an empty jar before taking up another sample.

I sat on the forest floor beside her, or walked with Badea, who was pacing a small circle out around us, watchfully. Occasionally she would unsling her scythe-blade, and then put it away again, and once she brought down a mottie, a small lemur-like creature. I say lemur because there is nothing closer in my experience, but it had none of the charm of an Earth-native mammal; I rather felt an instinctive disgust looking at it, even before she showed me the tiny sucker-mouths full of hooked teeth with which it latched upon a victim.

She had grown a little more loquacious, and asked me about my own homeworld. I told her about Terce, and about the seclusion of women, which she found extremely funny, as we can only laugh at the follies of those far from us which threaten us not at all. The Melidans by design maintain a five to one ratio of women to men, as adequate to maintain a healthy gene pool while minimizing the overall resource consumption of their population. "They cannot take the wings, so it is more difficult for them to travel," she added, with one sentence dismissing the lingering mystery which had perplexed earlier visitors, of the relative rarity of seeing their men.

She had two children, which she described to me proudly, living presently with their father and half-siblings in a village half a day's travel away, and she was considering a third. She had trained as a forest ranger, another inadequately translated term which was at the time beginning to take on a military significance among them under the pressure of the Esperigan incursions.

"I'm done," Paudi said, and we went to catch up Renata and find a nearby ant-nest, which looked like a mound of white cotton batting, rising several inches off the forest floor. Paudi introduced her small group of infected survivors into this colony, and after a little confusion and milling about, they accepted their transplantation and marched inside. The flow of departures slowed a little momentarily, then resumed, and a file split off from the main channel of workers to march in the direction of the mine.

These joined the lingering crowd still upon the mine, but the new arrivals did not stop at inspection and promptly began to struggle to insinuate themselves into the casing. We withdrew to a safe distance, watching. The mine continued on without any slackening in its pace for ten minutes, as more ants began to squeeze themselves inside, and then it hesitated, one spindly metal leg held aloft uncertainly. It went a few more slightly drunken paces, and then abruptly the legs all retracted and left it a smooth round lump on the forest floor.

## THE FIFTH ADJUSTMENT

They showed me how to use their communications technology and grew me an interface to my own small handheld, so my report was at last able to go. Kostas began angry, of course, having been forced to defend the manner of my departure to the Esperigans without the benefit of any understanding of the circumstances, but I sent the report an hour before I messaged, and by the time we spoke he had read enough to be in reluctant agreement with my conclusions if not my methods.

I was of course full of self-satisfaction. Freed at long last from the academy and the walled gardens of Terce, armed with false confidence in my research and my training, I had so far achieved all that my design had stretched to encompass. The Esperigan blood had washed easily from my hands, and though I answered Kostas meekly when he upbraided me, privately I felt only impatience, and even he did not linger long on the topic: I had been too successful, and he had more important news.

The Esperigans had launched a small army two days before, under the more pleasant-sounding name of expeditionary defensive force. Their purpose was to establish a permanent settlement on the Melidan shore, some nine hundred miles from my present location, and begin the standard process of terraforming. The native life would be eradicated in spheres of a hundred miles across at a time: first the broad strokes of clear-cutting and the electrified nets, then the irradiation of the soil and the air, and after that the seeding of Earth-native microbes and plants. So had a thousand worlds been made over anew, and though the Esperigans had fully conquered their own continent five centuries before, they still knew the way.

He asked doubtfully if I thought some immediate resistance could be offered. Disabling a few mines scattered into the jungle seemed to him a small task. Confronting a large and organized military force was on a different order of magnitude. "I think we can do something," I said, maintaining a veneer of caution for his benefit, and took the catalog of equipment to Badea as soon as we had disengaged.

She was occupied in organizing the retrieval of the deactivated mines, which the ants were now leaving scattered in the forests and jungles. A bird-of-paradise variant had been *adjusted* to make a meal out of the ants and take the glittery mines back to their tree-top nests, where an observer might easily see them from above. She and the other collectors had so far found nearly a thousand of them. The mines made a neat pyramid, as of the harvested skulls of small cyclopean creatures with their dull eyes staring out lifelessly.

The Esperigans needed a week to cross the ocean in their numbers, and I spent it with the Melidans, developing our response. There was a heady delight in this collaboration. The work was easy and pleasant in their wide-open laboratories full of plants, roofed only with the fluttering sailcloth eating sunlight to give us energy, and the best of them coming from many miles distant to participate in the effort. The Confederacy spy-satellites had gone into orbit perhaps a year after our first contact: I likely knew more about the actual force than the senior administrators of Melida. I was in much demand, consulted not only for my information but my opinion.

In the ferment of our labors, I withheld nothing. This was not yet deliberate, but neither was it innocent. I had been sent to further a war, and if in the political calculus which had arrived at this solution the lives of soldiers were only variables, yet there was still a balance I was expected to preserve. It was not my duty to give the Melidans an easy victory, any more than it had been Kostas's to give one to the Esperigans.

A short and victorious war, opening a new and tantalizing frontier for restless spirits, would at once drive up that inconvenient nationalism which is the Confederacy's worst obstacle, and render less compelling the temptations we could offer to lure them into fully joining galactic society. On the other hand, to descend into squalor, a more equal kind of civil war has often proven extremely useful, and the more lingering and bitter the better. I was sent to the Melidans in hope that, given some guidance and what material assistance we could quietly provide without taking any official position, they might be an adequate opponent for the Esperigans to produce this situation.

There has been some criticism of the officials who selected me for this mission, but in their defense, it must be pointed out it was not in fact my assignment to actually provide military assistance, nor could anyone, even myself, have envisioned my proving remotely useful in such a role. I was only meant to be an early scout. My duty was to acquire cultural information enough to open a door for a party of military experts from Voca Libre, who would not reach Melida for another two years. Ambition and opportunity promoted me, and no official hand.

I think these experts arrived sometime during the third Esperigan offensive. I cannot pinpoint the date with any accuracy, I had by then ceased to track the days, and I never met them. I hope they can forgive my theft of their war; I paid for my greed.

The Esperigans used a typical carbonized steel in most of their equipment, as bolts and hexagonal nuts and screws with star-shaped heads, and woven into the tough mesh of their body armor. This was the target of our efforts. It was a new field of endeavor for the Melidans, who used metal as they used meat, sparingly and with a sense of righteousness in its avoidance. To them it was either a trace element needed in minute amounts, or an undesirable by-product of the more complicated biological processes they occasionally needed to invoke.

However, they had developed some strains of bacteria to deal with this latter waste, and the speed with which they could manipulate these organisms was extraordinary. Another quantity of the ants—a convenient delivery mechanism used by the Melidans routinely, as I learned—were adjusted to render them deficient in iron and to provide a home in their bellies for the bacteria, transforming them into shockingly efficient engines of destruction. Set loose upon several of the mines as a trial, they devoured the carapaces and left behind only smudgy black heaps of carbon dust, carefully harvested for fertilizer, and the plastic explosives from within, nestled in their bed of copper wire and silicon.

The Esperigans landed, and at once carved themselves out a neat half-moon of wasteland from the virgin shore, leaving no branches which might stretch above their encampment to offer a platform for attack. They established an electrified fence around the perimeter, with guns and patrols, and all this I observed with Badea, from a small platform in a vine-choked tree not far away: we wore the green-gray cloaks, and our faces were stained with leaf juice.

I had very little justification for inserting myself into such a role but the flimsy excuse of pointing out to Badea the most crucial section of their camp, when we had broken in. I cannot entirely say why I wished to go along on so dangerous an expedition. I am not particularly courageous. Several of my more unkind biographers have accused me of bloodlust, and pointed to this as a sequel to the disaster of my first departure. I cannot refute the accusation on the evidence, however I will point out that I chose that portion of the expedition which we hoped would encounter no violence.

But it is true I had learned already to seethe at the violent piggish blindness of the Esperigans, who would have wrecked all the wonders around me only to propagate yet another bland copy of Earth and suck dry the carcass of their own world. They were my enemy both by duty and by inclination, and I permitted myself the convenience of hating them. At the time, it made matters easier.

The wind was running from the east, and several of the Melidans attacked the camp from that side. The mines had yielded a quantity of explosive large enough to pierce the Esperigans' fence and shake the trees even as far as our lofty perch. The wind carried the smoke and dust and flames towards us, obscuring the ground and rendering the soldiers in their own camp only vague ghostlike suggestions of human shape. The fighting was hand-to-hand, and the stutter of gunfire came only tentatively through the chaos of the smoke.

Badea had been holding a narrow cord, one end weighted with a heavy seed-pod. She now poured a measure of water onto the pod, from her canteen, then flung it out into the air. It sailed over the fence and landed inside the encampment, behind one of the neat rows of storage tents. The seed pod struck the ground and immediately burst like a ripe fruit, an anemone tangle of waving roots creeping out over the ground and anchoring the cord, which she had secured at this end around one thick branch.

We let ourselves down it, hand over hand. There was none of that typical abrasion or friction which I might have expected from rope; my hands felt as cool and comfortable when we descended as when we began. We ran into the narrow space between the tents. I was experiencing that strange elongation of time which crisis can occasionally produce: I was conscious of each footfall, and of the seeming-long moments it took to place each one.

There were wary soldiers at many of the tent entrances, likely those which held either the more valuable munitions or the more valuable men. Their discipline had not faltered, even while the majority of the force was already orchestrating a response to the Melidan assault on the other side of the encampment. But we did not need to penetrate into the tents. The guards were rather useful markers for us, showing me which of the tents were the more significant. I pointed out to Badea the cluster of four tents, each guarded at either side by a pair, near the farthest end of the encampment.

Badea looked here and there over the ground as we darted under cover of smoke from one alleyway to another, the walls of waxed canvas muffling the distant shouts and the sound of gunfire. The dirt still had the yellowish tinge of Melidan soil—the Esperigans had not yet irradiated it—but it was crumbly and dry, the fine fragile native moss crushed and much torn by heavy boots and equipment, and the wind raised little dervishes of dust around our ankles.

"This ground will take years to recover fully," she said to me, soft and bitterly, as she stopped us and knelt, behind a deserted tent not far from our target. She gave me a small ceramic implement which looked much like the hair-picks sometimes worn on Terce by women with hair which never knew a blade's edge: a raised comb with three teeth, though on the tool these were much longer and sharpened at the end. I picked the ground vigorously, stabbing deep to aerate the wounded soil, while she judiciously poured out a mixture of water and certain organic extracts, and sowed a packet of seeds.

This may sound a complicated operation to be carrying out in an enemy camp, in the midst of battle, but we had practiced the maneuver, and indeed had we been glimpsed, anyone would have been hard-pressed to recognize a threat in the two gray-wrapped lumps crouched low as we pawed at the dirt. Twice while we worked, wounded soldiers were carried in a rush past either end of our alleyway, towards shelter. We were not seen.

The seeds she carried, though tiny, burst readily, and began to thrust out spiderweb-fine rootlets at such a speed they looked like nothing more than squirming maggots. Badea without concern moved her hands around them, encouraging them into the ground. When they were established, she motioned me to stop my work, and she took out the prepared ants: a much greater number of them, with a dozen of the fat yellow wasp-sized brood-mothers. Tipped out into the prepared and welcoming soil, they immediately began to burrow their way down, with the anxious harrying of their subjects and spawn.

Badea watched for a long while, crouched over, even after the ants had vanished nearly all beneath the surface. The few who emerged and darted back inside, the faint trembling of the rootlets, the shifting grains of dirt, all carried information to her. At length satisfied, she straightened saying, "Now—"

The young soldier was I think only looking for somewhere to piss, rather than investigating some noise. He came around the corner already fumbling at his belt, and seeing us did not immediately shout, likely from plain surprise, but grabbed for Badea's shoulder first. He was clean-shaven, and the name on his lapel badge was *Ridang*. I drove the soil-pick into his eye. I was taller, so the stroke went downwards, and he fell backwards to his knees away from me, clutching at his face.

He did not die at once. There must be very few deaths which come immediately, though we often like to comfort ourselves by the pretense that this failure of the body, or that injury, must at once eradicate consciousness and life and pain all together. Here sentience lasted several moments which seemed to me long: his other eye was open, and looked at me while his hands clawed for the handle of the pick. When this had faded, and he had fallen supine to the ground, there was yet a convulsive movement of all the limbs and a trickling of blood from mouth and nose and eye before the final stiffening jerk left the body emptied and inanimate.

I watched him die in a strange parody of serenity, all feeling hollowed out of me, and then turning away vomited upon the ground. Behind me, Badea cut open his belly and his thighs and turned him face down onto the dirt, so the blood and the effluvia leaked out of him. "That will do a little good for the ground at least, before they carry him away to waste him," she said. "Come." She touched my shoulder, not unkindly, but I flinched from the touch as from a blow.

It was not that Badea or her fellows were indifferent to death, or casual towards murder. But there is a price to be paid for living in a world whose native hostilities have been cherished rather than crushed. Melidan life expectancy is some ten years beneath that of Confederacy citizens, though they are on average healthier and more fit both genetically and physically. In their philosophy a human life is not inherently superior and to be valued over any other kind. Accident and predation claim many, and living intimately with the daily cruelties of nature dulls the facility for sentiment. Badea enjoyed none of that comforting distance which allows us to think ourselves assured of the full potential span of life, and therefore suffered none of the pangs when confronted with evidence to the contrary. I looked at my victim and saw my own face; so too did she, but she had lived all her life so aware, and it did not bow her shoulders.

Five days passed before the Esperigan equipment began to come apart. Another day halted all their work, and in confusion they retreated to their encampment. I did not go with the Melidan company that destroyed them to the last man.

Contrary to many accusations, I did not lie to Kostas in my report and pretend surprise. I freely confessed to him I had expected the result, and truthfully explained I had not wished to make claims of which I was unsure. I never deliberately sought to deceive any of my superiors or conceal information from them, save in such small ways. At first I was not Melidan enough to wish to do so, and later I was too Melidan to feel anything but revulsion at the concept.

He and I discussed our next steps in the tiger-dance. I described as best I could the Melidan technology, and after consultation with various Confederacy experts, it was agreed he would quietly mention to the Esperigan minister of defense, at their weekly luncheon, a particular Confederacy technology: ceramic coatings, which could be ordered at vast expense and two years' delay from Bel Rios. Or, he would suggest, if the Esperigans wished to deed some land to the Confederacy, a private entrepreneurial concern might fund the construction of a local fabrication plant, and produce them at much less cost, in six months' time.

The Esperigans took the bait, and saw only private greed behind this apparent breach of neutrality: imagining Kostas an investor in this private concern, they winked at his veniality, and eagerly helped us to their own exploitation. Meanwhile, they continued occasional and tentative incursions into the Melidan continent, probing the coastline, but the disruption they created betrayed their attempts, and whichever settlement was nearest would at once deliver them a present of the industrious ants, so these met with no greater success than the first.

Through these months of brief and grudging detente, I traveled extensively throughout the continent. My journals are widely available, being the domain of our government, but they are shamefully sparse, and I apologize to my colleagues for it. I would have been more diligent in my work if I had imagined I would be the last and not the first such chronicler. At the time, giddy with success, I went with more the spirit of a holidaymaker than a researcher, and I sent only those images and notes which it was pleasant to me to record, with the excuse of limited capacity to send my reports.

For what cold comfort it may be, I must tell you photography and description are inadequate to convey the experience of standing in the living heart of a world, alien yet not hostile, and when I walked hand in hand with Badea along the crest of a great canyon wall and looked down over the ridges of purple and grey and ochre at the gently waving tendrils of an elacca forest, which in my notorious video recordings can provoke nausea in nearly every observer, I felt the first real stir of an unfamiliar sensation of beauty-in-strangeness, and I laughed in delight and surprise, while she looked at me and smiled.

We returned to her village three days later and saw the bombing as we came, the new Esperigan long-range fighter planes like narrow silver knife-blades making low passes overhead, the smoke rising black and oily against the sky. Our basket-journey could not be accelerated, so we could only cling to the sides and wait as we were carried onward. The planes and the smoke were gone before we arrived; the wreckage was not.

I was angry at Kostas afterwards, unfairly. He was no more truly the Esperigans' confidant than they were his, but I felt at the time that it was his business to know what they were about, and he had failed to warn me. I accused him of deliberate concealment; he told me, censoriously, that I had known the risk when I had gone to the continent, and he could hardly be responsible for preserving my safety while I slept in the very war zone. This silenced my tirade, as I realized how near I had come to betraying myself. Of course he would not have wanted me to warn the Melidans; it had not yet occurred to him I would have wished to, myself. I ought not have wanted to.

Forty-three people were killed in the attack. Kitia was yet lingering when I came to her small bedside. She was in no pain, her eyes cloudy and distant, already withdrawing; her family had been and gone again. "I knew you were coming back, so I asked them to let me stay a little longer," she told me. "I wanted to say goodbye." She paused and added uncertainly, "And I was afraid, a little. Don't tell."

I promised her I would not. She sighed and said, "I shouldn't wait any longer. Will you call them over?"

The attendant came when I raised my hand, and he asked Kitia, "Are you ready?"

"Yes," she said, a little doubtful. "It won't hurt?"

"No, not at all," he said, already taking out with a gloved hand a small flat strip from a pouch, filmy green and smelling of raspberries. Kitia opened her mouth, and he laid it on her tongue. It dissolved almost at once, and she blinked twice and was asleep. Her hand went cold a few minutes later, still lying between my own.

I stood with her family when we laid her to rest, the next morning. The attendants put her carefully down in a clearing, and sprayed her from a distance, the smell of cut roses just going to rot, and stepped back. Her parents wept noisily; I stayed dry-eyed as any seemly Terce matron, displaying my assurance of the ascension of the dead. The birds came first, and the motties, to pluck at her eyes and her lips, and the beetles hurrying with a hum of eager jaws to deconstruct her into raw parts. They did not have long to feast: the forest itself was devouring her from below in a green tide rising, climbing in small creepers up her cheeks and displacing them all.

When she was covered over, the mourners turned away and went to join the shared wake behind us in the village square. They threw uncertain and puzzled looks at my remaining as they went past, and at my tearless face. But she was not yet gone: there was a suggestion of a girl lingering there, a collapsing scaffold draped in an unhurried carpet of living things. I did not leave, though behind me there rose a murmur of noise as the families of the dead spoke reminiscences of their lost ones.

Near dawn, the green carpeting slipped briefly. In the dim watery light I glimpsed for one moment an emptied socket full of beetles, and I wept.

## THE SIXTH ADJUSTMENT

I will not claim, after this, that I took the wings only from duty, but I refute the accusation I took them in treason. There was no other choice. Men and children and the elderly or the sick, all the wingless, were fleeing from the continuing hail of Esperigan attacks. They were retreating deep into the heart of the continent, beyond the refueling range for the Esperigan warcraft, to shelters hidden so far in caves and in overgrowth that even my spy satellites knew nothing of them. My connection to Kostas would have been severed, and if I could provide neither intelligence nor direct assistance, I might as well have slunk back to the embassy, and saved myself the discomfort of being a refugee. Neither alternative was palatable.

They laid me upon the altar like a sacrifice, or so I felt, though they gave me something to drink which calmed my body, the nervous and involuntary twitching of my limbs and skin. Badea sat at my head and held the heavy long braid of my hair out of the way, while the others depilated my back and wiped it with alcohol. They bound me down then, and slit my skin open in two lines mostly parallel to the spine. Then Paudi gently set the wings upon me.

I lacked the skill to grow my own, in the time we had; Badea and Paudi helped me to mine so that I might stay. But even with the little assistance I had been able to contribute, I had seen more than I wished to of the parasites, and despite my closed eyes, my face turned downwards, I knew to my horror that the faint, curious feather-brush sensation was the intrusion of the fine spiderweb filaments, each fifteen feet long, which now wriggled into the hospitable environment of my exposed inner flesh and began to sew themselves into me.

Pain came and went as the filaments worked their way through muscle and bone, finding one bundle of nerves and then another. After the first half hour, Badea told me gently, "It's coming to the spine," and gave me another drink. The drug kept my body from movement, but could do nothing to numb the agony. I cannot describe it adequately. If you have ever managed to inflict food poisoning upon yourself, despite all the Confederacy's safeguards, you may conceive of the kind if not the degree of suffering, an experience which envelops the whole body, every muscle and joint, and alters not only your physical self but your thoughts: all vanishes but pain, and the question, is the worst over? which is answered *no* and *no* again.

But at some point the pain began indeed to ebb. The filaments had entered the brain, and it is a measure of the experience that what I had feared the most was now blessed relief; I lay inert and closed my eyes gratefully while sensation spread outward from my back, and my new-borrowed limbs became gradually indeed my own, flinching from the currents of the air, and the touch of my friends' hands upon me. Eventually I slept.

## THE SEVENTH ADJUSTMENT

The details of the war, which unfolded now in earnest, I do not need to recount again. Kostas kept excellent records, better by far than my own, and students enough have memorized the dates and geographic coordinates, bounding death and ruin in small numbers. Instead I will tell you that from aloft, the Esperigans' poisoned-ground encampments made half-starbursts of ochre brown and withered yellow, outlines like tentacles crawling into the healthy growth around them. Their supply-ships anchored out to sea glazed the water with a slick of oil and refuse, while the soldiers practiced their shooting on the vast schools of slow-swimming kraken young, whose bloated white bodies floated to the surface and drifted away along the coast, so many they defied even the appetite of the sharks.

I will tell you that when we painted their hulls with algaes and small crustacean-like borers, our work was camouflaged by great blooms of sea day-lilies around the ships, their masses throwing up reflected red color on the steel to hide the quietly creeping rust until the first winter storms struck and the grown kraken came to the surface to feed. I will tell you we watched from shore while the ships broke and foundered, and the teeth of the kraken shone like fire opals in the explosions, and if we wept, we wept only for the soiled ocean.

Still more ships came, and more planes; the ceramic coatings arrived, and more soldiers with protected guns and bombs and sprayed poisons, to fend off the altered motties and the little hybrid sparrowlike birds, their sharp cognizant eyes chemically retrained to see the Esperigan uniform colors as enemy markings. We planted acids and more aggressive species of plants along their supply lines, so their communications remained hopeful rather than reliable, and ambushed them at night; they carved into the forest with axes and power-saws and vast strip-miners, which ground to a halt and fell to pieces, choking on vines which hardened to the tensile strength of steel as they matured.

Contrary to claims which were raised at my trial *in absentia* and disproven with communication logs, throughout this time I spoke to Kostas regularly. I confused him, I think; I gave him all the intelligence which he needed to convey to the Esperigans, that they might respond to the next Melidan foray, but I did not conceal my feelings or the increasing complication of my loyalties, objecting to him bitterly and with personal anger about Esperigan attacks. I misled him with honesty: he thought, I believe, that I was only spilling a natural frustration to him, and through that airing clearing out my own doubts. But I had only lost the art of lying.

There is a general increase of perception which comes with the wings, the nerves teased to a higher pitch of awareness. All the little fidgets and twitches of lying betray themselves more readily, so only the more twisted forms can evade detection—where the speaker first deceives herself, or the wholly casual deceit of the sociopath who feels no remorse. This was the root of the Melidan disgust of the act, and I had acquired it.

If Kostas had known, he would at once have removed me: a diplomat is not much use if she cannot lie at need, much less an agent. But I did not volunteer the information, and indeed I did not realize, at first, how fully I had absorbed the stricture. I did not realize at all, until Badea came to me, three years into the war. I was sitting alone and in the dark by the communications console, the phosphorescent after-image of Kostas's face fading into the surface.

She sat down beside me and said, "The Esperigans answer us too quickly. Their technology advances in these great leaps, and every time we press them back, they return in less than a month to very nearly the same position."

I thought, at first, that this was the moment: that she meant to ask me about membership in the Confederacy. I felt no sense of satisfaction, only a weary kind of resignation. The war would end, the Esperigans would follow, and in a few generations they would both be eaten up by bureaucracy and standards and immigration.

Instead Badea looked at me and said, "Are your people helping them, also?"

My denial ought to have come without thought, leapt easily off the tongue with all the conviction duty could give it, and been followed by invitation. Instead I said nothing, my throat closed involuntarily. We sat silently in the darkness, and at last she said, "Will you tell me why?"

I felt at the time I could do no more harm, and perhaps some good, by honesty. I told her all the rationale, and expressed all our willingness to receive them into our union as equals. I went so far as to offer her the platitudes with which we convince ourselves we are justified in our slow gentle imperialism: that unification is necessary and advances all together, bringing peace.

She only shook her head and looked away from me. After a moment, she said, "Your people will never stop. Whatever we devise, they will help the Esperigans to a counter, and if the Esperigans devise some weapon we cannot defend ourselves against, they will help us, and we will batter each other into limp exhaustion, until in the end we all fall."

"Yes," I said, because it was true. I am not sure I was still able to lie, but in any case I did not know, and I did not lie.

I was not permitted to communicate with Kostas again until they were ready. Thirty-six of the Melidans' greatest designers and scientists died in the effort. I learned of their deaths in bits and pieces. They worked in isolated and quarantined spaces, their every action recorded even as the viruses and bacteria they were developing killed them. It was a little more than three months before Badea came to me again.

We had not spoken since the night she had learned the duplicity of the Confederacy's support and my own. I could not ask her forgiveness, and she could not give it. She did not come for reconciliation but to send a message to the Esperigans and to the Confederacy through me.

I did not comprehend at first. But when I did, I knew enough to be sure she was neither lying nor mistaken, and to be sure the threat was very real. The same was not true of Kostas, and still less of the Esperigans. My frantic attempts to persuade them worked instead to the contrary end. The long gap since my last communique made Kostas suspicious: he thought me a convert, or generously a manipulated tool.

"If they had the capability, they would have used it already," he said, and if I could not convince him, the Esperigans would never believe.

I asked Badea to make a demonstration. There was a large island broken off the southern coast of the Esperigan continent, thoroughly settled and industrialized, with two substantial port cities. Sixty miles separated it from the mainland. I proposed the Melidans should begin there, where the attack might be contained.

"No," Badea said. "So your scientists can develop a counter? No. We are done with exchanges."

The rest you know. A thousand coracles left Melidan shores the next morning, and by sundown on the third following day, the Esperigan cities were crumbling. Refugees fled the groaning skyscrapers as they slowly bowed under their own weight. The trees died; the crops also, and the cattle, all the life and vegetation that had been imported from Earth and square-peg forced into the new world stripped bare for their convenience.

Meanwhile in the crowded shelters the viruses leapt easily from one victim to another, rewriting their genetic lines. Where the changes took hold, the altered survived. The others fell to the same deadly plagues that consumed all Earth-native life. The native Melidan moss crept in a swift green carpet over the corpses, and the beetle-hordes with it.

I can give you no first-hand account of those days. I too lay fevered and sick while the alteration ran its course in me, though I was tended

better, and with more care, by my sisters. When I was strong enough to
rise, the waves of death were over. My wings curled limply over my shoulders as I walked through the empty streets of Landfall, pavement stones
pierced and broken by hungry vines, like bones cracked open for marrow.
The moss covered the dead, who filled the shattered streets.

The squat embassy building had mostly crumpled down on one corner, smashed windows gaping hollow and black. A large pavilion of simple cotton fabric had been raised in the courtyard, to serve as both hospital and headquarters. A young undersecretary of state was the senior
diplomat remaining. Kostas had died early, he told me. Others were still
in the process of dying, their bodies waging an internal war that left them
twisted by hideous deformities.

Less than one in thirty, was his estimate of the survivors. Imagine
yourself on an air-train in a crush, and then imagine yourself suddenly
alone but for one other passenger across the room, a stranger staring at
you. Badea called it a sustainable population.

The Melidans cleared the spaceport of vegetation, though little now
was left but the black-scorched landing pad, Confederacy manufacture, all
of woven carbon and titanium.

"Those who wish may leave," Badea said. "We will help the rest."

Most of the survivors chose to remain. They looked at their faces in
the mirror, flecked with green, and feared the Melidans less than their
welcome on another world.

I left by the first small ship that dared come down to take off refugees, with no attention to the destination or the duration of the voyage.
I wished only to be away. The wings were easily removed. A quick and
painful amputation of the gossamer and fretwork which protruded from
the flesh, and the rest might be left for the body to absorb slowly. The
strange muffled quality of the world, the sensation of numbness, passed
eventually. The two scars upon my back, parallel lines, I will keep the rest
of my days.

## AFTERWORD

I spoke with Badea once more before I left. She came to ask me why I was
going, to what end I thought I went. She would be perplexed, I think, to
see me in my little cottage here on Reivaldt, some hundred miles from
the nearest city, although she would have liked the small flowerlike lieden
which live on the rocks of my garden wall, one of the few remnants of

the lost native fauna which have survived the terraforming outside the preserves of the university system.

I left because I could not remain. Every step I took on Melida, I felt dead bones cracking beneath my feet. The Melidans did not kill lightly, an individual or an ecosystem, nor any more effectually than do we. If the Melidans had not let the plague loose upon the Esperigans, we would have destroyed them soon enough ourselves, and the Melidans with them. But we distance ourselves better from our murders, and so are not prepared to confront them. My wings whispered to me gently when I passed Melidans in the green-swathed cemetery streets, that they were not sickened, were not miserable. There was sorrow and regret but no self-loathing, where I had nothing else. I was alone.

When I came off my small vessel here, I came fully expecting punishment, even longing for it, a judgment which would at least be an end. Blame had wandered through the halls of state like an unwanted child, but when I proved willing to adopt whatever share anyone cared to mete out to me, to confess any crime which was convenient and to proffer no defense, it turned contrary, and fled.

Time enough has passed that I can be grateful now to the politicians who spared my life and gave me what passes for my freedom. In the moment, I could scarcely feel enough even to be happy that my report contributed some little to the abandonment of any reprisal against Melida: as though we ought hold them responsible for defying our expectations not of their willingness to kill one another, but only of the extent of their ability.

But time does not heal all wounds. I am often asked by visitors whether I would ever return to Melida. I will not. I am done with politics and the great concerns of the universe of human settlement. I am content to sit in my small garden, and watch the ants at work.

*Ruth Patrona*

Ian McDonald's work has been nominated for every major award in the genre. His first novel, *Desolation Road,* was published in 1988, and his most recent, *Luna: Wolf Moon,* came out in 2016 from Tor in the US, and Gollancz in the UK. He currently lives in Northern Ireland, just outside Belfast.

# VERTHANDI'S RING

## *Ian McDonald*

After thirteen subjective minutes and five hundred and twenty-eight years, the Clade battleship *Ever-Fragrant Perfume of Divinity* returned to the dying solar system. The Oort cloud web pulled the crew off; skating around the gravity wells of hot fat gas giants and the swelling primary, the battleship skipped out of the system at thirty percent light-speed into the deep dark. Small, fast, cheap, the battleships were disposable: a football of construction nanoprocessors and a pload crew of three embedded in the heart of a comet, a comet it would slowly consume over its half millennium of flight. So cheap and nasty was this ship that it was only given a name because the crew got bored five (subjective) minutes into the slow-time simulation of Sofreendi desert monasticism that was their preferred combat interface.

The Oort cloud web caught the crew, shied them to the construction yards skeined through the long, cold loops of the cometary halo, which flicked them in a stutter of light-speed to the Fat Gas Giant relay point, where the eight hundred habitats of the new Clade daughter fleet formed a pearl belly chain around the planet; then to the Cladal Heart-world herself, basking in the coronal energies of the senile, grasping, swollen sun, and finally into fresh new selves.

"Hi guys, we're back," said the crew of *Ever-Fragrant Perfume of Divinity* as they stepped from the bronze gates of the Soulhouse, down the marble staircase into the thronged Maidan of All Luminous Passion. Irony was still a tradable commodity on this innermost tier of the hundred concentric spheres of the Heart-world, even if not one woman or man or machine or beastli turned its head. Battleship crews knew better than to expect laurels and accolades when they resouled after a hundred or a thousand or ten thousand years on the frontline. Word of *Ever-Fragrant Perfume of Divinity*'s victory had arrived almost three centuries before. A signal victory; a triumph that would be studied and taught across the Military Colleges and Academies of the Art of Defense for millennia to come. A classic Rose of Jericho strategy.

Early warning seeds sown like thistledown across half a light-millennium had felt the stroke of the Enemy across their attenuated slow senses and woke. Communication masers hastily assembled from the regoliths of cold moons beamed analyses back to the Heart-world, deep in its centuries-long task of biosphere salvation: eighty thousand habitats on the move. The Clade battle fleet launched instantly. After two hundred and twenty years, there was not a nanosecond to lose. Thirty-five ships were lost: systems malfunctions, breakdowns in the drives that kept them accelerating eternally, decades-long subtle errors of navigation that left them veering light-years wide of the target gravity well, loss of deceleration mass. Sudden total catastrophic failure. Five hundred years later, *Ever-Fragrant Perfume of Divinity* alone arrived behind the third moon of the vagrant gas giant, which wandered between stars, a gravitational exile, and began to construct the rain of antimatter warheads and set them into orbit around the wanderer. A quick plan, but a brilliant one. A Rose of Jericho plan. As *Ever-Fragrant Perfume of Divinity* accelerated away from the bright new nebula, its hindward sensors observed eighty thousand Enemy worlds plow into the bow wave of accelerated gas at forty percent light-speed and evaporate. Twenty trillion sentients died. War in space-time is slow and vast and bloody. When the species fight, there is no mercy.

In the dying echoes of the culture fleet, the three assassins of *Ever-Fragrant Perfume of Divinity* caught a vector. The fleet had not been aimed on a genocidal assault on the Clade Heart-worlds clustered around the worlds of Seydatryah, slowly becoming postbiological as the sun choked and bloated on its own gas. A vector, and a whisper: *Verthandi's Ring*.

But now they were back, huzzah! Harvest Moon and Scented Coolabar and Rose of Jericho, greatest tactician of her flesh generation. Except that when they turned around on the steps of the Soulhouse to bicker among themselves (as they had bickered the entire time-slowed twenty-six minutes of the transtellar flight, and the time-accelerated two hundred years of the mission at the black wanderer) about where to go and do and be and funk first:

"Where's Rose? Where's the Rose?" said Harvest Moon, whose rank approximated most closely to the historical role of Captain.

Only two resouls stood on the marble steps overlooking the Maidan of All Luminous Pleasure.

"Shit," said Scented Coolabar, whose station corresponded to that of engineer. A soul-search returned no trace of their crewmate on this level. In this innermost level, the heart of the heart, a sphere of quantum nano-processors ten kilometers in diameter, such a search was far-reaching—the equivalent of every virtual mouse hole and house shrine—and instantaneous. And blank. The two remaining crew members of *Ever-Fragrant Perfume of Divinity* understood too well what that meant. "We're going to have to do the meat-thing."

Newly incarnated, Harvest Moon and Scented Coolabar stood upon the Heaven Plain of Hoy. Clouds black as regret bruised the upcurved horizon. Lightning fretted along the edge of the world. Harvest Moon shivered at a fresh sensation; stringent but not unpleasant—not in that brief frisson, though her new meat told her that in excess it might become not just painful, but dangerous.

"What was that?" she commented, observing the small pimples rising on her space-black skin. She wore a close-to-species-modal body: female in this incarnation; elegant, hairless, attenuated, the flesh of a minimalist aesthete.

"I think it was the wind," said Scented Coolabar who, as ever, played against her Captain's type and so wore the fresh flesh of a Dukkhim, one of the distinctive humanesque subspecies that had risen after a mass-extinction event on the world of Kethrem, near-lost in the strata of Clade history. She was small and broad, all ovals and slits, and possessed of a great mane of elaborately decorated hair that grew to the small of the back and down to the elbows. The crew of the *Ever-Fragrant Perfume of Divinity* was incarnate mere minutes, and already Harvest Moon wanted to play play play with her engineer's wonderful mane. "Maybe you should have put some clothes on." Now thunder spilled down the tilted bowl of the world to shake the small stone stupa of the incarnaculum. "I suppose we had better get started." The Dukkhim had ever been a dour, pragmatic subspecies.

Harvest Moon and Scented Coolabar spent the night in a live-skin yurt blistered from the earth of Hoy. The thunder cracked, the yurt flapped and boomed in the wind, and the plain of Hoy lowed with storm-spooked grazebeastlis, but none so loud or so persistent as Harvest Moon's moans and groans that her long black limbs were aching, burning; her body was dying dying.

"Some muscular pain is to be expected in the first hours of incarnation," chided the yurt gently. "As muscle tone develops these pains generally pass within a few days."

"Days!" wailed Harvest Moon. "Pload me back up right now."

"I can secrete general analgesia," said the tent. So until the lights came up all across the world on the sky roof ten kilometers overhead, Harvest Moon suckled sweetly on pain-numb milk from the yurt's fleshy teat, and, in the morning, she and Scented Coolabar set out in great, low-gravity bounds across the Heaven Plain of Hoy in search of Rose of Jericho. This innermost of the Heart-world meat levels had long been the preserve of ascetics and pilgrim souls; the ever upcurving plain symbolic, perhaps, of the soul's quest for its innate spiritual manifestation, or maybe because of its proximity to the virtual realms, above the sky roof, where the ploads constructed universe within universe, each bigger than the one that contained it. Yet this small grassy sphere was big enough to contain tens of thousands of pelerines and stylites, coenobites and saddhus, adrift in the ocean of grass.

"I'm sure we've been this way before," Scented Coolabar said. They were in the third monad of their quest. Eighty days ago, Harvest Moon had discovered beyond the pain of exercise the joy of muscles, even on this low-grav prairie, and could now be found at every unassigned moment delightedly studying her own matte black curves.

"I think that's the idea."

"Bloody Rose of Jericho," Scented Coolabar grumbled. They loped, three meters at a loose-limbed step, toward a dendro-eremite, a lone small tree in the wave-swept grass, bare branches upheld like prayers. "Even on the ship she was a damn ornery creature. Typical bloody selfish."

Because when Rose of Jericho went missing after the routine postsortie debrief, something else had gone missing with her. Verthandi's Ring, a name, a galactic coordinate; the vector upon which the Enemy migration had been accelerating, decade upon decade. In the enforced communality of the return flight—pload personalities intersecting and merging—Captain and Engineer alike had understood that their Mistress at Arms had deduced more than just a destination from the glowing ashes of the annihilated fleet. Soul etiquette forbade nonconsensual infringements of privacy and Rose of Jericho had used that social hiatus to conceal her speculations. Jealous monotheistic divinities were not so zealous as Clade debriefings, yet the Gentle Inquisitors of the Chamber of Ever-Renewing Waters had swept around that hidden place like sea around a reef. A vector, and a name, confirmation of the message they had received three hundred years before: Verthandi's Ring.

Even before they saw the face framed in the vulva of living wood, Harvest Moon and Scented Coolabar knew that their small quest was ended. When they first met on the virtual desert of Sofreendi for the Chamber of Ever-Renewing Waters' mission briefing (as dense and soul-piercing as its debrief ), a closeness, a simpatico, suggested that they might once have been the same person; ploads copied and recopied and edited with mash-ups of other personalities. Empathy endures, across parsecs and plain, battlefronts and secrets.

"Does that hurt?" Scented Coolabar said. Greenwood crept down Rose of Jericho's brow, across her cheeks and chin, slow and certain as seasons.

"Hurt? Why should it hurt?" Wind soughed in Rose of Jericho's twigs. Harvest Moon, bored with this small world of grass, surreptitiously ran her hands down her muscled thighs.

"I don't know, it just looks, well, uncomfortable."

"No, it's very very satisfying," Rose of Jericho said. Her face was now a pinched oval of greening flesh. "Rooted. Slow." She closed her eyes in contemplation.

"Verthandi's Ring," Harvest Moon said suddenly. Scented Coolabar seated herself squatly on the grass beneath the wise tree. Beastli things squirmed beneath her ass.

"What is this game?" With life spans measurable against the slow drift of stars, millennia-long games were the weft of Clade society. "What didn't you tell them, couldn't you tell us?"

Rose of Jericho opened her eyes. The wood now joined across the bridge of her nose, her lips struggled against the lignum.

"There was not one fleet. There are many fleets. Some set off thousands of years ago."

"How many fleets?"

Rose of Jericho struggled to speak. Scented Coolabar leaned close.

"All of them. The Enemy. All of them."

Then Rose of Jericho's sparse leaves rustled and Scented Coolabar felt the ground shake beneath her. Unbalanced, Harvest Moon seized one of Rose of Jericho's branches to steady herself. Not in ten reconfigurings had either of them felt such a thing, but the knowledge was deeply burned into every memory, every cell of their incarnated flesh. The Clade Heart-world had engaged its Mach drive and was slowly, slow as a kiss, as an Edda, manipulating the weave of space-time to accelerate away from bloated, burning Seydatryah. Those unharvested must perish with the planet as the Seydatryah's family of worlds passed beyond the age of biology. Calls flickered at light-speed across the system. Strung like pearls around the gas giant, the eight hundred half-gestated daughter-habitats left their birthing orbits: half-shells, hollow environment spheres; minor Heart-worlds of a handful of tiers. A quarter of the distance to the next star, the manufactories and system defenses out in the deep blue cold of the Oort cloud warped orbits to fall into the Heart-world's train. The Chamber of Ever-Renewing Waters, the military council, together with the Deep Blue Something, the gestalt übermind that was the Heart-world's participatory democracy, had acted the moment it became aware of Rose of Jericho's small secret. The Seydatryah system glowed with message masers as the call went out down the decades and centuries to neighboring Heart-worlds and culture clouds and even meat planets: after one hundred thousand years, we have an opportunity to finally defeat the Enemy. Assemble your antimatter torpedoes, your planet killers, your sun-guns and quantum foam destabilizers, and make all haste for Verthandi's Ring.

"Yes, but what is Verthandi's Ring?" Scented Coolabar asked tetchily. But all that remained of Rose of Jericho was a lignified smile, cast forever in bark. From the tiny vacuum in her heart, like a tongue passing over a lost, loved tooth, she knew that Rose of Jericho had fled moments before the Chamber of Ever-Renewing Waters' interrogation system slapped her with an unbreakable subpoena and sucked her secret from her. Scented Coolabar sighed.

"Again?" Harvest Moon asked.

"Again."

In all the known universe, there was only the Clade. All life was part of it, it was all life. Ten million years ago, it had been confined to a single species on a single world—a world not forgotten, for nothing was forgotten by the Clade. That world, that system, had long since been transformed into a sphere of Heart-world orbiting a sun-halo of computational entities, but it still remembered when the bright blue eye of its home planet blinked once, twice, ten thousand times. Ships. Ships! Probe ships, sail ships, fast ships, slow ships, seed ships, ice ships; whole asteroid colonies, hollow-head comets, sent out on centuries-long falls toward other stars, other worlds. Then, after the Third Evolution, pload ships, tiny splinters of quantum computation flicked into the dark. In the first hundred thousand years of the Clade's history, a thousand worlds were settled. In the next hundred thousand, a hundred times that. And a hundred and a hundred and a hundred; colony seeded colony seeded colony, while the space dwellers, the Heart-world habitats and virtual pload intelligences, filled up the spaces in between which, heart and truth, were the vastly greater part of the universe. Relativistic ramships fast-tracked past lumbering arc fleets; robot seed ships furled their sunsails and sprayed biospheres with life-juice; terraforming squadrons hacked dead moons and hell-planets into nests for life and intelligence and civilization. And species, already broken by the Second and Third Evolutions into space-dwellers and ploads, shattered into culture dust. Subspecies, new species, evolutions, devolutions; the race formerly known as humanity blossomed into the many-petaled chrysanthemum of the Clade; a society on the cosmological scale; freed from the deaths of suns and worlds, immune, immortal, growing faster than it could communicate its gathered self-knowledge back to its immensely ancient and powerful Type 4 civilizations; entire globular clusters turned to hiving, howling quantum-nanoprocessors.

New species, subspecies, hybrid species. Life was profligate in the cosmos; even multicellular life. The Clade incorporated DNA from a hundred thousand alien biospheres and grew in richness and diversity. Intelligence alone was unique. In all its One Giant Leap, the Clade had never encountered another bright with sentience and the knowledge of its own mortality that was the key to civilization. The Clade was utterly alone. And thus intelligence became the watchword and darling of the Clade: intelligence, that counterentropic conjoined twin of information, must become the most powerful force in the universe, the energy to which all other physical laws must eventually kneel. Intelligence alone could defeat the heat-death of the universe, the dark wolf at the long thin end of time. Intelligence was destiny, manifest.

And then a Hujjain reconnaissance probe, no bigger than the thorn of a rose but vastly more sharp, cruising the edge of a dull little red dwarf, found a million habitats pulled in around the stellar embers. When the Palaelogos of the Byzantine Orthodoxy first encountered the armies of Islam crashing out of the south, he had imagined them just another heretical Christian sect. So had the Hujjain probe doubted; then, as it searched its memory, the entire history of the Clade folded into 11-space, came revelation. There was Another out there.

In the six months it took the Seydatryah fleet—one Heart-world, eighty semi-operational habitats, two hundred twelve thousand ancillary craft and defensive systems—to accelerate to close enough to light-speed for time-dilation effects to become significant, Harvest Moon and Scented Coolabar searched the Tier of Anchyses. The world-elevator, which ran from the portals of the Virtual Realms through which nothing corporeal might pass to the very lowest, heavy-gee Tier of Pterimonde, a vast and boundless ocean, took the star-sailors forty kilometers and four tiers down to the SkyPort of Anchyses, an inverted city that hung like a chandelier, a sea urchin, a crystal geode, from the sky roof. Blimps and zeps, balloon clusters and soaring gliders fastened on the ornate tower bottoms to load, and fuel, and feed, and receive passengers. Ten kilometers below, beyond cirrus and nimbus, the dread forest of Kyce thrashed and twined, a venomous, vicious, hooked-and-clawed ecosystem that had evolved over the Heart-world's million-year history around the fallen bodies of sky dwellers.

The waxing light of tier-dawn found Scented Coolabar on the observation deck of the dirigible *We Have Left Undone That Which We Ought to Have Done*. The band of transparent skin ran the entire equator of the kilometer-long creature: in her six months as part of the creature's higher-cognitive function, Scented Coolabar had evolved small tics and habits, one of which was watching the birth of a new day from the very forward point of the dirigible. The Morning Salutationists were rolling up their sutra mats as Scented Coolabar took her place by the window and imagined her body cloaked in sky. She had changed body for this level; a tall, slightly hirsute male with a yellow-tinged skin, but she had balked at taking the same transition as Harvest Moon. Even now, she looped and tumbled out there in the pink and lilac morning, in aerobatic ecstasy with her flockmates among the indigo clouds.

Dawn light gleamed from silver wing feathers. Pain and want and, yes, jealousy clutched Scented Coolabar. Harvest Moon had been the one who bitched and carped about the muscle pain and the sunburn and the indigestion and the necessity to clean one's teeth; the duties and fallibilities of incarnation. Yet she had fallen in love with corporeality; reveled in the physicality of wind in her pinions, gravity tugging at the shapely curve of her ass; while Scented Coolabar remained solid, stolid, reluctant flesh.

She could no longer remember the last time they had had sex; physically or virtually. Games. And war was just another game to entities hundreds of thousands of years old, for whom death was a sleep and a forgetting, and a morning like this, fresh and filled with light. She remembered the actions they had fought: the reduction of Yorrrt, the defense of Thau-Pek-Sat, where Rose of Jericho had annihilated an Enemy strike-fleet with a blizzard of micro–black holes summoned out of the universal quantum foam, exploding almost instantly in a holocaust of Hawking radiation. She watched Harvest Moon's glider-thin wings deep down in the brightening clouds, thin as dreams and want. Sex was quick; sex was easy, even sacramental, among the many peoples and sects that temporarily formed the consciousness of *We Have Left Undone That Which We Ought to Have Done*. She sighed and felt the breath shudder in her flat, muscled chest. Startled by a reaction as sensational, as physical, as any Immelman or slow loop performed by Harvest Moon, Scented Coolabar felt tears fill and roll. Memory, a frail and trickster faculty among the incarnate, took her back to another body, a woman's body, a woman of the Teleshgathu nation; drawn in wonder and hope and young excitement up the space elevator to the Clade habitat that had warped into orbit around her world to repair and restore and reconstitute its radiation shield from the endless oceans of her world. From that woman of a parochial waterworld had sprung three entities, closer than sisters, deeper than lovers. Small wonder they needed each other, to the point of searching through eighty billion sentients. Small wonder they could never escape each other. The light was bright now, its unvarying shadow strict and stark on the wooden deck. Harvest Moon flashed her wings and rolled away, diving with her new friends deep through layer upon layer of cloud. And Scented Coolabar felt an unfamiliar twitch, a clench between the legs, a throb of something already exposed and sensitive becoming superattuned, swinging like a diviner's pendulum. Her balls told her, clear, straight, no arguments: she's out there. Rose of Jericho.

Twenty subjective minutes later, the Clade fleet was eighty light-years into its twelve hundred objective-year flight to intercept the Enemy advance toward Verthandi's Ring, the greatest sentient migration since the big bang. Populations numbered in logarithmic notation, like outbreaks of viruses, are on the move in two hundred million habitat-ships, each fifty times the diameter of the Seydatryah Heart-world. Of course the Seydatryah cluster is outnumbered, of course it will be destroyed down to the last molecule if it engages the Enemy migration, but the Deep Blue Something understands that it may not be the biggest or the strongest, but it is the closest and will be the first. So the culture cluster claws closer toward light-speed; its magnetic shield furled around it like an aurora, like a cloak of fire, as it absorbs energies that would instantly incinerate all carbon life in its many levels and ships. And, nerve-wired into an organic ornithopter, Scented Coolabar drops free from the *We Have Left Undone That Which We Ought to Have Done*'s launch teats into eighty kilometers of empty airspace. Scented Coolabar shrieks, then the ornithopter's wings scrape and cup and the scream becomes *oooh* as the biological machine scoops across the sky.

"Where away?" Scented Coolabar shouts. The ornithopter unfolds a telescope, bending an eye; Scented Coolabar spies the balloon cluster low and breaking from a clot of cumulus. A full third of the netted balloons are dead, punctured, black and rotting. The ornithopter reads her intention and dives. A flash of sun-silver: Harvest Moon rises vertically out of the cloud, hangs in the air, impossibly elongated wings catching the morning light, then turns and tumbles to loop over Scented Coolabar's manically beating wings.

"That her?"

"That's her." *You are very lovely,* thought Scented Coolabar. *Lovely and alien.* But not so alien as Rose of Jericho, incarnated as a colony of tentacled balloons tethered in a veil of organic gauze, now terminally sagging toward the claspers and bone blades of Kyce. The ornithopter matched speed; wind whipped Scented Coolabar's long yellow hair. A lunge, a sense of the world dropping away, or at least her belly, and then the ornithopter's claws were hooked into the mesh. The stench of rotting balloon flesh assailed Scented Coolabar's senses. A soft pop, a rush of reeking gas, a terrifying drop closer to the fanged mouths of the forest: another balloon had failed. Harvest Moon, incarnated without feet or wheels, for her species was never intended to touch the ground, turned lazy circles in the sky.

"Same again?" Scented Coolabar asked. Rose of Jericho spoke through radio-sense into her head.

"Of course."

Foolish of Scented Coolabar to imagine a Rose of Jericho game being ended so simply or so soon.

"The Deep Blue Something has worked it out."

"I should hope so." The balloon cluster was failing, sinking fast. With the unaided eye Scented Coolabar could see the lash-worms and bladed dashers racing along the sucker-studded tentacles of the forest canopy. This round of the game was almost ended. She hoped her ornithopter was smart enough to realize the imminent danger.

"And Verthandi's Ring?" Harvest Moon asked.

"Is a remnant superstring." A subquantal fragment of the original big-bang fireball, caught by cosmic inflation and stretched to macroscopic, then to cosmological scale. Rarer than virtue or phoenixes, remnant superstrings haunted the galactic fringes and the vast spaces between star spirals; tens, hundreds of light-years long. In all the Clade's memory, only one had ever been recorded within the body of the galaxy. Until now. "Tied into a loop," Rose of Jericho added. Scented Coolabar and Harvest Moon understood at once. Only the hand of the Enemy—if the Enemy possessed such things, no communication had ever been made with them, no physical trace ever found from the wreckage of their ships or their vaporized colony clusters—could have attained such a thing. And that was why the Chamber of Ever-Renewing Waters had launched the Heart-world. Such a thing could only be an ultimate weapon.

*But what does it do?* Scented Coolabar and Harvest Moon asked at once, but the presence in their brains, one humanesque, one man-bat-glider, was gone. Game over. A new round beginning. With a shriek of alarm, the ornithopter cast free just in time to avoid the tendrils creeping up over the canopies of the few surviving balloons. The tentacles of the forest clasped those of the balloon cluster and hauled it down. Then the blades came out.

How do wars begin? Through affront, through bravado, through stupidity or overconfidence, through sacred purpose or greed. But when galactic cultures fight, it is out of inevitability, out of a sense of cosmic tragedy. It is through understanding of a simple evolutionary truth: there can be only one exploiter of an ecological niche, even if that niche is the size of a universe. Within milliseconds of receiving the inquisitive touch of the Hujjain probe, the Enemy realized this truth. The vaporizing of the probe was the declaration of war, and would have given the Enemy centuries of a head start had not the Hujjain craft in its final milliseconds squirted off a burst of communication to its mother array deep in the cometary system on the edge of interstellar space.

In the opening centuries of the long, slow war, the Clade's expansion was checked and turned back. Trillions died. Planets were cindered; populations sterilized beneath a burning ultraviolet sky, their ozone layers and protective magnetic fields stripped away; habitat clusters incinerated by induced solar flares or reduced to slag by nanoprocessor plagues; Dyson spheres shattered by billions of antimatter warheads. The Clade was slow to realize what the Enemy understood from the start: that a war for the resources that intelligence required—energy, mass, gravity—must be a war of extermination. In the first two thousand years of the war, the Clade's losses equaled the total biomass of its original prestarflight solar system. But its fecundity, the sheer irrepressibility of life, was the Clade's strength. It fought back. Across centuries it fought; across distances so vast the light of victory or defeat would be pale, distant winks in the night sky of far future generations. In the hearts of globular clusters they fought, and the radiant capes of nebulae; through the looping fire bridges on the skins of suns and along the event horizons of black holes. Their weapons were gas giants and the energies of supernovae; they turned asteroid belts into shotguns and casually flung living planets into the eternal ice of interstellar space. Fleets ten thousand a side clashed between suns, leaving not a single survivor. It was war absolute, elemental. Across a million star systems, the Clade fought the Enemy to a standstill. And, in the last eight hundred years, began to drive them back.

Now, time dilated to the point where a decade passed in a single heartbeat, total mass close to that of a thousand stars, the Clade Heart-world Seydatryah and its attendant culture cluster plunged at a prayer beneath light-speed toward the closed cosmic string loop of Verthandi's Ring. She flew blind; no information, no report could outrun her. Her half trillion sentients would arrive with only six months forewarning into what might be the final victory, or the Enemy's final stand.

Through the crystal shell of the Heart-world, they watched the Clade attack fleet explode like thistledown against the glowing nebula of the Enemy migration. Months ago those battleships had died, streaking ahead of the decelerating Seydatryah civilization to engage the Enemy pickets and, by dint of daring and force of fortune, perhaps break through to attack a habitat cluster. The greater mass of the Clade, dropping down the blue shift as over the years and decades they fell in behind Seydatryah, confirmed the astonished reports of those swift, bold fighters. All the Enemy was here; a caravanserai hundreds of light-years long. Ships, worlds, had been under way for centuries before *Ever-Fragrant Perfume of Divinity* located and destroyed one of the pilgrim fleets. The order must have been given millennia before; shortly after the Clade turned the tide of battle in its favor. Retreat. Run away. But the Enemy had lost none of its strength and savagery as wave after wave of the cheap, fast, sly battle-ships were annihilated.

Scented Coolabar and Harvest Moon and Rose of Jericho huddled together in the deep dark and crushing pressure of the ocean at the bottom of the world. They wore the form of squid; many-tentacled and big-eyed, communicating by coded ripples of bioluminescent frills along their streamlined flanks. They did not doubt that they had watched themselves die time after time out there. It was likely that only they had died, a million deaths. The Chamber of Ever-Renewing Waters would never permit its ace battleship crew to desert into the deep, starlit depths of Pterimonde. Their ploads had doubtless been copied a million times into the swarm of fast attack ships. The erstwhile crew of the *Ever-Fragrant Perfume of Divinity* blinked their huge golden eyes. Over the decades and centuries, the light of the Enemy's retreat would be visible over the entire galaxy, a new and gorgeous ribbon nebula. Now, a handful of light-months from the long march, the shine of hypervelocity particles impacting the deflection fields was a banner in the sky, a starbow across an entire quadrant. And ahead, Verthandi's Ring, a starless void three light-years in diameter.

"You won them enough time," Scented Coolabar said in a flicker of blue and green. The game was over. It ended at the lowest place in the world, but it had been won years before, she realized. It had been won the moment Rose of Jericho diverted herself away from the Soulhouse into a meditation tree on the Holy Plains of Hoy.

"I believe so," Rose of Jericho said, hovering a kiss away from the crystal wall, holding herself against the insane Coriolis storms that stirred this high-gravity domain of waters. "It will be centuries before the Clade arrives in force."

"The Chamber of Ever-Renewing Waters could regard it as treachery," Harvest Moon said. Rose of Jericho touched the transparency with a tentacle.

"Do I not serve them with heart and mind and life?" The soft fireworks were fewer now; one by one they faded to nothing. "And anyway, what would they charge me with? Handing the Clade the universe on a plate?"

"Or condemning the Clade to death," said Scented Coolabar.

"Not our Clade."

She had been brilliant, Scented Coolabar realized. To have worked it out in those few minutes of subjective flight, and known what to do to save the Clade. But she had always been the greatest strategic mind of her generation. Not for the first time Scented Coolabar wondered about their lost forebear, that extraordinary female who had birthed them from her ploaded intellect.

What is Verthandi's Ring? A closed cosmic string. And what is a closed cosmic string? A time machine. A portal to the past. But not the past of *this* universe. Any transit of a closed timelike loop led inevitably to a parallel universe. In that time-stream, there too was war; Clade and Enemy, locked in Darwinian combat. And in that universe, as the Enemy was driven back to gaze into annihilation, Verthandi's Ring opened and a second Enemy, a duplicate Enemy in every way, came out of the sky. They had handed the Clade this universe; the prize for driving its parallel in the *alternate* time-stream to extinction.

Cold-blooded beneath millions of tons of deep cold pressure, Scented Coolabar shivered. Rose of Jericho had assessed the tactical implications and made the only possible choice: delay the Chamber of Ever-Renewing Waters and the Deep Blue Something so they could not prevent the Enemy exiting this universe. A bloodless win. An end to war. Intelligence the savior of the blind, physical universe. While in the second time-stream, Clade habitats burst like crushed eyeballs and worlds were scorched bare and the Enemy found its resources suddenly doubled.

Scented Coolabar doubted that she could ever make such a deal. But she was an Engineer, not a Mistress of Arms. Her tentacles caressed Rose of Jericho's lobed claspers; a warm sexual thrill pulsed through her muscular body.

"Stay with us, stay with me," Harvest Moon said. Her decision was made, the reluctant incarnation; she had fallen in love with the flesh and would remain exploring the Heart-world's concentric tiers in thousands of fresh and exciting bodies.

"No, I have to go." Rose of Jericho briefly brushed Harvest Moon's sexual tentacles. "They won't hurt me. They knew I had no choice, as they had no choice."

Scented Coolabar turned in the water. Her fins rippled, propelling her upward through the pitch-black water. Rose of Jericho fell in behind her. In a few strong strokes, the lights of Harvest Moon's farewell faded, even the red warmth of her love, and all that remained was the centuries-deep shine of the starbow beyond the wall of the world.

# Publication History

# About the Editor

Neil Clarke is an award-winning editor and anthologist. As the editor of *Clarkesworld Magazine,* he has won three Hugo Awards and a World Fantasy Award. His anthologies include The Best Science Fiction of the Year series, *Upgraded,* and several *Clarkesworld* anthologies. Neil currently lives in New Jersey with his wife and two sons. You can find him online at neil-clarke.com.